T. Csernis & Julia Bland

DEMON'S BANE
NUMEN CHRONICLES VOLUME FOUR

ORIGINAL EDITION

NUMENVERSE

DEMON'S BANE
Numen Chronicles | Volume Four

For more information on the world, this series, other books, or to contact the author, head to: https://www.numenverse.com/

Cover designed by Tate Csernis
Cover drawn by Simon Zhong
Cover edited by Julia Bland

ISBN – Paperback: 978-1-917270-04-5
ISBN – Hardcover: 978-1-917270-05-2
ISBN – E-Book: 978-1-917270-06-9

THE NUMEN CHRONICLES is a collaborative work written by

Tate Csernis (T. Csernis) and Julia Bland (Julia B.)

GLOSSARY

Ethos [ee-thos] - The energy within someone that can be used to create or manipulate other energies

†

Dor-Sanguis [door-san-goo-wis] - Translates roughly to Pain *[Portuguese]* and blood *[Latin]* (aka, Romania)

†

Nefastus [neh-fas-tus] – Translates to Unlawful *[Latin]*
(aka, the Americas)

†

Eltaria [el-tar-ia] – Zalith's homeworld

†

Numen [noo-men] - God-like beings that chose to show themselves to the world rather than remain anonymous

†

Aegis [ee-gis] - The Dragon Gods, children of Letholdus

†

DeiganLupus [day-gan-loo-pus] - Translates roughly to 'refused to turn to the wolf' *[Icelantic, Latin]*
(aka, UK)

†

Lumendatt [loo-men-dat] – Numen crystals containing the power to create life

†

Obcasus [ob-cass-us] – Knives capable of putting Numen in a frozen statis

†

Proselytus [pros-elly-tus] – A heart-like organ which creates ethos inside a body

†

Scion [skee-on] – ethos-crafted children of the Numen

†

Înfățișare [in-fuh-tsee-SHAH-reh] – vampires able to shift into animal forms

†

The Seven Realms:

Aegisguard [ee-gis-guard] - The world
(aka, Earth)
Mareaeternum [Mar-ay-ter-num] Translates to eternal tide *[Latin]*
Glaciaqua [Glass-ee-aqua]
Letholdus [Lee-fold-us]
Tengetso [Ten-get-so]
Celitrianas [Sel-it-ree-a-nas]
Yilmana [Yeel-mana]

The Months and Currency

Months

January – Primis
February – Cordus
March – Tertium
April – Aprilis
May – Quintus
June – Iunius
July – Quintilis
August – Tria
September – Novem
October – Decem
November – Undecim
December – Clausula

Currency

Copper – Equivalent of $0.01
Bronze – Equivalent of $0.20
Silver – Equivalent of $2
Gold – Equivalent of $10
Coronam – Equivalent of $100
Cidaris – Equivalent of $1 million

CONTENTS

ARC ONE | | YULE

ARC TWO | | THE PLAGUE

ARC THREE | | THINGS LOST, THINGS STOLEN

ARC FOUR | | TO UZLIA

ARC ONE
†
YULE

Understanding Alucard's Accent

Alucard's dialogue in this edition of the story has an accent. He doesn't pronounce Hs, THs and some Rs. Below are some examples to help you understand his dialogue:

You'll see words like 'ead (head), 'ere (here), and 'owever (however), missing the H.

THs are often ZHs, such as zhat (that), zhis (this), zhe (the), and zhere (there). In other cases, you'll see ozzer (other).

Ws become Vs, such as vhat (what), vhere (where), and vhy (why).

Some Ds become Zs, such as Zamien (Damien), zon't (don't), and Zetlaff (Detlaff).

Fs also become Vs, such as vollow (follow), vriend (friend), and vor (for).

And some Rs become Vs, such as vest (rest), Veiner (Reiner), and Remont (Vemont).

Prelude

—⊰ † ⊱—

Baron Crowell

| **Crowell, *Thursday, Clausula 29th, 959(TG)—Fort Rudă de Sânge*** |

Deep within the dark walls of the fort hidden inside the mountain island off Dor-Sanguis, Crowell sat at the head of the large round table. He eyed the five people who shared the hall's space with him; three Paladins, The Vampire Lord's most efficient footmen, and Rasmus and Cyril, two demons whom Alucard invited into Crowell's council. Crowell wasn't used to having demons around, especially since Alucard had been so repulsed by them before; but a lot had changed lately, and two demons were the least he'd seen in the same room.

The fort, once a safe haven for vampires too afraid to live among the humans, now doubled as a place for Alucard and Zalith's people to carry out the work given to them, work regarding their latest mission to destroy the Numen. And for Crowell, it was where his new office sat. Since Luther's removal as Alucard's second-in-command, *he* had been promoted to Baron, and he couldn't feel prouder. He never liked Luther, and he felt their new positions were much deserved. But he didn't have time to sit there and bask in his victory. There was work to be done.

Five months had passed since Alucard and Zalith told their most trusted subordinates that they had set their sights on Lilith and Damien; everyone had been working non-stop to find them the answers and logistics they needed, and Crowell was determined to please his Lord. But as the year came close to its end, he suspected that the war that his boss had been expecting might not be so far away.

Crowell had gathered the deridiuz, and his colleagues obtained the information requested. However, he wasn't aware of Attila's whereabouts and whether he'd been keeping track of the Numen for Alucard, but he could only assume that he had. He only needed to focus on the tasks *he* had been given.

"Following their current course," Rasmus' voice echoed through the hall, "the cult will reach Nefastus within the next month or so."

"They've been very thorough, too. Burning towns and villages, conducting manhunts in the cities, driving people out, overthrowing law enforcement. They've captured anyone who has even so much as *heard* of Lord Alucard and Apex Zalith," Cyril added.

With a deep sigh, Crowell leaned back in his seat. The Lilidian cult had been sweeping Aegisguard country by country in search of Alucard and Zalith, and they were moving *fast*. "And you're sure of this?" he asked.

"Completely," Rasmus answered.

Of course, Crowell knew that his superiors had both taken precautions to make sure that nothing and no one would stumble upon their residence, but the Lilidian cult was very thorough, and he didn't want to delay getting this news to Alucard. But he'd not dare disturb his Lord at this time; he was busy with his personal life, so he'd send a letter instead. He looked at one of the Paladins. "You will personally deliver my message to our Lord's residence," he instructed. Then, he pulled a piece of paper from beside him and started hastily writing the necessary information.

"I think you should mention that the Diabolus is still executing vampires in an attempt to draw our Lord out," Paladin Marius called from across the table.

"Yes," Crowell agreed.

"When will the killing stop?" Paladin San asked, glancing around the table. "It isn't like our Lord to sit idly by and let his people—"

"Like our Lord, we cannot let this get to us; it's what the enemy wants," Paladin Marius interjected. "The Diabolus are the least of our concerns right now. Every vampire knew what they were getting themselves into when they agreed to stay behind in Dor-Sanguis. Our Lord offered them sanctuary, and those who chose to stay knew of the risks."

Crowell stopped writing to look at the Paladins. "Our Lord has chosen to focus on Lilith and Damien at this time. The last thing *any* of us need is to let the Diabolus become any more involved than they already are. They are distracted trying to lure our Lord out to notice what is really afoot here, and we should do our best to make sure it stays that way."

"How long until they start targeting the Nosferatu?" San asked.

"They won't," Paladin Marcel, who had been quiet up until now, called with an assuring tone. "The Diabolus are weak; their numbers currently only consist of humans, or have you forgotten that every single demon in their midst was eradicated?"

San looked over at him. "I haven't forgotten, but what we don't know is *why*; *why* were all the demons loyal to the Diabolus so suddenly killed?" he asked, setting his eyes on Rasmus and Cyril. "I don't suppose *you* would know, would you?"

"We weren't given *any* task involving the Diabolus. That's Aleksei's business, and both he and Zalith have told us specifically to stay away from anything involving them," Rasmus answered.

"Aleksei has somebody on the inside; if there is something we need to know, we'll be told," Cyril added.

San snarled irritably and looked at Crowell. "To think we'd be working with demons. Why—"

"Because," Crowell interjected, "we all have our jobs, San. Our Lord doesn't expect us to sit around asking questions. We do what we are told when we are told. Marcel is right; the Diabolus won't attack the Nosferatu. Their numbers are wearing thin by the day. Lord Alucard has a reason for everything, and whatever his reason is for not stopping the Diabolus, I'm sure he will soon inform us. Forget about the Diabolus and focus on your orders," he said, finishing his letter.

Rasmus stared at Crowell. "There is a high chance that won't be seen until the new year," he informed. "Of course, you are aware of tonight's events and of the fact that both Aleksei and Zalith have many a thing to do involving their personal lives."

"I'm aware," Crowell said, sealing his letter into an envelope before holding it out towards Marcel, "and remember, it's highly likely that the Lilidian cults won't reach Nefastus for at least a month. A single day or two won't make any difference."

Nodding, Rasmus took his eyes off Crowell and stared aimlessly ahead.

"Take this to them," Crowell repeated, handing the letter to Marcel. "Make sure you give it either directly to our Lord himself or to the butler of their residence—and tell him to let our Lord know it is urgent."

Marcel took the letter and slipped it into his blazer pocket as he stood up. Then, without a word, he morphed into a raven and departed the meeting hall through a gap between the foggy bricks.

"We will take our leave now, too," Cyril said as he and Rasmus stood up.

"Go," Crowell said with a sigh, waving dismissively at them.

Both demons left through one of the side doors.

"If you don't mind me being candid, sir... those demons are just as condescending as our Lord has been saying they are for the last few hundred years," Paladin San mumbled.

Crowell leaned back in his seat and tapped his chin. "But we must learn to get along with them. Our Lord has mated with a demon, so I'm very sure that we will soon be seeing a lot more of them in our midst."

"Tch," Paladin Marius uttered.

Just then, someone burst through the doors.

"Baron Crowell, sir!" a vampire called in panic, staring across the hall at him.

A shiver of trepidation danced down Crowell's spine as he stood up. "What is it?"

"Hostiles are moving in on Dor-Sanguian territory. We've started defensive procedures, but they just keep coming!" the woman shouted.

The Paladins stood up and looked to Crowell for orders.

There was no time to contact Lord Alucard and wait for his response. Crowell was made his second-in-command for a reason, and he was going to prove himself worthy of that title. "Let's move!" he commanded, heading for the door. "We do whatever is necessary to defend Nosferatu territory."

"Yes, sir!" the Paladins replied.

Crowell morphed into a raven, darted out through the gaps in the bricks, and raced towards Dor-Sanguis. Whoever the hostiles were and whatever they planned to do, he'd put an end to it. It was his job to protect Lord Alucard's land and people, and once he got a chance, he'd inform his superiors. For now, though, *he* would handle the situation as best as he could.

Chapter One

Good Morning

| **Alucard,** ***Friday, Clausula 30th, 959(TG)—Nefastus*** |

It was happening again—that same dream. Alucard found himself shrouded in darkness, nothing but black in every direction. The sound of murmuring, suffering voices echoed through the emptiness, some far, some close, and every time, he felt only desperation.

He was searching... looking. But for what? For someone? Something? He didn't know—he never knew. Every time he sunk into this dream, it was never any different than before.

Birdsong woke him as usual. The sunlight crept in through the curtains as he slowly opened his eyes to the real world. He smiled when he felt Zalith move his arm around him, pulling him closer.

As he rested the side of his face on the side of Alucard's, Zalith sighed tiredly and contently. "Good morning, darling," he mumbled and kissed the side of Alucard's forehead. "Happy eleventh day of Yule," he laughed.

Alucard gripped the demon's hand, pulling it closer so that he could rest the side of his face against it. "'Appy Yule," he said.

Alucard hadn't experienced Yule before, a twelve-day holiday celebrating the arrival and births of the gods. Each day had a different ritual, most of which consisted of eating particular foods and lighting fires with specific herbs. Where Zalith was from, *everyone* celebrated Yule, so Alucard thought he'd join in. After all, they hadn't been able to do much last year because of Damien. Now, however, both he and Zalith felt safer than ever.

They had a party planned tonight, and Alucard was looking forward to it. Tomorrow, on the last day of Yule, they'd be giving gifts to one another, and Alucard was excited about that, too, despite his shyness when it came to gifts.

With his free hand, Zalith slowly dragged his fingers over the vampire's chest. "Did you sleep okay?"

"I did," he mumbled, although he once again dreamt that same dream of dark and desperation. But he'd not let it distress him. The moment he woke to Zalith's touch, he already felt a growing desire for his attention, and *that* was something he'd become a lot less nervous about expressing over the past five months.

"Good," Zalith said with a smile, hugging him tightly.

Alucard's lips curled into a slow, satisfied smile as he clasped Zalith's hand, pressing it to his face, savouring the warmth of the demon's touch. Each glide of Zalith's fingers over his chest sent a ripple of pleasure through him; he longed to voice his desire for Zalith's affection, but the words tangled in his throat, replaced by a flutter of nervous anticipation.

Instead of speaking, Alucard let his body do the talking. He arched his back slightly, and slowly and deliberately, he began to press his ass against the hard heat of Zalith's crotch. The contact was electric, a silent plea that spoke volumes, his movements teasing, coaxing a response from the demon that made his pulse race.

Zalith smirked and laughed softly as he stopped dragging his fingers over the vampire's chest to pull him closer. The demon then started kissing his neck, gently grinding his arousal against his ass.

Satisfied that Zalith understood his silent request, Alucard exhaled softly, letting his hand slip behind him to wrap around the demon's hard dick. The heat of it sent a thrill through him, and as he began to stroke, Zalith's grip tightened on his shoulder. The demon turned him just enough to claim his lips in a deep, hungry kiss, their bodies aligning as Alucard continued to caress him, his anticipation growing with every passing moment.

Their kisses grew intense, each one more passionate than the last, until Zalith reached over to the nightstand. Their lips parted for just a heartbeat while Zalith retrieved the lube, and Alucard's pulse quickened at the anticipation of what was to come. As Zalith slicked the lube over his ass, his fingers massaging with a firm, practised touch, Alucard couldn't help the quiet gasp that escaped him.

The demon's lips found his again, and while they kissed, Alucard relaxed into Zalith's touch, his body melting into the sensation as the demon pulled back slightly, only to slowly guide his shaft into his body. A contented sigh escaped Zalith as he filled Alucard inch by inch until he was buried as deep as he could go. The feeling was intoxicating, a shiver of pleasure coursing through Alucard as Zalith moved within him, his breath hot against the vampire's neck. The anticipation that had been building within Alucard reached a fever pitch, every nerve ending alive with the electric thrill of their connection.

With a mix of a struggled grimace and a pleased sigh, Alucard tilted his head, exposing his neck to Zalith's eager lips. The demon's kiss ignited a slow burn of pleasure that made Alucard exhale in contentment, a quiet moan escaping him as Zalith began to move his shaft, thrusting in and out with a deliberate, enthralling rhythm. Zalith's hand gripped his waist firmly, each motion sending ripples of delight through Alucard's body. Waking up to Zalith's attention was one of the things he cherished most, especially when the demon knew exactly how to push him to the edge of ecstasy.

Zalith always knew what he wanted, and he knew exactly how to give it to him. As their bodies moved in sync, Zalith's lips trailed slowly, sensually, along Alucard's neck, the anticipation building with each kiss. When he finally reached the back of Alucard's neck, he lingered there, teasing him with the proximity of his fangs. The pause was almost unbearable, but then Zalith sank his fangs into the tender flesh between Alucard's neck and shoulder.

Alucard moaned quietly, a surge of pleasure spiralling through his body as the demon's venom spread, electrifying his senses. The bite was both pain and pleasure, a perfect blend that left Alucard craving more, and when Zalith groaned in satisfaction, the sound reverberated through him, pulling him deeper into the demon's intoxicating embrace. Every sensation was heightened, every touch magnified as Zalith's venom ensnared him completely, binding them together in a moment of pure bliss.

His heart raced, his body trembled, and when Zalith slowly pulled his fangs from his skin, he moved his hand to Alucard's throat, gripping it tightly. The demon thrusted faster as Alucard's struggled breaths became desperate, quiet moans of delight. The harder Zalith gripped, and the harder he plunged his dick, the closer Alucard neared to his climax.

The demon moaned in Alucard's ear, kissed the side of his face, and nuzzled his neck as he gripped tighter. He knew how Alucard enjoyed his aggression—his *assertion*. Alucard didn't want him to stop, but he could feel his peak approaching, and Zalith would follow not long after, he was sure. And he wanted it despite his desperation for no end.

With his body shivering and enthralled in euphoria, Alucard quickly reached his limit, and when the demon's hard, deep thrust pushed him over the edge, he whined pleasurably, climaxing with a feverish cry, unable to keep himself quiet. He then gripped Zalith's wrist as the demon kept hold of his throat, still thrusting, still panting against his neck as he started moving a little faster. And with a final, muffled moan of satisfaction, the demon plunged his hard, throbbing dick as deeply into Alucard's ass as he could, tightening his grip on the vampire's waist as he came *hard* into the vampire's body. His shaft convulsed, and as Alucard felt the warmth of the demon's cum fill his ass, he hummed in delight.

Zalith exhaled and relaxed as he wrapped his arms around Alucard, kissing his neck. "Fuck," he groaned.

Alucard sighed contently, calming down, and once Zalith pulled his dick from him and rolled to lay on his back, Alucard turned over and moved his arm around Zalith, resting his head on the demon's chest.

"Is that what you wanted?" Zalith asked with a smirk, caressing the vampire's crimson hair.

With a pout, Alucard tightened his embrace around Zalith. "Yes," he muttered. "Is zhat vhat *you* vanted?"

"It's what I always want," the demon answered quietly and kissed Alucard's head. "Do you want blood?" he then asked, gently guiding his hand over the fang marks he'd left on Alucard.

Did he? He felt content enough already. Zalith's affection always made him feel so happy. But Zalith just drank his blood, and if he didn't take some of Zalith's, he'd feel tired all day, and he didn't want that. Alucard didn't want to miss the party because he needed a nap. Not only would he get to drink and spend time with Zalith, but he'd also get to dance with him, too.

So, as he slowly dragged his fingers over the demon's chest, he said, "Yes. Vank you."

He knew the demon smirked. "Come and get it, then," he said with an unseemly tone in his voice.

With a quiet sigh, Alucard leaned his arm on Zalith's chest and stared down at the smirking demon's face. He glanced at Zalith's neck, but he didn't want to bite there. He thought that he'd tease Zalith today; after all, Zalith always took whatever chance he could get to tease *him*, so why wouldn't Alucard do the same?

As Zalith moved his head aside slightly, inviting Alucard to bite, the vampire frowned and denied his invitation. Instead, he kissed Zalith's shoulder, and his pec, and then made his way under the cover and kissed the demon's waist. He didn't give him much warning, either; right after kissing his waist, he savagely sunk his fangs into it. He felt Zalith flinch and heard him grunt quietly, but that only gave Alucard more satisfaction as the demon's blood poured into his mouth.

He felt Zalith's hand move over his head, and when the demon sighed contently, he tensed up. "You're going to make me hard again," he laughed from above the covers.

Alucard pulled his fangs from Zalith's body.

"Oh," Zalith then said with a disappointed frown as he lifted the cover to look down at Alucard. "Do you not want me to get hard again?" he asked, smirking.

Pouting, Alucard made his way back out of the cover and rested his head on the demon's chest. "Ve zon't 'ave time. Ve're supposed to be 'aving breakvast vith zhat voman to talk about zhe party, and I vant to shower bevore ve do zhat."

Zalith laughed quietly. "So what if we're a little late?"

The vampire sighed. "She'll make a 'uge ving out of zhat and I zon't vant to deal vith zhat today," he complained as he sat up, tore the cover away from Zalith, and grabbed his wrist. "Shower," he mumbled, climbing out of bed, pulling Zalith with him.

"Yes, sir," the demon said amusedly, following behind him. He tapped Alucard's ass with his free hand and grinned when Alucard glared back at him in response.

Alucard led the way into the shower. As he and Zalith stepped inside, the demon switched the water on and stood in front of Alucard, gazing at him with a smirk on his face.

For the first short while, they washed. Zalith, as usual, shampooed and washed Alucard's hair for him, and once they were done, Zalith pulled Alucard closer and started to kiss him.

Although they had to be downstairs already, Alucard felt no rush to leave. He was content standing in Zalith's arms, kissing the demon as he kissed back. But when he felt Zalith's hand sliding down his wet body, he stopped kissing him to stare at his face, watching as a grin crept across it. As the demon then started to caress his crotch, Alucard's frown became a conflicted pout, and he took his eyes off Zalith. Despite the fact that he'd just got the attention he needed, the chance for more felt inviting. He couldn't resist it. He gripped Zalith's waist and slowly stepped back until his back was against the wall, pulling Zalith with him. The demon then started kissing him again, caressing his quickly growing arousal—

A sudden knock came at the door. "Sir, Lady Varana sent me up to let you know that she's waiting in the dining room," Edwin called.

Zalith stopped kissing Alucard and glanced at the door. "Okay, thank you," he called. Then, once the butler's footsteps disappeared down the hall outside, the demon smirked and started to kiss his way down Alucard's body until he was on his knees.

Alucard leaned his head against the wall, a sigh of anticipation escaping his breath as the demon slowly sucked his dick. He lost all care about being late; right now, he just wanted Zalith.

Chapter Two

Of Showers and Baths

| Varana |

In the dining room, Varana waited in the breakfast nook for Zalith and Alucard. The sunlight shone on her face as she scowled sourly. How long was she supposed to sit there? They planned to meet at precisely ten o'clock, so where the hell were they?

She glanced at her blonde maid, who was standing not too far from where she was sitting. "How long have we been waiting?" she asked bitterly.

The nervous woman looked at Varana. "A-about twelve minutes, my lady."

Varana scoffed and rolled her eyes. "I should go up there and yell at them. I *know* why they're taking so long—it's Z," she said, pouting. "He's always on time unless he's being a whore," she snarled in revolt.

"I—"

"Can you sit down?" Varana snapped. "You're irritating me!"

Without a word and a very anxious look, the woman sat in the closest seat across from Varana. And then, for a few moments, they sat in silence.

But Varana's impatience became worse. "He *knows* I'm waiting. How dare he treat me like this!" she exclaimed.

Her maid nodded slowly. "I'm sorry, miss."

"And you know what? I'm sure that if I were to go up there right now and open their bedroom door, I'd get an eyeful." She finally heard Zalith and Alucard approaching the dining room and quickly looked at her maid. "Get away from the table!" she shooed, waving her hands at the maid, who instantly stood up and scurried off to stand in one of the corners.

And then the dining room door opened, and as Zalith and Alucard walked in—both with damp, scruffy hair—Varana crossed her arms and glared at them. She was right as always.

"Good morning," Zalith said as he and Alucard sat on the opposite side of the breakfast nook.

She scoffed slightly. "Oh, is it morning? I've been waiting here for God knows how long," she complained.

Zalith smiled slightly. "Sorry."

Varana rolled her eyes, and as she did, Edwin made his way into the room with breakfast platters. The butler placed them both down, took the glasses off the platters, and placed one in front of each of them.

"Sir, an important letter has arrived for you," the butler said, looking at Alucard. "I was told to inform you of its deliverance."

"Vight," Alucard mumbled. "Vank you."

"Do you need to go and read it?" Zalith asked.

"No," he said with a shake of his head. "If vas dire news, zhey'd send an owl directly to vhatever voom I vas in. I'll vead later."

Zalith nodded in response, and as Edwin placed everything down, the demon sighed quietly in relief. "I'm so hungry," he mumbled, dismissing the butler, who silently left the room.

Varana scoffed as she took her glass and filled it with water. "I sincerely doubt that," she muttered, having *not* been able to ignore the sounds she heard coming from upstairs.

Zalith took his eyes off Alucard and smiled at her. "You're right; I already ate upstairs."

Disgusted, she rolled her eyes and sipped from her water.

"And it was *so* much better than anything from the kitchen," he added.

"Stop," she said with a scowl, placing her glass down to snatch her mimosa from the platter in front of her.

Laughing, Zalith took his eyes off her and then started mumbling to Alucard, taking items of food from the platter and putting them on his plate for him.

Varana's irritancy grew as she glared at them. Zalith smiled, Alucard smiled, and as Zalith kissed his forehead, Varana tutted and scowled down at her empty plate. Why did Zalith have to be so touchy and gross with *him* all the time? Why couldn't they just keep their hands off one another for a single minute?

Rolling her eyes again, she picked up a piece of toast and started eating it.

As he smiled at Alucard, who started eating his breakfast, Zalith glanced at Varana. "Are you looking forward to the party tonight?" he asked her.

"I don't know," she sneered. "Are you two going to be this gross *all* night?"

"Probably," Zalith answered, placing his hand on Alucard's thigh while the vampire continued eating.

"Well, maybe I shouldn't go," she then said, sipping from her drink.

He scoffed quietly in response.

"What?" she growled.

"You never miss the opportunity to have a ballroom full of people stare at you in whatever revealing dress of the season you've found yourself wearing," the demon said, watching as her aggravated frown thickened.

She retorted, "I'm not going to hide away my beauty."

"Of course not," he answered, "so I suppose we'll be seeing you there."

Varana took her eyes off him and glared down at her drink. "Whatever," she snapped.

After a few moments of eating in silence, Alucard then looked at Zalith. "Vhat time are zhey arriving again?"

"Between seven and eight, baby," Zalith said with a smile.

Varana groaned quietly and focused on her breakfast. She was sure that they were going to be disgusting and touchy all morning, and she'd prefer *not* to see it. But she wanted to be able to spend time with Zalith...and if that meant putting up with it, then she'd try her best.

| Luther |

As the morning grew later, Luther stood under the shower's warm water, where he'd been for the last twenty minutes. He'd left Danford waiting in his bedroom, and he didn't feel any motivation to go to him. He had *so* much on his mind. It was all focused around Alucard, of course—it always was.

Tonight, Alucard was hosting a Yule party at his home. Luther hadn't received an invitation, but he assumed that he was just supposed to turn up. That was how it usually went with all of Alucard's parties before. Alucard was his best friend; he didn't need an invite.

But he had to be careful. He didn't want to be seen by Zalith; he didn't really want to be seen by anyone, he just...wanted to see Alucard. He hadn't seen him in so long, and it caused him such pain. Part of him was beginning to think that Alucard had forgotten about him or didn't want anything to do with him because Zalith somehow convinced him to stay away from him. But he wasn't going to let that demon take Alucard from him; he'd already decided over the past five months that he was going to do whatever it took to save him from Zalith and show him that *he* was so much better for him.

And he had a plan.

He *needed* Alucard…and he was shamelessly desperate for even an ounce of attention. How could he go on without it? Without seeing him? Tonight would be the first time he'd seen Alucard in months, and he wasn't going to waste a chance like this to show him how he felt. He wouldn't waste the opportunity to get what *he* needed from Alucard. He was tired of waiting around; he was done dealing with that revolting demon. He felt as if he had but one option left to get Zalith away from Alucard, and he wasn't afraid to do it.

If Alucard wouldn't leave Zalith, then Zalith would leave Alucard. He was sure that an egotistical bastard like Zalith would *hate* to see Alucard so much as looking at another man, and Luther planned to be the very man that Alucard had unknowingly chosen instead of Zalith. How would that revolting demon feel to catch him and Alucard alone together? Of course, Luther had much more planned than to be caught alone with Alucard; he wasn't only going to use tonight to pry that demon from Alucard's soul but to also use it to get the attention he deserved.

Luther let out a slow, shuddering breath, bracing his forearm against the shower wall as he leaned in, pressing his forehead to his arm. The water cascaded over his face, trailing down his neck and chest, but its warmth was nothing compared to the heat building within him. His hand slid down, wrapping around his hardening dick, and he almost gasped as pleasure rippled through his body. His thoughts were consumed by Alucard—every touch, every taste—until all he could think of was how badly he needed him. Imagining Alucard's hands on him, his lips, his mouth—it wasn't enough anymore. His breath hitched as he remembered the moment he'd tasted Alucard's blood, the intoxicating sweetness he couldn't get out of his head. But even that memory wasn't enough to quench the hunger gnawing at him now. He needed more—something real, something raw. For all the years of loyalty, all the sacrifice, he felt he deserved it. He was owed that moment, that touch, the one thing that could make the fire inside him finally burn itself out.

He gritted his teeth, a low groan rumbling in his throat as he stroked his shaft, the pressure building with every touch. He had no intention of stopping, not with the vivid images of Alucard dancing in his mind, each thought of that tantalizing smile and sharp gaze driving his desire higher. The fantasy of Alucard's hands on him, the taste of his skin—it was enough to keep him throbbing with need, but what truly sent a thrill through him was the thought of what he had planned for tonight. He'd been waiting, biding his time, and there was no better opportunity than a party full of people too drunk to notice. It would be effortless to slip in, blend into the crowd, and get Alucard alone. His lips curled into a sly smile as he thought about his plan—all he had to do was whisper that he had crucial information about the mysterious Charlotte woman Alucard had been obsessing over. He knew Alucard wouldn't be able to resist. And then, he'd finally have the chance to make his fantasies a reality.

And then he'd tell him how he felt; he'd get the outcome he wanted, and he was certain that it would all work out. Luther *did* feel a little bad about his plan, but it had to be done—for Alucard. He had to protect him; he had to show him that he didn't need Zalith, and tonight would be the last that Alucard had to spend with that demon.

With a quiet, hushed moan, Luther gritted his teeth, climaxing abruptly at the thought of so much as kissing Alucard. But he'd get more than that. He was convinced that after tonight was over, it wouldn't take Alucard long to realize that Luther was who he needed, and he'd come running to him, and Luther would be waiting to give Alucard every inch of his body and soul. That was all he wanted.

He finished washing his hair, turned off the water, and wrapped his hair up into a bun after drying it until it was damp. He pulled his bathrobe on and left the bathroom; he set his eyes on Danford, who was still in bed waiting for him with a smile on his face.

"Good morning," Danford called.

"Hey," he mumbled. He'd much rather see Alucard waiting for him, but after tonight, he wouldn't have to settle for Danford any longer. He still liked the guy…he was nice. But he had become so focused on his quest to woo Alucard that he'd found himself just using Danford to alleviate his stress.

He knew that Danford deserved better, and Luther knew he could be better, but…he just couldn't right now. He had to have Alucard…and he couldn't let petty feelings of guilt and maybe even a crush stop him. Not only that, but he wouldn't allow himself to lose the only guy around here who was actually good at giving head…and he listened, too. But he shouldn't be thinking about that. He didn't *want* Danford the way he wanted Alucard.

"Are you okay?" Danford asked, watching Luther as he made his way over to his desk and pulled a cigarette out of his box.

Clamping it between his lips, he glanced over at him. "Yeah, why?" he muttered, striking the match he took from the side of the table.

Danford frowned as Luther lit his cigarette. "You just didn't seem too happy when I said good morning."

Sighing, Luther flicked the used match out of his window, leaned back on his desk, and looked at Danford, who sat up in bed. "I'm fine," he mumbled, "I'm just…thinking about the party tonight."

"Oh yeah. Do you not want to go anymore? We can stay here if you want…or go out and do something instead," he suggested.

Luther was going to the party and nothing was going to change his mind, but Danford would be there, too, and the last thing he needed was to be seen with him. He needed to be left alone, and he had to make sure that neither he nor Zalith or Varana would bother him and mess up his plans. "I'm still going," he confirmed. "Listen, though. You and I can't be seen together," he warned, pointing at him with his cigarette. "Varana's suspicious of us already, and the last thing either of us wants is drama, right?"

Sadness warped Danford's face as he looked down at his lap. "Oh…" he mumbled, "so…we're just supposed to ignore each other?"

Did Luther feel guilty? Yes—he always did when it came to Danford—but he couldn't let that jeopardize his plans. He pulled a look of regret, dropped his half-finished cigarette into a nearby ashtray, and made his way to Danford. He sat beside him, placed his hand on his shoulder, and quietly said, "It's only for tonight. The last thing I want is for that crazy woman to attack you because she saw us together. You know she's jealous that I chose you over her. I love you, and I don't want to risk you getting hurt." He moved his hand to the side of Danford's face.

Danford didn't lose his hurt frown. "Are you ever gonna stop seeing her?"

Luther sighed. "If I do that, you know the first thing she's going to do is suspect you have something to do with it, and she's gonna come over here and hurt you. I'm only seeing her to keep her sweet—to protect *you*."

"But it's *Yule*. I just wanna spend some time with you."

Becoming irritated by his persistence, Luther huffed and took his hand off Danford's shoulder. "We see each other pretty much every night, and it's not like I won't be there, we just can't be seen together."

"I don't know," Danford said, shrugging. "I guess I was just looking forward to spending time with you outside of this ship. We never get to do anything fun like that together," he said sadly.

Luther scoffed as he looked over at him. "What's so fun about a party? It's just a bunch of drinking and dancing. We can do that pretty much anywhere, anytime."

"When?" he asked.

"Whenever."

Danford went quiet for a few moments but then looked at him again. "When the party's over, are you going home with her or with me?"

Scoffing again, Luther smiled. "With you, duh."

"Okay," Danford mumbled.

"I'm gonna get ready now, though. I have to go and run a few errands, but I'll see you tonight, all right?"

"Sure," he said, nodding.

"Hey, don't be sad," Luther said as he pulled Danford into a hug. "I promise we'll do something together before Yule's over. We got the whole of tomorrow still, right?" He smirked and kissed his lips. "We'll go…have dinner or go watch a show."

Danford sighed and nodded. "Okay, sounds good. I love you."

Relieved that he gave up, Luther smiled and started pulling his trousers on. "I'll see you later."

"Okay," Danford uttered.

Luther then picked up his shirt and swiftly pulled it on before grabbing his blazer and heading for the door. He was already late to his meeting with Varana, and he didn't want to make it worse. So, as soon as he slipped his shoes on—which were outside his door—he hurried up to the deck and raced off towards Varana's house.

| Varana |

Varana settled into a bubble bath while her mousy maid read aloud from the novel in the corner of the room, but she wasn't doing her best, and that brought an unpleasant look to Varana's face. She didn't have the energy to snap at her, though. Her mind was elsewhere.

She glared up at the ceiling mirror above the bathtub. She already had to deal with one instance of people being late this morning, and now Luther was late, too. How could he be so inconsiderate and ungrateful? What could he be doing that was so important that he'd be late?

With a huff, she shifted her glare to her maid. "Do you have a boyfriend?" she snapped, interrupting the woman.

"Um…yes, miss, I do," she answered.

Varana sighed. "What's *he* like?" she muttered. She was sure that no standard maid could have it better than her. Her anger was still festering, becoming worse the longer she had to wait.

"Oh…he's wonderful," the maid answered. "He works at the mill in the next town. He's so attentive and—"

"I just don't understand why it's so hard for Luther to show up on time!" Varana then interjected. "It's not like he's in another country!"

"M-maybe he got held up?" her maid suggested.

"No, he's just rude and inconsiderate," she grumbled. "Which is why I'm sleeping with Tyrus on the side," she added with a devious smile.

Her maid didn't say anything.

Irritated, Varana sharply turned her head and glowered at her. "What?!" she exclaimed, sure that the woman was judging her. "You'd do the same thing if your little bread boy was treating you like this!"

With a nervous frown, the maid stuttered. "I don't—"

"Keep reading," Varana grunted, not at all interested in hearing what she had to say, and as the maid did so, she relaxed in her bath and glared up at the ceiling.

After a while of listening to her maid's irritating voice, Varana heard the door to her house open. She waited as footsteps made their way down the hall, and when her bathroom door was pulled open, an aggravated pout clung to her face.

"Hey, sugar," Luther called, closing the door behind him. "Sorry I'm late."

"Where were you?" she asked as she scowled over her shoulder at him, watching him make his way to her.

He didn't answer her right away. First, he shooed her maid out of the chair, and once she retreated to a corner not too far from the bath, Luther sat down. "I woke up a little late," he answered.

Varana rolled her eyes. "I don't know why you keep insisting on sleeping on that godforsaken boat when you could be sleeping with *me* in my nice, shiny house in my nice, comfy bed."

Luther laughed slightly and smirked at her, clearly trying to get a glance at her chest, which was hidden beneath the bubbles. "You know I would if I could," he said, his eyes slowly averting to her face. "But I still gotta keep an eye on the people staying there. But hey, I heard the complex is pretty much finished now, and once Yule is over, I'll be free," he said, slouching back in his seat.

She scowled at him. "Do you intend on spending tomorrow on that boat?" she asked. Tomorrow was the most important day of Yule, and if he chose to miss that with her, she wasn't sure what she might do.

"Actually…I have a thing," he said, staring at her as she started washing her legs. "I uh…gotta keep an eye on the boat. It's docked up in a city, after all. Who's to say some drunk idiots ain't gonna wreck the place?"

She stopped washing and glared at him for a few moments before scowling. "He can just buy a new boat!" she exclaimed.

Luther shook his head. "I don't wanna risk my job."

She scoffed, offended. "So, I'm expected to spend tomorrow all on my own like some filthy, unwanted orphan?" she asked, continuing to clean her legs.

Sighing, Luther shrugged and rested his elbows on his knees. "I don't know what you want me to say. If I could, I would, but I can't."

"Just quit your job."

He laughed. "Why would I do that?"

"So you can spend more time with your loving girlfriend."

Luther sighed deeply. "That's not even an option, either. Nobody walks away, and I'd rather not be sent to wherever it is vampires go when they die."

"You don't want to risk your life for me?" she asked, smiling at him.

He didn't answer. He just sat there like an idiot and laughed nervously.

Rolling her eyes, Varana turned her attention back to washing her legs. She wasn't mad; she didn't expect him to risk his life for her, she would have just liked it if he did.

Once she was done with her legs, she looked at Luther to see that he wasn't gawping at her anymore and was staring out the window at Zalith's house. "Well," she said, snatching his attention, "at least we can spend some time together at the party tonight."

"Uh, about that," Luther then said.

She snarled at him—she *knew* he was about to wriggle his way out of it.

"I don't…think it's a good idea for us to be seen together—"

"Excuse me?"

"Zalith threatened me, girl," he exclaimed. "I don't want to have my arms ripped off or something. He doesn't like the fact *at all* that you're dating me, so I'm gonna have to keep my distance. I'll still be there to admire you from across the hall, though," he said, grinning.

"*When* did he threaten you?"

"When people were being invited to this thing," he grumbled. "He knew Alucard would invite me—business reasons—and took it upon himself to tell me I'd do well to *not* be seen with you," he explained.

She scowled. "Well, I'm going to talk to him right now because that's redic—"

Before she could stand up and finish her sentence, Luther almost darted over and sat on the side of the bathtub, placing his hand on her shoulder to stop her from getting out. "No, it's all right, babe," he said, smiling. "Don't do it now. I wanna spend time with you," he said, moving his hand from her shoulder to the side of her neck. "And it'll probably only make things worse, you know. I want today to be peaceful. I don't want him to ruin what time we *do* have together."

Staring up at him, she sighed quietly. It would be nice to have someone to spend time with, so she put it out of her mind for now. She'd confront Zalith later. "Fine," she mumbled, looking down at the bubbles.

Luther then smirked as he started slowly moving his hand down over her chest. "So, what are we doing today?"

"That's up to you. I just have to start getting ready at five. I thought it would be nice to start my day off with a relaxing bath."

His smirk didn't fade. "Is there room for one more?"

"There is," she confirmed.

As he smiled, Luther stood up and started undressing. "Maybe we can take a walk after?" he suggested.

"Maybe. Just around the property, though. I don't feel like going far."

He nodded as he took the last of his clothes off.

She still wasn't impressed by him, but he *was* her boyfriend, so she'd just have to deal with it.

When he climbed into the bath and almost immediately started to grope her, she sighed quietly and rested her head on his shoulder. She was still mad at him for being late *and* his ridiculous excuses, but he was here now, and she didn't want to let it ruin her day. She felt grouchy, and she knew Luther was hoping to have sex with her; maybe *that* would make her feel a little less angry. So, as his gropey hands wandered all over her body beneath the water, she relaxed and let him get on with it.

Chapter Three

Those Left Behind

| Alucard |

Zalith and Alucard sat on one of the couches in the lounge, and in front of them, the two lead organizers of tonight's party were making sure for the *third* time that everything was prepared.

"Guests will be arriving between seven and eight," the planner with a list in his hand said, and as Zalith nodded, the guy glanced at his papers. "The band will arrive to set up at six."

Zalith nodded again, glancing at Alucard to see if he was content with what was being said, and as the vampire also nodded, he looked back up at the planner.

"Something went wrong with the salmon pâté, so we opted for shrimp tartlets instead," the second man explained.

"That's fine," Zalith said and glanced at Alucard again.

Although Alucard had no idea what shrimp tartlet was, he nodded.

Zalith set his eyes back on the planners. "Is that everything?"

Both men nodded.

"Yes, sir," the first said.

"Thank you," Zalith then dismissed.

As the planners left, Alucard turned to face Zalith. The demon might be good at hiding it, but Alucard could see the sadness in his eyes. He knew something was wrong, and he highly suspected that it was the fact that Zalith missed his family. He knew how much the demon loved and missed them, and a time like this could only make him feel worse.

Alucard didn't really know what to do or say… but he didn't want him to be sad. He didn't want to leave Zalith to sink into his despondency. If there was a way for his family to be there, Alucard would do whatever it took to make it happen, but they were gone, and all he could do was try to be there for him.

With a concerned frown, he slowly moved his hand over Zalith's leg to grip his hand, both of which were in his lap. "Are you okay?" he asked as the demon looked at him.

Zalith smiled as he took hold of Alucard's hand. "I'm okay."

He didn't believe that. "No, you're sad."

Sighing quietly, Zalith moved his arms around Alucard and lay down with him, resting the side of his head on Alucard's. "I'm okay," he repeated. "I just miss my family."

Hearing it made Alucard feel more desperate to try and come up with something that might help Zalith. It wasn't often that he saw him so down, and whenever he did, Alucard always felt guilty. All he could do was try whatever he thought up and hope it helped. Zalith was always there for him when *he* needed it.

But before he started trying to think of something that might distract Zalith from his sorrow, he wanted to give him the option to talk about how he was feeling. Alucard would listen, and he'd try to understand despite his lack of experience with spending holidays with family, and he'd try to comfort him. But if Zalith didn't want to talk about it, he'd not force him.

The vampire lightly gripped Zalith's wrist as he lay there with his arms around Alucard. "Do you vant to talk about zhis?" he asked quietly.

Zalith didn't immediately answer. He fiddled with Alucard's crucifix chain while he clearly debated whether he wanted to talk about it. With a quiet hum of pondering, he hugged Alucard a little tighter. But he soon sighed and buried his face in the side of the vampire's neck. "It makes me too sad," he muttered.

Although Alucard didn't want to insist, he didn't want to just leave Zalith to feel miserable. He wanted to know what was wrong, he wanted him to talk about it, and he wanted to understand so that he could help him. "Von't talking 'elp?"

"Maybe," he mumbled.

"Tell me," Alucard invited, taking hold of Zalith's other hand as he stopped fiddling with his chain.

The demon thought to himself for a moment again and then huffed sadly as he rested the side of his face against Alucard's. "This time of year is always hard because I miss my family. Every year, we'd always have a party like this but with more people. I'd help my mother plan everything, and then I'd listen to my parents argue about the ridiculous and unnecessary amount of money my mother was spending on the party. Then Xurian and I would play these stupid little drinking games, and the day after, we'd all huddle up in the morning with hot drinks and open our gifts. I just…miss them," he explained sullenly. "But I'm glad that I have you, and I'm thankful you're here; I love you so much," he assured him, kissing his neck.

"I love you, too," Alucard replied, but he was deep in thought. Maybe doing the things that Zalith used to do with his family would help? "Maybe ve can do zhose vings togezzer?"

Zalith laughed a little. "Spend too much money, argue, and play drinking games?"

"Vell…maybe not argue, but ve alveady spent a lot of money. Ve can alvays spend more; zhere are many vings I could list." He smiled, trying to entertain him. "And ve can dvink. Zhe only dvinking game I've ever played vas zhe vone Tobias 'ad us do at Elvin's party, but you can teach me," he offered.

The demon sighed quietly. "Yeah."

Alucard didn't know what else to say. Zalith didn't sound too enthusiastic, and it didn't seem like he wanted to say anything else. He *did* hug Alucard a little firmer, though, and that made him think that Zalith just wanted to lay there. So that's what they did.

But Alucard couldn't stop trying to think of what he might be able to do for Zalith. He didn't want him to be sad; he didn't want him to feel lonely. He wanted to cheer him up. But what would cheer Zalith up? He didn't sound so thrilled when Alucard offered to do the things with him that he said he missed, so he had to think of something else. Maybe they could go out; maybe they could go shopping or watch an opera or get lunch somewhere. What if Zalith just wanted to lounge around, though?

Sighing, Alucard slowly silenced his thoughts. He'd wait until Zalith let him know that it was time to get up to suggest they do something. He didn't want Zalith to think that he *had* to just to make *him* happy; he wanted Zalith to do what *he* wanted to do.

"Do you want to have sex?" Zalith suddenly asked.

Alucard always felt flustered when he was asked that question—when that word was used—but he'd not let it show. He'd become surprisingly better at hiding the fact that he was nervous and embarrassed.

But the question still remained: did he want to? They had sex before heading to breakfast, but considering he'd had some of Zalith's blood, Alucard didn't feel as tired as he usually might. He knew that Zalith needed sex for a reason—for many reasons—and not only would he say yes because of that, but he also felt enticed by the opportunity.

He nodded as best he could with Zalith's head on his.

"Are you sure?" the demon asked.

"Yes," he replied quietly, still fighting his nervousness, but it didn't have as much power over him anymore.

The demon lightly dragged his hand up over his waist and placed it on Alucard's chest. "Where?"

"Ve…can stay 'ere or…go to our voom."

"Can we do it outside?" Zalith asked, still with his sullen tone.

Conflicted and anxious, Alucard frowned—

"No, wait…let's go upstairs," the demon said.

Alucard nodded. He liked the sound of that much more.

Before he could get up, however, Zalith held him tighter. "Can you suck my dick for a bit?" the demon asked quietly.

Now he felt nervous—the type of nervousness that would surely show on his face. But Zalith couldn't see his face, so maybe he wouldn't notice. Of course, he knew *how* to do what Zalith asked because the demon taught him over the past few months, but despite the practice, he still wasn't entirely confident. But it was what Zalith wanted, and what *he* wanted was to make Zalith feel better. He'd also not deny the fact that he liked the idea of pleasing the demon, especially when he *really* needed it.

So he asked, "Vight 'ere…or…upstairs?"

Zalith clearly pondered for a few moments but then exhaled deeply as he rested the side of his face on Alucard's again. "Upstairs."

Alucard nodded slightly. "Okay."

The vampire stood up, his grip on Zalith's hand firm yet tender as he led the demon out of the lounge, his heart beating a little faster with each step they took towards the stairs. A familiar nervousness twisted in his chest, growing stronger the closer they got, but he steeled himself, determined not to let it show. Zalith had always been patient, always understanding, and Alucard trusted that this time would be no different. But as they reached the stairs, he felt Zalith hesitate. Alucard glanced over his shoulder, meeting the demon's gaze. Zalith's hand tightened around his, a silent command that sent a shiver down Alucard's spine as Zalith gently redirected them towards his office.

Zalith's intentions were clear, and Alucard willingly followed, his pulse quickening with a mix of anticipation and desire. As soon as they crossed the threshold into the dimly lit office, Zalith shut the door behind them and pushed Alucard back against it with a deliberate yet gentle pressure. The solid wood at his back was cool, a stark contrast to the heat of Zalith's body as he closed the distance between them. Zalith's fingers trailed over Alucard's collarbone; although the demon's sullen expression remained, his touch conveyed a deep yearning that sent sparks of electricity through Alucard's veins.

When Zalith leaned in to claim his lips, Alucard's breath caught in his throat, his earlier worries momentarily forgotten. The kiss was slow, almost tender, but there was an undercurrent of intensity that made Alucard's body respond instinctively. He melted into Zalith's embrace as the demon's hand slid up his neck, fingers tangling in his hair before tracing a possessive line to the back of his head. The sensation sent a thrill through Alucard, and his own hands moved almost of their own accord, finding their place at Zalith's waist, pulling him closer.

The kiss deepened, and Alucard could feel Zalith's warmth seeping into him, grounding him even as it ignited a hunger he couldn't ignore. His worry lingered in the back of his mind, but it was overshadowed by the desire to be consumed by Zalith, to give himself over completely to the demon's touch.

But then Zalith's expression darkened, his lips pulling away from Alucard's with a sullen frown. The shift in mood sent a ripple of uncertainty through the vampire, but before he could react, Zalith's gaze dropped to his shirt. Slowly, almost deliberately, Zalith's hand slid from the back of Alucard's neck, fingers brushing over his skin before gripping the top button of his shirt. He began to unbutton it, each release of fabric making Alucard's breath hitch slightly as the anticipation built.

As Zalith slipped the shirt from his shoulders, letting it fall to the floor, Alucard felt a shiver of excitement run through him. Zalith's eyes roamed over his now-exposed chest, taking in every detail, every contour. The intensity of Zalith's gaze sent a warm flush through Alucard, and when the demon rested his forehead against his, the gentle sigh that escaped Zalith's lips was like a whispered promise. Slowly, Zalith's fingers traced over his skin, following the lines of his abs with a tender, almost reverent touch that left Alucard yearning for more.

In response, Alucard's hands moved to Zalith's shirt, his fingers deftly working the buttons open one by one. When he finally pulled it off, he placed his right hand on Zalith's chest, feeling the steady rhythm of the demon's heartbeat beneath his palm. He opened his mouth to ask if Zalith still wanted this, to make sure they were both on the same page, but before the words could form, Zalith leaned in and captured his lips in another searing kiss. The question died on his tongue, replaced by the undeniable heat of their connection. If Zalith didn't want to continue, he would say so—there was no need to ask. Yet, as much as Alucard was content to fulfil Zalith's desires, the firm press of the door against his back made him crave something more intimate.

Their kiss deepened, and with a gentle nudge, Alucard began to guide Zalith away from the door, leading him towards the couch. When they reached it, Alucard urged Zalith to sit, the demon's grip on his waist tightening as he did. Alucard straddled Zalith's lap, the closeness of their bodies amplifying the heat between them. For a moment, the vampire simply stared into Zalith's eyes, letting the anticipation build as he absorbed the intensity of the moment, knowing that whatever came next, they were both ready for it.

Zalith gazed at him, slowly moving his hands around Alucard's waist and up to his abs. "You have such a nice body," he said quietly, a saddened tone still in his voice.

Placing his hand on the side of Zalith's face, Alucard smiled. "Vank you. So do you—and I veally love your vace, too," he said with a smirk.

With a smile breaking through his despondent frown, Zalith kissed his lips a single time before gazing at him. "Thank you," he said, and then he started kissing him again. But he paused to stare at him once more. "I really like it when you sit on me, and I really love *you*."

Smiling, Alucard rested his forehead against Zalith's. The demon seemed to be slowly feeling a little less upset, and Alucard would keep doing what he was doing to try and banish all of Zalith's sadness. He still felt his angst creeping in as he thought about what he was about to do for him, but he'd not let it stop him. He just wanted to give Zalith what he needed. "I veally love you, too," he said. "And I veally like to sit on you."

The demon smiled once again and resumed kissing him, dragging his hands over his body.

Alucard suspected that Zalith was waiting, though, and despite his own worry, he wasn't going to *keep* him waiting. As they kept kissing, he slowly guided his hand down the demon's body to grip the bulge in his trousers. Zalith inhaled sharply, tightening his grip on Alucard's waist; he was obviously getting excited, and Alucard wasn't going to disappoint. He unbuckled the demon's belt and started to unbutton the demon's trousers, and when Alucard gripped Zalith's arousal, he felt the demon tense up, and he lightly bit Alucard's bottom lip.

After a few more moments of kissing and caressing, Alucard felt his angst returning, but he ignored it and pulled his lips from Zalith's. He didn't spare a look at his face, though; he was sure Zalith was smirking, and that would only fluster him. So he made his way down to the demon's waist and rested his knees on the floor, and as he gipped the demon's dick and pulled it from the demon's trousers, Zalith shifted his hand to the back of Alucard's head and started fiddling with his crimson hair.

Alucard slowly dragged his tongue over the demon's tip. Zalith sighed quietly in satisfaction and relief, leaning his head back and gripping Alucard's hair; the vampire eased the demon's dick into his mouth, his tongue tracing each inch, and when he heard Zalith moan quietly, a consuming feeling of contentment raced through him. Knowing that he was pleasing the demon was satisfying enough, and he hoped that this would hopefully make Zalith feel better.

He sucked a little faster, the demon's sighs of enjoyment becoming quiet moans of pleasure as he fidgeted slightly in his seat. Alucard wasn't sure whether Zalith wanted him to keep going until he climaxed or if he was going to get him to stop soon; he said he wanted to have sex, but if he changed his mind, then that was okay. Alucard would keep doing what he was doing.

Zalith soon sighed pleasurably as he guided his hand from Alucard's head and gently stroked it around his face to lightly grip his chin. "Stop," he breathed.

Alucard did as the demon asked, and as the vampire straddled his lap, the demon started kissing him again. The longer they kissed, the more convinced Alucard became that Zalith *was* feeling better; the demon was kissing him more intensely, breathing quicker as he did. Alucard began to become swarmed with anticipation and excitement as Zalith gripped his crotch. But the demon then stopped kissing him and stared into his eyes.

"Can you go and get the lube, please?" Zalith requested, smirking.

Flustered, Alucard got up. He made his way over to Zalith's desk, pulled the top drawer open, and located the bottle Zalith asked for. The vampire went back over to Zalith, and as he handed it to Zalith, the demon pulled him into his lap again and kissed him as he began unbuckling Alucard's belt.

When Zalith pulled the vampire's trousers off, he smirked at him and instructed, "Lay down."

Excitement shot through Alucard, and as his heart beat a little faster, he got out of Zalith's lap and rested on his back on the couch. Zalith moved over him, pulling his own trousers off while Alucard waited, staring at him. The demon hastily smothered his dick in the viscous lube, and then he leaned closer to start kissing Alucard. As he moved his leg over Zalith's back, Alucard gripped a fistful of his hair, and to his relief, Zalith didn't keep him waiting.

The demon nuzzled Alucard's neck and exhaled deeply against his skin as he eased his dick into the vampire's ass. Alucard hummed in delight and gently pulled on Zalith's hair as the demon moaned quietly into his ear, each thick inch urging him to whine louder. And when Zalith began thrusting lightly, pushing his shaft deeper with each movement, they moaned into one another's mouths, kissing desperately.

As Zalith got faster, Alucard turned his head to the side, exhaling deeply as his body quickly became enthralled in delight. He listened to the demon's quiet moans of satisfaction as he nuzzled the vampire's neck, but despite that, Alucard wanted to know whether he was *actually* helping Zalith feel better. So he concentrated as best as he could with pleasure electrifying through his body; he focused on the connection that he and Zalith had through their imprints, hoping to discover feelings of happiness, and that's exactly what he found. Zalith was content; he *was* enjoying himself. His main thought seemed to be just how much he loved Alucard, and just how thankful he was for him. That made Alucard smile.

However, Alucard soon felt the urge to take more control. He knew that Zalith liked it when he did, so he turned his head to look up at Zalith, gripped his arms, and swiftly moved Zalith onto *his* back. As Alucard straddled his lap, Zalith exhaled and laughed playfully. Alucard could tell Zalith was excited through both his face and their imprint connection, and he smiled nervously in response as he started slowly guiding the demon's dick into and out of his body.

Zalith reached up and placed his hand on the side of the vampire's neck, and as Alucard leaned forward to kiss him, the demon frowned with a struggled look of pleasure. "I want you to take some of my blood," he insisted, pulling Alucard's face to his neck.

It was what Zalith wanted, and the idea *was* very inviting. The vampire leaned closer to Zalith's neck but gripped the demon's wrist and made him place his hand on his waist.

And without falter, he sunk his fangs into Zalith's neck. The demon moaned quietly, gripping Alucard's waist, making him move his body a little faster, and as Zalith's blood oozed into his mouth, Alucard groaned contently.

He didn't want to take too much of his blood, though. He already had enough this morning, but he knew from Zalith's thoughts that the demon wanted him to take just as much blood to compensate for the energy the demon was currently draining from him… but Alucard found that he *liked* something about the fact that Zalith had to take his life force to maintain his own strength. But this wasn't about him or what he wanted. So he gulped the demon's blood down, and the euphoria quickly made him feel a little lightheaded.

As he soon pulled his fangs from Zalith's neck, the demon grasped the vampire's dick and started to caress it. With the euphoria of both Zalith's shaft and his blood consuming him, Alucard moaned pleasurably and rested the side of his head on Zalith's, dragging his cheek over his as he kept moving back and forth.

"I love you," Alucard breathed, a frown of struggle beginning to appear on his face as he felt his peak approaching.

Zalith smiled and kissed the side of Alucard's face. "I love you, too." He then moaned as he fidgeted beneath the vampire, moving his hand faster over Alucard's dick.

The vampire grimaced in anticipation, tightening his grip on the demon's wrist as his trembling, euphoria-enthralled body began to shiver. Zalith started kissing his lips again, and as the demon moved his hand over the tip of the vampire's shaft, Alucard moaned in relieved satisfaction, falling over the edge of his peak. But as he climaxed, with each drop of cum that oozed from his dick, complete and utter exhaustion struck him like a fist to his face.

It wasn't over, though. Zalith breathed frantically, turning his head to the side to stop their kissing as he took his hand off the vampire's shaft. He smirked at Alucard and dragged his tongue over his hand, licking the vampire's climax off his palm with a satisfied groan. The demon then hastily grasped Alucard's waist with both hands and started pushing him back and pulling him forward with more force. Alucard's heart raced, and his breaths were frantic; any moment now, he felt as though his trembling, intoxicated body might collapse. But it felt so good—*he* felt so good—and so did Zalith. He could feel how much the demon loved him and how much he loved *this*.

The demon moaned and grimaced, pulling on his body as Alucard kissed him. And not long after, Alucard felt Zalith's body tense up beneath his, and the demon moaned feverishly in pleasure, tightening his grip on the vampire's body as his dick throbbed inside him, filling Alucard's ass with warmth—and *then* it was over.

Alucard exhaled deeply and rested his forehead against Zalith's. He enjoyed every moment like this; every moment they kissed, touched, and cuddled. It always made him feel so much closer to Zalith, and it made him feel so euphoric and satisfied. It was like a blood high but so much more intoxicating, and he let it devour him.

The vampire smiled as he slowly slid himself to the side and off Zalith's body. He rested beside him and nuzzled his neck. "You make me veel so good," he breathed, placing his hand on Zalith's chest as the demon turned onto his side to face him.

Zalith laughed through his calming breaths. "Yeah?"

The vampire nodded, closing his eyes as he sunk deeper into his high. "Do you veel good?"

"You always make me feel good, baby." Zalith smiled, moving his arms around him. "Thank you for having sex with me."

Alucard's smile became a shy one as he stared into Zalith's dark eyes. "Is okay," he said, placing his hand on the side of Zalith's face. "Do you veel better now?"

"Yeah," he answered, and then he kissed his lips.

But Alucard hadn't yet severed the imprint link, and he *knew* that Zalith was still upset. It might only be a hint of sadness, but it was still there, and Alucard didn't want him to be sad *at all.* What could he do to help him, though? He knew sex would help, but he didn't have the energy to go again. His first thought was to leave the house; getting outside helped them before, and he felt it might help this time.

He frowned in concern. "Do you vant to go out?"

"Where?" Zalith asked curiously.

"To zhe Citadel. Mary-Bev told me about zhese cakes zhey do every Yule. Zhey're only sold vor zhe twelve days, and I vant to try zhem."

"What kind of cakes?"

He thought to himself, trying to recall what Mary-Beth said. "Zhey're…a box of six…and zhey all 'ave zhese little icing pictures on zhem—pictures velating to Yule. Two of zhem are chocolate, two are red velvet, and zhe ozzer two are plain sponge cake. I vant to try all of zhem."

Zalith smirked. "And maybe one day, if they're good enough, we can get our wedding cake from there once I make an honest man out of you," he teased, gently tapping the vampire's nose with his finger.

Alucard pouted and frowned at him, trying to hide his fluster. It had been a while since Zalith said anything about getting married, and it made him feel excited, nervous, and eager. He already knew he wanted to marry Zalith, and he was sure Zalith wanted to marry him, but the demon might not be ready. If he was, he would have proposed, wouldn't he? Alucard was content either way. But when he thought about it, was *he* ready? He wasn't sure, but he didn't need to lay there and think about it right now.

He sighed and shrugged. "If zhey even do vedding cakes."

"What good cake store doesn't?" Zalith asked. "When do you want to go?"

Alucard wanted to say *right now*, but he didn't want to make Zalith think they had to go immediately. "Vhenever you're veady."

Smiling, Zalith kissed his lips. "Let's get dressed," he said, sitting up.

Nodding, Alucard sat up, and as Zalith handed him his trousers, he pulled them on and made his way over to the door where his shirt was. Once they were both dressed, they left his office and headed upstairs to get ready to head for the Citadel.

Alucard worried that he left it too late, though. There were only two days of Yule left, and for all he knew, the cakes could have sold out. Either way, he was glad that he was getting Zalith out of the house.

Chapter Four

A Trip to the Citadel

| Zalith |

Zalith followed Alucard into the carriage and sat beside him after pulling the door shut. The demon hadn't bothered combing his hair back and left it loose; he didn't have the motivation to do much at all right now. He just wanted to be with Alucard—as close as he could be. His sadness quickly returned after they finished having sex, but Alucard always made him feel better, and he needed him more than ever.

When the carriage started moving, he leaned his head on Alucard's shoulder; he eased his right hand into his fur-collared cape and under his shirt and placed it on his chest, sighing quietly as he closed his eyes. He had to resist the urge to ask the vampire for anything else. Alucard was clearly already tired and the last thing Zalith wanted was to make him miss the party tonight. It would be the *first* Yule party Alucard got to experience and he didn't want to ruin it for him.

Alucard moved his arm around Zalith, resting the side of his head on Zalith's. The demon was sure that Alucard would soon ask him if he was okay, but he didn't want to talk about his feelings anymore. He knew Alucard would want to try and help, but there wasn't really anything he could do. Zalith just needed him where he was right now. He didn't want to explain his sadness, he didn't want Alucard to worry more than he already was, and he didn't want to spoil the holiday for either of them. So, he sat in silence, holding onto his vampire.

But the silence didn't bring him peace. His family had been taken away from him so easily and so quickly, and he couldn't keep himself from panicking. What if Alucard was taken away, too? What if he lost Varana? Where would he be without them? They were the only family he had left, and the familiar fear of losing them returned. He shuffled as close as he could get to Alucard, his distress starting to make it a little harder to breathe. What if Alucard died? What would he do? What *could* he do?

"Zaliv," Alucard then said worriedly. "Are you okay?"

"I'm okay, baby," he confirmed.

Alucard obviously wasn't convinced, though. He leaned forward a little so that he could see the demon's face, and as they stared at each other, the vampire said, "No, you're not." His look of concern grew as each moment passed. He moved his hand over Zalith's shoulder, fiddling with his turtleneck sweater.

Zalith frowned slightly. "Yes, I am," he mumbled sullenly.

"Is…zhis about your vamily?" he asked quietly.

The demon shrugged.

"Tell me," he pleaded.

As Zalith stared at him, the distress weighing in his heart intensified. "I don't want you to die."

"I von't die," he insisted, pulling Zalith into a hug. "Noving vill take me vrom you."

Burying his face in Alucard's cape, nuzzling the vampire's neck, Zalith shook his head. "I don't like thinking about it; it makes me feel so empty and lost. I thought that no one would ever take away my brother and my parents, but they're gone, and I'm *so* afraid to lose you, too."

"You von't," Alucard assured him. "Ve're safer zhan ve've ever been, and ve're veady in case anyving dangerous like zhat does ever 'appen. I told you bevore zhat I vant to spend my life vith you, and zhat's vhat I vill do," he said sternly, hugging the demon tightly.

But Zalith didn't respond. He sat there in Alucard's embrace, breathing deeply on his neck. His throat was tightening, and the pain in his chest worsened. He'd been so sure that he wouldn't lose his family, and he wouldn't be so naïve as to let himself believe that he and Alucard were safe. Anything could happen.

"I love you," Alucard then said.

"I love you, too," Zalith replied quietly.

"Is zhere anyving zhat vill 'elp? Anyving you vant to do?"

"No," Zalith mumbled. "I just like sitting with you." He knew that sex would help, but he had to keep fighting it. He'd taken too much energy from Alucard already today.

Alucard nodded and held him, falling silent.

When the carriage left the forest, Zalith lifted his head from Alucard's neck and stared at the vampire's face for a few moments. However, Alucard frowned despondently and looked away. Zalith was convinced that the vampire was blaming himself for how he felt, and he didn't want to let him think that he was to blame. He lightly gripped Alucard's chin and made him look at him, and then he kissed him before he could say anything.

They kissed for a while, and although Zalith knew that he should stop, Alucard didn't push him away. He kept kissing him back, almost as if he *wanted* Zalith to take his energy.

But he didn't want to take advantage of him or his endearingly kind nature. So after a few more kisses, Zalith chose to cuddle up with him instead, resting his head on Alucard's chest.

"Zaliv?" Alucard then asked.

"Hmm?" the demon murmured.

"Do you…vant to do someving avter ve get vhat ve came vor?"

"Like what?"

Alucard shrugged. "Ve could…get lunch, or…just valk or maybe ve could vind a show to go and vatch," he said nervously. "Zhey probably do a lot of zhem zhis time of year, vight?"

Zalith pondered. He didn't want to be around other people any longer than he had to, and he'd rather spend time *alone* with Alucard. He sighed and started to slowly rub his hand over Alucard's chest beneath his shirt. "I kind of want to go to the lake once we're done here, but we really don't have to; the lake isn't going anywhere."

Alucard hugged him a little tighter. "No, ve can do zhat."

"Okay," the demon replied, and then he kissed his lips a single time before returning his head to the vampire's shoulder.

And for the rest of the journey, he tried to contain his sadness without Alucard's help.

| Alucard |

Once they arrived in the Citadel, Alucard and Zalith climbed out of the carriage. The coach house was full of carriages, but all their occupants were nowhere to be seen, and as Zalith clearly noticed that, the demon took hold of Alucard's hand.

Alucard smiled at him and led the way to the street. "Do you vant anyving vrom zhe bakery? Mary-Bev told me zhe cakes are veally good."

Zalith glanced at him. "No, thank you. Perhaps we should get something for the staff, though."

The vampire nodded, and as they approached the street, Zalith let go of his hand and walked beside him as closely as he could. Alucard knew why he let go; he couldn't afford to let the people of the city know he was gay. So, they walked side by side down the busy street as they made their way to the bakery.

Once an electric streetcar passed by, followed by a horse-drawn carriage, Alucard set his eyes on the place, which sat on the other side of the road; a large sign over the glass double doors read Dale's, and the windows were decorated with paintings of cakes. It was a lot larger than he had expected—in fact, it looked almost as if it might have once been a showroom. Every window was lined with all kinds of sweet snacks and cakes, some as tall as him. There were many sets of glass doors, too, but only one had been opened, making sure too many people didn't pile into the store at once.

He saw the long line outside leading into the store, but that wasn't his main concern. What if the cakes he came for were gone? There were so many people… and many more inside, too. He frowned irritably, joining the end of the line, and as Zalith stood beside him, he glanced at him.

But Zalith had an impatient look on his face. He tugged lightly on Alucard's cape and said, "Come on," as he stepped out of line.

The vampire followed him along the line, ignoring the irritated, questioning mumbles of the people they passed. Zalith led the way into the store and over to the counter, where a tall, chubby man was serving a well-tailored aristocrat.

As Alucard followed, he diverted his eyes to the displays of cakes and snacks—there were so many things he had never seen or tried before—and he became so distracted by the rows of colourfully decorated cakes that he almost walked into Zalith when he stopped by the counter.

"Be careful, darling," the demon said quietly with a smirk, placing his hand on his shoulder.

"Sorry," Alucard mumbled, embarrassed.

Zalith took his hand off him and looked at the chubby man, who was serving the tailored patron. "Good afternoon, Dale," the demon called.

The server instantly took his eyes off the patron and sharply turned his head to look at Zalith. His once-vacant face lit up, and as he smiled brightly, he shook his head in what might be disbelief. "Zalith?" he called. "I didn't expect I'd see you here. Come, come," he invited, shooing away his current customer and inviting Zalith and Alucard to cut in line.

As the tailored man exclaimed in disbelief, Zalith made his way over, and Alucard followed.

"Well, we heard about the delicious Yule cakes from Norman's wife, and we simply couldn't stay away," the demon said with a smile, resting one of his arms on the counter.

"Ah, yes, yes." Dale nodded, reaching over to a table behind him lined with white boxes. He picked one up and placed it on the counter. Inside were six cupcakes, and all of them were decorated with frosting and little pictures made out of icing sugar. "They've been quite popular this year. Is this all you've come for?" he asked, clearly sure that Zalith must have come for more than one box of cakes.

Zalith looked at Alucard. "Did you want anything else?"

Alucard glanced around, and despite there being so many things, he didn't actually want any of it. "No," he answered.

The demon then looked back at Dale. "I'd like…four dozen of your assorted Yule cookies, six croissants, six chocolate-covered croissants, and a cherry loaf, please," he said. "Oh, and four of those chocolate eclairs," he added, nodding at a display full of chocolate eclairs.

"Of course," Dale said excitedly. "Just give me a moment to bring it all over, please."

Nodding as Dale wandered off, Zalith turned his attention back to Alucard.

"Vhat's all zhat vor?" Alucard asked.

"Well, the cookies are for the staff, *we* can have the croissants for breakfast over the next few days, and the cherry loaf and eclairs are for us. Two eclairs are for Varana, though," he explained.

Alucard smiled in response and glanced around the room again, waiting for Dale to return with their items.

"Alucard," Zalith then said, tapping his arm.

"Vhat?" he asked, looking at him.

Smirking, Zalith glanced at something. "Look, they *do* have wedding cakes."

Alucard took his eyes off the demon to look at a tall, six-tier wedding cake on display in its own glass cabinet. It was as white as the walls, decorated with icing sugar and flower-shaped fondant. The longer he stared, however, the wider Zalith's smile seemed to grow, and the more embarrassed Alucard felt. He took his eyes off both the cake and looked away. "Zhey do," he mumbled.

Clearly amused, Zalith laughed quietly.

Dale then returned with everything Zalith asked for and started packing it into a large box.

Alucard wanted to get Zalith something. "Are you sure you zon't vant anyving?"

Zalith glanced at him, sighed, and looked around the room. "I don't know."

Alucard stared at the display in front of them. He knew Zalith wasn't exactly keen on sugary snacks and sweets, but there had to be *something* here that he'd like. It took him a moment, but he set his eyes on something that the demon would surely eat. "Vone of zhem, too," he said to Dale, pointing at a row of apple fritters.

"Sure thing." Dale grabbed one and packed it up.

"I'd like you to have this sent over to my carriage, please," Zalith then said. "It's parked in the east coach house."

"You got it," Dale said—

"Vait, I vant zhat now," Alucard said, pointing to the apple fritter.

Smiling, Dale handed the wrapped-up apple fritter to Alucard.

"Vank you."

"Will that be all?" Dale asked, setting his eyes back on Zalith.

"It will, thank you," Zalith said, placing both the payment and a tip for Dale on the counter. "Happy Yule," he said with a smile before turning around to leave.

"You, too!" Dale called, waving goodbye.

They left the store, ignoring the side-glares and annoyed mutters from the crowd waiting to get inside.

Alucard walked beside Zalith as they traversed the busy street. He held the wrapped-up fritter, waiting for the right moment to give it to him. A small snack probably wouldn't cheer Zalith up, but that didn't stop him from wanting to at least try.

When they turned onto another street, one that wasn't as busy as the last, Alucard held the pastry out to the demon. "Zhis is vor you," he said quietly.

Zalith looked at him, glanced down at the wrapped apple fritter, and then smirked. "Thank you, baby," he said, taking it from him. He then opened it, tore it in half, and offered a piece to Alucard. "Where are we headed next?"

The vampire took a bite of the fritter and pondered. He wanted to pick up a few more gifts, and upon noticing a pet store, he said, "Zhe pet store."

Zalith frowned anxiously. "What do you need from there?"

He shrugged and teased, "I zon't know…maybe a cat, or…anozzer dog—maybe an 'amster, who knows?"

Zalith's stare of dread thickened—

"I'm joking," Alucard laughed and took another bite of the apple fritter.

With a smile slowly appearing on his face, Zalith nodded slightly. "I was scared you might *not* have been joking for a moment. If you do want another pet, though, it's okay…I'd get over myself."

Alucard shook his head. "I zon't need anozzer pet vight now. I vant to get some vings vor Sabazios," he said, remembering that he only got two things for his hound.

Zalith laughed a little. "What a lucky dog he is," he said, finishing his half of the apple fritter.

"Do you need to go anyvhere vhile ve're 'ere?" Alucard asked as they approached the pet store.

"I don't think so."

"Okay," Alucard answered, stopping outside the pet store. For a moment, he had to tell himself that he was only there to get a few things for Sabazios; he knew how he was…how he'd see one cute animal and end up buying three of them. He wasn't going to do that today. Zalith was already stressed out, and he didn't want to add to that by bringing another animal home.

While Zalith followed behind him, Alucard walked through the pet store. The walls were lined with shelves of pet accessories, treats, and foods. A pungent smell of sawdust and straw lingered in the air, and the clicks and chirps of each animal on offer travelled through the open space of the centre of the shop, where the owner was sitting in the middle of a circular desk. The tired-looking pensioner had a parrot perched on a makeshift branch to his left, and as he scribbled into a small book, the parrot crunched loudly on a piece of kibble.

Alucard glanced at Zalith and saw that he didn't look particularly happy to be there, but Alucard wasn't going to take long. He already got Sabazios a collar—something he thought was mandatory now that he was a house dog—but he also wanted to get him some treats.

"Afternoon," the store owner called, setting his eyes on them both. "Do you need help with anything?"

"No," Alucard called back. "Vank you."

Nodding, the man went back to writing as Alucard led the way through the store to the dog section.

"Did you get someving vor 'im?" the vampire asked, looking at Zalith.

When they stopped in the dog section, Zalith frowned in confliction. "Admittedly, I didn't think about it. But I'll get him something now. What does he like?" he asked, glancing at the many shelves of dog toys, treats, and accessories.

"Hmm," Alucard murmured, looking around. "You could just get 'im someving vrom zhere," he said, pointing at a shelf of small dog treat packets.

The demon looked at the shelf for a few moments but then set his eyes back on Alucard and frowned unsurely. "What would he like the most?"

Alucard wouldn't lie that he found it endearing that Zalith really didn't know what he was doing when it came to animals and pets; the demon was so good with people, reading them and working them, but when it came to animals, he didn't know much at all. Alucard loved that, and he loved to be able to teach Zalith something once in a while.

He stopped looking at the accessories and escorted Zalith over to the shelf of treats. "Alzhough 'e is old in age, 'is body is still zhat of a puppy, so…zon't get 'im anyving zhat says is vor any older zhan two years. 'E's just over vone year," he started, pointing to a row of small treats. "'E also zoesn't like duck, so zon't get vones vith zhat. 'Is vavourite vight now is turkey, but 'e changes 'is mind a lot."

Staring at the dog treats, Zalith kept his perturbed frown and reached for one of the smaller bags—

"Zhose pieces are too small vor 'im; 'e von't eat zhem," Alucard said before Zalith could pick it up. He then watched as the demon chose a larger bag of turkey-flavoured treats from the shelf and looked at him for confirmation. "'E'll like zhose," the vampire told him.

Zalith smiled in relief as he turned to face him.

Alucard also smiled but looked down to hide his nervous face. "I vink is cute zhat you zon't veally know a lot about animals but know so much about people."

The demon laughed slightly as he moved his free hand to Alucard's shoulder. "Thank you. You're right though," he said, his smile becoming a smirk, "the closest thing I have ever had to a pet is you; I make sure you have everything you need, I feed you, I groom you, and I enrich you," he teased.

Pouting in embarrassment, Alucard scowled at him. "I'm *not* your pet," he grumbled, "I'm your boyvriend."

Zalith laughed quietly. "Thank God I'm your boyfriend because I do a lot of other things to you that one shouldn't do to a pet."

As his fluster grew, Alucard turned his back on Zalith and glared at the dog toys. He was still trying to feel more confident about receiving compliments and saying nice or cute things to Zalith, but he still hadn't gotten used to the fact that most of Zalith's responses made him feel like this. But he'd get used to it…someday. "Get vone of zhese vor 'im, too," he mumbled, looking down at the toys.

Still laughing quietly, Zalith lightly gripped Alucard's jaw and made him look at him. Then, after making sure that they couldn't be seen from where they were standing, he kissed the vampire's lips. But he didn't stop with one; the demon continued kissing him for a few moments.

When the store door opened, however, and the entry bell rang, Alucard flinched in startle and stopped kissing the demon, pulling away from him as he looked over his shoulder to make sure whoever came in hadn't seen. As much as he enjoyed kissing Zalith, he didn't want to risk him losing his reputation because he'd been caught kissing a man in the back of a pet store. So, he turned his attention back to the dog toys.

But Zalith moved his hand to the side of Alucard's face and smiled at him, and as Alucard stared back, he smiled, too.

"Get zhis vor 'im," the vampire said, handing Zalith a dog ball. "Zhen you can play vetch vith 'im, no?" he said, smirking.

"Okay," Zalith agreed. "Thank you."

Alucard picked up a few different dog snacks and treats and then started leading the way to the counter to pay. On his way, though, a flicker of white in the corner of his eye caught his attention. He stopped walking, stared to his right, and watched as a white-bellied, dull-yellow python slowly slithered up the glass of its enclosure, searching for an escape.

The moment he set his eyes on it, Alucard knew he had to get closer; he changed course, heading towards the snake enclosure instead of the counter as Zalith followed behind him.

He stood in front of the glass. The snake stopped for a moment, flicking its purple tongue, eyeing him up and down before returning to searching for a way out. Alucard told himself that he wasn't going to get any more animals, but…the snake's dull-yellow body, its dark green eyes, and the way it slithered through the leaflitter of its home so effortlessly *enticed* the vampire.... He wanted it.

He looked at Zalith. "I vant zhis."

Zalith glanced at the snake and then frowned at Alucard. "What are you going to do with it?"

"Look avter 'im," he answered.

He smiled slightly. "Where are you going to *keep* it?"

"In...zhis," Alucard said, tapping the wooden enclosure. "In my ovvice."

Zalith nodded slowly. "What does it eat?"

Alucard looked down at the snake as it moved through its enclosure. "Mice," he said.

"Where are you going to get mice from?"

"Zhis store."

Staring at him, Zalith obviously thought to himself for a few moments but then nodded. "Okay, I'll get it for you, but I don't want it or mice running around the house."

"You zon't 'ave to get 'im vor me," Alucard said with a frown. "I can get 'im."

Zalith smiled slightly. "Are you sure? I like getting things for you," he said contently.

Taking his eyes off Zalith, Alucard looked back down at the snake. He felt terrible that Zalith was paying for everything, but he did know that Zalith liked to buy things for him and pay for whatever they did, and right now, Alucard still wanted to do whatever he could to help Zalith feel better. So, he looked back at him and nodded. "Okay," he agreed.

Smiling, Zalith discreetly tapped the vampire's ass with his hand and led the way to the counter. "Let's pay for everything."

With a pout, Alucard followed the demon. He wasn't sure if they'd go anywhere else before heading home, but he was overall content with their day so far and was sure that it was going to get better for them both once they headed home and went to the lake as Zalith requested. He was certain that the party tonight would be fun, too, but after hearing how Zalith felt about Yule, Alucard would keep doing his best to make sure he was okay.

Chapter Five

Feelings

| Alucard |

Alucard and Zalith relaxed on the patio bench outside Zalith's office. They hadn't yet gone to the lake; Alucard wanted to wait for the staff to move his new pet enclosure into the house, and he also wanted to give the demon a little time to rest before heading out again.

The vampire lay on his back with his head against one of the cushions, and Zalith was resting on top of him with his head against his chest. Alucard enjoyed it when Zalith clung to him, but he knew that the demon was still sad, and the more he thought about it, the more he tried to figure out what to do for him. All he knew, though, was what Zalith said he needed him to do, and that was to lay there and be there for him. So he didn't say anything. He wasn't going to persist. Zalith would talk to him when he was ready.

He moved his hand to the back of the demon's head and gently caressed his hair. Worry wasn't the only thing he was currently feeling, though. The moment they got home, Alucard's fatigue became harder to fight. He'd managed to ignore it throughout their trip to the Citadel, but now that they were relaxing, he was beginning to realize just how exhausted he was.

"Are you looking forward to the party?" Zalith asked, snapping the vampire out of his thoughts.

Alucard did his best to try and banish his fatigue. "I am. Are you?"

"I can't wait to start drinking," the demon said with a quiet laugh, "and I'm looking forward to dancing with you."

"I'm looking vorvard to dancing, too; ve varely get to do zhat."

"Well, we should do it more but there's never any music playing."

Alucard *did* like the idea of being able to dance with him more; it was one of his favourite things to do with Zalith. "Maybe zhere should be music playing, zhen ve'd dance more," he mumbled. He was sure that his tiredness made him sound as though he was grumpy even though he wasn't…was he? He sighed quietly and turned his head to stare at the gardens.

"Should we hire a pianist to play a few times a week?" Zalith suggested.

The vampire shrugged lightly. "Ve can."

Zalith fiddled with Alucard's hair. "Are you sleepy, baby?"

Alucard pouted stubbornly. "No," he grumbled despite the fact that he *was* tired. But he didn't want to sleep the day away. It was Yule, and he wanted to spend all day with Zalith, especially before the party; they might not be able to be as clingy once their guests arrived. But as each moment passed, Alucard felt himself sinking deeper and deeper into his fatigue. It seemed as though drinking Zalith's blood to make up for his lost energy hadn't helped as much as it did the first time.

Laughing quietly, Zalith rested his chin on Alucard's chest and looked up at him. "Do you need a nap?"

"No," he answered. "Ve vere going to zhe lake."

"You're tired, baby. Let's just go upstairs and take a nap. I don't mind if we don't go."

With his stubbornness lingering, Alucard sighed and glared up at the afternoon sky. "I zon't vant to sleep all day. I vant to spend all day vith *you.*"

Zalith sat up slightly, leaning over Alucard so that he could stare down at him. "We can nap together just for a few hours, and then we can spend the whole party together. And later, we'll even get to sleep in the same bed," he said, smirking.

Alucard frowned reluctantly. He felt selfish; he knew he couldn't help that he was tired—after all, it *was* because of Zalith that he was so exhausted—but he wasn't doing much to try and keep himself from giving in to his fatigue. Zalith said he wanted to go to the lake, and Alucard wanted to make sure he got to go, but he was sure that once they got there, he might fall asleep.

He exhaled with a quiet huff and turned his head to the side again—

"Okay, come on," Zalith said, getting up. "Nap time."

Alucard groaned reluctantly as Zalith moved his arms under him and started picking him up. But he didn't fight or refuse. As the demon scooped him up, he moved his arms around Zalith's shoulders and nuzzled his neck.

Zalith carried the vampire into the house, through his office, and upstairs to their bedroom. He gently put Alucard in bed and then started helping him undress. Once Zalith was also undressed, he climbed into bed with him and rested his head on Alucard's shoulder.

Alucard's exhaustion grew heavier now that he was resting somewhere more comfortable. He rolled onto his left side, and when Zalith wrapped his arms around him, the demon rested the side of his head on Alucard's.

"Thank you for being here for me, Alucard," Zalith said quietly. "I know I'm frustrating to deal with sometimes."

"You're not vrustrating to deal vith," Alucard mumbled.

The demon fiddled with the vampire's hair again. "You're very sweet, Alucard. I love you."

Alucard smiled. "I love you, too."

Zalith huffed and said, "I feel guilty. You're tired because of *me*—because we had sex twice within an hour. Even now I feel like I want more; it's the only way I know to deal with my emotions for a little while when I get like this. And…I wish I *wasn't* this," he lamented. "I wish I didn't need to take your energy or have sex all the time just to feel okay, and I don't want you to feel like you *have* to have sex with me."

"Zaliv, is okay, I promise. I vant to 'elp you, and I vant to 'ave sex vith you," he replied, trying to keep himself from becoming flustered.

The demon sighed and tightened his embrace around him. "It's probably going to be like this every Yule. I'm sorry. I want to try and control myself for your sake, but I just…I—"

Alucard squeezed Zalith's hand. "Sleep vith me," he said as he felt himself giving in. "I love you just zhe vay you are, and you zon't need to change, okay?"

He nodded in response.

Then, Alucard let himself sink. His fatigue consumed him, and he slowly drifted off to sleep.

↞❖↠

Alucard woke to a familiar darkness. The same murmurs of suffering echoed around him, and he found himself searching again. But for what? For who? He still didn't know. All he knew was that was why he was here…to search, to long, to wander. The desperation strangled his heart, inflicting a feeling of loss so deep that he was sure he'd been crying before he came here. But why? Why did he keep returning to this place? And this feeling…. What did it mean?

This time, however, he was able to move. And so he did. He walked forward, searching the dark for any sign of why he might be there…for any sign that he wasn't alone.

He stopped when a hum broke through the bitter wails of hopelessness. As he looked over his shoulder, he set his eyes on something other than darkness—a window, perhaps? A wall that appeared to be glass, revealing a glimpse of a world outside the endless black. Through it, all Alucard could see were brick walls and white marble floors. He'd not seen such a place before, but he'd not have any time to try and work out where it might be.

With a quiet exhale, he opened his eyes to the warmth of his bed and Zalith's arms around him. For a moment, he gazed aimlessly; the weight of his fatigue hadn't waned as much as he'd like, but he felt better than earlier, and that was all that mattered.

"Alucard?" Zalith asked quietly.

He murmured in response.

"Are you okay?"

The vampire nodded and glanced at the window, seeing that the once bright blue sky had become dull and grey. "Vhat's zhe time?"

"It's about five," the demon answered, hugging him a little tighter.

Alucard rolled onto his right side, turning to face Zalith. "Do you veel better?" he asked as Zalith stared into his eyes.

Zalith placed his hand on the side of Alucard's face after moving a strand of his crimson hair away from his eye. "Mostly," he answered.

Alucard frowned. "Vhat do you mean?"

He smiled slightly. "That most of me feels better."

"Vhy only most?" Alucard asked, staring at him. Although a smile was on Zalith's face, he could see the sadness in his dark eyes.

Zalith kept his hand on the side of Alucard's face. "I don't feel completely better, but I feel *mostly* better."

Alucard's concern worsened. He wanted to know why Zalith didn't feel totally better; he wanted to try and understand so that he could help him. If the situation were reversed, Zalith would know *exactly* what to do for him. Of course, Alucard knew he was sad because he missed his family, but Zalith had only really touched on the subject and refused to tell him anything more. Why? Alucard wasn't sure, but he had to *try* and get him to talk about it. How else would he understand? He was tired of sitting around trying to work out why Zalith wouldn't tell him these things—why Zalith wouldn't completely open up to him. He *always* told the demon everything he'd need to know to understand, so why wouldn't Zalith do the same?

"Do you vant to talk about vhat's vrong?" the vampire asked.

The demon, however, smiled and said, "No."

Alucard pouted irritably. "Vhy?"

He shrugged a little. "Because I don't want to."

"Vhy?" he asked again as his irritancy started becoming anger, but he tried his best not to let it get to him. He felt guilty for feeling so angry at him… for feeling so frustrated that Zalith refused to explain to him why he wouldn't talk about his sadness. How else was he supposed to understand if Zalith wouldn't tell him?

"Because it feels wrong," the demon answered as his smile faded.

Alucard frowned strangely. "Vhy does veel vrong?"

"Because I never really talk about how I feel…other than feelings that are obvious to others."

"Zhen…vhy von't you tell *me*? I vant to know 'ow you veel—'ow you *veally* veel," he said, moving his hand to the side of Zalith's neck.

The demon continued to stare at him but with distress in his eyes. "Because…I'm not allowed to."

"Vhat?"

"It's not really that, but…I grew up under the impression that no one wants to hear it, and I shouldn't be burdening people with my emotions, so I just…never do," he explained, "and because of that, it doesn't feel right when I do it because I don't want to make a fuss."

Alucard tried to work out what to say. He didn't know enough about how a parent raised their child to comment on Zalith's upbringing, but if there was one thing that Zalith taught him, it was that someone shouldn't suppress their emotions, especially one such as sadness. Alucard spent his entire life hiding his sorrow, and it turned him into a cold, lonely creature, something he was only just beginning to break free from, and that was thanks to Zalith. He didn't want Zalith to feel the way he had; he didn't want Zalith to live thinking that he had to ignore his emotions. He wanted Zalith to know that he could tell him *anything*.

"Vell, I *vant* you to tell me. I vant to know 'ow you veel because…zhis matters. You matter to me, and so does 'ow you veel. You're not making a vuss or burdening me or anyving like zhat because I *vant* to know. Is zhe same as vhen you ask me 'ow *I* veel. I zon't vant to say, but you vant to know, so I tell you because I know zhat matters to you. I zon't know vhat's vrong, and I zon't know vhat to do ozzer zhan keep asking you to tell me," he insisted softly.

The demon frowned hesitantly. "I understand…and I can try, but I'm old as hell, and I've been living like this for a long time, Alucard."

"And I lived a similar vay vor all my life, too, but you 'elped me get over zhat, and I vant to try and 'elp you."

Gazing at him, Zalith donned a sullen expression and started fiddling with Alucard's hair.

"So…tell me," Alucard urged.

For a moment, Zalith hesitated. It looked like he was pondering…but then he stared into Alucard's eyes. "I feel like…I've done so many things I shouldn't have done and hurt so many people; I feel that karma has finally started catching up with me. I lost my home, my family, and my friends. The vast majority of the people I was supposed to protect have died, and now I'm worried that I'll lose the rest of them. I'm worried that I'll lose the house, V, and *you*. It's a feeling that I just…can't shake," he explained as the anxious tone in his voice thickened.

Alucard frowned despondently and guided his hand to the side of the demon's face. "Vell, everyvone 'as done vings zhey shouldn't 'ave—vings zhat zhey vegret—but your past zoesn't devine you, Zaliv. Zhe vings zhat 'ave 'appened to you 'aven't 'appened because you deserve zhem, zhey just 'appened…" he said. Then, he moved as close as he could and rested his forehead against Zalith's. "I'm not going anyvhere. No vone vill take me vrom you, no vone vill take you vrom me, and ve vill keep each ozzer and everyving ve care about safe *togezzer*. I zon't like Varana, but I know zhat…you love 'er, and I vill 'elp you to protect 'er if ever comes to zhat. You deserve to be 'appy, and I vill do vhatever I can to make zhat 'appen. I love you so much, and zhere isn't anyving I vouldn't do vor you."

Staring at him, Zalith smiled and kissed Alucard's lips. "Thank you," he said, moving his hand to the side of his face, but he still looked upset. He sighed quietly and said, "I'll be right back—stay here," and kissed the vampire's forehead.

As Zalith got out of bed and pulled on his trousers, Alucard remained where he was, watching as the demon smiled back at him before leaving their room. Alucard wasn't sure where he might be going, but he'd wait. And he wasn't sure if what he said had actually made Zalith feel better, but…what more could he do? He said what he said, and he meant it with all his heart. He loved Zalith, he deserved to be happy, and Alucard would do whatever it took to make sure he knew that.

Chapter Six

Stories

| Alucard |

Zalith returned to the bedroom not long later. Alucard smiled at him as he walked over to their bed, and when the demon sat down and shuffled closer to him, he held out one of the cupcakes they bought earlier.

"I got you a snack," Zalith said with a smirk.

Alucard took it from him and said, "Vank you." He glanced down at the white icing-covered cupcake. "Do you vant some?"

"I do," Zalith said, taking the cake from him. He pulled the paper from the bottom of the cake, placed it on his nightstand, and took a bite of the cake. He smiled contently, glancing at Alucard. But as his smile became an unseemly smirk, the demon dragged his thumb over the icing. He then held his thumb out to Alucard. "It's really good," he said, waiting for him to try it.

The moment Zalith adorned that same flirty smile he always did when he had sex on his mind, Alucard felt his once tired, irritated thoughts begin to wither. His nervousness increased—it always did, and Alucard knew it always would no matter how confident he was. But he liked the fact that Zalith's intentions made him feel anxious because he never knew what to expect.

Alucard leaned in, his breath hitching slightly as his fingers curled around Zalith's wrist, guiding the demon's icing-covered thumb towards his lips. He parted them slowly, clamping down on the thumb with a teasing pressure, his eyes locking onto Zalith's as he drew the sweet taste into his mouth. His tongue swirled against the icing, savouring the flavour, but there was no denying the heat beneath the playful act. Slowly, deliberately, he pulled Zalith's thumb back, dragging it out of his mouth with a soft, slick sound that sent a shiver down his spine.

Zalith's smirk widened, clearly enjoying the moment. Without breaking eye contact, the demon pushed his thumb back in, the gesture slower this time, more intimate.

Alucard's embarrassment deepened, a scowl forming on his lips, but it only fuelled the fire between them. The subtle tension was electric, and Zalith's quiet laugh sent a thrill through him.

The demon removed his thumb, fingers brushing against Alucard's cheek as his hand shifted to cradle the side of his face. In the next instant, Zalith's lips were on his, capturing Alucard in a hungry kiss before he even had time to swallow the sweet remnants of icing still lingering in his mouth. The kiss was firm and demanding, and the vampire felt his control slipping as the demon's touch sent sparks of heat through his body.

But Alucard wasn't about to let Zalith have all the fun. While the demon's focus was on the kiss, Alucard moved swiftly, snatching the remaining cupcake from Zalith's hand in one fluid motion. He broke the kiss, pulling back with a teasing scowl that only deepened the tension between them, the lingering taste of icing still clinging to his lips as he met Zalith's gaze with a challenging gleam in his eyes.

Zalith laughed amusedly in response. "You're so cute." He edged his face closer to Alucard's as the vampire took a bite of the cake. "But you shouldn't eat in bed."

Alucard pouted. "You just gave zhis to me in bed. Do you vant me to go over zhere and eat?" he protested, glancing at the window.

The demon rested his forehead against Alucard's and smiled. "I'm joking," he said, tucking a loose strand of the vampire's hair behind his ear.

The vampire finished the cupcake and laid back down, exhaling quietly. Zalith got back into the blankets and rested beside him with his head on his chest. For a short while, they lay in silence as the sky darkened; Alucard wasn't sure if Zalith might want to talk or not, but he seemed to be content relaxing with him, so he'd wait and continue enjoying Zalith's embrace.

But the demon soon glanced up at him. "Will you tell me a story, baby?"

Alucard glanced down at him. "Vhat kind of story?"

The demon shrugged. "Something…nice."

Looking back up at the ceiling, Alucard thought to himself for a few moments. Nothing came to mind…but he didn't want to disappoint him, and he also wanted to amuse Zalith; perhaps making him laugh would help him to forget his sadness for a little while longer.

He moved his arm around the demon. "Vell…a vhile ago, I met zhis zemon outside a tavern in Dor-Sanguis," he started. "I vanted noving to do vith 'im, so I told 'im to fuck off. Zhat same night, I vas called to meet Zamien, and I zon't know vhy I zidn't suspect zhat vould 'ave someving to do vith zhat same zemon. Anyvay, I vent zhere, ve met again, and I knew immediately zhat I vasn't going to like 'im. 'E vas as all zemons are, no? Vude, arrogant, and vhought 'e vas better zhan everyvone else."

Zalith laughed quietly. "Demons are truly awful," he agreed.

Alucard smiled. "But Zamien vanted me to vork vith 'im, so I 'ad no choice," he continued, and Zalith started slowly dragging his fingers over the vampire's chest. "I vasn't content; I vas angrier zhan I 'ad been in a long time because Zamien knew I zidn't vant to vork vith *anyvone*, let alone zemons, but I guess 'e vhought zhat vas vunny to expose me like zhat. I kept my secrets 'idden vrom zhis zemon, zhough; but vor some veason, zhis zemon started to talk to me as if ve vere more zhan vork partners," he said, frowning as Zalith's fingers started moving from his chest to his abs. "I vasn't intervested, and I made zhat clear, but 'e still zidn't get zhat I zidn't vant to be anyving more zhan associates."

"What did he do?" Zalith asked with what seemed like curiosity and concern in his voice, almost as if he wasn't sure whether or not Alucard was actually talking about him.

But that only made Alucard smile more. "'E vould just insert 'imselv into my life, show up at my 'ouse…and zhen vone day, I decided to stop being so standoffish and let 'im in. Ve vent on a date."

Zalith gently stroked his fingers down past Alucard's abs. "Oh, wow," he said, "that's a big step. How did it go?"

Anticipation quickly shivered through Alucard's body the moment the demon's fingers reached his inner thigh. "Vent…okay," he answered, staring up at the ceiling. "I still vasn't sure 'ow to veel, but I vas starting to like 'im."

"What was he like?" the demon asked, trailing the tips of two of his fingers over Alucard's crotch.

Still frowning, Alucard tried to ignore his arousal. "'E vas…divverent," he answered. "'E zidn't look down on me, 'e zidn't belittle me, and 'e devended me in vront of Zamien," he said, noticing that Zalith's affection was rushing him to bring his story to an end. "And…'e taught me zhat I zidn't 'ave to spend my entire life alone."

"He sounds very kind and very handsome," Zalith said, stroking Alucard's shaft.

The vampire laughed quietly in amusement, trying to ignore his growing angst; he knew Zalith wanted to see him react, and he wasn't going to give him the satisfaction. "'E is…zhe kindest, most 'andsome man I know," he agreed.

"How did everything work out?"

Pouting, ignoring Zalith's touch, Alucard shrugged. "Vell…ve started dating," he said, tensing up as the caress of Zalith's fingers became harder to dismiss. "Ve…spent a lot of time togezzer, and zhen…ve moved in togezzer," he said with a frown of struggle. "And 'e spends an awvul lot of time trying to vrustrate me," he snarled, reaching below the blanket and snatching Zalith's wrist.

The demon laughed. "Maybe it's because you're so cute—I mean, that's why *I* do it," he said with a smirk, and then he leaned closer and kissed Alucard's lips.

Pouting, Alucard glared back up at the ceiling. "Vhatever," he mumbled.

"Did you like it?" the demon then asked.

His embarrassment didn't settle, so he shrugged and kept glaring ahead. "Maybe."

"Maybe? Well, maybe *I* should just stop if it's that underwhelming," he said with a dramatic sigh. "I'm losing my touch, I see…I just might never be intimate with you ever again," he said sullenly, but Alucard knew there was a smile on his face.

He frowned, unsure of how to respond. "Is…not undervhemling," he said quietly. "Just…makes me veel *over*vhemled…and I zon't know vhat to say—but I *zidn't* say stop," he grumbled, moving Zalith's hand back to his crotch.

Smirking, Zalith leaned over Alucard so that he could stare down at his face, and as he gripped the vampire's dick in his hand and started to gently caress it, he began kissing the vampire.

As they kissed, Alucard moved his hand to the back of Zalith's head. What was once growing anticipation was now excitement; despite the fact that he knew the energy he'd regained from his nap would disappear if they continued, Alucard felt eager for Zalith's affection.

They hadn't been kissing very long when Alucard decided that Zalith's hand wasn't enough; he pushed Zalith's face away from his and down under the blanket. Alucard kept his hand on Zalith's head, sighing impatiently because the demon didn't immediately take his shaft into his mouth. Instead, Zalith slowly dragged his tongue over it, and as both angst and desperation shivered through Alucard's body, he scowled in struggle and huffed impatiently.

He heard Zalith laugh beneath the covers, but the demon didn't make him wait a moment longer. As the demon moved his mouth over the vampire's dick, Alucard exhaled deeply in relief. His irritancy faded, and the warmth of Zalith's soothing lips around his shaft alleviated him. He murmured pleasurably as he lay there, allowing himself to become enthralled in the moment, but the moment didn't last as long as he might like.

Zalith soon stopped sucking the vampire's dick and kissed his way back up his body until he reached his face. He stared at Alucard's perplexed expression, gently stroking his cheek with his thumb. "Fuck me," he said, but his request sounded more like a demand.

It was a demand, however, that Alucard would oblige to. He nodded shyly and watched as excitement accompanied Zalith's smile.

"Where do you want me?" the demon asked with a grin.

Alucard wasn't sure, but he didn't want to lay there and think about it for an unnecessary amount of time. So, he gripped Zalith's arms and sat up; as the demon smiled curiously, Alucard made Zalith lay on his side. He thought such a position would be easier on his own body; he already felt his regained energy waning as each moment passed, but he didn't want to ignore his desires, nor did he want to disappoint Zalith. He wanted to do whatever he could for the demon, and he knew he needed this, so he'd not let his body stop him.

As Zalith pulled his trousers off, Alucard lay behind him and moved his arms around him. He kissed the demon's neck, making Zalith sigh in both anticipation and relief, and as he slowly dragged his hand down to grip Zalith's waist, the demon reached over to his nightstand and swiftly handed Alucard the small bottle of lube that he kept inside. Alucard eagerly smothered both his own dick and the demon's ass with it, and as he started to ease his shaft inside the demon, Zalith hummed pleasurably.

Alucard thrusted slowly, gripping Zalith's waist with his left hand as he nuzzled the side of his neck, breathing deeply. He pulled Zalith's body back every time he moved his own forward, listening to the demon's quiet sighs of pleasure. His own enjoyment, however, didn't feel as intoxicating as it usually would, and he was sure that had something to do with his disappearing strength. But he enjoyed it, nonetheless; drowning, alleviating pleasure made its way through his body as he continued moving his dick into and out of Zalith, and as the demon moaned, he gripped hold of Alucard's hand and held it against his chest.

With his heart racing, Alucard exhaled deeply on the demon's neck. He felt as if he might bite, but he could only seem to focus on one thing at a time, so he didn't. He started thrusting a little faster as Zalith let go of his hand and caressed his own shaft. But Alucard didn't want him to have to do anything himself. He might not be able to make him climax like this, but he was going to do it *somehow*. He pulled Zalith closer, sighing pleasurably into the demon's ear. But Zalith then laughed through his moans when Alucard snatched his wrist to stop him from touching himself.

The vampire pouted and moved faster; a grimace of struggle stole his pleased expression as he sunk deeper into the delight. But the closer he came to his peak, the more fatigued he began to feel. His body was trembling, his heart was racing, and in an attempt to ignore his tire, he gripped Zalith's waist a little *too* hard, and his claws cut his skin. But the demon seemed to enjoy it; he moaned contently as he grasped Alucard's wrist, and when he gritted his teeth in struggle, Alucard buried his face in Zalith's neck. As the vampire climaxed, he whined pleasurably, but a strange feeling of discomfort followed. He could feel his body succumbing to his fatigue, and his eyes were getting heavy.

As Zalith moved his palm over Alucard's hand, the vampire frowned and sat up, denying himself rest. He wasn't done yet. The vampire gripped Zalith's arm and turned him so that he was on his back and then disappeared beneath the covers before Zalith could say a word. He gripped Zalith's waist once more with his right hand, and with his left, he took hold of the demon's thick, hard dick. Ignoring his exhaustion, he moved his mouth over its tip, dragging his tongue over its length as he listened to Zalith's content, somewhat exhilarated moan.

Zalith moved his hand beneath the covers and lightly gripped a fistful of Alucard's hair as the vampire continued sucking him. Alucard felt the very last of his strength waning, but he enjoyed knowing that he was satisfying Zalith. He *wanted* to keep going, but he felt he might not be able to ignore his exhaustion much longer.

He held on, though, listening to Zalith's pleasured mumbles. The demon's body was tensing up; Zalith gripped Alucard's hair a little tighter, his frantic breathing accompanied by pleased moans. And then he stopped fidgeting and whined loudly in satisfaction, climaxing as Alucard groaned in satisfaction. He felt the demon's warm cum ooze into his mouth, and as he swallowed it, a great sense of relief washed over him. But when he went to drag himself up to rest his head on Zalith's chest, he felt like he wasn't going to make it that far, so he instead rested it against the demon's stomach and sighed deeply, relaxing at last.

However, his fatigue hit him like a fist to his face. It pulled him further and further from the world, and he didn't fight it. He let himself drift off to sleep, giving in to what his body had been pleading for him to do since the moment he woke up.

| Zalith |

Zalith felt so overwhelmingly satisfied. But guilt started warping his relief as he lay there, staring up at the ceiling while he waited for his racing heart to calm. He knew that Alucard was exhausted; he'd done so much for him today. The vampire seemed to have pretty much collapsed, and he might have even decided to let himself fall asleep the moment he stopped.

"Alucard?" Zalith asked, lifting the blanket to look down at what he could see of the vampire.

He didn't respond.

Zalith frowned worriedly. "Alucard?"

The vampire murmured a sound in response.

"Hey," he said with a relieved smile, caressing the vampire's hair as he pulled the blanket aside so that he'd not have to hold it up to see him. "I want you to have some of my blood."

But Alucard didn't respond. He lay there, his grip on Zalith's waist slowly loosening as he sighed quietly.

"You've been through a lot today, baby." Zalith frowned in worry. "Please?" he pleaded. "I want you to feel better."

Alucard took a moment but slowly dragged his face closer to Zalith's waist and bit down close to where his claws had cut into his skin. Zalith flinched, trying his best not to utter a sound in response to the euphoria that Alucard's bite gave him, but Alucard didn't bite for long. After a few seconds, he pulled his fangs from Zalith's body and rested his head back on his stomach.

Zalith's guilt grew. He knew he'd exhausted Alucard; he'd asked so much of him and taken a lot today that he couldn't *not* feel guilty—selfish, actually. Even after he'd told himself he'd not ask for anything intimate from Alucard again today, he'd just initiated something *again*, and Alucard seemed to be struggling a whole lot more than he had before.

"I'm sorry you feel so tired baby," he said sullenly. "It's my fault."

Alucard didn't say anything in response.

"Alucard?" Zalith asked, moving his hand over his head as concern began to enthral him.

The vampire—to Zalith's relief—uttered a quiet sound in response.

"Will you be okay for the party?" the demon asked. "We don't have to go. We can cancel it if you'd—"

"No," Alucard mumbled. "Zon't cancel. I just…vant to sleep vor a bit longer," he said, dragging himself away from Zalith and to his side of the bed. He slumped down on his front, exhaling deeply as he gripped the blanket and tried to pull it over himself.

Zalith moved the blanket over Alucard and then rested his head on his back, wrapping his arms around him. "Are you okay?" he asked. Of course, he knew Alucard *wasn't* okay, but he'd ask anyway.

Alucard was breathing unsteadily. "I'm vine," he murmured, slowly moving his arm under his pillow. "'Ow…long until people get 'ere?"

Hugging him tightly, Zalith stared over at the wall. "Around two hours."

"Are you going to dance vith me tonight, Zaliv?" Alucard then asked with what sounded like a quiet laugh.

Amused, Zalith smiled as he started lightly guiding his fingers down Alucard's back. "Of course I am," he confirmed. "I've been looking forward to it all day."

"Me too," Alucard said quietly. "Vill you stay 'ere vith me?"

Zalith nodded. "Of course," he said quietly and kissed Alucard's back.

And then, as the vampire slowly drifted off to sleep once more, Zalith lay with him, trying to focus on the contentedness that he felt while in Alucard's presence. Alucard made him feel so happy; he did so much for him, and he loved him endlessly. *That* was what he wanted to focus on, and for however long Alucard would sleep, Zalith would stay there with him.

Chapter Seven

Arriving Guests

| Zalith |

Zalith lay beside Alucard with his head on the vampire's back and his arm around him. It had been a while—over an hour, at least—since the vampire fell asleep; despite his slowly returning dismay, Zalith found comfort in laying there with the man he loved. But the longer he rested, the duller the sky got, and the closer it came to the time when he and Alucard would have to start greeting their guests.

The demon got up earlier and put his and Alucard's evening attire on the couch next to their dressing rooms. Now, he just had to wake his vampire up because he was sure that if he didn't, he'd sleep right through until morning. However, he was confident that Alucard didn't want to miss the party—Zalith didn't want him to miss it either. He'd been looking forward to it for weeks.

He hugged the vampire a little tighter. "Alucard?" he asked quietly. "We have to get up and get ready soon."

Alucard murmured irritably in response.

Zalith smiled and started to caress his hair. "I laid our clothes out already."

The vampire stayed silent.

"Come on," he said, sitting up a little to look down at what he could see of the side of Alucard's face.

Alucard grumbled quietly, turning his head to bury his face in his pillow.

Amused, Zalith laughed quietly. He had to wake him up. As his smile faded into a smirk, he leaned closer to Alucard and lightly bit the back of his shoulder. But all that made Alucard do was groan irritably once more. So, Zalith started to slowly and gently bite his way down the vampire's back, disappearing beneath the cover once he reached it. Alucard then flinched in surprise as Zalith lightly bit his ass and chuckled.

But the vampire still didn't show any sign of getting up. So, as Zalith smirked, he started to rhythmically pat the vampire's ass with his hands. "It's time to get up," he said, patting Alucard's ass with each word he said.

That sparked more of a reaction. Alucard uttered a sound of tired complaint and started shuffling around as Zalith made his way out of the cover.

When Alucard rolled onto his back, Zalith leaned over him and gazed down at his tired face. "Hey."

Staring up at him, Alucard sighed quietly.

Zalith shuffled closer, straddling Alucard's lap while keeping his eyes on his tired face. "You can be lazy for a bit. I already have everything we need."

Alucard stared at him for a moment, but he soon sighed again and started to sit up. "No, I'll probably vall back asleep," he mumbled.

Still sitting in his lap, Zalith rested his forehead against Alucard's as the vampire sat in front of him. "I'm sorry again… for stealing all your energy."

"Stop saying sorry," Alucard said with a pout, moving his hand to Zalith's waist. "I vant you to take vhat you need vhen you need."

Zalith fiddled with Alucard's tousled hair and smiled sadly. "Thank you, but I don't want to do it at the cost of your well-being. I promise I won't ever have sex with you more than twice a day ever again—unless it's a special occasion, and you've had a lot of sugar that day," he said, smirking.

Alucard didn't laugh, however. The vampire frowned in what looked like discontent. "You zon't 'ave to limit yourselv. I vould say no if I zidn't vant to 'ave sex."

Zalith smiled, unsure of what to say in response. He'd already decided that he was going to stop being so needy.

But Alucard clearly knew that he wasn't going to say anything else. The vampire huffed and looked over at the couch where Zalith had laid their clothes out. "Ve should get veady."

Smiling, Zalith slowly took his hand off the vampire's face. "Okay," he said. Then, he climbed off Alucard and got out of bed, and as Alucard followed, he made his way over to the couch and picked up the shirt he chose for Alucard. As the vampire stood in front of him, he started to help him dress.

"'Ow long do ve 'ave until people get 'ere?" he asked as Zalith straightened the collar of his white shirt.

"Hmm… maybe twenty minutes," he answered, handing Alucard his trousers.

"Did zhe band get 'ere?"

"They finished setting up not too long ago," he confirmed, helping Alucard into his blazer. "Everything's ready." He looked around for Alucard's bowtie, but he couldn't find it. "I can't find your bowtie," he said and then glanced at the dressing room door. "I'll go get you another one. One minute," he said and then kissed Alucard's lips.

He turned around and headed into the dressing room, hoping he'd find another bowtie inside. But as he searched, his guilt grew heavier. All it took was one glance at Alucard's face to see that he was exhausted, and Zalith felt awful about it. He didn't want to ruin the night, though. He'd do his best to hide his dismay from Alucard *and* their guests, and hopefully, everyone would have a fun night.

| Alucard |

Alucard waited by the couch, attempting to fight his fatigue. He could feel his eyes trying to close, but he wasn't going to give in again. He'd been looking forward to this party for *weeks*.

When Zalith came out of the dressing room with a new bowtie—and still naked—Alucard smiled and let him put it on for him. Once Zalith had finished, Alucard sighed and slipped his hand into Zalith's. He thought he wanted to say something, but he wasn't sure what it was. All he knew right now was that despite his exhaustion, he was looking forward to spending the night with Zalith—and for a moment before their house would fill with guests, he wanted to enjoy a last minute of solitude with his demon.

He pulled Zalith closer and moved his left hand to the demon's waist as Zalith gazed curiously at him. As he slowly let go of Zalith's hand, Alucard dragged his palm down from the demon's shoulder and over his chest and started to move his fingers between the defined lines of Zalith's abs. "Do you veel…okay?" he asked, taking his eyes off the demon's naked body to stare into his eyes once more.

Zalith smirked and placed his hand on the side of Alucard's face. "Yeah."

Alucard smiled. "Okay," he said. Then, he reached behind Zalith, snatched his white shirt from the couch, and handed it to him. "You're not going like zhat."

"I could," he suggested. "It'll be a little Yule treat for everybody—"

"No," Alucard said, pouting. "Is only me zhat gets to see you like zhis," he said possessively, and once he realized how possessive he sounded, he looked away in embarrassment. He'd never really said something like that before, but it felt…right. Zalith *was* his, and he was Zalith's. He was sure that Zalith wouldn't like anyone else to see him naked. "Stop staring at me," he then grumbled—he didn't even have to look at the demon to know he was staring at him with an unseemly smirk.

Zalith laughed and said, "I like it when you boss me around," as he trailed his hand to the side of Alucard's face. The vampire pouted, but Zalith started kissing him, and after a few moments, he stopped. "Tell me what to do again," he requested.

"Get dressed," Alucard mumbled, pushing the demon's shirt against his chest. "People vill arrive soon."

Zalith grinned amusedly. "Yes, sir," he replied, starting to pull his shirt on as the quiet house filled with the sound of the band tuning their instruments downstairs.

While the demon got dressed, Alucard slumped down on the end of their bed. He felt irritable, drained, and extremely sluggish, but he wasn't going to let that ruin the party for him. He didn't regret giving up his energy to help Zalith, and he didn't regret that he felt so tired because of it. He'd still be able to enjoy the party; he just needed something to help him wake up a little.

Zalith sat beside him, buttoning his blazer. "Is there anything I can do for you?" he asked, moving his arm around Alucard's shoulders to pull him closer. "I could get Edwin to make you some tea…or some coffee. Maybe something sugary?"

Alucard glanced at him and shrugged. "Maybe…some ice cream," he said, looking down at his lap as Zalith hugged him tightly. "I vink zhere's some levt."

The demon smiled and kissed Alucard's forehead. "I'll go and tell Edwin."

As Zalith stood up, so did Alucard. "I'll come, too. If I stay 'ere, I'll probably vall asleep," he admitted, taking hold of Zalith's hand.

Zalith smiled and led them out of their room, through the hall, and downstairs. The ballroom doors were wide open, and the staff were rushing in and out to make sure that everything was ready before people started arriving. Alucard was sure that both he and Zalith didn't want to stand around while the staff did what they needed to do, and he felt relieved when the demon led them towards his office.

"You wait here, and I'll go get your snack," Zalith said, opening the office door.

As Alucard walked inside, Zalith pulled the door shut. The vampire walked to the nearest couch and sat down, sighing deeply as he relaxed. People would start arriving any moment, and as excited as he was, he started to feel dread now that he thought about the fact he'd have to mingle. Right now, he felt as though he just wanted to hang around the snack tables and dance with Zalith. But it was a party, and he knew pretty much everyone who was coming—or he knew *of* them through Zalith—so he thought he should at least greet them before wandering off.

The door to Zalith's office then opened once more, and as the demon walked in with a tub of chocolate ice cream, Alucard sat up and watched him make his way over.

"Here you go, baby." Zalith smiled, sitting beside him as he handed it to him.

"Vank you," Alucard replied, and as Zalith gave him a spoon, he immediately opened the tub of ice cream. But he didn't start eating it right away. Instead, he looked at Zalith. "Do you vant some?"

"I'll have a bite," he said.

Alucard scooped some ice cream onto his spoon and then frowned, holding it out to Zalith. The demon liked feeding things to him, and he didn't really know why…but he thought he'd try it in an attempt to see what Zalith found so enjoyable about it.

Smirking, Zalith ate the ice cream and then smiled at Alucard as he stared back down into the tub. "It's good," he said.

Feeding Zalith didn't give Alucard an answer, so he was going to have to ask. "Vhy…vhy do you like…veeding me vings?" he mumbled as he ate some of the ice cream.

"I like to do it because I love you, and I like to take care of you. Sometimes, though, I do it because I like your mouth," the demon answered.

Alucard pouted and continued eating. "Vhat…do you like about my mouth?"

The demon rested his forehead on the side of Alucard's. "Well, I like your tongue," he said quietly, "and the things it can do. You also have very nice teeth," he added with an amused tone in his voice.

Alucard finished eating, losing interest in the ice cream. As the band across the hall started playing, the vampire placed the ice cream on the table beside him and turned to face Zalith. The demon kissed his lips once and then kissed his forehead before a knock came at his door.

"Yes?" Zalith called.

"Sirs, the first of your guests are arriving," Edwin said as he opened the door and peered inside.

"Thank you. We'll be out momentarily."

The butler left the room, closing the door.

Zalith looked at Alucard. "Are you ready to go?"

Alucard stared at him for a moment, debating whether or not he was ready to leave the quiet, peaceful office and begin a night of socializing. He felt sluggish *now*, but perhaps he'd start to wake up as the night progressed. So, he stood up. "I'm veady," he confirmed.

Zalith took his hand. "Let's go," he said, leading the way to the door.

As Alucard and Zalith emerged into the hall, they set their eyes on Idina, who was standing by the front door with a small white box in her hand. She was dressed in a mauve ballgown, and beside her, she had a blonde-haired, female companion in an olive green ballgown. They turned to face Zalith and Alucard and smiled when they noticed them approaching.

"Hey," Idina said contently as they reached them. "This is for you both," she said, handing Zalith the small white box.

"Thank you so much," the demon said with a smile, taking it from her. "We'll put this under the tree."

Nodding contently, Idina then placed her hands on Zalith's arms and kissed the side of his face. "I'm sorry if we're a little early."

"You're right on time," Zalith said.

Idina then set her eyes on Alucard and very lightly placed her hand on his arm as she leaned in to greet him the same way she always greeted Zalith. But Alucard felt okay with her contact; she'd been living in his and Zalith's house for quite some time now, and he knew her a lot more than he had before. When she kissed the side of his face, he set his eyes on her quiet companion.

"Oh, this is Elena," she said as she stepped back and held her hand towards her blonde friend, who was in fact an elf.

Zalith said to her, "It's nice to meet you."

Elena smiled. "You, too. You have such a lovely home," she said, glancing around.

"Thank you," Zalith replied.

Idina then looked at Alucard and frowned in what looked like worry. "Oh, Alucard, are you okay?" she asked. "You look a little under the weather."

Alucard frowned strangely. "Vhat?" he asked, looking at Zalith. "Do I?"

Zalith smiled as he tucked a strand of Alucard's hair behind his ear before looking back at Idina and Elena. "We've both just had a long day."

"Oh, I hope everything's okay," Idina said with a concerned expression.

"Everything's perfect," Zalith assured her. "You can both head into the ballroom if you like; the refreshments have been laid out, and the other guests will be arriving shortly."

Idina smiled and nudged her companion's arm. "Okay, we'll see you in there," she said, and then, as Elena followed, she left Zalith and Alucard and headed for the ballroom.

Once they were gone, Zalith summoned Edwin over and handed him the gift Idina gave him. Then, he turned to face Alucard and kissed his forehead before hugging him tightly. Alucard wasn't sure when everyone else would start arriving, but he *was* sure that he and Zalith were going to be waiting around to greet them all.

And they *did*.

Alucard remained at Zalith's side, greeting everyone as they all started turning up one by one. The demon directed all of them to the ballroom, handing the gifts they brought to Edwin, who moved back and forth between the hall and the lounge where the gifts had been kept over the month. It wasn't until close to half an hour had passed that everyone arrived, and Zalith and Alucard finally made their way into the ballroom.

It was going to be a long night.

Chapter Eight

The Party

| Alucard |

Alucard stuck with Zalith from the moment they left his office. Despite the fact that he wasn't included in the conversations that the demon had with his guests, he clung to his side and tried his best to stay awake.

Most of the guests Zalith spoke to were people who either worked for him or wanted to work for him. Alucard understood, of course. His own parties often consisted of people whom Dirk invited to form business relations.

Amongst the crowd, Alucard spotted Erwin talking to one of Zalith's subordinates who often patrolled the grounds of their home. Tyrus was present, as was Orin, and he saw Margo and the rest of the city council, too, all nosing around the room and mingling with the other guests. He caught sight of Varana a few times waltzing around until she found Mary-Beth, Selena, and Cadance, who she decided to stick with. Although those three women were known to Alucard—he might even say Mary-Beth was a friend—he didn't head over to them. Not only because Varana was with them, but because they seemed to have accumulated a rather large group of women around them who Alucard had never met. He didn't feel like trying to start a conversation with Mary-Beth anyway. The vampire was content with Zalith, nodding and occasionally agreeing when the demon looked at him. He wanted to ask him to dance, but he'd wait. Zalith was busy.

While Zalith conversed with a rather loud crowd of businessmen, Alucard glanced at each of them, trying to listen so that he might engage, but he felt so tired and disassociated that all he could do was nod when one of them looked at him. He thought, however, that it wasn't necessary that he knew what they were talking about; they were Zalith's guests. He'd leave Zalith to his business and remain at his side if he needed him. After all, he didn't feel like wandering off.

"Hey, buddy," Greymore suddenly said, snapping Alucard out of his thoughts as he appeared beside him. "How you been?"

Alucard took his eyes off the businessmen and looked to his left, where the black-haired wolf-man was standing. Without his usual casual attire, Greymore looked uncomfortably different, and he didn't look all that content with the suit he was wearing.

"Vhat?" he asked with a frown but then sighed and shrugged. "Eh," he mumbled before sipping from his drink. He didn't feel like telling Greymore that he felt like absolute shit, so he'd change the subject. "You are…velieved to vinally leave my ship, no?"

"Yeah," he said, smirking. He sipped from his glass of mead and said, "I'm excited as heck. I haven't touched grass in what feels like thirteen years."

Zalith then looked at Alucard. "Hey, I'm going to be right back," he said with a smile, squeezing Alucard's free hand. Then, he wandered off with the group of men he was talking to.

Alucard felt despondent the moment Zalith left his side, but he didn't want to make a huge deal out of it. It was a party, and he knew that he should stop clinging to the demon. He sighed and turned to face Greymore. "Good," he muttered. "I 'ope you like zhe place Zaliv put a lot of money into vor you."

Concern flickered in Greymore's eyes but he kept a smile on his face. "Hey, you all right, man?" he abruptly asked. "You look a little under the weather."

Why did everybody keep saying that? "I'm vine."

"Did Zalith drain all your energy?" he asked, winking as he lightly nudged Alucard's arm with his elbow.

As embarrassment started to consume him, Alucard pouted. "No," he grumbled. He had no idea what he looked like right now, but he obviously looked terrible enough for people to notice. Perhaps he should head to one of the bathrooms and try to make himself look a little better.

Laughing, Greymore shook his head. "Yeah, okay," he bantered. "Were you two going at it all day? Just based on the look of you, I'd say you're lucky to be alive."

Scowling, Alucard glanced down at what he could see of himself, and as far as he could tell, he looked presentable. "Do I veally look zhat bad?" he questioned, setting his eyes back on Greymore. "You're not zhe virst person to say someving."

Greymore patted Alucard's shoulder. "Well, it's fortunate you're a good-looking guy because fatigue on you just makes you look haunted and mysterious. On someone like me, though? I look like roadkill."

Amused, Alucard laughed quietly. "I'm sure is not zhat bad."

"Trust me," Greymore insisted. "You don't want to see this face in the morning. Why do you think I've been single for so long?" he jested. "I may be married to Freja, but let's face it, I'm still single."

Alucard scoffed and replied, "No. Maybe is because you vish in a lake zhat 'asn't 'ad vish vor centuries."

Greymore laughed again. "It's a *massive* lake. There *has* to be something in it—"

"No," Alucard argued, shaking his head.

"There's no way there's no fish living there, man. What do those dolphins eat if not fish?" he challenged smugly.

"Zhey eat zhe eels," Alucard answered.

"But what do the eels eat? Fish," Greymore stated.

"Actually, zhey eat crustaceans and small eels—"

"No, man…it's fish," he chuckled.

"And zhe smaller eels eat smaller crustaceans, and zhe crustaceans eat zhe vater-vlora. No vish," he told him matter-of-factly.

"Nah, there's—"

"You are *not* going to vind a single vish in zhat lake, Zhomas," he said sternly and sipped from his drink, and as Greymore pouted, he felt confident he'd won the argument—again.

But Greymore sighed deeply. "You can try to break my spirits, Alucard, but I'm not gonna give up."

Alucard shook his head as he finished his wine.

"What are the logistics of bringing in lake fish from a different lake and setting them loose to breed in the Citadel's lake?" Greymore then asked.

"Zhe vaters around zhe Citadel are polluted," Alucard said sadly. "Zhe vish vould die or sooner svim out to sea and become a meal to vhatever vinds zhem virst."

Greymore chortled and gulped down what was left of his mead. "I don't know. I still think there's a way. But it doesn't matter if there is or isn't, because there *has* to be fish in that lake," he repeated. "And I will die on this hill—"

The vampire sighed quietly. "As I leave 'umans to believe zhe gods vill save zhem, I vill let you believe zhat vish live in zhat lake."

"One day, I'm going to show up knocking on the door to this very house with a *lake fish* in my hand and a grin on my face," Greymore said with a wide grin.

"If you say so," Alucard mumbled, glancing at him.

"I do," he laughed. But then he glanced around the room. "I need another drink…."

"Luca," Mary-Beth suddenly called, making her way out of the crowd and over to him. "The girls and I have been waiting *all* night to talk to you—come, come," she insisted, linking her arm with his and escorting him away from Greymore, who uttered words of disapproval, but he didn't dive into the crowd after him.

Mary-Beth swiftly guided him away from his friend, through the party, and to one of the far back corners to the right of the band. A large group of women had congregated there, along with Varana, Cadence, and Selena.

The moment Mary-Beth arrived with Alucard, all the women set their eyes on him and bombarded him with so many questions and compliments that he could barely work out half of what was being said.

"Oh, hi Luca," Selena cheered.

"How are you?" one of the new women asked, reaching for his hand—

But his hand was swiftly grabbed by another woman. "The party is fantastic—"

"You look very handsome," someone else giggled.

While they continued greeting and asking him how he was, Alucard glanced at Mary-Beth, who adorned an apologetic look. Then, he looked around at all the women as they awaited his response. "I'm…vine," he said. "Vank you."

"Where's Zalith?" Mary-Beth asked, smiling at him.

Alucard looked over his shoulder at where Zalith had been taken by the men he was talking to. "Over zhere—"

"You two are *so* cute together," one of the women blurted.

"Very cute," another agreed. "I'm glad you two aren't hiding away anymore—"

"Yes, it was very brave of you both to come out," Mary-Beth concurred.

Varana, who Alucard could see lingering beside Selena, rolled her eyes and sipped from her martini with a sour look on her face.

"So," one of the women said, "who's the man and who's the woman in the relationship?"

"What? They're both men," Varana grunted irritably.

"Zhere's…no voman," Alucard said with a frown, speaking at the same time as Varana.

He and Varana then glared at one another as the women giggled.

"Yeah, but…there's always the two roles in every relationship, so one *has* to fill that of the woman," the woman insisted.

"Which one of you does the shopping, for example?" the woman beside her asked.

Alucard frowned. "Ve pay people to do zhat vor us."

One of the other women then sighed and shook her head. "I think what Doreen is trying to say is…which one of you…which one of you lays down in bed?" she asked with a hushed voice.

Varana grunted irritably and sipped from her drink again as Alucard's frown swiftly became a confused, embarrassed scowl.

"You can't just ask that, Maybelle," Mary-Beth snapped.

"How do you even…have sex?" one of the women asked. "How does that work?"

"Oh, my God," Mary-Beth groaned.

"How do you think?" Varana scoffed.

"Well, I don't know," the woman said with a frown.

"You're all *so* ridiculous. I'm getting another drink," Varana mumbled, walking off.

"Oh," one of the women then giggled, "if you two…get married," she said with a confounded look on her face, "which one of you is the one that's supposed to get down on one knee and ask the question?"

"You don't have to answer them," Mary-Beth said, leaning closer to him.

Alucard took his eyes off the group of women and looked at her. "Vell…Zaliv 'inted a vew times zhat…'e vould be zhe vone to ask."

All the women giggled and mumbled to one another.

Regretting that he answered, Alucard scowled and stared down at his empty glass.

"Aw, that's so sweet," Mary-Beth said. "Do you think you two will start a family?"

Looking at Mary-Beth again, he shrugged. She was probably the only person he would answer. "Vell…'e spoke about zhat a vew times."

She smiled. "That'll be nice for you two—"

"How would you two even have children?" Doreen asked. "I suppose you'd have to adopt," she said with a sigh.

Alucard frowned, glancing at Doreen as she and the other women waited for him to answer. But he didn't know how to respond. He hadn't thought about how he and Zalith would have a family; all he knew was that both he and Zalith wanted to have one someday.

"Adoption is good," Mary-Beth said with a nod. "There are lots of children out there who don't have homes."

"Would any orphanage let two *men* adopt a child, though?" Maybelle questioned.

"Oh…" Mary-Beth drawled. "I'm not sure."

"Luca, how did you know you were gay?" another woman interjected, swiftly changing the subject. "Was it a lifelong thing, or did you realize when you met Zalith?"

Then, all the women stopped muttering and stared at him, waiting for him to answer.

Alucard shrugged. "Vell…I never…'ad any vomantic intervest or attraction to anyvone until I met Zaliv."

All the women smiled and murmured, "Aw," to one another.

"If I were a man, I'd probably feel the same," one of the others then said with a nod.

Alucard scowled at her, but before he could say something, Zalith appeared at his side, moved his arm around his waist, and pulled him closer.

"There you are," the demon said with a smirk and kissed the side of his face.

Once again, all the women chortled.

"You two are so adorable," Mary-Beth said.

"I know," Zalith agreed, holding Alucard in a tight side embrace. "Unfortunately, ladies," he then said, "I have to take him to speak to Wilfred, but thank you for keeping an eye on him."

"That's okay," Doreen giggled.

"Bye-bye," another called as the women waved in farewell, letting Zalith walk off with Alucard.

As Zalith escorted him away, Alucard sighed deeply in relief. "Vank you," he mumbled.

"Of course," Zalith said with a smile, stopping by a table lined with beverages. He turned to face Alucard. "I heard they were being intrusive, so I felt the need to come and rescue you," he said, smirking as he lightly dragged his thumb over the side of Alucard's face. "I also missed you," he added with a more intimate tone.

"I missed you, too," Alucard said, moving his hand to Zalith's waist.

"It's nice to have my arm candy back," the demon said with an unseemly smile.

Unsure of what he meant, Alucard took his eyes off Zalith's waist and stared at him. "Vhat?"

He smirked amusedly. "It means that just having you on my arm makes everyone jealous because you're the most beautiful and handsome person in this room—in *any* room."

With a nervous frown, Alucard looked down again and smiled. "I vouldn't say zhat."

"But *I* would," the demon said, "and with certainty." Then, he kissed Alucard's forehead.

Still smiling, Alucard leaned closer, moved his arms around Zalith, and rested his head on his shoulder.

Reciprocating his hug, Zalith started fiddling with the vampire's crimson hair. "Are you feeling any better?" he asked quietly.

"A little," he mumbled.

"Good," the demon said. "Do you have enough energy to dance with me?"

Alucard leaned back so that he could see Zalith's face and nodded. "I do," he confirmed. He'd been looking forward to dancing with Zalith all night, and he wasn't going to pass up the opportunity to do so.

He took Zalith's hand, and as Zalith led the way, Alucard followed him to the middle of the room, where couples were dancing. And as the music played slow, he and Zalith danced just as so.

The demon placed one hand on Alucard's waist and the other on his shoulder. Alucard did the same, but in Zalith's company, he felt a whole lot more relaxed; he decided to rest his head on the demon's shoulder once more. As long as they got to dance like this for a short while, then he'd feel content.

His fatigue was catching up with him the longer he stood there with Zalith, but he didn't care. They held one another tightly, and as the night went on, they danced their slow, silent dance.

Chapter Nine

Amongst the Guests

| Luther |

Luther glared across the room with such animosity, watching as Zalith danced with Alucard—as he danced with a man he didn't deserve.

Every time he saw them together, every time he so much as *thought* of them together, Luther *seethed* with anger. Knowing what he knew, having seen what he'd seen. Convincing Alucard to leave Zalith hadn't worked, and Luther was left with one last option. He'd get what he wanted—*who* he wanted—and he'd win. Zalith would lose, and nothing could make him happier.

He sipped from his drink as a smirk crept across his face. After tonight, his suffering would be over. He'd not have to think about Zalith touching Alucard anymore; he'd not have to sit around dwelling on the fact that Alucard was with a man who didn't deserve him, a man who wouldn't love him forever.

Luther would no longer be Alucard's subordinate. Alucard would be *his*, and he would be Alucard's. Something he wanted for a long time, something he craved from the moment he'd laid eyes on him. He still strongly resented the fact that he hadn't been the one who Alucard discovered his sexuality with, but it didn't matter. He'd surely be his once the night was over.

However, he couldn't focus on Alucard for very long—which was confounding, considering he was on his mind all day every day. Right now, though, Luther's thoughts clung to the desire to enact revenge against Zalith. That demon ridiculed him, belittled him, and made him suffer far too many times, and taking Alucard from him simply wouldn't be enough. No…he wanted to hurt Zalith *physically*. He wanted to make that demon understand how much he hated him and just how much he deserved to suffer for the things he'd done.

But what could Luther do without endangering his plans for Alucard and having everyone in this room attack him at once?

He sighed, sipping from his drink as he glowered at Zalith and Alucard. It should be *him* dancing with Alucard. But then again, Luther felt like he wasn't the dancing type. Was Alucard? Would Alucard expect him to dance with him once he had him? If that were the case, it was something Luther would probably have to talk to him about. He didn't feel so content with such a thing. Dancing.... He'd never learnt, and he thought he never would. He was sure that Alucard would be okay with that, though.

"I was wondering if you'd show up," Varana suddenly said, appearing beside him.

Luther took his eyes off Zalith and Alucard and sharply turned his head to stare at her. His thoughts were still bitter, and seeing Varana despite telling her *not* to approach him only made him madder. "I told you we can't be seen together."

She scoffed. "I'm not allowed to say hi?"

He didn't want to argue with her; the last thing he needed was to cause a scene. So he tried to banish his irritated frown. "Hi," he said.

Varana glared at him, clearly waiting for him to say something more, but he had nothing to say.

The woman scoffed, tutted, and glared at him in frustration. "Whatever," she snarled, pushing him back a little. Then, she turned around and stormed off.

Rolling his eyes, Luther set his sights back on Zalith and Alucard, watching...waiting for the moment the vampire left the demon's side.

| Danford |

On the other side of the room, Danford watched as Varana made her way over to Luther, and the smile on her face made him feel so grief-stricken. He knew that Luther was still seeing her, and as much as he hated to admit it, he was almost certain that Luther would never stop seeing her and settle with him.

And he couldn't just go over there and ask him what was going on because Luther told him that they couldn't be seen together. Varana would hurt them *both*. Danford didn't want that, but he didn't want to be there anymore. It hurt too much to know that he'd never be the only person Luther gave his attention to.

Trying to hold back his sadness, he abruptly turned around to head for the door—

"Watch it!" Freja snapped as he unintentionally collided with her.

He stumbled back, holding out his hands. "Oh-oh, my God, I'm so sorry—a-are you okay?" he stuttered, staring at her irritated face—a face that almost instantly transformed his sadness into fear. He'd just crashed into Freja, his recently extended pack's Luna, and he was sure that he was about to receive a scolding for it.

Freja eyed him for a moment but then sighed and shook her head. "It's fine," she muttered. But she frowned in what looked like concern. "Where are you going looking so sad?" she questioned.

"Home," he said sullenly. "O-or I mean…to the boat," he corrected. "I'm sorry I bumped into you," he said, moving to step past her.

But Freja crossed her arms and stepped aside so that he couldn't walk past. "Why? Because of him?" she asked, nodding over his shoulder.

Danford frowned and looked back there, seeing that she was referring to Luther.

"Don't waste your time," she told him. "That man's worse than Zalith used to be from what I've heard."

He looked down at the floor as his sadness started to grip him tightly. "I don't know," he said with a shrug. "He's not perfect, but…I thought we had something special."

"He makes everyone think they have something special with him. I've been working with Luther for a few years now, and the amount of people I've seen him go through is astonishing, even for someone like him. Don't let him break your heart."

Her words filled his heart with more pain. He tried his best to be what Luther wanted—what he *needed*. But nothing ever seemed to be good enough for him, and it was only now that Danford was starting to wake up. Freja's revelation made him feel embarrassed because he didn't want to end up being played again; he just wanted someone to love who loved him back the same way, not someone who loved him when it suited them. Luther wasn't who he thought he was; he wasn't who Danford tried so hard to believe he was. He was using him, wasn't he? And he had been from the start.

He didn't want to stay there a moment longer. It was a party, and he didn't want to be crying—and it was also Yule, a time of year that *everyone* spent with their loved ones. He didn't have anyone, really…so maybe he would be better off alone on the ship.

"Oh," he said sadly in response to what Freja said. "I should…get going," he said, moving to walk past her again—but as she had the first time, she stopped him.

"Are you looking forward to moving off the boat?" she asked, changing the subject.

Danford stared at her for a moment. He didn't want to be rude; she was actually being a lot nicer to him than he thought she might be. He stopped trying to leave and nodded. "Yeah, it'll be nice. I'm getting tired of being on the water all the time."

She smiled. "Do you miss the forest? The grass?"

He nodded shyly as he glanced at her curious face. "Yeah, I really do. I used to love going out into the woods to find somewhere nice to sit down and draw for the day."

"Oh, I've seen you sitting around drawing from time to time, but I've never actually seen any of your stuff. Maybe you can show me sometime," she suggested, still smiling at him.

Danford felt surprised and confused; had someone sent her over to talk to him because they'd seen that he looked sad? Had Greymore sent her? What would someone like her want with someone like him?

He then realized that he was just staring at her and hadn't replied. "U-uh…yeah, sure, I can show you whenever," he agreed. "I have a lot of drawings in my room—n-not that we have to go to my room or anything," he then insisted, his heart starting to race as angst gripped him tightly. He didn't want her to get the wrong impression. "I can show you up on the deck…o-or in the bar—b-but you don't have to get a drink or anything, I probably won't drink, I'll just be…at the table, or something," he said so quickly that he had to take a deep breath once he was done.

But Freja giggled, holding her hand over her mouth as she did.

She probably thought he was an idiot, didn't she? He lowered his head and stared sullenly at the floor below. "Sorry," he said.

Freja frowned and stopped giggling. "Why are you sorry?"

"Because I'm embarrassing."

She laughed again but placed her hand on the side of his arm. "You're not embarrassing. You're actually the most tolerable out of everyone I've spoken to tonight," she said with a sigh.

As his eyes widened in shock, he glanced at her hand. Why was she touching him? She was so nice—but why? He was just a measly Omega. A nobody. He frowned and looked at her. "T-thank you. Are…are you not having a nice time?"

Taking her hand off his arm, she sipped from her drink and shrugged. "I'm having a nice time, it's just hard to find someone who isn't so loud. You'll find that a lot of the men here are not only too loud for their own good but really don't know how to hold a conversation, either."

"They're not *so* bad once you get to know them," Danford said. "But I agree…I just keep to myself mostly—n-not because I think I'm better than them, though. I'm just more introverted," he said quickly, once again having to take a breath after.

She giggled in response. "I've been here long enough to get to know what I need to know about everyone, but all I really know about you is that you're a bit of a quiet one and one particularly good at drawing. If you still want to leave, I won't stop you, but I think I might actually enjoy a little more of your time."

Danford so very swiftly became enthralled with confliction. He looked back over his shoulder to where Luther had been standing, but he wasn't there anymore, and he wasn't anywhere to be seen, either. He wasn't by any of the refreshment or food tables, nor was he near the door or talking to anyone or dancing. He was gone, and Danford suspected that he must have wandered off with Varana, who was also now nowhere to be seen.

He felt as if he'd like to stay and talk to Freja; they could be friends…or something…whatever an Omega could be to a Luna. But he didn't want Luther to see them—if he came back, that was. He might get mad and jealous—but…maybe he deserved to see how it felt to deal with those feelings in *silence* whenever he saw Luther with Varana.

But then he scowled. It wasn't like anything was ever going to happen between him and Freja; she was an Alpha and better than him in so many ways. She was *far* out of his league, and the most they would probably ever be was friends. But that was okay because he actually liked the idea of that.

Sighing, he shrugged. He wanted to go back to the boat and dwell in his sadness, but…he was also having a nice time talking to her and thought that maybe it would be better to stay in the company of someone who somehow made him feel better. So, he nodded. "I'll stay," he agreed.

"Great," she said with a smile, taking his arm in hers. "Let's go over here and get a drink."

"O-oh, okay, sure," he agreed, following as she dragged him off into the crowd. Maybe he didn't have to spend all night in a pit of depression after all.

| Alucard |

Zalith and Alucard slowly danced in the centre of the dancefloor. But as the night grew later, he sunk deeper and deeper into his thoughts. He couldn't stop thinking about how Mary-Beth's friends had laughed at him when he'd said that he and Zalith would get married, and it was starting to get to him.

Why did they find it so funny? He couldn't help but think that everything they said and asked was all an attempt to ridicule him. It almost felt the same as when Attila tried to tell him *not* to pursue anything with Zalith. Was his and Zalith's relationship a joke to them?

He frowned and lifted his head from Zalith's shoulder, glancing at the demon's face as he stared at him and smiled. *Would* he and Zalith get married? Zalith had spoken about it on various occasions, and he convinced Alucard that the time would come…so why did that seem humorous to those women? Would it be something laughable to everyone here if and when he and Zalith got engaged? Would it even happen? Were they laughing because it wouldn't?

Alucard scowled sullenly and quietly asked, "Vill ve get married?"

Zalith kept his smile but frowned a little as they kept dancing. "Of course we will—if you'll still have me," he said.

Freja and Danford's story can be read in the Numenverse Companion Story, FORBIDDEN BOND

The vampire nodded, staring down at the floor—

"Why do you ask? Is something wrong?"

Alucard shrugged. "No," he mumbled. "I just said someving to Mary-Bev and 'er vriends about zhat and zhey laughed."

"They *laughed*?" Zalith questioned.

He nodded, slowly lifting his head to see that Zalith didn't look as content and relaxed as he had before he said something about it. The demon appeared conflicted… gazing for a moment as Alucard stared back.

But then an aggravated expression appeared on the demon's face. "I'm going to say something," he decided, glancing around the room, and when he set his eyes on Mary-Beth and her huddle of friends, he let go of Alucard and started making his way over to them.

Alucard frowned in confliction. He didn't want to cause drama tonight; not only was he tired as hell, but it was their Yule party—it was supposed to be fun and stress-free. But what Mary-Beth's friends made him feel had stuck with him, and he'd let Zalith say whatever he was about to say.

The vampire swiftly hurried after Zalith and followed him to Mary-Beth and her friends.

Once Zalith reached the huddle of bickering women, he donned a smile, and Alucard was sure that he was about to say *a lot* to these women.

"Sorry, ladies," Zalith started as they all turned to face him. "I hate to interrupt."

Most of them giggled.

"Oh, no, it's no problem, Zalith," Doreen said.

He kept his smile and eyed them all. "I'm just going to cut to the chase here because there's something I don't really understand," he said as Alucard stood behind him, watching as the smile on each woman's face slowly faded. "So, despite the fact that we have welcomed each and every one of you into our home to attend our wonderful Yule party as a heartfelt thank you to you, our dear friends, for sharing your lives with us in one way or another, you decide that it would be a wonderful idea to, again, in our *home*, laugh when Luca says that we plan on getting married one day?" he questioned, keeping his smile. "What was the thought process there? I'd love to know."

All of them looked close to horrified, looking around at each other.

One of them frowned, however. "We—"

"Listen," Zalith interjected, "I understand that our relationship isn't the norm, and maybe it makes you uncomfortable or upset, but the fact of the matter is that I love this man with every inch of my heart, and what we have is very real," he stated sternly. "If I *ever* hear another word that any of you disrespected him or our relationship ever again, consider my immense financial contributions to each of your husbands' companies terminated. Luca is far more important to me than your money, and I'm sure that you can see that neither of us really even needs it," he said as *all* the women frowned in dread.

"Zalith, I'm so sorry, we—"

"This conversation is over," Zalith interjected once more, silencing the panicking women. "If you can't keep your opinions to yourself, please do me the favour of laughing your way to the door. Have a great night," he said, smiling.

As the women started uttering their apologies, Zalith turned around, took hold of Alucard's hand, and wandered off into the crowd.

Alucard followed behind Zalith and didn't even try to hide the small smile that found its way to his face. He loved it when Zalith stood up for him—not that he didn't know how to stand up for himself, he'd just rather let Zalith do it, not only because he liked it, but because these were all technically Zalith's guests, and he didn't want to start drama with them. But everything Zalith said made Alucard's despondency fade, and for a moment, not even his fatigue could keep him from enjoying the contentedness that Zalith gave him.

But then, before Alucard could comprehend, Zalith swiftly turned around, moved his hand to Alucard's back, and tilted him back, leaning over to stare down into his eyes. He gazed at him for a few moments, and as Alucard stared up at him, the demon smiled and kissed his lips.

Gripping Zalith's arms with both his hands, Alucard closed his eyes and allowed himself to become lost in their small moment of affection before Zalith stopped and smiled down at him.

"Do you feel better?" the demon asked.

Alucard nodded.

Zalith smiled, kissed him again, and stood them both up straight. He then tucked a strand of Alucard's hair behind his ear and placed his hand on the side of his neck.

"Vank you vor saying someving," Alucard mumbled.

"You're welcome, baby. I just hope they keep their mouths shut next time—for their sake," Zalith grumbled.

Alucard nodded, smiled, and gripped his hand. He didn't want to spend a moment longer talking about them. He wanted to continue enjoying his time with Zalith. So, as the demon smiled, Alucard led them back through the crowd towards the dance floor.

Chapter Ten

Ysmay

| Varana |

Varana left the party. She was irritated with Luther, and she felt as if she wasn't enjoying herself as much as she could be. And she felt…lonely. Zalith had Alucard now…*him*…and Luther was the worst excuse for a boyfriend she'd ever had. She didn't want to talk to any of the other women either; *all* of them were annoying her. So, she retreated to her small, silent reading room and slumped down in her armchair.

Was this how it was going to be now? Would she always be alone?

Varana sighed, staring out of the window at the gardens. She caught sight of a few guests chattering away with drinks and cigarettes in their hands over by the hedges. If only she could have invited Ysmay…then she'd be hanging out with *her*. She missed her sister; however…because of *Alucard*, not only could her sister not come to these things, but she also couldn't even tell her sister where she lived.

"I was concerned, Ronnie," came Ysmay's sly, suspicious voice—

Horrified and startled, Varana instantly jumped to her feet and turned around to set her eyes on her bitter-faced sister, who stood in the same dress that *she* was wearing.

"I thought something happened," Ysmay said with a frown, dragging her clawed fingers over the table she was standing beside. "Why else would you have avoided inviting me here *two* years in a row when it had become quite the tradition to have me over for this stupid human holiday?" she questioned.

"What are you doing here?" Varana asked with a laugh, trying to act as casually as possible.

Ysmay scoffed, gritted her sharp teeth, and dug her claws into the table, splintering the wood. "*You* were the last of us I'd suspect to betray our Father! How long have you been hiding him, dear sister?"

"Who?" Varana asked. She was sure that Ysmay was talking about Alucard, but…maybe she was talking about someone else—someone Varana wasn't aware of. If she acted as though she didn't know what her sister was talking about, perhaps it would lessen the amount of trouble she knew that she was in.

Snarling, Ysmay abruptly flung herself forward and slammed into Varana, forcing her back against the wall, where she held her hand against her chest to keep her in place. "Who?!" she exclaimed. "Don't you *who* me!" she growled, keeping her voice hushed. "How long have you been protecting that foul, ugly little spawn we were *all* sent up here to look for?!"

"Get off of me," Varana snapped, trying to push her sister off—

"Do you know how *disgusted* Father will be when he has to hear from *me* that you've been deliberately hiding Caedis from him?"

Varana's fear instantly became overwhelming as she stared at her furious sister. "Please don't say anything, Y—it's not my fault!" she insisted.

"Not your fault?" she scoffed, her anger thickening. "How is this *not* your fault?! You could have told Father at *any* point that he was here, but did you?! What the *fuck* is wrong with you?!"

Varana burst into tears; she had no idea what to say. She didn't want her sister to tell their Father. She loved him so much, and if he found out that she'd been helping hide Alucard, he'd disown her at the very least, and that terrified her.

Ysmay snarled in revolt. "Varana!" she growled. "Stop fucking crying!"

"I did it for Z!" she bawled, sniffling as tears streamed down her face.

"Of course you did," Ysmay uttered. "You'd do anything for that disgusting excuse for a man—a man who will *never* love you the way you want him to. He lies, manipulates, and uses *everyone* around him. Do you think you're some kind of exception?" she scoffed. "He doesn't care about anyone but himself. He'd probably toss you away again the moment you hurt his little boyfriend's feelings! How many times do I have to tell you, V?! Yet here you are, betraying even our *Father* because of him.... I don't know what to do with you anymore."

"I tried to break them up so I could tell everyone where he was, but it didn't work!" she insisted, still crying. "And Z cares about him, and I don't want to hurt Z because I love him! And I didn't want you to get in trouble too, so that's why I didn't tell you!"

"Do you love him more than you love Father?!" Ysmay yelled.

Varana frowned in struggle and tried to work out whether or not she *did* love Zalith more than her Father. But she quickly became distressed. She didn't want to have to choose between them—she didn't want any of this.

Scowling, she tried to push Ysmay off of her once again. "Get off me," she complained sadly.

"Answer the question," Ysmay demanded.

Varana scowled and whined quietly. "Why are you doing this?" she wailed.

"Because despite the fact that you've betrayed our Father, you're my sister, and I want what's best for you. I know that Father will kill you if he finds out... and although you deserve it, for some reason, I still feel convinced that you'll come to your senses. Father is closing in; he *will* find Caedis with or without you, but I think it would be in everyone's best interest right now if it were you who handed him over. After all, Daddy's been wondering why he hasn't heard from you in so long."

"But what about Z?" she cried. "He's not going to let anybody take Caedis away from him! He's gonna fight back, and I don't want him to get hurt—I don't want him to hate me," she bawled.

Ysmay snarled in revolt. "I don't give a *shit* about him, and neither should you. It's high time you worked out where your loyalties lie, and this time, you'll have no choice but to make an actual decision, Varana," she warned, placing her hand on the side of Varana's face. "You'll have exactly *one* month to decide whether or not you're still your Father's daughter—"

"What the hell are you talking abo—"

"—OR if you're going to throw away everything that you have and follow around a man who won't ever love you," she stated, cutting her off. "And don't even think about trying to run and tell Zalith about *any* of this. Not only will it be impossible, but if I find you tried squealing... I'll hurt him, I'll hurt *you*, and I'll make sure *no one* will *ever* love you," she snarled, digging her claws into the side of Varana's face—

Varana screeched in anger and tried to push her off. "Get the fuck away from me!" she demanded, but Ysmay snarled and fought back, overpowering her sister.

She pinned Varana against the wall. "Our Father is the *only* one you need to love you, and if you continue to betray him, you'll lose *everything*."

Varana stared at her sister in horror—in astonishment. She knew what she was doing—she could *feel* the silencing curse slowly enthralling her body. Now that she knew what Ysmay meant when she said she wouldn't be able to say a thing about what was happening. Her sister was silencing her, and Varana felt as if she was frozen.

She didn't know what to do. She loved her sister—she loved her family—but she loved Zalith, and she didn't want to have to choose between them. But Ysmay was making her choose... and she had one month to decide whether to stay with Zalith or return to her family.

Why was Ysmay doing this? Why was she acting out of hatred? She was her sister—she was supposed to love her. Why didn't she understand? Why would she do something so cruel as to make her choose between their family and Zalith? She couldn't—she wouldn't. Varana tried to fight her sister off, she tried to resist the curse, but it burrowed so deep inside her mind that she had no chance to even attempt to escape.

And there it sat…in the very centre of her mind. She'd not be able to tell Zalith about this—about *any* of it. She'd not be able to warn him or help him, and what was she to do? She could only choose…but how could she?

Her ability to fight faded, her body felt numb, and as Ysmay took her hand off her face, Varana slowly sunk to her knees, staring ahead in dismay. What was going to happen now? She had a month to choose between Zalith and her family. If she chose her family and gave up Alucard, Zalith would hate her—he'd disown her. But if she chose Zalith, her *family* would disown her, and her Father would probably hunt her down. How could she choose between them? She couldn't…she wouldn't…but she had to.

"I'm *so* disappointed in you, V," Ysmay said, glowering at her as the wounds on her face slowly healed. "To think that *you*, my own sister, would do something so vile as hide Caedis…and for the sake of a disgusting man who will never treat you the way you deserve. What's happened to you? Have you spent too long in a world of soft, petty humans? Does our Father need to teach you what it is to be a demon again?"

Overwrought with so many different feelings, Varana stared at her sister. "Why can't you just let me be happy?" she asked, her anger seething, and her heart breaking.

"You'll thank me for this one day soon, V," Ysmay said. "You'll make the right choice."

"You're such a bitch!" she screeched in agonized anger, picking up the closest book and launching it at Ysmay.

Scowling, Ysmay moved aside and dodged the book. "You have a month, V—and remember what I said: I'll hurt your precious Z if you so much as even *think* about trying to tell him—not that you'll be able to, though."

With tears streaming down her face, Varana shrieked in frustration and despair and started chucking books at her sister as she turned around and headed for the door. "I hate you!" she yelled. "Get the fuck out!"

Without another word, avoiding all the books being thrown at her, Ysmay left the room.

And Varana was left silenced and distraught.

Chapter Eleven

Risk

| Alucard |

As the night grew later, Alucard and Zalith found themselves on the dancefloor once more. They rested their foreheads together, holding each other tightly while the vampire gazed into Zalith's eyes, and the demon stared back with a smile. Zalith placed a soft, passionate kiss on his lips every so often, and each time he did, Alucard's content feeling grew.

Alucard couldn't feel any happier—well…the only thing that would make him feel utterly euphoric would be if Zalith asked him to marry him, but he was sure that wasn't going to happen for a while. And now that he was thinking about it again, he couldn't stop. Every time it was so much as mentioned, he'd remember how excited he felt to think that one day he and Zalith would be married, and they'd start a family of their own.

But tonight wasn't about marriage; tonight was about enjoying what they had right now, and he couldn't be any more grateful to have Zalith.

Alucard moved the side of his face against Zalith's; he was sure that a shy expression now clung in place of his smile. He'd already given in to the fact that the demon *always* made him feel so nervous no matter how long they'd been together. But that was okay. It was just a part of who and what they were.

Zalith exhaled quietly and guided his hand down from Alucard's shoulder and to his waist. "Are you excited about the presents tomorrow?" he asked, leaning into his ear.

Alucard smiled. "Yes," he confirmed, nuzzling the side of Zalith's face. "Are you?"

"I am. What did you get me?"

The vampire frowned slightly. "Is a surprise."

Laughing, Zalith kissed the vampire's neck. "Perhaps you could give me a hint?"

Smiling once more, Alucard shook his head. "No."

"What if I'm really good?" the demon asked, leaning back so that he could stare at Alucard's face.

"I still von't tell you," Alucard said, smirking.

The demon smirked, too. "What if I ask you very nicely…and give you a kiss?"

"No."

"What if I cry?"

Alucard frowned again. "You're not going to cry."

"But what if I do?"

Staring at him as they continued dancing slowly, Alucard searched Zalith's eyes for any sign of seriousness, but he was joking—of course he was. Why would he cry as if he were a child? The vampire rolled his eyes and shook his head. "I'm not telling you."

The demon laughed and sighed. "I guess I'll just have to be patient, won't I?"

"Yes, you—"

Before Alucard could finish his sentence, Varana grabbed his arms and *ripped* him away from Zalith. She instantly wrapped her arms around the demon, and as the woman cried, Alucard's relaxed composure withered, and anger filled his heart.

Zalith asked the woman what was wrong as he tried to push her off, but she clung on tighter and cried and cried and cried, and Alucard so very quickly lost his patience.

Snarling, the vampire snatched Varana's arm and yanked her off Zalith, but she pulled free and latched onto him again. Alucard didn't want to start a scene, but he wasn't at all content with the way this woman just pulled him off *his* demon and threw herself in his place. So, he gritted his teeth and snatched her arm again—

"Hold on," Zalith interjected before Alucard could try and pull her off.

Hold on? Alucard scowled at them both, watching as Zalith looked down at the bawling woman and frowned.

"Varana, what's wrong?" Zalith asked sternly, placing his hands on her shoulders as he managed to pull her off.

But the woman just stared up at him with tears streaming down her face. Then, she wailed and threw her arms around him, and Alucard had to resist the urge to try and pull her off once again.

Zalith then glanced at Alucard with a look of concern on his face. "I'm going to take her upstairs; I don't want to do this in front of everyone," he said quietly.

Of course he was going to take her upstairs. Of course *something* was going to happen to cut their time short, and *of course*, it was going to be Varana who was responsible for it.

Alucard didn't know what to say, do, or feel. All he knew right now was that he had very little patience and even less energy, and he didn't have the motivation to argue. He'd been enjoying his and Zalith's intimate, stress-free time together, but he felt like he should have known it wouldn't last much longer. And he felt…disheartened.

The vampire gave up without putting up a fight—after all, what would be the point? He didn't want to cause a spectacle, he didn't want to irritate Zalith, and he didn't have the strength he knew he needed to bicker with that woman. So with a distressed huff, he turned around and walked off into the crowd, leaving Zalith and Varana to do whatever it was they did when that needy woman came over crying.

He ignored Zalith's quiet call of his name, and he didn't care to sit around waiting for him to come back, either. He was tired and disappointed, and he just wanted to sit somewhere he'd not be stared at.

Alucard left the party and made his way to his office. With a sullen frown, he closed the door and dragged himself over to the alcohol cabinet. He poured himself a glass of brandy and then walked to his desk, where he slumped down in his seat. He took a sip of his drink and swivelled around in his chair to stare out the window. And then his thoughts started to louden. Why was Zalith always so quick to dismiss *anything* for that woman? All she had to do was come over with tears in her eyes and Zalith would baby her. Alucard understood that Zalith cared about Varana, but there were times when he found that he felt as if he wished the demon didn't. He'd been looking forward to tonight for so long; he and Zalith were supposed to spend the entire night together, but there was no telling how long he'd be gone consoling Varana.

He scowled at the darkness outside, trying to keep his anger focused on Varana and away from Zalith. He didn't want to be mad at him; he was just looking out for his friend. Why did Varana have to come over and ruin everything all of the time? She always had something to say, she always had to insert herself, and she was *always* there to complicate everything. Even though she didn't live in their house anymore, she was still such a prominent issue, and it was probably going to stay that way forever. Alucard was sure she'd also make a fuss when he and Zalith got married, but he wasn't going to let her ruin *that* party for them.

Why was he even thinking about that again? He didn't want to sit there and ponder about marriage or weddings. He was mad, tired, and upset. He just wanted to sit there for a while and try to calm down. The last thing he wanted to do was head back to the party and snap at Zalith or someone else. He needed to spend a little time on his own and wait until he either heard Zalith come back downstairs or until the demon came to find him.

| Luther |

Luther took a deep breath as he crossed the hall and headed for Alucard's office. He knew what he had to do, but he couldn't help but feel nervous.

He knocked on the door.

"Vhat?" came Alucard's irritated voice.

Luther pushed it open and stepped inside—

"Vhat zhe fuck are you doing 'ere?" the vampire snarled, standing up as he placed his hands on his desk.

"It's important," Luther insisted, shutting the door behind him. "Look," he said, holding out his hands before Alucard could tell him to leave. "I know I'm not meant to be here, and I know I could most probably lose my head for it, but I had to come. I have news," he said, moving closer to the desk.

Alucard growled in hostility. "I zon't care if you 'ave news—send a fucking letter. Get out of my 'ouse—"

"It's about Charlotte," Luther said.

Alucard's angered expression started fading. He sat down and said, "Speak."

Luther moved to sit on one of the seats in front of his desk—

"I zidn't say sit, I said speak."

Looking down at him, Luther nodded. But he felt very anxious all of a sudden. He was finally alone with Alucard, and now he had to follow his carefully thought plan step by step. He had to be careful, though. Alucard wasn't stupid; he was skeptical, aware, and pragmatic. If Luther were to achieve what he'd come to achieve, he would have to be very prudent.

First, the information. "I discovered that, despite her allegiance to the Diabolus, Charlotte was, in fact, a disciple of Erich. Unlike others, though, she turned her back on such a following a long time ago. This…Charlotte woman was just as much Diabolus as any other agent we've come across. She was killed by Lilith, and nobody knew that it happened, but it was written in one of the ancient, badly damaged diaries I found. Not only did Lilith kill her, but apparently, she *loathed* her. Something to do with uh…Charlotte was given the responsibility to do something Lilith wanted to do—"

"I alveady know *all* of zhis," Alucard said with a frown.

Luther stuttered a little. "Uh…oh…well, I didn't know."

Alucard rolled his eyes. "Next time, vrite to me, and zhen ve can avoid zhe embarrassment, no?" he snarled and sipped from his drink.

Gawping at him, Luther's thoughts halted for a moment. He'd come here *sure* that Alucard wasn't aware of what he'd just told him, and now…he had nothing. How was he going to do it? How was he going to get Alucard to let his guard down?

"Leave," Alucard grumbled. "Bevore Zaliv vinds out you're 'ere."

Luther didn't fail to notice the sheer exhaustion in Alucard's voice—and not only that, but he also *looked* fatigued. That didn't surprise him, though, and it only made him think back to earlier when he and Varana had been walking the grounds. He'd not forget what he saw happening in Zalith's office, and he was convinced that had something to do with why Alucard looked so…dead.

Varana mentioned that Alucard's precious boyfriend spent this time of year *every year* bedding so many different people in an attempt to escape his loneliness, and he suspected that Zalith was trying to keep up with his old ways but with solely Alucard. Luther hated to think about it—to think about how many times today that demon had used Alucard. It only motivated him more to save his boss from this life he'd obviously settled for.

He had to think of an excuse to stay; he had to come up with something that would yield the same results he envisioned. "Detlaff's been talking a lot more lately," he said—and it wasn't a lie because Alucard's guest *had* been saying a lot, but most of it seemed like gibberish. However, maybe it would interest Alucard. The vampire never really said why it was so important to keep an eye on that Detlaff guy, nor why it was so important to have so much security around him. He was evidently important, wasn't he?

"Saying vhat?" Alucard mumbled.

"Talks about Lucifer a lot. Reminds us at least once every ten minutes that Lucifer is coming to rescue him and that all of us are going to pay for hurting him. He also yaps on about vampires and how pathetic we are. He likes to ask about you and insult you, too. Strange little man."

"None of zhis is news to me," Alucard uttered. "Get—"

"He talks about Zalith, too."

Alucard's attention seemed to have been grasped. The Vampire Lord took his eyes off his desk, scowled, and glared at Luther. "I gazzer 'e just vants on about 'ow much 'e 'ates 'im, too?"

"That, and he also likes to tell us that he, like you, will suffer immensely for the things he's done. According to Detlaff, Lucifer has quite a few reasons to hate him."

Alucard sighed and rested his arms on his desk. "And zhese veasons are?"

"Well, Lucifer doesn't yet know that Zalith's harbouring you, but that's one reason. Another is that he upsets your sister so much—"

"Zon't call 'er my sister," Alucard snapped.

Luther held up his hands. "Sorry. Anyway... apparently, he tried to get Lucifer's followers involved in some war a long time ago and tried to get Varana to convince Lucifer for him. Didn't work out. He also wiped out a lot of Lilidian demons a few years back, and that's got like... half the Numen up in arms."

"I alveady know about zhe Lilidian zemons. 'E killed zhem because zhey vere all lined up to take 'is place vhen Zamien killed 'im. So, he got vid of zhem so zhat Zamien 'ad no choice but to keep 'im alive."

"Oh," Luther said with a frown. He was running out of infor—

"'E said zhat Luciver is looking to kill Zaliv vor zhis?" Alucard asked.

Luther shrugged. "Sure sounded like it."

Still frowning, the vampire looked down at his desk.

"He also talks a lot about Damien," Luther added.

Both anger and discomfort flickered across Alucard's face. He snarled and swivelled in his seat, turning his back to Luther. "Vhat 'e 'as to say about zhat creature does not matter. You've told me vhat you came to tell me, so get out bevore Zaliv vinds you 'ere," he warned him.

Luther frowned anxiously. Alucard had his back to him, and the opportunity he'd been waiting for was right in front of him. He knew that mentioning Damien would make Alucard uncomfortable enough to hide his expression, and Luther wasn't going to waste what little time he might have. He reached into his pocket, pulled out a small vial of surripio, and leaned over the table. He swiftly poured the black powder into Alucard's brandy, and as the drug quickly dissolved into the drink, Luther stood up straight and sighed deeply. "I saw what happened…with Zalith and Varana—"

"I said get out," Alucard repeated.

"Whenever you realize that you'll never be his first priority, you might actually begin to understand that you deserve better," Luther snapped.

Alucard swivelled around in his seat and glared up at him with a look of such animosity in his eyes that Luther knew it was time to go…at least for now.

Without another word, he turned around and left The Vampire Lord's office—and now, he'd just have to wait.

Chapter Twelve

Delusion

| Alucard |

As his door shut, Alucard huffed irritably. Listening to Luther try to convince him that he didn't need Zalith had become normal, and if he felt anything at all about what Luther said, it was that he had insulted Zalith by practically calling him a liar. Zalith had said and continued to say on multiple occasions that Alucard was his first priority, and Alucard had no reason to doubt him. He might have left him to go and talk to Varana right now, but that was because he didn't want to do it in front of the guests, not because she was more important…right?

He rolled his eyes, picked up his drink, and took another sip. He didn't want to sit around thinking about how much Varana irritated him and how much he wished Zalith wouldn't just immediately jump to her call. Luther told him that Lucifer was most likely looking to kill Zalith, too, and that brought deep concern to his heart. Zalith already put himself in so much danger for his sake, and he felt guiltier about it every day. Now, to hear that he was probably in more danger made him feel worse.

Once Zalith was done with Varana, he'd tell him what Luther said, and he'd tell him that Luther decided to step foot in their home again. While he felt too exhausted to punish him, he was sure that Zalith might enjoy the opportunity.

Sighing, he sipped from his drink once more and slumped back in his seat. He silenced his thoughts, sinking into his fatigue. He wasn't sure how long Zalith might be, and he wasn't sure what he wanted to do in the meantime, but the longer he sat there, the more he began to feel as though he wanted to call it a night. He was tired, he was irritated, and he had dealt with enough people for one night.

While he sat there, though, he began to feel his fatigue growing. He wasn't even sure if it was his exhaustion causing him to feel so…suddenly disorientated. Frowning, he placed his drink down and sat up straight, trying to dismiss the strange feeling, but as each moment began to pass a little slower than the last, Alucard could tell that something wasn't right.

His mind went blank, his body began to feel numb, and he felt his ethos fading, leaving him feeling as though a dagger had been plunged through his chest. And as his head spun, the only thing he could think of was Zalith. He didn't know what was wrong, but he knew he needed help, and the moment his dizziness started feeling as though it was dragging him into a state of unconsciousness, he pulled himself from his seat and headed for the stairs that led up to his study.

But everything felt odd…*wrong*; he was so dizzy and confused. It hit him so abruptly that he had to grip the wall beside him to keep himself on his feet. However, he couldn't feel the wall. His eyes and body were heavy, and whatever was happening, he couldn't even try to fight it.

As the world around him began to appear as nothing but a strange, blurred discombobulation, Alucard struggled to keep his balance, and all he could do was hope that Zalith would find him before whatever this was consumed him entirely.

| Luther |

Five minutes should be more than enough time.

Luther stopped waiting by the bathroom and headed into Alucard's office again. When he got inside, he saw Alucard attempting to climb the stairs to his study. Luther shut the door behind him and rushed to the vampire. He gripped Alucard's shoulder and pushed his back against the wall, and when the vampire lifted his hand in what might be an attempt to attack, Luther snatched his wrist and pinned his arm at his side.

However, now that he had Alucard where he wanted him, he found himself once again acknowledging how wrong this was. But…it was the only way he'd get what he *needed* and what he wanted. *He* deserved this, and so did Alucard—so did *Zalith*. And the thought of having to let Alucard crawl into bed with that demon tonight banished his hesitation.

As Alucard scowled at him in confusion, Luther kept his hand on his right shoulder, keeping his back against the wall. The vampire stopped resisting, so Luther let go of his wrist and reached into his trouser pocket. What he put in Alucard's drink was only somewhat sedating him; what was inside the syringe that he pulled out of his pocket would help him get what he had come for. He didn't hesitate as he pierced Alucard's neck with its needle, and he watched the vampire's face as his look of confusion faded into something of a vacant, disorientated stare the moment he injected him with the hallucinogen.

Luther placed the needle on the desk beside him and stared at Alucard for a few moments, waiting for his panicked breaths to calm, waiting for his taut body to settle. He kept his hand on Alucard's shoulder, and as the vampire slowly frowned, his eyes shifted and met Luther's gaze.

"Alucard?" Luther asked.

Alucard stared at him for a few tense seconds. But as his frown thickened, and he leaned his head back against the wall, he asked, "Zaliv?"

Luther's plan was working. Although he still felt guilty, the thought of finally touching Alucard sent his hesitation far, far away. He'd not waste a moment. He slowly lifted his hand and moved it towards Alucard's face, and as the vampire frowned in discontent, Luther placed his hand on the side of his face. He leaned closer, and as his lips *finally* touched Alucard's, Luther felt relieved. He'd devoted his life to Alucard, and he wasn't going to stand around anymore as if he was some unimportant employee. He'd known Alucard for decades; he deserved this more than Zalith ever would.

Alucard didn't kiss back despite the hallucinogen making him think that Luther was Zalith. But Luther didn't care. As long as he didn't start fighting, he wasn't concerned.

However, Alucard quickly moved his hand to Luther's shoulder. At first, Luther's heart skipped a beat as the thought of Alucard reciprocating his intentions filled his mind, but he soon understood that Alucard was trying to push him away. Luther didn't want to stop, though. His first kiss felt so right that after taking a moment to stare at Alucard's confused face, he leaned in for another.

Alucard suddenly shoved Luther, who growled irritably. He wasn't going to let *anything* ruin this or take away what little time he might have. He grabbed both of Alucard's wrists and pinned his arms against the wall as Alucard grunted and snarled, but the drug was doing its job, keeping the vampire disorientated and weak.

As Alucard frowned, exhaled, and calmed down again, Luther slowly let go of his arms. He wanted to kiss him, and he so sorely wished Alucard would kiss back, but to his dismay, the hallucinogen wasn't working as effectively as the sedative.

He dragged his hands down Alucard's clothed body and quickly started unbuttoning his blazer. Luther pulled it off him and smacked the vampire's hands away when he tried to tell him to stop, his words slurred and quiet. But he couldn't stop; he was so close, closer than he'd ever been. And after this, this whole thing Alucard had going on with Zalith would *have* to end…and then, he'd belong to Luther.

With angst building inside him, Luther chucked Alucard's blazer on the floor and started unbuttoning his shirt. Alucard still tried to stop him; the vampire seemed to have gathered enough strength to try and pull away from the wall, but Luther frowned in desperation, gripped his arms, and pushed him back against it.

"It's okay," Luther breathed. "You need this just as much as I do."

Alucard scowled in what looked like distress, gripping Luther's wrist as he continued to unbutton his shirt, and once all the buttons were undone, he pulled the shirt apart and revealed Alucard's body.

Luther gawped at Alucard's muscles as fascination shivered through him. He'd never seen him without a shirt, and he wasn't surprised to see how fit and attractive he was beneath it. Overpowering excitement ensnared him.... How could he *not* touch? He placed his hand on the vampire's naked chest, staring at his pecs and abs. He stroked his hand down his body, glancing at Alucard's face to see that his confounded look had become utter discomfort.

With a scowl on his face, Luther set his eyes back on Alucard's body and slowly dragged his hand down to his stomach. He then hastily gripped Alucard's belt, but that was when the vampire disapproved with a lot more strength than before. He must have been gathering his strength; he snatched Luther's wrist so tightly that Luther winced painfully, and as he shifted his eyes to Alucard's face, he saw his glower of hostility.

But Luther wouldn't stop—not now. He fought back, struggling with Alucard for a moment. Alucard managed to pull himself away from the wall and snarled angrily, but Luther swiftly snatched the vampire's throat and slammed him back against the wall.

Luther's calm, relaxed curiosity became a forceful, irritated insistency. Why couldn't he just cooperate? Why did he have to make everything so hard? He'd always hated how Alucard chose to make things difficult, and right now, his refusal to do something so simple as stand there made Luther feel infuriated.

The last thing he wanted to do was hurt Alucard, though; he wanted to show him that he was better for him than Zalith. So when Alucard snarled and tried to pull free, Luther moved his hand to the side of his face and stared at him. The drugs seemed to be working on and off, and surely enough, as Luther waited, it started to take hold of Alucard once more, forcing him to calm down.

Luther guided his hand down from the side of Alucard's face and to his shoulder, where he gripped his shirt and started to pull it off him. However, when he pulled it over Alucard's shoulder, he noticed something peculiar. Creeping over the vampire's left shoulder was a faint, raised scar, one Luther had never seen before. He felt curious, so he leaned closer, peering down Alucard's back as he eased the shirt over his arm.

But what Luther saw made him feel...repulsed. Alucard's back looked like it was *covered* in raised and deep scars so horrific that Luther couldn't take his eyes off them. Alucard then suddenly gripped his wrist again, and this time, he had no trouble forcing Luther back since he'd become so overwhelmed with confusion.

Luther wished he hadn't seen those scars; it turned him off a whole lot, but... it made him think. There was no way Zalith had seen that and ignored it; there was no way someone like him could love something like that about Alucard, and Luther felt that if he could forget those scars, that would already make him so much better for Alucard. Alucard was clearly insecure about them—that had to be why he always kept his back covered—and as horrific as they were, Luther would do his best to ignore them.

He pulled Alucard's shirt back over his shoulder and set his eyes on his distressed face. As he placed his hand on Alucard's chest, Luther frowned in confliction. "Alucard?" he asked quietly.

Alucard's conflicted scowl thickened.

Luther moved closer and kissed the side of Alucard's face. Maybe he was being too hasty. Perhaps he was trying to move things along too fast. Zalith was nowhere to be seen, and Alucard was still sedated. Luther felt as if he should slow down a little...and maybe Alucard would stop being so reluctant.

So he kissed his face again and moved his hands around Alucard's waist to pull him closer—but that was when Alucard attacked. Before Luther could comprehend, Alucard swiftly reached over to his desk, snatched whatever was closest, and stabbed it into Luther's side, sending several things on top of his desk to the floor in the commotion. With a startled wince of pain, Luther let go of Alucard and dropped to his knees as he gripped whatever had been stabbed into his side.

Alucard moved past him—

Luther couldn't let him get away. He wasn't done yet. Zalith hadn't found them, Luther didn't feel content, and if Alucard got away, he'd *never* get another opportunity like this. Leaving whatever was in his side in place, he hurried to his feet, turned around, and darted after Alucard, who was heading for the stairs. Luther was sure that he was running to get to Zalith, and that made him feel furious.

With an infuriated snarl, Luther snatched Alucard's arm, pulled him back, and threw him against the wall before Alucard could try to defend himself. To Luther's relief, the sedative was still working—if it weren't, Alucard would have surely executed him by now.

But that didn't scare him. He wasn't afraid, he was *angry*, impatient, tired. He was *done* with *never* getting what he wanted, and as he watched Alucard struggle to his feet, he glowered down at him. Alucard always took what he wanted, Zalith clearly did the same, and Luther wasn't going to remain some unimportant little bottom feeder anymore. He'd take what he wanted, and not even Zalith or Alucard would stop him.

The moment Alucard climbed to his feet, Luther threw himself at him, gripped his arms, and pinned him against the wall. Alucard snarled and grunted in struggle, but any hint of hesitation that Luther might have had disappeared long ago. He yanked the letter opener Alucard had stabbed him with from his waist, threw it to the floor, and glared at Alucard's confused, distressed face. He tried to be patient with him, but he had already waited years, and he wouldn't wait a moment longer.

He eagerly unbuckled Alucard's belt, pulled it from around his waist, and tossed it aside. Anticipation raced through him as he unbuttoned the vampire's trousers, and his racing heart became enthralled by desperation. Once the buttons came away, he eased his fingers inside, and when his tips brushed against Alucard's crotch, he exhaled shakily onto Alucard's neck.

Alucard winced in distress. "S-stop," he slurred, trying to break free.

Luther shook his head as he murmured, "It's okay. You want this."

With a grunt and a grimace, Alucard gritted his teeth. "No."

He didn't want to risk anyone hearing him, so Luther clamped his other hand over Alucard's mouth, silencing him. Then, he wrapped his fingers around the vampire's dick, groaning as he felt its soft length. He wasn't expecting him to be hard, but he'd make short work of that problem. As he kissed Alucard's reluctant lips, he stroked his shaft, becoming more and more eager as each second raced past.

"Don't fight it," Luther whispered, caressing his crotch a little faster. "You *know* you want it, you know I'm better for you than he could ever be."

Alucard winced again, trying to push Luther away—

Luther snarled frustratedly and slammed Alucard against the wall. "I said you want it!" he growled, turning Alucard to face the wall. He held him against it, ignoring his panicked grunts and confused whimpers. And then he stroked the back of the vampire's neck, trying to calm him. "Just relax," he muttered as he tugged on his own belt, unbuckling it.

His anticipation became unbearable, and as he pulled his trousers down, he exhaled excitedly. *Finally*, he'd have Alucard.

Chapter Thirteen

Death Penalty

| Zalith |

While he sat on the edge of his and Alucard's bed, Zalith let Varana cry on his shoulder with her arms around him. He wasn't sure what was wrong with her, but he could feel that she was not only distraught but also deeply *disturbed.* Something happened, and the longer she took to tell him what it was, the more his concern grew.

He held his arm around her and lightly patted her back in an attempt to console her. "If you don't want to talk about it, I can just read your mind instead," he offered.

"No," she said with a pout, shaking her head.

"So what happened?" he asked for the *fifth* time.

Varana sniffled and held him tightly. "My sister's a huge bitch," she complained.

Zalith sighed quietly. That made him feel much more relaxed; Varana and Ysmay fought *all* the time, so it wasn't new. But then he frowned and looked down at her again. "You were talking to your sister in the middle of the party? She's not here, is she?" he asked with a quiet, nervous laugh.

"We talked in the mirror—she was just saying happy Yule," she answered.

The demon nodded. "Well, what happened between you two to make you so upset?"

Once again, she shook her head, buried her face in his shoulder, and sulked.

Zalith huffed lightly and then sat in silence while he let Varana wail into his shoulder. He wanted to give her time to calm down, but he felt like he should probably be downstairs with Alucard and his guests. He didn't want to leave Alucard alone for too long; he saw that his vampire was upset when he said he was going to go and talk to Varana, and he knew how Alucard tended to sink into his emotions. He didn't want him to be sad tonight, and he also didn't want his guests to think that he was rude.

He waited a few moments and said, "We can stay here for a few more minutes but I need to get back downstairs." But then something hit him. His instincts told him that something was wrong—either that or it was the connection he had with Alucard through their imprints. But whatever was warning him, he *knew* that something was wrong with Alucard. He felt distress, struggle, and something like a plea for help. It made Zalith feel desperate, confused, and overwrought with worry. He had no idea what was happening; all he knew was that he had to get to Alucard right away.

Zalith stood up and headed to the door as quickly as he could—

"Where are you going?" Varana asked, standing up.

"Alucard," he said, leaving the room. He rushed downstairs and towards Alucard's location as quickly as he could, and when the smell of blood smacked his face, he started panicking. But he didn't have time to think; he just had to get to him.

The demon followed Alucard's aura, and when he pushed the door to the vampire's office open, he set his eyes on Luther, who had Alucard pinned against a wall with his trousers down. Alucard looked distressed and confused, and Luther's grin faded to a scowl when he turned his head to glare at Zalith.

He didn't even think about it. As horror and rage burned through him, Zalith burst forward, gripped Luther's arms, and pulled him off Alucard with a vicious snarl, making the vampire drop to the floor as if he had no strength at all. Zalith let his fury rule him. He savagely extended his claws and grabbed Luther's crotch, and as he tore the man's dick and balls off with an enraged yell, Luther screamed and wailed, his blood spraying onto the carpet. The demon then shoved the bloody mess into Luther's mouth and threw the ugly, disgusting little man across the room and as far away from Alucard as he could get him; he didn't even want to think about what might have happened if he hadn't gotten there in time, but he was going to make sure that Luther regretted every moment of what he'd done.

Zalith threw himself at Luther, his disgust and hatred burning so intensely that he felt as though he would kill Luther... but not yet. He was going to make him suffer, he was going to make him beg and wail and plead for death. Luther *assaulted* Alucard—he was clearly about to try and rape him—and Alucard looked like he had no idea what was going on. Zalith had no words to explain his feelings; he just wanted to *kill*. And so he grabbed Luther and crashed his fist into his face so hard that his skull broke with a loud crack, and as Luther made some feeble, pathetic attempts to fight back, Varana raced off in what Zalith assumed was an attempt to get help.

The demon felt nothing but anger—nothing but sheer fury. He knew that he could beat Luther to death in a mere moment, and as much as he'd like to do that, he wouldn't grant Luther such mercy. No, he was going to make this atrocious man suffer for everything he had done and everything he thought about doing, and he was sure that once he spoke to Alucard and found out what happened, his anger would only become worse.

"Take him out of here," Zalith snarled, standing up to glower down at Luther as Varana returned with Tyrus.

Without a word, Tyrus dragged the wailing, writhing, dickless man out of Alucard's office, and Varana followed him, closing the door behind them to leave Zalith alone with Alucard.

Zalith quickly wiped his bloody hands on his suit and rushed to Alucard, who was huddled up in the corner behind his desk, where he must have fled to in the commotion. He looked lost, almost as if he had no idea what was going on. But Zalith was still overwrought with anger, and his worry was quickly increasing as he crouched at Alucard's side.

He moved to help Alucard get up. "Are you—"

Before he could finish his sentence, however, and before he could grip Alucard's arms, the vampire panicked and fought him off, snarling in hostility as he shoved Zalith away.

Confused, Zalith stared at him. "What's wrong?"

"Zon't touch me," Alucard growled, glaring up at him as Zalith slowly crouched back down beside him.

"Okay," he agreed warily. "I won't touch you." He stared at Alucard's distressed face. "Are you okay?"

But Alucard just glared at him with a look of such confusion in his eyes that it almost seemed as though he didn't recognize Zalith.

"What happened?" the demon asked, trying to resist the urge to touch him while he searched for any physical injury.

There didn't seem to be any surface wounds. The vampire sat there with his shirt undone and his belt unbuckled, and Zalith refused to picture what Luther had done to him. But why did Alucard look so disoriented? Did he even know where he was? Did he have any idea of what happened or what was happening?

"Alucard?" he asked slowly, staring into the vampire's confounded, conflicted eyes. "Do you…know where you are? Do you know who I am? Who *you* are?"

Alucard glowered at him but didn't answer.

"Alucard?"

The vampire then frowned and looked like he was trying to concentrate. "Vhat…vhat do you vant?" he asked, and he sounded exhausted.

Zalith was starting to feel just as distressed as his vampire looked. He wanted to touch him—to just put his hand on his arm or something comforting, but he said he wouldn't, so he resisted. "I want to make sure you're okay, Alucard. I left you for five minutes, and I came down here to see Luther holding you against a wall…and you're acting strange. What happened?" he asked again, hoping he'd get an answer this time.

Alucard scowled. "Luther?"

"Yes," he answered sullenly. "What happened?"

The vampire took his eyes off Zalith and glanced around the room. "I zon't...know," he answered, searching until he set his eyes on his desk. "I vas...dvinking."

"Drinking what?"

Alucard shrugged and muttered, "Vas...someving."

Zalith's concern intensified. Alucard couldn't have drunk so much that he'd become intoxicated enough to be acting like this in the space of five minutes—Alucard never even got drunk—and Zalith could only assume that Luther did something...perhaps even put something in Alucard's drink. But he didn't want to jump to conclusions. He didn't know what was wrong and sitting there trying to get Alucard to tell him wasn't helping. He needed help, and coincidently, someone who he knew could assist him was already there.

He stood up and hurried to Alucard's door, pulled it open, and searched the hall for Edwin. The butler immediately saw Zalith and made his way over.

"Go and get Erwin—the blue and red-haired elf," Zalith instructed.

Edwin nodded and hurried into the ballroom.

Zalith then returned to Alucard's side—

"Vhere is Zaliv?" Alucard demanded.

Frowning as he crouched beside him, Zalith stared at his confused face. "*I'm* Zalith."

Alucard glared at him, staring into his eyes, looking him up and down.

Did he not recognize him? How? Why?

Slowly, Zalith moved his hand towards Alucard's shoulder. "Alucard, it's me," he said despondently, and as he placed his hand on him, he felt the vampire tense up.

Alucard glowered at him for a few moments as though he was considering what Zalith said. Then, when a frown appeared on his face, he slowly lifted his hand and placed it over the hand that the demon had on his shoulder. However, when the door to his office then opened, Alucard panicked and let go. It looked like he was preparing to defend himself.

"It's okay," Zalith said softly and looked over his shoulder at the door.

"What can I help you with?" Erwin asked as they entered the room with Edwin.

"I don't know what you're capable of right now, but I think he's been drugged," Zalith answered. "Or at the very least concussed. I don't know what happened."

"Ali?" Erwin frowned in worry and rushed over. "Was he alone?" they asked, looking at Zalith as they crouched beside him.

"No," Zalith answered. "Luther was in here with him, but he's been apprehended."

Erwin gained a look of skepticism as they stood up and glanced around the room.

"He said he was drinking; maybe Luther put something in his drink," Zalith said.

The elf made their way to Alucard's desk, picked up his glass of dark liquor and stared into it. "I wouldn't put it past him," they said, swishing the liquid around. "I don't have anything on me to tell whether or not there was something put in this; if that's what happened, Luther would have known to use something Ali wouldn't detect."

"Could you perhaps go and get something that you can use to tell?" Zalith snarled irritably.

The elf looked at him as they placed Alucard's drink down. "Of course... I'll see what I have in my carriage," they said. Then, they swiftly left Alucard's office.

Zalith set his eyes back on Alucard, who stared at him in confusion. He wanted to find out what exactly had been done to him; he wanted to help him feel better... but could he? Alucard had just been through something that no one should ever have to experience, and the longer the demon sat there and stared at him, the more his heart hurt. He shouldn't have left him alone. He was supposed to protect him, and he'd almost let one of the most terrible things happen to the man he loved.

Chapter Fourteen

— ⊰ ✝ ⊱ —

The Night's Conclusion

| Zalith |

Zalith slowly slipped his hand into Alucard's and took hold of it. Alucard remained wary, but he let the demon help him to his feet and lead him to one of the couches, where Zalith sat him down. The demon sat beside him, keeping hold of his hand and staring at his confused face. He watched as Alucard's eyes occasionally darted around the room as if he was still trying to work out whether or not this was happening, and it made Zalith feel dismayed.

But he had to focus on Alucard and make sure that he was okay. Erwin hadn't long left to see if they had anything to help find out what happened to Alucard, and while Zalith waited, his concern was accompanied by despair. Alucard evidently had no idea what happened or what was going on, and Zalith didn't know what else to do other than try to comfort him until they could work out how to snap him out of his confusion.

The demon slowly moved his hands towards Alucard's shirt; although the vampire seemed to have accepted that he was actually Zalith, he still frowned defensively and snatched the demon's wrists when he lightly gripped each side of his shirt. They stared at one another for a moment, but Alucard gradually let go, allowing Zalith to start buttoning his shirt back up.

"How are you feeling?" the demon asked quietly.

Alucard stared aimlessly. "I zon't know," he answered.

With a sullen frown, Zalith finished buttoning Alucard's shirt and pulled him closer. "I'm here with you now, baby. You're safe," he said as he moved his arms around the vampire and pulled him into a tight embrace, and when he felt Alucard's tense body begin to relax, he tightened his grip around him.

They sat there in silence for a while. Eventually, Alucard lightly pushed Zalith down so that he'd lay on the couch; Zalith complied, and when Alucard rested atop him and buried his face in his chest, the demon moved his right arm around him and started caressing his hair with his left hand. He knew Alucard was exhausted, and if they weren't waiting on Erwin, he'd carry him up to bed. But he wanted to know what had been done to him…just in case it was something that required medical attention.

The elf soon returned to Alucard's office and carried their briefcase to the desk. They placed it on the table and then started rummaging through it while Zalith kept a close eye on them.

Erwin muttered to themself, flipping through a notebook as they picked up Alucard's drink in their other hand. They then laid out tiny strips of paper, filled a small pipette with the drink from Alucard's glass, and started adding a drop to each piece of paper. Clearly, they were trying to determine what had been put in Alucard's drink, if anything at all. And Zalith waited…glaring at them, waiting as patiently as he could manage for the moment Erwin would tell him what happened.

But once Erwin stopped and stared down at the papers for a few moments, they seemed to notice something on the floor. Zalith watched skeptically as the elf crouched; he had no idea what Erwin might be doing, but as he watched them stand up, the demon frowned impatiently.

Erwin turned to face him and held up what appeared to be a small syringe. "Unless Ali chooses to medicate himself in such a manner, I would suspect that this might have something to do with his current state."

Staring at it, Zalith's anger became rage once again—but he'd not show it. He had to be calm for Alucard. "Is there any way to tell what was in it?"

"Unfortunately not," Erwin answered. "If we want to know, I'll have to test Ali's blood. As for the drink…" they said, glancing over their shoulder to look down at the papers, "it appears that Luther managed to slip a sedative into it—surripio, a kind of sedative that would cause Ali to lose control of seventy-to-ninety percent of his body. I understand from our past that Ali's body burns through things a lot faster, so I imagine that he'll fully recover from the surripio in roughly…twenty minutes," they explained, looking back over at them. "However, this kind of sedative would not leave Ali disorientated and confused like this. I suspect this syringe contained a hallucinogen, but I still want to check just to be safe."

That name—Ali…. Zalith *hated* it, and he knew Alucard did, too. If he didn't need Erwin's expertise right now, he'd warn them to stop saying it. But he had to be reasonable. He wanted to know what was in that needle, but he'd not force Alucard to agree to something that he might not be comfortable with.

"Alucard," he said quietly, nudging the vampire a little.

"Vhat?" he grumbled sleepily.

"Erwin needs to look at your blood to see what's in your system, okay?"

Alucard tensed up. "No," he denied.

Zalith frowned sullenly. "They need to do it so that we can figure out what happened," he said, caressing the vampire's hair. "And so that we can help you feel better. It's going to be okay. If Erwin does anything they shouldn't be doing, I'll kill them right where they stand," he added as Erwin frowned anxiously.

Alucard remained silent for a moment, clearly debating whether or not he wanted to let Erwin do what they needed to do. But eventually, he sighed heavily and sat up. Zalith helped him sit and rolled up his sleeve once he unbuttoned his cuffs.

Zalith kept his arm around Alucard, watching closely as Erwin took a syringe from their case and then began taking some of Alucard's blood with it.

"This will take a little longer than the drink," Erwin said. "Especially since his blood isn't human, and it's humans I specialize in."

"How long?" Zalith asked.

"Five-ten minutes," they answered, carefully pulling the needle from Alucard's arm.

Alucard's small wound immediately healed, so Erwin didn't have to cover it with anything. The elf returned to Alucard's desk to start testing his blood as Zalith rolled his eyes impatiently.

Zalith laid back down with Alucard, but when the vampire nuzzled his neck, he felt him tense up again—and that made him worry more. Was something wrong? Was he getting worse?

"Zaliv?" Alucard suddenly asked.

Frowning, he held him tightly. "Yes?"

Alucard shuffled around ever so slightly, resting his forehead on Zalith's shoulder as he exhaled deeply. "I veel vunny," he mumbled.

"Funny how, baby?" he asked worriedly, caressing his crimson hair.

Alucard didn't answer, though. He tensed up so much that he felt *frozen*, and then he abruptly sat up, revealing a nauseous look on his pale face.

"Alucard?" Zalith asked, placing his hand on his shoulder as he sat up, too.

The vampire scowled but then hurriedly got up, raced out of his office, and darted into the closest bathroom.

Zalith followed but stopped when Alucard slammed the door. He wouldn't barge in; Alucard obviously wanted to be alone. So when he reached the door, he stopped outside and waited. He wanted to comfort and help him, but what could he really do right now? Waiting and trying to keep his worry from forcing him to open the door was just about it.

But his anger started to claw its way to the surface. Alucard was in pain—he was confused, uncomfortable, and now he was being sick... all because of Luther. The things Zalith wanted to do to that disgusting little man—he couldn't wait to kill him.

He didn't want to think about it, but how could he not? He left Alucard alone for *five* minutes and Luther used that time to try—once again, and in a much more despicable way—to try and take Alucard away from him. He would have thought Luther had learnt his lesson when he'd had both his hands broken, but he clearly hadn't, and this time, Zalith was going to do more than break his hands.

When Alucard finally opened the bathroom door, Zalith took his hand and pulled the vampire into a light embrace, afraid that it might make him feel worse if he hugged him too tightly.

"Are you okay?" the demon asked.

Alucard rested his head on Zalith's shoulder and exhaled deeply. "I vant to sleep," he muttered.

"Do you want to go and lie down? I'll be up once Erwin has found out what happened."

The vampire nodded.

Zalith carefully scooped him up in his arms and then carried him to their bedroom. When he reached their bed, he gently placed Alucard down and sat beside him. "Do you want to take these off?" he asked, fiddling with the collar of Alucard's shirt, and as the vampire started unbuttoning it, Zalith helped.

Once his shirt was off, though, Alucard lifted the blanket and crawled beneath it, exhaling deeply as he rested his head on his pillows.

Zalith knew he was exhausted, and although he wanted to know exactly what happened, he wasn't going to try and get the vampire to talk about it. For now, he'd let him rest. He helped Alucard into the covers, pulled them over him, and made sure that he was comfortable before kissing his forehead. "I'll be back soon—"

"Vait," Alucard said with a frown, snatching his wrist before he could move away. "Zon't go."

Zalith frowned sadly and shuffled closer to him. "Okay, but I don't want Erwin coming up here, so we can go back downstairs for a moment," he suggested, "and then we can both come back upstairs and rest."

Alucard frowned hesitantly and gradually let go of his wrist. "I zon't vant to get up."

Staring down at him, Zalith smiled slightly and moved his hand to the side of Alucard's face. "I'll stay here with you for a few moments," he said, and as the vampire turned onto his side and made himself comfortable, Zalith stayed with him, gently caressing his hair.

Zalith gazed at him, watching as he slowly drifted off. Alucard had already dealt with so much today, and now this, too? Zalith felt so guilty. Alucard didn't deserve anything like this, and he couldn't help but feel like this was his fault. He should have killed Luther *months* ago.

He still didn't want to think about Luther, though. That grotesque man wasn't a problem anymore.

The demon waited until Alucard was asleep and glanced at his pocket watch. Twenty minutes had passed, and he was sure that Erwin must be coming close to discovering what Alucard had been drugged with.

Zalith kissed Alucard's forehead and then stood up. He made his way out of their room, downstairs, and back into Alucard's office.

Erwin took their eyes off whatever they were working on when Zalith stepped in.

"How much longer?" the demon asked impatiently.

The elf looked back down at their work. "A few moments. I've narrowed it down already—it *was* a hallucinogen," they said, glancing at Zalith—

"What?" he snarled, his rage returning. Luther not only drugged Alucard once with a sedative but then again with a hallucinogen. He had no words to describe how he felt, nor those to explain what he was going to do to Luther.

"I suspect..." Erwin said, gawping down at their work, "yes...he used a rather popular one—this drug," they said, looking at Zalith. "Noctryl, also known as Gloomshade; a lot of people use it around the Citadel, and I hear that it's travelled far out of Nefastus. Depending on the dosage, it can cause dizziness, nausea, sedation, drowsiness, confusion, memory loss, amnesia, hallucinations, confusion, and a dissociative state where the victim feels detached from reality. It can also result in memory loss and immobilization. Its most popular use is in bars and brothels. Say someone was committing sexual acts, this drug would often allow them to see the person they *actually* want to be involved with. I get cases of it all the time; people often overdose. This is probably why Ali is so confused; he might have had no idea that it was Luther in here with him, or if he did, it was likely that he couldn't fight him off. To be honest, if Ali was human, a dose of noctryl and surripio would have killed him," the elf explained sympathetically.

Zalith growled quietly, clenching his jaw and fists. At least Alucard was safe now. He'd got to him before Luther managed to force himself on him. But everything that Luther had already done made Zalith think about skinning what was left of him alive.

It was over, though. Alucard was okay...at least Zalith hoped he was.

"How long will the effects last?" the demon asked.

"It depends how much he gave him. Anywhere from an hour to twelve hours. But...Ali threw up not long ago, right?"

Zalith nodded.

"Then I think that most of what he was drugged with has left his system. I'd say...a few hours."

"Okay," Zalith said, reaching into his pocket. "Thank you." He pulled out a handful of Coronam papers and held them out to Erwin.

Erwin made their way over, took them from him, and slowly flicked through them as they glanced up at Zalith. "Is there…something else you want from me? This is an awful lot for a simple determination of substances."

"Your discretion," Zalith answered.

"Of course," Erwin agreed, tucking the money into their pocket. "I shall clear up my things and be on my way, then."

"Thank you," he said once more.

Erwin cleaned their things off Alucard's desk, putting everything back into their briefcase while Zalith watched. "Oh, and I feel I should warn you. I travelled a lot with Ali once upon a time, and I saw a lot, learned a lot. I suspect that the Vampire Council may come calling. Any and all incidents of this…nature…involving vampires are often dealt with by them, so don't be surprised if a group of Inquisitors turns up on your doorstep."

"Inquisitors?"

"Judges. The vampires who determine the punishment for crimes committed."

Zalith frowned *hard*. He didn't want to hand Luther over to some vampire judges, he wanted to kill him himself.

"Although you're Ali's mate, so it's quite possible that they may hand his punishment over to you to decide; you just have to ask," Erwin explained. "It is your right, after all."

He didn't want to deal with a Vampire Council, nor did he want to let Luther be taken from the cell he was being tossed in, but if that was the way things worked with vampires in this world, he'd do his best to comply—they were Alucard's rules, after all. One thing was for sure, though: he wasn't letting *anyone* near his vampire.

Once the elf left, Zalith called over Edwin, who had been lingering in the hall.

"Go and tell my guests that something work-related has come up, and Alucard and I will be absent for the rest of the night. Everyone is welcome to stay and enjoy the party but keep an eye on them for me," Zalith told him.

The butler nodded. "Of course, sir."

As Edwin headed to the ballroom, Zalith sighed and made his way back upstairs.

When he returned to their bedroom, Zalith undressed and climbed into bed with Alucard. He cuddled up beside him, holding him tightly…and tried to keep himself from sinking into his anger.

But he couldn't stop thinking about how much he wanted to kill Luther—how much he couldn't wait to make him suffer endlessly. But Alucard needed him right now, and he wasn't going to leave his side. So with a quiet sigh, he did his best to relax and held his vampire in his embrace. He wanted Alucard to know that he was safe; the last thing he'd do was let him wake up alone.

He'd deal with Luther in the morning.

Chapter Fifteen

Sentenced

| **Zalith,** ***Saturday, Clausula 31st, 959(TG)—Nefastus*** |

The hours ticked by, and Zalith couldn't sleep. All he could think about was what he'd seen and what might have happened to Alucard if he hadn't reached him in time. Pure rage burned inside him, intensifying with each tick of the clock's hands. He didn't want to leave Alucard alone, but he didn't want to wait any longer to deal with Luther. The thought of tearing that man apart, making him suffer in ways his pathetic, tiny little brain could never imagine…it was consuming him.

He glanced at Alucard, who slept silently. Then, he looked at the clock. It was 3 a.m., and he'd heard the last of the party guests leave over an hour ago. He was sure that Alucard wouldn't wake any time soon, but he quietly summoned an izuret and told it to watch over his sleeping vampire just in case. While the izuret took its position on one of the dressers, Zalith carefully climbed out of bed and pulled some clothes on.

Swiftly and silently, he moved through the house; left through the patio doors, crossed the gardens, and walked into the dark forest. When he reached the limestone boulder that hid the entrance to the caves, he rolled his sleeves up and flexed his extended claws; he headed down below, navigating the darkness until he found the cell where Tyrus had locked Luther.

There he was…that disgusting, atrocious little creep, cowering and whimpering in the corner, his trembling, shackled hands covering the gory mess between his legs where his tiny dick had once been. He'd cried so much that his tears had become blood, a sign Zalith knew meant that a vampire was starting to starve. But he wasn't going to let starvation or blood loss end Luther. No. *He* would be the one to decide when and how he rotted away.

"Do you want a kit, sir?" Tyrus asked, emerging from the shadows.

"No," he muttered, unlocking the cell door.

With a nod, the allocer demon returned to his post.

Zalith scowled in revolt as he stepped into the cell; he watched Luther try to back up into the corner, but there was nowhere for him to go.

"Y-you can't... do this to me!" Luther cried, whimpering.

The demon closed the door behind him, and then he prowled towards Luther.

"V-Varana... will n-never forgive you!"

With a disgusted snarl, Zalith snatched Luther's throat and pulled him to his feet, pinning him against the wall. "The only thing Varana won't forgive me for is not giving her the chance to tear you apart herself," he growled, and then he dragged Luther over to the chair in the middle of the cell. He threw him in it, chained him down, and glowered at him for a moment.

Luther squirmed and struggled, trying to break free; bloody tears trickled down his broken, bruised face, and blood oozed from the gaping wound left in his crotch. "Y-you can't," he breathed, scowling up at him. "Alucard w—"

Zalith grabbed Luther's jaw, silencing him. "Don't you *dare* say his fucking name!" he roared in his face.

As he grunted and choked, Luther scowled at Zalith, his vampire fangs slowly extending almost as if it were a warning.

But Zalith felt nothing but fury. He wasn't patient enough to send Tyrus to fetch him a pair of plyers, so he harshly gripped Luther's left fang with his fingers and yanked it from his mouth.

Luther yelped and cried out in agony, writhing in the chair. He tried biting when Zalith gripped his other fang, but there wasn't anything he could do. The demon ripped it out, leaving Luther wailing and shrieking as blood oozed from his mouth.

Zalith sent both fangs up in white flames—they wouldn't grow back; he destroyed the healing ethos inside them that linked them to Luther's body. And the pathetic little man didn't take long to realize that. His cries grew louder, thickening with anger and despair, and as he continued attempting to break his chains, Zalith just glared at him, breathing deeply as his heart thumped. The urge to tear Luther apart was getting stronger; he wanted to claw and tear and slash and rip... but he wanted him to suffer. He wanted to take his time.

He started with his hands. Zalith snatched Luther's right wrist, and when he broke his fingers one by one, Luther screamed and howled—and those screams got even louder when the demon *ripped* each finger off, snapping their joins, tearing their flesh as Luther wailed and cried, shaking his head, begging, pleading.

What a pathetic cretin. What a weak, disgusting little rat of a man.

Zalith moved onto his left hand, but when he was about to start breaking Luther's fingers, he heard voices outside the cell, voices clashing with Tyrus' confused, firm refusal to let whoever was out there any deeper into the caves.

The demon snarled as he let go of Luther, and then he stepped outside the cell.

Four vampires stood in front of Tyrus, who looked over his shoulder at Zalith. The two men and two women wore long, dark robes, and their auras were strange, different to any vampire Zalith had encountered. It felt as if they were all the same person…or all part of the same consciousness.

"You are…Zalith?" one of the men asked, his voice thick with an accent almost like Alucard's, only weaker—perhaps not as old.

Zalith nodded. "And you are?"

"Inquisitor Ludovicus," said the tallest, dark-skinned man with hair as silver as the metal itself, bone-straight and reaching his waist, tied with a small black ribbon. This vampire had the strongest aura—he was over three hundred years old, and he was likely their leader.

"Inquisitor Sanchia," the smaller woman said, her eyes as red as blood, glowing in the darkness. She looked barely old enough to be considered an adult, but her aura suggested that she, too, was over three hundred.

"Inquisitor Emelina," the second woman said, her voice almost reminiscent of a snake. Her curled, silver hair was tied behind her head, and in her ears sat shimmering diamond earrings, sparkling as they caught the very dim light of the lanterns.

And the last man, also with silvery hair and blood-red eyes, said, "Inquisitor Wymond."

"We have been made aware of crimes committed by Luther Harcourt," Ludovicus said to Zalith. "As Inquisitors, is our job to assess serious crimes committed by vampires, and our job to issue punishment."

"Who made you aware?" Zalith questioned.

"No message necessary," Ludovicus said. "We are…connected to all vampires. It is like…grim reaper hive mind…in a way."

"Where is Luther?" Sanchia asked.

Despite having been expecting these vampires to show up after Erwin's warning, Zalith felt very defensive. He wasn't done hurting Luther; what if they wanted to take him and lock him in some vampire prison? No, he didn't deserve that mercy. He just hoped that Erwin was right when they suggested that the inquisitors might hand over the responsibility of Luther's punishment to him.

The demon nodded to the door of Luther's cell. "He's in there."

With complete disregard for Tyrus' presence, the four vampires glided past, pushing the allocer demon aside, and followed Zalith into Luther's cell.

A look of relief struck Luther's face when he saw the four Inquisitors, though. "Th-thank…God," he cried. "Y-you have…have to get this psycho away from me! He—"

"Luther Harcourt," Inquisitor Ludovicus said, ignoring Luther's cries of relief, pulling a scroll from the inside of his robes. "You are charged with assaulting our very own Lord, the sentence for which is death by sunlight."

"W-what are you talking about?" Luther stammered as if he had no idea why he was locked up or facing the Inquisitors.

"However, being a day walker, this method of execution is not possible. Therefore, death will instead be carried out by any means seen fit by our Lord's fated demon mate, Zalith," Inquisitor Ludovicus said, gesturing to Zalith with one arm.

"A-are you fucking c-crazy?!" Luther cried.

Sanchia handed Zalith a scroll tied with a red ribbon. "You have permission to execute him however you see fit; however, once he *is* dead, or at the very least mummified, please mark this death certification, thus banishing him from any realm that might await him after his soul leaves this body."

Taking the scroll, Zalith kept his eyes on Luther, who was panicking. Seeing the sheer horror on his face made the demon smile discreetly; he was going to enjoy dragging his death out for as long as he could.

"Y-you can't l-leave me with him!" Luther pleaded as Inquisitors Sanchia, Wymond, and Emelina left the room. "H-he's a ffffucking lunatic! Take me to the dungeons, starve me, anything!"

Ludovicus glowered at Luther as if he were a mere insect. "You are disgrace to our kind," he said firmly. "May your pathetic existence soon come to a much-desired end." And then he turned around and left.

"Wait!" Luther cried. "Th-this isn't right! Y-you're supposed to take me to-to the dungeons!"

Zalith closed the cell door once the vampires had left, and then he turned to face Luther. "You're not going anywhere," he snarled, tucking the scroll into his pocket as he prowled towards him.

Luther started crying again. "Alucard would ne—"

With a revolted, *furious* snarl, Zalith burst forward and snatched Luther's throat again. "What did I fucking say about his name?!" he yelled.

"A-all right!" Luther wailed.

But Zalith didn't let go. He glared into Luther's bloodshot eyes, going over in his head the hundreds of ways he'd hurt him, bleed him, and subject him to the worst kind of suffering any living or undead thing could experience. He'd make him suffer for every fucked up thought he'd ever had about Alucard, every disturbing, insane little fantasy that he'd dreamed up in his head.

"Tyrus," the demon called.

His subordinate appeared on the other side of the door. "Yes, sir?"

"Bring the roaches."

An amused smirk crept across Tyrus' face as he turned around and walked off.

Luther's eyes widened. "W-wh—"

Zalith tightened his grip on the man's throat, silencing him.

Moments later, Tyrus returned, stepping silently into the cell and handing Zalith the glass jar filled with writhing, dark mutagen roaches—a particular Eltarian torture method Zalith had come to favour. The bugs inside squirmed and scratched at the glass, their chittering noises thickening the tension in the air.

"Hold his mouth open," Zalith instructed, releasing his grip on Luther.

Tyrus nodded, and before Luther could react, he firmly seized his jaw and head, forcing his mouth open and tipping his head back. Luther's eyes widened in terror as he caught a glimpse of the roaches in the jar, their bodies pulsing with eagerness. Zalith unscrewed the lid, pausing briefly to let Luther absorb the sight of the writhing insects before tipping the jar.

The first roach slipped out, clinging to the edge of Luther's lip before skittering inside, quickly followed by a cascade of others, each one chittering as they plunged into his mouth. The moment the roaches hit the warm, damp space, they sprang to life, gnashing their tiny mandibles as they spread across his tongue, biting and burrowing. Luther gagged, his muffled screams vibrating through his throat as the creatures clawed and chewed at the sensitive flesh inside his mouth.

Once the last bug had slipped out, Tyrus clamped Luther's mouth shut and strapped a muzzle over his face, sealing in his muffled cries. The roaches, seemingly emboldened, began their relentless journey deeper into his body, gnawing their way down his throat. Zalith watched with grim satisfaction as Luther's muffled cries grew more desperate. Inside, the bugs burrowed and feasted, leaving trails of rot and decay in their wake. They weren't just consuming his flesh; their mutagen-infused bodies injected a toxin that spread the rot even faster, ensuring that every bite would fester, every inch of damage would throb with infection.

Luther's vampire body strained to heal itself, his veins pulsing as his regenerative abilities fought against the relentless spread of decay. But as each new wound was inflicted, it became clear that his powers would be overwhelmed. The bugs dug further, slipping past his throat into the deeper recesses of his body, leaving a trail of rotting tissue as they went. His skin paled further, a sickly pallor spreading as his body struggled in vain to repair the damage.

Zalith crossed his arms, watching as the roaches' venomous decay and relentless appetite began to take their toll, the dark satisfaction within him growing as Luther's cries reverberated off the cold stone walls, a haunting symphony of agony that he knew would continue long into the night.

"Send Danford an izuret," the demon said, handing the empty jar to Tyrus. "Tell it to tell him that Luther's been sentenced by the Vampire Council and locked up. He doesn't need the specific details."

With a nod, Tyrus left the room to do as he'd been told.

Zalith stood over Luther, watching as the mutagen roaches continued their merciless feast, burrowing deeper into his flesh, gnawing their way through tissue and muscle with ravenous abandon. Each muffled scream that escaped Luther's throat echoed through the dimly lit cell, reverberating off the cold stone walls like a twisted symphony of pain. For a moment, satisfaction filled Zalith, a dark sense of triumph knowing that this despicable man was enduring agony beyond comprehension, his body being eaten alive from the inside out.

But that satisfaction was fleeting, like a cold wind that quickly passed. The initial thrill of watching Luther's torment began to fade, and as it did, an unsettling hollowness crept in. He wanted this man to suffer—he deserved it tenfold—but with each passing second, Zalith's thoughts drifted further from the scene before him. His rage, the all-consuming need for vengeance, began to loosen its grip, and in its place, a more pressing concern took hold.

Alucard.

Alucard still needed him.

Zalith clenched his fists, his jaw tightening as he fought to reign in the torrent of emotions. Luther's suffering was satisfying in a way, yes, but it couldn't be his focus—not now. Alucard was still healing, still recovering; his well-being and his safety were far more important than this momentary vengeance. Luther's punishment wouldn't change the past, and it certainly wouldn't heal Alucard's wounds.

And then, another thought gnawed at him. It was still Yule. A time meant for celebration, for togetherness. He had promised himself that he wouldn't let the darkness that clung to his past ruin the present. Yet there he was, letting his desire for vengeance shroud everything else, festering in a rage that was, ultimately, only taking more from him than it gave.

Zalith exhaled slowly, his eyes narrowing as he looked at Luther one last time. The man's suffering would go on—there was no need for Zalith to linger in it. He had someone far more important waiting for him, someone who mattered infinitely more than this worthless life writhing in pain before him.

He turned away from the pitiful sight, determined to focus on what truly mattered: Alucard, their future, and the Yule celebration that still awaited them. There was no more room for vengeance today.

With a deep sigh, he stepped out of the cell. "Once the roaches are done, let him starve," he told Tyrus.

"Understood," the allocer demon said.

And then Zalith headed back to the house, his desire to be there for Alucard far more intense than his need to see Luther suffer. He wasn't going to bring any of that into the new year; it was dealt with, it was done. Luther would die for what he'd done—a slow, agonizing, miserable death. And Alucard wouldn't have to worry about him anymore.

Chapter Sixteen

Buried Trauma

| Alucard |

Alucard didn't remember getting into bed, nor did he remember how he got there. He was just…there. He opened his eyes—and they *ached.* His head was pounding, his limbs were sore, and something so very tightly constricted his body. He scowled, staring over at the closed curtains, listening to the sound of birdsong. He was sure that it was dawn, maybe a little later…. Where had the night gone? Why did he feel so…dead?

He slowly looked down, seeing Zalith's arms around him, and the demon was also nuzzling his neck. His body felt strangely sensitive—strangely irritated. Was he hungover? He frowned, struggling to remember much past the moment he'd gone to his office. He remembered pouring himself a drink; had he gotten drunk? He hardly ever got drunk…. He remembered Luther had come to talk to him and told him something about Zalith being in possible danger…and after Luther left, he kept drinking.

Frowning, he started to give in to the possibility that he must have drunk a little too much. He wasn't entirely sure, but maybe Zalith would know—then again…did he even want to know? What if he'd done something embarrassing? Maybe it would be better *not* to remember. Whenever he got drunk, he always ended up doing something that made him feel stupid, and perhaps this time, it was a blessing that he didn't recall much.

With a quiet sigh, he carefully rolled over to face Zalith, and as he did, the demon woke and smiled, opening his eyes. For a moment, Zalith just gazed at him, moving his hand to the side of his face.

"Hey," the demon said. "Good morning."

Alucard smiled, and the longer he spent awake, the more he began to notice that his fatigue wasn't as bad as it had been yesterday. He still felt as tired as he normally felt whenever he woke up, and he admittedly still felt a little weary, but it wasn't so severe that he felt like he didn't want to leave their bed any more than usual.

"How are you feeling?" Zalith asked quietly.

"I'm okay," he answered.

"Do you still feel sick or dizzy?"

Sick or dizzy? Alucard frowned. "Vhat?"

Zalith adorned a look of concern. "Do you not remember anything from last night?"

Staring at him, Alucard hesitated. Seeing the worry on Zalith's face *and* hearing it in his voice made him wonder if something terrible had happened. Had it? "No," he answered.

The demon exhaled quietly, tucking a loose strand of Alucard's tousled hair behind his ear. "It's probably for the best."

Alucard's frown became a confused one. "Did I… do someving stupid?" he asked as his embarrassment started growing.

Zalith shook his head and caressed his hair. "You didn't do anything stupid baby, don't worry."

He began to suspect that he must have done *something*; why else would Zalith seem so concerned about him not remembering? "Zhen… vhat did I do?"

"Not much," he answered. "You were just a little confused."

"Convused 'ow?"

"Well," the demon said with a look of what might be hesitation on his face, "you just didn't recognize me… and took a few moments to come around."

That didn't sound like him. On the odd occasion when he *had* become so drunk that he couldn't even walk, he still recognized Zalith. *Nothing* would be able to make it so that he didn't recognize him, so his confusion intensified. "Vhat?" he muttered. "Vhat vas I drvinking?"

Zalith's despondent expression deepened as he stopped caressing Alucard's hair and slowly dragged his hand down to the side of his neck. "Luther drugged you. He gave you a sedative, but that wasn't what confused you. He also gave you a hallucinogen—"

"Vhat?" Alucard asked as his frown contorted into a look of disbelief.

"I stopped him before he could do anything else, though," he said.

Utterly confounded, Alucard scowled in confliction and took his eyes off Zalith. Luther drugged him? Why? How? He frowned… all he remembered was Luther leaving his office. But… Zalith stopped him before he could do *anything else*? What did that mean? Did he even want to know? His scowl returned, as did a familiar discomfort. A sedative and a hallucinogen? It didn't take him long to work out why Luther would give him such things… and he knew what Luther wanted with him, but would he go so far as to drug him to get it?

He scowled uncomfortably, glaring down at the sheets. "Vhat…did 'e do bevore you stopped 'im?"

"I don't know," Zalith answered. "Your shirt was unbuttoned…and your belt was off when I got to you; Luther had his trousers down, and…he had you against the wall. But that was all I saw."

It all started coming back to him. In flashes, in fragments of memory, he recalled what happened. He remembered Luther touching him…kissing him…and telling him that he wanted it. Luther groped him, Luther tried to…. He scowled and turned his head away, hiding his sickly, disgusted look from Zalith. He wanted to throw up, but that was when his past crept up on him. A memory he'd tried to forget—*memories* he'd managed to bury deep inside his mind. Luther wasn't the first person to touch him without his consent, to do things to him that he didn't want. And as his nausea grew, he closed his eyes and tried to dismiss it all—all the dismay, all the despair and pain and horror. He didn't want to let it consume him. He didn't want to relive it.

He took a deep breath and sat up. "I vant to shower."

"Okay," Zalith said, placing his hand on Alucard's back. "I'll be here."

The vampire got out of bed and made his way into the bathroom. He closed the door, pulled off his trousers, and got into the shower.

He hoped for the same relief that he always got when the hot water poured over his body, but his discomfort didn't fade. Alucard stood there, staring down at the marble floor as the water graced his skin. He should have known Luther wouldn't let it go; he shouldn't have allowed him to come into his office. He should have known that he'd try something despite Zalith's warnings. But why? Why hadn't Zalith's threats and his own denials been enough? What had driven Luther so far as to drug him?

The vampire scowled and leaned back against the wall, resting his head against it. As he stared up at the ceiling, he let out a deep sigh. Zalith probably already killed Luther. There was no way he'd let him live after finding him…doing that to him. But Alucard couldn't help but wonder…had something more happened, and Zalith wasn't telling him to spare him the trauma? No…Zalith *would* tell him, and he was sure that he'd know, too. He didn't recall Luther doing more than pinning him against the wall and trying to take his trousers off…and he was sure that Zalith would be acting differently if there was more to it.

Alucard sighed again and started washing his hair. As for Luther…*had* Zalith killed him? He didn't care. He didn't want to stand there and overthink, nor did he want to let it ruin the last day of Yule. Last night hadn't been as wonderful as Alucard hoped, and he didn't want that to be the case today. He wanted to enjoy it, and he wanted Zalith to have fun, too.

So, he did his best to dismiss his thoughts and continued with his shower. But he knew that his traumatic past and the dismay that came with those memories would be lurking in the back of his mind all day.

Once he was done, he shut the water off and got out. He wrapped a towel around his waist and used another to dry his hair while standing in front of the mirror. When the bathroom door opened, though, he pulled the towel away from his head and watched Zalith walk in.

The demon was wearing only a pair of trousers, and he smiled when their gazes met. He made his way over to Alucard and grabbed a towel from the rack on his way. Then, he wrapped the towel around the vampire's shoulders and hugged him. "Do you feel better?" he asked, nuzzling the side of his face.

Alucard shrugged as Zalith started drying his body for him. "Somevhat," he said.

"We can go for breakfast once we're done here if you're hungry," Zalith said as he moved closer and rested his forehead against Alucard's.

"Okay," he mumbled, trying to fight the embarrassment and despair that last night and his past were still inflicting. He turned to face the mirror and started brushing his hair in an attempt to distract himself and hide his feelings.

Zalith started brushing his teeth but paused to say, "Unless you'd like to open gifts first."

"I zon't mind."

The demon smiled and continued brushing his teeth.

Alucard picked up his toothbrush once he was done with his hair and started to brush his teeth. He continued fighting the dismay, ignoring what he remembered, trying to bury it all. He just wanted to concentrate on today and have a nice time with Zalith.

He glanced at the demon, watching as he brushed his teeth. He was both nervous and excited to head downstairs and start opening the gifts they got for one another. But what if he couldn't enjoy it? What if his thoughts pulled him into misery?

Zalith glanced at him and smiled when he caught him staring. "What?"

"Noving," Alucard mumbled, continuing to brush his teeth.

With a quiet laugh, Zalith finished and then turned to face him, watching him as he washed his toothbrush and put it away. The demon then placed his hands on either side of Alucard's waist and pulled him closer, staring into his eyes for a moment before kissing his lips a single time.

As Zalith went to move back, though, Alucard kissed him and moved his hand to the side of Zalith's neck. He didn't want just one kiss; he'd left their bed almost immediately after waking up, skipping past the time he and Zalith would usually spend lying beside one another kissing or talking or hugging. It was one of his favourite things, and felt a little desperate for the demon's affection. Despite the fact that Zalith was right in front of him, he missed him, and he just wanted to be close to him. So, he pulled him closer, continuing to kiss the demon as he kissed back.

And maybe it would help him forget.

He slowly rested his free hand on the demon's shoulder and dragged his fingers down the demon's chest, over his abs, and to his waist. He felt the demon smile as they continued to kiss one another, and Zalith placed his hand on Alucard's body. It didn't take very long for Alucard's simple desire for affection to become close to desperation for sex, and without much thought at all, his hand wandered down to Zalith's crotch.

Zalith smirked as Alucard kissed him a little more aggressively, gripping his waist tighter as he pulled him closer. The demon laughed quietly in response, taking a moment to breathe through their kissing. "This wasn't one of the options I gave you," he told him softly.

Alucard stopped, leaning back ever so slightly so that he could stare at his face. He felt embarrassed…and his desperation quickly withered beneath his nervousness. He looked away, trying to hide his anxious face—

"Wait," Zalith insisted sadly. "I didn't mean I wanted you to stop. I'm just concerned. I took so much of your energy yesterday—"

"I'm vine," Alucard mumbled.

"Are you sure?"

The vampire nodded.

Zalith smiled. "Okay," he said, and then he started kissing him again.

Alucard gave in to his need for Zalith's attention and gripped the demon's belt. He knew what he wanted, what he *needed*, and he was sure that Zalith knew, too. The demon kept kissing him and stroked his hands down his body when he began kissing his neck. But to Alucard's despair, it made him think about Luther's hands on him.

"Vait," he mumbled uncomfortably, gripping Zalith's wrists and pulling his hands off him.

"Are you okay? We don't have to do this if you're uncomfortable. I understand."

He took a deep breath, looking the demon up and down, focusing on *him* and *his* body. He wanted him, but what if he was going to be forced to think about Luther and is past every time Zalith touched him now? He didn't want that; the thought made him want to huff and snarl and cry. So he shook his head and put Zalith's hands back on his body. "I'm okay."

"You're sure?"

He nodded and exhaled quietly, leaning back against the countertop behind him, and as Zalith unravelled the towel around his waist, Alucard gripped the demon's sides. When the towel fell to the floor, Alucard's anticipation returned. The demon placed several soft kisses on his neck as he stroked his hand down his body and gripped the vampire's arousal.

But Alucard didn't want to wait much longer; he didn't want to give his trauma time to creep in again. He turned around to face the mirror, resting his back against Zalith's chest. Zalith kept his hands on Alucard's waist, gently rubbing his arousal against the vampire's ass. Alucard rested his hands on the countertop, his anticipation growing, his excitement even more so as Zalith let go of the left side of his waist to move his hand around his body to start caressing his shaft.

Zalith guided his free hand up Alucard's body and lightly gripped his jaw. He then looked up from the vampire's neck, his eyes meeting with Alucard's in the mirror. He smirked, watching as the vampire's eager stare became a nervous one. Alucard knew that Zalith loved to watch him struggle to hide how he felt, but he couldn't look away; he kept his eyes on Zalith's seductive face as he caressed his shaft, teasing him by rubbing the tip with his thumb.

Alucard wanted to scowl in disapproval, but he couldn't. He took his eyes off Zalith as a quiet, pleased moan escaped his breath, and the longer he had to wait to feel the demon inside his body, the more eager he began to feel.

Something relieving shivered through Alucard when he heard Zalith unbuckle his belt; the demon let go of the vampire's dick and gripped his waist as he reached into one of the counter drawers with his free hand. And then, Zalith leaned back in to kiss his neck, gripping Alucard's jaw again to make him stare into his eyes in the mirror.

The demon gazed at him as a smirk crept across his face, a smirk that Alucard was sure was a response to his struggled expression when Zalith carefully eased his lube-smothered fingers into his ass. Alucard looked away, closing his eyes as he exhaled quietly. Zalith kissed his neck and slowly eased his hard dick inside the vampire's ass, causing a scowl of struggle to appear on Alucard's face as he gripped the counter. Alucard hummed quietly in pleasure, and as the demon moved his hand back up to grasp his jaw, he made Alucard stare at his reflection again.

Zalith stared at Alucard's nervous face, but the longer Alucard stared back, the more anxious he felt—but seeing the demon helped him grasp onto the moment; it helped him bury his trauma. He moaned quietly as the demon started thrusting his dick into and out of his body, as pleasurable shivered through him, and as his mind quickly became blank, overwhelmed by the sheer delight. The demon was moving a little faster than usual, but Alucard enjoyed it; it made him feel a whole lot more enthralled in a rapture that so quickly devoured him.

Alucard exhaled in both contentedness and struggle, leaning forward, avoiding glancing in the mirror because he was sure that Zalith was looking for the opportunity to see his face. But *he* wanted to see *Zalith's*. He listened as the demon moaned quietly into his ear, tightening the grip he had on his body, and moving his dick into and out of his ass as his limbs began to tremble.

However, the vampire soon started noticing his fatigue. It began with his trembling body beginning to ache; he slouched forward, resting his forearms on the counter as he hung his head to exhale deeply. Zalith moved his hand and gripped his jaw once again, and with a struggled grimace, Alucard glanced at the demon in the mirror. Zalith stared back with a smirk breaking through his pleasured frown.

The demon abruptly sunk his fangs into the left side of Alucard's neck. Alucard flinched and grunted painfully; it hurt a whole lot more than usual, and he was almost sure it had something to do with his returning exhaustion.

Zalith pulled his fangs from his neck and almost immediately stopped thrusting. "Sorry," he breathed, nuzzling the side of his face.

When Alucard took a moment to try and calm down, Zalith gently kissed all over his neck and his shoulder and wherever he could reach on his back. Zalith's bites never really hurt that much, and the pain would *never* linger. But this time, the demon's venom didn't seem to be doing anything for Alucard. It didn't numb the bite's pain, nor did it enthral him in euphoria. Instead, it sent a cold shiver down his spine as it coursed through his veins.

Alucard wouldn't deny that it panicked him. Why wasn't it doing anything? And why did his body ache and hurt more than it usually did? He could only assume that it was because of yesterday—because he'd become so drained and exhausted. Or could it be because of whatever Luther drugged him with? He didn't want to think about it. He wouldn't. He just wanted to enjoy his time with Zalith, and he wouldn't let it stop them. Despite his confusion, and despite his discomfort, he was still enjoying the sex.

So he ignored his fatigue as Zalith started slowly thrusting again. His once calming heart began to race as the demon hummed pleasurably into his ear, moving a little faster as each moment passed by. Alucard was quickly enthralled by Zalith's movements; he grimaced and moaned as the demon tightened his grip on his hand, breathing frantically onto his neck as he clearly approached his peak. But Alucard felt somewhat grounded. The pleasure wasn't so intense anymore, and neither was his enjoyment. He felt tired, and not even Zalith's intimate affection seemed to be able to pull him out of it.

Alucard tried to relax when Zalith climaxed, moaning quietly as he nuzzled the vampire's neck. Alucard's heart continued to race, and his body still trembled and ached while the enthralling pleasure of Zalith's warm cum filled his ass. That feeling always brought a delighted smile to his face, and when the demon slowly pulled his dick from his body, the vampire turned to face him, leaning back against the counter as he exhaled deeply.

Zalith frowned, placing his hands on either side of Alucard's waist and resting his forehead against his as he stared into his eyes. "Are you okay?" he asked quietly.

"I'm vine," he lied. He didn't want to worry Zalith, nor did he want to sit around overthinking. He and Zalith were supposed to be opening each other's gifts soon, and he wanted to enjoy today. He wasn't going to let anything ruin it.

The demon adorned a concerned look but pulled him into a tight hug. "We're not going to do anything at all for three days."

Alucard moved his arms around Zalith, holding him as tightly as his aching body would allow. He wanted to disagree because he knew that Zalith would start to feel exhausted and riddled with sorrow if they didn't have sex for three days, and also because he didn't want to have to deny himself Zalith's affection. But maybe it was a good idea; perhaps he should take some time to completely recover before doing anything else.

"Maybe five," Zalith then said.

Frowning hesitantly, Alucard leaned back and stared at the demon.

"Do you want blood?" he asked before Alucard could tell him he'd be fine.

He did. The moment Zalith offered, Alucard felt his heart race a little in what might be excitement—desperation, even. He nodded, his eyes wandering down to Zalith's neck. As Zalith then moved his hand to the back of Alucard's head, he leaned closer to the vampire. Alucard slowly dragged his hand up Zalith's body, over his shoulder, and to the back of his head, where he lightly gripped a handful of his hair.

But Alucard hesitated. He felt so exhausted…so drained that he thought he might struggle a little to stop once he started. It wasn't often that he battled with his bloodlust, but he felt as if he might this time. His body needed it—he craved it—and the longer he waited, the more intense his desire became.

He didn't want to wait. He didn't want to continue to hurt and ache and feel so tired that he could just fall asleep anywhere. As abruptly as Zalith had, Alucard sunk his fangs into the demon's neck, latching on so tight that he felt the demon fidget a little. But Zalith didn't stop him. He stood there, caressing his hair while he drank the demon's blood. The moment it poured into his mouth, Alucard began to feel relieved, and the more he gulped down, the better he felt. And he didn't want to stop.

But he had to. He didn't want to drain Zalith, so he'd only take what he needed.

After a few moments, Alucard pulled his fangs from Zalith's neck and lifted his head to stare at him. He was already sinking into the euphoria, and he was *glad* of it. He'd rather feel high as fuck than tired as fuck.

The demon smiled and rested his forehead against Alucard's again. "Did that help?"

When Alucard smiled in response, Zalith dragged his thumb over his bottom lip, wiping his blood from it.

"Good," the demon said, starting to caress the vampire's hair. As he stood there with him, he frowned curiously, staring at Alucard's back in the mirror as the vampire rested his head on his shoulder. "What does my blood taste like?"

Alucard laughed a little. "Veally…good. Is sveeter zhan anyving else."

Amused, Zalith laughed, too. "Is mine your favourite blood you've ever tasted?"

"Yes," the vampire said with a smile, nuzzling his neck. "And I zon't ever vant any ozzer blood."

Chuckling, Zalith hugged him tightly and then made him lift his head so that he could kiss his lips. "Yours is the only blood I'll ever want, too," he said, gazing at him. Then, he dragged his hands down Alucard's body and gripped either side of his waist. "What do you want to do next?" he asked with a smirk. "Do you want to have breakfast, or do you want to open gifts?"

"Ve can…" he stopped and thought to himself for a few moments. "Open givts."

"Okay," Zalith said, smiling. "Should we go down there like this, or should we get dressed?" he asked, glancing at the vampire's naked body.

Alucard frowned slightly. "*You* can go like zhat if you vant," he mumbled. "*I'm* getting dressed."

Zalith laughed amusedly as he stopped Alucard from trying to walk off. "I thought you were the only one allowed to see me like this."

The vampire then frowned irritably. "I vorgot zhat voman is joining us," he grumbled, taking his eyes off him.

Zalith turned his head to look at Alucard in the mirror. "So, I should probably get dressed."

"Vine," Alucard muttered, taking hold of his hand.

Then, the vampire led the way out of the bathroom.

Chapter Seventeen

Gifts

| **Alucard** |

Once they were dressed, Zalith gripped Alucard's wrist and pulled him closer. For a moment, the demon gazed at him and smiled as the vampire stared back, and then Zalith kissed him a few times.

The vampire smiled when they stopped kissing, but he didn't really know what to say; he wasn't sure if he even *should* say anything. He was still enthralled by the euphoria that Zalith's blood gave him, and he was trying to keep himself from asking a collection of stupid questions, such as why did he find Zalith so attractive when he wore a turtleneck sweater? Why was he wearing one right now? Why did his eyes shimmer red in the light? Why was he smirking? Why was he holding his wrist? What time was it?

Alucard scowled, trying his best to concentrate as Zalith led the way to the door. Maybe he'd get answers to his questions one day.

The vampire followed Zalith out of their room, down the stairs, and into the lounge, where the Yule tree stood with a collection of wrapped gifts beneath it. Zalith sat him down to the right of the tree, and the demon sat to the left, smiling at him as they both made themselves comfortable. Varana, however, wasn't yet present, and Alucard was sure that she wouldn't be absent much longer.

When Edwin came into the room, Zalith took his eyes off Alucard and looked over at the butler. "Could you fetch Varana, please?" he asked.

"Of course, sir," the butler said and left silently.

The moment Edwin left, Zalith looked back at Alucard, who hadn't taken his eyes off the demon. How could he? He loved when Zalith wore casual clothes, and when he let his hair sit naturally, too; the demon hadn't combed it back, and Alucard was trying to resist the urge to lean forward and start playing with it. But he couldn't fight it, so he smirked, leaned forward, and flicked the demon's fringe with his fingers.

When Zalith laughed amusedly, Alucard shuffled closer and slowly guided his fingers through the demon's hair. Zalith moved his hand to the back of Alucard's head and pulled him closer; he started kissing the vampire again, but as the door to the lounge opened, Alucard pulled away from Zalith and glanced at Varana, who made her way over to them. She sat on the couch in front of the tree.

It wasn't Varana his attention was focused on, however. He spotted Edwin outside and called, "Vait."

Edwin stepped into the room, "Yes, sir?"

"Bring zhe vings," Alucard ordered.

The butler nodded. "Of course, sir," he said before leaving once again.

Zalith looked at Alucard as the butler disappeared. "Things?" he asked curiously.

"Someving," Alucard mumbled. He didn't want to ruin the little surprise he'd planned.

The demon smiled but then looked at Varana. "Good morning," he said to her.

She huffed, resting her arm on the couch's arm. "Good morning."

"Are you feeling any better?"

Varana shrugged, glancing around the room.

Zalith frowned in concern. "Do you want to talk about it?"

"No, I'm fine," she muttered. "Let's just open presents."

Sighing, Zalith took his eyes off her and looked at the presents. "All right—"

"Vait," Alucard insisted.

"For what?" Zalith asked, smirking.

"Vor Ezvin."

Zalith stared at him for a moment but then waited patiently for the butler to return.

When the lounge door opened *again*, Alucard's confidence waned a little as his nervousness kicked in. Along with Zalith and Varana, he watched as the butler made his way over with a tray. The demon glanced at Alucard but then set his eyes back on Edwin as he handed Varana a white mug and a small plate with two cookies on it. The butler then gave the same to Zalith and Alucard, but Alucard's dish had one of his cupcakes on it.

"Thank you," Zalith said as Edwin bowed humbly. "And thank *you*," he said with a smirk, looking at Alucard. He then kissed the vampire's lips before glancing at the butler again before he could leave. "Edwin, come sit," he said, holding his hand out towards the couch beside the one that Varana was sitting on. "There are a few gifts here for you, too."

With a surprised expression, the butler walked over and sat down, his look of astonishment increasing as the demon handed him a small box before handing a gift each to Varana and Alucard.

They started opening their gifts as Zalith handed them out one by one, making sure that everyone had one to open at a time. Everyone received many things from one another, except Alucard and Varana, who only got each other a single item. But that was to be expected, considering they weren't exactly on the best of terms and might never be.

From Zalith, Varana was so delighted to receive a new hand mirror, as well as many new outfits, a few pieces of jewellery, and some small things for her new home, as well as a brand-new series of novels written by an author Zalith once said she was fond of. Alucard went out of his way to get her a rather expensive bracelet that she might never admit she liked, but he caught her glancing at it from time to time as everyone took the time to appreciate their gifts.

Varana gave Alucard a decently sized chocolate horse, one Alucard was sure he might end up eating in a single day if Zalith wasn't there to stop him. From Zalith, the vampire had also been given several new pieces of clothing, a new book in which he could write sheet music—for he had already used up the space in all his others—and a few other Deiganish-written novels; Zalith knew that he was still trying to improve his understanding of the language. After much hesitation, the demon also helped Alucard into the black turtleneck sweater he'd gifted him. Zalith had also given Alucard a new gold earring to replace the gold loop he'd been wearing for decades.

Alucard got Zalith some new clothes, as well as cufflinks, a few things for his office as well as some new books—books he'd had to make sure that the demon didn't already have—and a pair of tickets to see a show with him in the new year. He'd also given him a pair of rings he made himself. They were rings that would allow them to know when the other was thinking of them, so long as they were both wearing one, and Zalith had been admiring them for a while since opening them.

Everyone seemed content and spent the next short while finishing their cocoa and cookies whilst conversing with one another about their given and received gifts.

However, as Alucard admired one of the books Zalith had given him, the demon leaned over and kissed the side of his face. "I'll be right back," he said, and as Alucard smiled at him, the demon stood up and made his way out of the lounge.

Alucard missed him *already*. He wasn't about to try and start a conversation with Varana, and he knew that she wasn't even thinking about it, either. So, he sat there…staring at the books while he waited for Zalith to come back.

Moments later, the demon returned. Alucard lifted his head and watched as he made his way over with a large gift box in his hands. When he sat beside the vampire, he handed it to him, kissed his cheek, and smiled contently.

"Be careful. It's fragile," Zalith told him.

With an intrigued frown, Alucard looked down at the box, glanced at Zalith again, and then set his sights back on the box. "Vank you," he said, unsure of what might be inside. But when he heard a quiet shuffle from within, he felt more eager to open it. He slowly lifted the lid and peered inside, and when he set his eyes on it, disbelief, surprise, and happiness gripped hold of him. He let the lid fall to the floor, reaching inside to pick up the tiny, hairless kitten that had been waiting inside, staring up at him with a confused look on its small, bald face.

Alucard smiled so happily as he hugged the small sphynx kitten. Its ears were larger than its head, and its pink body was dotted with darker, grey splotches. Her eyes were a bright blue, much like his own when the sun hit them, and her skinny, hairless tail was the most adorable thing he'd ever seen.

He so swiftly became overwhelmed with excitement that he didn't know what to do or say, all he could do was sit there, hug the kitten, and bury his face in its head in an attempt to hide the fact that he was about to cry from Zalith.

"Do you like it?" the demon asked.

Alucard nodded, hugging the tiny hairless kitten as it clung to him. "I love 'er," he mumbled, struggling to hold his tears of joy back. "Vank you."

Zalith smiled. "You're welcome, baby."

"I vhought…you zidn't vant me to 'ave vone," he said, turning his head a little so that he could glance at Zalith's face.

"I thought about it for a long time because I knew you really wanted a cat. I still wasn't so sure about it, but then I decided to figure out what it is that I don't like about them, and I realized that most of my issues come down to the fur. So, I decided to get you one without fur," he explained.

With an appreciative smile, Alucard looked down at the kitten again and then leaned over to Zalith. He kissed the demon's lips, the demon kissed him back, and then he shuffled closer so that he could lean on Zalith while he cuddled with his new feline friend.

"I love you," Alucard said.

"I love you t—"

"I vas talking to zhe cat."

"Oh…" Zalith said with a disappointed frown.

But Alucard then looked up at him and smiled. "I also love *you*."

Smiling down at him, Zalith started caressing his hair and said, "Good."

Chapter Eighteen

Dire News

| Zalith |

The day had been a long but enjoyable one. Zalith, Alucard, and Varana finished dinner not too long ago, and while Varana chose to return to her own home, Zalith and Alucard relaxed on the couch in the lounge. Alucard had his new kitten curled up on his chest and his head rested in Zalith's lap; the demon slouched back lazily on the couch with him, caressing the vampire's hair.

Zalith smiled down at Alucard, who lay there with a relaxed look on his face, his eyes closed, and one hand over his sphynx kitten. He hadn't parted with that cat all day, and Zalith was glad that he loved it. He knew how much Alucard wanted a cat, and as uncomfortable as they often made him, Zalith couldn't help but compromise. Alucard was happy, and that was all that mattered to him.

As well as relaxed, however, Zalith was concerned for Varana. She hadn't said much all day and seemed somewhat depressed. She more or less said yesterday that she and her sister argued *again*, but Varana had never been this upset before. Usually, she'd be up in his face ranting about how much she hated Ysmay, calling her every name she could think of. But this time, Varana was secluding herself.

Zalith was sure that she wasn't entirely alone over in her house, but that wasn't any of his business. Who she chose to spend her time with—as long as it wasn't Luther—didn't bother him. What *did* bother him was how sad she seemed. He felt as though he should go and talk to her again, but not yet. He wanted to spend more time with Alucard.

But the mere thought of Luther made his anger return. A part of him wanted to go back down into that dungeon and torture him some more himself, but that wasn't how he was going to spend the last day of Yule. He'd probably just check in on the people he had making him suffer.

He sighed quietly and moved the vampire's fringe away from his face. "Did you think of a name for her yet?" he asked, glancing at the kitten as Alucard opened his eyes to stare up at him.

Alucard looked down at his sleeping kitten and shrugged lightly. "Not yet," he admitted—which was strange because he always seemed to have a name for something just moments after deciding that it would be his pet.

"That's okay," the demon said with a smile. "Take your time. I'm sure it'll come to you."

The vampire nodded, closing his eyes again as he sighed deeply and relaxed.

"I was going to get Varana a cat, too," Zalith mumbled. "But I wanted your present to be special; I didn't want to get you both the same thing. I'm sure she'll buy her own if she wants one."

"Hmm," Alucard mumbled. "I suppose all vitches are meant to 'ave cats, or so people say," he said with a smirk.

Amused, Zalith laughed a little but shook his head. "That's not funny," he said, fiddling with Alucard's fringe as the vampire opened his eyes to look up at him. "I'm actually worried about her; she seemed really down today."

"Down 'ow?" Alucard asked.

"She was unhappy all day and barely said a word."

Alucard frowned slightly. "Did someving 'appen?"

"I think she got into an argument with her sister. They always argue, so I wasn't surprised to hear it, but it's never really affected her this much before."

The vampire sighed as he looked down at his sleeping kitten again. "Maybe you should go and talk to 'er or someving," he mumbled.

Zalith sighed deeply. "Yeah, I should," he agreed. "Hopefully it's nothing serious. She normally bounces back quickly from these things, so it's probably something bad. I might be talking it out with her for hours."

Alucard huffed but then moved and sat up straight beside him. "Zhen I guess you should go and talk to 'er now bevore ve vant to go to bed," he suggested, but there seemed to be a conflicted tone in his voice.

The demon hesitated. He didn't want to go over there and listen to Varana cry for hours upon hours, but he knew he had to. She mattered to him, and despite not wanting to listen to her bawl, he would because how she felt was important. He looked at Alucard as he stared down at the sleeping kitten. "I don't really want to right now, but I should."

"Okay," Alucard said with a shrug.

But Zalith didn't want to get up. He wanted to stay where he was with Alucard, so he moved his arm around the vampire and pulled him closer, fiddling with his hair again as he rested his head on his chest. He then sighed and said, "I'll probably be gone a while—not just because of her, but because I also want to pay a visit to Luther," he said, revealing that he'd stored Luther somewhere.

Alucard shuffled around uncomfortably, and when he looked at Zalith, there was a perturbed expression on his face. "'E's 'ere?"

"He's in the caves," he answered.

"Zhe…vhat?" Alucard asked with a confused frown.

"There's a cave system not too far away. I've been using it for a few different reasons. As well as it being the place where I store my money and some of my possessions, there are also a few cells down there for situations such as this—situations where I would need to detain someone," he explained.

"Vight," Alucard said as his confused expression lifted. "I store mine in a similar place, so…makes sense. But you zidn't kill 'im? Zhe Vampire Council came, no? I assume zhey gave you control of 'is sentence."

Zalith nodded. "Yeah, they came. I plan to kill him, I just want to hurt him first."

A discomforted frown made its way onto the vampire's face. "Can't you just kill 'im? Knowing 'e's alive is making me veel…I zon't know," he said sullenly.

"I'm sorry," Zalith said quietly. Why didn't he think of that? He felt like an idiot. "I'll kill him, don't worry. I was just so…*angry* when I saw him…" he stopped himself and exhaled deeply, trying to dismiss the rage that was quickly ensnaring him. "He'll be dead before tomorrow, I promise. I just have to go and see Varana first."

The vampire nodded as he stared at his kitten. "Okay. I'll just…vind someving to do vhile you do zhat."

"You're welcome to come with me," the demon invited, caressing his hair. "But I wouldn't blame you if you didn't want to—especially with Varana."

Alucard sat up, pulling away from Zalith. "No," he said. "I'll stay 'ere and…vink of a name vor 'er," he muttered, looking down at his kitten.

"Okay, that's fine," Zalith said, gazing at him. "Hopefully I won't be talking to her for too long."

Watching his kitten as she woke up and yawned, Alucard nodded. "I'll be 'ere."

"Are you okay?" Zalith asked.

"I'm vine," he grumbled, standing up as he held his kitten in his right arm.

"Then why are you walking away?" the demon asked, staring up at him.

"I'm not valking avay," he said. "I'm going to vind someving to do vhile you talk to 'er and do vhatever vith Luther."

"Okay," Zalith said, standing up. He knew when Alucard was avoiding talking about something, and considering what he'd just said about Luther, Zalith didn't want to push him. Instead, he moved over to the vampire, placed his hand on the side of his face, and kissed his lips. "I'll be back later."

Alucard nodded.

Then, the demon left the room and headed for Varana's house. As worried as he was about her, he was now also worried about Alucard. Knowing Luther was alive had obviously upset him, and Zalith wanted to dispose of that disgusting little man before the night was over.

| Alucard |

Alucard wasn't sure if Zalith was mad at him for dismissing his concern or not, and now that the demon was gone, he felt despondent. He didn't want to be alone right now, but Zalith had things he wanted to do, and Alucard wasn't going to stop him.

"I don't want to go yet," Zalith suddenly said, somehow having entered the room again without Alucard realizing.

When Alucard turned to face him, Zalith was already in front of him and gently pushed him back against the wall. He didn't give Alucard any time to reply and immediately started kissing him.

Holding his kitten in one arm, Alucard gradually moved his free hand to Zalith's waist and let his conflicted thoughts wither. He kissed Zalith as Zalith kissed him, dragging his hand up his body and to the back of Zalith's head. In that short moment, any dismay that he'd been feeling swiftly faded.

But as it always did, the kissing came to an end, and Zalith sighed as he rested his forehead against Alucard's. "I love you," he said quietly, staring into Alucard's eyes.

Staring back, Alucard moved his hand from the back of Zalith's head and to his shoulder. "I love you, too," he said with a smile. "'Ow long vill you be?"

"Maybe an hour or two," the demon answered.

"Okay, vell... I'll vait up vor you."

Zalith smiled and tucked a strand of the vampire's hair behind his ear. "Okay," he said and then kissed him again. "I'll see you later," he said, and then he left the lounge once again.

As Zalith left, Alucard looked down at his kitten and sighed, trying to work out what he was going to do with his alone time. He scowled, glancing around, and when he set his eyes on the gifts that he hadn't yet put away, he placed his kitten on the floor and made his way over as she followed. He picked up his new books and the small box in which his new earring was, which he slipped into his pocket before turning around and leaving the lounge.

His kitten followed him through the hall and into his office. He closed the door behind him and glanced at the new snake tank; the serpent was watching him as he made his way over to his desk and placed his books on it. He then sighed, slumping down in his seat, and not too long after, his kitten climbed up his leg and curled up in his lap.

For a moment, Alucard sat there in silence, glancing down at the things on his desk which were where he hadn't left them. He didn't want to think about what happened yesterday, but it seemed as though someone had been cleaning his office; among the cleaning chemicals, he could still smell the blood—*Luther's* blood. He didn't want to wonder, though.

He grabbed one of his new books, but as he opened it and started reading, he began to feel irritated. He couldn't concentrate, so he placed the book back down, sighed, and rested his arms on his desk as his kitten pounced up onto it and sat in front of him.

As she stared at him, he smiled. "Vhat should I call you?" he asked, petting the kitten as she purred quietly. He was admittedly struggling to name her; he often found it easy to come up with names for his animals, but he had nothing. She was so unique and new that he had no idea where to start. It would come to him eventually, though.

Alucard looked at where his pens had been placed. He pouted and moved them to where they *should* be but then set his eyes on a white envelope sitting beneath a paperweight. He didn't recall seeing it yesterday, but he remembered Edwin telling him that an important letter had arrived for him when he and Zalith had breakfast. He wasn't doing anything right now, so he thought he might as well open it.

He picked it up, but when he searched for his letter opener, he couldn't find it. The vampire tutted irritably, sure that whoever cleaned his office had put it somewhere stupid. Instead of searching for it, he opened the letter with one of his claws and pulled the paper out. It was written in Dor-Sanguian—updates from Crowell. Just as he started reading, though, an owl landed on the ledge outside his window and tapped at it with its beak.

Alucard opened the window to let the bird in, and it handed him the rolled parchment in its beak. When the vampire unrolled it and read the Dor-Sanguian written on *that*, though, his irritancy faded into dismay. The moment he read that his castle in Dor-Sanguis had been destroyed and that the Diabolus *and* unknown forces that could be Lilith's were overpowering his vampires, he felt as though a part of him had been torn away. That castle was the only thing he had left of his mother, a woman he hadn't even had the chance to get to know, and just as she had been, the one thing she'd left him was torn from him.

His immediate thought was to head back there and salvage what he could, but to top it off, half his council had been wiped out, the Diabolus were still killing his people in an attempt to draw him out, and those of his council who were left were currently debating whether they would continue to put their faith in him. The only good news the letter conveyed was that Crowell had managed to get most of his vampires to safety.

Alucard knew he had to do something—he'd spent so much of his time lately in Nefastus with Zalith that it didn't surprise him that his people were wondering whether he actually still cared for them. Before, he'd been so dedicated to creating a safer place for his people to exist that they never questioned how long he took to do it, but now, he'd more or less abandoned Dor-Sanguis, hadn't he?

He scowled, slowly placing the letter down. But Dor-Sanguis wasn't safe for *him*; he'd been working with Zalith to create something here in Nefastus, and eventually, more of his people could leave Dor-Sanguis and live here with those he already invited. His people knew that... but they hadn't seen a glimpse of him in so long—of course they would worry.

And then there was the Diabolus. Alucard gritted his teeth and dug his claws into his desk. They were *still* attempting to kill his people to try and draw him out; it obviously wasn't working, and he would have thought they'd give up by now, but clearly, they hadn't, and he wasn't going to sit there for a moment longer and let his people suffer.

However, he had Zalith to consider, too. He couldn't just up and leave without telling him—without considering his feelings on the matter. He knew how much Zalith worried about him, and currently, they were both hiding from the Numen and their cults. It wasn't safe anywhere but in Nefastus, and Dor-Sanguis was one of the most dangerous places he could head to.

But he had to. He couldn't leave his people a moment longer.

Chapter Nineteen

To Dor-Sanguis

| Varana |

Varana lay silently in her bed, not paying much attention at all to the maid, who was reading one of her new books to her. All she could think about was the situation she found herself in because of her bitchy twin sister.

She had a month to decide whether she would do what her Father wanted, to turn Alucard in or choose Zalith and abandon her family. She wasn't going to betray Zalith…but she didn't want to betray her Father, either. In fact, she just didn't want to pick a side. Why couldn't she continue to love both her Father and Zalith? Why couldn't she remain on the outside of all of this conflict—why did *she* have to choose?

Varana frowned hopelessly. Of course, if she didn't choose Ysmay's side, then her sister would think that she was choosing Zalith and Alucard—*him*. None of this would be happening if that little red-haired vampire hadn't come along and wriggled his way into Zalith's life. She scowled again because she knew that wasn't what happened. She knew Zalith better than anyone, and she was certain that *Zalith* pulled Alucard into their lives. And now she was paying for it.

But there she was…being made to choose between the two people she loved most. They were both family to her, and she didn't want to lose either of them. She had no idea what to do, and the only thing that seemed to come to mind was to just run away from it all…but she couldn't even do that, could she?

Just then, a knock came at her door, and Varana anxiously tensed up. She immediately assumed that it was Ysmay, but as she quickly sat up and stared at her door, she realized that it was actually Zalith.

"I thought I'd better come and check on you," the demon said as he made his way into her room.

With a deep sigh, Varana laid back down. She didn't want to say anything.

Zalith frowned in concern, but he quickly shifted his gaze to the maid, who had stopped reading the moment he entered the room. The girl stared at him, clearly unsure of what to do.

The demon set his eyes back on Varana. "I hope I'm not interrupting anything."

"You're not," Varana muttered. She then sat up and looked at her maid. "Get out," she ordered.

The girl hurried to her feet. "Y-yes, ma'am," she said, scurrying past Zalith and out of the room

Zalith leaned back against the wall close to the door. "How are you feeling?" he asked her.

"Horrible," she answered.

He frowned harder. "Is there anything I can do for you to help you feel better?"

"Put me out of my misery," she lamented.

"Why are you so upset? Is this about your sister?"

She didn't immediately answer; her despondent frown worsened. "Yes."

"What happened between you two?"

Varana opened her mouth to speak but then struggled to say what she needed to. The curse that Ysmay had put on her kept her from mentioning a single word about her warning. She buried her head under her pillow as frustration enthralled her.

"Varana..." Zalith drawled.

"It's nothing," she grumbled, her voice muffled beneath her pillow.

"Obviously it's not nothing, Varana. Look at you."

"I'm fine!" she insisted.

"Why won't you just tell me?" he asked, now becoming irritated.

She didn't answer. She *couldn't.*

"Hello?" he asked.

She huffed irritably and held her pillow over her head a little tighter. "There's nothing to tell! I'm just sad, okay? Have you never been sad before?" she exclaimed, trying to hide the fact that she was quickly becoming overwhelmed by her dismay. "I have *one* off day for the first time in eighty years, and suddenly it's like the world is ending! I'm entitled to my emotions, you know!"

Ignoring her fit of anger, Zalith sighed. "What did she do to you?" he asked skeptically.

"No one did anything to me."

"Is there a secret you're supposed to be keeping?"

"No!" she snapped.

Zalith calmly suggested, "Should I read your mind so that you don't have to say it out loud?"

"Go away!" Varana complained.

He sighed. "What if we—"

"Zaliv—" Alucard suddenly interjected.

Varana pulled the pillow away from her head and glared at Alucard, who was standing in her doorway with his kitten in his arms.

Surprised, Zalith took his eyes off Varana and looked over at him. "Oh, hello," he said with a smirk.

"I need to talk to you," the vampire said, but with an almost dismayed look on his face.

"Go away!" Varana yelled, launching her pillow at him.

However, Alucard caught the pillow in his free hand and threw it right back at her, snarling as he did, and as the pillow hit Varana, she snarled back—

"Varana," Zalith warned, and as he scolded her, she pouted and started crying, burying her face in her pillows. He took his eyes off her and asked Alucard, "Is it urgent?"

"Yes," he answered.

Of *course* it was. Alucard was *always* taking Zalith away from her, and it made her cry harder. Why couldn't he just leave them alone? If he wasn't there, then none of this would be happening!

"Okay," Zalith said, looking back over at Varana. "I'll be right back—"

"Go away!" she screeched. Zalith had obviously chosen him *again*, and she didn't want to see either of them.

Zalith scowled irritably, but without another word, he followed Alucard out of Varana's room.

Alone, Varana shrieked and punched her pillows as tears fell down her face. She didn't know what to do anymore. How could she choose? Why couldn't she just remove Alucard with Zalith's consent? Why couldn't Alucard just accidentally trip and fall into a hole that took him down to Hell?

She wailed and sniffled, sinking deeper into despair. Who was she supposed to choose?

| Alucard |

As they emerged outside into the gardens, Alucard stopped walking and turned to face Zalith. He didn't want to waste any time. "I 'ave to go to Dor-Sanguis—vight now."

"Why?" Zalith asked worriedly.

"I just vound out zhat my castle 'as been destroyed, 'alf my council are dead, and zhose who made out of zhere need my 'elp," he explained with a huff of both irritancy and distress.

Zalith frowned sympathetically as he placed his hand on the vampire's shoulder. "Do you know who did it?"

"Zhey zon't know if vas zhe Diabolus or Liliv's people—eizer vay, I 'ave to do someving," he insisted.

"Okay, I'll go with you," Zalith said. "You can leave the cat with Edwin while we're gone—"

Alucard shook his head. "No, I 'ave to go alone," he refused. "Zhey're convinced I've abandoned zhem vor you and vor zemons, and I need to show zhem zhat's not zhe case. If you come vith me, zhat might convirm zheir suspicion, and I zon't vant to 'ave to deal vith zhe discord zhat's going to cause," he explained, trying his best to word everything Crowell had written to him in the first letter without causing unnecessary conflict.

His people believed that he was abandoning them, and the recent alignment of his and Zalith's people wasn't helping. Demons and vampires had never gotten along, and right now, he needed to take that into consideration. If he showed up with Zalith, that would probably make them all think it was true. His people were only familiar with him working alone, and now really wasn't the time to change that—for their sake.

Zalith frowned in what looked like confusion. "What if something happens to you?"

He didn't know what to say; what if something *did* happen to him? But then... what if he didn't go? He had to go. So many of his people had died already, and Alucard couldn't let it happen anymore. He was their leader—their creator—and he had to do something to save them. He wasn't sure if it was the Diabolus or Lilith's people—or Damien's—but whoever destroyed his castle, and whoever was slaughtering his people, he had to stop it.

"Noving vill 'appen," he said. "Crowell said is just zhe cults—'umans and veak zemons. I zon't even 'ave to get too close to scare zhem off, and zhen I'll take my people somevhere safe."

"Where?" Zalith asked, his concerned frown thickening.

"I zon't know," Alucard said with a sigh, dragging his hand over his face in frustration as he realized that he was only losing more time. "I zon't know," he repeated. "I'll vind somevhere, I just... 'ave to get zhem avay vrom Dor-Sanguis virst."

Zalith stared at him, and it looked like he was trying to decide whether or not he wanted to argue. But after a few tense seconds, he sighed and said, "Okay." But then he hesitated before he let Alucard go. "Can't I just come with you and stay completely out of the way so that I'm not *there*, but close if you need me?" he asked desperately.

Alucard frowned as his thoughts became so erratic that it was hard to weigh his options. All he could think about was the fact that every second he spent here with Zalith was another second his people were dying—another second he could be using to help them. With half his council dead and the other half in peril, the Diabolus and Lilith's people could kill *everyone* back in Dor-Sanguis. His people had no one to protect them now, and *he* was the only one who could do something—he... and Zalith.

Admittedly, he wanted Zalith to go with him; if he had to fight, having Zalith there to help would mean that he could focus on helping *more* of his people than he would be able to if he were alone. He also didn't want to leave Zalith at home to worry and panic, either—he knew how that felt, and he would never wish it upon Zalith.

He'd not waste another moment thinking about it. "Vine," he said, leading the way away from Varana's house. "But zon't let any of zhem see you."

"Thank you," Zalith said with a relieved sigh. But the demon then caught up to him and grabbed his arm. "Alucard, you can't take the cat."

Realizing that he was still carrying his kitten, Alucard frowned slightly. "Vight..." he said. He turned to face his and Zalith's house. "Sabazios," he called.

Moments later, the white hellhound came running out of the house and over to where he and Zalith were standing. Alucard placed the hairless kitten on the huge dog's back and patted his head.

"Take 'er inside and vait vor me in my ovvice," he instructed but then swiftly pulled off his new sweater, too, and placed that over the dog's back. "And zhis," he said. He didn't want to damage it.

With a quiet bark, Sabazios turned around and carried the kitten and Alucard's sweater back into the house.

Alucard then faced Zalith. "Are you veady?" he asked, preparing to dematerialize.

"I'm ready," the demon confirmed.

"Okay..." Alucard said, moving a little closer. "Zon't move."

The vampire moved his arms around Zalith as if he was hugging him. Then, without any hindrance, Alucard swiftly dematerialized himself and Zalith into vermillion smoke and disappeared into the night sky, heading for Dor-Sanguis.

Chapter Twenty

The Fallout

| Alucard |

Alucard and Zalith's journey came to an end just over an hour later. He'd flown himself and the demon to Dor-Sanguis so quickly in hopes of being able to intervene, but as he stood before the burning ruins of his castle, his dismay burned as deeply in his heart as the fire engulfing his old home. There wasn't a single vampire in sight, nor could he detect any in their immediate area. There was nothing, no one…nowhere.

As Zalith frowned sadly and placed his hand on Alucard's shoulder, the vampire scowled in anger and *hatred*; the Diabolus had to have done this—*they* were the ones killing his people to try and draw him out, and *they* had to be the ones who attacked his castle in an attempt to wipe out his council.

But his thoughts weren't entirely with them right now. As he stared at his burning birthplace, his concerns stuck with who and what was locked up down beneath the surface.

Detlaff.

Alucard couldn't detect him, but he was sure that he nor Zalith could see *anything* with the amount of silver, rhodium, and platinum shimmering on the ground around them. Seeing such a combination of poisonous metal led Alucard to believe that it could be Lilith's people who attacked—they were the only ones who knew Zalith was susceptible to rhodium. But it didn't precisely matter right now. What mattered was finding Detlaff. If he'd escaped, then there was no telling how much more danger he and Zalith would be in.

Without a word, he hurried towards his burning castle. Zalith followed beside him, scouring the area around them for danger as they approached the entrance.

When they reached the door, though, Zalith grabbed Alucard's shoulder and pulled him back. "Alucard, we should go," he said, looking around at the metal-smothered ground.

Alucard looked back at him and frowned, staring at Zalith's paranoid face. "No," he said. "I 'ave to vind Zetlaff."

Zalith gripped Alucard's shoulder a little tighter; it looked like he was about to try and convince Alucard to return home...but he shook his head instead and slipped his hand into Alucard's. "Okay," he said, and immediately, Alucard turned around and led the way into the burning building.

Alucard glanced around in despair as he led the way through the burning hall. The bodies of half his council were scattered over the place—the bodies of Diabolus *and* Lilith's people were among them. What were Lilith's *and* Lucifer's people doing in the same place at the same time? Alucard was sure that it wasn't good news, but he couldn't focus on that right now. He needed to find Detlaff—if he hadn't already escaped.

But as he and Zalith approached the door to the dungeons, his eyes found something he wished they didn't. Pip—one of Alucard and Zalith's main messenger izurets—lay dead at the foot of one of the windows with a large shard of blue glass impaled through his tiny body.

Alucard stopped walking and stared down at the little lifeless demon. His fury only worsened; he scowled, turning away from the izuret. He couldn't let his anger get to him; it had been so long since he'd felt so furious before, and he knew that if he allowed himself to become any less composed, he'd start to sink into the rage that he always tried so hard to bury.

He gripped Zalith's hand a little tighter, turning around and heading towards the dungeon door. Corpses of both his men and the Diabolus stretched down the stairs and throughout the smoke-filled corridor; while the fire had no effect on him or Zalith, they both still struggled to see through the smoke. The unbelievable amounts of poison in the air made it impossible for him to use his sensory ethos, and he was certain that the case was the same for Zalith, who was looking around frantically. But Alucard knew exactly where Detlaff's cell was and swiftly led the way through the corridor.

However, when they emerged into the smoke-filled cell, Alucard's prisoner was nowhere to be seen. He let go of Zalith's hand and made his way over to where the ugly demon should be lying but found only his empty shackles on the stone floor.

As panic and anger gripped him tightly, Alucard snarled in frustration and kicked the metal chains across the floor, turning around to frantically search the room for anything that might tell him where Detlaff had gone. But the walls were intact, and there were no signs of struggle—the door, however, had been forced open from the *outside*.

Had the Diabolus attacked solely to free Detlaff, or had their goal been to kill his people, and finding Detlaff was a mere coincidence to them? He didn't know.

He dragged his hands over his face in frustration, turning back to face Zalith. He didn't know what to do now. Detlaff had escaped; he knew how to find Alucard, despite his and Zalith's defences—they were going to have to relocate, and that thought forced his anger to wither into distress. Why now? Why did this have to happen *now*?

Zalith frowned worriedly as Alucard made his way over to him.

But Alucard was too late when he felt someone moving behind him—

Detlaff lunged at him, laughing maniacally as he did. Alucard quickly turned around to defend himself, but Zalith pushed him aside and threw himself at Detlaff, who shrieked in fear the moment he noticed that Alucard wasn't alone.

With a snarl and a growl, Zalith grabbed Detlaff's throat in one hand and his left wrist with his other. The man yelped and struggled as Zalith forced him back against the closest ash-covered wall, but the moment they hit the bricks, Detlaff wailed in panic and impaled something deep into the side of Zalith's body—

"You're always in the way!" Detlaff stropped, struggling to try and escape from Zalith's weakening grip. "That wasn't meant for you—"

Before Detlaff could speak another word, and before Zalith could react, Alucard ripped Detlaff from the demon's grip. But when he saw Zalith grip his side the moment Detlaff's knife was torn from his body, he watched the demon's blood pour through his fingers. Zalith grunted as a confused look appeared on his face, and as he leaned back against the closest wall and slowly slid down to the ash-smothered ground, Alucard became ensnared by panic and fear.

But he had to deal with Detlaff.

Alucard roared with fury as the pitiful creature of a man screamed in cowardice. He didn't hesitate—grabbing the filthy demon by the throat, he hurled him against the back wall with a sickening thud. Detlaff barely had a chance to react before Alucard slammed into him again, pinning him hard against the cold, unforgiving bricks. The man's pathetic pleas for mercy fell on deaf ears; without a shred of remorse, Alucard seized a fistful of his hair, brutally smashing his face into the wall again and again and again, the sound of bone cracking against stone filling the air. Over and over, he struck until Detlaff was a bloody, unconscious mess, his face reduced to a grotesque smear of flesh and blood.

The vampire didn't linger. His attention snapped back to Zalith, slumped on the ground, clutching his side as blood poured from the wound in his torso. Panic surged through Alucard as he dropped to his knees beside him. His breath caught at the sight of Zalith growing weaker with each passing second; the wound was deep, unnatural in its severity, and Alucard cursed himself for not stopping Detlaff sooner. Whatever that man had used, it wasn't a normal blade. He'd heard Detlaff say that it was meant for Zalith, but he'd taken the blow in Alucard's place—and now, something far worse than a simple wound was ravaging him.

Alucard's hands trembled as he pressed down on the wound, desperately trying to stem the bleeding, but he knew it wasn't enough. Time was running out.

He took his eyes off the hand that Zalith had over his wound and stared at the demon's pain-smothered face. "Zaliv," he insisted, pulling the collar of his shirt away from his neck as he moved closer, "you need to—"

The demon shook his head, turning his head away from Alucard. "No," he uttered painfully. "I don't want it."

Alucard frowned in distress, glancing down at Zalith's bloody hand again. He could see that he was losing his strength, his hand slowly slipping away from the wound in his side. With an almost desperate scowl on his face, Alucard moved his hand over Zalith's to help him keep it over his wound. "You von't 'eal vithout," he insisted. "Vhatever Zetlaff did is stopping you vrom 'ealing."

"I've…already taken too much from you," the demon refused. "What if…*you* need it?"

"I'll be vine, Zaliv. Please," he insisted sullenly.

The demon stared at him in confliction, and as each moment passed, he looked weaker and weaker. But he eventually moved his hand to the side of Alucard's neck and pulled him closer. Then, he kissed him, moving his hand to the back of his head.

Alucard knew being an incubus meant that Zalith could get whatever energy he needed even through kissing him, and if he preferred that to blood right now, then that was what Alucard would do for him. As Zalith kissed him, he kissed back; the demon pulled him closer so that Alucard was sitting in his lap, and as his body started to heal, Zalith slowly dragged his hand down from the back of Alucard's head, over his side, and under his shirt to lightly grip his waist.

After what felt like only a few moments, Zalith brought their kissing to an end and leaned his head back against the wall to stare sadly at Alucard's face.

"Do veel okay now?" Alucard asked, glancing down at the place where Zalith's wound had been to see that it had healed.

"I'm okay," he mumbled, moving his bloody hand to the side of Alucard's face.

However, Alucard felt reluctant about letting Zalith accompany him beyond this point. He needed to find Crowell and whoever was left, but Zalith had been hurt, and although he may say he was okay, Alucard's worry wouldn't wane. "I need to vind Crowell. I vant you to vait somevhere safe vith Zetlaff—"

"No," he insisted, starting to get up. "Let me go with you."

As he stopped Zalith from getting up, Alucard frowned in hesitation. "You just got stabbed, Zaliv," he said. "You need to vest."

"I don't want anything to happen to you," he said, gripping his hand.

"I'll be vine," Alucard insisted.

But Zalith tried to get up again—

"Zaliv..." Alucard said firmly, keeping him down. "Stay 'ere vith Zetlaff. I'll be vight back—no vone vill vind you 'ere."

The demon stared at him in despair but soon sighed a deep, sullen sigh and scowled in confliction. "Fine," he uttered. Then, he moved his hand to the side of Alucard's face again, pulled him closer, and kissed him one last time. "Be careful," he pleaded.

"I vill."

Alucard stood up and looked at Detlaff, and after one final glance at Zalith, he turned around, headed for the door, and left, hoping to find his people as quickly as he possibly could.

Chapter Twenty-One

Retaliation

| Crowell |

Dargamoore had become a battlefield. Since yesterday, Crowell and what remained of his men had been fighting off the enemy, grasping whatever rest they could get as the Diabolus' reinforcements flooded in. Anyone weaker would have fled by now, but this was Alucard's city—Alucard's *land*, and Crowell would defend it with his life.

But the end might very well be what was coming for the last survivor of Alucard's council. The leading Paladins were dead, as were the vast majority of vampires Crowell had fighting at his side, and now, all that remained within the darkness of a fallen tavern were Crowell and six vampires, one of which was currently bleeding out due to a silver-inflicted wound in his thigh.

This time, the Diabolus might win, and as they had been before, vampires would be thrown back into the despair that once enthralled them, hiding in the shadows, treated like pests—like *rats*; hunted for their blood, their venom, and their cold, staggering hearts. They'd become nothing but a commodity again.

Crowell anxiously stared out into the fog-ensnared city. Fires burned in the distance; the cries of helpless people carried upon the warm breeze. He'd done all he could. He'd saved a measly six vampires; he'd let *all* of Alucard's Paladin leaders die, and wherever his Lord may be, Crowell wished that he could have left behind more for Alucard to find.

With a pained grunt, he slowly looked down at his blood-covered hand as he pulled it away from his stomach. The wound hadn't healed, the poison was spreading, and soon, his time in Aegisguard would be over. And for what? What did he have to show for his time here? He looked over at the six vampires he'd managed to pull from the carnage that hadn't long gripped the city. Only *one* of them was a fighter, and he was going to die soon, too, leaving five hapless civilians to fend for themselves.

He scowled, moving his hand back over his wound and glaring out at what remained of the city. In the distance, a patrol of seven Diabolus troops hurried past, searching the ruins for anyone who might have made it out. It was only a matter of time before they were discovered, and Crowell wasn't going to be able to do much either way. If they found him and these vampires before he died, he would be useless defending them; his ethos was fading, as was his strength, and very soon, he'd join the forever-dead.

All he could do was stand there and hope that Alucard received his message. Alucard needed to know that the Diabolus were closing in; they'd soon know that Alucard wasn't in Dor-Sanguis anymore, and surely the Diabolus had found Detlaff, and from what Crowell had been told, he knew that Detlaff knew how to find Alucard.

Did Alucard receive his message? What if the owl was seen and killed? If Alucard *had*, then surely he would have shown up by now. Crowell wasn't concerned about himself, though; his worries remained with his Lord. If he hadn't received his message, he'd not know what was happening here, and he and Zalith would be in danger. Crowell didn't want that… but what more could he do?

"What are we gonna do?" one of the vampires asked, appearing beside Crowell.

Crowell took his eyes off the outside and glanced at him. Just like the others, this vampire had splotches of ash and blood on his face, and in his dark green eyes, despair lingered so profoundly. But Crowell didn't have an answer for him—well, he didn't have a solution that would give him hope. Dargamoore was lost—Dor-Sanguis was lost.

"Baron, sir?" the man asked impatiently.

Frowning, Crowell sighed deeply, but it caused pain to slither through his body, and as he gritted his teeth, he shook his head. "We stay here. Patrols are everywhere, and we can't move him," he said, gesturing to the dying vampire with his free hand.

The man scoffed, glanced back at the shot vampire, and then set his eyes back on Crowell with a look of desperation on his face. "Just leave him!" he insisted quietly. "He's done. What about the rest of us? There were hundreds of us yesterday; are we all that's left?"

"It looks that way," Crowell answered, staring back out at the city. "Sit down and be quiet. The Diabolus are still patrolling the area. If by any luck they leave soon, we'll move out and head for Lord Alucard's castle. I'm confident he has a ship there—"

"A ship?" the man asked. "Where are we gonna go? This is the only place we know—"

"Lord Alucard will find somewhere for us; he's been setting up something in Nefastus, so maybe you can go there—"

A deafening explosion shook the ground and broke the quiet, the darkness lighting up a bright orange for a few short moments. The vampires all stared in fear as dust fell from the cracked roof, and as yells and weapons fire echoed in the distance, the man gripped Crowell's arm and frowned anxiously.

"You really think so?" the guy asked, ignoring the commotion. It wasn't the first battle they'd heard since sheltering in the fallen tavern. "Is it safe there? Most of us stayed behind because *everyone* knows it's not safe for people like us over in Nefastus."

"Lord Alucard and Zalith have been making it safe," Crowell muttered. "And if we make it out of this, then... we'll go there."

"*If* we make it out?" he panicked, moving closer to him, and as he moved, the rubble beneath him shifted.

"Be quiet!" Crowell snapped, pulling him out of the way of the window as he spotted yet another patrol of Diabolus making their way through what was left of the buildings across the street.

As he held the man, Crowell's anxiety increased. He heard the patrol mumbling, and as one of them called out for backup, Crowell scowled. They were surely headed their way, and he wasn't going to be able to do *anything*. But he had to try.

Silently, he let go of the man and pointed over at the rest of the vampires, instructing him to join them. As the man soundlessly crept over to join the others, Crowell leaned back against the wall beside the window and glanced outside, seeing that the Diabolus patrol was slowly creeping nearer.

He wasn't sure what he was going to be able to do. His body was becoming weaker, and the more he moved, the quicker the poison in his bloodstream would spread. He was aware that he didn't have very long left, but he wasn't going to die without a fight—without doing something that mattered. If he ran, he could lead the patrols away from the vampires; he wouldn't get far, but it would give them time to get away and head for the docks.

With a fatigued huff, Crowell closed his eyes, let go of his wound, and yanked the door open—

But then came fire.

Fire as red as blood rained down from above and spewed across the rubble-covered ground, engulfing the Diabolus before they could react to Crowell's appearance. Crimson light broke the darkness, and the horrified, agonized screams of the burning Diabolus broke the eerie silence.

Crowell stared in disbelief as he watched the people burn into nothing—not even a trace of ash was left as the blood-red flames disappeared, and from above, landing over where the Diabolus had once stood, was Alucard.

The ash beneath The Vampire Lord pounced into the air as he landed, rematerializing as he set his eyes on Crowell—and he didn't waste a moment. Alucard immediately made his way over and glared at him.

"M-My Lord?" Crowell asked, but as he noticed the holes and tears in Alucard's bloodied shirt, he frowned in panic. "Are you—"

"'Ow many of you are zhere?" Alucard asked.

Frowning, Crowell looked over his shoulder and then back to Alucard. "Seven…but one of them isn't going to make it."

"And you?" he asked, looking him up and down as a colossal explosion of orange flames burst up into the sky a few yards behind him.

"It's hemlock, My Lord," Crowell answered, looking down at his wound, maintaining the calmest composure he could. "I have moments before I can no longer speak—"

"Zhen shut up," Alucard ordered. "Zhis street is clear; stick to zhe alleys and get zhem to my castle," he said, snatching Crowell's wrist. Alucard then swiftly used his claws to cut Crowell's wrist and then his own palm. He let his blood drip down onto Crowell's new wound and said, "You'll veel better in a vew moments. Zaliv is at my castle; vait vith 'im. I'll join you all soon."

The other vampires climbed to their feet, and they all adorned the same look of relief and surprise as they stared at their Lord. The only one who didn't stand was the vampire currently bleeding out from a wound in his leg.

"Are you all right?" Crowell asked Alucard again, looking him up and down.

Scowling irritably, Alucard glanced at him. "Are zhere any more people 'ere?" he asked, ignoring his question. "Zhere's too much silver in zhe air vor me to be able to sense anyving very var."

Crowell shook his head. "I don't know, My Lord. Maybe—"

"Go," Alucard insisted, turning his back on him, preparing to dematerialize again.

With a nod, Crowell ushered everyone out of the building. Then, he helped the hurt vampire to his feet. He knew that Alucard couldn't help him—the silver had spread beyond repair—but Crowell wasn't going to leave the guy to die in the rubble.

And once everyone was outside, he did as Alucard said and began leading the way to the castle. He'd get them all to that ship, and he'd get them somewhere safe.

| Alucard |

Alucard didn't have time to wait around. There could be more vampires among the ruins who needed his help. He'd come only for Crowell, but he'd make one last sweep before he returned to Zalith. There were only human Diabolus here, as far as he had seen, so there wasn't much to worry about—and he wasn't yet done killing them.

Wordlessly, Alucard dematerialized into vermillion smoke and raced into the night sky, glowering at the ruins that had once been his city. Anger burned inside him, and his desire to kill wasn't sated. The enemy was still here, and he didn't want to leave until every single one of them was dead.

But he wouldn't leave Zalith for too much longer. He swept the city, searching for signs of more trapped vampires... or other civilians, but as far as he could tell, there was no one. So, he headed back to where he'd left his demon, but he'd kill whatever he could on his way.

He swiftly sped over the destroyed city and set his eyes on a group of patrolling Diabolus. He'd already been scathed enough times by their pathetic little knives, and he didn't have the patience for it to happen again. So instead of landing to tear them apart with his hands, he instead rained crimson fire down on them. He did, however, swoop down and tear off the head of one man who tried to run.

There was *nothing* left of Dargamoore, and from what Alucard had seen, Crowell and those he'd taken with him were the last of his vampires who opted to stay in Dor-Sanguis. The thought dismayed him; once, he had hundreds of vampires staying in this city, and now, there were but six left.

And the Diabolus: they were surely going to move on to the rest of Dor-Sanguis' towns and cities, and Alucard had to send out a call for evacuation. He wasn't going to abandon his birth country, though. As he was doing right now, he'd kill *all* the Diabolus until they retreated into their holes—but such commotion would surely alert the Numen, so Alucard had to be wary.

He swooped down and rematerialized in the midst of a group of startled Diabolus. They all knew who he was, and they charged at him as if they thought they actually had a chance. Humans—so inept, so moronic. They came at him with their weapons, and without mercy, he tore them limb from limb.

From a distance, a man and his bow aimed at the vampire, and he fired—it wouldn't be the first arrow Alucard had been hit with since getting here, but this time, he decided to catch the arrow and launch it back at the man, and as it burst through the human's face, Alucard rolled his eyes and grabbed the throat of his next victim. The man cursed and yelled but fell silent once his throat was torn from his body.

And then Alucard took off once more.

As he flew towards the city exit, he tried to decide what to do. He could hunt down the entirety of the Diabolus, but that would entice larger, deadlier troops to move in—and considering that he hadn't yet seen a single member of Lilith's cult, he was certain that they'd soon turn up, too; he was also surprised to see only humans and not a single demon, werewolf, or whatever else the Diabolus had recruited. Not only that, but mass-killing Lucifer's cult would most likely attract the attention of the other cults or their Numen leaders. Alucard wasn't going to risk that—he wasn't going to risk Zalith, himself, or their lives together. He and Zalith weren't ready to face Lilith and Damien, and he'd not bring that upon themselves prematurely.

But what about the rest of his vampires, those living elsewhere in Dor-Sanguis? Half his council was dead; Crowell looked to be the only one left, and he wasn't enough to send out and evacuate those of Alucard's people who remained.

Zalith then came to mind, however. Maybe Crowell could work with Tyrus or Orin or someone who could assist him in getting the rest of Alucard's people to safety before the Diabolus found them. And one day, when he and Zalith were ready to fight the Numen, Alucard could reclaim his land once again. To think that it had only been his for a few years after killing Ada and to lose it so suddenly to the Diabolus—he should have known this would happen, though. The moment Zalith had pretty much declared war on the Numen, he should have known that what he'd built here and through Aegisguard would be in danger.

He didn't have time to dwell on what had been done. He'd left Zalith with Detlaff, and he didn't want to take much longer getting back to him. Dargamoore was lost. But Nefastus was still safe. *That* was where he and Zalith were building, *that* was where he and his people were safe. But…would it stay that way once they started fighting the Numen?

Alucard scowled, setting his eyes on his fallen castle in the distance as he edged closer. His and Zalith's home was the safest place Alucard had ever been; not only did they live in a country made up only of humans—the last place any Numen would look for them—but the house was also protected by so many different shielding and boundary ethos'…but Alucard couldn't help but wonder…would that continue to be enough once Damien and Lilith themselves came looking for them?

That was something to think about later. After all, he and Zalith didn't plan on directly attacking Lilith or Damien just yet. They needed to increase not only their numbers but their resources, too—something that was moving along at a reasonable pace.

But right now, he had to focus on getting back to Zalith. He'd work everything else out once he and his people were safe.

| Zalith |

In the castle dungeons, Zalith waited with a conflicted, dismayed frown. He sat with his back against the wall, the pain from his recently healed wound still lingering. But he didn't care about himself; he fiddled with the ring on his right index finger—the ring

Alucard had given him today. The metal had been warm to the touch ever since Alucard left, letting Zalith know that his vampire was not only okay but also thinking of him.

He wasn't sure how much longer Alucard might be, but the longer he took, the more Zalith's concern grew. He couldn't *not* worry about him, especially after what just happened.

His eyes then fixed themselves on the knife that Detlaff attacked them with, and as he stared, he focused on the unusual, *cold* pain he felt. Detlaff said that the knife was meant for Alucard, and he couldn't stop thinking about what that meant. It had to mean more than the fact that he simply got in Detlaff's way—he seemed so very distraught about it. So, Zalith frowned and leaned over to grab the knife, grimacing as the pain from his healed wound worsened.

As he leaned back against the wall again, he stared down at the knife in his hands, examining it. The mahogany hilt looked to be made of glass—or perhaps a type of crystal he'd never seen before, and he highly suspected it to be the latter as he watched a stream of black light flicker through it. And the blade—it was silver, but it had many different runes and patterns carved into it. That wasn't what brought deep dismay to Zalith's heart, however. As he turned it around, he noticed something written on the small, rounded cross-guard: Caedis—Alucard's demon name. Part of him suspected that maybe this knife belonged to Alucard…but then what would Detlaff be doing with it? Why had he seemed so desperate to impale Alucard with it?

Zalith scowled, taking his eyes off the knife to slowly look over at Detlaff. He had to find out what this knife was, why it hurt *him* so much, and why it was intended for Alucard.

Gripping his side, the demon grunted irritably and slowly lurched to where Detlaff lay. He grimaced in revolt at the stupid little man's face but placed his fingers on it to read his mind. And then, he searched for answers—answers that so very quickly came to him, and they made his paranoia and dismay increase. An Obcasus…a blade specifically created to terminate someone like Alucard—a Numen, or someone with Numen blood. Detlaff's thoughts told Zalith that this knife would have *killed* Alucard—it would have killed him in a way he wouldn't be able to come back from. It had been created upon Alucard's first death—*first death?*

The demon took his hand off Detlaff's face, taking a moment to collect his thoughts. He felt his heart racing a little faster as panic consumed him. While he and Alucard were creating weapons to weaken and maybe even kill the Numen, *they* already had a weapon to kill Alucard. And that mortified Zalith. But his despair would have to wait. As he heard footsteps echoing down the corridor, he slipped the knife into his trouser pocket and looked back over his shoulder.

Alucard entered the cell. Zalith frowned in distress and climbed to his feet; he immediately wrapped his arms around his vampire, holding him tightly. But he wasn't alone. Behind him, Crowell and a few other vampires stood, staring and waiting.

"Are you okay?" Zalith asked, gazing at Alucard, seeing that he was covered in blood and ash, and many tears existed in his shirt.

"I'm vine. Ve can talk vhen ve get 'ome," he said as Zalith slowly moved his hands down to grip the vampire's waist.

Obviously, Alucard didn't want to talk in front of his subordinates, and Zalith respected that.

Alucard continued, "Crowell vill take zhese vampires to a ship I 'ave in zhe docks and sail zhem to Nevastus. Ve vill take Zetlaff," he said, glancing down at the ugly, unconscious gremlin of a man. Then, he looked back at Crowell. "Bind 'im vith zhose vor me," he instructed, nodding at the steel chains at the other end of the room.

Zalith knew that Alucard couldn't have Detlaff bound in silver because then he'd not be able to use his ethos to carry them home with him. And if Detlaff woke mid-flight, then Zalith was sure that Alucard would just beat the shit out of him again until he fell unconscious—that was if Zalith didn't do it first.

"Yes, My Lord," Crowell answered with a nod, making his way over to the chains.

Alucard then set his eyes back on Zalith. "Are *you* okay?" he asked quietly.

Zalith nodded. "I'm okay," he said, moving his hand to the side of Alucard's face.

"M-My Lord," one of the other vampires then interrupted before Zalith could kiss Alucard. "What…what are we to do?"

With an irritated huff, Alucard looked at him. "Crowell vill take you to Nevastus vhere you vill be safe—"

"What about everyone else?" he interjected worriedly, stepping closer. "Are we all that's left?"

"You're all I could vind 'ere, but zhe ozzer covens vill be evacuated, too," Alucard answered. "Zhere's an old manor in zhe vedvood vorest; vonce you arrive at zhe docks, I'll send somevone to take you zhere and guide you," he said to Crowell. He then looked back at Zalith. "Are you veady to go?"

Zalith nodded. The sooner they could leave this place, the better. He just wanted to be back home where it was safe.

Alucard glanced at Crowell, gripping hold of Zalith's hand as he watched his subordinate wrap Detlaff's wrists in the steel chains. Once Crowell was done, Alucard turned around and led the way out of the cell with Zalith at his side. Crowell followed along with the other vampires, dragging Detlaff with him.

As they made their way up the stairs and out into what was left of the hall, however, Zalith stopped walking and looked down at Pip. "We should take his body back so that his family can mourn him properly," he said.

Staring at the dead izuret, Alucard frowned sullenly. "'E zidn't deserve zhis."

Zalith squeezed the vampire's hand. "I know. I'm sorry."

"Zhis attack vas just so…vandom. Ve zidn't know…and so many people are dead because of—"

"It's not your fault, okay? Like you said, this was random, and we couldn't have known," Zalith said softly.

"But I *should* 'ave known," Alucard insisted sadly. "Zhe Diabolus 'ave *alvays* caught up to me sooner or later."

Zalith shook his head. But it didn't look like Alucard wanted to be consoled. He watched the vampire pick up Pip in his arms, and then he wordlessly continued leading the way.

Once outside, Alucard turned to face his vampires. "Go to zhe ship," he ordered. "In vree days vhen you arrive in Nevastus, somevone vill be vaiting vor you at zhe docks to escort you to vhere I 'ave zhe vampires staying."

Crowell nodded humbly and took the people he'd saved away towards the docks, leaving Detlaff with Alucard and Zalith.

"Will you be okay?" Zalith asked, placing his hand on the vampire's arm. He knew how tired Alucard was already, and flying three people all the way from Dor-Sanguis to Nefastus was going to take a lot out of him.

Alucard nodded. "I'll be vine," he confirmed, glancing down at Detlaff. He then handed Zalith the lifeless izuret; he gripped Zalith's other hand and walked over to Detlaff. With a revolted grimace, he snatched Detlaff's wrist and sighed deeply. "Are you veady?" he asked Zalith.

The demon nodded. "I'm ready."

And then Alucard dematerialized himself, Zalith, the izuret, and Detlaff into vermillion smoke, racing up into the sky and towards Nefastus. All Zalith wanted to do the moment he got home was crawl into bed with Alucard, but there was going to be a lot to do before that could happen.

Chapter Twenty-Two

A long, Dismaying Night's End

| Alucard |

As the late night became early morning, Alucard and Zalith arrived home and landed in the back gardens. The moment they rematerialized, though, Alucard felt a headache scratch its way to the surface. It had been a while since he'd used so much ethos in one night, and the fact that he'd given his energy to Zalith twice today didn't help. But he'd be fine. To his relief, he'd not used enough of his own ethos to have to tap into his Numen ethos—he'd rather keep that dormant unless he absolutely had to use it; a headache wasn't going to make him do that.

"Are you okay?" Zalith asked as he placed his hand on Alucard's shoulder, holding Pip's body in his other arm.

Alucard nodded and said, "I'm vine. Are *you* okay?"

"I'm good," he answered. Then, he shifted his gaze to the vast garden. "The caves are this way. We'll take Detlaff down, and then we'll call for Pip's friends," he said, glancing at the izuret.

With a deep sigh, Alucard reached down and snatched Detlaff's wrist—to his relief, the ugly man was still unconscious. Then, he followed Zalith, dragging Detlaff along with him.

Neither of them said a word while they made their way through the gardens and past the tree line. Alucard walked with Zalith to a large limestone boulder, and once they moved around to the other side of it, Alucard set his eyes on the entrance to what could only be the caves Zalith had spoken about. The entrance was concealed by brush and a few trees and probably wouldn't be noticeable unless one knew where to look.

The vampire pulled Detlaff down, following Zalith past the two demons guarding the entrance, one of which he handed Pip's body to, telling the man to hold him for a few minutes. They walked to the bottom of the stairs and through a long, narrow cavern; the cave was deep—they travelled for a few minutes before reaching a slightly wider area with several barred steel doors lined along the walls.

However, as they came closer to the end of the cavern, the doors became silver, and from the cell at the very end of the cavern, Alucard could hear what was unmistakably Luther.

Behind the silver door, the foul little man pleaded miserably, his weak, pain-ridden voice echoing down the cavern. "Hello?" he cried, obviously aware that *someone* was headed his way. "Let me just…just *see* Alucard," he begged and sniffled. "Let me just…tell…him I'm sorry—he won't let Zalith do this to me," he insisted, whimpering painfully.

Once he reached the door, Alucard let go of Detlaff's wrist, stopped walking, and glared inside. He set his eyes on Luther, who was chained to a chair in the middle of his bloody cell. His naked body was covered in deep gashes, slashes, and puncture wounds, and his crotch had been torn apart—maybe even *off* completely.

The moment Luther lifted his head and saw Alucard, relief and desperation broke through his agonized scowl. "A-Alucard!" he cried, trying to get up, but the chains binding him sizzled against his skin, making him whimper and groan. "I-I knew…knew you'd come," he said, grimacing and sniffling. "You…you gotta…g-get me out of here!"

Alucard glowered at him as discomfort and anger devoured him the longer he stared at Luther. He'd been trying to ignore what he remembered of last night…and what he remembered of his past, and despite the fact that seeing Luther was making it harder for him to bury it all, he couldn't look away. Seeing someone who'd tried to take advantage of him suffer…it satisfied him a little. But not enough to make him want to take in the remnants of Luther's torture for much longer.

"It's Z-Zalith…he's f-f-fucking crazy," Luther insisted, tears streaming down his face. "All I…I was doing…is drinking with you, and h-he comes in a-and…and just…attacks me!" he wailed, still trying to escape, but as his melted skin peeled from the shackles while he writhed, spreading like glue between both surfaces, he shrieked and stopped struggling, lowering his head. "He…*hates* me b-because I…*I* know things," he continued, glancing up at him. "Things about him…that h-he doesn't want me to know—things he d-doesn't…want me to tell y—" he explained but then went silent, his eager look fading into dismay as Zalith stood beside Alucard, glaring in at him with a smile on his face.

Alucard had nothing to say to Luther. He glanced at Zalith and turned his back on the cell, snatching Detlaff's wrist. He started dragging him away—

"A-Alucard!" Luther wailed. "P-please!"

Ignoring him, Alucard dragged Detlaff into the unoccupied cell opposite Luther's and left him in the middle of the room. He'd need silver to bind him to ensure that he didn't break out through the walls, but of course, he couldn't touch the metal, so he'd have to go back out there and ask Zalith to do it.

He made his way back out of the room and stopped beside Zalith.

"A-Alucard!" Luther pleaded again, his look of desperation growing.

Still ignoring him, Alucard scowled as Zalith looked at him. "I need you to bind Zetlaff," he muttered.

Zalith nodded and followed Alucard back into the cell. While the demon started binding Detlaff with some silver shackles from the corner of the cell, Alucard sighed deeply and leaned against the wall. He was so tired that he couldn't think about anything else other than getting this over with and then heading to bed; sleep was all he wanted right now—sleep and to lay with Zalith. A day that was supposed to be relaxing had turned out to be a whole lot more demanding than Alucard could have imagined.

When he finished, Zalith joined the vampire by the door and slipped his hand into Alucard's. "Come on," he said quietly, leading the way out of the room. He locked the cell door behind them.

"W-wait!" Luther begged as they walked past without sparing him a glance. "A-Alucard! You can't…l-leave me down here! I-I didn't do anything! Alucard?!"

Scowling, Alucard walked at Zalith's side, leaving the cavern and heading up the stairs into the forest. Zalith took Pip from the guard he'd left him with before continuing towards the house.

"I'm going to get his family to come and take him," Zalith explained, glancing down at the izuret, which he carried in his left arm.

They stopped walking a few yards from the house, and after Zalith let go of Alucard's hand, the vampire watched him summon what he assumed was Pip's family. A group of five izurets quickly appeared in front of them and gawped at Zalith.

"I have some bad news," the demon said quietly, and as the izurets noticed their fallen comrade in his arm, they all frowned despondently and floated towards Pip. "I'm sorry."

The izurets chirped sadly to one another, watching as Zalith placed Pip's body on the grass. Then, the small creatures glided down and placed their tiny hands on the body, muttering their farewells before they picked up their fallen friend and disappeared once again, leaving Zalith and Alucard alone.

After the izurets left, Zalith took hold of Alucard's hand. "I just want to go to bed," he mumbled.

Alucard nodded in agreement as they headed inside the house through the patio doors. He followed Zalith upstairs, and as Zalith led the way into their bedroom, the demon reached into his pocket with his free hand and pulled out his pocket watch. The vampire peeked at it and saw that it was almost two in the morning.

Zalith sighed and turned to face him. "Let's get ready for bed," he murmured, guiding his hand over Alucard's shoulder. "I'm going to go and brush my teeth."

The vampire nodded and let go of his hand. He slumped down onto the end of their bed and watched Zalith head into the bathroom, leaving the door ajar behind him. He listened as Zalith began brushing his teeth; he knew that he should get ready for bed, too, but first, he wanted to go and check on his kitten.

He got up and walked across the hall to his study. When he found her curled up on his couch, and as he smiled, he carefully scooped her up. He didn't want to leave her to sleep alone—she was just a baby. So, he carried her through to his bedroom. Zalith was going to disapprove, but Alucard would try to convince him to let her stay.

Once he hid her under the bed, giving her a cushion from the couch to rest on, he stood up and looked over at the bathroom door. He heard Zalith switch the shower on, and he was certain that his leaving the door ajar was an invitation. Alucard was going to take it; he wouldn't miss an opportunity to shower with his demon, and he also wanted to make sure that Zalith was okay after Detlaff's attack.

He pulled off what was left of his shirt, and as he made his way into the steamy bathroom, he took off his trousers and wasted no time climbing into the shower with Zalith, who smiled at him the moment he turned to face him.

"Hey," the demon said with a smirk. He moved his hands to Alucard's waist and pulled him closer after Alucard shut the shower doors.

Alucard smiled, guiding his right hand over Zalith's shoulder as the water poured over them.

"Where did you go?" Zalith asked curiously.

"To check on zhe kitten," he answered.

Zalith kissed his lips and rested his forehead against Alucard's. "How's she doing?"

"She's sleeping."

"That's good," the demon said, and then he started to kiss him again, pulling him even closer.

But as Alucard trailed his hand up his side, Zalith grunted painfully; Alucard realized he'd moved his hand over Zalith's wound and frowned in dismay. "I'm sorry," he said, hoping he hadn't caused him too much pain.

"It's okay," Zalith said, resting his forehead back against Alucard's. He then frowned in what looked like distress, staring into Alucard's eyes. "Do I have a scar?"

Alucard looked down at the side of Zalith's chest; his wound hadn't healed entirely yet, but it *had* closed, and the skin and tissue were gradually repairing itself, so he couldn't really tell whether he'd be left with a permanent scar. "I zon't know," he answered. "Is not 'ealed yet."

Zalith sighed quietly as Alucard stared back into his eyes. "Okay," he said, guiding his hand to the side of Alucard's face. "Hopefully the energy I took from you at the castle will help it heal nicely, and if not…well, at least I got to make out with you," he said amusedly.

Pouting, Alucard glanced down at the wet marble floor. He was glad that Zalith was okay—or as okay as he could be after getting stabbed. Any ordinary man would have died; maybe a weaker demon would have, too, but Zalith was okay, and all Alucard wanted to do was help him feel better…and he knew *exactly* how to do that.

He did his best to keep an awkward frown off his face as he lifted his head to look into Zalith's eyes again. He moved back, pulling Zalith with him, and as he leaned against the wall, he slowly dragged his hand down the demon's wet body. "You can do more zhan make out vith me now zhat ve're 'ome," he invited, taking his eyes off Zalith's face to glance down at his body.

The demon laughed quietly as he rested his forehead against Alucard's. "I can, can I?" he asked and continued kissing him for a few moments. He smirked at him again and said, "I said no more." But then he resumed kissing him.

Alucard returned each of Zalith's kisses, and as their tongues entwined, he frowned slightly. Zalith didn't really seem to want to stick to what he said earlier about no more sex for a few days—if he *had* meant it, then why was he still kissing him? Why was he still moving closer, pulling as much of Alucard's body against his own as he could? And as the demon's hand wandered down past his waist and gripped his ass, Alucard was sure that Zalith hadn't meant what he said at all—and that relieved him. All he wanted was to be close and give Zalith what he needed to feel better.

However, after a few more minutes of kissing, Zalith stopped and smiled at him. "It's bedtime," he said, reaching over to turn the water off.

Alucard couldn't help the flicker of disappointment as Zalith stepped out of the shower, but he followed when the demon took his hand, the lingering warmth of the water still clinging to his skin. Zalith handed him a towel, and Alucard wrapped it around his waist before grabbing another to dry his damp hair. The rhythmic motion of the towel through his hair was soothing, but his attention kept drifting back to Zalith, who was calmly drying himself off with that effortless grace he always carried.

Once Alucard finished, Zalith's eyes met his, a playful smile tugging at the corner of his lips. The demon stepped closer, placing his hands on either side of Alucard's waist, pulling him into a slow, teasing kiss. It was gentle but charged with an underlying tension, and when Zalith's hands drifted lower, slipping under the towel wrapped around Alucard's waist, Alucard felt his anticipation stir. But just as the towel slipped free, Zalith didn't do what he expected.

Instead of the touch that Alucard craved, Zalith smirked and began methodically drying him off, running the towel over Alucard's body in slow, deliberate strokes. The demon's smirk grew as Alucard's pout deepened, the vampire's body tensing with frustrated anticipation. Each pass of the towel was a tease, an unspoken promise that left Alucard's skin tingling, his disappointment turning quickly to impatience.

Zalith was enjoying this, wasn't he? He was just going to keep teasing him. But as frustrated as it made Alucard feel, he wouldn't make the demon feel guilty. Zalith was hurt and worried, and the last thing Alucard wanted was to make it worse. So, he exhaled quietly and did his best to ignore his growing eagerness for Zalith's affection. He'd be there for whatever Zalith needed.

Chapter Twenty-Three

Obcasus

| Alucard |

Once they were both dried off, Alucard and Zalith climbed into bed and pulled the covers over themselves. But before the vampire could get comfortable, Zalith gripped his waist and pulled him over to his side of the bed. He made Alucard straddle his lap and smiled up at him, tucking the loose strands of his tousled hair behind his ears. Alucard glanced down at the demon's healing wound, worried that he might be hurting him, but Zalith seemed fine, so he set his eyes back on his face and guided his hand over Zalith's shoulder.

Zalith slowly dragged his hand down Alucard's body, gazing up at him. But he then sighed and leaned his head back against the headboard. "We need to talk about what happened in Dor-Sanguis—unless you'd rather talk tomorrow," he said.

Alucard scowled in confliction, looking to his side; he hadn't forgotten what he'd left under the bed, but he was sure that Zalith wouldn't discover it. He wanted to talk, after all, and he wasn't going to be getting up any time soon. So, he looked down at Zalith and said, "Ve can talk."

Zalith exhaled deeply. "The knife that Detlaff attacked with: it's called an Obcasus, and from Detlaff's memories, I found out that it was created specifically to kill you—permanently," he explained as an anxious stare stole his relaxed one.

Alucard wasn't surprised. He knew what an Obcasus was.

"Did…you already know?" Zalith asked with a frown.

"Vell…vhat I attacked Liliv vith back vhen she 'ad us vas an Obcasus—I know zhat zhey existed, but…I zidn't veally vink I vould 'ave vone vor myselv," he explained.

"Well, at least *we* have it now. It's still in my trouser pocket in the bathroom." But he frowned and asked, "If these things are meant to kill Numen, then why didn't Lilith die when you attacked her with the same kind of knife?"

"Zetlaff vas clearly misinvormed," Alucard grumbled. "Zhe Obcasus' zon't kill us, zhey just…comatose us. Zhey keep us in a suspended state zhat ve can't escape vrom; zhe Obcasus' are supposed to be paired vith a Pandorican, vhich is a prison. Zhat's vhat I sent Crowell to vind so zhat ve could lock Liliv avay—is zhe same vay zhe Numen stopped Luciver all zhat time ago. But zhe longer vone stays in a Pandorican vithout zhe Obcasus, zhe veaker zhe prison gets."

Zalith nodded slowly as a conflicted expression appeared on his face.

Alucard continued, "Zhat's vhy Luciver 'as been able to talk to Zetlaff and zhe Diabolus, and 'ow 'e vas able to cveate me. 'E's still locked up in zhere, but 'e can do vings vhrough zhe Astral Plane—zhe 'umans call zhat limbo. Luciver levt 'is physical body in zhe Pandorican and is able to appear as an essence…or…someving like a ghost. 'E can't do anyving vhile in zhis vorm. Does zhat make sense?"

"It makes sense," Zalith said, nodding. "Can we destroy the one with *your* name on it?"

"No," he answered. "Zhere's no vay to destroy zhem."

Sighing despondently, Zalith dragged his hand down Alucard's body. "How do you feel about it?"

Alucard shrugged, glancing away from Zalith's saddened face. "I zon't know," he admitted. "I guess…I should 'ave known zhis vould 'appen; zhe Numen 'ave zhem, so vhy vouldn't I?" he muttered. "But ve 'ave zhe ving now, so…ve can keep zhat avay vrom zhe enemy."

The demon nodded. "We'll take it down to my vault tomorrow. That's the safest place I know."

"Okay," the vampire said.

"What about the situation with Dor-Sanguis?" Zalith then asked.

"Vell," Alucard mumbled. "Dargamoore is noving but vubble now. My castle is gone, and zhe Diabolus is probably going to 'unt down every single last vampire zhat's out zhere. If I start mass-killing zhe Diabolus, vone of zhe Numen is surely going to vealize, so all I can veally do is tell my people to leave zhe country."

Zalith frowned sympathetically and rubbed Alucard's arm.

"I zon't know if zhis vas just zhe Diabolus, zhough; zhey vouldn't do zhis. Zhey're discreet—zhey zon't just…blow up cities and castles. Eizer Luciver 'as changed 'is tactics, or somevone else is telling zhem vhat to do. Considering zhat zhere vere poisons at my castle zhat only Liliv knows you are susceptible to, I suspect she is involved. But…Dor-Sanguis isn't safe vor me or vor my vampires. I 'ave to leave be'ind vor now. I'll take back vone day, zhough," he grumbled, slowly sinking into sadness as he realized that Dor-Sanguis really was lost. If he wanted to keep himself, Zalith, and both their peoples safe, he had to let it go. They didn't have the time or the resources to take it back right now.

Zalith guided his hand to the side of the vampire's face. "I'm so sorry, baby," he said quietly and pulled him into a tight hug. "I'll help you take it back one day."

As he felt his sadness growing, Alucard sighed deeply and tried to dismiss it. He just had to accept that he lost his home a very long time ago and that reclaiming it just wasn't meant to happen. Maybe he was supposed to move on; after all, where he was right now felt more like home than anywhere else ever had.

He sat up straight, looking down at Zalith's gradually disappearing wound. "'Ow do you veel now?" he asked, changing the subject.

"I'm okay. I'm happy to be home…and in bed with you…naked," he said with a smirk, looking him up and down.

Smiling slightly, Alucard glanced at his side of the bed again. He was tired, and he was sure Zalith was, too. He wasn't certain if anything else needed to be said, so he looked back at the demon. "Me too," he murmured.

Zalith stroked his hand to the side of Alucard's neck. "Can we still do more than make out or is that off the table?"

Alucard did his best to avoid becoming flustered and looked away from him. "Ve…can."

The demon laughed. "Okay," he said, guiding his hand to the side of Alucard's face and making him look at him. He then started slowly kissing him, dragging his hands down Alucard's body to grip his waist. "Are you going to be okay? You seemed pretty tired this morning, and you just flew us to and back from Dor-Sanguis."

He nodded. He didn't care that he felt tired; he just wanted Zalith's affection. "I'm vine."

"Okay," Zalith said with a smile, caressing Alucard's hair, "but we're taking a break after this."

Alucard stared at him for a moment; he'd said the same thing this morning, but there they were…. He smirked slightly. "Vight," he said doubtfully.

Zalith laughed. "We *are*," he said sternly.

"Okay," Alucard said with a shrug. "Ve vill see."

"Oh, you'll see all right," Zalith insisted. "In fact, maybe we should start right now."

"Okay," Alucard said with another shrug, moving to get off Zalith's lap—

Zalith grabbed his waist, stopping him. "No, wait," he pleaded, moving his hand to the side of Alucard's face. He kissed him again and sadly murmured through their lips, "I take it back."

Amused, Alucard trailed his hand to the side of Zalith's neck and returned his kisses.

Their tongues entwined with an urgent rhythm, every movement sparking a deeper hunger. Alucard could feel the heat rising between them as Zalith's hand traced a slow, tantalizing path over his skin, sending shivers in its wake. When Zalith's fingers finally settled on the side of his neck, the touch was electric, a promise of what was to come.

When Zalith's lips left his mouth and moved to his neck, Alucard tilted his head to give him more access, his breath escaping in a soft, anticipatory exhale. The moment Zalith's lips pressed against the sensitive skin of his neck, a sharp tremor of pleasure shot through Alucard's body, tightening every muscle with anticipation. His breath hitched, and instinctively, he pressed closer, nuzzling into Zalith's neck, his lips brushing the demon's skin as his pulse quickened. Each kiss was a tease, a slow burn, and Alucard felt the tension coil firmer with every second.

But the longer he spent so close to Zalith's neck, the quicker a familiar craving for the demon's blood enthralled him. He'd usually wait until they were both lost in the moment to bite—or until Zalith offered—but he wanted it *now*.

The demon placed another soft kiss on Alucard's neck; in response, the vampire leaned closer to Zalith's throat. And he didn't wait to bite down. He sunk his four fangs into Zalith's skin, humming in satisfaction when Zalith flinched and grunted quietly as his blood poured into Alucard's mouth. However, Alucard didn't want to take too much; Zalith had already lost a lot earlier, and he'd drunk some this morning, too. So after a few small gulps, he pulled his fangs from Zalith's neck and licked his lips, ensuring he didn't make a crimson mess. Then, he leaned back, allowing the demon to start kissing his chest as the euphoria of his blood quickly consumed him.

However, *that* was when the quiet was disturbed by *purring*.

Zalith immediately stopped kissing him. "Is the cat up here?" he questioned.

Alucard shuffled around in his lap. "I zon't know," he muttered, but he'd never been able to lie to Zalith.

"Alucard…" Zalith drawled disapprovingly as an uncomfortable frown appeared on his face. He then lifted Alucard off himself and rolled over onto his back with a huff. "Please get the cat out of the bed."

Sitting on his knees beside him, Alucard pouted down at the demon. "Vhy?" he muttered. "She von't get vur anyvhere; she 'as none."

"Because it's been walking around a dirty litterbox all day, and I don't want it in the bed," Zalith said, and he was clearly trying to keep himself from becoming too angry.

"No, she's clean," the vampire insisted. "I checked."

Zalith sighed again. "I got her beds for Yule. Can't you leave her in one of those?"

"No," Alucard denied stubbornly. "She's just a baby. She zidn't vant to be levt alone."

The demon huffed and didn't say anything else for a few moments. But he soon rolled onto his back and glanced up at Alucard. "She can stay for tonight," he said. "But tomorrow, you need to figure something out because we both agreed that she wasn't going to come on the bed."

"I zon't vemember agreeing to zhat," Alucard mumbled.

"Well, *I* remember. I told you when you brought her to dinner."

Alucard didn't want to argue with him. He knew that cats made Zalith uncomfortable, and it would be selfish of him to ignore that. So, he got up and scooped his kitten out from under the bed. He took a pair of trousers from the drawer and started pulling them on. He'd take her downstairs to one of her beds and get Sabazios to look after her for the night.

"Wait," Zalith then said.

Alucard turned around and watched as Zalith got out of bed and went over to the couch by the dressing rooms; he grabbed one of the cushions before making his way around to Alucard's side of the bed. The demon pulled open Alucard's nightstand drawer and took the two books out from inside. He pushed the cushion into the drawer, walked over to one of the closets and pulled out a black fleece blanket, and put that into the drawer, too.

Zalith then made his way over to the door and left the room; his footsteps faded down the hall and the stairs. Where was he going?

Alucard sat on the edge of the bed and looked down at his quietly purring kitten while he kicked his trousers off. He didn't want to make her sleep alone, but he also didn't want Zalith to be uncomfortable or irritated because he didn't want the cat in the bed. But from what he was seeing right now, it seemed as though Zalith was making his kitten a bed. So, he waited, listening as Zalith eventually made his way back upstairs and into their room.

Zalith walked back over to the nightstand and placed one of the kitten's mouse toys inside. He then looked down at Alucard with an expectant expression. With a quiet huff, Alucard tucked the kitten into the makeshift bed. He might not be able to have her in *their* bed, but at least she was close enough that he could still pet her.

Once the kitten was comfortable, Zalith crawled back into bed beside Alucard and pulled the covers over them. He wrapped his arms around Alucard again, which relieved the vampire. At least Zalith wasn't mad enough to not want to hold him.

"I'll leave 'er downstairs tomorrow," Alucard mumbled despondently.

The demon kissed his back. "It's okay. I got her a bed so that she can sleep in the room without being on the bed. We can bring it up tomorrow."

Alucard reached into the drawer to pet his kitten goodnight. "Okay," he said sleepily.

"I love you, baby," Zalith then said. "I'm sorry I'm so frustrating."

He'd not lie and say that it *wasn't* frustrating to have to get used to the fact that Zalith didn't love animals like he did; he was going to have to make a lot of compromises. But it was Zalith, and Alucard loved him more than enough to make those changes. "Is vine," he said, dragging his hand back under the covers after petting his kitten. "I love you, too."

As Zalith then hugged him tight and kissed the side of his face, Alucard closed his eyes, relaxing as he started to drift off. The day had been long and strenuous, and it wasn't what he'd imagined, but it was over, and tomorrow, he hoped that he wouldn't have to abruptly fly off somewhere to kill Diabolus.

Chapter Twenty-Four

Loose Ends

| **Zalith,** ***Sunday, Primis 1st, 960(TG)—Nefastus*** |

The gentle dawn light of the new year streamed through the single open window, casting a warm, golden glow that stretched across the quiet landscape and into the room. Zalith blinked slowly, adjusting to the soft, almost ethereal brightness—a soothing contrast to the darkness of the year that had just ended. Through the open window, the first notes of birdsong drifted on the cool morning breeze, echoing faintly from the woods beyond and filling the air with a sense of renewal, of a beginning untouched by shadows.

In his embrace, Alucard lay peacefully, his face softened in serene slumber. Zalith's gaze lingered, tracing every familiar curve and line with a quiet, consuming relief, his arms instinctively holding his vampire a little tighter. This was a new beginning, a chance to leave behind the torment and scars that had haunted them both. Alucard's presence was a balm to his own soul—a reminder of all they'd survived and all they'd fought to protect.

But as much as he wanted to lose himself in this moment, to savour the purity of dawn with the man he loved, he knew that some remnants of the past year still clung to him, unresolved and festering. There were loose ends—shadowed things that needed to be severed if he truly wanted this new year to be a clean start. Before he could fully step into the light, he had to cut away everything that no longer served them, everything that threatened to drag him back into the darkness he wanted to leave behind.

He took a slow, deep breath, feeling the resolve settle within him. This year would be different. This was the dawn of something better, brighter, and he would clear every obstacle, rid every shadow, for Alucard's sake as much as his own.

Zalith brushed a soft kiss onto Alucard's forehead, a silent promise as the new light bathed them both. And with that, he knew what he needed to do. Before he could fully embrace the new year, he'd make sure no part of their past would haunt their future.

The demon carefully climbed out of bed, making sure not to wake his vampire. He wanted Luther to suffer more than he already had, but the mutagen roaches would have done a thorough job right now. It was time to kill him and leave him in the past.

He quietly pulled on some new clothes, but as he was about the leave the room, he remembered the Obcasus knife he'd taken from Detlaff last night. He wanted to put that in his vault, safe from anyone who wanted to do Alucard harm. So he went into the bathroom and grabbed his bloody, torn trousers from the previous night. When he searched the pockets, though…they were empty.

Zalith's heart started racing as panic enthralled him—he desperately searched the floor, the rest of his torn clothes, and the entire bathroom, but the Obcasus was *gone*. A million things raced through his mind—who had it? Were they coming to kill Alucard? He wouldn't give his thoughts the chance to overwhelm him. He left the bathroom and hurried over to the bed, where he gently shook the sleeping vampire's arm.

"Alucard?" he asked.

The vampire frowned and murmured confusedly as he woke.

"Alucard?" he insisted.

"V-vhat?" Alucard questioned, staring up at him wide-eyed and confused.

"The knife's gone—I can't find it. We need—"

Alucard sighed deeply and sat up as he said, "Zon't panic."

Zalith frowned. Don't panic? The very knife that could comatose him was *gone*.

"Zhese knives veturn to zheir sheaths avter going so long vithout living contact."

"Okay…so where's the sheath?"

That was when Alucard looked concerned. "I…vould imagine zhat Zetlaff still 'as…or could be in zhe vuins of my castle."

"We have to find it," Zalith insisted, letting his worry start to devour him. He wasn't willing to take any risks; they needed to find the Obcasus before someone else did.

Alucard climbed out of bed and hurriedly got dressed. Zalith then protectively grasped his hand and raced out of their room, downstairs, and outside. He took his vampire to the caves, the journey through the gardens and forest a blur—he only snapped out of his panic-driven trance when the darkness of the underground tunnels struck his senses. The smell of damp and blood, wet soil and moss, dripping water, rotting flesh, and the distant chitters of mutagen roaches.

But Zalith pulled Alucard past the cell where Luther was rotting and took him to Detlaff's cell. "Wait here," he pleaded, turning to face his vampire.

With a nod and a worried frown, Alucard said, "Okay."

Zalith reluctantly let go of Alucard's hand as he turned to face the cell door. When he unlocked and pushed it open, he set his eyes on Detlaff, who lay unconscious in the corner. He cautiously approached, unsure whether Detlaff was actually still out or was pretending and planning an attack or attempt to escape—he wouldn't get very far if he was, though; his shackles would keep him exactly where he was. When the demon reached him, he slowly edged closer, leaning forward; he saw the outline of a blade in his left trouser pocket, so he extended his arm—

Detlaff sprung to life and lunched with a desperate snarl, but Zalith pulled his arm away and stepped back, avoiding his attack.

The demon snarled irritably and harshly kicked Detlaff's face, knocking him back out cold. Then, he reached into his trouser pocket and yanked from it what was thankfully the Obcasus safe within its sheath. Zalith let out a relieved sigh, and when he looked over his shoulder at Alucard, he smiled at his vampire.

"I'm glad *'e* 'ad," Alucard said with a huff. "I zidn't vant to 'ave to go back to Dor-Sanguis…not avter last night."

Zalith tucked the knife into his own pocket and left the cell, locking the door behind him before he pulled Alucard into his embrace. "We don't ever have to go back there until you're ready," he told him softly. He kissed the vampire's forehead, tidied his crimson hair a little, and then caressed the side of his face. "Let's go and put the Obcasus in my vault, and then we can decide what to do with the rest of our day." He still wanted to kill Luther, but he wouldn't do it in front of Alucard. He'd figure out how he was going to do it once the knife was safe.

"I should 'ave said someving last night," Alucard mumbled as Zalith began leading the way to where he kept his money and valuables. "I vas just so…I zon't know—"

"I know," Zalith said understandingly. "You've been through a lot these past days." He squeezed Alucard's hand, holding the Obcasus firmly in his other. Although he didn't want to overwhelm Alucard, he *did* have questions. "Alucard…."

The vampire glanced at him.

"When I was looking through Detlaff's mind, he knew something about…the knife being created upon your first death. What…what does that mean?"

Alucard sighed quietly. "Vell, zhe short story is zhat…." He paused and shook his head. "Vorgive me, vings are still blurry avter ve vecovered my memories."

"It's okay. If it's too much, then—"

"No, is vine. I just…need a moment."

Zalith nodded, and when they reached the warded, guarded door to his vault, he signalled the two demons protecting it to open it. When he led the way inside, though, he turned to face Alucard as the door closed behind them.

"Zhe…Numen 'ave zheir own sort of savety measures, I guess—zhose ve know, and zhose ve zon't."

"Other Numen?"

"Mm. Vone law zhey collectively agreed upon vas zhat, in zhe event of a Numen-blooded being's virst death and veturn to life, a veapon vould be born to ensure zhe indevinite ending to zhat being. So…vhen I virst died—"

"When did you…I mean…how?" Zalith asked, almost horrified hearing the words from Alucard's own lips.

Alucard's gaze drifted to the ground. "Vas such a long time ago. Maybe avound zhe year 580. I vas struggling a lot back zhen vith trauma and loneliness; I lost Vanessa, I couldn't keep any vriends because I zidn't know 'ow to control myselv. I vinally vhought I made a vriend, zhough—Anselm. 'E vas an alchemist vorking out of a small store in a Lupanese city. 'E knew vhat I vas bevore I even vigured zhat out vor myselv, and 'e knew 'ow to 'elp me stop myselv vrom losing control avound people I zidn't vant to 'urt." He paused and scowled sullenly. "But vone night, 'e vas mugged in an alley, and instead of getting 'im 'elp, I…dvained 'im," he said with a shrug. "I killed zhe longest vriendship I'd ever 'ad, and I velt like I'd never get zhat close again. I vent avter zhe people who mugged 'im, let my vage consume me. Zhere vere a lot more of zhem zhan I vhought, but I zidn't care. I only vealized zhe extent of my vounds vonce I'd killed zhem all. Zhese people vere prepared for zemons and verevolves and vhatever else, so zhey knew 'ow to poison me. And I vas young, so my body vasn't as strong. I succumbed to my un'ealing vounds, and I died." He looked at Zalith and shrugged again, clearly trying to hide just how upset he was. "I voke up I vink…a veek later. All zhe blood vrom zhe ozzer bodies buried avound me slowly revived me. My Obcasus vas likely vormed vight zhere in zhat graveyard, but I zidn't know at zhe time. I zon't know 'ow Zetlaff knew, or anyvone, veally, but zoesn't surprise me zhat zhe people who vant to kill me 'ave dug so deeply into my past zhat zhey vound zhe knife."

As sadness and sympathy ensnared Zalith's heart, he pulled Alucard into his embrace. "I'm so sorry you had to go through that," he murmured, tightening his hold around him.

The vampire explained deeply, nuzzling Zalith's neck. "I 'ave a lot of ghosts and a lot of guilt. Not vemembering most of zhis stuff makes everyving vorse because vhen I *do* vemember, is like is all 'appening again—like…a vresh vound."

He didn't know what to say other than, "I'm always here to listen, and you know that I'll always do whatever I can to help you."

Alucard nodded, relaxing in the demon's embrace. "Alzhough…'urts, I *am* glad zhat my memories are mine again."

Zalith kissed his head and then leaned back, gazing into his eyes. "I'm sure there's good memories in there too, right?"

The vampire smiled at him. "You vant to 'ear a good vone?" he asked amusedly.

He smiled, too. "I do," he said, linking his arm with Alucard's as he turned to face his vault.

Instead of immediately answering, though, Alucard glanced around at the piles of gold bars, old jewels and coins, magical artifacts, the pieces of furniture which Zalith had managed to salvage from his childhood home, as well as the few priceless outfits that once belonged to his mother; dusty books, beloved heirlooms, the gold statue of his mother's most beloved horse, the ornaments carved out of precious gems and stones, each representing almost-perfectly every one of his mother's cats, his brother's guitar, a precious collection of his father's hand-crafted contraptions, and the only, single painting of his family that he'd managed to save from the wreckage of his old life, its golden frame melted on the left corner as a result of the ethos-infused fires that took his home.

"This is all I really have left of my family," the demon said, stopping in the centre of the vault. "It's all I could save." He pointed to the old vanity. "That was my mother's." He nodded at the dollhouse, which had lost most of its pink paint. "And that belonged to my nieces. So did they," he added, gesturing to the collection of wooden animal toys and three dolls. "The guitar was my brother's, and all those little things over there were my dad's; he loved fiddling with old fog watches and trinkets like that," he said with a sad smile.

Alucard placed his hand on the side of Zalith's face, and then he kissed his lips. "Is good zhat you vere able to save some vings. At least you know zhey'll be safe 'ere vorever, no?"

He nodded, stroking his fingers through Alucard's hair. "Yeah." He took hold of Alucard's hand again. "Come on, let's put this away," he said, lifting the Obcasus in his other hand.

The demon led Alucard through and to the back of the vault; he stopped in front of the weapons cabinet, inside which were all the dangerous, magical weapons he, his family, and his people had accumulated over the past six hundred years. The cabinet opened at the touch of his middle finger, and he put the Obcasus inside next to the very knife that had once cut off one of his hands.

"Zhat's a Nether Blade, no?" Alucard asked, pointing to the knife.

"Yeah. Some asshole cut my hand off a while ago," he chuckled, locking the case.

"'Ow long did zhat take to grow back?"

He shrugged, turning to face him. "A little over a month."

"Vighting a war vith vone 'and couldn't 'ave been easy."

"I managed," he said with a shrug and a smile. "Now, tell me about that good memory."

Alucard smiled, too. "Vell, about two 'undred or so years ago, I vitnessed somevone playing a violin. Vas my virst time 'earing zhis music, and I vas vascinated. I started talking to zhe voman who vas playing—'er name vas Cecily. She told me zhe best place to buy vone, vhere to learn zhe basics. I could never veally pinpoint in my life vhen I started playing, but now I know," he said fondly.

"What happened to Cecily?" he asked curiously.

"Eh, like all 'umans, she grew old, but she 'ad a good life. She 'ad…eight children, and some of 'er descendants are still avound today—vone plays vor a vamous orchestra."

"Oh?" Zalith replied as he started leading Alucard through the vault once again. "Perhaps we should go and see them in concert."

"Maybe. Could be a nice little break avay vrom 'ome."

When they reached the door, which opened in response to a wave of his hand, he stepped outside and stopped by the guards. He still had to deal with Luther. "I'm going to take care of the cretin occupying the other cell. Do you want to head up to the breakfast nook and wait for me there?"

Alucard glanced at Luther's cell, frowned uncomfortably, and nodded. "Okay. 'Ow long vill you be?"

"Not very long at all, don't worry," he assured him. He then kissed his lips, and as the vampire left his side, Zalith watched him go. As much as he already missed him, though, he wanted to tie up the last loose end.

Once the guards closed the vault door, he headed over to Luther's cell and glared in through the bars. Unlike last night, Luther wasn't saying much anymore. The roaches had clearly finished their job, leaving his skin rotting and peeling, blood oozing from every tiny bite mark and gash on his body. His aura was weakening, and the smell was so disgusting that it burned the insides of Zalith's nose.

Did he really want to put him out of his misery? He knew that he should, but…he wouldn't. Despite having come down here intending to end it and leave Luther in the previous year, he didn't think that creature of a man deserved such mercy. He'd leave him to starve, to mummify, and then he'd mark the scroll that the Inquisitors had given him. Right now, he just wanted to head back to Alucard and enjoy their first day of the new year together.

| Alucard |

The kitchen staff came and went, placing Alucard and Zalith's breakfast on the table. Every time the vampire glanced over his shoulder and out the window, he hoped to see Zalith walking through the gardens on his way to join him, but the demon was nowhere to be seen. Alucard wasn't going to let himself wonder what was taking him so long, though. He knew what Zalith was doing.

Instead, he sipped from his coffee and picked up the small pot of dried rice that Edwin had delivered as requested.

A knock then came at the door.

Alucard frowned and looked over there.

It was *her*. Varana.

He stifled a scowl—he didn't want the first day of this new year to be ruined.

"Where's Z?" she asked him.

"Dealing vith Luther."

"Oh…" she mumbled, stepping into the room and closing the door behind her. She didn't approach the breakfast nook, though. "Well, I thought that I'd just…say that Luther got what he deserved."

He was admittedly surprised to hear her say anything to him that didn't contain an insult, but he was skeptical. What was she after? "'E did," he mumbled.

"And, well…I have to go and meet my friends, but Happy New Year."

His skepticism grew, but he kept it hidden behind his neutral expression. "'Appy New Year," he replied.

Varana then turned around and left the room.

Alucard sighed and leaned back in his seat. Just as he was about to take a sip of his coffee and glance over his shoulder again, though, the door on the other side of the room opened, and Zalith stepped in.

"Was that Varana?" the demon asked worriedly, walking towards the breakfast nook.

The vampire nodded. "She vas just saying 'Appy New Year."

"Oh…." He looked relieved. "Okay, good." He sat beside Alucard and shuffled closer so that their thighs were touching.

"Ezvin brought zhe vice, so ve can scatter zhat avter," he told him, showing him the pot of dried rice.

"Is this little ritual something you've done every new year?" Zalith asked as he started buttering some toast.

"'Ere and zhere," he said, taking one of the doughnuts. "Vhat about you and zhis doughnut stuff, hm?"

The demon chuckled. "Yeah, it's an Eltarian thing. We eat certain foods on New Year's Day; it's meant to bring luck and prosperity for the coming year."

Alucard took a bite of the doughnut. "Vell, tastes very good."

Zalith smiled and pulled the plate of éclairs closer. "I had the staff give us these, too," he said, offering one to him.

The vampire put the doughnut down and took one of the éclairs. He curiously bit into it, and when the cold cream met his tongue, he shivered a little but smiled. "Is veally good," he murmured.

A flirtatious, devious little smile appeared on Zalith's face as he took one of the éclairs and gently squeezed it. The cream from inside oozed out, and the demon grinned and said, "This kinda reminds me of your ass."

Alucard pouted embarrassedly and looked away, trying to hide his face, which he was sure had turned red.

Zalith laughed and took a bite of the éclair. "I love your ass," he said and wetly kissed Alucard's cheek. "Now, tell me more about this rice ritual."

With a quiet sigh, Alucard took another bite of his éclair. "Is Dor-Sanguian tradition; ve vhrow zhe grains of vice inside our 'ouse as a blessing—encourages abundance, vealth, and vertility vor zhe coming year."

"Fertility?" Zalith asked with a smirk. "Are you thinking about having our daughter?"

Alucard pouted again but didn't shy away. "Someday."

Zalith smiled and kissed his cheek again. "We can finish up breakfast, and then we'll get started."

As Alucard finished his éclair, he glanced at Zalith. "I've been vorking on your birvday," he said excitedly.

The demon laughed a little. "Oh?"

"I vas vondering vhat kind of cake you'd prever."

"Hmm…" Zalith pondered. "Well, nothing too sweet. I'm not really a fan of fondant or sugary icing, but I do love fruit cakes."

Alucard smiled at him. "Noted."

Zalith then leaned a little closer. "What are you planning?"

"You'll just 'ave to vait and see," he teased.

"You're going to make me wait?" he questioned amusedly.

"Mm-hmm. You're going to 'ave to be patient."

The demon laughed softly, taking some bacon from the plate. "Can't I have one tiny little hint?"

"No," Alucard refused, smirking at him.

Zalith sighed and said, "Okay, I guess I'll just have to try my best to be patient."

"You vill," the vampire said firmly. "But vill be vorth zhe vait."

"I know it will," Zalith said and kissed Alucard's head.

Alucard smiled contently and continued eating his breakfast. He hoped that the new year would be better for everyone—him, Zalith, and his vampires. They should be arriving in the Citadel at dusk, and he trusted Crowell to get them all to safety. His Obcasus was also in one of the safest places that he and Zalith knew, so they didn't have to worry about that *or* Detlaff anymore. All they had to focus on was their lives together…and their fight against the Numen.

Chapter Twenty-Five

A New Home

| Crowell |

As the ship approached the Nefastian docks, Crowell stood on the forecastle deck, watching the sun set over the horizon, as the rain started trickling before pouring. Once the burning star had disappeared completely, giving way to the six rising moons, he called the surviving five vampires up onto the deck. They were all still healing, their injuries closed but not gone; Vasilica's wounds would likely take the longest to heal, though—she'd lost Costache, her husband, and Crowell couldn't help but feel like he could have done more to help him. The fact that Lord Alucard had been able to save him from hemlock but not Costache from silver made him feel worse. But he had to be strong. He had a job to do; he couldn't let the guilt devour him.

"Look," Drăguța said, pointing up at the clouds.

The vampires looked up, and when Crowell spotted the silhouette of a shark above the grey clouds, a brief moment of awe fell over him, shrouding his guilt and grief. He'd seen skyfish before, of course, but in all his years, he'd never seen a shark.

"Do they come below the clouds?" Răzvan asked, shifting his unsettled gaze from each observing vampire.

"No," Costin answered. "They hunt above the clouds; it's rare to see them."

"Not as rare as whales," Drăguța said matter-of-factly.

While the survivors began discussing skyfish, whales, and sharks, Crowell set his eyes back on the docks. He saw Lord Alucard's galleon in the shipyard, and the people on its deck seemed to be partying. It was then that he realized: it was the new year, wasn't it? *Everyone* was celebrating. But not him. Not the five surviving vampires behind him. All they wanted was a safe, secure home—they'd just lost *everything*.

"Does Lord Alucard have somewhere for us to stay?" Vasilica quietly asked him, her voice thick with despair.

"A manor in the redwoods. Those trees will provide plenty of shade from the sun."

"Will he go back to Dor-Sanguis and look for more survivors?"

"He sent some of our strongest from Fort Rudă de Sânge. If there's anyone left, they'll find them," he assured her. Then, he turned his body to face her, placing his hand on her shoulder. "I'm really sorry about Costache."

She scowled sadly, looking away from him. "He's in the Eternal Rest now. I'll see him again someday."

"Baron Crowell?" Costin called.

Crowell looked down at him.

"There are only six of us. Does Lord Alucard plan to create more?"

"I'll receive orders and updates once I've told him that we've arrived. Someone will be waiting for us once we dock to take us to the new coven house, so they may have more information," he explained.

"He's getting everyone out, right?" Drăguța asked. "Not just the vampires from Dargamoore."

Crowell nodded. "Dor-Sanguis isn't safe for us anymore. I expect that we'll eventually start seeing vampires from across the country."

Răzvan groaned. "Including the Hatre vampires?"

"Yes," Crowell answered, hiding a grimace. The vampires of Hatre Manor were *very* stubborn and stuck up—they were Lord Alucard's very first fully-formed coven.

"That means we'll be seeing Knight Lăcrămioara," Ancuța mumbled.

Several groans followed her statement.

Crowell wasn't going to lie—he wasn't a fan of Lăcrămioara either; she might be one of Lord Alucard's best fighters, but she had a stick up her ass. In his opinion, she seemed to think that she was as mighty as their Lord himself. She needed knocking down a peg or two.

"Have you heard from Păzitoarea?" Vasilica suddenly asked him.

"No," he answered, unable to hide a worried frown. But his wife was strong, she was one of the most powerful vampires, and he just *knew* that she was alive. He could feel it. "Get ready," he then said, heading down the steps onto the deck. "We're almost at the shipyard."

The vampires converged on the deck, and when the ship eased into the dock, they worked together to moor it. Once it was secure, they followed Crowell down onto the docks, where a woman with hair as orange as fire approached.

"Safta, Baron Crowell," she said respectfully with a small bow of her head. "Lord Alucard sent me from the Fort to escort you to the Redwood Manor. There's a coach waiting just outside the shipyard."

"Thank you," Crowell said and glanced back at the vampires. "Let's go."

Safta took them through the docks and across the shipyard; they stepped onto the Citadel's icy streets, and just across the road, a horse-drawn coach was waiting.

"In," Crowell instructed as he pulled the back door open.

One by one, the five vampires got inside and took their seats. Safta got in next, and Crowell last, pulling the door shut behind him. Safta tapped on the wall, signalling the coachman to get going, and the carriage started moving.

"What's this place like?" Drăguța asked.

"Generous," Safta answered. "An old, unused estate on Lord Alucard and Zalith's land. It's a twenty-minute horse ride from their home, and forty from the compound being built for the werewolves. The shade of the redwood trees will allow those of you who cannot day walk to step outside during daylight hours, but you must be cautious; not all areas of the forest are permanently sheltered. I will, however, be there to guide you all for the first month."

"Thank you, Safta," Crowell said. "Is Păzitoarea okay?"

She nodded. "She's helping the others evacuate vampires from across Dor-Sanguis."

Relieved, Crowell let out a deep sigh and leaned back in his seat.

"I expect that she'll be arriving at the Redwood Manor this time tomorrow," Safta continued. "She's evacuating the Avluoywood Coven with Teodora."

That made Crowell feel *even* better. Teodora was one of the best înfățișare vampires, so at least his wife had capable allies at her side.

"You know, I've heard stories about this place," Costin said as the carriage left the city roads and headed into the woods. "The humans don't take very well to anybody but elves. It's not going to be easy to feed, is it?"

"Lord Alucard will arrange something," Safta assured them. "There are always humans willing to do anything for money."

"Fresh blood always beats farmed blood, paid for or not," Ancuța mumbled.

"Blood is blood at the end of the day," Crowell said. "We should appreciate what we have, and what we've been given."

All of the vampires adorned guilty and apologetic stares.

"Will we get to see Lord Alucard soon?" Drăguța asked.

"Our Lord is going to come by tomorrow evening once Păzitoarea and Teodora have arrived with the Avluoywood Coven," Safta told them. "He'll make sure that you're comfortable, and he'll instruct you regarding feeding and travelling."

Răzvan then sighed, staring out the window at the passing trees. "I miss Dor-Sanguis already. Everything here looks different, it all smells different. The blood probably tastes different, too."

"Fruity," Costin suggested, almost salivating. "I hear the aristocrats drink a lot of wine and eat a lot of pineapples."

"But they smoke a lot, too," Vasilica muttered. "Their blood is probably putrid."

The thought of putrid blood reminded Crowell of the first time he'd tasted the *worst* kind of blood in his long life. "I don't think anything could ever taste as disgusting as the blood of the humans during the bubonic plague that swept through Ripperton. So many vampires starved because no matter how much of it they managed the stomach, it was contaminated; it didn't feed us, it just made us hungrier—it made a lot of Fledgelings sick, too. It was a very sad time."

"How did you live through it?" Răzvan asked.

Crowell shrugged and said, "Lord Alucard pulled us through. He'd spend days finding humans who weren't infected just so that we could feed."

"Well, I suppose we all better hope that nothing like that happens here," Drăguța said uncomfortably. "Just the idea of contaminated blood makes me want to puke."

"Human medicine is much more advanced now, especially here," Safta said. "I'm certain that we're all perfectly safe—so long as we follow the rules, of course. Things will be much stricter here."

While Safta continued detailing the complexities that lay ahead, Crowell's gaze drifted to the window, where the first shadowy outline of Redwood Manor loomed against the dusky sky. The manor was emerging like a ghost from the mist that clung to the towering redwoods around it, their ancient trunks dense and foreboding, stretching upward to obscure the sky. The thick canopy above seemed to filter what little light remained, casting a dim glow over the manor's weathered facade.

The house itself stood proud and brooding, with dark, stone walls cloaked in creeping vines that twisted and tangled as though alive, woven into the manor's very foundation. Tall, narrow windows, dusty and dark, lined the walls, their shapes sharp and angular like watchful eyes gazing out over the landscape. The peaked roofs were edged with intricate wooden trim, casting dramatic shadows that fell across the ivy-strewn stone, giving the manor an air of ominous elegance.

As they drew closer, Crowell could make out the manor's grand entrance—a pair of heavy, ornately carved doors that seemed to dare visitors to enter. Above the doors, a stone archway bore worn engravings, their meanings long since obscured by time, lending an air of mystery to the place. Crowell felt a strange thrill rise in his chest, as though Redwood Manor itself pulsed with secrets, each twist of the surrounding forest a silent guardian, shielding its mysteries from all who ventured too near. It was perfect.

"Woah, is that it?" Drăguța drawled, also staring out the window.

The other vampires set their sights on it, too, all adorning equal looks of surprise and awe.

"It's like a mini fortress," Costin said.

"Lord Alucard said that the place will need fixing up a little," Safta explained. "But it's liveable. There are enough rooms for us all and the Avluoywood Coven to have our own rooms, but eventually, it's likely that some of us will have to double or triple up; the rooms are large enough for at least three beds or coffins, though."

"Do we get to choose new coffins?" Drăguța questioned.

"Some have been supplied for now, but I'm sure that you'll be allowed to personalize them or purchase new ones as more vampires begin arriving," Safta answered.

As the carriage came to a creaking halt in the courtyard, Crowell could feel the damp chill of the night clinging to the air as he stepped out, followed by Safta and the other five vampires. The sound of boots meeting cobblestone echoed softly as each vampire alighted, the quiet forest seeming to absorb their presence. Up close, the Redwood Manor loomed with an even darker, more imposing presence than it had from the distance. Crowell glanced up at the stone structure—aged but steadfast, the manor seemed to peer down at its new inhabitants with an almost sentient curiosity.

The manor's façade, weathered by time and the weight of the forest's shadow, was an intricate tapestry of ivy and moss, each crack and crevice speaking to decades of solitude. Massive arched windows lined the walls, their glass cloudy with age and partially obscured by sturdy, folding shutters that would soon protect them from the coming daylight. Worn carvings adorned the stone around the entrance, faint but visible, like traces of old ethos etched into the very bones of the manor. The doors themselves were tall and formidable, thick slabs of ancient oak, weathered yet resilient.

Safta led the group forward, pushing open the heavy doors with a low groan. As they stepped inside, a stillness settled over them. The entry hall was dim, lit by the soft glow of oil lamps affixed to the walls, their brass fixtures casting faint halos against the wood-panelled walls. The hall smelled faintly of dust and old wood, with a lingering hint of something sweet—perhaps remnants of perfumes long since dissipated clinging to the fabric of the place.

The ceiling stretched high above them, supported by heavy beams, and the walls were decorated with faded portraits and tarnished mirrors. Safta began her tour with an air of casual authority, leading them from the hall to an adjacent lounge. The lounge was sparsely furnished with low, upholstered chairs and a fireplace, its stone mantle decorated with timeworn carvings of flora and fauna. A few candles rested on the mantle, unlit but ready for use. Crowell noted that this room, like every other they had passed so far, had tall windows fitted with those same protective shutters, prepared for the sun's intrusion at dawn.

Next, they moved into a study. Dust motes floated in the air, stirred up by their entry, and Crowell observed the bookshelves lining the walls, filled with leather-bound tomes of all shapes and sizes. A large desk dominated the centre of the room, its surface cluttered with scattered papers and a few glass vials that hinted at past experiments or concoctions. An old, high-backed chair sat behind the desk, its fabric threadbare in places, as though waiting patiently for its next occupant.

Safta then guided them into another lounge, slightly smaller than the first but furnished with a few more chairs, a coffee table, and an empty glass cabinet along one wall. This room felt darker, less welcoming; its windows were narrower, and the walls bore faint stains from a previous leak, though the overall structure remained sound. Safta's assurance that repairs could be made quickly gave the group a sense of relief.

They moved through to the kitchen, where Crowell spotted the large stone basin for water and the ample counter space. Cabinets lined the walls, many of them fitted with ethos preserving seals ready for bottles and vials of blood; those enchanted cabinets could keep farmed blood fresh for weeks, ensuring that they'd not have to hunt frequently in the nearby city.

Lastly, Safta led them up a grand staircase with creaking steps to the manor's upper floors. There, she opened the doors to multiple rooms, each intended for the vampires' daytime rest. The rooms were simple but functional, with each containing a coffin nestled into a corner, ready for the daylight hours. The beds, for the rare occasions any of them might use one, were covered in dusty linens, and the windows were all fitted with heavy shutters, ensuring total darkness for sleep.

The manor was old indeed with cracks in the walls and patches of peeling paint, but it was sturdy. To Crowell, it felt like a place brimming with secrets and stories, a sanctuary built to endure the march of time. As Safta concluded the tour, Crowell felt a strange, tentative sense of belonging settle over him. This manor, with its creaks and shadows, would be their haven, and with a few repairs, it would feel like home.

"I want the room at the end of the hall," Răzvan announced. "I like the paintings."

Crowell nodded, and the man departed.

"I'll take the one next door," Costin said.

"And I guess I'll take the one with the mahogany coffin," Ancuța said as she left the room with them.

As Drăguța left, she said, "I'm taking the one with the vanity."

Vasilica let out a deep sigh. "I'll take the one by the stairs."

Once the vampires had left to explore their chosen rooms, Crowell set his eyes on Safta. "Where are you staying?"

"There's a study in the loft; I had a coffin put up there."

"All right. I'll take the master bedroom since I'm the only one who can walk in the sun. I've never really been one for coffins."

Safta nodded. "I'll see you later."

He watched her leave the room, and when he heard the creaking of the steps that must lead up to the loft, he headed towards his own room. It had been a long journey—a long week, actually. The destruction of Dor-Sanguis still weighed heavy on his mind, and although Lord Alucard may have healed him, there were moments when he felt like he could still feel the hemlock in his bloodstream. He brushed it off, though—there was no room for discomfort.

When he got to his room, he closed the door and fell onto the bed, sending a cloud of dust up into the air. He groaned but didn't move; he was far too exhausted. For a few moments, he lay there, staring up at the ceiling. There was a lot of work ahead of him; helping vampires settle into a new coven house was one thing, but an entirely new country, too? It was going to be tiring, but he was ready for it—at least he would be once he got some rest. Lord Alucard was relying on him, and he wouldn't let him down. Not again.

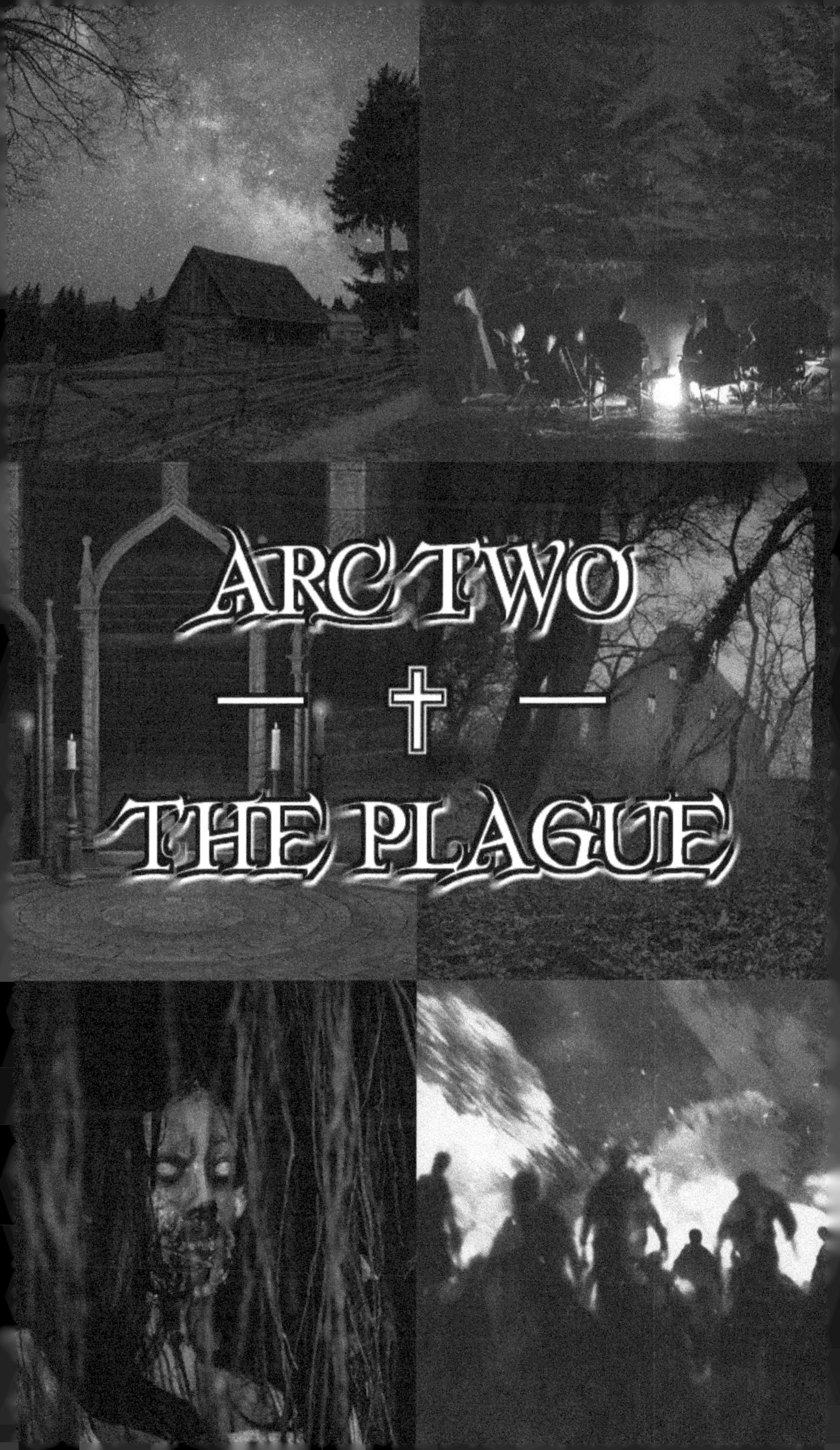
ARC TWO
†
THE PLAGUE

Chapter Twenty-Six

Zalith's Birthday

| **Alucard,** ***Wednesday, Primis 18th, 960(TG)—Nefastus*** |

Zalith's birthday seemed to come so fast, and Alucard was excited. He made sure to wake before the demon; as much as he wanted to go back to sleep, he had plans, and he wasn't going to mess them up.

While the demon lay asleep beside him, he quietly got out of bed, pulled on his trousers and a shirt, and crept over to the door. He silently left the bedroom, made his way across the hall, and headed downstairs. Last night, he'd told the kitchen staff to prepare Zalith all his favourite things for breakfast, and he hoped that it was ready for him to take up to him.

He went into the kitchen, and to his relief, the staff were finishing up plating the eggs and bacon. Upon the tray sat a bowl of fruit salad, some toast, and a small cupcake that Alucard sent Edwin to the Citadel to pick up yesterday.

Once the staff were done with Zalith's coffee and placed it on the tray, Alucard picked it up. "Vank you," he said and left the kitchen.

The vampire walked through the house once more, and when he reached the stairs, Sabazios greeted him with a happy bark. Alucard smiled and patted the dog's head, and then he continued up the stairs as the hellhound wandered off towards the kitchen, searching for his own breakfast.

Alucard stepped back into the bedroom, setting his eyes on Zalith, who was still sleeping soundlessly. He made his way over, placed the tray of food on the demon's nightstand, and sat on the edge of the bed beside him. "Zaliv?" he asked, placing his hand on the demon's shoulder.

Zalith murmured a tired sound in response.

The vampire smiled. "'Appy birvday," he said, stroking his hand up to the side of Zalith's face.

With a slight smile, Zalith turned his head to nuzzle Alucard's hand. "Thank you," he mumbled sleepily.

"I got you breakvast."

The demon smiled again. "Thank you, baby."

Alucard frowned a little; he had so much planned for today, and there wasn't really much time for them to lounge around, as much as he liked to do that. He tried his best to contain his excitement, though; he guided both his hands to Zalith's arm and shook him gently. "Come on," he encouraged with a quiet, playful laugh. "You 'ave to get up; ve 'ave vings to do today."

Zalith laughed quietly as he opened his eyes to glance up at him. "Like what?"

"Is a secret," Alucard answered with a smirk. "But you 'ave to eat your breakvast and zhen ve can go."

"What if I want to eat you instead?" the demon flirted.

Alucard pouted a little. "I'm *not* breakvast."

"I can make you my breakfast," the demon said, trailing his hand up Alucard's arm.

Trying to keep an embarrassed frown off his reddening face, Alucard looked away. "Vell…I guess is your birvday," he said with a shrug, slowly looking back down at him. "You can 'ave vhatever you vant." He wanted to make sure that Zalith was as happy as he could be today.

"I don't know what I'd do without you," he said with a smile and then looked at the breakfast tray. "I suppose I'll eat the food for now."

"I 'ad zhem make all your vavourite vings," Alucard said proudly as Zalith sat up and leaned his back against the headboard.

Zalith took a small cube of melon from the fruit salad. "Thank you," he said. "The little cake is cute," he added. "Did *you* eat?"

Alucard shook his head. "No. I vanted to 'ave everyving veady vor you…and I'm not veally 'ungry vight now."

"If you need blood, you know where to get it," the demon said, smirking as he slowly chewed on the melon.

He wanted it—he *always* wanted Zalith's blood—but he didn't want to do anything that would weaken the demon, not today. "Is okay, vank you," he mumbled. "I can 'ave someving later."

Zalith nodded and continued eating his breakfast.

"Ve 'ave to leave in two hours, so vill be time vor you to eat and velax…and vor us to get veady."

"Where are you taking me?" Zalith asked as he took a bite of his toast.

Alucard shrugged. "You'll see."

"Do I have to get dressed up?"

"Not yet," he said, smirking.

"Not yet?" Zalith asked, finishing the first piece of his toast. "Should we bring clothes along?"

The vampire thought to himself for a moment. "Hmm…no. Ve'll be coming back 'ere again later."

"Okay," the demon said.

Alucard smiled and sat there for a little while as Zalith ate his breakfast, and once he was done, the demon picked up the small cupcake.

"Do you want half?" Zalith offered.

"Is yours," Alucard said—but he *did* want some, and it made him feel guilty.

"I'm pretty full…I don't mind sharing."

The vampire shrugged slightly. "Vell…okay," he agreed.

Zalith carefully tore the cupcake in half horizontally. Then, he flipped the bottom half and pressed it down over the top of the cake, sandwiching the icing in the middle. "My brother used to eat these like this all the time," he said, holding the cake out to Alucard.

Alucard frowned curiously as he leaned forward and took a bite. "I zon't know vhy I never vhought of zhat. Is a good idea."

The demon nodded. "As stupid as he was, sometimes he did have some very good ideas."

Once he finished eating his half of the cupcake, Alucard pondered. Zalith talked about his brother a lot—Xurian. Alucard enjoyed hearing the stories of Zalith's past and his family; he found it intriguing hearing about not only what life was like for somebody who wasn't raised by Damien, but he loved learning more about the man he loved. He had so many questions, but he knew talking about these things often upset Zalith…so he tried his best not to ask them all at once. "Vhat…did 'e look like? Your brover," he asked, looking at him.

"We had similar features," Zalith said, finishing his half of the cake. "Except he had my mother's blue eyes and my father's hair, which was brown."

Alucard smiled. "Is good zhat you got along. I vish I 'ad a brover who vasn't devanged," he grumbled. "I guess creating children vrom ethos drastically changes 'ow zhey turn out, no?"

Zalith shrugged and said with a quiet laugh, "I'd use Varana as an example of things going right, but she's certainly had her moments where I've found myself wondering why she is the way she is."

The vampire smirked slightly. "If I 'ad a brover vhrough blood, do you vink 'e vould look just like me? Or…maybe more like Zetlaff?" he wondered.

As he smiled, Zalith moved his hand over the side of Alucard's face. "He would probably look like you…but maybe different hair. He'd definitely *not* be as pretty, though."

With a flustered smile, Alucard looked away and pouted. "I'm not pretty."

"You *are*," he teased. "But I suppose the acceptable term is handsome if it makes you feel better."

"Zhat does."

The demon chuckled. "I'll take note of it." Then, he took a sip of his coffee and sighed. "Do you want to take a bath?"

He smiled and nodded. "Ve can do zhat."

"Can you do stuff to me when we're in there?" Zalith asked.

Alucard frowned a little in embarrassment. "Vhat stuff?"

"I don't know," he said with an unseemly tone in his voice. "Hand stuff…mouth stuff, maybe. But I'd prefer if you didn't do that underwater; I don't want you to drown."

The vampire mumbled, "Only if you ask nicely."

Zalith adorned a pleading look. "Can you please do sexy stuff to me in the bathroom, Alucard?"

Alucard smiled amusedly and fought off his nervousness. "Okay."

"Thank you," the demon said and kissed his lips. "Let's go right now," he said excitedly, taking Alucard's hand.

Without hesitation, Alucard followed him out of bed and into the bathroom, eager to give Zalith everything he wanted.

⤛❖⤜

Their day outside of the house started with a relaxing shopping trip in the Citadel. Zalith picked out some new clothes, cufflinks, ties, and a wristwatch. He also got Alucard a pair of cufflinks matching a pair he'd brought, as well as a few extra toys for Peaches. Once they were done, they handed everything off to one of Zalith's shadowing guards and made their way through the Citadel to a small café, where they decided to sit.

On their table sat a plate of sandwiches, and they each had a coffee in front of them. As Zalith Gazed at the vampire, he smiled curiously and rested his arms on the table.

"So," the demon said, "where are you taking me next?"

Alucard shrugged. "You'll see."

"Is it far?"

"Vell…ve vill 'ave to vly zhere."

"For how long?"

The vampire shrugged again as he took a sip of his coffee. "About tventy minutes—I can go vaster if you vant, zhough."

"Twenty minutes is fine…unless you can't handle it," the demon said, smirking.

Alucard pouted. "I *can* 'andle zhat."

"Are you sure? I don't want you to wither away," he teased.

"Vell, maybe *you* can vly us zhen, hmm?" Alucard suggested.

"But it's my *birthday*. I'm not supposed to lift a finger, let alone a fully grown man."

The vampire smiled a little in amusement. "You zon't 'ave to do anyving," he assured him. "Ve 'ave to 'ead 'ome to get veady virst, zhough."

"Okay," Zalith said. "When should we head back? Is what we're doing time-sensitive?"

"Not veally," Alucard said. "Ve should probably 'ead back soon, zhough, so ve 'ave time to get veady."

The demon smiled and said, "Okay."

After finishing their lunch, they left the café and walked back to their carriage. They climbed inside, and when it started moving, Alucard sighed quietly and rested his head on Zalith's shoulder. The day was close to half done, but what Alucard had planned next was what he was most excited about. He knew that Zalith was going to love it.

The demon moved his arm around Alucard and hugged him firmly. "You smell good," he mumbled, nuzzling the vampire's head.

With a curious frown, Alucard guided his hand over Zalith's body and up to the side of his neck. "What do I smell like?"

"The bath…and cedarwood…hmm…warm amber, roses, and cinnamon."

The vampire laughed quietly. "You veally like smelling me, zon't you?"

"Amongst other things," the demon answered with a smirk.

"Vhat ozzer vings?" Alucard asked.

Zalith kissed Alucard's head. "I like experiencing you through *all* my senses, like smelling you, hearing you, seeing you…*feeling* you," he murmured seductively. "Tasting you."

Alucard was beginning to feel flustered. "Vhich is your vavourite?"

"It depends on my mood, but I'm particularly fond of the last three," he mumbled, stroking Alucard's back. "Although hearing you can be very nice, too, especially when you're moaning and arching your back," he flirted.

The vampire's face turned a little red as he buried it in Zalith's shirt. "Vell, you know exactly 'ow to make me do zhat."

"I'm very talented, aren't I?" Zalith said with a quiet laugh.

"You are," the vampire agreed. "You know…ve 'ave some time bevore ve 'ave to leave," he hinted.

"To do what?"

He shrugged lightly. "Vor you to make me moan and arch my back."

"What if I want *you* to make *me* moan and arch my back?"

Admittedly, that made him feel a little intimidated, but it was Zalith's birthday, and he wanted to do whatever it was that the demon wanted. "I can try," he said with a curious smile.

The demon kissed his head again. "Good boy," he said. "But actually, I'd rather fuck you right now and make some good use of this space we're in."

Alucard smiled shyly. "Zhat sounds like a good idea."

"I think so, too," the demon said as he lightly gripped Alucard's jaw with his hand. He lifted the vampire's head and pulled his face closer to his own… and kissed him.

Alucard returned Zalith's kiss, and they quickly began kissing eagerly, their tongues entwining with one another. The vampire could feel his desperation increasing; he moved a little closer to Zalith, and as the demon guided his hand to the back of Alucard's head, the vampire started to unbutton Zalith's shirt.

Zalith laughed quietly and gripped a fistful of Alucard's hair; he pulled him a little closer, but once the vampire unbuttoned his shirt, Alucard pulled his face away from Zalith's and kissed the centre of the demon's chest. Zalith let out a quiet hum of delight, and as Alucard started to kiss his way up Zalith's chest, the demon leaned his head back against the carriage window.

Alucard kissed his way to the side of Zalith's neck, and when he reached the space between Zalith's neck and shoulder, he nuzzled it, trying to resist the urge to sink his fangs into the demon's skin. While he inhaled the demon's intoxicating scent, Zalith grasped Alucard's wrist and moved the vampire's hand down into his trousers, where Alucard lightly gripped the demon's crotch.

As Zalith hummed contently and kissed the side of his face, Alucard continued to nuzzle the demon's neck. His desire for Zalith's blood increased with each passing moment, and the longer he stayed where he was, the harder it became to ignore the sound of Zalith's beating heart. But he didn't want to take his blood, least of all without his permission. The last thing he wanted was for Zalith to feel any discomfort today. So he slowly dragged his tongue up the demon's neck… exhaled quietly, and then pulled away.

But when he moved his face back towards Zalith's to kiss him, the demon lightly gripped Alucard's jaw again. He stared into the vampire's confused eyes and smirked. "Bite me," he said demandingly.

Alucard didn't need convincing. The moment Zalith let go of his jaw, the vampire returned his face to the demon's neck. He placed a single, soft kiss on his skin and then sunk his four fangs into him. Zalith flinched but groaned pleasantly, and Alucard murmured contently as the demon's warm, sweet blood seeped into his mouth. It was then that Zalith started caressing the vampire's arousal over his trousers, and as he moved his hand inside, Alucard tensed up and hummed in delight.

After a few more gulps of the demon's blood, Alucard pulled his fangs from his neck and exhaled deeply. "'Ow are you going to fuck me?" he asked quietly, still tending to the demon's arousal with his hand.

The demon smirked as he took his hand out from Alucard's trousers and started unbuckling his belt. "So hard that the people in the street are going to know what's going on in here."

With a quiet laugh, Alucard nuzzled the side of Zalith's face. "Vell, ve only 'ave until ve get 'ome."

"If we have to tell the driver to take a few laps, we will."

The vampire laughed again. "Zhat sounds like a plan."

Their lips collided again with feverish intensity, the air in the carriage thick with urgency. Alucard's fingers worked furiously at Zalith's clothes, feeling the demon do the same, their movements rushed, almost desperate. Fabric tore and fell away, their bodies pressing closer with every second, the world outside the carriage forgotten in the heat of the moment.

With a growl, Zalith spun Alucard around, guiding him onto the seat. Alucard braced himself, his hands gripping the leather while his knees sank into the cushion. The sensation of the cool afternoon air hitting his skin made his breath catch, but it was the feel of Zalith's firm grip on his waist that sent a wave of anticipation surging through him. Behind him, Zalith knelt, one knee planted on the seat and the other foot steady on the floor for leverage, his hands moving possessively over Alucard's hips, pulling him back just enough to close the space between them.

Alucard's heart raced, the heat of Zalith's body pressing into his own, his anticipation building with every slow, deliberate breath. He tensed up a little more as the demon started to massage lube into his ass, and when Zalith hastily eased his hard dick into his body, Alucard let out a quiet, pleased moan.

The demon thrusted assertively, moaning contently as he plunged his shaft into Alucard's body. Alucard dug his claws into the leather seat, humming in delight as he was swiftly enthralled in pleasure. He moaned and whined as Zalith thrusted harder and faster; his heart raced, his body trembled, but as the carriage jolted over a rock outside, Zalith pulled Alucard back abruptly—

Alucard grunted in startle, but he didn't want him to stop. He leaned forward onto his forearms, arching his back inwards as Zalith continued thrusting. He could feel himself approaching his peak as sheer euphoria pulsed through him, and as his body was swiftly overwhelmed with pleasure, he moaned and grimaced in struggle. Each thrust pushed Alucard nearer and nearer to his limit, and he wanted to reach the edge so badly. He moaned again, trying to whine the demon's name, but his frantic breaths wouldn't allow him. And as the vampire approached his peak, Zalith took his left hand off the side of Alucard's waist and lightly gripped the tip of the vampire's dick, a devious smirk striking his face in response to Alucard's whining, pleased cry. Pleasure pulsed through the vampire's shivering body as he climaxed, making him groan in relief and delight.

Zalith then pulled his hand from Alucard's shaft and dragged his tongue his palm, humming contently as he licked the vampire's cum from his skin. "Fuck, you taste so good," he hummed and started moving faster, tightening his grip on Alucard's waist. He grunted, he groaned, and then with a pleased, relieved whine, he thrusted his shaft deep into Alucard's ass and climaxed.

Alucard moaned in response to the sensation of the demon's throbbing dick. He felt the warmth of Zalith's cum fill his body, and he couldn't help but push back a little, taking Zalith's shaft as deeply as he could.

Zalith slowly took his shaft from Alucard's body and then pulled the vampire into his embrace. He exhaled deeply, both their trembling bodies slowly calming down, as were their frantic breaths.

"I'm having a nice birthday so far," Zalith said with a quiet laugh.

The vampire smiled. "Tell me if I can do anyving else vor you," he offered.

"I'm sure I'll think of something, but I'll give you a break for now."

"Okay," the vampire mumbled, nuzzling Zalith's neck. "Ve're going to be pretty busy vor zhe next vew hours or so, zhough."

"Doing what?" Zalith asked curiously.

"Is a surprise."

"What kind of surprise?"

"Vone you'll veally love... or at least I 'ope so," he laughed.

"I'm sure I will. You've always had good taste," the demon said with a smile.

Alucard lifted his head from Zalith's neck, smiled, and kissed the demon's lips. "I love you."

"I love you too, baby."

Chapter Twenty-Seven

The Castle

| Alucard |

In their bedroom, Alucard and Zalith got ready to head out. They put their black waistcoats on, and while Alucard chose to wear his red velvet blazer, Zalith chose his black pinstripe one. Then, they headed to the bathroom.

"Where are we going?" the demon asked again as if he was expecting a different answer this time.

"Is a surprise," Alucard repeated, smirking at him.

"Can I have a little hint?" he asked, combing his hair in front of the mirror.

Alucard glanced at him and said, "You 'ave to dress up vor zhis."

An exaggerated unamused look struck Zalith's face. "What else?" he asked, finishing with his hair.

The vampire thought to himself for a moment as he tidied his own hair. "You'll need zhis," he said, reaching into his pocket. He pulled out a tie he'd taken earlier while they were getting dressed and held it out to Zalith.

"I already have one picked out," the demon said, straightening the tie around his neck.

"Is not vor your neck," Alucard said. "Is vor your vace."

Zalith frowned a little and smiled. "My mouth or my eyes?"

Alucard pouted. "Vhy vould zhis go on your mouth?" he asked, confused.

"To keep me quiet when you whisk me away."

The vampire stretched the tie out. "No," he mumbled. "Is vor your eyes so you can't see vhere I'm vhisking you avay to. Are you done getting veady?"

"I am," he confirmed.

Alucard took the demon's hand and held the tie in his other. "Zhen let's go."

"Okay," Zalith said, and as Alucard led the way, he followed him out of the bathroom.

Alucard took him across the hall, downstairs, and outside the house.

Once they'd walked a small distance from the front door, Alucard let go of Zalith's hand and turned to face him. "I 'ave to put zhis on you bevore ve leave," he said, holding up the tie.

"What are you going to do to me when it's on?"

Alucard shrugged. "You'll 'ave to vait and see."

The demon smiled. "Okay."

Alucard moved closer and gently wrapped the tie around Zalith's eyes, keeping him from being able to see anything. He tied it behind the demon's head, took his hand, and laughed amusedly. "You can't see anyving, no?"

"I can't," he confirmed.

"Good," the vampire said. "I vill vly us now. Zon't take zhat off," he warned him.

"I promise," the demon said with a smile.

Alucard didn't immediately dematerialize, though. For a moment, he kept a smirk on his face while he stared at Zalith. He actually enjoyed this. Zalith couldn't see anything, which made him seem a little powerless. Alucard didn't feel like he had to look away to hide his embarrassment after staring at his face for so long; Zalith's steely eyes weren't able to stare into his and fluster him.

The demon then frowned slightly. "Hello?" he asked, confused.

"Vhat?" Alucard said with a pout, taking his gaze off him.

"Are you just standing there?"

"Maybe," he mumbled. "Are you veady?"

"Wait, why were you just standing there?" Zalith asked, his confused frown becoming a curious one.

Alucard shrugged. "No veason," he lied.

"Were you staring at me?"

"No," he grumbled, looking away.

Zalith laughed quietly. "Okay. Let's go."

"Okay," the vampire said and wrapped his arms around Zalith. He dematerialized them both into vermillion smoke and sped up into the air, heading for their final destination.

| Zalith |

Around twenty minutes later, Alucard slowed and landed. As the sound of the vampire racing through the sky faded, Zalith could hear the sea crashing against rocks; the smell of salt and brick sat on the gentle breeze, and birdsong echoed from every direction. He had no idea where they were, but he was eager to find out.

"Where are we?" he asked.

"Guess," the vampire said amusedly.

Zalith frowned. "The…ocean?"

"Zhere's a lot of ocean avound us, yes."

"Are we at a resort?"

"No."

"Am I allowed to look?"

"No," Alucard denied. "Not yet." He took hold of Zalith's hand and led him a short distance forward. "Vait…" he mumbled, pulling him with him as he walked in another direction.

Zalith had no idea what he was doing or where he was taking him, but he laughed quietly and waited patiently while Alucard redirected him again…and again…and once more until they finally stopped.

"Okay," Alucard said, letting go of his hand. "You can look now."

"Are you sure? I don't think you spun me around enough times," he laughed.

"I'm sure," Alucard grumbled.

With a curious, excited smile, Zalith pulled off his blindfold, his breath catching as the world came into view. He stood in a meadow of soft, blue-green grass, dotted with vibrant, jewel-toned flowers swaying gently in the breeze. To his left, a stone pathway wound through the landscape, flanked by a few apple trees whose branches sagged with ripe fruit, the air tinged with their sweet scent. But it was what lay ahead that truly held his gaze.

Perched majestically atop a towering hill, a vast castle of black and white brick loomed against the sky, its presence both imposing and awe-inspiring. The roofs, a slate-dark grey, sloped sharply, framing large arched windows, some of which glimmered with intricate stained glass designs that caught the light. High above, crowning the tallest tower, a golden rod shimmered brilliantly, reflecting the sunlight like a beacon of power and prestige. The entire structure seemed to pulse with history and secrets, inviting him to explore its every corner.

Zalith smiled as he looked at Alucard. "It's very beautiful. I love the windows and the colours. Is this where we're going?"

Alucard frowned slightly. "Vell…yes, but…is yours."

"What is?"

The vampire looked at the castle and then back at Zalith. "Zhe castle…is your birvday givt."

Zalith stared amusedly at him for a moment, sure that he was joking. But the vampire didn't lose his frown. "Are you serious?" he questioned as disbelief struck him.

Alucard looked away. "Yes," he mumbled shyly. "I've 'ad people vorking on vixing up ever since Decem, and zhey just vinished last veek. I vanted everyving to be pervect."

A bright smile made its way onto Zalith's face. "What?" he asked, still in disbelief. "Really?"

The vampire nodded. "Veally."

Zalith set his gaze back on the castle. "The whole thing is for *me*?"

Alucard nodded again and looked around. "Vell…zhis whole island, actually. Zhis is Usrul," he said, gesturing to the space around them. "And zhis collection of islands is called Uzlia."

Unsure of how else to express how happy he was, Zalith pulled Alucard closer and kissed his lips. Then, he kissed him again…and again…and again. "Thank you," he said quietly and rested his forehead against Alucard's.

The vampire smiled. "Is okay. Do you vant to see inside?"

"Yeah, let's go," the demon said excitedly.

Alucard took his hand, dematerialized with him, and headed towards the castle. He swiftly landed on the white brick ground of the courtyard in front of a large fountain and led the way towards a pair of dark oak doors.

"I 'ad zhe doors enchanted so zhat only you and I can open zhem—and Ezvin, too. You can also change zhat and give whoever you vant access," Alucard explained as they reached the doors. "Zhis is vor you," he said, handing Zalith one of two gold keys that he pulled from his trouser pocket.

Zalith smiled as he took the key from him and stared down at it. "I love it already," he said, slowly setting his eyes on the doors. He felt overwhelmed; it was a whole lot to take in, but he was doing his best. A *whole* castle? Alucard had surprised him *yet again*, and he loved it. He loved *him*.

The vampire smiled, too, and tucked his key back into his pocket. "You can lead zhe vay in," he invited.

"Do I need to invite you in?" the demon asked as he eased the key into the lock.

"You vill vhen you sign zhe lease," Alucard confirmed, following Zalith in once he pushed the two doors open. "I 'ad in my name vhile vas being vixed up, but now is done, vill become yours, and you vill need to tell me I can come in—unless…you zon't vant me in your castle," he said with a smirk, following Zalith into the entrance hall.

"Maybe I want it all to myself," Zalith said as he stepped inside, his boots echoing softly against the gleaming white marble floors. The stark contrast of the space struck him immediately—the walls, a deep black accented with sleek grey panelling, added a bold, dramatic feel to the vast interior. Above him, the rib-vaulted ceiling soared, adorned with an intricate mural depicting hunting dogs in mid-chase, their forms frozen in motion alongside galloping horses as though the scene might spring to life at any moment.

Directly ahead, a grand staircase swept upward, its bannisters carved with ornate designs that glimmered in the low light. To his left and right, large open archways beckoned, leading to unknown chambers, while two heavy, imposing doors flanked the base of the staircase, guarding whatever secrets lay beyond. The air inside was cool, still, and charged with the weight of the castle's history, every detail meticulously crafted to exude power and refinement.

"Zhen zhat's okay," Alucard said, closing the front door. "Is *your* castle, so…you can do vhat you vant vith zhis," he said, joining Zalith in the centre of the hall.

The demon laughed quietly as he glanced at him. "Well, what's mine is yours, so you're welcome to visit any time."

Alucard smiled amusedly. "Vell, bevore ve start, I actually got vivteen divverent vards and protection spells put avound zhe whole island, so…no vone vill ever know zhis place is 'ere. Zhe big vendite vod on zhe tower is vhat keeps zhem all in place. Ve can add more if you vant, too."

Zalith nodded. "Thank you. Which wards did you use?"

The vampire took his hand. "Levt or vight virst?" he asked.

"I don't know where anything is, so you can just lead the way."

He shrugged. "Okay." Alucard then led the way into the first room on the left. "I 'ired a vizard I knew vor a long time. 'E used zhe same vards you put avound zhe 'ouse back in Nevastus, and zhen some of zhe vones I 'ad avound my own castle. Zhey keep anyvone vrom being able to see zhe castle; zhey keep zhe building and everyvone inside zhe vard 'idden—so…zhis is zhe safest place anyvone could ever be."

They stopped in the middle of the first room, and Zalith glanced around.

"Zhis is zhe vaiting voom," Alucard said, and then he led Zalith through the door to the right of a couch. "And zhis could be an art gallery…and zhen vhrough zhere is zhe centre 'all," he explained, pointing to another door. "Zhere's a door to a porch in zhere. Zhen zhis vay…" he said, leading the way to the left again, "…zhat goes into vone of zhe towers," he said, pointing to the bottom of a staircase on the sidewall. "And straight a'ead takes us past zhe doors to a courtyard—zhe kitchens are zhat vay, too."

"I want to see the courtyard," the demon said.

Alucard nodded and led the way through to a large glass door. He pushed it open and took Zalith out into a small garden area sheltered under a dome-like glass roof three floors up. In the middle of the garden sat a small pond with a bench beside it; flowerbeds of roses and orchids sat around the edges, and a small tree leaned over the pond.

"I zidn't veally know vhat else to tell zhem to do 'ere. I zon't veally do gardens. I only know vineyards."

Zalith smiled contently. "It's beautiful. You did a good job."

The vampire smiled at him. "Zhere's still more," he said and led the way back inside.

"I'm excited to see it all," Zalith said.

Alucard toured him around the rest of the left side of the castle. He showed him the kitchens, the dining rooms, and the spare and guest rooms upstairs, all waiting to be fully furnished. Once they were done, he took them back down to the entrance hall and prepared to show Zalith the *right* side of the place.

"So, do like so var?" the vampire asked when they stopped in the entrance hall.

"I love it," Zalith said, fiddling with Alucard's hair. "You have very good taste."

He smiled and shrugged as he looked down at the marble floor. "I based off zhe 'ouse in Nevastus."

Zalith laughed quietly. "That was a good idea because *I* have good taste, too."

"You do," the vampire concurred. "Zhis vay," he said, leading Zalith through the archway on the right and into a large lounge. "I vhought zhis could be zhe lounge," he said, looking around.

The rich scent of polished wood filled the air; the dark wooden floors gleamed beneath his feet, their deep hues complemented by the shimmering mahogany walls, which seemed to glow in the warm afternoon sunlight streaming through the tall, arched windows on the left. The light cascaded down in golden shafts, catching on the sleek black curtains that framed the windows, casting long, dramatic shadows across the room.

Against the black walls with grey panelling, rows of empty shelves lined the space, waiting to be filled with books and trinkets that would one day give the room a sense of life. Overhead, a glimmering crystal chandelier hung from the pristine white ceiling, its facets catching the sunlight and casting scattered prisms of light across the floor. To the left, two doors, each carefully placed about four feet from the corners, added an air of mystery. Another door stood directly ahead on the back wall, offering an invitation to explore further into the depths of the grand castle.

"Zhis vone goes into anozzer voom—maybe a study or someving," Alucard said, pointing to the first door on the left wall. "Zhat vone goes out into a 'allvay, vhich leads into anozzer 'all, and zhat vone goes into vhat I vink vould be a nice library," he said, pointing to the door on the back wall.

Gazing around, the demon smiled again. "Can we see the library?"

Alucard nodded and led him to the end of the room. He pushed the door to the library open, and as they stepped inside, he pointed at the door that led outside. "Zhere's a terrace out zhere…and zhen zhis goes to zhe 'all I said zhe ozzer door does," he explained, pointing to the door next to the one which led out to the terrace. "Zhere's a lot of shelves in 'ere, so…is vhy I vhought vould be a good library."

"It's beautiful," the demon said.

"Zhis vay," Alucard said excitedly, leading him out of the library and into the main hall.

As his smile grew wider, Zalith walked with him, eager to see the rest of the castle. He loved it already, and he was going to ensure that he made that clear to Alucard later. For now, though, he wanted to focus on the tour.

↞❖↠

About forty minutes later, Alucard led Zalith back into the lounge, where they relaxed on the couch.

"I really love it all. Thank you," the demon said as he pulled Alucard into a tight hug. "I don't think I'll be able to thank you enough, to be honest."

The vampire smiled as he nuzzled Zalith's neck. "I'm glad you like zhis. And if zhere's anyving you vant to change, zhen you can."

"I might add a few things here and there, but it's pretty much perfect already."

"Okay," the vampire said. "I 'ave zhe lease if you vant to get zhat signed."

"Sure," the demon said with a smile.

"Ve 'ave to go outside, zhough."

"Why?" Zalith asked, smirking. "Will you be banished from the castle?"

Alucard frowned. "Yes…and I'm sure is someving you zon't vant to see."

"Why?" the demon asked amusedly.

"Because I vill start bleeding," Alucard revealed with a pout.

"Oh…well, we don't want that," Zalith said. "Let's go."

"Agreed," the vampire said, and as Zalith got up and started leading the way out of the lounge, Alucard followed.

Once they returned to the courtyard, Alucard took a few pieces of paper from his coat's inside pocket. He unfolded them, handed them to Zalith, and took a pen out of his pocket, too. "You just 'ave to sign zhere," he said, pointing to a blank line at the bottom of the parchment, and then he flipped to the last piece. "And zhere," he said, pointing to another line.

As he signed his name, Zalith glanced at Alucard. "I want your name on it, too," he said, holding the papers out to him once he was done.

The vampire looked a little startled. "Veally?"

He nodded and laughed amusedly at the vampire's surprised face. "Yeah, really."

"Okay," he said shyly and then signed his name.

"There," Zalith said with a content smile. "Now it's *ours*, and you can come and go as you please."

Alucard smirked as he handed the parchment back to Zalith. "I zon't know…maybe you'll vegret zhat vhen you vake up vone night and you're missing 'alf of your blood."

"As long as you're fed, I'm happy," the demon said.

Turning to face him, Alucard smiled and pulled Zalith closer. "I vould never do zhat vithout your permission."

"Thank you, baby," the demon said and kissed his lips.

Alucard kissed him back, and as he dragged his hand around from the back of Zalith's head and to the side of his face, he smiled shyly. "So...do you vant to go back inside vor a bit? Or...'ead 'ome?"

The demon smirked suggestively. "Maybe we can make use of the bed upstairs," he said quietly, staring into Alucard's eyes. "But I don't want you to be exhausted, so...maybe we shouldn't."

"I'll be vine," Alucard said with a shake of his head. "And ve 'ave time bevore ve 'ave to be back 'ome anyvay."

"Why do we have to go home?" the demon asked curiously.

Alucard shrugged. "I 'ave vone more ving planned vor you."

"Am I allowed to know what it is?"

"No," Alucard teased.

"Well, can we come back here for a few days and enjoy it?"

"Ve can do zhat," he said with a nod.

"Okay," the demon said. "Lead us to the bedroom," he said, taking Alucard's hand.

The vampire smiled, and without any hesitation, he led the way into the castle, heading for the bedroom.

Chapter Twenty-Eight

Zalith's Party

| Alucard |

It was almost 8 p.m. when Alucard and Zalith got home. The vampire landed in the gardens, and once he rematerialized himself and the demon, he led the way up to the front door. He was just as excited as he was nervous, but he was confident that Zalith was going to enjoy what was waiting for him.

"How are you feeling?" Zalith asked him. "Are you tired?"

Alucard shook his head. "I'm okay. Vhat about you?"

"I feel good. I should probably stop by V's house before it gets too late."

The vampire shrugged as they reached the front door. "I guess, but…maybe ve can just sit down vor a little virst," he suggested, trying his best not to be too obvious.

"That's fine," the demon said with a nod. "Do you want to come with me when I go over?"

"I can," he said, unlocking the door. "If you vant me to."

"I don't mind either way," Zalith said, following him into the house. "But I don't want you to get cranky if you do come and we're there for a little longer than you thought we'd be," he said with a quiet laugh.

Alucard pouted and shut the door behind them. "I von't get cranky," he grumbled.

"You *always* get cranky when she's around," he teased and followed Alucard through the hall.

"Because she pisses me off," the vampire mumbled.

Zalith chuckled amusedly in response. But when he saw that they were approaching the ballroom, he frowned and asked, "Why are we heading towards the ballroom?"

"No veason," Alucard said dismissively.

"Okay," Zalith dragged out the word. "If you say so…."

Alucard then pushed the doors open—

A flurry of enthusiastic voices shouted, "Surprise!"

Zalith stared in startle and smiled, and as Varana and Idina emerged from the crowd of guests and made their way to him, the demon moved his arm around Alucard's waist and pulled him closer.

But Alucard didn't share a look of content. His smile faded as he looked around the room to see that *nothing* he'd organized was set up. The first thing he noticed was that the white and light green décor was absent, and in its place sat *gold* and white. He then set his eyes on the three-tier chocolate cake topped with strawberries and blackberries that he'd had made for Zalith, seeing that blueberries, raspberries, and grapes had been added to it. The wine he'd ordered had been replaced by a totally different brand, as had the champagne, and the band he'd hired weren't present—in their place sat a different troupe.

He scowled at Varana, watching as she hugged Zalith.

"Happy birthday," the crimson-eyed woman said and kissed Zalith's cheek. Her lipstick left a bright red smudge on his skin.

"Thank you," Zalith said. "You look nice."

She glanced down at her dress and smiled. "Thank you; it's new."

Alucard wordlessly took the handkerchief from Zalith's pocket and cleaned the lipstick off his face while Varana watched with a bitter scowl and then rolled her eyes.

Zalith headed to the nearby table and picked up a glass of champagne, and as everyone started heading over and said their happy birthdays, Alucard glared around the room again.

Varana had changed pretty much *everything* he'd spent the last week setting up, and as furious as it made him, he did his best not to react. Today was supposed to be about Zalith and he wanted the demon to be happy…but he couldn't help but feel upset and maybe even a little disappointed. If Zalith was enjoying this, it wasn't because of him, and the demon wouldn't even get to see the work *he'd* put in. All he was seeing right now was what Varana had done.

And of course, if he reacted, he knew he'd ruin it for Zalith. He didn't want to think about how Varana probably wouldn't even be scolded. So, while Zalith received his birthday wishes from the room of guests, Alucard stood there in silence, trying to appear as calm as he could. But inside…he wanted to slap Varana's ugly face.

Once everyone wandered off to enjoy the party, Zalith placed his empty glass on the table behind them. As one of the staff passed by, he took two glasses of red wine from his tray and handed one to Alucard.

"Are you okay?" the demon asked.

"I'm vine," he grumbled, taking the glass from him, but he didn't want to drink it.

"You look upset," the demon said with a concerned look on his face.

He didn't want to look upset, nor did he want to make tonight about him. So he dismissed his irritated frown and smiled. "I'm okay," he assured him.

The demon smiled. "Well, thank you for this party. The ballroom looks very nice," he said, pulling Alucard closer.

His bitter stare returned. "You're velcome," he mumbled.

Zalith took a sip of his wine. "Is this *your* company's wine?" he asked with a confused frown.

"No," he grumbled. "Vas supposed to be."

"What happened?"

He sighed quietly, but when he set his eyes on Varana and watched her turn away the staff who were bringing in the food that he'd had them prepare, he scowled and snarled irritably. "Zhat voman is changing *everyving*," he growled.

"What?" Zalith questioned.

"None of zhis is vhat I planned. She changed zhe décor, she changed zhe cake, zhe drvinks, zhe band, and now she's sending zhe vood avay, too," he complained, glaring at her as she shook her head at the next pair of staff carrying trays of food.

The demon sighed quietly. "I can talk to her."

"Zon't vorry," he dismissed with a sigh. "All zhat veally matters is zhat *you're* 'aving a nice time."

He rubbed Alucard's back. "I'm not going to have a nice time if you're not having a nice time, so we're better off saying something."

Alucard wasn't going to argue with him. "Okay," he mumbled. He didn't want to start an argument, but he *did* want to see Varana get scolded. So, as Zalith started heading over to where Varana was standing, Alucard followed.

"Varana," Zalith said when he reached her.

She turned to face him and smiled. "Yes?"

"Why are you changing things?"

Varana frowned. "Because things needed changing."

Alucard scowled irritably. "Noving needed changing. Everyving *I* put togezzer vas pervect."

"Well if it was perfect, I wouldn't have needed to change it," she sneered at him. "Green, Alucard? Really? It's his birthday; we're not celebrating a harvest—"

"Is 'is vavourite colour," he snarled, trying to keep himself from lunging at her.

"And my favourite colour is purple, but you don't see me shouting it from the rooftops," she said with a roll of her eyes. "I did leave *some* green accents here and there," she said, waving her hand over at the nearby table.

The only green Alucard could see were a few silk flowers that she mustn't have had time to clear away. "Did zhe cake look too 'arvesty? Vas zhe vine too green? Zhe *vood*?" he questioned, losing his patience. "And zhe band? Vere zhey too green? Did zhey look like zhey should be at a 'arvest?"

She scoffed rudely. "Excuse me for wanting to have a piece of my best friend's birthday party."

Alucard's scowl thickened. "You changed everyving!" he exclaimed, raising his voice. "I vorked on zhis vor veeks—" he cut himself off and took his furious eyes off her. He wasn't about to start an argument and ruin Zalith's birthday. Instead, he shoved the glass of wine he was holding against Varana's chest, turned around, and walked off. "*Cātea*," he snarled, leaving her with Zalith.

"Grow up," she called.

He rolled his eyes and kept walking. The last thing he wanted was to show that woman just how mad he was. For the sake of Zalith's happiness, he'd hold back. So, he found an empty chair by the wall, slumped down, and glared at the band as they energetically played the boring music that Varana had evidently instructed them to.

| Zalith |

Zalith sighed quietly. He understood why Alucard was frustrated, and it made him feel bad. The vampire had worked hard on everything for him, and Varana took over without so much as telling him. So, he frowned at her and said, "You really should have asked first, Varana."

"It's not fair," she stropped. "I never see you anymore; he didn't even ask me if I wanted to help with the party, and I just wanted to do something nice for you."

"I understand, but it doesn't change the fact that you should have at least said something."

Varana scowled irritably. "Why do you always take *his* side?"

"Because it would seem that you're always in the wrong—"

She exclaimed angrily and shoved Alucard's wineglass into one of the staff, but it splashed all over the man. With an infuriated snarl, the woman then stormed off.

Zalith looked down at his drink and exhaled deeply. He was tired of the fact that no one was ever happy around here…and he hated that he had to keep picking sides. The only two people he really wanted to spend today with were mad and hated each other, so it looked as though he'd not get to be with both Alucard and Varana this evening.

He placed his drink down on the nearby table and left the ballroom. He didn't want to be there anymore.

| Alucard |

Alucard saw Zalith leave the ballroom, and it made him feel worried and guilty. All of this was supposed to be about Zalith…and up until now, everything went to plan. But *of course*, something had to ruin it.

He got up and headed over to the door, shooting an irritated scowl at Varana, who joined Idina by the drinks table. With a roll of his eyes, Alucard stepped outside and set his sights on Zalith, who was leaning against the wall beside the doors.

"Vhat's vrong?" he asked sullenly, standing in front of him.

The demon smiled weakly. "Nothing. I just needed a minute."

But Alucard knew something was wrong…and he had a pretty good idea of what it was. "I'm sorry," he said, placing his hand on Zalith's chest. He leaned a little closer and sighed quietly. "Today is supposed to be about you."

"It's fine. You have every right to be upset with her."

He shook his head. "But I should 'ave just levt zhat until avter zhe party—and I *vill.* I just vant you to 'ave a nice time."

The demon hesitated for a moment. "I just…" but he didn't finish what he was going to say. "Never mind, let's just go back—"

Alucard stopped him from moving away from the wall and frowned sadly. "Tell me," he pleaded.

Zalith huffed and lamented, "You and V are all I have, and I feel like my relationship with her is slowly slipping away…and I understand that she can be terrible, and I respect that you and her might never get along—I'm not asking that you let her get away with things—but I don't want to keep losing the people I love. It's just…difficult for me."

Alucard understood what he was saying, and the sadness in Zalith's eyes made him feel worse. The vampire looked down at the floor as his guilt started consuming him. He *hated* that woman and there was no way in hell he'd ever see himself becoming her friend or even learning to tolerate her. She purposely did things to upset and anger him, and he knew that she enjoyed seeing him react; she reminded him of Lucifer and Damien, she reminded him of the fact that he'd always been and would always be an outcast. He didn't want to have to back down or accept the shit she threw at him…but he didn't want Zalith to be mad or upset, either.

The vampire tried to dismiss his anger. "Okay," he mumbled. "I'll try not to get so annoyed by 'er."

"Thank you, I appreciate it," the demon said, moving his hand to the side of Alucard's neck. "But it's not entirely on your shoulders."

Alucard shrugged. "Maybe if *I* try, zhen…she vill try."

"Maybe."

"But if she tells me to fuck off zhen I'm not trying again," he warned, pouting.

Zalith nodded. "I understand," he said and kissed Alucard's cheek. "Thank you for today. I'm sorry she changed everything."

"Zoesn't matter," he said with a shrug, trying to disguise his anger with light-heartedness. "As long as you like zhis, zhat's all I care about."

"I do," the demon said. "I'm sure that the green looked really nice, too."

Alucard smiled and took Zalith's hand. "Come on," he said, and as Zalith followed, he led the way back into the room.

He saw Varana standing with Idina and Elena. Although he was hesitant, he let go of Zalith's hand, and while the demon waited by the food table, Alucard made his way over to the woman.

"Oh, hi Alucard," Idina said when she spotted him approaching.

Varana didn't turn to face him.

Alucard looked at Idina and Elena. "I need a moment vith Varana, please."

"Of course," Idina said as she took Elena's hand. Then, she wandered off with her.

Varana finally decided to face Alucard. "What?" she snarled.

Her bitter attitude already made him want to leave, but he'd told Zalith he'd try…so that was what he was going to do. "I zon't like you," he started, scowling at her. "And I vill probably *never* like you, but—" he said, raising his voice a little before Varana could interrupt, "—Zaliv cares about you, and I care about *'im*. 'E knows 'ow ve veel about each ozzer and zhat upsets 'im; 'e's lost everyvone but us, and if ve 'ave to try and tolerate each ozzer vor 'is sake, zhen *I* vill try. But zhe next time you decide to erase all my 'ard vork, ask me. I get zhat you 'ave probably been doing zhis longer zhan me, but zhat's my point; you've 'ad 'undreds of years to do zhis vor 'im, and I vanted just *vone*. Zhat vas evidently too much to ask vor, no?"

She frowned irritably at him. "You should have at least come to me and said you were throwing a party so I didn't have to find out on my own like some commoner and throw everything that *I* was planning out the window," she argued. "But of course, you didn't tell me because *no one* seems to give a shit or even notice that I'm around anymore. You have him *all* day *every* day and I never get any time with him *at all*—even now!"

He had so many things to say to her; she knew that Alucard was there and probably suspected that he was planning something for Zalith, so why didn't she come and talk about it when she'd received her invitation a few days ago? And the reason he spent so much time with Zalith wasn't only because they were together; he felt like that was the case because Zalith was also choosing to spend so much time with him. But he knew that if he said *any* of that, Varana would kick off like a child, and he didn't want the drama.

Alucard set his anger aside, but the scowl on his face didn't fade away. "You 'ave time. I'm not vith 'im vight now, am I?"

"No, but I'm sure you'll go marching right back over to his side the moment we're done here, as per usual."

"I'm not going to apologize to you vor spending all my time vith zhe man I love; maybe if you zidn't act as zhough you 'ave some sort of claim over 'im, zhen I'd veel inclined to zhe vree of us spending more time togezzer. Zhe vact is you're not zhe only person in 'is life anymore, and if you zon't like zhat, zhen zhat's not my problem. And vhy zidn't I tell you vhat I vas doing? Is because I *know* you vould 'ave done zhis anyvay, or you vouldn't 'ave let me get a vord in at all," he muttered.

"Well it's hard to do that when I can barely understand what you're saying," she said with a roll of her eyes.

He growled quietly, trying his very best to keep himself from snapping at her. "Maybe if you actually took a moment and listened and stopped daydreaming about fucking my boyvriend, zhen you'd understand."

Varana gritted her teeth and splashed her drink in his face—

Alucard snarled and clenched his fists but resisted the urge to hurt her. He wasn't going to let her paint him as the antagonist, nor was he going to ruin Zalith's party. So, as he wiped his red wine-covered face with his blazer sleeve, he turned around and headed for the door.

He left the ballroom and went to the closest bathroom, and when he heard Zalith call for Edwin to fetch a towel—having followed him out of the ballroom—the vampire scowled irritably and started pulling his blazer off.

"I'm sorry, Alucard," the demon said as he stood in the bathroom doorway.

Alucard stood in front of the mirror. "I zon't even know vhy I tried," he grumbled, unbuttoning his wine-covered shirt. "She zidn't even listen to anyving I said. Is *alvays* about 'er."

Zalith frowned sullenly, watching him as he took his shirt off, threw it into the nearby laundry basket, and took the towel from Edwin, who appeared beside Zalith. "I think I might just go to bed," the demon mumbled as the butler left them alone.

Alucard stopped patting his face with the towel and looked at him. "Vhy?" he asked—but he knew the answer to that. "You zon't 'ave to, I can just…stay avay vrom 'er or someving," he muttered, drying his hair. "If she vants to spend time vith you, I vill just…go and sit vith Zhomas."

The demon shrugged. "I'm just not feeling very sociable anymore. But I can go back; I know you worked hard, and I don't want to spoil the night even further."

With a quiet, guilty sigh, Alucard turned to face him. He reached out, grabbed Zalith's hand, and pulled him closer. "Is *your* night, zhough. Zoesn't matter 'ow I veel. I just vant *you* to 'ave vun."

Zalith caressed his crimson hair. "Okay. I'll have someone get you a new shirt."

Alucard shrugged as his anger swiftly faded. "Or…ve could take advantage of alveady being off," he suggested, smirking through his shyness.

"We're not supposed to have sex more than twice a day," the demon reminded him.

"But is a special occasion," Alucard said, remembering what Zalith had said about the rule they'd made.

"Maybe to the calendar, but not to your body."

He shrugged again. "I vill just 'ave extra cake—vor zhe sugar."

"I'm not really feeling it right now, sorry," the demon said with a shake of his head. "But maybe later tonight."

The fact that he was saying no to sex and wasn't even flirting back made Alucard certain that he really *had* ruined Zalith's night. He should have just left it alone instead of confronting Varana, shouldn't he? He nodded sadly and let go of him. "You zon't 'ave to go back in zhere," he mumbled. "I know you zon't vant to. But if you vant to spend some time vith Varana, zhen I can go and tidy myselv up and do someving else."

"I want to spend time with the both of you," Zalith said sadly.

Alucard knew that, but he didn't know what to do about it. He'd tried to talk to Varana, but she'd thrown it in his face—literally. Despite that, though, he still wanted to do whatever he could to ensure that Zalith had a good rest of his birthday. So, he relented…again. "You *can* spend time vith zhe both of us…but she zoesn't vant me avound *at all*. I can be civil, but if I get anozzer vace vull of vine, zhen I'm not going to give 'er any more chances," he mumbled.

The demon stared at him for a moment. It looked like he was pondering. But after a few moments, he nodded. "Okay," he said with a hesitant, sullen frown.

Smiling, Alucard placed his hands on Zalith's chest and started pushing him back out of the bathroom. "You go in zhere and I'll meet you. I 'ave to get changed."

The demon moved his hands to either side of Alucard's waist and pulled him closer. He kissed his lips, and with one final stare at him, he turned around and headed for the ballroom.

And while he waited for Edwin to bring him a new shirt, Alucard hoped that Zalith would be able to enjoy what was left of his birthday.

Chapter Twenty-Nine

The Compound

| Zalith, ***Wednesday, Cordus 1st, 960(TG)—Nefastus*** **|**

As the evening grew late, Alucard and Zalith prepared to head out to the compound where Zalith's people were staying. Greymore had invited them to celebrate the construction's completion, and Zalith was glad that his people didn't have to live on Alucard's ship anymore. *Everyone* was relieved that Aegisguard was well and truly their home.

While Alucard combed his hair, Zalith smirked at him and watched for a while—he enjoyed staring at him—but he soon smiled amusedly and teased him, "Are you making yourself look good for your boyfriend Greymore?"

Alucard scowled at him. "'E's not my boyvriend," he mumbled and looked back into the mirror.

"If you say so."

With a sigh, Alucard rolled his eyes a little and continued.

But Zalith wasn't done playing with him just yet. He moved a little closer. "It's a good thing that he's not your boyfriend because then I might have to kill him, and I really don't want to do that—I like him," he said with a smile and a casual tone. "But I *do* like that you two are friends; it's very cute," he added, leaning over and kissing him.

Alucard smiled at him and placed his comb down. "Are you veady to go?"

Zalith moved his hands to each side of Alucard's waist and pulled him closer. In all honesty, he didn't really feel like going out; he just wanted to stay at home with his vampire, but he *did* want to celebrate this new beginning with all of his subordinates because *at last*, everyone was settled and safe. So, he nodded. "I'm ready," he answered.

The demon took Alucard's hand and led the way out of the bathroom, through the hall, downstairs, and outside into the courtyard, where their horses were waiting for them. Once they mounted their steeds, they made their way through the gardens and towards the property gate. The compound was only fifteen minutes away.

While they rode, Zalith smiled at Alucard and curiously asked, "Are you going to try and keep up with Greymore tonight?"

Alucard laughed slightly. "I could drvink 'im under zhe table."

Amused, Zalith laughed, too. "I don't know about that," he said with a sigh. "He drinks *a lot.*"

"Ve'll see."

"Are Dimitri and I going to have to carry you home?" he then asked, glancing down at his horse as they followed the path.

The vampire pouted. "No," he grumbled.

"If we do, it's okay; we won't judge you," Zalith teased as he leaned over to him and nudged his arm.

"Vhat makes you so certain zhat I von't beat Zhomas?"

"Oh, I don't doubt you, I just don't know if you're aware of how much he drinks."

"I can take a guess," Alucard muttered. "Every time I vent to my ship, 'e vould be out on zhe deck drvinking vhiskey at ten in zhe morning, so…I 'ave a pretty good idea."

Zalith laughed, amused to hear about Greymore's morning drinking, but then looked at Alucard and asked, "Has he managed to catch a fish out there yet?"

"No, and 'e never vill," Alucard said with a shrug.

"Perhaps he'll have better luck in the creek near the compound."

"Maybe."

The demon faced ahead, and as Alucard rode beside him, he headed for the compound. He was sure that it was going to be a loud, lively night, but he was looking forward to enjoying it with Alucard. *Any* time he got to spend with his vampire made him content, even if he had to deal with rowdy werewolves and campfire songs. He also liked watching Alucard interact with other people; it was endearing, and he also loved that Alucard had friends. He used to be so secluded and shy, but he'd changed so much, and Zalith adored him for how far he'd come.

| Alucard |

When they reached the compound, they dismounted and hitched their horses to a nearby fence. Then, they followed the gravel path into the gated area. There were around forty-five houses lined around the large glade, and some were tucked behind others. At the very end of the opening was a barn, and a few horse-filled stables were scattered here and there, too.

A bonfire raged in the centre of the place, and a small crowd of people were sitting around it. To the bonfire's left, another smaller fire burned, but the people crowded around *that* were cooking food rather than drinking and laughing obnoxiously.

Zalith took Alucard's arm in his as the vampire looked at him.

"Is bigger zhan I vhought," Alucard admitted, glancing around.

The demon laughed quietly as an unseemly smile appeared on his face. "I've had that thought before," he said with a sultry tone.

But before Alucard could reply, Greymore cheerfully called their names from over by the bonfire. He made his way towards them, holding his arms out with an enthusiastic smile on his face. "I'm glad you two could make it."

Zalith smiled when Greymore stood in front of them and shook both their hands before leading them to the bonfire. Once they reached it, Greymore shooed away three men sitting on a log and invited Alucard and Zalith to sit. As they did, Greymore enthusiastically clapped his hands together.

"You have a nice set-up over here," Zalith said.

"Yup," Greymore agreed with a grin, crossing his arms. "We got some food going over there," he said, glancing at the smaller fire, where a large crowd of people were conversating and laughing loudly. "I guess the party's over there," he laughed. "Are you guys hungry?"

"No," Zalith answered.

"What about you, Alucard?" Greymore asked, looking down at the vampire.

"No, vank you," Alucard denied; he wasn't interested in eating anything, especially something brewed over a campfire. He was certain that Zalith felt the same.

"Are you sure?" the beefy man laughed. "We're grilling up some steaks with Randy's homemade seasoning blend," he said with a smirk, trying to convince him.

Alucard shook his head. "I'm sure. I'm not 'ungry."

"Okay," Greymore said with a shrug. "Your loss, man. We also have some sort of stew going over there if you'd be interested in that instead," he said, gesturing towards the smaller campfire again. "I think it was turkey or something. Nelson caught it earlier."

Still not interested, Alucard shook his head. "No, vank you," he repeated.

"Really?" He scoffed amusedly. "Did you just come to ogle me, then?" he asked and flexed his muscles.

Zalith deadpanned. "We'll just have drinks, Greymore," he muttered, unimpressed.

Amused, Alucard smiled at Zalith.

"What do you want?" Greymore asked, clapping his hands together again.

"Anything," the demon grumbled.

"Okay. What about you, Alucard?"

"Vhat do you 'ave?"

Greymore smirked and posed again. "Well…."

"Oh, my God," Zalith uttered and sighed irritably.

Laughing, Greymore crossed his arms and stood up straight. "I'm kidding. We have some mead…some whiskey…uh…I think that's it—or you can have some water from the creek," he offered.

Shaking his head slightly, Alucard said, "Vhiskey."

"Sounds good. I'll be right back." Then, he wandered off, leaving Zalith and Alucard alone with whoever else was sitting around the bonfire.

Once Greymore was gone, Alucard turned to face Zalith, who smiled at him. Before either of them could say a word to one another, however—

"Thank you so much to the both of you for this," one of the people sitting around the fire called. "This place is perfect."

"We appreciate everything you've done for us," one of the women added.

"It feels so good to finally settle down," the man beside her said.

"You're all very welcome," Zalith said, but he then set his eyes on Tyrus, who was making his way over with two glasses in his hands.

"Hey," Tyrus said when he reached them. He handed them each a glass of whiskey. "I saw that Greymore got distracted," he said, glancing back over his shoulder at Greymore, who was among a large crowd of jeering people, all of whom laughed as Greymore playfully strung the strings of a man's guitar, stopping him from playing his quiet song several times.

"Thank you," Zalith said and then smiled amusedly. "You're not being a kiss-ass, are you?"

Tyrus chortled as Alucard took his drink from him. "Well, I know I'm already your favourite, so what's the point?"

Zalith laughed again, sipped from his drink, and sighed. "How's everyone settling in?"

"Good," Tyrus answered, glancing around at the congregations of people scattered across the field. "People are glad to finally have a place to call home."

"Let's hope it lasts," the demon muttered.

Tyrus chuckled. "I'm sure it will," he said confidently, raising his glass, and everyone downed their drinks. He then sighed contently. "Let me take your glasses," he offered, holding his hand out towards Zalith and Alucard, and once they both handed them to him, he wandered off again.

Zalith smiled and leaned closer to Alucard as he moved his hand to the side of his face. He then started to kiss him, enjoying what might only be a few moments of solitude—

"Aleksei," came Freja's voice.

Irritated, Alucard scowled and turned his head away from Zalith, catching a glimpse of the demon's face, and he looked just as annoyed as the vampire felt.

Freja stopped in front of them, and Danford lingered behind her almost as if he was her shadow. It seemed as though he didn't want to be seen and avoided even looking in Alucard's direction.

"Vhat?" Alucard snarled, staring at her.

"It's good to see you here," she said, smiling. "Everyone seems to have settled in all right. It's nice…to have a place to live now. I mean…it's not the same as living out in the caravans back home, but…I'm getting used to it. How *is* Dor-Sanguis?"

The very mention of Dor-Sanguis brought pain to Alucard's heart. A month ago, he'd lost the country where he was born and spent most of his life. Many of his vampires had been evacuated to Nefastus, and while some were given jobs in his and Zalith's new castle, others were now staying on his ship and in towns scattered around the country. He had to make somewhere safe for them to exist, but right now, he had to focus on the inevitable war that was soon to come their way.

But he didn't want to think about any of it; tonight was supposed to be about celebrating the completion of the compound.

Zalith obviously noticed Alucard's sadness; he kissed his cheek and took hold of his hand.

Freja then blurted, "So…Danford and I are dating." She glanced over her shoulder at Danford, who looked as though he'd seen something ghastly.

Uninterested, Alucard stared up at them. "Okay."

Zalith laughed quietly. "So, things didn't work out with you and Greymore, did they?"

Freja took her eyes off Alucard and looked down at Zalith as she sighed quietly. "No. I mean…he's a great guy, just…not my type—too loud," she grumbled, rolling her eyes as Greymore's boisterous laugh came from halfway across the field. "Of course, arranged marriages like these happen a lot, and it isn't strange for the people involved to find their true mates eventually."

"So, you're not just dating?" Alucard questioned. "You are…vated?"

Freja smiled at Danford. "We are." She then rolled her eyes when Greymore's laughter echoed loudly again.

Alucard glanced in Greymore's direction and watched as he chortled and conversed with a crowd, *still* holding the drinks that he was supposed to be bringing over for him and Zalith.

"At least we're all settling down now," Freja said with a sigh. "Everyone's very thankful."

Nodding, Alucard sighed. "Good. Go and…see if Zhomas is actually bringing us our drvinks."

"All right. Nice seeing you, though," she said with a smile, waving slightly as she wandered off with Danford.

"I guess 'e moved on vrom Luther," Alucard mumbled as Freja disappeared into the crowd Greymore was humouring.

"It must have been pretty easy," Zalith muttered, moving as close to Alucard as he could get. He then leaned nearer and nuzzled the vampire's neck. "You smell really good," he murmured.

Alucard smiled and went to reply—

"There you are," Greymore interjected, appearing in front of them with the drinks he'd left to get twenty minutes ago.

Zalith glared up at him as he and Alucard took their drinks.

Greymore slumped down onto the grass in front of them. "So, how have things been lately?" he asked, looking at Alucard.

"Devine 'vings'," Alucard said.

Greymore laughed. "Life."

Alucard shrugged, sipping from his drink. "Is good," he said, but he was more interested in finding out what Zalith's intentions towards him were before Greymore interrupted.

"As good as mine?" Greymore asked with a content sigh, leaning back and relaxing.

"Better," Alucard said with a smirk.

"Yeah?" he challenged.

"Did you vind a girlvriend yet or are you still dvelling on zhe vact zhat you look like voadkill vhen you're tired?"

Greymore guffawed. "I don't dwell, buddy. I have to beat off the ladies with a stick *every day*."

Convinced that was a lie, Alucard shook his head and sipped from his drink. "Is zhe pack okay vith Vreja and Danvord?" he then asked.

He nodded and said, "Yeah, they don't give a shit, which suits me just fine because Freja and I were *not* meant to be." He sighed and took a gulp of his drink. "Sometimes, you wind up in a business marriage, though, and that's fine by me, as long as everyone does their job and I can be with whoever I want, I don't really care." He finished his drink. "How are things with the two of you?" he then asked with a curious smile.

Zalith moved his arm around Alucard and pulled him closer. "Wonderful," he said.

Greymore laughed quietly. "So, are you two engaged yet or not?"

"Soon," Zalith said, staring at Alucard.

Soon? Angst gushed through Alucard's tensing body, and he was sure that there was an expression on his face to match his growing nervousness. Engaged…*soon*? Was Zalith serious?

"*How* soon?" Greymore questioned.

"Soon," Zalith repeated irritably.

Greymore widened his eyes in response. "Very mysterious," he drawled before looking at Alucard. "Why don't *you* just propose?"

Alucard's nervousness was accompanied by embarrassment. He didn't know what to say. He'd been waiting for Zalith to propose all this time; should he have just proposed to Zalith instead? He *did* want to marry him; he wanted an eternal life and family with him... but there was a part of him that was still afraid that Zalith might not want the same thing.

"*I* want to do it," Zalith said.

As he quickly became flustered by the demon's answer, Alucard tried to hide his face by sipping from his glass.

"When?" Greymore asked with a grin.

Aggravated, Zalith rolled his eyes and sipped from his drink, finished with the conversation.

"I'm joking, obviously," Greymore laughed. "Take your time. You're already old as fuck; these days must fly by for you two," he said with a sigh. But then he slapped his hands on his knees. "Okay, I'm hungry," he announced, standing up. "Don't go anywhere." He wandered off towards the crowd congregating around the smaller fire.

Once Greymore left, Alucard looked at Zalith and frowned. He didn't seem to be having a good time, and he began to wonder if the demon even wanted to be there. "Are you okay?" he asked him.

Zalith smiled. "I'm okay, I'm just a little tired," he said, moving his hand to the side of Alucard's neck. Then, he softly kissed his lips.

"Do you... vant to go?" Alucard asked. "Ve zon't 'ave to stay if you zon't vant to."

"And miss all of this?" Zalith laughed, looking around at everyone and everything, frowning as he set his eyes on Greymore, who was holding a steak in his bare hands, gnawing on it like an animal.

Also spotting Greymore, Alucard shook his head and smirked at Zalith. "Vhat? You zon't vant to eat a 'alf-cooked steak vith your bare 'ands, Zaliv?"

The demon chuckled and leaned nearer. "Only if you feed it to me," he said with a smirk, and then he pulled Alucard's face closer and started kissing him. After a few moments, though, he stopped and rested his forehead against Alucard's. "I can't wait to see how they eat their stew," he mumbled.

"Maybe zhey... dip zheir vaces in... as vone vould do vhen bobbing vor apples," he suggested unsurely.

Amused, Zalith snickered and dragged his hand down from Alucard's neck to his chest. "That sounds eerily similar to something I want to do to you later."

Alucard frowned, trying to work out what he meant as the demon softly kissed his neck. The feeling of his lips against his skin sent a shiver of delight through his body, and knowing that Zalith had plans for him later made him feel a little aroused. He lost his frown and moved his hand to the back of Zalith's head, sighing quietly and contently as the demon continued kissing him.

"Hey!" bellowed Greymore's voice from across the field.

Zalith sighed and looked over his shoulder.

Alucard huffed away his aggravation and set his eyes on Greymore, too. The man was waving at them, standing in front of a small crowd, all cooking food at the campfire.

The vampire smiled and looked at Zalith. "Let's go. Ve should enjoy zhe night a little, no? Ve'll 'ave time vor ourselves later." He might be enjoying Zalith's attention, but he *did* want to spend some time with his new friend.

Zalith sighed again and stood up as Alucard took his hand. And as they started heading over, he quietly grumbled, "I hope he doesn't make us eat anything."

Chapter Thirty

Truths, Dares, and Challenges

| Alucard |

As soon as Zalith and Alucard joined Greymore, he handed them each a shot of whiskey. "We're playing truth or dare," he announced, casually lifting his own drink. Alucard glanced around as Greymore's friends quickly gathered in a loose circle, their curiosity palpable as they closed in on the trio.

"Are we thirteen?" Zalith asked with a hint of amusement, raising his left eyebrow.

Greymore laughed. "Come on—it'll be fun, right Alucard?" he asked, looking at the vampire.

Alucard shrugged. "Maybe," he mumbled, unsure whether he was interested in playing.

"It *will*," Greymore insisted, smirking. Then, he nudged Alucard's shoulder. "Truth or dare?"

The vampire pondered for a few moments. He didn't want to be put on the spot and asked something he might not want to share, so he sighed and said, "Dare."

Greymore grinned. "I dare you to try and talk in our accent for the remainder of the game."

But Alucard scoffed and scowled. "I can't do zhat," he admitted.

"Fine, then drink," Greymore laughed.

Rolling his eyes, Alucard downed his shot.

"Now *you* gotta ask someone," Greymore said, handing him another shot.

Alucard almost immediately set his eyes on Zalith. "You, truth or dare."

Zalith simpered and replied, "Dare."

The vampire glanced at the grill over the fire; several steaks had been left on it. He hadn't forgotten Zalith's comment about not wanting to eat anything on offer. "Eat vone of zhose steaks," he said with a smirk.

Smiling, Zalith rolled his eyes and laughed a little as he glanced down at one of the steaks. "Fine," he said.

"What's wrong with the steak?" Greymore asked.

"Noving," Alucard said with a shrug. "Zaliv just zidn't vant to eat vith 'is 'ands."

Watching Zalith as he picked up one of the steaks off the grill and glowered at it, Greymore laughed slightly. "Ah, Mr Money-Bags doesn't wanna get his counting hands dirty, I see," he said as everyone around them laughed.

Amused, Zalith sighed and took a bite out of the steak, keeping his eyes on Alucard the entire time. He didn't eat the whole thing, though. After a single bite, he handed it to somebody who was walking by with a drink in their other hand. "Get me a napkin," he said, and the guy hurried off with the steak in his hand to do so. The demon then eyed the crowd for a moment before setting his eyes on Idina. "Idina," he said, and when she stared at him, he asked, "Truth or dare?"

"Um…truth," she said as her blonde companion giggled, the same woman she'd shown up with to both the Yule party and Zalith's birthday party.

"Who here do you want to punch the most?" Zalith asked.

Her eyes widened in astoundment. "N-no one!" she exclaimed.

Amused, Zalith laughed with everyone else. "Who?" he asked again.

"Nobody!" she insisted.

"Is it Greymore?" he questioned.

She thought to herself for a few moments but then sighed. "Yes."

Everyone laughed—

"But I don't know why, and I'd *never* do it—I'm sorry," she said, looking at Greymore as she placed her hand on his shoulder.

Greymore shook his head. "No, no, I see how it is," he said with a saddened frown on his face.

"It doesn't mean I actually want to hit you!" she told him.

He sighed despondently and shook his head again. "Nah, it's cool, I get it," he said with what was clearly fake offence.

With an embarrassed frown on her face, she sighed at Greymore. "Truth or dare?"

"Truth," he said, grinning.

"Okay…who do *you* want to punch the most?"

Greymore chortled loudly, thought to himself, and then set his eyes on Danford. "Danny," he said with a shrug.

Everyone laughed again, even Danford, but he looked upset.

"Okay, wait though," Greymore laughed, "you have to understand that if I hit them," he said, pointing at Alucard and Zalith, "I'm dead, and honestly if I hit her," he said, nodding at Idina, "I'd wish I was dead—and I can't hit her friend because she's a guest and that's rude, and I'm certainly not going to hit Tyrus or Freja," he explained. "So, that leaves you, buddy," he said, gesturing to Danford.

"That's fair," Danford said.

"Okay," Greymore laughed, nodding at him. "Truth or dare?"

"Uh…truth," he said nervously.

Greymore grinned widely. "Why are you afraid of Alucard?"

The crowd went quiet, glancing at Alucard and then Danford, who stared in what looked like horror.

Alucard huffed irritably, tempted to just down his shot out of irritancy. He didn't care to know; he was already confident that he knew why Danford was so cautious and nervous around him, and he felt as though hearing it might only make him feel aggravated.

"B-because…he's scary," Danford stuttered. "No offence," he added, managing to look at Alucard for a moment without trying to hide his face from him.

The vampire rolled his eyes, and as he did, Danford took a step back with a cautious expression.

"*I* don't think he's scary," Zalith said as he guided his arm around Alucard's waist and pulled him closer to hug him.

"That's because *you're* scary," Greymore laughed.

Zalith nodded slightly in agreement.

Danford then looked at Freja. "T—"

"Let's do something that involves more drinking," she interjected before he even had a chance to ask her.

Greymore sighed loudly. "Like what?"

Tyrus shrugged. "Let's just throw back some shots, and then we can—"

"And then I'll play some guitar for everyone," Greymore said enthusiastically.

They all groaned in disapproval, but Greymore chuckled and poured more shots for everyone.

As he handed Alucard another shot, however, he smiled excitedly. "You can play with me."

Not exactly interested in performing, Alucard shook his head. "No, vank you."

He nudged Alucard's arm. "Come on, man. How about we arm wrestle, and if I win, you play?" he suggested.

Amused, Alucard crossed his arms. "You von't vin."

"You never know. I might have a few tricks up my sleeve."

Shaking his head, Alucard sighed and followed Greymore to a nearby table. "Vine."

When they reached the table, Greymore sat on the left side and Alucard sat on the right; everyone grouped around them to observe, and as Greymore started rubbing his hands together and rolled his sleeve up, Alucard sighed and placed his elbow on the table, ready to humiliate him.

Greymore didn't hesitate. He slammed his hand into Alucard's, gripped it tightly, and frowned determinedly as Tyrus stood beside them.

"Okay," Tyrus said. "Three…two…one—go," he said, tapping the table.

On his word, Greymore immediately put what felt like *all* of his strength into trying to force Alucard's hand down onto the table, but Alucard's arm didn't move at all. The vampire sat there, staring vacantly at Greymore's struggled face as he frowned and glanced at him with disbelief in his eyes. The man huffed, grunted, and gritted his teeth as he shuffled around in his seat, trying what was evidently his hardest to overpower him.

Alucard let him struggle for a short while, listening as Greymore's friends laughed quietly in response to his desperation, but it was probably better to put him out of his misery. So, after a few more moments, Alucard stopped humouring the crowd and forced Greymore's arm aside without much effort at all.

The moment the back of his hand hit the table, Greymore jumped to his feet, started rubbing his elbow, and scoffed in astonishment. "How strong *are* you, man?" he laughed, staring down at Alucard.

With a shrug, Alucard rested his arms on the table. "Stronger zhan you, obviously."

Greymore howled amusedly but then pointed at Zalith. "Okay, now let's see you two arm wrestle."

Alucard looked over his shoulder at Zalith, who shrugged and made his way around to where Greymore had been sitting. He sat down, smiled at Alucard, and leaned over the table; he kissed the vampire's lips before he rested his elbow on the wood, holding his hand out towards Alucard. The vampire took hold of Zalith's hand, preparing for what he knew would be a more intense battle, but this time, he found himself wondering…who would actually win? Zalith might be thinking the same thing despite his smirk, and Alucard could see the confliction in his eyes. But they were both about to find out, weren't they?

"Go easy on me," Zalith said.

Staring at him, Alucard frowned. He wanted to win; he didn't want to spend the night playing music, least of all in front of a field of people he didn't really know. And he was almost certain that Zalith knew that.

Tyrus stood beside them again and placed his hand on the table, and once he counted down, both Zalith and Alucard gripped each other's hands a little tighter and began their battle. But Alucard wasn't using *all* of his strength because he could feel that Zalith wasn't using all of his. They struggled a little against one another, but neither of them attempted to overpower the other—either that or they were simply equal.

However, that was when Alucard felt Zalith slowly moving his knee along the inside of his thigh. The vampire scowled, convinced that Zalith was trying to distract him so that he'd lose—he wasn't going to lose. He started using a little more of his strength, and he began to ever so slowly overpower Zalith.

But Zalith smirked and laughed amusedly—without any warning, he leaned over the table and kissed Alucard, catching him off-guard. Alucard wasn't expecting it, and as the demon's lips touched his, he frowned and unintentionally allowed his composure to wither; as the back of his hand hit the table, he scowled and pushed Zalith away, embarrassment smothering his face as the crowd laughed.

Greymore's laughter faded as he patted Alucard's shoulders. "Looks like you're coming with me, buddy."

Alucard scowled at Zalith, who sat there with a snide grin. He couldn't believe that he'd just used a move like that to beat him. He didn't even have the words to explain how astounded and flustered he felt—how *embarrassed* he was. Now, because of Zalith's conniving little move, he would have to hang around and play music with Greymore when he'd much rather hang around and do nothing. He wasn't going to whine his way out of it, though—he wasn't a coward. He was just going to spend the next while feeling aggravated.

When Alucard stood up, Zalith also got up and followed him and Greymore, leaving the crowd.

"I'm sorry, baby," Zalith said quietly with a smile. "Are you mad at me?"

"No," Alucard said with a pout, glaring ahead.

"I'll let you touch my inner thigh and distract me with your mouth later if you want to get even," he flirted.

Alucard glared at him. "If I vanted to get even, I vould make you play vith Greymore," he sneered.

The demon laughed quietly. "That's not a very nice thing to say."

Rolling his eyes, Alucard glared ahead again. "Go avay," he grumbled. "You're not playing vith us."

Zalith laughed again. "That's okay. I just plan on watching anyway."

"Vhatever," Alucard mumbled.

The demon kissed the side of Alucard's face but then stopped following them.

Alucard then looked at Greymore, who quickly turned his head to stare up at the sky, obviously trying to make it look like he hadn't been listening. The vampire sighed, rolled his eyes, and asked, "Vhat zhe 'ell am I supposed to be playing? I can't play zhe guitar."

"What do you play again?" Greymore questioned. "The violin?"

"Yes," Alucard grumbled.

He smirked. "I got you covered," he said as he stopped walking.

While Alucard waited, Greymore rushed over to one of his men, muttered to him, and then made his way back to Alucard as the man hurried into one of the houses. He swiftly returned to Greymore with a fiddle, handed it to him, and scurried off again.

"Here you go," Greymore said, handing the fiddle to Alucard.

Without taking it from him, Alucard glowered at it. "Veally?"

Making him take the fiddle, Greymore winked. "Take a seat, pal," he invited, nodding at the bench where Greymore's guitar sat.

Alucard sighed deeply but walked over to the bench and sat down. He was sure that the next while would be draining, and he didn't feel very enthusiastic about it. It wasn't that he didn't like hanging out with Greymore, he just didn't really want to perform in front of people—especially not with a fiddle. But what choice did he have? He wasn't going to cower out of it; he'd already refused Greymore's dare, so he'd not refuse something else and let people think that he was boring. He could have fun, and he would…or at least he'd try to.

Chapter Thirty-One

Tour

| Alucard |

It felt like a century had passed. Alucard had long lost track of how many hours ago he'd started playing the same hapless little tunes Greymore insisted upon. He couldn't even recall when the first song had begun. But the crowd around them seemed to relish their duet, and so, despite his growing fatigue, Alucard pressed on. Greymore had already coaxed him into 'just one more song' four times, yet in his enthusiasm, he seemed blissfully unaware of Alucard's desire to stop. Just one more, Alucard promised himself, and then he'd tell Greymore he was leaving.

He continued playing, staring vacantly across the compound. Greymore was enjoying himself, as were those dancing around the fire. Alucard wasn't one for this sort of setting, but he did appreciate time outside of the house with Zalith, and he also liked hanging out with Greymore, so he'd make it through.

And surely enough, what Alucard wished to be their final duet came to an end.

Greymore started cheering and hollering with the clapping crowd but then placed his guitar down and exhaled deeply. "Time to break out my baby," he said, smirking.

"Vhat?" Alucard asked with a frown.

Still smirking, Greymore waved over at one of his people. "My accordion," he said.

Alucard felt a slither of dread creep through him; he didn't want to play anymore. He just wanted to sit somewhere and rest. But Greymore seemed to have other plans.

However, Alucard's saving grace came when Zalith appeared beside them, smiling down at Greymore as he looked up at him. "I'm going to borrow Alucard for a few minutes," he said, taking hold of Alucard's hand as the vampire placed the fiddle beside him.

Shrugging, Greymore rested his arms on his knees. "No worries."

Alucard immediately got up and followed Zalith away as Greymore called someone else to take over in his absence. And then, he and Zalith walked back to where they'd been sitting.

"Vank you," Alucard said when he sat down in front of the bonfire.

As he sat beside him, Zalith smiled. "Did you have a nice time at least?"

"Yes…until about vour songs in," he mumbled.

Zalith laughed slightly and pulled him closer, kissing his forehead. "Sorry baby."

Alucard shrugged and sighed quietly. "Vhat vere you doing vhile I vas vith Zhomas?"

"Talking to Idina and watching over you."

"Vhat vere you talking about?"

"Oh, just about how handsome you are," he said with a smirk, moving Alucard's fringe away from over his face. "And about Elena."

"Are zhey a couple?" Alucard asked.

"I think so," Zalith said. "But she's being very hush-hush about it."

"I vink zhey are."

The demon exhaled and said, "Well, she'll let us all know in her own time, I suppose."

Nodding, Alucard moved a little closer to Zalith and rested his head on his shoulder. "Vell, vhat should ve do now?"

"Drink," the demon said with a smirk, "and enjoy the night."

Alucard had no quarrels with that. "You might 'ave to vrestle a bottle off Zhomas, zhough," he said, nodding in Greymore's direction, watching as he started downing a bottle of whiskey as his friends cheered him on.

Zalith laughed slightly. "I don't want anything with his spit on it. I'll be right back," he said and kissed Alucard's lips.

As Zalith wandered off to get them something to drink, Alucard slouched forward, resting his arms on his legs. He watched as the demon made his way over to a collection of crates, where Greymore had left a few bottles of whiskey and some glasses; Zalith took one of the bottles, poured two drinks, and then headed back to the vampire.

The demon handed one of the glasses to Alucard as he sat close to him. "There wasn't much there in terms of variety, but I got us the best I could get my hands on."

Glancing at the whiskey, Alucard shrugged and shifted his gaze to Zalith. "I'm sure von't matter vhat zhis tastes like vhen ve're drvunk enough."

"I hope we don't get too drunk," Zalith said, guiding his free hand to the side of Alucard's face, "because then we can't do this." He smirked and pressed his lips against Alucard's. They kissed for a few moments but then stopped when Zalith laughed quietly. "At least not as well."

Alucard smiled. "Ve can still do zhis, zhough."

"Well, I—"

"I, um…" Danford interjected, appearing in front of them. "Sorry," he said, clearly aware that he'd interrupted them. "I just…wanted to say sorry," he said as they looked up at him. He shifted his nervous gaze to Alucard, who wasn't pleased to see him this close. "Uh…to say sorry for saying you were scary. Y-you're not scary," he said, trying to put on a brave face as he looked down at the ground. "You're just…intimidating—sorry," he stuttered.

With a vacant stare on his face, Alucard rolled his eyes. "Is basically zhe same ving."

"Y-yeah…." Danford frowned, glancing at Alucard and then back down at the ground. "But what I mean is…you're not…um…you're not ugly or scary-looking or anything—you're just…I just didn't want you to think I was trying to offend you or anything," he said with a cautious look on his face.

All Alucard really got from his fumbling rant was the word ugly. Who said he was ugly? Did Danford think that? The vampire scowled up at him; Danford wasn't much to look at himself, so who was he to say something like that? "Who said I vas ugly?" he asked as calmly as possible.

A look of horror smothered Danford's face. "O-oh, n-no, no, I just mean that you're not scary-looking or anything like a witch or something; you're just intimidating to be near," he tried to explain. "S-sorry, I didn't mean it to come across that way. I don't think you're ugly."

Zalith then frowned. "So, you think he's hot, then?"

Danford stared in distress. "I…no," he answered.

"So you *do* think he's ugly?"

Alucard kept his scowl on Danford as the guy shook his head, stammered, and struggled to answer.

"N-no, not at all, I-I just—"

"Okay, so you think he's hot, then?"

"Well…I—"

"Do we need to step aside and have a conversation, Danford?" Zalith asked and sipped from his drink.

Alucard sipped from his drink, hiding his amused smile.

"N-no," Danford quavered. "I'm just…gonna go, if-if that's okay."

Zalith took his eyes off Danford and looked at Alucard.

As amusing as it was, Alucard wouldn't be cruel and bully Danford. So, he waved his hand in dismissal. "Go and do vhatever," he muttered.

"O-okay," Danford said with a nod. "Sorry again. A-also, I wanted to say thank you, Zalith, for building this place for us; we all really appreciate it," he added.

The demon replied, "You're welcome."

Danford then took a few steps back. "Uh…okay…bye," he said, and then he turned around and scurried back over to where Freja was waiting.

Alucard rolled his eyes. He always felt irritated when he saw Danford, and he was sure that was primarily because of his and Zalith's past—and because of what Varana said and the fact that Alucard thought Zalith was seeing Danford again through the months he'd ignored him. He was over it, though. He didn't feel any insecurity or jealousy; he just hated having to see a man who Zalith had slept with before.

Zalith obviously hadn't failed to notice his aggravation. The demon lightly gripped the vampire's chin with his thumb and index finger. "What's wrong, baby?"

"Noving," he mumbled and finished his drink as he turned to face Zalith again.

"Are you sure?" he asked, caressing the vampire's hair.

Alucard nodded. "Can I get anozzer drvink, please?"

"Okay," Zalith said, smiling. He kissed Alucard's lips and walked to where the drinks were. However, this time, he returned with an entire bottle rather than a glass each.

As Zalith sat back down, Alucard held out his empty glass. "Vank you," he said as the demon filled it.

"Of course," he said, pouring his own drink. He then placed the bottle on the ground and moved closer to Alucard. He started fiddling with his hair again. "You look very handsome in the firelight," he said contently. "I just might ask you to come home with me," he said with a sultry tone.

Alucard smiled as he stared down at his drink but then slowly shifted his gaze to Zalith's dark eyes, watching as the light of the fire reflected crimson in them. "Good, because I'd like to go 'ome vith you."

Zalith laughed quietly as a flirty smile appeared on his face. "You would?"

Alucard rested his forehead against Zalith's. "I'd also like to go to your bedvoom vith you."

"That can be arranged," Zalith said as he moved his hand to the back of Alucard's head, and then he started kissing him. But after a few moments, he stopped and rested his forehead back against Alucard's. "Do you want to dance?"

The vampire glanced at the people who were dancing rather strangely to the music that Greymore and his new friend were playing; they were flailing their arms around and wriggling their bodies like they were on fire. "Vell…as long as ve zon't 'ave to dance like zhat," he said, watching as a couple stumbled over one another's feet, waving their arms around like what could only be described as…a pair of crabs.

Zalith nodded, fiddling with Alucard's crucifix. "Well, I know another dance we could perform, but it mostly involves us lying down…and there are normally fewer people involved," he said seductively.

Alucard smiled and glanced down at his lap. "I like zhe sound of zhat."

The demon started kissing him again but paused to say, "I think they might think we're rude if we leave right now, though." He kissed him for a few more moments. "It's not good for morale."

As Zalith's lips met his once more, Alucard felt frustration grip him. He hated being offered Zalith's affection, only to be told that he couldn't have it moments later. But he wasn't going to argue. "Vine," he grumbled.

Zalith kept his smirk and stroked his hand down the vampire's body. He gripped his hand and said, "Come on, Mr Grumpy. I want to give you a tour."

Alucard sighed and followed as Zalith led him past the strangely dancing crowd and over to the very first house, which stood beside the compound entrance. Zalith took him past each building; they all looked the exact same, and Alucard's interest was very quickly lost.

"What's wrong?" Zalith asked.

"Noving," he mumbled. "I'm vine."

"You seem grumpy," the demon teased.

"I'm not grumpy."

"If you say so," Zalith said, dragging out his words. He then nodded at the house that they were approaching. "So, that's where your boyfriend lives," he said with a smirk.

Alucard shook his head, sighing quietly as Zalith laughed amusedly. He didn't want to fight with him, nor did he wish to insist that Greymore was nothing more than his friend. He knew that would entertain Zalith, so he felt like it was time to change the subject. Greymore mentioned them getting engaged earlier, and Alucard actually had some questions about that. "If ve get married, who vill take whose name?" he asked but then he frowned in confusion. "Vhat even *is* your last name?"

"Well, I don't have a last name, so I'll be taking yours—unless you don't want a last name, too," he said while he kept leading the way past the houses.

"Vell…." Alucard frowned, staring ahead. "Do *you* even vant a last name?"

"I want *yours*," Zalith said, smirking.

The vampire smiled, trying to keep a shy look off his face. "You can 'ave vhenever."

Zalith moved his arm around Alucard's waist and pulled him closer. "Thank you. I look forward to it," he said and kissed the side of the vampire's face.

Smiling as Zalith linked arms with him, Alucard continued following at the demon's side while he led him from house to house, telling him who lived where.

Eventually, Zalith took him away from the houses and towards one of the barns. "There's something behind here that I think you'll find very interesting," he mumbled, pulling him along as he walked around to the back of the barn.

What could possibly be so interesting behind a barn? All Alucard could think of was maybe a horse or some animal that Zalith knew he'd like to see, but he didn't feel like that was the case. "Vhere are you taking me?" he asked.

"Just back here, don't worry." Zalith pulled him behind the barn to reveal that there wasn't anything there other than a few stacked crates.

Zalith stopped walking, giving Alucard a moment to search the area with his eyes, but he didn't give him much time to ask what was going on. The demon stood in front of him, placed his hand on the side of his neck, and started kissing him. Zalith gradually moved forward as they kissed, making Alucard step back until his back hit the barn wall.

When his back hit the wall, Alucard turned his head aside, inviting Zalith to start kissing his neck so that he could take a moment to breathe. The demon did as he wanted, and as he did, Alucard stared at the forest to his right. "Are ve going to do zhis 'ere?" he asked quietly. What if somebody saw them?

"Not if you don't want to," Zalith murmured into his ear.

A shiver of anticipation spiralled through Alucard's body. He wanted it—of course he did. He craved Zalith's affection as if it were a drug. There *was* the risk that someone might see them, but so what? It didn't put him off. Not only were these Zalith's people—people who wouldn't care if they saw—but it also wouldn't be the first time he'd let Zalith touch him in a public place. He didn't care. His desperation won.

"No, I vant to," he answered.

Zalith guided his hand under Alucard's shirt. "Then you should stop asking questions," he said with a smirk and started kissing him again.

Alucard leaned his head back against the wall, trailing his hand to the back of Zalith's head as their tongues eagerly entwined. Zalith dragged his hand over the vampire's abs, eventually reaching his waist; he didn't waste time unbuckling the vampire's belt and reached into his trousers.

As Zalith caressed Alucard's shaft, the vampire gripped a fistful of the demon's hair, exhaling deeply as Zalith softly kissed his neck. But he didn't want to wait. His anticipation quickly became overwhelming; Zalith already teased him earlier, and although it had irritated him, it made him feel a whole lot more desperate. So he moved his hand to the top of Zalith's head and hastily pushed him down.

Zalith grinned excitedly and got down on his knees as he unbuttoned Alucard's trousers. The moment he took the tip of Alucard's dick into his mouth, the vampire sighed quietly in relief, gripping hold of Zalith's hair again. He closed his eyes, sinking into the euphoria that the feeling of Zalith's warm, wet tongue stroking his length gave him. Nothing else seemed to matter; all he could focus on was Zalith and how satisfied he made him feel as he slowly eased his shaft deeper into his throat.

Alucard moaned quietly as Zalith sucked a little faster, caressing his balls with his free hand. Despite the loud party behind them, Alucard didn't put much effort into quieting his groans of pleasure; he was sure that no one would hear.

The vampire held out for as long as he could—he didn't want it to end—but the gentle yet enthralling strokes of the demon's tongue brought him to his peak. He moaned in delight and abruptly pulled Zalith's face against his crotch as he climaxed, each pulse of pleasure lightening his pleased expression. He felt the demon's throat tightening around his throbbing dick as he swallowed his cum, and it made Alucard hum contently. And then he let out a relieved sigh as he relaxed and let go of Zalith's hair; the demon pulled Alucard's shaft from his mouth and wiped his lips and chin before he kissed his way back up the vampire's body.

When Zalith reached Alucard's neck, he kissed it and murmured, "I love it when you cum down my throat." Then he kissed his neck a few times while he buttoned Alucard's trousers up and buckled his belt for him. Once he'd done that, he moved his hand to the side of Alucard's face and made him look at him. "I'm sorry I cheated at arm wrestling," he mumbled.

Alucard sighed and shrugged. "Is vine. Ve'll vematch vone day, no?"

"I look forward to it," the demon laughed as he lightly dragged his fingers over the side of Alucard's face. Then, he started kissing him as he moved his hands down past Alucard's waist and gripped his ass tightly. But Zalith stifled their next kiss and grunted in startlement as he slapped his hand over his own neck. "Ow," he snarled angrily.

Alucard frowned, staring at him as he lifted his hand from his neck. "Vhat?"

Zalith held out his hand, revealing what looked like a dead mosquito on his palm. "Disgusting," he muttered, glaring down at the dead bug.

The vampire laughed a little in amusement. "Is just a mosquito," he said, looking at Zalith's revolted face as he wiped his hand on the barn behind him. "Zhey get 'ungry, too."

As he wiped the dead mosquito away, Zalith smirked a little. "You're the only thing I want sucking my blood, vampire," he said and leaned closer as if he was going to kiss him. "We're lucky it wasn't a moth, or I'm sure I'd be spending the entire night convincing you it's gone," he teased, tapping Alucard's chin.

Pouting, Alucard looked away from him. "You zon't need to make zhis personal," he complained.

The demon laughed quietly. "I'm sorry," he said, tucking a loose strand of Alucard's hair behind his ear. But then he sighed deeply and rested his head on Alucard's shoulder. "Should we go back now?"

Alucard thought about it for a few moments. Of course, he enjoyed the time that he and Zalith got to themselves, but they *had* come here to celebrate with Zalith's people—or to at least be seen by them. They couldn't hang around behind a barn all night, could they? The night was also late, and surely enough, the party wouldn't continue much longer, so he and Zalith could soon return home to their bed.

"Yes," he answered, taking hold of Zalith's hand.

With a quiet exhale, Zalith lifted his head from Alucard's shoulder, kissed his lips again, and started leading the way back from behind the barn.

Chapter Thirty-Two

Swarm

| Alucard |

Alucard walked back towards the field with Zalith. But when they approached the fire, Greymore's enthusiastic music halted, and the man's irritated grunt echoed across the glade. Zalith and Alucard watched as the beefy man slapped his own neck, as did several other people.

Convinced that they, like Zalith, had just been bitten by mosquitos, Alucard glanced at the demon and shrugged. "I guess you're not zhe only vone who got eaten."

Zalith frowned as he nodded at the fire. "It's odd that the smoke isn't keeping them away."

"Zhere are so many people 'ere; maybe zhey zon't vant to miss zheir chance to snack."

"Maybe," the demon agreed.

They made their way back to where they were sitting and made themselves comfortable. Zalith poured himself and Alucard another drink before resting his head on the vampire's shoulder.

And for the next while, they sat there, enjoying one another's company.

But Alucard hadn't forgotten Zalith's invitation to dance. Since they'd left for the barn, many more people had started dancing, and Alucard began to feel like he wanted to accept Zalith's invitation. Of course, he wasn't going to dance around like some crab as everyone else seemed to be... and he was sure that Zalith wasn't going to do that either. He just wanted to enjoy Zalith's embrace, and slow dancing with him was one of his favourite ways to do so.

He frowned shyly and asked, "Do you... vant to dance now?"

"Do *you* want to?" Zalith asked.

Alucard nodded. "As long as ve zon't 'ave to be crabs."

Zalith laughed and finished his drink. Then, he slipped his hand into Alucard's and stood up. "We can dance however you'd like."

With a sigh of relief, Alucard stood up and followed Zalith a short distance from the bonfire, where they then started to slow dance. He rested his head on Zalith's shoulder, closing his eyes as he allowed himself to become lost in the demon's embrace. It was within moments like these that he felt most at peace—when he and Zalith could simply enjoy one another's embrace, the moments where they didn't have to spare a single thought about what might happen tomorrow or in the weeks to come. The moments where they could just be silent and know that they couldn't be without each other.

But Alucard couldn't be so naïve. He'd done his best all night not to think about it, but…how could he not? He and Zalith had pretty much declared war on the Numen last year, and it had been relatively silent up until Yule. And Freja reminded him about the devastation that warped his homeland; the Diabolus had taken Dor-Sanguis from him, and they tried to take his people. He'd managed to get some of them out of the line of fire, but so many vampires had died.

The worry that the Diabolus was working with Lilith or Damien lingered in the back of his mind ever since that night, but nothing his or Zalith's people had found had confirmed their suspicion. No one had found out whether Damien and Lilith were *actually* working together again or if the Diabolus were working with either of their cults, either. He wouldn't be surprised if the Numen were creating truces with one another to find him and Zalith…but Lucifer would never work with Damien, and Damien would never work with him. Something was going on, but…what?

He tried to think of a logical answer. The Numen wanted him for their own reasons, and they also wanted Zalith; why would they work together when they wanted their own, singular victory? They wouldn't share Alucard with each other, and they sure as hell wouldn't all settle for killing Zalith together. So why was there evidence of the Diabolus and Lilith's people in the same place?

Could Lilith have somehow shared information with Lucifer regarding Zalith's weaknesses? It was now a well-known fact that Lilith and Lucifer had something going on between them before Damien interjected. But the bottom line was that if Damien, Lilith, *and* Lucifer were working together, it only meant that things for Alucard and Zalith would become much worse. To fight three cults at once was one thing, but three Numen? Even with the knowledge of the Obcasus and Numen prisons, they might not stand as much of a chance as they might have before.

"Hey," Zalith said, breaking his train of thought. "Are you okay?" he asked, staring into his eyes.

Alucard frowned, realizing he'd let their silence force him into his thoughts. So, he sighed and said, "I'm okay. I just…can't stop vinking about Dor-Sanguis."

Zalith moved his hand to the side of Alucard's face and frowned sadly. "I'm sorry," he said quietly. "As soon as things are safe enough, we can work on taking it back," he assured him.

Nodding, Alucard stared down at the grass. "I know," he said but then shook his head and sighed deeply. "I zon't vant to talk about zhis vight now. Ve're supposed to be 'aving vun."

The demon pulled him into a tight hug. "Okay, baby."

But now that he'd given into his thoughts, Alucard couldn't ignore his concern; he couldn't ignore the anxiety and desperation that their lack of answers was making him feel. "Ve still 'aven't 'eard if zhe Diabolus is vorking vith Liliv, and ve still zon't know if zhe cults are vorking togezzer—if zhe *Numen* are vorking togezzer. Vhat if vhat 'appened in Dor-Sanguis 'appens 'ere? Ve zon't know enough to be prepared," he said, starting to feel distressed.

Zalith's despondent frown thickened. "Why are you so worried all of a sudden, baby?" he asked in concern. "Where is this coming from?"

As he took his eyes off Zalith, Alucard huffed and stared down at the ground. Now that he thought about it, he didn't really have much of an answer. Yes, Freja's mention of Dor-Sanguis made him think about what happened, but why did he feel the sudden need to worry about what might happen *here*? He knew Nefastus was safe—*no one* knew that he and Zalith were there—so…why did something feel…wrong? Why did he feel as though his fear of losing their home wasn't random?

He frowned in confliction and slowly lifted his head to look at Zalith's concerned face. "I zon't…know," he admitted. "I just…avter losing Dor-Sanguis, I guess I've started vorrying a lot more about our 'ome 'ere. Zhis is zhe only place I veel safe, and zhe only place I vant to be. Vhat if I lose zhis place, too? I zon't know vhat zhis is," he said, and he was sure that there was an expression on his face to match the way he was feeling. He was overwhelmingly distressed, and he didn't understand why. "I know ve're safe 'ere…but vhat if ve're not? Ever since Dor-Sanguis, I've ovten vound myselv vorrying zhat vouldn't be long until ve lost Nevastus, too," he explained.

Zalith stared at him as he moved his hand to the back of the vampire's head. "I worry about that as well. But as long as we have each other, we'll be okay. We *are* safe here, and no one knows where we are or how to find us."

"I know." Alucard sighed and looked down at the grass again. "And even zhough I know zhat, I just…can't stop vorrying—is like a veeling almost…a veally bad vone. Like I know someving vill 'appen, but…I zon't know vhen, 'ow, or vhat to do," he explained as best he could, staring into Zalith's conflicted eyes.

An anxious expression stole Zalith's concerned face. "What do you *feel* we should do?"

They stopped dancing, and as they gazed at one another, the world around Alucard seemed to slow down a little, and that feeling of worry and angst…it grew into a sudden realization, the kind of feeling that would strike him when he realized that he was too late.

And they *were* too late, weren't they?

Alucard's eyes shifted from Zalith's angst-smothered face to the dark cloud heading towards them over the trees in the distance. It stretched for miles, getting closer and closer, and despite the loud music and the burning fire, Alucard could hear the rustling—the chirping. He stared in utter horror; he had no idea what was heading their way, but he knew that it was what he'd been fearing.

Zalith sharply turned his head and stared in the same direction, and when the demon saw the cloud racing towards them, he gripped Alucard's hand tightly and pulled him along with him as he started hurrying towards the crowd.

"Take cover!" the demon yelled, and he was clearly doing his best to keep a calm composure as he hurried towards the closest building, pulling Alucard with him.

As Zalith's people stopped partying and set their eyes on the incoming cloud, Alucard snapped out of his state of horror. Everyone started running, and as he was pulled along by Zalith, he kept his eyes on the cloud. It was getting closer…faster…and it spread far beyond even *his* eyes could see—and what his eyes *could* see was what made up the incoming darkness. Insects—billions of them. Tiny, clicking, winged insects racing in their direction. They would arrive in just moments, and Alucard had even less time to think of a plan.

But he had something.

"Vait," he insisted, yanking back on Zalith's hand to make him stop. The demon stopped and stared at him with a conflicted, distressed frown. "Ve von't 'ave time," he insisted, taking his eyes off the incoming darkness to stare at Zalith. "Zhey're insects—too many of zhem. If zhey're coming vor vood, zhen zhey'll make easy vork of zhese buildings. Ve need to get everyvone into vone area, and zhen you and I can create a barrier of vire avound zhem. Ve'll 'ave to keep up until zhey pass," he explained.

Zalith immediately nodded and yelled out to his people, relaying Alucard's plan, and as his people started rushing towards them, the vampire set his eyes back on the approaching darkness. Alucard wasn't certain what he was looking at; it was obviously a swarm of insects, but…why? There wasn't time to ponder. His priority was protecting Zalith and his people.

As Zalith's people huddled around them, Alucard shifted his gaze to the demon. He wasn't sure whether what was coming was just a swarm of hungry insects or something sent for them, but the latter was screaming at him, and if the incoming swarm had been sent, then there was a possibility that it wasn't going to be so easy to destroy. So, if they both combined their abilities, it would increase their chances of destroying the enemy.

"You can draw ethos vrom me," he said, gripping Zalith's hand tightly. "Ve'll combine our vire ethos and destroy vhatever zhe fuck zhat is," he said, glaring out at the incoming darkness once more. It was seconds away.

They had no time to think and no time to discuss it. But they trusted one another, and they knew each other well enough to know what they had to do. They held their tightly grasped hands up above their heads; Alucard focused his ethos, Zalith focused his, and just as the swarm of buzzing, winged insects approached, an immense circle of white fire burnt into the grass around the huddled group of people. From the grass, the flames swiftly rose, curved inwards, and formed a dome, concealing everyone inside.

As the wave of insects hit the white fire, the creatures screeched and perished, but despite Alucard sharing his ethos, Zalith's white flames began to thin. Alucard knew he had to do more, and Zalith knew that, too. As he shared his ethos with Zalith, Zalith began to share his with *him*. Alucard then summoned his own fire and combined it with Zalith's, and the moment he did, the shield of white flames strengthened and darkened to a dark yet vibrant orange, and it singed the insects before they could get within ten feet of it.

Zalith and Alucard kept their fire burning, waiting while the swarm thinned. The people's panicked voices started to quieten, and when there wasn't a single insect left, Alucard began to slowly let go of Zalith's hand.

"What the hell was that?" Freja asked as the fiery dome withered and disappeared.

Ignoring Freja's question and those of everyone else, Alucard set his eyes on Zalith. The demon looked horrified; Alucard *felt* horrified. He had no idea what to think or say. He looked over his shoulder, watching as what remained of the insect swarm raced towards the city. *They* were safe, but the same couldn't be said for the Citadel, and Alucard didn't know whether they should hurry to the city and help or if he and Zalith should decide if it was safe to stay in Nefastus a moment longer.

"Zaliv," he said, moving his hand to the demon's shoulder—but that was when his feeling of despair returned.

This time, he had no chance to warn Zalith—

A blinding light hit the ground behind them, and as a horrific, deafening boom exploded through the air, *everyone* was thrown off their feet.

It all happened so fast. Alucard felt Zalith's fingers slip from his grasp, he felt Zalith disappear from his reach, and as his back hit what he presumed to be the ground, agonizing pain surged through his body.

Everything went still and silent.

And darkness enthralled his senses.

They were under attack.

Chapter Thirty-Three

Protocol

| Zalith |

Ash fell onto Zalith's face, and the ringing in his ears was so loud that it made him feel sick to his stomach. The confusion, the disorientation—the pain in his right side. But none of that mattered. Where was Alucard? What happened? What was going on?

He opened his eyes but saw nothing but light—shining…white light. Adellum—*the Light*…. Dread gripped his heart, soul, and being as he did his best to sit up wherever he'd fallen. But as he moved, the light obstructing his vision faded. It wasn't Adellum—it wasn't *anyone*; it was simply his own concussion, which slowly withered as his body healed itself.

But that didn't calm his paranoia. He stared ahead, watching as a crowd of faceless people stepped out of the smoke surrounding the glade. *His people* were on the ground; some had recovered and were shifting into their wolf forms and charging at the faceless men. Zalith didn't recognize a single one of them, though. But he *did* know that they were the enemy—that *they* had attacked. Why else would they be battling his people?

Where was Alucard?

Zalith looked around as frantically as his stiff body would let him, and when he dragged his hand down his right side to locate the cause of his pain, his hand met a large wooden splinter embedded in his waist. He yanked it from his body and snarled irritably as he struggled to his feet; his disorientation was taking a little longer than he'd like to fade. But he didn't care about himself; his people needed help…and Alucard…where was he?

The demon stumbled forward as his concussion and disorientation slowly faded. His vision began clearing, and as he glared ahead, the people who emerged from the smoke became recognizable—but not as people he knew. They were demons. Their ethos was demon…and their faces…they looked familiar, especially that of the man leading and commanding the others as they threw themselves at Greymore's wolves. His hair was ashen, his eyes a very light red—and the dent in the guy's ego became clear the moment he set his sights on Zalith and scowled in resentment. *That* man...that was one of Lilith's scions, the very same scion Zalith had beaten into submission on multiple occasions when he and Alucard were trapped in Lilith's domain.

Alucard—he had to find him. His mind was racing, and his body was still lagging, but his instincts were urging him forward. He didn't care about the scion—of course, he cared about his people, but they were already getting up and following Greymore's orders. Zalith knew that they could handle themselves.

However, the scion called, "You!" just as Zalith recovered enough of his focus to begin searching for his vampire.

He turned in the direction of the scion, who reached Zalith in the blink of an eye and gripped his throat, pushing him back as his feet dragged along the ground. Zalith's back slammed against the fence of one of the houses, and as he gripped the scion's wrist, the man leaned into Zalith's face and snarled aggressively.

"You have no idea how long I've waited for this," the scion hissed.

"I have a pretty *good* idea," Zalith replied with a matter-of-fact tone.

Irritated, the scion growled and tightened his grip. "You'll not humiliate me this time. I'm stronger...better—I consumed *all* my brothers to be ready for this moment, the moment I'd make you regret *everything* you did to me," he stated.

Staring almost vacantly at him, Zalith frowned. "Who are you again?" he asked condescendingly, watching as the guy's look of fury became one of humiliation.

But the scion slammed his fist into the side of Zalith's face, sending him tumbling across the grass. He was a lot stronger than before, but it didn't unsettle Zalith.

"Who am I?!" the scion yelled, reaching Zalith before he could get up, snatching his throat once again. "*I'm* Lilith's son—and *you*?! Who are *you* compared to that? Some pathetic little pest who should have died *centuries* ago," he roared furiously, slamming Zalith's back against the closest tree.

Amused, Zalith kept his vacant glare. "And yet, I didn't. I guess you'll just have to kill me then, won't you?" he said with fake sorrow.

The scion scowled, gritted his teeth, and moved closer to him. "Oh, I will, and I'm going to have so much fun d—" Something cracked and squelched, silencing him as a look of startlement smothered his face, and he convulsed violently. He choked when blood started to spew from his mouth, and he slowly averted his eyes down to his chest. But before he could utter another sound, he flinched violently and dropped to the ground, his hand slipping from Zalith's throat.

Zalith took his eyes off the scion and set his sights on who stood in his place. With a revolted look on his bloody face was Alucard, and he was holding the dead scion's heart in his hand. Relieved to see him, Zalith smiled through his relieved sigh and moved closer to him. He placed his hands on the vampire's shoulders as he let the dead man's heart drop to the ground—

"Is Liliv," Alucard said before Zalith could ask him if he was okay. "I zon't know 'ow she vound us, but she knows vhere ve are now," he said hopelessly with a despondent scowl.

Seeing Lilith's scion had clarified that, but Alucard's confirmation only made Zalith feel more anxious. Lilith knew where they were, and they couldn't stay there a moment longer. He had to leave with Alucard and his people. Nefastus wasn't safe anymore.

"We have to leave—now," the demon said sternly. But Varana…she was still back at the house and probably had no idea what was going on. They had to leave for the closest rendezvous point, but he didn't want to leave without her. Someone had to go back for her—there was no question about *that*—but who? "We…need to get Varana," he panicked.

Alucard turned to face the battle, and Zalith took his eyes off him to stare, too. Greymore was commanding what was left of his pack to assist those who needed it so that they could retreat, following the protocol discussed months ago. But it was taking more than two of Greymore's wolves to hold back just one demon as those who couldn't fight hurried into the cover of the trees. Zalith knew that Alucard was trying to decide whether he should help, and if that was what he wanted to do, then Zalith would get Varana alone.

But as they began heading towards the battle, Alucard said, "I can go and get 'er, and you can 'elp everyvone get to zhe rendezvous point."

Zalith stopped and grabbed Alucard's arm before he could hurry off. He wanted to protest, but he took a moment to consider his options. They couldn't both leave; one of them needed to stay behind and help Greymore hold off their attackers while everyone else retreated. Someone had to make sure everyone got away…but he didn't want to send Alucard off on his own without backup in case something happened. He'd let Alucard go, but he wanted to send someone with him, someone who Varana was likely to listen to because he was certain that she'd refuse to believe Alucard.

He frowned in confliction, frantically searching for who remained. He set his eyes on Tyrus and decided. "Okay, but take Tyrus with you," he pleaded.

Alucard didn't hesitate. "Vine. I'll meet you zhere in ten minutes."

The demon hesitated, tightening his grip. He didn't want to let go; ten minutes was *too* long, but…he wasn't going to leave Varana. "Okay," he said reluctantly.

"I'll be vine," Alucard insisted. "You need to get everyvone to safety."

Zalith stared at him and refused to let go. Everything within him told him to keep hold of Alucard's hand—to not let him leave. He didn't want to risk losing him, but he didn't want to abandon Varana, and his people needed his help. He had to let go; he trusted Alucard, and Tyrus would be going with him. He'd be fine…Zalith was just going to spend every moment without Alucard worrying. "Okay," he said again. "Just make sure you come back to me," he begged in distress.

Alucard nodded as he moved his hand to the side of Zalith's face. "I vill."

He still didn't want to let him go; he wanted to stay with him, but he owed his people his assistance—he had to let Alucard go, as much as he didn't like it. There was no time for any further debate. He slowly loosened his grip on Alucard's arm and watched as the vampire hurried over to Tyrus and told him to go with him; the orange-eyed allocer demon looked over at Zalith, and Zalith nodded in confirmation. And then Alucard dematerialized with Tyrus, leaving the battlefield which had once been his people's home. But no longer was it that. It was no safer than Eltaria, and Zalith had to get his people away.

Without further falter, he hurried over to Greymore and his wolves and began fighting off the demons that Lilith had sent, doing his best to set aside his overwhelming worry that something might happen to Alucard.

| Alucard |

Alucard landed in front of Varana's house and let go of Tyrus' wrist. The man was clearly doing his best to keep a vacant stare; Alucard knew that the allocer demon was probably suffering from nausea—everyone who he dematerialized *always* suffered the first time. But he wasn't concerned about Tyrus. He ignored his thoughts, anger, and worry, and focused on his task.

Tyrus followed behind him as he made his way into Varana's house. He knew where she was—her repulsive, Lucifer-like scent was so tough to ignore—and navigated his way to the woman's lounge. He set his eyes on her while she lay on her couch with a wet towel over her eyes.

"Ve 'ave to leave," he announced.

Varana flinched in shock and pulled the towel off her face; she turned onto her side as she dropped it on the floor and glared at him in revolt. "What? No!" she denied confusedly. "Where's Z?"

"Liliv's people attacked zhe compound, and Zaliv is leading 'is people to zhe rendezvous point. I've come back vor you. Stop vasting time, let's go," he snarled.

Her eyes widened. "Lilith?!" she exclaimed.

"Yes, Liliv," Alucard grumbled impatiently.

"Why?!" she shouted. "And you just left him there all alone?!" she screeched, jumping to her feet. She then set her eyes on Tyrus. "And *you*, too?! How dare you!"

With an aggravated sigh, Alucard turned his back on her and headed for the door. "Zaliv chose to stay and 'elp 'is people. 'E is…'eading vor zhe meeting point now," he said, focusing on the connection they had through their imprints to find out where Zalith was.

"Oh, so he chose to help a bunch of people but didn't come to help me?" she questioned, taking a few steps forward. "That doesn't sound like him."

Alucard stopped walking and glared over his shoulder at her. "'E sent me to 'elp you."

"Why didn't he just come himself if it was so important?!"

Losing his patience, Alucard clenched his fists but did his best to keep his anger at bay. "You 'ave vive minutes to get vhataever zhe fuck you vant to bring vith you, and zhen ve are leaving. Tyrus vill stay vith you, and you vill meet me outside zhis 'ouse," he said, not interested in listening to anything else she might have to say. He had his own things to grab before he and Zalith had to leave their home behind.

Varana scowled, picked up her wet towel, and launched it at Alucard. "Fine," she snapped as the towel flew towards him.

Alucard caught the towel and snarled as he handed it to Tyrus. Then, he left Varana's lounge. He had nothing else to say to her.

The vampire left Varana's house and hurried towards his and Zalith's. As he did, all he could think about was how he didn't want to leave it behind. The house where he and Zalith lived had become so important to him; it had become the one place where he felt truly safe. But that couldn't be the case anymore. Lilith had found the compound, and the compound was only fifteen minutes from the house. They couldn't come back—they couldn't stay there anymore—and the plan had always been to retreat if any of the Numen ever found them.

There was no saving their home, but they could save each other, and Alucard had but minutes to gather whatever he could for himself and Zalith.

"Ezvin!" he yelled as he entered through the back door, heading for his office.

The butler came running and walked at Alucard's side as he made his way into his office.

"Ve've been compromised," the vampire explained, heading to his snake's tank. "You know vhat you 'ave to do," he said, taking his snake out of its home and placing it into a cardboard box which he then closed and handed to Edwin. "Take Dante. Vind and take Sabazios, and vhatever you can gazzer vrom Zaliv's office in zhe next vive minutes. Zhen, go to Uzlia, and vait vor us zhere. Ve might be a vhile, zhough. Go to Crowell vhen you get zhere and share zhe news."

"Of course, sir," Edwin replied, nodding. "What of Peaches?"

Alucard frowned as he looked around his office for his hairless cat. She was nowhere to be seen, and he suspected that she must be upstairs. "I'll take 'er." He didn't want to be without his cat, and although Zalith might disagree with his decision to bring her, he had already decided it would happen. "Go," he instructed.

Edwin nodded and hurried out of Alucard's office with the box.

The vampire rushed up his office stairs to his study. Peaches was sitting on his desk, staring curiously at him. He had no time to tell her what was going on and scooped her up in his arms as he walked past. He left his study and made his way into his and Zalith's bedroom. He only had a few minutes to grab whatever he could; he wouldn't lug anything with him, so he'd just send it to the vault where he kept his valuables.

He went into the dressing rooms and started snatching his and Zalith's clothes, dematerializing them and sending them off the vault below their new castle. Then, he glanced out of the window, seeing that Varana and Tyrus had just left her house and were waiting for him. So, he snatched his fur-collared cape from the cupboard beside the door and ran through his and Zalith's house for what might be the last time. He didn't want to think about how despaired that made him feel. It was time to go.

With his kitten in his arms, Alucard emerged back into the gardens. Tyrus was holding three rather large suitcases and looked a little embarrassed about it, and Varana scowled at Alucard as he made his way over.

"Are you veady?" the vampire asked hastily.

"What am I supposed to do with my girls?" Varana questioned.

By girls, Alucard assumed she meant her maids. "Zhey'll go to Uzlia vith Ezvin."

She kept her scowl. "Well did you even ask if they'd like to go before you get some man to drag them halfway across the globe?!"

"Zhey vere invormed of zhis protocol vhen zhey vere 'ired," he snarled.

"By *who*?" she questioned. "I certainly didn't tell them."

"One of my men runs through the contracts with the new hires," Tyrus said.

Varana looked at him, scowled, and crossed her arms. "Hmph."

"Let's go," Alucard grumbled, moving closer to them, preparing to dematerialize.

"I want Santana," Varana said.

"Ve zon't 'ave time. Ezvin vill—"

"What if something happens to her while we're gone?!" she exclaimed. "Where's *your* horse?!"

"Zaliv 'as 'er and Dimitri," he said.

"So, you're allowed to take your horse, but I can't take mine?!"

"Mine vas alveady zhere!" he snapped, losing his patience.

"Okay, so why can't we just take mine there, too?!"

Alucard gritted his teeth; she was the most irritating, insufferable woman he'd *ever* met. He didn't want to argue, and he didn't want to waste any more time, so he dematerialized, raced over the house and to the stables, snatched the reins of Varana's horse, and dematerialized it. Then, he swiftly made his way back to where she and Tyrus were waiting, rematerializing with her horse.

"See, that wasn't so difficult," she sneered.

"'Old 'is fucking 'and," he growled, nodding at Tyrus.

Varana scowled but did as she was told.

"And take 'er," he said, reluctantly handing his kitten to her.

Then, in his right hand, he snatched Tyrus' wrist as the man clung to Varana's suitcases. He placed his left hand on the horse's neck and dematerialized everything and everyone. He wouldn't waste another moment. He wanted to get back to Zalith.

| Zalith |

Roughly a mile from the glade, Zalith leaned against a tree in the cover of an old ruin. His people were all around him, mumbling, crying, arguing, and panicking—nobody knew why their home was gone. Zalith wanted to know *how* Lilith knew where he was, and he'd already searched the minds of everyone here to see if any of them had anything to do with it, but nobody was guilty. Nobody knew anything. And his anger *seethed.*

Why did this have to happen? Why *now*? His people were *finally* settling down, everything was finally okay…and now it wasn't. Lilith had somehow found out where his people were, and Zalith wasn't sure if she knew where his and Alucard's home was. Could it have just been a coincidence that he and Alucard so happened to be at the compound when Lilith decided to send her pawns to attack? He gritted his teeth, glaring into the darkness, waiting for Alucard to come back to him. He had no idea, and he *hated* not knowing what was going on.

But…Alucard—he'd been right. He'd expressed his fear more than once to him—his fear of their home becoming lost to them, his fear that one day they'd be found. Zalith knew he should have taken him a whole lot more seriously back then; he took *everything* Alucard said seriously, but he hadn't chosen to look into this particular concern, and now, here they were. Lilith had attacked, she knew they were in Nefastus, and his life on the run was starting all over again.

This wasn't the first time Alucard mentioned that sort of feeling, though, a feeling that something was coming. It might have been different from the dreams he'd explained—dreams he said came true. But maybe it *was* the same; perhaps Zalith should take everything he said as if it were like those dreams. They'd both speculated that Alucard might have some kind of ability to see ahead of time—a sort of premonition-like sense—and it would make sense since he was the son of a Numen, and the Numen often spoke of prophecy.

He wasn't going to debate Alucard's feelings of impending danger anymore. He was going to treat all of his worries as if they would come true.

"How are you doing?" Idina asked in concern, having made her way over.

Zalith sighed deeply, keeping his eyes on the darkness. "I don't know," he answered.

"Hopefully they'll get here soon. I'm sure everything's okay," she said.

The demon nodded, but his worry about Alucard and Varana didn't fade.

Idina stared at him for a few moments but clearly understood that he wasn't interested in talking. So she turned around and returned to Colt and Elena.

Zalith waited, glaring into the dark. There were so many things on his mind; he didn't know what to focus on. However, he kept a very strong focus on his imprint, glancing down at his ring, making sure that Alucard was okay, and from what Zalith could tell, he wasn't too far away.

His people kept asking each other for answers. He knew that they were all devastated; they had finally been given a safe place to live, and it was taken from them, and Zalith didn't have the words to describe his fury. But he kept his anger hidden as well as he could. He couldn't afford to act upon it right now. He had to wait for Alucard, and then they had to leave.

The moment Alucard's vermillion shadow came into view, Zalith felt his dread fade just enough to allow him to stand up straight and lose his scowl. The smoke hit the ground a few feet from him, and when it faded, it revealed Alucard, Varana, Tyrus, and Varana's horse, which Tyrus took to join the other horses. Alucard immediately rushed to Zalith, and the demon threw his arms around him, hugging him tightly.

"Are you okay?" Zalith asked quietly, squeezing him a little tighter.

"I'm vine," Alucard confirmed.

Zalith moved his hands to his shoulders, kissed him, and frowned worriedly.

"Are you?" Alucard asked.

"I'm okay. I was just worried about you two," the demon said sadly. Then, he made his way past Alucard and closer to Varana, and he hugged her, too.

"What's happening?" she asked. "Are we running again?"

"We still have things to figure out," he said, looking down at her.

Varana sighed sadly and handed Alucard his kitten before she joining Idina.

As she left, Zalith frowned in dismay and moved his arms back around his vampire. Everything felt like it was falling apart again. For a moment, he just wanted to hold Alucard; he wanted to go home to their bed, but they couldn't go back there anymore. It wasn't safe, and it might never be until the Numen had been eradicated. However, he didn't have time to stand there and mourn. They had to get moving before Lilith's people caught up with them.

But first, he asked, "What about your vampires? Have you contacted them and told them to evacuate?"

Alucard sighed heavily. "I can't visk sending an owl; zhe insects zhat got avay could kill zhe ving. Can I use an izuret?"

"Of course," Zalith said with a nod and summoned one of the small creatures.

"Go to Crowell in Vedvood Manor. Tell 'im zhat ve're under attack, and 'e needs to evacuate zhe vampires," Alucard told the izuret.

With a nod, the izuret disappeared, heading off to do as it was told.

"We have to move," Zalith then murmured, staring into Alucard's eyes.

Alucard nodded.

"We're moving," Zalith called to his people.

They all swiftly climbed to their feet, ready to leave. And then, without falter, Zalith took hold of Alucard's hand and started leading the way through the forest.

What would they do next? He wasn't the only one wondering that, was he? He looked at Alucard as the vampire looked at him with a look of distress on his pale face. "We're going to have to keep moving…for a few weeks at least. We need to make sure Lilith's people aren't on our trail anymore. We'll head for the next rendezvous point."

Alucard frowned. "Avter ve're sure ve've lost zhem, ve can 'ead vor Uzlia—zhe castle, vight? Is safe zhere."

"I don't want to go there," Zalith denied sadly.

"Vhy?"

"Because I don't want to lose that, too," he said sullenly. "Especially with all of these people depending on me."

Still frowning, Alucard looked down at the ground as they continued through the dark. "Zhen vhere vill ve go? Is not safe back 'ome…ve can't stay in Nevastus at all, and Dor-Sanguis is gone."

Zalith thought to himself…but he didn't know. Where *could* they go? He shook his head, dragging his free hand over his face. "I don't know," he admitted, looking at Alucard. "But we have to focus on moving right now. I'll think of something."

Alucard nodded in response.

The demon tried his best to come up with something. But he was so overwhelmed with anger and grief that he couldn't think. He didn't know what to do. Like Eltaria, Nefastus was lost, and all he could do was run and try to keep everyone alive.

But where would they go this time?

Chapter Thirty-Four

The Ranch

| Alucard |

Alucard sat with his kitten in his lap on a small broken wall in the middle of an abandoned ranch. A few hours had passed, they'd walked a few miles, and everyone needed rest. The ranch was one of the locations they'd set up months ago in case something like this happened, and they'd be spending the night here before setting out tomorrow for the next safe location. All of Zalith's people were huddled up in small groups, either sitting in total, despair-filled silence or chatting despondently with one another.

Did Zalith have a plan yet? The castle in Uzlia was the safest place Alucard knew, and he understood how Zalith felt—*he* didn't want to lose it either—but he'd fortified the island that their castle stood on so well that it would never be found; it was in the middle of the ocean, after all, and no one had any idea that it was there. But he wasn't going to try and convince Zalith right now.

It was all catching up to him. Lilith's people had attacked; she had to know that he and Zalith were living in Nefastus, and because he killed her scion, he was certain that she'd soon send reinforcements to search the country. They *had* to run; they'd have to keep moving, hiding, and avoiding Lilith's people until Zalith felt it was safe enough to leave Nefastus to wherever they'd go next.

Alucard didn't want to leave. Nefastus had become his home—*his* and Zalith's home. He and Zalith had built so much here. Were they just…leaving it all behind?

He scowled in confliction, glaring into the forest. He had so many questions. How did Lilith find out they were in Nefastus? Did Damien know? Did Lucifer know? Alucard knew this wasn't the end of it, but…what would happen next? He and Zalith weren't yet ready to face any of the Numen, and running was the only option.

When *would* they be ready? He *did* have Lilith's Obcasus, but he nor Zalith were sure whether she was working alone or not. If she turned up with Damien, Alucard wouldn't stand a chance, Zalith most certainly wouldn't, and their people would perish. As much as Alucard wanted to fight for the place he'd come to call his home, he knew it wasn't possible. Just as he had with Dor-Sanguis, he'd have to leave Nefastus behind, and as much as that pained him… at least he still had Zalith. Without him, Alucard knew all of this would be a whole lot more of a struggle—he didn't even want to think about the possibility of losing him or not having him right now. Zalith was there with him, which was all that mattered.

Alucard observed silently as Zalith moved among his people, checking on each one with quiet reassurance. The weight of devastation hung thick in the night air, palpable even to him. Faces were etched with sorrow, eyes hollowed by despair. After years of running, of hoping for peace, Zalith and his people had once again lost the place they had hoped to call home. Alucard could sense the calm façade Zalith tried to maintain for their sake, but beneath it, the demon's torment was unmistakable. He could see the flickers of anger in his eyes, the bitter reminder of a past Zalith loathed—a past that had now resurfaced to become his present once more.

The vampire didn't know what to say to him right now. He looked down at his kitten and sighed despondently. It wasn't just Zalith who would now be living his life on the run once again; *Alucard* would be living that life, too. A life he knew too well—one he'd also thought was behind him. But it was happening again; he was running and hiding, and the longer he spent thinking about that, the less safe he began to feel. His and Zalith's home had given him security—it had made him feel safe and content and gave him hope of a life free of the Numen and their pursuit. But he couldn't go back there, and he was beginning to feel the weight of its loss.

His scowl thickened with distress. All he wanted to do was go home with Zalith; he wanted to crawl into their bed and lay there for hours with his demon, but… he couldn't. He'd be spending his days moving from place to place just as he had to do so many years ago, and he'd have to be constantly looking over his shoulder for any sign of danger. He didn't want to live that life again; he'd become so used to living a life of freedom, a life where he didn't have to sleep with one eye open, a life where he actually *got* to sleep. But all of that was over, wasn't it? The calm, serenity-filled life he'd come to love so deeply… it was no more.

He took his eyes off his kitten and looked over at the demon again. He still had Zalith, and *he* made him feel safe; Zalith made him feel content and loved, and *he* was home to Alucard. But nothing was really going to be the same, was it? Danger could be anywhere, the enemy could be anywhere, and he and Zalith were going to have to keep their guard up *all* the time. They wouldn't have time to have fun or mess around; they were going to be stressed and aggravated… and it felt like their peaceful, playful little life was over.

The vampire scowled again. They needed to find out how Lilith found them; they still had no idea whether any of the Numen were working together, and now more than ever, they needed to know. Luckily, Lilith hadn't shown up herself—if she had, getting away would have been a whole lot more complicated. And no one was killed. People may have been hurt, but they hadn't lost anyone. Greymore, Freja, and Zalith managed to get everyone away, and they also managed to lose their enemies. Alucard couldn't detect anyone for miles, and he was sure that if Zalith could, he wouldn't have stopped here. He just hoped that Crowell was able to get his vampires to safety.

Alucard turned his attention to Freja, who was making her way over to him, having just left Danford with her sisters. The vampire sighed quietly, and when she reached him, he looked up at her.

"Does anybody know what happened?" she asked with a hint of distress in her voice. "How they just…knew where we were?"

"No," he grumbled, looking back at Zalith, who was now talking to Varana, Idina, and Tyrus. "But ve'll vind out."

Freja crossed her arms and slowly sat down beside him. "Do you think they…I don't know…have a mole or something? Wasn't that the case with Adellum back in Eltaria?"

Having not told her this information himself, Alucard frowned at her.

"Oh, Greymore told me," she said. "He filled me in on a lot of what's happened—he told me about Addison—"

"None of zhat matters," Alucard mumbled. "Is over. No, zhere's no vay Liliv could've planted a spy among us; ve 'ave people vatching everyone alvays. Ve also 'ave people vatching all of our land, and zhey vould 'ave seen if anyvone suspicious vas lingering avound, so zhere's no vay vone of Liliv's people could 'ave vound out vhere ve vere," he explained quietly. "Zaliv and I are also undetectable, and so is Varana."

She nodded slowly but didn't say anything; she probably didn't know what to say. Instead, she looked down at her lap and sighed quietly. "Idina's told everyone we're heading out for the next rendezvous point tomorrow—"

"At dawn," Alucard confirmed. "And ve'll keep moving until ve're convident zhat Liliv and 'er people 'ave no idea vhere ve are. Avter zhat…Zaliv and I still 'ave to discuss vhere ve'll be going vonce ve veel is safe to leave Nevastus."

"How long are we going to be moving for? Idina said a couple of weeks, but—"

"A couple of veeks," Alucard said. "Ve 'ave to be sure is safe."

Freja nodded. "I understand. Okay, I'll leave you to it," she said as she stood up.

When Freja walked off, Alucard set his eyes on Zalith, who was already heading over. The moment the demon reached him, he took hold of his hand; Alucard stood up, holding his kitten in his other arm as he followed Zalith away from the wall and his people and into the only standing building. The place was empty; hay was scattered over the wooden floors, the windows were just small gaps in the walls, and the door hung on by a single nailed hinge.

Once they got into the building, Alucard let his kitten down onto the ground; Zalith immediately wrapped his arms around the vampire and held him tightly, resting the side of his face against Alucard's.

"How are you feeling?" Zalith asked quietly.

Alucard frowned, holding Zalith just as tightly. His heart was ensnared by angst, and his instincts were telling him to keep running, but he needed to be there for Zalith. Despite his own anxiety, he cared more about making sure that the man he loved was okay. "I veel…overvhelmed," he admitted. "Like everyving is just vrong, and I zon't know vhat to do. I still vant to go 'ome, even zhough I know ve can't," he mumbled despondently.

Zalith squeezed Alucard. He didn't say anything, and Alucard felt like he knew exactly what the demon was thinking.

"Are you blaming yourselv? Is not your vault, Zaliv. Ve knew zhis vould 'appen in vone vay or anozzer; ve knew vould 'appen zhe moment ve decided zhat ve vere going to kill zhe Numen. If anyving, is *our* vault vor getting too comvortable."

He shook his head and mumbled, "I could have done more."

"Vhat more could ve 'ave done?" he asked sadly. "Ve kept ourselves 'idden, ve 'id in zhe vone place *no vone* vould look vor us. Ve 'ad all zhe people possible looking vor our enemies, looking vor answers, and keeping an eye on everyving and everyvone zhat matters. Zhere vas only so much ve could do vith vhat ve 'ad—and vhat matters vight now is zhat everyvone got avay and zhat ve 'ave a plan in place to make sure everyvone vemains safe," he insisted, trying to convince him.

"I let everyone down," he uttered, his voice a little strained. "This is…it's *all* my fault *again*."

The vampire shook his head and leaned back a little so that he could see Zalith's face. It looked like he was trying to hold back tears, and seeing Zalith so shaken and despondent made his heart hurt.

"I just want you to be safe," the demon lamented.

Alucard was trying his best to comfort him; he could only guess how distraught Zalith felt, and he knew that the demon needed him, just as he needed Zalith. "I'm alvays safe as long as I'm vith you."

Zalith frowned in distress as he nodded in response. "I can't lose you," he uttered through his pained scowl. "What if I can't protect you? I've lost everyone I love, and I can't stop thinking about how I failed them." He pulled Alucard closer and buried his face in his shirt.

The vampire didn't know what else to say. Maybe they just…needed to grieve. They'd lost a lot tonight—everyone had—and there wasn't any making it better, was there? He rested his head on Zalith's shoulder, closing his eyes. "I love you," he mumbled, his voice muffled against the demon's shirt.

"I love you too, baby," Zalith murmured. He then fell silent for a few moments before sighing sadly. "We need to start gaining numbers as soon as we can... because this is only going to keep happening."

Alucard nodded in agreement. One advantage the Numen had over them was their numbers. The Numen had cults of people who followed and worked for them, and he and Zalith... well, they only had a few hundred people between them. A lot of Alucard's vampires had already been killed since their hunt for information, and many had lost their lives whilst hunting and killing the Numen's cultists. They *did* need more numbers, and Alucard knew that he and Zalith would come up with ways to get what they needed. But for now, it was late, and he thought they ought to rest.

"I know," he replied. "But ve can vigure out tomorrow. Is late; ve should just vest vor now."

Zalith sighed again but nodded. "Okay."

Alucard then stepped back and looked around. "Vhere... do ve sleep?"

Zalith frowned despondently as he glanced around the abandoned shack. He shrugged and watched Alucard's kitten pounce onto a stack of straw as he said, "On the grass, I suppose."

Alucard took hold of his hand and sighed quietly. "Ve'll be okay," he assured him. "Is only vor a little vhile, vight? Zhen... ve'll vind somevhere."

"Yeah," he said with a quiet sigh, but it didn't sound like he believed it.

Alucard led the way outside as his kitten followed. Everyone seemed to have made themselves as comfortable as they could, using what supplies were stored in the ranch to make beds on the ground.

The vampire took Zalith over to the wall that he'd been sitting on and let go of the demon's hand as he took off his cape. He laid it on the grass, gripped Zalith's hand again, and sat down, pulling Zalith with him. He thought his cape might be a little more comfortable to sleep on than the grass, and as he laid back, resting his head on its furred collar, Zalith did the same.

As he lay beside Alucard, Zalith rested his head on the vampire's chest. "Thank you," he said, trying to make himself comfortable.

Alucard moved his arm around Zalith and held him as he exhaled deeply. Tomorrow was going to be exhausting; he and Zalith needed to work out what they were going to do, but he wouldn't overthink it now. He needed to sleep.

| Varana |

Varana—who had been watching Zalith and Alucard the moment they'd come out of the shack—sighed sadly and buried her face in Tyrus' shirt. She sat with him under a tree, crying quietly as Tyrus rubbed her back. She had no words to explain how she felt. She didn't want to do this again—to move from place to place, house to house, running away from the enemy.

This was Zalith's fault—*all* of it was—and he'd ruined her life. She understood that he was in love with Alucard… and she wanted him to be happy even though it aggravated her, but he shouldn't have decided to challenge the Numen. He shouldn't have declared war on them because *exactly* this was going to happen. Of course they were going to be chased from their home, a home they hadn't even had that long. And now, because of Zalith, it was all ruined, and they were back to where they had been before they left Eltaria.

Not only was she now homeless, but her sister was also going to think that she'd run away from her to try and escape her threat. *That* was only going to make things worse, and she had no idea what to do. She didn't want her sister to turn up and kill everyone or get killed herself…and Varana felt so lost, confused, and isolated. She couldn't talk to *anyone* about it, not even Tyrus.

She scowled a little; she was tired of Tyrus; she didn't want him touching her anymore, so she sat up and pulled away from him.

"What's wrong?" he asked.

"Nothing," she muttered sadly, staring down at the grass.

"It can't be nothing…you've been crying this whole time," he said sympathetically.

"I'm tortured!" she exclaimed irritably. "Leave me alone."

Wide-eyed and confused, Tyrus backed off a little "Okay…."

But Varana didn't want to be left alone. Of course, Tyrus didn't know that because he was a man and men were stupid…. That wasn't true. He wasn't stupid; he just didn't know her well enough to know what she wanted.

With a hushed sigh, Varana moved back over to him and rested her head on his shoulder. There wasn't much that she could do right now, was there? She couldn't tell anyone; she knew her sister wouldn't reconsider…and she was just…trapped. No one could help her, and she would lose either way. If her sister came for her, she would lose her and her family…or she'd lose Zalith and the people who slept in the ranch. She didn't know what she wanted. Why *couldn't* she just have both?

She closed her eyes and tried to silence her thoughts. She might as well sleep, and if they didn't get to sleep somewhere with a roof tomorrow…she was going to make sure that *everyone* knew just how furious she was.

Chapter Thirty-Five

Archway

| **Alucard, *Thursday, Cordus 2nd, 960(TG)—Nefastus*** |

An eerie voice pulled Alucard from the silence of his sleep. It called his name, and it was so familiar—so dreadfully familiar. He opened his eyes to find himself standing in endless darkness, a place he was sure he'd been to before. And he woke with that same feeling of desperation; he frantically searched the black with his eyes... like he was looking for something. But what?

This time, he started to move forward, his footsteps rippling through the inch-deep water beneath him. He wasn't sure where he was going or what he was looking for—what even was there to look for? As far as his eyes could see, there was nothing but gloom.

The vampire stopped and took a moment to collect his thoughts. This place... he'd been here before—in his dreams, and in a fit of rage.... Was this his mind? His subconscious, maybe? He wasn't sure, but he felt that in some way this place was a part of him—like it was connected to him. If that were the case, though, why did he feel so... confused?

He stared ahead, focusing on the feeling of loss... of emptiness, and the desperation that he experienced; it felt like he'd lost something, and he kept returning here to find it. But what had he lost that he couldn't find? All that came to mind was his home, but... this feeling felt deeper than simply having something taken from him. It felt as though what had been lost was gone forever, erased, torn away... extracted like threads from a sewn quilt.

What had been taken, though? Memories?

The moment that thought came to mind, the darkness ahead of him began to brighten. Three tall black-stone archways formed beside one another around the outsides of a magic circle cutting into the thin blanket of water; the circle hummed and sparked, and as the archways rose from below, Alucard watched curiously. He didn't sense danger; he just felt... perturbed. What was he looking at?

Alucard made his way forward once the archways had formed in their entirety, standing a few meters off the ground, and inside them, he saw... light. He still had no idea what he was looking at, and once he reached them, he stopped in front of the middle one. He waited, staring into the white; something started to form within—someone, maybe. He waited a few more moments until it became clearer, revealing the inside of what looked like a tent. Alucard could hear the mumbles of people outside and the pouring of rain as it pitter-pattered against the fabric. And lying on a bed made up of quilts and furs was Zalith, who gripped onto Alucard's cape tightly, using it to keep warm.

The demon didn't look well. He was as pale as ice—paler, even—and an irritated, agonized expression clung to his face. He was breathing frantically, almost as if he was trapped in a dream that he couldn't escape. Alucard knew that feeling too well. But as far as he was aware, Zalith didn't experience such nightmares... so what was wrong with him? Why was he so pale and in so much pain? Why was he shivering?

With his concern intensifying, Alucard went to step forward, but the sound of a battle stopped him in his tracks. He stepped back and stared into the left archway; inside, he saw the field where he, Zalith, and the demon's people had chosen to spend the night. He flinched when fire hit the ground, and his eyes widened in trepidation as ethos-charged attacks collided with the running, panicking people. Zalith was nowhere to be seen, and neither were Varana or Tyrus or anyone who might defend them.

What the hell was he seeing?

He edged nearer; he wasn't sure whether this was a dream or an illusion or something else... but whatever it was, he knew that he had to help Zalith's people.

But before he could step into the left archway, a rumbling voice echoed from the right one. He froze up; fear spiralled through him as the voice called him by his demon name—the same voice he heard the moment he'd woken in this strange place. But... it couldn't be, could it? How had he found him?

Alucard scowled, trying to banish his fear as he looked over his shoulder at the last archway, the light within having faded to darkness. He watched anxiously as a pair of hellish, fiery eyes appeared inside. And the archway... it began to crack, crumble, and break. Claws emerged, breaking out through the murk to grip the frame. The creature's voice echoed, snarled, and laughed, and a wicked, smiling row of teeth cut through the black as the eyes moved closer—as who they belonged to moved closer. Alucard's instincts told him to run—to leave. He couldn't stay here—he wouldn't stay here.

Without hesitation, he leapt into the archway leading to the ranch and landed on the grass. He tumbled across it until he came to an abrupt halt, gripping the ground below to slow himself. Zalith's people ran around him, panicked, trying to avoid the rain of fire falling from the sky.

Alucard stood up and frantically searched for Zalith. Demons of red and black manipulated flames in every direction, and from the trees, charging creatures began to erupt. The vampire set his eyes on Greymore and Freja as they commanded what remained of their united pack to fight off the enemy. Zalith was there fighting, too, as was Varana, but the creatures and demons kept flowing into the glade.

The voice called again, sharper this time, pulling Alucard's attention as he spun to face the archway leading back into the murk. His eyes locked onto the hulking beast as it dragged itself from the shadows. Its claws gripped the frame with an unnatural force, pulling its massive form into the open. For a fleeting moment, Alucard's heart quickened, fear surging through him. Despite his best efforts, he couldn't summon the composure he normally commanded. The battle raging around him seemed insignificant now, dwarfed by the monstrosity snarling and creeping ever closer. Paralyzed with fear, he stood frozen, caught in the grip of terror as the creature advanced.

What did all of this mean? He knew that he was asleep... this wasn't the real world, and it didn't feel like a nightmare, either. So what was it? What were the archways he saw? Why had he never seen this before when he'd come to the darkness that creature was dragging itself out of? He had no time to try and work it out.

He turned around and raced towards Zalith, who was struggling against a group of demons. Reality or not, Alucard didn't want to see Zalith get hurt, and he knew... he knew that he needed help fighting the monster crawling into the light of the battle. But not even Zalith would be able to help him against his father.

| Zalith |

Zalith woke suddenly, his heart racing, his paranoia forcing a feeling of desperation on him as he opened his eyes. He heard Alucard mumble in what sounded like panic, and as he felt the vampire fidgeting beside him, he sat up to see that he was still asleep and most likely suffering another of his horrific nightmares.

His first thought was to wake Alucard up; he didn't want to leave him to suffer alone, especially not now. "Alucard?" he asked quietly as he placed his hand on the vampire's shoulder and turned him so that he was lying on his back. He stared at Alucard's distressed face and gently shook his shoulder as he worriedly exclaimed, "Hey?"

But Alucard still didn't wake up.

The demon shook his shoulder one last time, but still nothing, so he prepared to wake him up the only way he felt would work: within the dream itself. He placed his hand on the side of Alucard's face and closed his eyes—

However, the moment Zalith went to enter the vampire's mind, Alucard suddenly shot up so fast that Zalith flinched in startlement. As Alucard breathed frantically, looking around just as so, Zalith placed his hands on his shoulders.

"Are you okay?" Zalith asked; his concern was so intense that he couldn't banish the panicked look from his face.

Alucard stared vacantly while he breathed frantically.

Zalith waited and rubbed the vampire's shoulders—

But Alucard then sharply turned his head and gawped at him. "Ve 'ave to go."

Zalith's concerned frown thickened. "Why? What's wrong?"

"Zhey're coming," he insisted as he gripped Zalith's wrist. "Is like last night but vorse—zhe veeling zhat someving's coming." He pulled Zalith up with him as he stood up. "Ve 'ave to move."

"Who's coming?" the demon asked as Alucard picked up his cape and put it on.

"Someving!" he insisted desperately. "Liliv, Luciver, I zon't know! But ve can't stay 'ere anymore."

Zalith didn't need convincing. He'd already decided that he'd never second-guess Alucard's premonition-like feelings again. He swiftly nodded and started calling all of his people to wake up and get ready to move, and he watched as Greymore immediately got up and began waking his wolves with Freja. Tyrus woke Varana, and Idina scooped up Colt, and as soon as they were on their feet, everyone rushed over to Zalith and Alucard.

The demon called their horses over, and as the beasts came running, Greymore reached the pair.

"What's going on?" he asked, looking at Zalith and Alucard as they both mounted their horses.

"Ve 'ave to leave," Alucard said sternly.

Greymore clearly understood that there wasn't time to question. He nodded and hurried off to continue rounding up his pack.

Once everyone had grouped up behind them, Zalith and Alucard led the way towards the ranch exit and into the forest.

Zalith stared at Alucard as they moved through the trees. He watched the angst on the vampire's face slowly lift, but he still looked anxious, and Zalith's heart raced while he battled with his own paranoia. What had Alucard seen? What did he know was coming? And had they moved in time to get away from it?

"What's going on?" Varana abruptly asked as she rode beside Zalith.

"Alucard?" the demon asked.

The vampire frowned unsurely and glanced at Zalith. "I 'ad…a veeling," he said slowly. "Zhe same as last night."

Varana frowned. "What is *that* supposed to mean?"

Alucard rolled his eyes. "I velt like someving vas going to 'appen last night, and zhen Liliv's people turned up. I velt zhe same ving vhen I voke up, and I zidn't vant to stick avound and see if someving veally vas coming."

"Oh…" Varana said. "My Daddy can do that," she boasted.

She hadn't even been awake five minutes and Zalith could see that she was already angering Alucard. But the vampire didn't say anything. He remained silent and rode beside Zalith as they moved further away from the ranch.

The vampire glanced at Zalith again. "You…vemember vhen I told you zhat I 'ad dreams as a child zhat later came true, vight?"

"Yeah," he answered quietly.

"Vhat if…vhat if I *can* compre'end death or situations zhat involve death? If Luciver can do zhat…zhen maybe zhe ability is 'ereditary," he suggested. But then he shifted his sights to Varana. "'E can…veel zhat vings are going to 'appen, and zhen zhey 'appen, no?" he asked her.

"Yeah," she said, smiling proudly. "Like one time when Ephriel stuck her big, ugly nose into the Diabolus' business and tried to wipe them all out, but he had a premonition beforehand and could stop it from happening at just the right time," she explained.

Alucard went pale. He looked confused and upset, almost as if Varana's confirmation had made him realize something. But what?

"Zaliv?" Alucard then asked.

Zalith, who had admittedly zoned out a little, frowned when he heard Alucard say his name. He looked at his vampire and then glanced back at Varana. "Is it safe to assume that Lucifer will be able to tell every time we're making moves against his people?"

"I don't know," she said with a defensive tone in her voice.

Sure that she didn't want to reveal her father's secrets—either that or she didn't actually know—Zalith rolled his eyes and sighed.

"'E's never been able to tell vhen I vas making moves against zhe Diabolus," Alucard said. "And I suspect—because 'e zoesn't know vhere I am—zhat 'e can't see vings zhat 'ave me involved," he said confidently.

Nodding, Zalith stared ahead again. "Good," he said, relieved to know that they still had the upper hand against one of the Numen. But the question still remained: how had Lilith known where they were last night? He found himself wondering if perhaps they could harness Alucard's ability to comprehend incoming danger now that it had pretty much been confirmed that he had the ability.

However, his train of thought was quickly interrupted by the aching, overwhelming pain in his shoulder. Now that the adrenaline of rushing away from the ranch had waned, he felt increasing soreness in the right side of his neck. He frowned irritably and dragged his hand over his shoulder and to his neck; the moment he felt a small but noticeable swollen bump on his neck, his irritancy faded into confoundment—and shock, too. He *never* suffered from anything of the sort; he remembered he'd been bitten by a mosquito last night, but his incredibly responsive healing abilities should have stopped any form of irritation or swelling from occurring…but it was swollen, painful, and concerning.

He scowled and lowered his hand from his neck. Now wasn't the time to be fretting over a swollen wound. When they stopped later, he'd make sure to examine it if it was still there.

Clearly having noticed Zalith's perturbed scowl, Alucard gazed at him. "Are you okay?"

"I'm okay," he assured him.

Alucard looked worried but nodded in response.

In the silence, dismay started ensnaring Zalith. He still felt like this was all his fault; he should have had a better plan, one that didn't involve running *again*. But he'd let himself get too comfortable. He'd become far too confident that they'd never be found, and now, not only had he and Alucard been stripped of their home, but so had all the people who relied on him.

All he wanted to do was give Alucard a stable life where he didn't have to worry—a life where he didn't have to constantly look over his shoulder in fear of the Numen. But now they were running from them and knowing that running and hiding had been Alucard's life for the past hundred years made him feel distraught. He'd failed the man he loved, and he wouldn't blame Alucard if he turned around and berated him for causing this.

He tried to sigh his despair away and concentrate on getting far from the ranch. The next rendezvous point was half a day away. They had a long way to go, and Zalith hoped that they'd make it without running into danger. But he trusted Alucard to help them avoid it.

Chapter Thirty-Six

Riverbank

| Alucard |

The rhythmic crash of water broke the quiet as they neared the waterfall. It cascaded down from the towering limestone mountain, spilling into a narrow river that shimmered under the soft afternoon sunlight. Cypress and oak trees lined the riverbank, their gnarled roots twisting into the earth and casting dappled shadows across the water. The fresh, earthy scent of moss and bark mingled with the sharp tang of cigarette smoke drifting from the group; a few had lit up, their exhaled smoke curling lazily in the cold air.

Alucard and Zalith had been leading the group along the mountain's base for nearly two hours, winding through the dense groves of oak and cypress. The vampire could feel the afternoon's weight settling in, the sun hanging lower in the sky, signalling that it was time for rest. The ranch was far behind them, as were any hostiles that might have been in pursuit. For now, the steady rush of the waterfall and the tranquil shade of the trees offered a brief respite from the journey's strain.

As they came closer to the river, the vampire looked at Zalith. "Ve should probably stop 'ere," he said, glancing back at the following crowd, seeing that most of them looked exhausted. The liveliest of them all was Colt, who was dragging a stick along the limestone cliff wall, holding tightly onto his stuffed dolphin as Idina followed wearily beside him.

Zalith looked back at his people, nodded, and then stared ahead at the river. "Okay," he said. He made his horse slow, and as Alucard slowed, too, the demon called, "We're stopping here." His horse stopped a few feet from the river.

Relieved sighs came from the angst-ridden group.

When Alucard dismounted his horse, he took a moment to enjoy standing on his own feet again, letting his kitten down to run over to the river, which she immediately started to drink from.

Zalith, however, hadn't made his way over to Alucard as he expected. Instead, the demon walked a few feet away from everyone else, but before he disappeared behind a nearby tree, he made sure he caught Alucard's attention, urging him to follow. Unsure of why Zalith seemed to be acting so… discreetly, Alucard frowned in confoundment and slowly walked over, making sure that no one saw where he was headed—whatever Zalith wanted him for, he was confident that he didn't want anyone else following.

He went behind the cover of a few trees with him. He assumed that Zalith brought him there so that they'd get some time alone, so once they stopped walking, he moved closer and guided his hand over Zalith's shoulder, convinced that the demon wanted to kiss him.

Zalith *did* kiss his lips a few times, but then he used his right hand to pull away his shirt's collar from his neck. "Can you…look at the back of my neck for me?" he asked, and he looked concerned.

Alucard frowned, glancing at what he could see of Zalith's neck. "Vhy?"

"The mosquito that bit me last night—the bite hasn't healed," he said, turning his head.

Now he was worried. He moved around to Zalith's side so that he could check the back of the demon's neck; he was immediately able to tell where the insect had bitten him because there was a swollen, sore-looking wound. It was no bigger than an average mosquito bite, but what perturbed him were the faint, crimson vein-like marks on Zalith's skin, stretching from the wound and beneath the collar of his shirt. He gripped Zalith's collar and pulled it down a little more to see that whatever was infecting his wound was slowly spreading down his back and might eventually spread over his shoulder.

He didn't know what to make of it. "Looks…invected," he said, "but zhat's not meant to be possible."

Instead of reacting confusedly, Zalith sighed deeply, pulling his collar back into place. "Did you happen to get a look at the insects when we were killing them?"

Frowning, Alucard shook his head. "No. Do you…veel okay?" he asked as he moved his hand over Zalith's arm. "Maybe is just all zhe vunning about; maybe vill 'eal if you vest," he suggested, trying not to let his worry overwhelm him. But this wasn't meant to be possible; a demon's wounds couldn't become infected, and they healed moments after they were inflicted. Why was that bite still there, and why was it infected? Was something happening to Zalith? He hadn't seen the insects closely enough to tell whether they were different or not but considering that Lilith had most likely been behind that swarm…his worry turned into panic. "Liliv sent zhem," he said, pulling away Zalith's collar to look at his wound again. "Vhat if…zhey vere carrying someving poisonous to us—to *you*?"

The demon sighed again. "And this is the icing on the cake, I suppose," he said sarcastically.

"Vhat?" Alucard asked, letting go of the demon's collar, and Zalith pulled it back over his wound.

"It's just what we need," he muttered. "I'm being sarcastic," he said with a dry tone.

Alucard stared at him for a moment but then moved his shirt's collar once again so that he could stare at the wound, hoping to see something that he understood. But he'd never seen anything quite like it, and the fact that he didn't know what to do made him anxious. "Vhat do ve do?"

"What *can* we do?" Zalith mumbled hopelessly. "I don't want to risk searching for someone knowledgeable to look at it, either. It's too risky. Hopefully it'll just go away on its own."

"And vhat if zoesn't?"

"I don't know."

"So you're just…going to leave zhat and 'ope goes avay?" he asked, confusion smothering his face. "Ve need to vind someone to look—is impossible. Vhatever zhis is, is not someving you can just ignore, Zaliv," he insisted.

The demon shrugged, his almost hopeless, despondent look having not faded from his face. "No one here can help, and I'm more concerned with getting everyone to safety."

"Maybe not *'ere*, but zhere are people in zhe Citadel who might be able to 'elp."

"I don't want to go to the Citadel," he denied. "That's the first place they're going to be looking for us—it's too dangerous."

"Ve zon't all 'ave to go; I'll go—"

"I *especially* don't want you going there," Zalith interjected.

"But…ve 'ave to do *someving*. Vhat if zhis gets vorse?" he asked, glancing at the demon's neck. He'd not forgotten what he'd seen in his dream; he'd seen a very sick-looking Zalith suffering, and Alucard hadn't been able to see what the cause was then, but now, he was almost certain that this impossible wound had something to do with it. He didn't want to let that happen; Zalith didn't deserve that.

"Hopefully it'll be gone by tomorrow, and then we won't have to worry about it," the demon dismissed.

Alucard hesitated. He wasn't going to just sit around and hope he'd be okay; he had to do something. But Zalith was such a stubborn man—probably the *most* stubborn person he knew and had ever known. He was convinced that Zalith would continue to refuse his insistency to find someone, so he'd stop trying to persuade him. He'd not back down, though. He was going to find someone to help him, and no amount of hopelessness on Zalith's part was going to get him to stop. He understood Zalith's misery—his disappointment—and he was sure such dismaying feelings were causing him to forget that he mattered, too. But while he refused to take care of himself, Alucard was there to help him, even if he had to do it behind his back.

"Vine," he said with a sigh.

"I'll be okay," Zalith said as he guided his hand over Alucard's shoulder and to the side of his neck. He moved closer and kissed the vampire's forehead and then wrapped his arms around him, pulling him into a tight hug.

Not at all convinced, Alucard held Zalith tightly. "Are you sure?"

"I feel fine," he said, hugging him firmer. But after a few moments, he exhaled quietly and leaned back a little so that he could see Alucard's face. "We better get back."

Alucard frowned, knowing that Zalith was lying. He wasn't okay—not today, not yesterday. The distress and sadness were still painfully clear in his eyes, if not worse than before. Alucard recognized the feeling all too well, that crushing sorrow that made everything seem hopeless. He could see it gripping Zalith now, just as it had gripped him. The thought of leaving him to suffer through it alone was unbearable, especially since he knew that Zalith was blaming himself for everything that had happened. Alucard felt the urge to help, but how? What could he do?

Before Zalith could walk off, he gripped the demon's left arm and stopped him. "You're *not* okay," he said despondently, staring at his vacant expression as he turned to face the vampire. He focused, concentrating on the connection they had through their imprints. He was right—of course he was. Zalith was sinking deeper into his sadness, but he was trying to deny it—ignore it, even. And it wasn't just *that* that had Alucard feeling so distraught all of a sudden. He could *feel* the pain that Zalith's wound was causing him. It was as if the entire right side of his body was being crushed and on fire at the same time; the pain was making it hard for Zalith to control his conflicting emotions, and he was *so* exhausted. How could he ignore that?

"I'll be okay," Zalith said, trying to reassure him.

Alucard let go of Zalith's arm. He wasn't getting anywhere; what was he doing wrong? Whenever *he* didn't want to talk about how he felt, all Zalith had to do was ask him a few more times and he'd tell him, so why did it not matter how many times *he* asked? He wanted Zalith to talk to him—to tell him how he was feeling. Maybe it would help him, perhaps it wouldn't, but it would at least give Alucard some more insight so that he might be able to make him feel better. It was always so hard, though. Why wouldn't Zalith speak to him? Why wouldn't he tell him why he was so distressed?

The vampire shook his head and moved closer to Zalith. "I know zhat you're sad, and I know zhat you're blaming yourselv vor all of zhis. Zhere veally vasn't anyving else you could 'ave done. You got everyvone avay, Zaliv—is zhat not enough?"

"I shouldn't have had to get everyone away in the first place," he said, sadness still lingering in his voice.

"Zhere vas no vay vor us to know zhat Liliv vas coming; ve 'ad so many people out zhere looking vor 'er, but she managed to evade zhem all," he insisted.

"If I were more vigilant, they wouldn't have found us. And we still don't know *how* they found us," Zalith lamented.

Alucard shook his head. "Ve'll get answers soon. Vhat matters vight now is zhat everyvone is safe. You need to stop being so 'ard on yourselv, you did everyving you could," he said, still trying his best to convince Zalith that this wasn't his fault.

But then Zalith did what he always did when he wanted to stop talking about something. He nodded and looked away.

"I zon't know vhat else to say," Alucard mumbled. "No vone vinks zhis vas your vault, and no vone blames you. So vhy do you blame yourselv?"

"That's not true," he said sadly. "I know that some of them blame me." But then he sighed dismissively. "I'm sorry," he said quietly. "You shouldn't have to do this."

"Do vhat?" Alucard asked, frowning.

"Feel like you have to reassure me," Zalith said, setting his eyes on the vampire's confused face. "I don't like that I'm like this, but I am, and I don't want to put this all on you and cause you stress," he explained.

"I zon't veel like I 'ave to do anyving—I *vant* to 'elp you. I 'ate to see you upset and suffering, and I vant to do vhatever I can to 'elp you."

Zalith said once again, "I'm okay. You don't have to worry."

Alucard felt distressing frustration grip hold of him. It shot through him like anxiety, but he didn't feel desperate; he felt disappointed, irritated, and hopeless. He didn't know what else to say, and he feared that if he persisted, he was only going to annoy Zalith, and he didn't want to do that. Zalith didn't want his help—at least that was how it seemed. Whatever he said didn't appear to matter, and he was out of ideas. What use was he if he couldn't even comfort Zalith? If he couldn't even make him feel the slightest bit better about what happened?

He let go of Zalith's hand and exhaled quietly, taking his eyes off the demon to look over at the river. Zalith might tell him that he didn't have to worry, but that was all he did when this happened—when Zalith didn't want to talk to him. He was already panicking about the wound on the demon's neck; he didn't have the strength to persist and try to get Zalith to open up to him. It was always such a struggle, one Alucard couldn't fight through this time.

"Vine," he muttered. "I'll stop trying. Vhen you vant to talk, I'll be 'ere."

Zalith looked guilty and ashamed. "I'll fix this, Alucard."

Alucard did his best to bury his feelings. Despite his hopelessness, despite his irritancy, he'd still be there for Zalith. He moved closer, slowly pulling him into a hug. "Ve vill *both* vix zhis," he mumbled.

Hugging him tightly, Zalith kissed Alucard's forehead. And with that, their conversation seemed to end.

After a few moments, Alucard pulled free from Zalith's embrace and sighed. "Ve should 'ead back now. Zhey're probably vondering vhere ve are."

But Zalith kept his despaired frown and pulled him back towards him. He moved his hand to the side of Alucard's face and then started to kiss him. And each caress of the demon's lips made Alucard feel a little better.

Eventually, though, Zalith stopped and rested his forehead against Alucard's. "I love you," he breathed, closing his eyes.

"I love you too," Alucard mumbled, pulling Zalith closer.

But then Greymore cleared his throat loudly, and when Alucard and Zalith looked at him, he tapped the tree that he was standing beside with his knuckles. "Sorry. Is it all right if me and some of my guys head out and go hunting real quick? People are hungry."

Zalith adorned an irritated look. "Fine. You have ten minutes."

"No problem," Greymore said with a nod. "Thanks," he said before wandering back off to where the rest of Zalith's people were waiting.

Once Greymore left, Alucard huffed and took hold of Zalith's hand. He then turned around and led the way back to the river, where the demon's people were resting. He immediately searched the riverbank for his kitten, but he couldn't see her, and panic quickly enthralled him. However, before he could freak out, he set his eyes on Varana, who was sitting on a fallen tree trunk with his kitten in her lap, petting her furless body as she purred quietly.

What was that *woman* doing with his cat? He scowled in hostility, letting go of Zalith's hand as he stormed over to her and gently snatched his kitten from her lap. He held it possessively against his chest as Varana gasped and glared up at him. "Zon't touch my cat," he snarled.

"What the *hell* is your problem?!" she exclaimed.

"*You* are my problem," he growled as Zalith stood beside him, finally catching up. But the demon didn't say or do anything; he just stood in silence.

"I didn't even do anything!" she shouted. "Grow up!"

Alucard snarled irritably, but he didn't want to argue with her anymore. He already had far too much on his mind. So, with Peaches in his arms, he scowled at Varana one more time and then turned around.

"Asshole," Varana growled quietly.

Ignoring her, Alucard left, leaving both her and Zalith as he walked off to spend a little time in solitude. Maybe *that* would help him calm down and work out what he wanted to do.

The vampire stopped by the river and huffed angrily as he slumped down on the ground and let Peaches sit in his lap. He needed to figure out what he was going to do; Zalith had a wound on his neck—an *infected* wound—and it shouldn't be possible. Alucard needed to find somebody who could look at it, somebody who could help. There wasn't anyone *here* that could help, so he'd have to get a message to Crowell. He wasn't sure if Zalith was going to get worse but considering what he'd seen in his strange dream this morning, he wasn't going to take any chances.

He concentrated, telepathically connecting with Crowell the way he could with all his vampires, but it was a power he refrained from using often; it left his mind vulnerable to others around him who might be listening, but as far as he was aware, Zalith was the only person capable of telepathy.

"*Crowell,*" he spoke into his Bloodling's mind. "*Come to me zhe moment you've gotten zhe ozzers to savety.*"

And his Bloodling obediently replied, "*Yes, My Lord.*"

Alucard let out a deep sigh, closing his mind. All he had left to do was wait for Crowell to appear, and hopefully, he'd be able to get Zalith some help.

Chapter Thirty-Seven

Strife

| Zalith |

Where Alucard had left him, Zalith sighed quietly, sitting down beside Varana. Relief struck him, and he realized how strained he'd felt standing on his feet. But he didn't care about himself right now. He was sure that Alucard was irritated and probably wanted some time alone with his thoughts, so he'd let him have it.

The demon sat there, glancing around at all of his people as they rested and spoke indistinctively amongst each other. He heard a lot of them asking each other how long they'd be on the road for this time, and some were disappointed in not only Zalith but in themselves for trusting him to give them a better life.

Zalith took his eyes off them—he already knew how they felt and how he felt. He didn't need to know more. But he was determined to make it right—to fix it. None of them deserved this again, and he didn't care what it might take. He owed them a better life—he owed *Alucard* a better life, and he would do whatever it took to give it to him. He gazed over at his vampire, fiddling with the ring on his right index finger. Alucard was thinking about him, too—probably worrying about the wound on his neck and his decision not to talk to him about his feelings. What was the point? He didn't want to think about how despaired he was, let alone talk about it. And he was certain that Alucard was upset with him.

"You need to control your boyfriend," Varana muttered irritably.

Zalith rolled his eyes. He had nothing to say to her right now.

"Hello?"

"What, Varana?" he grumbled.

"I said, you need to keep your boyfriend under control!" she exclaimed.

"I heard you."

She scowled, glaring at him for a few moments, obviously hoping that he'd say something. But he didn't want to respond. Granted, Alucard's snatching of the cat had been a little rude, but he didn't care. He wasn't surprised that Alucard had done it—it was his cat, after all, and he also knew the vampire didn't like Varana.

Varana then tutted and made herself comfortable. "Have you figured out where we're going yet?"

"No."

She sat there with an expectant look on her face, obviously waiting for a 'but'. However, Zalith had nothing to add. Varana waited a little longer but then rolled her eyes, sighed irritably, and stood up, muttering to herself as she wandered off to where Tyrus and Idina were, the word 'useless' coming from her mouth a few times.

Resting his chin in his right hand, Zalith glanced over at Alucard again. He wanted to try and work out what to do, where to go. He didn't want to go to Uzlia; he didn't want to risk losing the castle, too. But where else did he know that would be safe for him, his people, and Alucard? Nothing came to mind, and he started to feel strangely disorientated the more he tried to think. He wanted answers—how had Lilith known where they were? Why wasn't his wound yet healed? How angry was Alucard with him? What was he going to do? How long would they be on the road again?

He sighed, taking his eyes off his vampire, staring down at the ground. It wasn't often he found himself without a plan, but there he was…unable to think of anything other than following the protocol set in place months ago. But he wouldn't be stuck travelling forever—not again. He had to find *somewhere* for everyone…after all, once they had everything that they needed to actually go up against the Numen, he and Alucard would need somewhere to work from—somewhere they could command and scheme and just be safe. Where was that now that their home was gone?

As Greymore returned with his packmates, all of whom were carrying dead rabbits, Zalith pulled himself from his thoughts and sat up straight, ignoring the ache in his neck. He watched as people prepared a fire—he wasn't going to be eating with them, though. He just wanted to leave—to continue onwards until they reached the next rendezvous point. Maybe then he'd be able to think straight. But his people needed rest, and truthfully…so did he.

| Alucard |

Alucard glanced over his shoulder, watching as everyone prepared some rabbits that Greymore had caught. He wasn't hungry himself—at least not for what was on offer, but his kitten had to eat, so he scooped her up and made his way over to the fire. He stopped beside Greymore, who was cutting the rabbits into portions for everyone with his hunting knife. "Can you cut some of zhat off vor Peaches?" he asked.

Greymore glanced up at him. "Of course," he said. He then cut a few pieces of meat off the rabbit and handed them to him.

"Vank you," Alucard muttered, wandering off with his kitten, who gawped at the meat in his hand.

The vampire made his way over to where Zalith was sitting and sat beside him, letting his kitten sit in his lap as he started to feed her. He stared down at Peaches, watching as she devoured the rabbit in just moments. Of course she was hungry; she'd missed dinner last night and breakfast this morning. He frowned as he fed her the last scrap of meat; at least she was safe, though. He might have sent her off with Edwin, but... he just couldn't let her go.

As his kitten started cleaning her paws, he glanced at Zalith. He didn't know what to say—he didn't even really want to say *anything*. He still felt annoyed; it always made him feel so vexed when Zalith did this, when he shut himself off. He knew that the demon was suffering. He was upset, distraught. And Alucard wanted to help, but how could he help when Zalith wouldn't talk to him?

He looked back down at Peaches, frowned, and set his eyes on Zalith's people. Everyone was relatively silent, and that was to be expected. Zalith wasn't the only one dealing with the depression of last night's events and their current reality. Everyone had dismay lingering over their heads like storm clouds; even Alucard felt the weight of it all. They couldn't leave the cover of this forest, they had to follow protocol, and they had to abandon Nefastus. But Zalith didn't want to go to Uzlia, and that was where Alucard wanted to go. Nowhere was safer, and he understood that Zalith didn't want to risk losing the only home they had left, but nobody knew where it was—it would be *impossible* for someone to find. Maybe he just needed to convince Zalith some more.

Alucard saw Zalith in the corner of his eye; he didn't want to irritate him, but he needed to persuade him that their castle was the safest possible place that they could go to, and he wasn't going to waste it. "I still vink ve should take everyvone to zhe castle vonce ve're sure is safe to leave Nevastus."

"I don't want to lose that, too," the demon refused. "Especially before we've even had a chance to properly enjoy it."

Alucard looked away, closed his eyes, and exhaled deeply before glaring ahead at the trees. He didn't want to risk losing it either, but there was no risk. He'd spent his entire life hiding from the Numen, and he had fortified their castle in every single way possible. Not even *he* would be able to find it if he didn't possess the key to its door.

He'd applied perception filter after perception filter; he'd piled shields upon shields, barriers upon barriers. As far as this world and any other was concerned, his and Zalith's castle—and everything and everyone inside—didn't exist. And he'd told Zalith that the day he'd gifted him his own key. So why didn't he trust him when he said it would be safe?

As much as he wanted to give up and walk off to be angry by himself again, he sighed and set his sights back on Zalith. "Ve von't lose zhe castle," he said firmly. "I told you bevore, is zhe safest possible place *anyvone* could be. Noving can penetrate zhe devences I put up zhere," he insisted.

"I don't doubt you, Alucard," Zalith said quietly, "but if they figure out that we're there, it's a risk."

"But zhey von't, Zaliv—zhat's vhat I'm trying to say. Is impossible vor zhem to vind, and vonce ve're inside, zhey von't be able to detect us, even vithout zhese," he said, raising his hand as he glanced down at the ring that hid him from the Numen's detection.

Zalith sighed; it looked like he was thinking. "I just need time," he then said.

Alucard's frustration returned. He didn't want to let it get any worse, and he was sure that there was no convincing Zalith right now. So why waste any more time trying? He scowled and picked Peaches up. "Vine. Take your time."

He then left Zalith and made his way over to his horse, where he'd wait until the time to leave came—and that time wouldn't be too long. As soon as people had seen Alucard mounting his horse, they'd climbed to their feet and started getting ready to go, some of them still eating as they got ready.

Alucard wasn't opposed to getting on with their journey already, so once he was comfortable atop his horse, he looked back at everyone. "Ve're leaving," he announced, and as they heard him, everyone else got up and prepared to get going.

The vampire glanced over at Zalith, who sighed and got up. Alucard glared ahead, taking his eyes off the demon as he made his way over and mounted his own horse. He felt so mad at him right now that he just wanted to continue forward in silence.

And that was what he'd do. Once everyone was ready, he started leading the way over the flowing water and into the forest once more.

| Zalith |

As the sky became darker, Zalith scowled into the forest, following behind Alucard as he trailed the limestone mountain, which was now leading them up a hill. He knew that their next rendezvous point was just a few more minutes away, and he tried to focus on *that*, but the wound on his neck was beginning to cause him pain that he couldn't ignore anymore. He felt drained and exhausted, yet he hadn't done much today except sit on a horse. His entire body ached, and the more he tried to ignore it, the worse it became. But he didn't want to make a fuss. He was sure it would fade; he just needed to lie down and rest.

He glanced at Alucard as they began slowing down. He was convinced that the vampire was mad at him, not only for disagreeing with him but for also not opening up to him. But he wasn't going to change his mind, nor did he want to talk about how he felt—it didn't matter…at least he didn't think it did. Finding somewhere safe was far more important, as was working out what to do…but…whenever Zalith tried to focus and think, he began to feel disorientated. His thoughts seemed slow, and he felt so tired, which angered him. He didn't have time to sit around frustrated. He had to *think*.

Once they reached a tiny glade in front of the mountain face surrounded by towering trees, Zalith sighed in relief. The side of the mountain had a large, gaping hole in it and inside, a hollow cavern. When he and Alucard had been preparing these safe locations, they made sure to have his people fill each area with supplies. The moment they arrived, Greymore and a few of his men immediately made their way over to the hidden cellar doors beside the cave entrance, took the supplies from within, and began setting up camp as everyone else relaxed against the limestone cliff face.

Ignoring his headache, disregarding the irritating fatigue, Zalith huffed and pulled on his horse's reins, making it stop beside Alucard's stallion. As soon as he dismounted it, though, he felt his condition abruptly worsen. His exhaustion intensified, and his legs betrayed him as his feet touched the ground. He stumbled back, his horse's reins slipping from his hands as both panic and confusion quickly consumed his once-aggravated thoughts. If it wasn't for Alucard catching him, he might have hit the ground; a cold shiver electrified through his entire body, and as it reached the wound on his neck, he gritted his teeth and grimaced, still trying to deny just how agonized he felt.

"Zaliv?" Alucard asked quietly, keeping him on his feet as those of his people who stood around them stared in alarm.

Zalith grunted painfully; it was all he could manage.

Alucard left his kitten atop his horse's saddle and moved his arm over the demon's shoulders. But before Alucard could move him anywhere, Varana's startled screech echoed through the opening.

The woman rushed over, pushing her way through the confused crowd; she gently grasped Zalith's chin and made him look at her. "Are you okay?!" she exclaimed, trying to pull him from Alucard's attentive grip.

"Get off 'im," Alucard snarled, lightly shoving her back with his free hand.

"Where are you taking him?!" she shouted.

Alucard wordlessly helped Zalith towards the cave.

"Hello?!" she demanded, following.

The vampire snarled irritably. "'E needs to lay down."

"Is he okay?!" she asked in panic, starting to cry.

"I zon't know," Alucard grumbled and helped Zalith sit against the cavern wall. "I'm going to go and get you someving to lie down on, okay?"

Zalith closed his eyes, trying to ignore the pain. He nodded in response, and he wanted to reach for Alucard's hand, but his vampire couldn't comfort him *and* fetch blankets at the same time. So, he let him go, and as everyone's worried voices drowned out around him, he tried his best to relax. But the pain was getting worse; he had no idea why, and he couldn't even try to ponder. All he could do…was sit.

| Alucard |

Alucard hurried out of the cave and to the supply crates. He snatched a few blankets and raced back into the cavern; he hastily laid the blankets down on the ground and then helped Zalith away from the wall; he laid him down, trying to make him comfortable. But his worry was beginning to overwhelm him. Why hadn't Crowell found someone to help him yet?

"What's wrong with him?" Greymore asked, standing beside Varana.

Varana wailed, "I don't know, he just…he just fell, and…I don't know!"

"Shit, man," Greymore uttered.

Sure that Zalith didn't want *either* of them in his space right now, Alucard pulled off his cape, placed it over Zalith so that he could use it as a blanket, and then stood up, facing Varana and Greymore. "Go and 'elp everyvone else. 'E just needs to vest."

"Okay," Greymore agreed. "Well…if you need anything, man, let me know."

"I'm not leaving!" Varana argued as Greymore left the cave.

Alucard sighed irritably. He really didn't have the patience for her right now. He was already irritated, and seeing that Zalith had gotten much worse wasn't helping at all. "Vhat could you possibly do vor 'im?" he snarled. "Zhe best ving *you* can do vight now is get out of my space so I can 'elp 'im," he said cruelly.

"Just because you're both fucking doesn't mean you're the only person he cares about!" she stropped.

"Zoesn't matter who 'e does and zoesn't care about vight now!" he yelled back. "Vhat matters is zhe vact zhat *you* can't do anyving to 'elp 'im!"

"And *you* can?!" she shouted. "None of this would be happening right now if you weren't in the picture! Everything would be *so* much easier!"

He didn't want to hit her, but what she just said not only provoked his anger but upset him, too—it made him want to hit her face so hard that she'd not utter another word his way. But he wouldn't…for Zalith's sake. Instead, he gritted his teeth and stepped closer, glowering down at her as she glared up at him. "So much easier vor *you*, you mean. Vhy do you 'ave to stick your nose into everyving? You're not entitled to know *everyving* zhat 'appens vith 'im, nor is everyving alvays about you."

"And *you* don't get to pick and choose who gets to be in his life—and if he didn't want me around, then I wouldn't be!" she screeched. "We've been best friends for hundreds of years—of course I'm sticking my nose into the situation; he looks like a corpse!" she exclaimed, pointing at Zalith, who was lying on his back, still, silent, and now sweating.

Alucard glanced back at him—

"Are you the one that's doing this to him?!" she then accused. "Is that why you're acting so secretive?!"

He sharply turned his head and glared down at her again. "Vhy zhe fuck vould I do anyving to 'urt 'im?!" he yelled. "Are you sure *you* zidn't 'ave anyving to do vith zhis? You still speak so 'ighly of Luciver, I vouldn't be surprized if you vere doing all of zhis vor 'im!" he accused.

"I would *never* hurt him!" she insisted, infuriated.

"Veally?" Alucard growled. "Maybe zhis is your vay of punishing 'im vor loving someone else zhe vay *you* vant 'im to love you."

Varana then snarled aggressively and slapped her hand harshly across Alucard's face with so much force that he turned his head to the side. Blood trickled from the small cut that her nails had made on his cheek, and he didn't even take a moment to think about how he wanted to react. She made him so furious that he couldn't stop himself from abruptly turning to face her and slamming his fist into her chest, sending her flying back towards the cave entrance as she screamed angrily.

Everyone stopped what they were doing, gasping and staring in shock as Varana tumbled out of the cave, tears streaming down her infuriated face. Idina rushed over to help, but Varana immediately got up and darted back into the cave, heading for Alucard with murder gleaming in her crimson eyes.

Alucard let his temper and hatred free; he felt no desire to hold it back anymore. She'd hit him, and now she was coming back for more—she pounced at him, her fist clenched, aiming for his face, but instead of attacking, he held out his hand and caught her fist in it. The force of the collision, however, pushed him back; his feet dragged along the ground as she screeched lividly at him. He wasn't really paying attention to his surroundings and tripped over something behind him. He fell back, growling furiously, and because he hadn't let go of Varana's fist, she fell with him, landing on top of him.

The moment his back hit the ground, Varana started punching him, screaming whatever insult came to her mind. Alucard wanted to fight back with as much animosity as her, but he didn't want to actually hurt her. He knew that would only upset Zalith, and he didn't want to be the reason behind his anger. So he snatched her throat through her constant punches and pinned her down, glaring at her as she squirmed and struggled beneath his grip, trying to escape.

"Calm zhe fuck down!" he yelled at her.

"Get off me!" she screamed, trying to push him off.

Alucard loosened his grip when he heard people rushing over; he snarled irritably as both Greymore and Tyrus gripped an arm each, pulling him off of Varana, who immediately climbed to her feet. The vampire's instincts told him to lunge at her—and he wanted to, but he didn't. Despite just how furious he was, he wouldn't hurt her. He pulled free from Greymore and Tyrus and prepared to defend himself as Varana flew at him, but Tyrus grabbed hold of her and tugged her away from him.

Varana kicked and screamed as Tyrus held onto her, and eventually, she stopped fighting and started bawling in his arms as he lugged her out of the cave. Alucard rolled his eyes, glaring at her as she cried, and as Tyrus led her out of the cave, Idina hurried over.

"Are you okay?" she asked anxiously.

"He won't let me see him!" she wailed, and as she cried, everyone who had been spectating started mumbling quietly to one another, sending a flurry of disapproving looks Alucard's way. He didn't care. She'd clearly gotten the attention that she wanted, but all that mattered to him was Zalith.

He turned his back on the drama occurring outside—

"Are you all right, man?" Greymore asked him.

"I'm vine," he snarled, glancing over at Zalith as he used the back of his hand to wipe the blood from his cheek.

"Okay, good," Greymore said, nodding. "We'll do our best to keep her away for now," he said before he turned around and left Alucard alone with Zalith.

For a moment, Alucard stood there, staring at Zalith as he lay still and silent upon the blankets. He frowned despondently and moved closer but realized that the demon must have passed out somewhere between his argument with Varana and their fight. He felt so stupid; Zalith was suffering, and he'd been too busy arguing with a woman who wasn't worth his time.

He sat beside the demon, his aggravated thoughts withering into ones of dismay. So many things were wrong with this; Zalith was sweating, and demons didn't do that—at least not either of their kind. He was breathing erratically, trembling beneath Alucard's cape, and he was almost as pale as he was. With panic enthralling him so very quickly, the vampire leaned over Zalith and pulled his shirt collar away from his neck, revealing the wound that was causing this. It was still sore and swollen, and the crimson vein-like marks had spread over his shoulder, edging closer to his chest. Whatever was doing this to him—whatever was spreading through him—it was working *fast*, and Alucard had to work faster to stop it.

But Crowell was yet to turn up, and he was beginning to feel as if he couldn't wait anymore. Zalith needed his help… and he didn't care what he had to do to make him better. He was sure that Zalith would be mad at him if he left to find someone, but what other choice did he have? The demon had struggled to stand and walk, and now he was unconscious. Alucard didn't want to see what might happen next.

With a scowl of worry, Alucard went to stand up—

"Wait," Zalith uttered wearily, snatching Alucard's wrist.

Surprised to see that he was actually conscious, Alucard frowned and stared down at him. "Zaliv?" he asked.

Zalith took a moment, holding onto his wrist, staring up at him. "Where are you going?"

Alucard frowned despondently. "To get 'elp."

The demon stared at him but then closed his eyes. He mumbled quietly, something Alucard couldn't make out, slowly letting go of his wrist.

"Vhat?" the vampire asked anxiously.

But Zalith didn't say anything.

Frowning, Alucard moved his hand over the side of Zalith's face. "Zaliv?" he asked again, but he seemed to have fallen unconscious again.

The vampire scowled in dismay, sitting back down, staring at Zalith's weary face. He didn't know what to do. Zalith didn't want him to go, and he didn't want to leave Zalith to wake up to find he wasn't there. But he couldn't just sit around and do nothing. What if Zalith suddenly *stopped* breathing altogether?

He glanced back at the cave entrance. It would take him at least fifteen minutes to reach the Citadel if he made haste… but what if Zalith woke up searching for him? He looked down at Zalith, huffing frustratedly as he tried to decide what to do. Nobody here would be as fast as he would—but somebody had to go. Who? Pip then came to mind—the izuret who died in the battle that had taken Dor-Sanguis from him. He'd use an izuret to contact someone—Erwin. They were a doctor; they'd have to know what to do.

Alucard knew that he wasn't really supposed to without asking Zalith, but he summoned an izuret using the words he'd once heard Ben use, and as the creature appeared in a puff of violet smoke, it floated down to the ground beside him with an angered look on its face. Alucard didn't know this particular izuret, and it didn't know him—which was probably why it looked as if it was about to scold him—but as it caught sight of Zalith beside him, it gawped at the demon and chirped in confusion.

"I need you to go to zhe Citadel—to Ervin. Zhey live above zhe Crystal Place—is a tavern. Blue 'air, elv. Bring zhem 'ere immediately," he ordered.

The izuret nodded and squeaked quietly, disappearing into violet smoke.

Alucard then sighed deeply and stared back down at Zalith. He took hold of his hand, which was cold and clammy. It made his heart hurt, and he wished that there was more he could do. But there wasn't, was there?

Chapter Thirty-Eight

Bite

| Alucard |

Alucard waited. It felt like an hour had passed, and the izuret *still* hadn't returned with Erwin. Zalith had been in and out of consciousness, asking for Alucard the moment he woke. The vampire stayed at his side but occasionally returned to where he was putting up the tent that Greymore had given him.

Once the tent was finally up, Alucard set up a much more comfortable bed for Zalith, but he didn't want to move him—not yet. The demon was still sleeping and had been for longer than he had since they'd got here. He didn't want to disturb his rest.

The vampire sat beside Zalith again, leaning his back against the cave wall. Crowell was yet to appear, and Alucard could only assume that his absence meant something had happened, so now he was worrying about his vampires, too. Had the insects killed everyone in the Citadel? Was that why the izuret hadn't come back with Erwin? Were *all* of his vampires dead?

He scowled despairingly and dragged his hands over his face. He didn't want to leave Zalith, but what if his vampires needed him? What if he left and Zalith woke up or got worse? His scowl thickened as the frustration intensified. He didn't know what to do.

With a sullen scowl, he glared at the cave entrance. Everyone outside had settled down, either sleeping in their tents or muttering quietly to one another around one of the few fires. He then looked down at Zalith. All of this felt strange to him…for him to be sitting there by himself, worrying, waiting for the next moment Zalith would wake so that he'd get to talk to him for a few moments. Any irritancy he felt towards the demon earlier had faded—if anything, Alucard felt terrible for being so annoyed at him. Seeing him so still, silent, and vulnerable—it distressed Alucard. He just wanted to crawl under his cape with Zalith, but he didn't know whether that might hurt or annoy the demon.

He sighed quietly, staring down at his lap, constantly glancing outside to see if the izuret or maybe even Crowell had arrived—but the longer he waited, the sadder he became. Why was this happening? In a single night, his and Zalith's life was turned upside down. Everything they had built together was crumbling; his *and* Zalith's people were homeless, and he'd heard their disappointment in Zalith. But none of this was the demon's fault.

Alucard dragged his hand over his face again, but when he scraped the cut earlier left by Varana, he grimaced and huffed, gazing at Zalith. When would he wake up? Was he even going to wake up? Even though Zalith was *right there*, Alucard missed him. He missed his voice, his aura—he missed his arms around him. He stared down at his lap again, fiddling with the ring he wore on his right index finger to match Zalith's. Then, he looked at Zalith again. He really couldn't sit there a moment longer.

He pouted and moved closer, carefully lifting his cape and crawling under it so that he could lay beside Zalith. Slowly, he moved his arm around the demon, rested his head on his chest, and exhaled deeply. Now he felt a little better.

For a while, Alucard lay there, listening to Zalith's slow but calming heartbeat. The demon still trembled, though. He breathed frantically, and sometimes so much slower than he should; his typically hot body heat had declined, and he was as cold as ice. Alucard wouldn't be able to warm him, though; he was just as cold.

"Ali!" came a sudden but familiar voice.

Alucard looked over his shoulder and set his eyes on Erwin, who hurried over to him with the izuret that had been sent to collect them. Relief flooded through the vampire as he carefully got out from under his cape and pulled it back over Zalith before standing up.

Erwin placed their briefcase beside them. "I'm so glad to see you're okay! And I'm so sorry about your little friend here," they said, glancing at the hovering izuret. "I moved outside of the Citadel to my country home in Brabus late last night."

Alucard didn't care for small talk. "Zaliv needs 'elp," he said, facing Zalith, standing beside the perplexed elf.

"Oh…my." Erwin frowned, staring down at the demon. "I…do you know what's wrong with him?"

"No, I zon't know vhat's vrong vith 'im," he snarled impatiently. "If I did, I vouldn't 'ave sent vor you."

Nodding, Erwin looked down at Zalith again. "I…at first glance, I'd say it was a fever—an infection, maybe. But Ali…he's a demon. You know I don't specialize in that type of healing, I…I'll take a look," they said as Alucard gritted his teeth in anger.

He watched the elf as they crouched beside Zalith, placing their hand over his forehead. They then pressed two fingers against his neck, presumably checking his pulse, and as they did, Erwin noticed the crimson vein-like marks spreading over Zalith's skin.

They frowned, pulling away Zalith's shirt collar—they gasped quietly as they set their eyes on the wound and then glanced up at Alucard.

"How long has he been like this?" they asked.

"Since zhis morning."

"It's definitely an infection," Erwin said. "I need to get a better look—do you mind…or…would *he* mind?" they asked, tapping the top button of Zalith's shirt.

Alucard wouldn't usually let *anyone* undress his demon, but now wasn't really the time to feel possessive. Erwin could help, and to do that, they'd need a better look. So, he pulled the elf aside and started to unbutton Zalith's shirt. The demon then murmured, making Alucard stop as he reached his fourth button.

"Zaliv?" he asked quietly.

But the demon frowned and fell silent once again.

The vampire pouted and continued unbuttoning his shirt, eventually removing it. He moved aside, giving Erwin space to take a closer look at the bite on the back of Zalith's neck. He still felt a little protective, watching closely as Erwin put their hands on Zalith to move his head aside so that they could see the back of his neck. The crimson vein-like marks had spread down over his shoulder and reached his right pec. Zalith had become ever so pale, still sweating, still trembling—Alucard waited anxiously for some kind of answer, but would Erwin even have one?

He glared at the elf, waiting as patiently as he could. "Vell?" he asked.

Erwin shook their head, sighing deeply. "I've never seen anything like this before, Ali—I'm sorry," they said, looking up at him. "Demons are supposed to be immune to disease and infection, but his wound is *definitely* infected—"

"Zhen vhat do you suggest ve do? Zon't you 'ave some sort of…anti-biotics or vhatever zhe 'umans call zhem? Someving to 'elp 'im?" he asked desperately.

The elf looked down at Zalith again as they stood up. "I mean…we can try, but…this sort of stuff just doesn't work on demons. I…we can try," they said, watching as Alucard's scowl of desperation became one of anger. "What caused his wound?"

"A mosquito."

"I see," Erwin said, nodding. They then scurried over to their briefcase, opened it, and rummaged through whatever they had inside. "Can you wake him to take something? Or will I have to use a syringe?"

Alucard didn't want to wake him up. "Use zhe syringe."

"I don't know if this will do anything," the elf said, filling a syringe with something amber.

The vampire snatched Erwin's wrist before they could return to Zalith, setting aside his desperation and worry so that he could take a moment to think straight. "Vhat…vhat vill 'appen—side evvects or…vill someving bad 'appen if you use someving intended vor 'umans on a zemon?"

Erwin shook their head. "It will either work or do nothing, Ali—this isn't meant for a demon's metabolism, so…either it'll somehow help a little, maybe more…or his body will simply burn it away."

Alucard was confident that Erwin knew what they were talking about—they always did. So, he let go of their wrist, nodded, and stepped back, watching as the elf crouched beside Zalith once again.

"Speaking as if he were human, this would battle the infection…clear it out, help the wound heal," Erwin explained slowly, carefully pressing the needle into Zalith's neck. Then, as they injected the amber liquid into him, Zalith exhaled deeply. "We should see results in a matter of moments."

Alucard waited, staring down at Zalith as Erwin backed away, returning to their briefcase. He watched the vein-like marks on the demon's neck, eager to see them recede.

"You can also try to make him a little more comfortable," Erwin said. "Put a hot towel on his forehead, maybe. He's sweating, but he's cold, so…you need to keep him warm and change his clothes. He'll need water—"

"'E's never avake long enough to drvink," Alucard mumbled.

"You need to convince him to stay awake," the elf said, taking a hand towel from their briefcase, which they then handed to Alucard. "And he may need to eat too—I assume…he eats?"

With a bit of hesitation, Alucard looked over at them and said, "'E's an incubus—is uh…a male succubus."

"Ah, I see," Erwin said, looking at Zalith again. "I don't…want to assume or impose, but…you may need to do something to give him some energy. He looks very fatigued, and I assume this infection is sapping away whatever energy he has. Ethos doesn't matter here, either. It's his body that's being attacked—his…cells, his blood. He needs what an incubus needs to regenerate—or…to at least keep him from slipping into a comatose state."

Alucard didn't want that to happen—he didn't want Zalith to be comatose. Now he knew that there was something he could do…he wanted to do it, but…he didn't exactly want to just start touching the demon without his consent.

But Erwin then sighed and said, "It doesn't look like it's doing anything. I can try a different dosage, but…I really don't think there's anything else *I* can do for him."

"Do you know anyvone who *can* 'elp 'im?" Alucard pleaded.

"Hmm…I have a few contacts in my notebook—I'll have a look; maybe one of them will know something. Give me a moment," they said, returning to their briefcase.

As the elf wandered off, Alucard frowned despondently and slumped down beside Zalith. He pulled his cape over him a little more, covering his neck. He'd do his shirt up once Erwin was gone—that was if they couldn't give him the name of someone else who might be able to help. He then moved his hand to Zalith's forehead, tucking back the strands of his hair that had come loose. He just wanted him to get better.

But as Alucard moved his hand away, the demon opened his eyes. Relief shot through Alucard even though he knew he'd only get to talk to him for a moment. However, Zalith didn't say anything. He just…stared up at him…and Alucard quickly noticed his eyes were bloodshot.

"Zaliv?" the vampire asked quietly—but panic started to enthral him. His eyes hadn't been like that before. "'Ow are you veeling?" he questioned, hoping he might be feeling better.

Zalith didn't answer, though. He frowned, and his distressed expression suddenly faded into one of malice. Alucard had no time to comprehend—to evade. With strength that had seemingly come out of nowhere, Zalith flung up out of bed and grabbed hold of the vampire, snarling savagely as he did. Alucard's eyes widened in startle, Erwin gasped loudly, and as Zalith dug his claws into his wrists, the vampire grunted painfully. His back hit the ground, his head hitting it a whole lot harder, and as the demon sunk his fangs into his neck, it all finally caught up to him.

Alucard grimaced and groaned painfully as Zalith pinned him down, biting harder, snarling like some sort of rabid beast. The demon's venom quickly entangled him in a flurry of confusion, panic, euphoria, and then disorientation. He tried to kick Zalith off—the demon only had his arms pinned down—but Alucard's strength quickly waned against the venom that was quickly infecting his body. He stammered, but he didn't even know what he was trying to say. Maybe he was going to call for help, maybe he was going to try and snap Zalith out of whatever trance he was in—but he had nothing. His voice was silent, his body fell still, and as the demon started to drain him of his blood, he began to feel himself slipping away.

But then Zalith stopped. He pulled his fangs from Alucard's neck, snarling once more as his blood dripped from his chin. Alucard stared up at what he could see of Zalith through his disorientated vision; the demon wasn't looking down at him—he was staring at something ahead of him, and considering he could hear Erwin's panicked mutters, Alucard assumed it was the elf who Zalith was staring at with such animosity.

He felt Zalith's grip loosen—the demon moved from over him, but Alucard couldn't let him attack anyone else. He gathered what little strength he had left and reached out, snatching the demon's ankle; Zalith growled in frustration as he tripped and fell—but he immediately rolled over, snatched Alucard's throat, and picked him up, pinning him against the cave wall as Erwin cried and hurried out to where a few of Zalith's people had grouped up.

Alucard choked, gripping Zalith's wrist with his hands, staring down at the demon—but he didn't see Zalith in his eyes. Something was very wrong—whatever was happening to him…Zalith looked to be some sort of starved, savage creature, blood trickling down his chin and his neck, and as he hissed furiously, he tightened his grip.

Struggling, choking, Alucard couldn't make out what Zalith's people were shouting. He could make out Varana's voice—Idina's, too. But they didn't matter. Grunting and panicking, he managed to lift his hand—he pressed his index and middle fingers against Zalith's forehead. "Sleep," he murmured painfully, and the savage scowl immediately vanished from Zalith's face. As the demon swiftly fell unconscious, Alucard dropped to his knees, catching Zalith as he fell with him. "Is okay," he insisted when Varana and Idina rushed towards him—he didn't want either of them to get too close, nor did he want any of them getting involved, either. They couldn't help him.

"What are you doing to him?!" Varana exclaimed.

"Is he okay?!" Idina panicked.

Alucard snarled and held onto Zalith a little tighter. To his relief, they had only heard Erwin screech and hadn't seen Zalith attack him—if they had, he was sure this would be a whole lot worse. The last thing he wanted was for everyone to panic thinking Zalith was out of control, attacking whoever got close. "I vas just…giving 'im blood—'e got carried avay," he lied.

"That's not what it looks like at all!" Varana scowled. "What's wrong with him—why were you trying to give him blood?!"

"Vell is vhat 'appened," he snapped, glaring up at her. "If you zon't mind, I'd like to get 'im back into bed now."

"I want to see him!" Varana argued, starting to cry yet again.

Alucard…he really, *really* didn't want to fight with her right now. Erwin was cowering over by the cave entrance, and no one else was putting up much of a fuss to see Zalith. Idina stared worriedly, but she didn't utter a word. And Varana—she glared at Alucard; he was sure that she wouldn't give up any time soon. So…he sighed, giving in—but only for a moment. "Vine," he breathed, his blood loss cursing him with such intense fatigue that he had no energy to argue a moment longer. "'Elp me get 'im in zhere," he said, nodding at the tent he'd set up earlier.

Surprised, Varana shook her head a little. But as Idina muttered something to her and left, she kept her scowl and hurried to help Alucard move the unconscious Zalith. Neither of them uttered a word to each other as they got the demon into the tent and laid him down in the bed that had been made up of several furs. Alucard then left, snatching his cape, and swiftly returned to lay it over Zalith as a blanket.

The vampire glanced at Varana, who had sat beside Zalith, a worried look on her face as she tried to wipe the blood from his chin with one of the spare blankets. Alucard felt the need to stop her—that was *his* job…*he* wanted to take care of Zalith, but after what had just happened…he felt…strangely hesitant. He moved his hand to his throat, rubbing it gently as the pain lingered. He didn't want to think about it. Erwin was outside, and Zalith still needed help.

"Is this *your* blood all over him?" the woman asked, glaring at him tearfully.

Alucard scowled, moving his hand from over his wound, covering it with his shirt. "Who else's vould zhat be?"

"I don't know," she said, frowning. "That little elf was screaming pretty loud."

"Zhat's because zhey are covard," Alucard grumbled, looking down at Zalith.

Varana frowned but then turned her attention back to Zalith, sniffling quietly as she cleaned the blood from his face.

With a deep sigh, Alucard let go of his hatred for Varana for just a moment—for Zalith's sake. "You can…stay 'ere vith 'im," he said slowly. "Vor a minute. I'm trying to vind someone to 'elp 'im."

"Who?"

"I zon't know," he muttered. "Somevone who can actually do someving."

"Okay," she said sadly, staring down at Zalith.

Alucard got up, stumbling a little, but to his relief, Varana didn't comment. He then left the tent, hoping that Erwin had a name in their contacts list who might be able to do more than give Zalith a useless anti-biotic.

Chapter Thirty-Nine

Plague

| Alucard |

Alucard slowly made his way towards Erwin, who was waiting by the cave entrance with a horrified look on their face. The moment they noticed Alucard, though, they scurried over.

"Ali! Are you okay?!" they exclaimed.

"I'm vine," he dismissed, smacking away the elf's hand when they reached out towards his wound. "Did you vind somevone who can 'elp?"

"I…I did," they said. "I think. Let me look at that," they insisted, reaching towards him again.

This time, Alucard didn't fight. Instead, he stumbled back, slumping down atop a nearby crate. He let Erwin move closer and pull away his shirt collar to examine the wound Zalith's bite had left.

"Does he do that often?" they mumbled. "What a scary man—"

"No," Alucard muttered.

Erwin sighed and let go of his collar. Then, they stared down at him, crossing their arms as Alucard slowly lifted his head to look up at them. "You sure have surrounded yourself with a different crowd, Alucard," they said sternly. "If anyone from a few years back had attacked you like that, you would have killed them. I guess…he's really important, huh?"

Alucard frowned at Zalith's tent. "'E is…everyving to me," he murmured.

Erwin smiled softly, but then they scratched their head and said, "Okay, I know somebody who might be able to help, but…you might not like him."

Alucard glanced up at them. "Vhether I vill like zhem or not zoesn't matter. If zhey can 'elp Zaliv, zhen zhat's all I vealy care about."

The elf nodded again. "Okay. Well, first, let me clean your wound. It's going to take a couple of days to heal, I imagine—that's how demon wounds work, right?"

"*Da*," he muttered, staring down at the ground. He then waited as Erwin rummaged through their briefcase. He was beginning to feel worse; he needed to sleep, and he'd need to feed soon or he'd start feeling absolutely dreadful. Zalith had just taken a lot of his blood—why had he just…attacked him like that? He frowned in dismay, looking over at Erwin. "Vould…an invection make 'im do zhat?" he asked.

Erwin sighed and shrugged, making their way back over to Alucard with a cloth that they'd just poured some water over. "I don't know," they admitted, standing in front of Alucard. "Things like this are unpredictable—it's new, so…for all I know, yes, this infection could have caused him to lash out—or maybe it was just his survival instincts…like you. Your instincts force you to search for blood when you're particularly exhausted, right?"

Alucard sighed, leaning his head aside so that Erwin could start cleaning his wound. "Vill zhis doctor I von't like be able to 'elp 'im?"

"I believe so," they said with a nod, getting to work. "He's…knowledgeable in many things, and he has also earned a name for himself in a world of experimental procedures. He works with ethos, though, so I don't have to worry about his competition," they said, smiling.

Glancing up at the elf, Alucard frowned. "Vhy *do* you decide not to vork vith ethos? Is so much easier zhan all zhis…'erbal stuff," he said.

The elf laughed a little as they cleaned away the blood from Alucard's neck. "Have you thought about the future, Ali? One day, ethos might not be so common. People rely on it a little too much, I'd say, and for all we know, it could become a little harder to come by in a few centuries, just as it was back when you were younger—and meaner," they said with a smirk.

Alucard rolled his eyes, glancing over at the tent again. "I'm no better zhan I vas back zhen," he muttered. "I simply like some people more zhan ozzers."

Erwin placed the bloody cloth down beside Alucard and pulled his collar back over his wound. "I'm glad to see that you're happy, Ali. It's a good look on you."

With a perplexed frown, Alucard looked up at them again.

"I'm going to leave you a sedative for Zalith; I'm sure your sleep spell will keep him down for a little while, but in case my contact doesn't arrive before he starts to wake, just give him one of these," they said, reaching into a satchel on their side and pulling out a small belt of three syringes containing something dark. "I may work with humans, but…it's always handy to have something stronger around now and then," they added, handing the belt to him.

"Vank you."

Erwin then sighed and stepped back, picking up their briefcase. "Okay, remember what I said about keeping him comfy. Keep him warm, and…if you can, give him what he needs. I'll do my best to find my contact, but…the Citadel isn't exactly…safe right now."

Alucard frowned. "Vhat?"

"Oh," Erwin uttered. "I…thought you knew."

"Knew vhat?" he asked, standing up.

"The…the plague?"

"Plague?"

The elf nodded, looking nauseous. "It's why I relocated to my country home. The first case popped up yesterday evening sometime. A man brought his wife to my office—she was…alive wouldn't be the best way to describe her—"

"Vait…." Alucard scowled, glancing back at the tent and again at Erwin. "Is…is zhat and vhatever is vrong vith Zaliv connected?"

"I…well, I don't know. I've only seen the plague in humans. Whatever is wrong with Zalith…it's…it doesn't actually seem entirely different, I suppose, but…it really isn't my area."

Taking his eyes off Erwin, Alucard looked over at the tent. It was far too coincidental *not* to be related. Zalith was bitten by that mosquito yesterday, and the swarm of insects that hadn't burned in their fire headed towards the Citadel. But…if it was the insects that caused whatever Erwin mentioned, then why was Zalith sick? Why hadn't Greymore—who had also been bitten—become sick? *Were* the cases linked, or had Lilith sent multiple attacks in different places?

He asked Erwin, "Do you know vhat caused zhis…plague?"

"No," Erwin said, frowning. "One case popped up, then another, another, and as I was leaving in my carriage, it looked like the Citadel had become overrun. A lot of people were barricading themselves in their homes because…because these people who got infected…they're like ghouls," they explained. "They kill everything they set their eyes on."

Yet *another* problem. Alucard scowled, shaking his head. He wasn't going to concern himself with that right now—he simply couldn't. Zalith was more important. "Go and get me zhe guy to 'elp Zaliv," he said. "Is…vill you need 'elp?" he asked, concerned now that he knew the Citadel wasn't as safe as it used to be.

"No, I'll be fine. Your little cat can take me where I need to go. If he's still in the Citadel, I'll send him your way."

Taking his eyes off Erwin, Alucard looked over at the izuret that hadn't actually left and was instead sitting upon a ledge close to the cave ceiling. "Get down 'ere," he called.

Without falter, the izuret floated down and hovered beside Erwin.

"Take Ervin to zhe city and 'elp zhem vind zheir associate. Zhen bring zhem 'ere," he ordered.

"And Ali," Erwin then said, "be careful."

"Go," Alucard dismissed, and without another word, the izuret disappeared with Erwin.

Alucard pulled his shirt back over his wound, grimacing as moving his arm caused pain to surge through his body. But he didn't care about that—he didn't care about his own fatigue. He just wanted to get back to Zalith.

Ignoring his tire and pain, Alucard made his way outside. He set his eyes on a flask, which he hoped contained water. As everyone slept silently, he quietly headed over to it, picked it up, and opened it. To his relief, it *was* water. He then hurried back into the cave as his kitten followed, snatching a cloth from a nearby crate as he passed it.

He moved back into the tent, sitting beside Zalith as Peaches crept in and curled up in the corner. He expected Varana to comment, to ask him where he'd gone, but she stayed silent, staring down at Zalith. Alucard held the flask of water in his right hand, heating it with his ethos, and once he felt it was warm enough, he carefully poured it onto the cloth, which he then placed over Zalith's forehead.

"I don't want him to die," Varana wept sadly, glancing at Alucard as he tried to make Zalith a little more comfortable.

"'E von't die," Alucard muttered firmly. "I von't let zhat 'appen."

"He has so many plans," she cried, placing her hand on the demon's shoulder.

"'E's not going to die," Alucard repeated.

"I know!" she sniffled. "I'm just talking."

Alucard sighed and leaned back on his hand, but it sent agony spiralling through his body, making him grimace and lean forward, resting his arms in his lap. He didn't really have anything else to say to Varana, he just wanted…actually, he didn't know what he wanted right now. He felt as if he wanted to lay beside Zalith, but…what if he woke up? What if he lunged at him again? He frowned in confliction, glancing at his kitten—

"Why are you so mean to me all the time?" Varana suddenly asked.

He rolled his eyes, exhaled deeply, and looked at her. "I'd ask you zhe same question if I cared to know zhe answer, but I zon't," he said before looking back over at his kitten.

She scowled. "Well, you should!"

"Vhy?" he muttered, uninterested.

"Because I'm tired of arguing and feeling bad all the time because of you two," she said sadly. "And Z wants us to get along…it's important to him."

With a shake of his head, Alucard huffed wearily. "'Ow could ve *possibly* get along? You 'ate me because you vink I came along and vuined vhatever you vhought you 'ad going on vith Zaliv, and you're Luciver's scion—you vere cveated to take me back to 'im. I'll never trust you, and is not ovten I choose to get along vith somevone I zon't trust. Is not vorth my time."

Despondency flickered across her face. "But I don't want to hate you, and I don't want to be mad at Z for it anymore!" she insisted. "All it's done is hurt me and everyone else."

Still uninterested, Alucard looked away, sinking into his fatigue. He was convinced that this was some ulterior approach to trying to worm her way in and make him rethink his relationship with Zalith. That was all she had ever tried to do, so why would now be any different? He was sure that soon, she'd start listing names at him, telling him that something like this had happened with someone Zalith had been with before and that he was doomed to suffer the same way they did.

"And I wasn't created to take you back to him," she said, frowning. "I was actually created and sent to Eltaria to merge the Lucidian and Lethidian demon bloodlines."

"Vhy are you suddenly telling me zhis?" he snapped irritably.

"Because things are getting bad again, and I'm tired of being miserable all the time," she retorted.

He kept his eyes on Zalith. "I'm sure ve're all tired of being miserable."

"Z does a lot for us, and I think he deserves to be happy, too," she said quietly, sniffling as she wiped away her tears. "We don't *have* to be friends, we can just…try to get along." She sniffled again and then mumbled, "And…I'm sorry for your face."

Unsure whether she was actually trying to form some sort of relationship or attempting to dig her way in again, he exhaled deeply and set his tired eyes on her. "Just skip to zhe part vhere you tell me zhis 'appened vith somevone else 'e vas vith, and zhat Zaliv is going to vake up and vealize 'e zoesn't vant me anymore," he invited.

"What?" she scoffed, glowering at him. "This has never happened before with anyone else—he's *never* been like this with *anyone*," she said irritably and pouted. "Why else would he have bought that stupid ring?" she muttered.

Alucard scowled irritably—at first, he thought she might be referring to the ring that Zalith had given him after they escaped Lilith, the same ring that had belonged to his father. But Varana had said *bought*, and as far as Alucard was aware, the ring was an heirloom. So he lost his irritated frown and instead glared at her confusedly. "Vhat stupid ving?"

Varana stammered, her eyes wide as if she'd said something she shouldn't have. But then she rolled her eyes and exhaled deeply. With a sigh and a shrug, she revealed, "Your engagement ring. He's had it forever."

Alucard's frown thickened. Engagement ring? He knew nothing about any engagement ring, and to hear that Zalith had actually bought one however long ago…. He pouted, looking away to hide his flustered face. He didn't know how to explain his feelings. He felt…relieved—he felt so very content to know that Zalith really did want to marry him. Of course, all this talk of it happening one day had to mean something, but he hadn't been aware of the fact that Zalith had already committed to it as much as to have already got a ring. But then that led Alucard to his next question—a question that lingered in the back of his mind every time Zalith mentioned marriage. Why hadn't he proposed yet? He had the ring…he always talked about how he wanted to do it…so…why hadn't he?

Maybe he just wasn't ready.

"He started working on it when you and Greymore would go fishing," she continued.

That was a little over six months ago—he'd had it *that* long? Why was she even telling him this? Was she trying to upset him? Was she trying to make him overthink? He scowled in distress but kept his face out of her view. "I zidn't know about zhe ving," he replied tonelessly.

"Sorry," she mumbled.

He didn't really know what to think *or* what to say. It made him feel content to know that Zalith had already made preparations, but he only sunk deeper into his despair knowing that they probably won't be getting married now for a long time. Their home was gone, Lilith was on their trail, and Zalith was sick. The Citadel was in ruins—he had only found that out a short while ago, and it was beginning to feel as though they might not be as safe and comfortable as they had been. There wouldn't be time for them to get married, would there?

Alucard shrugged, staring down at his lap. "Zhere probably von't be time vor zhat now. Too much is 'appening."

She frowned sadly.

But Alucard then sighed again, glancing at her. "Is late, and I zon't know 'ow long zhis doctor vill take to get 'ere. I need to vest, so…" he said, gesturing at the tent's opening with a nod.

Varana scowled hesitantly, and Alucard was almost certain that she was about to argue, but as she looked down at Zalith, she asked him, "Will you tell me if anything happens?"

"I vill," he muttered.

She lightly moved her hand over Zalith's hair, sighed, and stood up. "Thank you," she said, making her way out of the tent, and before leaving, she stopped and glanced back at Alucard. "Goodnight," she said.

"*Noapte bună*," he muttered, closing the tent.

As Varana left, Alucard sighed quietly and looked down at Zalith. The demon didn't look any better, and all he could do was wait until Erwin's contact arrived. The elf had suggested he do what Zalith needed to heal, but…not now. He felt so fatigued because of his blood loss, and he just wanted to rest for a while.

He moved closer, lying beside his demon. He wanted to ponder about what he'd just learnt—to think about how happy he was knowing that Zalith had already got him an engagement ring, but that would only make him feel miserable. The Numen situation was worsening, and once Zalith was better, they'd both need to focus their attention on that. He closed his eyes and moved his arm around Zalith, resting his head on his chest. But maybe one day…they'd have time to get married.

Chapter Forty

Angels

| Alucard |

It felt impossible to rest. Alucard lay there with his arm around Zalith and his head on the demon's chest; he wasn't sure how long it had been or how long it might still be until Erwin's contact arrived, and as each minute of silence passed, he felt his heart ache just a little more. His blood hadn't seemed to have done anything for the demon, nor had whatever Erwin had given him.

The demon suddenly murmured uncomfortably.

Alucard sat up. "Zaliv?" he asked, ignoring his headache as he watched the demon slowly open his eyes.

Pain smothered Zalith's face; his eyes were no longer bloodshot, nor did they possess a gleam of malice. He just looked tired, weak, and as if he wasn't sure where he was. "Hi," he said weakly.

Alucard felt a little relieved to see him awake again—although it might not last long, he'd make the most of what time he got to talk to Zalith. "'Ow are you veeling?" he mumbled, hoping that maybe his blood had actually done something. After all, Zalith no longer looked like a starved creature.

"I don't know," the demon said sadly. He tried to get up, but he struggled and quickly surrendered to his trembling limbs. "What's wrong with me?" he questioned desperately.

Keeping him down by placing his hand on Zalith's shoulder, Alucard explained, "I sent vor 'elp—somevone should be 'ere soon. Ervin came, but…zhey veren't able to do anyving."

The demon frowned confusedly. "When? I don't remember."

"About an hour ago."

Zalith lifted his hand, moving it to Alucard's collar. The vampire realized that he hadn't hidden the bite that Zalith had earlier given him and frowned hesitantly as the demon lightly moved his thumb around the wound. It hadn't yet healed, so Alucard grimaced and sighed quietly.

"What happened?" the demon asked worriedly.

Alucard was convinced that Zalith didn't remember attacking him, and he didn't want to tell him he had done so—he didn't want Zalith to worry or panic or punish himself. "I gave you blood," he lied, gripping Zalith's wrist and pulling his hand away from his neck.

"Why…does it look so bad?" the demon uttered sadly.

"Is vine," he said, making Zalith rest his arm back under the cover of his cloak. "You just…struggled a bit."

Zalith went silent for a moment as Alucard tried to make him comfortable. Then, he frowned and stared up at him. "I'm sorry," he said.

Alucard sighed and moved a few loose strands of Zalith's hair over his head. "Zhere's noving to be sorry vor."

He huffed and muttered, "Thank you…for taking care of me."

Sitting beside him with his hand now in Zalith's, Alucard smiled as best he could through his fatigue. "I vill alvays take care of you," he assured him.

After Zalith barely managed a smile, silence gripped them. Alucard stared down at the demon, who looked like he was about to pass out again, but the vacant stare on his face soon warped into an uncomfortable scowl.

He looked up at Alucard. "Can you help me get my shirt off? It's hot in here."

Alucard hesitated. Erwin told him to keep Zalith warm, so removing layers probably wasn't the best idea. "I'm…supposed to be keeping you varm."

"I feel gross," the demon said. "I just…want to take it off for a minute."

"Gross 'ow?"

"Sweaty," he muttered in discontent.

Alucard still felt hesitant. He didn't want Zalith to have to lay in the discomfort of his own sweat—something a demon's body shouldn't even produce—and he was sure that something as thin as a shirt wouldn't affect him that much. "Okay," he agreed, "but you 'ave to stay in zhe blanket—or…vell…my cape."

"Okay," Zalith agreed quietly.

The vampire leaned over him, helping him out of his shirt. Zalith struggled—Alucard could see him attempting to hide his pained frown as he moved his body. Alucard tried to be as careful as he could, and once the shirt was off, he threw it over to one of the tent corners and made sure Zalith was comfortable before sitting back beside him.

As Zalith went silent, Alucard stared despondently. How much longer would they have to wait until Erwin's contact got here? He scowled, glaring down at his lap.

"Where's V?" Zalith asked.

Alucard looked down at him again. The demon lay with his eyes closed, a look of struggle on his face. "She vas 'ere earlier, but zhen I vink she vent to go and sleep."

The demon nodded. "Okay," he mumbled before falling silent again.

With his sorrow and concern increasing, Alucard gazed at the demon. He had to do *something*. He hated sitting there feeling like he was unable to do anything, knowing that Zalith was suffering. But he was convinced Zalith wouldn't want to do anything intimate to get some energy back right now, and Alucard didn't really feel like it either. He sighed, taking the cloth from Zalith's forehead. He chucked it over to where Zalith's shirt was and reached behind him to grab another. There was still some water left in the flask from earlier, so he heated it, poured it onto the new cloth, and gently laid it over Zalith's forehead. Then, he reached over to where a few blankets had been piled and carefully pulled one over Zalith's legs. Once he was asleep again, Alucard would pull it over the rest of the demon's body—he just didn't want him to be uncomfortable through his short moments of consciousness.

But his worry didn't fade. Zalith needed his strength—he needed energy, but what could Alucard do? He'd ask…he'd make sure Zalith was comfortable. "You need energy," he said despondently, taking hold of Zalith's hand beneath the cover of his cape.

Zalith hesitated, keeping his eyes closed. "You're going to need it if something happens."

Alucard shook his head. "I'll be vine," he insisted. "You need to get better."

"I already had blood," Zalith then mumbled, turning his head as he opened his eyes to look up at him.

"But…blood zoesn't veally do anyving vor you," he said with a worried frown.

"But what if something happens? Neither of us will be able to help. I don't want to take your energy," he said sadly.

Clearly, there wasn't going to be any convincing him. Despite there being only so much that Alucard could do, he wouldn't let himself rest until he knew he'd done all he could. So, he frowned and leaned closer, placing his hand on the side of Zalith's face. He knew that kissing was one way Zalith could take his energy, so he'd do that. He closed his eyes and gently pressed his lips against Zalith's; the demon kissed him back, and as he moved his hand to the side of Alucard's face, they continued to kiss one another slowly.

Alucard felt relieved. Zalith might not be getting as much energy as he would if they were doing more, but he was still getting it…and he missed kissing the demon. But it didn't last as long as Alucard would have liked. After just a few minutes, Zalith moved his hand from the side of his face and to his chest, pushing him back a little. Alucard frowned, but Zalith then slowly moved his hand to the back of Alucard's head, pulling him closer so that he could rest their foreheads together.

"Thank you," Zalith mumbled, closing his eyes.

The vampire frowned a little, but…he'd done what he could, and he didn't want to make Zalith uncomfortable. So, he sighed quietly and closed his own eyes. "I love you," he uttered sadly.

"I love you too, baby," Zalith replied, the weariness upon his voice deepening.

"Is okay if I lean on you again?" Alucard asked.

"Yeah," the demon said, moving his arm so that Alucard could lay beside him.

Alucard moved slowly, making sure not to hurt Zalith, and rested his head on his chest. He then guided his arm around him, exhaling deeply as he let himself relax. He wasn't going to fall asleep, though. He wanted to comfort Zalith as *he* fell asleep. "Do you…vant to 'ear a story?"

"I do," the demon answered.

He took a moment to shuffle through his many memories and smiled when he came across something he thought Zalith might like. "Did I ever tell you about Ilia?"

"No, I don't think you did."

"Vas…a long time ago. I vas new to zhis vorld, and zhe vorld vas vather new, too. Vas during vone of zhe times Zamien just…let me go. I vent to Tāi Qiān in search of vone of zhe Aegis—zhe Dragon Gods. Zhe people of zhis land 'ad some intervesting believs; a visitor to zheir land vas very uncommon, and zhey believed zhat anyvone who could cross zhe terrivying ocean 'ad devied death and vas vorthy of zheir undivided attention. Zhey never veally let me be—zhey vould offer me everyving zhey 'ad, even zhe clothes off zheir own backs in exchange vor vive minutes of my time. A lot of zhem vanted to know about zhe vorld outside of zheir secluded country.

"I later assumed zhey might know vhere zhe Aegis vas—zhat being Ilia—so in exchange vor my time, I 'ad zhem tell me vhere she vas. I killed zhe dragon, but she vasn't vone of Levoldus' children—vather…vone of 'is children's children. Zhe people vere outraged; zhey claimed zheir land vould crumble vithout Ilia's 'elp. I knew zhat Levoldus vould send anozzer Aegis to investigate, and probably to veplace Ilia, so I stuck avound vor a vhile. Zhe people came up vith so many names and so many stories vor me. Is actually vhere zhe name Night Beast came vrom, vor I only veally came out at night. Zhat name travelled vith me vor a long time, all zhe vay to Dor-Sanguis. I'm sure zhe people zhere still tell stories about me," he said with a smirk. "I vhought about going back zhere at some point to see if Levoldus 'ad sent anozzer Aegis zhere, but Zamien 'ad me too busy."

Zalith didn't respond.

Alucard frowned and sat up a little, looking down at him to see he had fallen asleep. With a relieved but sad smile, the vampire sat up and rested his arms on his knees. He could feel himself slipping into dismay once again; the thoughts of what had been lost and the uncertainty of what might happen next caused pain in his head and his heart. But he'd not have to sit in silence much longer—he knew that when he saw a burst of purple light break the darkness outside the tent. It could only be the izuret returning, so he stood up—before he could hurry outside, though, an *awful* dizziness struck him like a fist. But he didn't care. Help had arrived—at least he hoped so—and he wasn't going to waste a moment.

He left the tent to see that the izuret had returned with not just *one* man, but…three? Alucard frowned as he reached into his pocket, summoning a coin from where he kept his money—he knew he'd have to pay the izuret, and the only shiny item he had access to right now was his money. So, he summoned a gold coin and made his way over to where the three men stood, looking around with condescending scowls. Alucard didn't care to look at them—he reached them, handed the izuret the coin, and *then* set his eyes on the three men that the little demon had delivered.

A grotesque, conflicting nausea enthralled Alucard as he realized that all *three* of these men were angels. The first—long, silky silver hair platted and styled, eyes as purple as a demon's blood—stood in expensive white attire, but it had streaks of dirt and blood all over; if he had come from the Citadel, then it was no surprise that he looked beaten up after what Erwin had informed Alucard of. The man on his left also possessed silky, silver hair, but it fell past his waist. He, too, possessed the same shimmering purple eyes, but he seemed to glare at Alucard in revolt, while the man in the middle stared vacantly. The last man was slightly taller than the others and dressed in white attire, but his eyes were a light, almost gold hazel, and his hair was sandy blonde.

Why were *three* angels here? Who were they? Erwin had said they'd sent one man—a *man*, not an angel, let alone three of them.

The first man stepped forward. "You must be…Aleksei, yes," he said, holding out his hand. "Erwin said that you needed my help."

Alucard frowned, but he didn't feel as though he had to be defensive. Clearly, this *was* the man Erwin had said they'd send his way. "Is not me who needs 'elp—is Zaliv," he said, looking back over his shoulder at the tent.

"I see…," the man drawled.

When Alucard turned back to face him, he failed not to notice that the man was discreetly moving his fingers at his side as if he was using ethos—Alucard could *feel* that this angel was summoning something, and that along with the now hostile looks on the other two angel's faces had Alucard's instincts immediately telling him that he either had to fight or retreat—but he wasn't going to run. He wouldn't leave Zalith.

Without hesitation, Alucard moved to defend himself, always ready to return to Zalith. But as he stepped forward, the man's two companions lunged at him. Alucard felt the weight of fatigue pulling at him, urging him to stop, but he pushed through it. The purple-eyed man charged at him, but Alucard was faster. His fist connected with the man's face before he could even react, sending him reeling backwards, his expression frozen in disbelief. The second attacker reached Alucard moments later, but the vampire's hand was already at his throat. Snarling, Alucard locked eyes with the man's stunned face before hurling him towards his fallen companion. As both men tumbled to the ground, Alucard's gaze shifted to the third figure—the one in the middle. His claws bared, lips curled back in a snarl, Alucard prepared for whatever the man's next move might be.

But he did nothing. He stood there, keeping his eyes on Alucard as if he was thinking—one might think he was reading Alucard's thoughts, but Alucard would know if that was happening—so what was he doing?

"I apologize for my companions' behaviour," he said calmly as the two men he had arrived with pulled themselves to their feet, remaining where they were, glaring over at Alucard.

At the same time, Tyrus and two of his men appeared at the cave entrance, watching closely, obviously ready to attack if need be.

"They seem to have greatly underestimated you, yes," the man added with a nod. "They often choose to attack before they take the time to work out what it is they are attacking."

Alucard scowled—he wouldn't let his guard down. But why *were* they attacking? Hadn't they been sent to help? He knew angels didn't particularly like demons, but surely Erwin had mentioned he and Zalith were such creatures. Not only that, but if this was the man Erwin had spoken of—the man they said was skilled in areas involving *demons*—then why was he attacking?

"I, however, am not known to make the same mistakes, yes," the purple-eyed man continued. "I can either force you to come with me to Purgatory, or you can come willingly, yes."

The vampire snarled—Purgatory; he knew that place. The place where the angels of death worked—grim reapers, they had come to be called, and he also knew they worked for Erich. Obviously, they had detected the death mark he had upon himself the moment they had arrived, and this man in front of him clearly thought he was going to be taking him away from Zalith—that wasn't going to happen, nor was he going to explain himself to this angel. "You're not zhe virst angel I 'ave 'ad to deal vith," he threatened him.

"I can imagine," the man said, nodding. "For someone as old as you, yes…I would be surprised if we were the first to cross your path."

Alucard glared at him, preparing to attack.

But the man just stared vacantly at Alucard for a few moments—he suddenly scowled, glanced at his companions, and then looked back at Alucard. "You must be wondering why nobody came searching for you after that mark was placed, yes?"

He didn't answer.

"Your shielding ethos could not hide you from us—after all, it was I who placed it upon the ring you wear. I can feel its aura from here. I am…Magnus, son of Erich. These are Ulric and Camael," he said, looking back first at the silvery haired man and then the blonde.

"I zon't care who you are," Alucard snarled.

"No, of course not. Erwin said you needed my help—forgive my companions' behaviour and my own, yes. We all sensed the mark, and as our instincts would have it, we attacked," Magnus explained.

Alucard *still* wasn't going to let his guard down. What mattered right now was protecting Zalith and himself. He wasn't going to let this man near Zalith without knowing what his intentions were, though.

"I will help you now—"

The vampire stepped into Magnus' path, stopping him from taking another step. "'Ow do you know about my ving?" he asked—everything else made sense. He knew that grim reapers could sense death marks others had placed; that was their purpose, after all…to mark them for *permanent*, painful death.

"Your…Zalith came to me a while ago, yes. He still owes me a debt for that…hmm…I hear it is *he* who needs my assistance, yes?"

Alucard hesitated—he didn't trust this man, but…the fact that Zalith needed his help still remained. He couldn't waste any more time, either. So he scowled, he sighed, and he nodded. "Is zhis vay," he said, starting to lead the way to the tent.

Magnus followed, leaving his two companions by the cave entrance where Tyrus remained, keeping a close eye on them.

And *Alucard* kept a close eye on Magnus.

Chapter Forty-One

Cure

| Alucard |

The vampire led the way into the tent and sat beside Zalith.

Magnus sat down opposite him, staring down at the demon. "Can you explain to me his symptoms, yes?"

"'E…said 'e veels veally 'ot, but…'e's cold. 'E's sveating, but zemons aren't meant to do zhat. 'E's veally veak—'e can't veally move much, and a vew hours ago, 'e just…collapsed vhen 'e got off 'is 'orse."

Nodding, Magnus held his hand a few inches above Zalith's chest. "Have you tried to heal him, yes? He is an incubus—"

"Not…veally," he admitted.

"You are his mate, are you not?" he asked, looking at Alucard. "You've imprinted on one another—"

"Vhat?" Alucard asked, confused.

"I can sense it…ethos," he said, smiling.

"No, I mean…vhat does zhat 'ave to do vith 'ealing 'im?"

Magnus nodded, reaching up to pull the blanket away from Zalith's neck, revealing his infected wound. "When mated demons remain close to one another, it begins a joint healing process—it increases both their healing abilities and your ethos as a whole. If you have remained at his side and noticed any improvements, that would be why, yes," he explained.

Alucard *had* noticed Zalith was slightly different earlier; he wasn't trembling anymore, and he had stayed awake a little longer than before.

"How long has this wound been infected?"

Snapping out of his thoughts, Alucard frowned at Magnus.

"What caused this?" the angel asked.

Looking at Zalith's wound, Alucard scowled despondently. "'E vas bitten by a mosquito yesterday night—but 'e only veally started showing symptoms a vew hours ago. 'E did show me zhe bite zhis morning, zhough."

"Has he shown any erratic behaviour—anything out of the ordinary, yes?"

Alucard felt discomfort grip hold of him as he thought back to the moment Zalith had attacked him. "*Da*," he said, hesitating to specify what had happened.

"Has he attacked anybody? Has he *bitten* anybody, yes?"

"Vhy?" he questioned.

Magnus looked down at Zalith again. "Erwin told me that you weren't aware of the plague that has swept the country, yes. The plague that has infected the Citadel was, in fact, spread by demons—it looks as though your mate has the original demon infection," he said, reaching into his pocket, "that which first incubated in demons and was soon spread to whoever they came close to. We currently know that it can be spread through bites and any exchange of saliva—although bites have been seen to spread the infection faster, yes," he told him, pulling out a syringe. "It is a good thing that you decided not to try to help him heal, yes," he said, glancing at Alucard.

That wasn't entirely true, though, was it? Not only had Alucard been kissing him, but Zalith had also bitten him. Did that mean that *he* had caught whatever Zalith had, or could it only be passed onto humans by a demon? Magnus had just said that it was a good thing he'd chosen not to help him heal, which surely would have involved him kissing Zalith either way. "Ve…vere kissing," he said.

Magnus stopped moving his syringe towards Zalith's neck and looked at Alucard.

"'E also…bit me," he said, pulling away his shirt collar to reveal the wound Zalith had given him.

"Then the infection is currently within your body, yes," Magnus said, placing the syringe down. "I can stop it from spreading any further so that you might not suffer the same as your mate—"

Alucard shook his head, covering his wound up again. "No—vocus on Zaliv."

The angel frowned. "I'm not going to lie to you; the chances of me saving him are a lot less than those I have of curing you, yes."

"I zon't care," Alucard snarled, glaring at him. "Vocus on Zaliv."

Magnus glanced down at Zalith and then back at Alucard. "Luckily, I have been working on a vaccine ever since the outbreak," he said, picking up the needle he'd not long pulled from his pocket. "I haven't been able to test it on a demon yet, but with a few alterations, I believe it will work, yes. I will need a sample of…clean demon blood, yes, and considering as yours is contaminated, you will have to find me another demon—preferably one as close to Zalith's age as possible."

Alucard didn't hesitate. He didn't spare a thought to the fact that he was infected, too; he just wanted to help Zalith—Zalith was more important, and he always would be.

He nodded and left the tent, exiting the cave as he passed by Magnus' companions, who eyed him closely, and Tyrus, who nodded at him. He made his way to the tent where he could detect Varana and stepped inside to see that she was sleeping in her own bed.

"Varana," he said, moving a little closer to her.

The woman groaned irritably, waving her hand at him as if she was trying to thwack a fly away.

He wasn't going to wait. "Ve can 'elp Zaliv... but ve need some of your blood."

"Who?" she mumbled sleepily.

"A doctor—'e arrived not long ago and 'e 'as a vaccine, but 'e needs zemon blood to make vork vor Zaliv."

"What doctor?" she asked, opening her eyes to scowl at him.

He frowned. "Magnus."

"I want to see him," she demanded, sitting up.

With nothing but Zalith on his mind, he nodded. "Vine, let's go," he said, turning around, not giving the woman much time to get up and follow him. He led the way through the camp, past Magnus' companions once more, and back into Zalith's tent as Varana followed, messing with her hair on the way.

As soon as Varana stepped into the tent, she set her eyes on Magnus and scowled. "Who are *you*?" she asked skeptically.

"I am Magnus, yes," the angel said, glancing at Varana.

She looked him up and down for a few moments before asking, "You're a doctor?"

"I am, yes," he confirmed, placing down his syringe next to a few items he must have taken from his pockets while Alucard was gone. "I assume you are the demon whose blood I will be taking, yes?"

"What are you going to do with it?"

"Well," he said, picking up the syringe again, "the vaccine I have made is meant for humans, and in order to make it effective for demons, I simply need some clean, uninfected demon blood to add to the vaccine. I will then use the demon blood to transform it into something that will work on a demon, yes—I can explain that process, but it will take more time than Zalith probably has."

"Wait, what?!" she asked in panic.

Alucard felt his own panic become overwhelming. "Just give 'im your blood," he insisted.

As tears started to form in her eyes, Varana held her arm out to Magnus. "What's happening to him?" she asked despondently as the angel hastily drew her blood.

"Zalith was bitten by a mosquito carrying a virus found in a few other demons I have come across over the last twenty-four hours, yes. For some reason, he has not yet passed into the stage that will completely erase who he is, leaving him as nothing but a starving creature whose thoughts tell him to kill whatever he sees. I believe that is because he has been rather close to his mate this entire time, which seems to have kept him from deteriorating. This vaccine should clear out the infection, thus curing him. If it works, I will also administer it to anyone else who has experienced symptoms, yes," he explained. Then, he looked at Alucard—

"'Ow long vill take to vork?" he asked, not exactly comfortable with him revealing that he was now also infected because of Zalith's bite.

"We should know within a few moments, yes," he said, pouring some of Varana's blood into a small vial. He added a strange amber liquid to the blood and gripped the vial with his hand. He used ethos to alter the vaccine, the purple aura around his hand glowing brightly, and after a few moments, he filled another syringe with the now violet concoction. "Once injected, it should only take a few seconds to tell whether it has worked or not—we will keep an eye on the wound, yes. I believe it will start to heal." He then injected the vaccine into Zalith's neck.

Alucard stared at Zalith's wound, his heart beating a little faster as his angst increased with each passing moment. Varana continued crying, but after a few minutes, Alucard could see the crimson vein-like marks starting to slowly fade.

"Is it working?" Varana asked desperately.

Magnus nodded. "I believe that it is, yes."

Relief enthralled Alucard as he leaned closer and placed his hand over Zalith's.

Varana also sighed in relief but looked at Magnus. "When will he be better?"

"Most of my human patients have regained consciousness, and some are even moving around—with assistance. I believe that within another day or two, they will be completely cured. So... a day, maybe two—but if his mate stays with him, maybe even sooner, yes," Magnus replied.

"Okay," she said, looking down at Zalith. "Thank you."

Magnus nodded but then started to prepare another syringe. "Has anyone else shown symptoms, yes?"

"No," Alucard said. "But I 'aven't veally levt Zaliv. Maybe you should go and ask Tyrus," he said, looking at Varana, "see if anyvone else 'as experienced anyving."

"Me?" she asked, shocked.

"Yes...."

She looked at Magnus with an expectant frown but then sighed irritably. "Fine," she muttered. "But it's late... should I just let everyone rest?"

"Just go and ask Tyrus," the vampire muttered irritably. "I'm sure 'e's been vatching everyvone."

"Fine," she grumbled, standing up. "Who are those two guys out there?"

Magnus smiled up at her. "Ulric, my brother, and Camael, my... relative, yes."

"Oh, okay," she muttered, rolling her eyes as she turned her back to him. She then left the tent, leaving Alucard with Magnus and Zalith.

"Would you like the vaccine now, yes?" the angel asked Alucard.

Alucard wasn't sure if he had experienced any of the symptoms yet, but he wasn't going to risk it. "Vine," he said, holding out his arm.

Magnus picked up the syringe he'd just filled with what was left of the vaccine. "I will need to inject it as close to the wound as possible, yes—it will work faster that way."

Rolling his eyes, Alucard made his way around Zalith and sat beside Magnus. He grimaced as the angel eased the needle right into the bite Zalith had left on his neck and then scowled irritably as he waited.

"I can also remove that death mark from the roof of your mouth if you would like, yes," Magnus offered.

"'Ow exactly are you going to do zhat?"

Taking the needle from his neck, Magnus placed the syringe down and watched Alucard back off a little. "I will simply have to touch you, yes. Or, if you'd prefer, it can remain upon you. No harm will come to you. Erich has told us through our hive mind specifically to ignore and avoid contact with *you*—"

"Zhen…vhy did you 'elp Zaliv?" he asked. It was no surprise that Erich wanted nothing to do with him. That Numen only cared about his grim reapers.

"Because…he and I have history, yes. He now owes me two debts, and a man such as Zalith can be very useful, yes."

Alucard didn't like the sound of that *at all*. Part of him wanted to threaten this angel and tell him that Zalith wouldn't be doing anything for him, but he wasn't sure if that was what Zalith wanted or not. So, he just scowled and held out his arm. "Get vid of."

Magnus gripped Alucard's wrist. "I feel I should also warn you since I cannot warn Zalith at this current time. Your…Tyrus…he is being tracked, yes."

"Tracked?" Alucard asked.

Letting go of the vampire's wrist, Magnus nodded. "I sensed the ethos upon him the moment I arrived. It is angelic ethos, and as far as I am aware, Erich nor any of my siblings have placed a tracker on this man. You might want to look into that, yes," he said, packing all of his things into his pocket. "I will remain here at your camp until Zalith has awakened. I am sure he will want to talk to me once he can."

The angel then stood up and left the tent, leaving Alucard alone with Zalith.

Alucard stared down at the demon. So many different things possessed his thoughts; how long would it be until Zalith was okay again? Was *he* going to suffer the way Zalith did because of the infection? And Tyrus—he was being tracked; Alucard needed to work out what to do about that. Magnus had said he had angelic ethos placed upon him, and if it hadn't been Erich or any of his offspring, it could only be Ephriel. Did that mean that *she* was involved in all of this now, too? The thought brought both dread and fatigue to Alucard's already tired body.

How much worse was this going to become? Their home was gone, the Citadel was overrun, Zalith could have died…and now they were being tracked—*Tyrus* was being tracked, and *he* had to be how Lilith's people had found them…and if that were true, that would mean Lilith was making deals with Ephriel. Why? He scowled over at the tent's wall. He could think about that later; right now, he had to get rid of Tyrus before Lilith's people caught up to them.

He leaned over and pulled another blanket over Zalith; he changed the warm cloth on his forehead, made sure that he was comfortable, and then left to find Tyrus.

The vampire walked through the hollow cavern, and once he stepped outside into the camp, he searched for the allocer demon. Everyone was still sleeping, and Magnus and his two companions were sitting by themselves not too far from the cave entrance. Tyrus was standing by a tree on the opposite side of the camp, keeping a close eye on the visiting angels, but he took his sights off Magnus as Alucard approached.

Alucard had to think of a reason to send Tyrus away and had to avoid giving him the real reason in case the people who were tracking him could see or hear through him. "I need you to travel to Vort Rudă de Sânge. Crowell 'asn't turned up, and I suspect zhat someving might 'ave 'appened. 'E may need assistance, so take some of your men," he instructed. "Vonce at zhe vort, ask vor Kristov; 'e'll be able to 'elp you track Crowell."

As he spoke, Tyrus donned a look of confusion. "I'm sorry, and I mean no disrespect, but I can't leave without Zalith's order," he said.

His answer made Alucard feel frustrated. Not only was there no time to waste, but Zalith was sick and trying to recover—Alucard wasn't going to wake him up because Tyrus wanted to be insubordinate. And his anger—it caused him to not only scowl at Tyrus but to snarl in irritancy, too—it might even be a threat. These people were supposed to listen to him.

But Tyrus didn't look at all threatened; of course, he frowned in concern, but he didn't seem to recognize Alucard as his superior—at least, that was how it felt. "Again, I mean no disrespect, but I can't do it without his direct order."

Alucard scowled harder and clenched his fist at his side. Did *anybody* here see him as their superior, or was he just…Zalith's boyfriend? He felt so aggravated that he could hit Tyrus, but he'd not do it. The last thing he wanted to do was cause discord among Zalith's people—he was sure that Varana had spread many a lie about him earlier, and he wasn't going to prove her ridiculous stories to be true. He'd have to set his anger aside and go and talk to Zalith.

As he turned around, he snarled and made his way back towards the cave. He tried setting aside his anger, but he also felt embarrassed…like he was some errand boy. He shouldn't have to ask Zalith if it was okay to send someone off to do something, should he? He thought all of Zalith's subordinates thought of him as their superior—as Zalith's partner or equal or something that wouldn't have him in the situation he was in right now. But clearly, that wasn't the case. Maybe his authority meant nothing—perhaps he didn't have any at all. Maybe everyone just saw him as some guy hanging around like the rest of Zalith's people. Tyrus might have said he didn't intend any disrespect, but Alucard felt all manner of disrespect right now.

He continued towards the cave, but when he heard a mumble and a snicker, he scowled, stopped in his path, and looked over at the three angels. They were still sitting upon creates not too far from the cave entrance; Ulric, the long-haired idiot, was snickering behind his hand, and Camael…he looked away to avoid Alucard's scowl. Magnus kept a smile on his face, though, staring directly at Alucard as he glowered at them.

Alucard was sure that in whatever language they were muttering, they were disrespecting him, too. But he didn't care about them—they meant nothing. He rolled his eyes and went to continue into the cave—

"I assumed you might be this pack's Alpha, yes," Magnus called, "I have been…watching, but for once in a very long time, I appear to have assumed wrong, yes."

Glaring at him, Alucard felt his anger intensify just a little more. He'd already had to deal with Tyrus' insubordination; he didn't need someone to point out what had just been made evident.

"You are…Zalith's mate, yes?" Magnus smiled. "I assume you haven't bonded—that would explain his insubordination," he said, nodding over at Tyrus.

Alucard wasn't about to admit that he had no idea what Magnus was on about. Instead, he wanted to know why he seemed so interested. "Vhy are you so intervested?" he snarled.

"Simply curious," Magnus said. "It's not often I get to see such powerful demons, yes."

"Not much to see," Ulric then interjected. "Angry…disdainful…boring," he said, looking Alucard up and down with an almost revolted look on his face. "Is this one even really a demon, Opus? I heard it has no wings."

The vampire growled through gritted teeth. He wanted to respond by beating that man's face until he was unrecognizable, but he hesitated. Not only was he supposed to be hurrying to get Tyrus away from here, but he didn't want to start problems. Instead, he looked Ulric up and down. "I vhought angels vere supposed to be attractive," he said, a disappointed look on his face, and as Ulric's jaw dropped in offence, Alucard scoffed and walked away, heading into the cave.

He made his way back into the tent, setting his eyes on Zalith, who had a lot more colour on his face than he had before he'd left; Magnus' vaccine was evidently working faster than Alucard had thought. He headed over to him and sat down—he didn't want to wake him up, but…what choice did he have? Tyrus wasn't going to leave unless Zalith said so, and Alucard didn't want to waste time arguing with him.

"Zaliv?" he asked quietly, staring down at the sleeping demon. But he didn't stir. Alucard frowned and gently placed his hand on Zalith's arm, nudging him lightly. "Zaliv?" he asked again.

The demon murmured in response, slowly opening his eyes to look up at him.

"Zhe angel zhat came 'ere and treated you said zhat Tyrus is being tracked vith angel ethos, and I vink might be Ephriel. I vent to 'im and tried to send 'im avay, but 'e von't listen to me," he grumbled, trying to hide just how irritated it made him feel.

Zalith frowned in confusion. "How is that possible?" he asked, sitting up—he struggled, so Alucard helped him lean his back against the crate behind him.

"I zon't know," Alucard admitted. "Maybe zhe Numen 'ave some'ow vorked out zhat 'e vorks vor…you; zhey couldn't track us, so zhey vhought zhey vould vind us vhrough vone of zhe people who vork vor you. Tyrus zoesn't seem to know anyving about zhis—vhy else vould 'e still be 'ere if 'e did?" he muttered. "Maybe…vone of Liliv's people or somevone tagged 'im vithout 'im vealizing."

"Where are you sending him?"

"To Vort Rudă de Sânge. My vampires 'aven't veplied, so I vhought I'd get 'im to vind out vhere zhey are; avter zhat, I'll get Kristov to send 'im somevhere to keep whoever's tracking 'im busy."

With a deep sigh, Zalith said, "Bring him in."

Nodding, Alucard left the tent and made his way back out to where Tyrus was. He set a hostile glare upon the man and did his best to hide his anger. "Zaliv vill see you."

"Okay," Tyrus said, following Alucard as he led the way back into the cave and the tent. The moment they got inside, Tyrus said to Zalith, "Aleksei said he needs me to head to Fort Rudă de Sânge; I just want to confirm that's what you want me to do."

Zalith scowled *furiously* at the allocer demon. "If he tells you to do something, you do it," he said firmly.

Tyrus nodded apologetically. "I'm sorry, I just wanted to make s—"

"Go," Zalith interjected irritably.

Without another word, Tyrus left the tent—and soon, he'd be leaving the camp, too.

Sighing quietly to himself, Alucard closed the tent's opening and made his way over to Zalith.

As he sat beside him, the demon moved closer. "It's bedtime, baby," he said sleepily.

Alucard wasn't going to deny that he was exhausted, and sleeping sounded so very inviting right now, especially since he'd get to do so beside Zalith. He crawled into bed with the demon, pulling his cape and the blankets over them both as they made themselves comfortable. They both lay on their left side, and as Zalith eased his arm around Alucard and rested the side of his face on the vampire's, Alucard exhaled deeply and gripped Zalith's hand.

"How are you feeling?" the demon asked.

"I'm okay," Alucard muttered, closing his eyes. "Vhat about you?"

"Tired," he replied sleepily, "but a little better."

"Do you need anyving?" Alucard asked—although he was exhausted, he still wanted to do whatever he could for Zalith.

"No, I'm okay," he said, kissing the side of his face. "You've done enough. Thank you."

"Okay," the vampire mumbled, exhaling deeply once more as he tried to relax.

"What about you?"

"No, I'm okay—vank you."

The demon held him a little tighter. "Can you have some blood anyway?"

Alucard opened his eyes to stare over at the tent wall. He didn't really want it…even though he knew he needed it—especially after having lost so much; he just…didn't want to take anything from Zalith right now. He was recovering, and the last thing he needed was to be giving up his blood.

Closing his eyes again, Alucard lightly shook his head. "I'm veally okay," he insisted.

Zalith fell silent for a moment but then muzzled Alucard's neck. "Tomorrow?" he asked tiredly, but it sounded more like a stern request.

"Maybe."

The demon exhaled quietly, relaxing as he held onto Alucard, and then, for a long while, they lay in silence together.

Alucard did his best to ignore his headache—his *entire* body was aching, but he was confident that it would pass once he got some rest.

"Are we safe?" the demon suddenly asked.

Alucard scowled in confliction. *Were* they safe? He didn't feel the kind of safety he felt when within their home, but Zalith always made him feel safe…and he didn't sense any sort of danger…not now, anyway. "I zon't…veel like ve're in imminent danger," he answered, "especially now zhat Tyrus is gone."

"Okay," the demon murmured. "I love you."

The vampire smiled as best he could through his fatigue. "I love you, too."

If Zalith were well enough to move, they'd continue their journey tomorrow. Alucard didn't want to think about tomorrow, though. He didn't want to drift off to sleep thinking about what might happen…he wanted to lay there and let himself sink into all the emotions that came with knowing that Zalith had bought an engagement ring—that Zalith would have proposed to him sometime soon…only if this hadn't happened.

He lay there, wondering what it might look like—he knew he'd love it. But while he thought about their wedding and their parties, everything that he and Zalith and maybe even Varana would have organized to celebrate, dismay ensnared him. None of that was going to happen now—at least not for a few long years. He knew that he and the demon would get back up on their feet—they'd fight back. They just…needed to get Zalith's people to safety.

Chapter Forty-Two

Recovering

| **Alucard,** ***Friday, Cordus 3rd, 960(TG)—Nefastus*** |

As the morning became light, Alucard woke to the warmth of Zalith's embrace; the demon was a lot warmer than he was yesterday—perhaps his body had even returned to its usual hot temperature. The vampire opened his eyes but swiftly held them shut tight once again as a searing headache electrified through his head and eyes. He grimaced painfully, the ache in his body not much better as he shuffled around where he lay—and where he lay didn't feel as comfortable as it had last night. Not even the layers of fur he placed down made him forget that they were sleeping on a cave floor.

He wanted to get up—he'd rather stand than lay there in such discomfort. But he didn't want to wake Zalith, nor did he want to leave the demon's embrace. Peaches had also curled up beside him, and as he started to move onto his back, the hairless kitten yawned, stretched, and sat up, staring at him. He was sure that she wanted food—he was rather hungry, too…but not for whatever he could smell cooking from the camp. However, just as he hadn't last night, he didn't want to take Zalith's blood. He could wait; he just…needed air.

Alucard carefully got out of bed. Zalith murmured sleepily, but he didn't wake. Peaches followed the vampire as he left the tent, making his way through the cave; as he approached its entrance, the sunlight hit his face, and surely enough, his headache worsened. He felt overwhelmingly disorientated as if he'd stood up too fast, and he had to take a moment to lean back against the wall while he waited for his body to catch up. He wasn't sure whether it was his blood loss or his hunger, but something made him feel like he was moments from passing out.

"Will you burn up?" came someone's voice—someone Alucard didn't recognize.

The vampire frowned, turning his head to set his blue eyes upon…Camael, the blonde angel who'd come last night. He was sitting on a boulder, tying his boot laces while Magnus and Ulric slept against the wall behind him.

Rolling his eyes, Alucard glared ahead aimlessly and muttered, "No."

Finishing with his boots, Camael stood up and wandered over to where Alucard was standing.

Peaches glared up at the angel, folding her ears behind her head as if she were ready to attack.

"How's your friend?" Camael asked.

Alucard already felt irritated, and his day hadn't even started yet. He just wanted some air…he didn't want to have to talk to anybody, least of all some condescending angel. "'E's *not* my vriend," he snarled, glaring at him. "'E's my *boyvriend*," he corrected.

"Oh, sorry," Camael laughed. He had a shoulder bag at his side, and he'd left what looked like a list on the boulder he'd been sitting on.

"Are you vinally leaving?" Alucard grumbled.

"No. I'm heading out to the closest village. We're still people down here, right? We need to eat," he said. "Opus gave me the *wonderful* task of heading out to bring back food—I guess we didn't imagine we'd be sticking around or we'd have brought supplies," he muttered as he shuffled back over to the boulder and snatched his list. "Do you want anything?"

Looking him up and down, Alucard thought about it. This guy was going to the closest village to get food, and Alucard knew that everyone here could probably use something nicer than a few wild-caught hares for breakfast, especially Zalith, who hadn't eaten at all since they'd had to flee. And with Zalith on his mind, there wasn't any question about it. "Yes," he said, snatching Camael's list. He read it, seeing what Camael's companions had requested. They'd asked for items that could only be found in a bakery…or a stall selling baked goods…and since Camael had said he was going to a village, Alucard assumed there might only be a small market. "Do you 'ave pen?"

Camael reached into his bag and handed him a quill.

Alucard wrote down a few things; he thought of Zalith first, noting down fruit and eggs that someone here could cook. Then there was everyone else—he wasn't sure what any of them would prefer, and he didn't care to ask, so he wrote what came to mind, referencing his and Zalith's usual breakfast. "Zhere," he muttered, handing the list back to Camael. "Is village, so zhey might not take zhe coronam papers," he said, reaching into his pocket and pulling out a few gold coins. He handed them to the man.

"Thank you," the angel said, taking the gold and slipping it into his bag. "I'll be back later," he called, turning around and heading towards the trees.

Alone once again, Alucard sighed and wandered over to a nearby log, just a short distance from the cave entrance. He sat down, and Peaches promptly leapt into his lap. Absentmindedly, he scanned the camp, his gaze lingering on the rows of tents. He wasn't sure if they'd be packing up and moving on today, but he could already imagine the irritation that might ripple through Zalith's people if they had to take everything down and set it up again.

But why did he care? His scowl deepened as he looked down at Peaches. He cared because they were Zalith's people, and whether he liked it or not, he found himself worrying. Did they truly not blame Zalith, as Alucard had tried to reassure him? Or was their faith in him beginning to waver?

He sighed and dragged his hand over his face, his eyes still aching in the morning sunlight. If only there were something he could do about it; he'd love to wake up and not have to hide in the shade for an hour or so until he felt ready to step into the light—but that was just another part of being Lucifer's son; his eyes weren't meant to see in this world—a world full of light.

Just then, he shifted his attention to the small party of people coming out of the trees led by Greymore; they must have been patrolling the area. As Greymore spotted Alucard, he muttered to his men and then headed in the vampire's direction.

"Hey, how ya doing?" the beefy Alpha asked, sitting beside him.

With a long, deep exhale, Alucard shrugged. "Eh," he muttered.

Greymore frowned. "Do you need anything?"

"I'm vine," Alucard muttered. "I'm just... 'ungry."

Nodding, Greymore glanced around the camp. "If you really need something, I'm sure someone here can give you blood."

"No. Von't do anyving vor me unless is zemon blood anyvay."

Greymore nodded again. "How's Zalith doing?"

"'E looks better," Alucard said, staring down at his kitten. "'E's not pale anymore, and 'e vas both speaking and moving a lot more last night."

"That's good. I'm glad to hear it," he said. "If either of you need anything, just let me know, man. Are those angel guys any help?" he then asked, nodding over to where Magnus and Ulric were sleeping.

"Zhe Magnus vone cveated a cure vor Zaliv, and zhe ozzer two zon't veally seem to do much—I zon't like any of zhem."

Greymore patted Alucard's shoulder. "I'll keep an eye on 'em for ya," he said, standing up. Then, as Alucard sighed and nodded, Greymore walked off to join his men over by one of the extinguished fires.

Alucard stayed where he was, staring down at Peaches again. Sitting out here, however, really didn't make him feel any better. The light was hurting his eyes, and his aggravation was gradually increasing. He didn't feel as uncomfortable anymore, so he decided to get up and go back into the cave, carrying Peaches with him.

As he retreated into the tent, he saw that Zalith was waking up—and Alucard felt guilt begin to outweigh his agitation. "I zidn't vake you up, did I?" he asked, sitting beside Zalith as he smiled at him.

"No," the demon said, starting to sit up. "Greymore's voice woke me up."

The vampire helped him sit and then frowned as he sat beside him, staring at his tired face. "'Ow do you veel?" he asked as Peaches made herself comfortable in his lap.

"A lot better," he answered, leaning his head back against the crate behind him. "How do *you* feel?"

"I'm vine," he mumbled. "Just zhe sunlight gave me a 'eadache."

Zalith frowned slightly in concern, moving his hand to the side of Alucard's arm. "Do you want blood?"

Alucard *did* want blood, and he needed it; he was already experiencing the symptoms that came with going without it for too long. The headache, the fatigue, the extra sensitivity to the sun. But he didn't want to take it from Zalith. The demon was still healing, and he needed it more. Alucard could bear the discomfort as long as Zalith was okay. "I'm okay," he insisted.

"Why not?" the demon asked. "I'm fine," he said with a smile.

"I zon't vant to take anyving vrom you."

"But *you* need it too, Alucard," Zalith mumbled, stroking his hand to the side of his face.

He didn't want to argue about it, so he sighed and nodded. "Maybe I vill later."

Zalith sighed, too. "As long as you have some today."

Nodding, Alucard moved closer and wrapped his arms around Zalith, resting his head on his shoulder. He closed his eyes, exhaling deeply as Zalith wrapped his arms around him. He'd been so worried about his demon, but…he was getting better, and he didn't have the words to explain how relieved he was.

"Is anyone else awake?" Zalith asked.

"No. Just Zhomas and a vew of 'is guys. Vhy?"

The demon glanced around the tent. "I just need some water."

"I'll get you some," Alucard said, but when he reached for the flask, it was empty.

"You don't have to. It's okay."

The vampire got up. "Is just a vew veet avay. I'll be vight back," he said, taking the flask with him.

"Okay. Thank you."

Alucard left the tent and stepped out of the cave. He spotted a few buckets of water by one of the extinguished campfires, so he went over there and filled the flask. As he headed back to the cave, he shot a skeptical stare over at Magnus and Ulric; he wished they'd leave, but he was certain that last night was only the beginning of them sticking their noses into his and Zalith's business.

| Zalith |

When Alucard returned to the tent, Zalith smiled at him. "Thank you," he said, taking the flask from him. After a few sips, he sighed quietly, wrapped his arms around Alucard, and held him tightly. The last two days had been dreadful—disheartening. But he didn't want to think about any of that right now—it would only pull him into despair. He wanted to focus on the fact that he was feeling better and that Alucard had taken care of him. If it wasn't for Alucard, he might have given up. "I love you," he mumbled, nuzzling his vampire's neck. "Thank you for taking care of me."

Alucard rested his head on Zalith's. "I love you, too."

Zalith then lifted his head, placing his hand on the side of Alucard's face. For a few moments, he just stared at the man he loved—the man he felt he owed so much to. But just as he didn't want to think about the depravity of the last two days, he didn't want to think about how guilty he felt. He leaned closer and pressed his lips against Alucard's. Right now, he just wanted to enjoy a few moments as best he could. So he kissed him once, twice, and for a short while, ignoring the world around him.

What he couldn't ignore, however, was that he felt so filthy and was in dire need of a shower. Of course, that wouldn't be possible, but…he knew there was a river nearby, and that would have to suffice. He stopped kissing Alucard, sighing deeply as he rested his forehead against his. "Can you take me to the river?"

Alucard frowned, a hesitant look appearing on his face. "Are you sure you vant to valk avound alveady? Zon't you vant to vest more virst?"

"I'm okay," he assured him. "I'm tired of laying around."

The vampire kept his hesitant stare but nodded and started to help him to his feet. "Okay," he mumbled as he did. "Do you vant a new shirt?"

"Yes, please," Zalith agreed—he wasn't going to put last night's shirt back on. As Alucard pulled one of his shirts from a small ethos tear in the air, the demon smiled slightly and said, "Thank you." Alucard helped him put his shirt on, and while he did, Zalith found himself trying to find the words to explain just how thankful he was to Alucard—*for* Alucard. His vampire did so much for him, and he didn't even have to ask.

"Are you veady to go?" Alucard asked once he buttoned Zalith's shirt for him.

"I'm ready," he said, sliding his hand down Alucard's arm to grip his palm.

They left the tent, leaving Alucard's kitten behind. Silently, they made their way out of the cave—but as they stepped out into the camp, Zalith set his eyes on someone familiar sleeping not too far from the entrance. Silver hair, white suit; he'd not forget someone like Opus so easily. Not because he was interesting, but because of how irritating he had been the night Zalith asked for his help. And he wondered…what was he doing *here*?

"What's Opus doing here?" he questioned, looking at Alucard.

"Ervin couldn't 'elp," he answered as they made their way towards the trees. "So zhey vent to zhe Citadel and sent…Opus 'ere—zhough 'e calls 'imselv Magnus."

Something about Opus had *always* made Zalith feel skeptical, as though there was something he was hiding—something he was up to. But he was sure that Alucard must be wondering how he knew Opus, so as they made their way into the forest, he explained, "He's the one I went to last year to enchant that ring for you—and then my chain and V's anklet."

Alucard nodded, glancing down at the ring Zalith had given him to hide him from the Numen. "'E did mention someving about zhat last night—is vhy I zidn't kill 'im zhe moment 'is two ugly vriends came at me."

"What happened with his friends?"

The vampire shrugged. "Zhey detected zhe death mark zhat I 'ad vrom killing zhat grim veaper last year—zhey vhought zhey vere going to take me to Purgatory," he said with a quiet, amused laugh. "I taught zhem a lesson, and zhen Opus decided to vork out zhat I vasn't actually of any intervest to Erich. 'E took zhe death mark avay—not zhat vas actually a vhreat anyvay," he muttered.

"Well, I'm glad the mark is gone, regardless."

Alucard nodded and then stared ahead, leading the way towards the river.

The demon gazed forward, holding onto Alucard's hand as they walked through the forest. He started thinking about the fact that he was feeling better. He didn't feel amazing, but he was definitely recovering with each passing moment. His body still ached, but it wasn't so stiff, nor did he feel as disoriented anymore. Whatever Opus had done had worked, but…*what* had he done? "What did Opus give me?" he asked Alucard.

"'E made a vaccine using Varana's blood. 'E'd alveady been making vone vor 'umans, so 'e just changed zhat a little so zhat vould vork on a zemon."

"That was convenient. I suppose we got lucky."

"Hmm," Alucard murmured in agreement. But then he looked at Zalith, and sorrow lingered in his blue eyes. "I vhought…I vhought I vas going to lose you," he muttered sadly.

Zalith stared despondently at him. He felt like he wanted to tell Alucard that he'd never lose him, but…his dismay made him think that Alucard would probably have a much easier time dealing with everything that was happening if he *had* died from that insect bite; Alucard would be able to just hide away as he had before without any of this additional baggage and the risk of having Zalith around. Everything…it would all just be so much easier for Alucard, and that was what Zalith wanted—for Alucard to be safe, for him to not have to deal with all this stress.

He sighed, pulling Alucard a little closer as the thought of losing him brought pain to his heart. "Thank you for helping me," he said and kissed the vampire's cheek.

"Is okay," he replied.

But Zalith wanted to change the subject. "Did anyone else get sick?" he asked, watching as what seemed to be confliction appeared on Alucard's face; he was sure that the vampire was wondering why he hadn't comforted him.

"No," the vampire said, taking his eyes off him to stare ahead as the river came into view through the thinning trees.

"Do you think it might happen again?"

"I zon't veally know. Opus and Ervin 'ave made clear zhat zhe Citadel is overvun vith people who are invected—zhat's vhy Opus vas making a vaccine in zhe virst place. Zhere's a possibility zhat might spread vrom zhe city if somevone or someving zoesn't get zhe situation under control, zhough."

Zalith sighed and said, "I'd like to see if Opus can give this vaccine to as many of us as he can."

"Ve can ask 'im vhen ve get back," he mumbled.

"We should also make sure no one goes to the Citadel in the meantime."

"I 'aven't 'eard vrom Crowell yet, but I do 'ave some vampires at zhe vort, so I vink I'll send some of zhem to zhe Citadel to 'elp clean up vhatever's going on," Alucard said as they stopped a few feet from the slowly flowing river. "And so zhat zoesn't spread. I zon't know if vas just zhe Citadel and zhe places nearby zhat got 'it by zhese insects, but I guess ve'll vind out sooner or later if vent vurther."

Zalith nodded in agreement. "Agreed," he said, also thinking about the fact that it would be good for the image that he and Alucard needed to create for themselves for Alucard's people to be seen helping the Citadel. Especially now, he and Alucard needed numbers—they, like the Numen, needed influence. They needed people who followed them, who would put their faith in them. This could be the first of many chances to get people's attention. But he could think about that later. For now, he wanted to bathe.

Chapter Forty-Three

Down by the River

| Alucard |

In the shade of the trees, Alucard watched Zalith unbutton his shirt. But when the demon glanced at him, he averted his gaze to the river. All he could think about was how hungry he was; not only had he lost a lot of blood to Zalith last night, but he hadn't had any in a few days either. He knew he needed it, and he wanted it, but he didn't want to take from Zalith while he was still healing—and there was no way he'd drink from anyone else.

"Are you going to get in?" Zalith asked.

Taking his eyes off the river, Alucard looked at the demon to see that he'd taken his shirt off and was smiling at him. "I zon't know," he muttered hesitantly.

The demon walked towards him, and when he reached him he guided his hand around Alucard's waist and pulled him closer. "Please?" he pleaded. "It'll be nice and warm…so long as your body is touching mine at all times," he said with a smirk.

Frowning, Alucard glanced over his shoulder in the direction of the camp. "Vhat…vhat if zhey see?" he asked embarrassedly.

Zalith laughed a little. "Who cares if they see?"

"I do," he mumbled, looking down at the ground.

"So, you're just going to stand here and watch me like a creep?" he asked amusedly.

Alucard scowled in both fluster and anger as he lifted his head to glare at Zalith. But as the demon smiled, he looked away—

"What's wrong?" Zalith asked, moving his hand from Alucard's waist and to the side of his neck.

"I zon't know," he admitted. What *was* wrong? The idea of undressing made him feel so uncomfortable right now, the same type of uncomfortable he used to feel years ago when he did his best to keep Zalith from seeing his scars. *That's* what it was. He felt insecure—he didn't want anyone to see his back. Not only had Opus' brother taken it upon himself to remind him just how disgusted demons were by others who had their wings stripped of them, but Tyrus had also played a part in how he now felt. Tyrus refused to listen to him, to see him as his superior, and at the time, it hadn't crossed his mind, but now that he was faced with the chance of being seen, it struck him like a cold, slithering breeze. Maybe Tyrus knew that he was Disavowed, and perhaps that was why he didn't want to listen to him, perhaps that was why none of Zalith's demons really seemed to look at him as though he was their superior. Because he wasn't, was he? They all probably thought less of *Zalith* for loving someone like him and even lesser of *him* for thinking that it was okay to be with someone like Zalith.

He looked at Zalith; he wanted to ask *why* Tyrus didn't listen, but…Zalith would want to know why he was upset about it, and Alucard didn't want to make this about himself. Today was about Zalith and making sure that he was recovering. He didn't want to burden him with his stupid feelings. Why should it matter so much? It wasn't like these demons were his, and it wasn't like they ever would be, even if he and Zalith *did* get married. He'd been cast out, so he'd never lead a pack of demons, nor would he get one to see him the way he wanted to be seen—the way he *felt* he should be seen. He'd become so comfortable with his scars around Zalith that he'd forgotten he wasn't the only demon there; yes, he was the only one who mattered to him, but…Zalith's people mattered to Zalith, and Alucard didn't want to be a reason why they questioned him or his judgment.

Why was he even thinking about it so much? It shouldn't matter—it never mattered before…but that was because everything demon about him had been suppressed by Damien's runes. He'd noticed changes in his attitude and desires since having the runes removed, and perhaps this new feeling of inferiority was one such change. He was Zalith's partner, and since Zalith was the demon Apex, he should be too, right? But then again, maybe not. Opus mentioned something—bonding, whatever that was. He'd said that might be why Tyrus hadn't listened because he and Zalith weren't bonded. But he had no idea what that meant. Would Zalith?

Alucard sighed, dismissing his thoughts. "I'm vine," he said. "Just tired."

"I'm sure you are," he agreed quietly, caressing his cheek with his fingers. "You've had a stressful two days."

The vampire nodded, looking down at the ground again.

"You should come in the water with me," Zalith then said sadly, starting to fiddle with the buttons of Alucard's shirt.

Alucard stared at Zalith for a moment. Maybe he was just overthinking. *No one* had made it seem like they had a problem with who he was, and maybe Tyrus' insubordination was simply because he was worried about Zalith's approval. It didn't have to be because he didn't respect Alucard. He didn't want to think about it anymore, though. Zalith clearly wanted him to join him, and he wanted to do whatever he could to make Zalith happy. Not only that, but he *did* feel somewhat uncomfortable in his clothes—the same clothes he'd been in for two days.

He nodded and started to unbutton his shirt.

"Why are you sad?" Zalith asked.

The vampire did his best to dismiss his despondent frown and replace it with a curious one. "Vhat…do you know vhat bonding is?"

"Yeah," he said, smiling. "It's basically demon marriage. Why?"

Surprised, Alucard shrugged and mumbled, "Zhe Opus guy just mentioned."

"What did he say?"

He scowled and sighed. "'E said zhat vas vhy Tyrus zidn't listen to me."

Zalith shook his head, making Alucard look at him. "Baby, it has nothing to do with that," he said reassuringly. "Even if we were married, he wouldn't have listened simply because of how loyal he is to me—and he doesn't want to get hurt," he said with a smirk. "But everyone respects you."

Nodding, Alucard sighed and continued to unbutton his shirt. "Okay."

"Why do I feel like that's not all that's wrong with you right now?" Zalith asked, lightly gripping his wrist, stopping him from unbuttoning his shirt.

Alucard exhaled deeply—he didn't want to delve into it. Instead, he moved his arms around Zalith and hugged him tightly. "I'm just vorried about you."

Zalith hugged him in return, kissing the side of his face. "I'll be okay," he said. "I love you."

"I love you, too," Alucard replied. But then he sighed and pulled his shirt off. "Let's get in zhe vater," he muttered, unbuckling his belt.

"Okay," Zalith smiled and pulled his trousers off.

Once he shyly pulled his trousers off, too, Alucard followed Zalith into the gently flowing river until they reached its middle. The cold water came up to their waists, and when Zalith turned to face Alucard, he stroked his hands down to the vampire's thighs and pulled him closer. Alucard shivered for a few moments, but the warmth of Zalith's body quickly banished the cold.

"Vhat do ve do now?" Alucard asked quietly as he rested his forehead against Zalith's. "Ve can't stay 'ere too long."

"I know," Zalith said sadly. "We can leave after everyone's eaten—that means *you* too, vampire."

Alucard felt a hesitant sigh trying to break free of his breath, but he kept it back. He knew Zalith wouldn't stop offering, and he was sure he'd only feel worse the longer he ignored his need. So, he huffed and gazed into the demon's expectant eyes. "Are you sure is okay?"

"It's okay," he confirmed. "You need it."

Alucard still felt reluctant, but the truth was, he needed blood—*Zalith's* blood—and Zalith wasn't going to stop offering until he took it. As he glanced down at Zalith's neck, he frowned in confliction but moved his face closer as the demon moved his hand to the back of Alucard's head. Before he bit down, though, he stopped to worry—was this going to hurt Zalith? If it did, he'd stop the moment Zalith uttered a whisper of discomfort, and he'd also do his best to make sure that Zalith felt only pleasure from his bite.

Setting aside his hesitation, Alucard widened his jaw and sunk his fangs into Zalith's neck. He felt the demon tense up in response, but he soon sighed in satisfaction, dragging his fingers through Alucard's hair. Alucard almost immediately felt his fatigue fading as he swallowed Zalith's warm, sweet blood. His aching body relented, his headache withered, and his feeling of sheer exhaustion left him as if he hadn't even been burdened with it.

But he soon stopped—he didn't want to take any more than he needed to feel okay, and he felt good—*more* than good. The euphoria of Zalith's blood so very quickly consumed him, and as he stood there, nuzzling Zalith's neck, he smiled contently.

"Do you feel better?" Zalith asked quietly.

Alucard lifted his face from his neck, nodding slightly. "Yes," he answered, sighing.

"Good," the demon murmured, moving his fingers through his hair.

But then he just stared at Alucard, gazing into his eyes, slowly stroking his hand to the side of his face. Alucard thought he might be about to say something, but instead, the demon pressed his lips against his and started kissing him.

For a long while, they kissed in the river; Alucard let go of all his conflicting, dismaying thoughts, allowing himself to become lost in the euphoria of Zalith's blood and his affection. It had only been two days since they'd left the safety of their home, and Alucard missed it—he craved to feel the comfort he felt within the walls of the place he and Zalith slept—but it was gone, and what they had right now was something he had to get used to. It wasn't so bad...he still got to kiss him, hold him. Zalith was still there, and he was getting better. *That* was all that really mattered.

Zalith then stopped, sighing as he rested his forehead against Alucard's. His eyes wandered down to Alucard's neck, staring at the side upon which he had left his bite last night. Alucard could see the discontent in the demon's eyes, and he was sure that he was about to ask him what actually happened. Alucard knew he was good at a lot of things, but lying wasn't one of them, and he was certain Zalith hadn't believed him when he'd said his bite only looked so bad because Zalith had struggled last night.

"How hard did I bite you?" the demon asked shamefully.

"No 'arder zhan usual," he mumbled.

The demon sighed, lightly trailing his finger around the bite. "I don't remember. I'm sorry for biting you, and I'm sorry for being sick," he muttered, looking ashamed.

"Vhy are you sorry?" Alucard frowned, staring into the demon's dismayed eyes. "Is not your vault—none of zhis is your vault."

He shook his head a little. "I'm sure this hasn't been easy on you, and I feel bad for making it worse."

Alucard's frown thickened. Why was Zalith so quick to blame himself? Why did he feel like he had to apologize for things that were out of his control? He didn't need to be sorry for being sick—Alucard felt no resentment or aggravation about having to take care of him. If *he* had been the one who got sick, Zalith would have done the same for him. He *wanted* to look after Zalith; he didn't feel like he had to, and that was how Zalith was making it seem. And as for making things worse…that wasn't the case at all. Zalith hadn't caused any of this—he couldn't help that he got sick; no one could have known those insects were carrying a plague that could infect demons.

He moved his hand to the side of Zalith's face. "You 'aven't made anyving vorse. And all of zhis vould be a whole lot 'arder if you *veren't* 'ere vith me."

Zalith gazed at him for a moment, his despondent expression not fading. But he then leaned closer and kissed him a single time before pulling him into a tight embrace.

"Vhat's vrong?" Alucard asked. Of course, he knew Zalith was just as devastated as he was about losing their home, but Alucard just felt like there was something more to it.

The demon nuzzled his neck. "I just want to go home," he uttered despondently.

"Me too," Alucard mumbled, his concerned frown contorting into a distressed one. "But ve 'ave to do zhis—ve 'ave to keep moving avound. Ve'll vind somevhere more permanent soon, zhough," he said, hoping to convince not only Zalith but himself that they wouldn't have to be moving from place to place for too long.

But Zalith only nodded in response, pulling out of their hug. He took hold of Alucard's hand, though, leading him over to a shallower part of the river, where Zalith sat down, the water reaching his shoulders. He pulled Alucard closer, making him sit in front of him as he rested his forehead against the vampire's. And that was where they sat in silence for the next short while.

Time alone, however, was something they were both going to have to get used to not having so much of anymore.

"Zalith," Idina soon called from the tree line.

Startled by her abrupt appearance, Alucard hid himself behind Zalith, who looked over his shoulder at her. Although she couldn't see his scars, he still felt uncomfortable—he still wanted to hide. Zalith remained the only person he felt comfortable enough to see him without his shirt, and it would probably always be that way.

"One of those angels came back with breakfast," Idina told them. "Do either of you two want some?"

Taking his eyes off her, Zalith looked at Alucard. "Do you want anything?"

Alucard shook his head.

"Are you sure?"

"I'm vine," he said, nodding.

Zalith then looked over at Idina. "Just me," he called back. "Thank you."

Nodding, Idina wandered back off into the trees, leaving them alone again.

As she left, Zalith turned to face Alucard and smiled. "Did she scare you?" he asked with a quiet, amused laugh.

Embarrassed, Alucard scowled, pouted, and looked away from him. "No," he muttered.

"Not even a little?"

Still pouting, Alucard glared at the other side of the river.

Zalith then laughed and started to fiddle with the vampire's hair. "It's okay. She surprised me, too."

Alucard sighed softly, turning his head to face him. "I told zhat guy to get you some vruit," he mumbled. "I vhought you might vant some."

The demon smiled. "I would. Thank you."

With a nod, Alucard moved closer and rested his head on Zalith's shoulder. For a moment, he relaxed as the demon fiddled with his hair. Now that he was in the water, he didn't really want to leave. The confines of his and Zalith's tent didn't make him feel very safe or relaxed, and neither did being surrounded by so many people. Out here, they were by themselves, and that was something he wasn't going to let go of so easily.

Alucard straightened, his hand resting on Zalith's shoulder as he locked eyes with the demon, who flashed him a slow, teasing smile. Zalith edged closer, their breaths mingling before he leaned in to kiss him. Alucard met him eagerly, guiding his hand to the back of Zalith's head, pulling him deeper into the kiss. He felt the heat rise as their tongues entwined together, each swirl pulling him further from the camp, from responsibility, until only Zalith remained.

But when Zalith's kisses drifted from his lips to his neck, Alucard felt the shift, the hunger deepening. He tilted his head, wordlessly inviting Zalith to continue, his fingers threading through the demon's hair. A shiver ran through him as Zalith's hand began its slow descent, trailing down his back and over his waist until it reached his inner thigh.

However, as Zalith's fingers slid purposefully over his crotch, Alucard's desire mingled with hesitation. His breath hitched, the moment thick with tension. His eyes darkened, and without a word, he gripped Zalith's wrist, stopping him. The want was there, but Alucard wasn't ready to lose control—not yet.

"Vhat are you doing?" the vampire asked with a flustered frown.

"Are you still scared?" Zalith mumbled, smirking.

Alucard scowled in embarrassment once more and looked away. "No."

The demon then started caressing his shaft beneath the water as he kissed his neck a few more times. "Are you sure?"

Nodding, Alucard hid his face against Zalith's neck. He felt nervous—of course he did. Anyone could walk out to the river at any moment and see them, but despite that, he didn't want to miss a moment of Zalith's affection. He sat there, gripping a handful of Zalith's hair as the demon continued to slowly pleasure him with his hand. He still feared someone might see them, but after a few moments, it didn't really seem to matter anymore. He exhaled deeply, nuzzling the demon's neck, a quiet moan of pleasure upon his breath as he dragged his hand down Zalith's neck and over his shoulder.

As Zalith moved his hand faster, the pleasure gripped Alucard a little tighter. He fidgeted, grimacing in struggle—he didn't want to make too much noise, but then again, he felt as if he didn't care. All that mattered was Zalith. The vampire moaned quietly, gripping Zalith's shoulder, delight enthralling him as the demon started to kiss his way down from his face to his neck. Zalith then widened his jaw, lightly biting Alucard's shoulder, pressing his fangs against his skin, but not enough to pierce it. And with one final moan, Alucard reached his peak and abruptly climaxed, gripping a handful of Zalith's hair as he did his best to hush his pleased whine.

Zalith kissed Alucard's neck again, making Alucard smile against the demon's neck' the vampire dragged his hands down Zalith's body, taking in the warmth of his soft skin. He felt a whole lot more relaxed now, but he wasn't quite sure if he wanted more or not. Did *Zalith* want more? He lifted his head from the demon's neck, smiling at Zalith as he smiled back.

Placing his hand on the side of Alucard's face, Zalith exhaled deeply and rested his forehead against his. "We should probably head back now," he suggested. "We'll be leaving once everyone's done eating."

Alucard felt a little disappointed to hear that, but…he was right. They couldn't stick around for too long, and he was sure Zalith was hungry. "Okay," he mumbled.

The demon took his hand and led the way out onto the riverbed, where he gathered their old clothes. Alucard used his ethos to send them to where he'd stored clean clothes and then summoned new clothes for them. Once they were dressed, they took each other's hand and headed back to the camp. Their peaceful solitude had come to an end, and Alucard wasn't sure when they'd get a moment alone again.

Chapter Forty-Four

Debts

| Zalith |

When they returned to camp, everyone was either eating or packing away their tents. Zalith set a skeptical gaze on the three angels; they, too, were eating, and the demon led the way over to them. He wanted to ask about the vaccine and giving it to as many of his people as possible.

Magnus smiled pleasantly as he caught sight of them making their way over; he stood up, handing his plate of eggs to Ulric, who rolled his eyes. "Ah, I see you are making a remarkable recovery, yes. I am not surprised—demons and their healing abilities are quite the marvel, yes."

Zalith offered his hand out. "I wouldn't be doing so if it wasn't for you. Thank you for coming all the way out here."

Magnus shook Zalith's hand. "Of course. But nothing is ever done out of the kindness of one's heart, yes. How are you feeling?"

"I feel fine," Zalith said, letting go of the angel's hand. "But I'll feel better once I know what it is that you want," he said, smirking.

"I'm sure we can talk about it," Magnus said, glancing at Alucard. "Alone…yes."

Alucard scowled, watching as Magnus set his eyes back on Zalith.

Zalith had no desire to leave Alucard alone, though. "He's very discreet," he said, gesturing to his vampire with his arm.

The angel frowned. "Whether one is discreet or not doesn't matter. I wish to talk to you alone, yes."

"Well, sometimes, we don't get what we wish for, do we?" he replied.

Magnus smiled at Alucard before gazing at Zalith. "I see you are attached to this…what are you?" he asked Alucard.

Zalith immediately crashed his fist into Magnus' wrinkled face. "Have some fucking respect," he warned him, watching as Magnus stumbled back into Ulric, who stood up to catch him.

Most of Zalith's people went silent, watching as the angel held his hands to his face, blood oozing from his now broken nose as he glared at Zalith in both startlement and anger.

"Get off your ass," the demon snarled at Magnus before taking hold of Alucard's hand and leading him into the cave.

Magnus followed, pulling free of Ulric after uttering something to him in a language that Zalith didn't understand.

"Speak," the demon then said as they stopped a few feet from his and Alucard's tent.

Magnus wiped the blood from his nose with a handkerchief before saying, "I had heard that demons are quite violent, yes…."

"So I suggest you start apologizing before you gain some more first-hand experience," Zalith growled.

The angel scowled but glanced at Alucard. "Forgive me, yes…I tend to forget to watch what I say."

Alucard rolled his eyes. "Vhat do you vant vrom 'im?"

Magnus eyed Alucard up and down but then looked at Zalith. "Erich had heard that somebody had stolen Lucifer's son from Damien—a Lilidian demon, the same Lilidian demon who killed most of Lilith's scions, yes. You are…Lilidian, and you match this demon's description. And obviously," he said, glancing over at Alucard, "you possess Lucifer's son. I'd like to know…what are your intentions? You must know that *all* of the Numen are willing to destroy entire civilizations to find…him," he said, looking at Alucard *again.*

Zalith scowled. "*Alucard* is a grown man; he isn't a piece of jewellery or a horse—he can't be stolen from anyone," he snarled. "And I don't have to answer or explain myself to *you*, of all people."

"Of course not—however, you *are* wrong, yes. He was created to be used as a weapon—nobody has ever seen him as a man; he simply walks in the skin of one, hoping to fool people like you," he said. "He will only bring destruction wherever he may go, yes."

"If that's the case, I suppose that's my burden to bear then, isn't it?" Zalith said with a smile, threat in his voice.

Magnus scoffed slightly, clearly aggravated that he wasn't getting to him. "Quite," he agreed. "I see. I should just get right to the point."

"That would be wonderful."

Magnus glared at Zalith. "You owe me for a total of two debts, both worth as much as a life, yes—and *you* owe me for saving *your* life," he said, glancing at Alucard.

Both Alucard and Zalith rolled their eyes, waiting for him to tell them what he wanted.

"Erich knows of your wish to undermine the Numen. He believes that you may be successful; you have the…tools," he said, shooting a glare at Alucard. "You have the knowledge, and the determination, I see, yes. There is nothing more powerful than one's love for another—one's desire to protect no matter the cost…." He smiled. "Lilith possesses something Erich wants; *you* will retrieve it and give it to me so that I can deliver it to Erich, yes."

"And what might this thing be?" Zalith asked.

"A Lumendatt…a crystal, yes. She stole it from Erich many centuries ago, and he has never been able to retrieve it—of course, you must both know that Erich isn't as powerful as his siblings. Unlike them, he isn't interested in obtaining…him," he said, glancing at Alucard again. "But, considering that you already have him, it would be foolish to waste such an opportunity, yes."

"What's a Lumendatt?" Zalith questioned, an aggravated tone in his voice.

"It does not matter. I didn't ask too many questions when you came seeking my assistance—I'd prefer you did the same, yes."

"I don't know how you expect us to get something for you without any specifics," Zalith uttered through his irritated scowl.

Magnus smiled. "It is on her person at all times, yes. It is what gives her the ability to adorn a human-like form, yes…to create scions, to enter the realms."

Zalith's aggravation was increasing. He didn't like the way Magnus looked at him…the way he smiled at him. And he didn't like the way he glanced at Alucard, talking about him as if he were a tool—an item. He had to refrain from hitting him again; he would have done so at least six more times already. He just didn't like Magnus *at all*. Fair enough, he owed the angel a debt, but there was no reason to be so skeptical, so arrogant and evasive. It was as if Magnus thought he was being slick and intelligent—but Zalith could see right through him. Whatever Magnus thought he was getting away with, Zalith wanted to let him know that he *wasn't* getting away with anything. There wasn't a *thing* Magnus would be able to hide from him or Alucard—Zalith would make sure of it. But he'd not let on that he knew—that he could see through him. That would only make Magnus try to hide his intentions better. Whatever he was *really* after, Zalith would find out. But he wanted to talk to Alucard about it first.

Glaring at Magnus, he extended his arm towards the cave's entrance, inviting Magnus to leave. "We'll get back to you," he said.

Magnus frowned, glancing at Alucard—

That was the last time Zalith would stand there and let this angel look at Alucard like that. He angrily gritted his teeth, forcing his arm against Magnus' chest as he pushed him back against the cave wall. "I don't care who you think you are," he snarled in his face. "Look at him like that again, and I'll send you back to Erich in pieces," he warned.

The angel stared at him, clearly startled—if Zalith didn't know better, he'd assume that Magnus wasn't used to this kind of treatment. He knew Magnus was the brains—or so he liked to act as though he was and assumed his brothers were his muscle, but…his brothers weren't stepping in; they were sitting outside watching.

Magnus gulped, glancing over at Ulric, who stepped into the cave, but he didn't call his brother over. Instead, he set his eyes back on Zalith. "Of course…my apologies," he said, and as Zalith loosened his grip, Magnus scurried away and left the cave.

As he left, Zalith sighed and turned to face Alucard. "We should talk about—"

"Woman outside said you were expecting this," Ulric suddenly called, making his way over to them with a smile on his face and a plate in his hand. He stopped in front of them as they turned to face him, holding the plate out—the plate that had eggs, toast, and a few pieces of fruit on it. "My brother is…not the most people-aware person. He does not understand emotion—how to…hmm, talk to someone."

"No amount of explaining him to me will make me like him, but thank you for the eggs," Zalith said, taking the plate from him.

Ulric smiled. "I remember you."

"I'm not easy to forget," Zalith said, uninterested.

"Quite," Ulric said. "Although I believe our last meeting was spent discussing whether or not one had problems with their…manhood." He smirked, looking Zalith up and down.

"Vhat?" Alucard snarled.

With a smile on his face, Ulric looked at him. "Oh, I didn't see you there."

"Well, your brother seems to like to stare—maybe he can teach you how to make better use of your eyes," Zalith interjected, taking Alucard's hand. Then, he ended their conversation, wandering off with his vampire and into their tent, leaving Ulric alone.

As he led the way into the tent, Zalith sighed and sat down on the blankets, smiling at Alucard as he sat in front of him.

"'Ow do you know zhat guy?" Alucard asked with a frown.

Zalith felt a little unnerved, he'd not lie. He wasn't sure whether Alucard was skeptical—did he think he'd cheated on him? He wouldn't blame him—Ulric had said what he'd said in a way that made it seem like something happened between them, but it hadn't. "He was there when I was waiting for Opus to enchant your ring," he explained. "He was being rather rude, and we got to talking about why I was there. He asked if I was there to figure out problems with my manhood, as that was apparently one of Opus' areas of expertise."

"Vight…" Alucard muttered.

Was Alucard mad at him? Zalith frowned. "Are you upset?"

Alucard set his eyes on him. "No," he said. "I vas just vondering vhether or not I needed to put 'im in 'is place."

Zalith laughed slightly, easing his fork into a piece of melon. "Are you going to beat him up?"

"If 'e vlirts vith you again, maybe," he confirmed.

Smirking, Zalith leaned over and kissed Alucard's lips before he started eating his food.

"Vhat do ve do about Magnus?" the vampire then asked. "Are ve going to look vor zhis crystal vor 'im?"

Zalith sighed deeply, picking up another piece of melon with his fork. "I don't know how I feel about it. His little shit-eating grin is a red flag."

"Do ve need 'im? Avter ve've got 'im to make more of zhe vaccine."

"Maybe it's worth keeping him around to keep tabs on Erich's side of things," he said.

Alucard nodded, leaning back against the crate behind him. "Is a lot to ask… vor zhat crystal," he mumbled. "Zhat ving is vorth more zhan our lives tvice over."

A curious smile met Zalith's lips. "What is this crystal? What does it do?" he asked—of course, he wasn't surprised to learn that Alucard knew what it was. The vampire had spent most of his life with the Numen, so of course he'd know things that he didn't.

The vampire shrugged. "Does many vings. Gives 'er access to Aegisguard's ethos, vhich is vhy she can valk in zhis vorld. Also 'elps 'er to look more 'uman. I've 'eard also gives 'er a voice zhat zhe people of zhis vorld can understand, and allows 'er to cveate scions," he revealed.

"Do all of the Numen have one, or just her?"

"Zhere are… seven of zhem. Zhey come vrom vherever zhe Numen came vrom. I know zhat Zamien 'as two, and Levoldus 'as vree. Luciver 'as vone, leaving Ephriel, Liliv, and Erich to vight over zhe last vone. Is vhy zhere isn't a constant vlow of Lilidian scions or Ephrian scions; zhey 'ave been… sharing zhe ability to cveate by stealing zhis crystal vrom each ozzer."

Zalith pondered for a few moments while he ate his food. It would appear that these crystals were a significant source of power to the Numen—the same power that allowed them to make scions. If he and Alucard were to acquire one or more Lumendatt, they'd have something else to use against their enemies. They were low on numbers, so to have something that could potentially help them increase their forces—that was something he'd not pass up. But he'd think about it more later when they were somewhere safer and could sit down and discuss their next moves.

"Interesting," the demon finally responded. "We'll talk about it more when we get ourselves and everyone else situated."

Alucard nodded. "Okay."

The demon then continued eating his breakfast, trying not to focus on anything too much. His thoughts, his feelings—everything was causing him to feel downhearted right now, and all he wanted to do was focus on Alucard. His vampire always gave him relief, escape. So he smiled, offering the piece of melon on his fork to him, and as Alucard gladly ate it, Zalith's smile grew. There wasn't a thing he wouldn't do for him, but…then came the imposing thoughts. Alucard deserved better—he didn't need any of this. Zalith just wanted Alucard to be safe, happy, and stress-free; Alucard wasn't getting any of that from him, was he?

Zalith sighed, finishing his food, and once he placed his plate aside, he laid down, exhaling deeply. "We should leave soon," he muttered, staring at the tent ceiling.

"Are you okay?" Alucard asked in concern.

"I'm just tired, but I know I shouldn't sleep."

Alucard laid down beside him, resting up on his arm so that he could look at Zalith, and as he did, Zalith turned his head and looked up at the vampire's concerned face. "Ve can vest vor a bit," he said. "If you vant to."

Smiling, Zalith rolled onto his side and pulled Alucard closer, wrapping his arms around him. He might not be able to get any more sleep now, but he *could* enjoy a short while cuddling with his vampire. There was nothing he loved more than to hold and to be held by his vampire…well, there was *one* thing, but…was now the time? He kissed Alucard's forehead and pulled him into a tight embrace.

Alucard smiled contently, resting his head against Zalith's chest.

Zalith started nuzzling his neck, fiddling with his hair; he kissed the side of his face but then stopped to kiss his neck. "Alucard," he said.

"Vhat?"

"Can you do mouth stuff to me?" the demon asked.

Alucard looked anxious, and as his face redenned, he looked away for a moment. But it didn't take him very long to nervously say, "Okay."

As excitement spiralled through him, Zalith kissed the vampire, dragging his fingers through his hair. Alucard guided his hand down the demon's body, gripping his inner thigh, and Zalith started kissing him a little faster, lightly biting his bottom lip; his anticipation was intensifying, and his desire for Alucard was quickly becoming overwhelming—and when the vampire trailed his hand from Zalith's inner thigh to grip his crotch and dragged his fingertips over his bulge, Zalith tensed and groaned quietly.

Alucard didn't seem to want to keep Zalith waiting. As their kisses became aggressive, the vampire dragged his hand up the demon's leg, over his waist, and under his belt. He gripped Zalith's arousal, unbuckling his belt with his free hand. They kissed just a few more times before Alucard gently pushed Zalith down onto his back, pulling his trousers from his body. Then, the vampire made his way down to Zalith's waist as the demon exhaled excitedly.

Zalith guided his hand to the back of Alucard's head, uttering a sigh of pleasure as the vampire slowly took his dick into his mouth. The demon tensed up, lightly gripping Alucard's hair as he dragged his tongue up his length; he moved teasingly slow, making Zalith murmur pleasurably, and with each passing moment, Alucard seemed to grow more confident, sucking a little harder, and eventually, faster.

The demon smiled contently, humming contently as he felt Alucard's warm tongue grace each inch of his dick. He didn't have the words to explain how much he enjoyed when Alucard did this for him; he knew how nervous the vampire was, but Zalith loved it—he loved him, and as he sunk deeper into just how pleasing it was, he moaned quietly, dragging his fingers through the vampire's hair.

But he ought to not let himself become too enthralled. As much as he enjoyed it, he wanted to have sex with him, too. So for a few moments longer, he let Alucard continue using his mouth, dragging his tongue over his shaft as the demon moaned quietly in response. And then Zalith guided his hand to the side of Alucard's face, looking down at him as he made him look up at him, taking his shaft from his mouth. "Do you want to fuck?" he asked, smirking.

Alucard's face went a little red—he looked so flustered, but he let go of Zalith's dick, making his way back up to his face to start kissing him as Zalith kissed back. Zalith was certain that this was his way of agreeing, and as Alucard lay on his back, pulling Zalith over him, the demon felt his excitement become overbearing. He focused on the fact that he now wanted to please Alucard—to make him feel better than just good, and he knew what he was going to do.

Zalith deepened their kiss, his hand sliding down the length of Alucard's body. His fingers moved swiftly, unbuckling the vampire's belt and tugging down his trousers with a hunger that matched the fire building between them. His palm graced Alucard's tense thighs, feeling the delicious response of his body, the way his muscles tensed and his breath quickened. He could sense the eagerness in Alucard's touch, each exhale betraying the excitement that matched his own.

Smiling against Alucard's lips, Zalith trailed his kisses down to the vampire's neck, relishing the way Alucard's body reacted to every brush of his lips. With a flicker of his ethos, he summoned the lube from his vault, wasting no time as he massaged it into Alucard's ass, his touch teasing and firm. As he playfully bit at Alucard's neck, he felt the vampire grip his hair, pulling him closer.

But Zalith wasn't ready to relinquish control just yet. He grabbed Alucard's wrists, pinning his arms above his head, his eyes locking onto the vampire's with a smirk. Slowly, he eased his dick into Alucard's ass, savouring every inch as he watched Alucard's expression shift—his usual composure giving way to a flustered, breathless need. The quiet moan that escaped Alucard's lips, the way he turned his face away in pleasure, only fuelled Zalith's desire. He leaned in, pressing a heated kiss to Alucard's neck, his smirk widening as the vampire's quiet resistance melted into raw, undeniable want.

The vampire moaned quietly—Zalith loved to hear him moan, to watch the struggled look on his face deepen as he tried to keep quiet. He slowly pulled back, breathing on Alucard's neck, dragging his right hand down Alucard's arm, over his pec, and then up to lightly grip his throat. He moved his dick back into him, gripping Alucard's wrists and throat a little tighter as they both moaned pleasurably. He wanted to move so much faster, but he also wanted to overwhelm Alucard with pleasure. He had to be patient. Careful. He couldn't lose control.

He let go of Alucard's throat, stroking his hand down his body as he thrusted his hard dick into and out of him, listening to his utters of pleasure. He was sure that he was about to hear more, though, as he placed his hand on Alucard's waist. Zalith focused, concentrating—he'd never done it to Alucard before, and he was admittedly excited to see how he might react. He focused on overwhelming Alucard with something intense, something so pleasing that the vampire wouldn't be able to hide just how satisfied he felt. The demon lightly pressed his index finger into Alucard's side, using an incubus ability that he didn't often use—and then he stared down at Alucard with a smirk on his face.

Alucard frowned, but his furrowed brow quickly lifted, giving way to a flustered yet relievingly pleased smile, his mouth gaping as he whined. He grimaced, he moaned, and he scowled, clearly struggling as Zalith's burning, *intense* pleasure surged through his body.

Zalith smiled in delight, moaning as he thrusted a little harder into the vampire's tight ass. He watched as Alucard held his eyes shut tight, digging his claws into Zalith's arms; he heard the vampire's racing heart, he felt his body shiver. The demon grew just a little more aggressive as he felt himself slowly approaching his peak; he didn't stop inducing the overwhelming state unto Alucard—he couldn't get enough of Alucard's pleasured expression.

The demon gently gripped Alucard's jaw and turned his head so that he could kiss his lips while he murmured and mumbled in delight. Zalith moved his hand from Alucard's wrists and to his throat, thrusting hard as the vampire fidgeted and trembled. His own heart was racing, any fatigue that he'd felt before now gone; he felt the vampire's warm, tight walls ensnare his dick, and as the vampire struggled to moan his name when he climaxed, an intense rapture gripped Zalith. He loved hearing Alucard's pleased moans, and he loved to hear him cry his name—both together satisfied him profoundly, urging him closer to his own peak.

Zalith took his hand from Alucard's waist, freeing him of the overbearing pleasure he'd bestowed upon him. He kissed the vampire's neck, thrusting faster, breathing harder; he grimaced in struggle, tightening his grasp on his vampire, getting nearer and nearer to his limit—and when tipped over the edge, he climaxed *hard*, making him moan loudly in pleasure against the side of Alucard's neck. He panted as his dick throbbed inside Alucard, listening to the vampire's pleased hum, and as the waves of sheer delight travelled through Zalith, he dragged his tongue up Alucard's neck and groaned in relief.

With a satisfied exhale, Zalith then eagerly pulled out and kissed his way down Alucard's body. He trailed his tongue along Alucard's sensitive dick, making the vampire fidget as he licked up Alucard's warm cum with a delighted hum. And as he swallowed it, his contentedness grew, leaving him feeling utterly appeased.

The demon lay beside Alucard, moving his arm around him and pulling him closer. As he sunk into the gratification, he smiled and nuzzled Alucard's neck, breathing in his sweet, intoxicating scent. He just wanted to lay there with him, hold him, have him—he loved him so much, and that was all he wanted to think about.

Chapter Forty-Five

Departing

| Alucard |

Alucard exhaled deeply as he lay with his head on Zalith's chest, pulling his cape from beneath them and moving it over them. Despite the fact that it was over, he still felt pleasure lingering through his sensitive, trembling body, pulsating from where Zalith had placed his finger. It was almost like a quiet, discreet climax, ever so slowly coming to its end as he lay in the demon's embrace, his eyes closed, his thoughts bare.

Nothing else mattered. Of course, Alucard's thoughts were never truly silent, though. He felt…curious. Zalith had shown him so many new things, he'd made him feel so many new things. He wondered…was there anything Zalith hadn't done before? Was there…anything Zalith had done with him that he hadn't done with or for someone else? It didn't bother him—why would it bother him? If he weren't comfortable with the fact that Zalith had been with people before, he wouldn't still be here. He just wanted to know…would Zalith be experiencing anything new with him, as *everything* he was experiencing with Zalith?

He then frowned. If none of this was new to Zalith, was he…actually enjoying it as much as he said? Alucard didn't want to think about that—he didn't want to lay there and worry about doing something wrong or not doing something the way Zalith wanted. Zalith had said that he was content, and Alucard trusted him. He didn't want to overthink it. But…his curiosity didn't exactly wane.

Zalith turned his head to look at Alucard. "Are you okay?" he asked quietly, sounding worried.

Opening his eyes, Alucard glanced up at him, nodded, and looked back over at the tent's wall. He was okay; he was just…wondering. "Zaliv," he mumbled.

"Yeah?" the demon asked, fiddling with his hair.

"Is zhere…vell…I'm just curious about zhis, but…is zhere…anyving you 'aven't veally…done bevore?" he questioned nervously.

"What do you mean?"

"I mean…like…intimately."

"Oh…" the demon replied, fiddling with Alucard's hair. "Like…sex or in general?"

Alucard shrugged. "Sex," he mumbled.

"I don't know," he admitted, and he sounded ashamed. "Well…I've never had sex with a woman," he added.

His answer made Alucard uncomfortable, but he wasn't about to let *that* trauma devour him. "Oh," he muttered in response, fighting the surfacing memory of…*that.* "Okay. I vas just curious."

"I'm sorry," Zalith uttered despondently.

"Vhy are you sorry?" Alucard asked, concerned. "I'm not upset."

Zalith shook his head. "You deserve better," he mumbled.

Confused, frowning, Alucard leaned onto his side and stared down at Zalith. "Vhy are you saying zhat?"

"I don't know," the demon said shamefully, looking away, a saddened look on his face.

It was an expression that brought heavy sadness to Alucard's heart. He didn't mean to upset Zalith—he didn't want that at all. He was just curious, but that had led to Zalith looking and sounding depressed, and Alucard as if felt he couldn't feel any worse than he now did. He didn't know how to make it better, but he'd try. "I zon't vant anyvone but you," he said, gazing down at Zalith as he looked back up at him.

"I don't want anyone but you, either," the demon said, guiding his hand to the side of Alucard's face.

"I'm sorry I asked," he said sadly.

"It's okay," Zalith replied, stroking his fingers down from Alucard's face, over his shoulder, and down his arm to his hand. "You were just curious. It's a reasonable question."

Eager to banish the sullen mood, Alucard shrugged and smiled as best he could. "You can ask me anyving you vant…if you vant," he offered.

Zalith stared up at him for a few moments, tracing his fingers up and down Alucard's bicep, but he then wrapped his arms around him, pulling him closer into a tight hug.

"Are you okay?" Alucard asked sorrowfully, laying on Zalith's chest, holding him.

"Yeah," he sighed deeply. "I just love you a lot."

"I love you a lot, too," Alucard said with a pout, nuzzling the demon's neck.

For a short while, they lay there, but Alucard's questions weren't going to wait to be answered. He'd already asked one; he might as well ask another. As awful as he felt for upsetting Zalith, he knew that the demon would rather him ask than sit around wondering.

So he asked, "Is zhere…anyving new I do vor you…anyving you 'aven't velt bevore?"

The demon held him tighter. "You love me like no one else ever has, even when I probably didn't deserve it. You make me happy like no one else has, and you make my life worth living," he mumbled sadly, burying his face in his neck. "You're everything to me."

Alucard smiled widely, moving his hand up to the side of Zalith's neck. "I vill alvays love you, no matter vhat. You make my life vorth living, too—and you make me 'appier zhan I ever vhought I might be. I still vant to spend my life vith you, and I still vant to 'ave a vamily vith you. Noving vill ever change my mind," he said quietly.

"I want that too," the demon muttered.

Still smiling, Alucard thought back to when Zalith mentioned their future, when they spoke about having a family. But the thought quickly brought sadness to his heart; now that they had lost their home and were running from Lilith's people, it would most likely be a long while until they could actually have a family. "Ve probably 'ave to put zhat on 'old vor now, zhough, huh?" he mumbled sadly.

"Some of it," the demon agreed sullenly, "but things will get better."

"I know zhey vill," Alucard agreed, moving his hand closer to Zalith's hair and starting to fiddle with it. "But I'm okay as long as ve're togezzer."

The demon nodded, stroking his fingers through Alucard's hair. "We'll figure it out."

Also nodding, Alucard sighed and closed his eyes. "I know ve vill."

| Varana |

Sitting on a log on the outskirts of the camp, Varana finished her breakfast and frowned down at her lap. Why did she still feel so sad and hesitant? The same way she'd felt last night when she and Alucard were watching over Zalith. It wasn't very long ago that she had purely hated Alucard—he'd ruined so much for her. But now that she actually thought about it…she didn't want to hate him. Maybe it was because she faced a situation where she had to choose either her family or Zalith. She didn't want to pick sides—she wanted to be happy on both sides. But when it came to Zalith, all she really felt was sadness, and that made her wonder…what if she picked her family because of how unhappy she currently was here? What would happen? She'd lose Zalith, and she didn't want to lose him, she didn't want to pick a side…she just wanted to be neutral, just as she had been before things escalated.

She sighed deeply, placing her plate aside. In the situation she found herself in right now, she realized that neutrality required her to be happy with both Zalith and her family—and if she was to be happy with the part of her life that involved Zalith, she had to get along with Alucard. It was going to be a struggle, admittedly, here and there, but…she'd try—for her own happiness and Zalith. They'd managed to talk last night for a short while without going for each other's jugular, so…maybe that was a sign that they *could* get along.

A twig then snapped, pulling her from her thoughts. She set her eyes on Idina, who was pacing back and forth a few feet from where she was sitting, muttering to herself and looking more conflicted than Varana had ever seen her.

"I should go and see if we should leave soon," the woman said, looking over at the cave, but then she shook her head and paced again. "No, I don't want to bother him; he's sick…" she murmured, but as she turned to face the cave again, she sighed deeply. "Maybe I should…no…I don't know."

With her limited patience thinning, Varana rolled her eyes and stood up, sighing a deep, annoyed sigh. "Oh, my God, I'll just do it!" she exclaimed, leaving Idina and heading towards the cave.

However, as she approached the cave entrance, she noticed the sandy-blonde, hazel-eyed angel who arrived last night set his gaze on her and ceased eating his food. He handed the plate to one of the others and swiftly hurried over to catch her before she entered the cave.

"Hey," he said with a smile, stopping in front of her.

She frowned, halting in her tracks to stare at him for a moment. "Hi," she said—yet another man flirting with her… though she wasn't surprised. But at least this one was attractive—he was, however, an angel. She found it strange since angels and demons were natural enemies, but everything had become strange lately. She didn't care.

"I'm Camael," he said.

She nodded slightly. "I'm Varana." She waited for him to respond, but he just gawped at her with an awkward smile on his face—she didn't have time for this. She went to walk away—

"W-wait, uh…how was your breakfast?" he asked, stepping in front of her. "I brought the food back."

"It was fine…" she answered, becoming aggravated. "Bye." She headed for the cave.

He didn't try to stop her this time; either he didn't know what to say, or the fact that his two angel companions were laughing at him stopped him.

Rolling her eyes, Varana made her way over to Zalith's tent.

| Zalith |

Zalith lay on his back with his arms around Alucard, who was lying on top of him, his head resting on his shoulder. He didn't feel any better—thought-wise, anyway. He sunk deeper into his sadness and despair the longer he lay there, and Alucard's questions drowned him further. He wished that he could be the most perfect version of himself for Alucard; he wished he wasn't the way he was and the way he had been before he met Alucard. Alucard deserved better.

He scowled, trying to hold back his misery. He sorely wished that he could give Alucard the things he was unable to give him; the joy of mutually experiencing new things together, a stable home life—he couldn't do that for Alucard, and it hurt. Everything was falling apart, and Alucard didn't deserve to go through it. He didn't deserve any of this, and Zalith didn't deserve *Alucard.* The vampire might tell him that he loved him, he might think that he loved Zalith, but Alucard had only ever been with him. If Alucard met someone else, he might love them more and see that Zalith wasn't worth his time or energy…because he wasn't, was he?

"Hello?"

Varana's voice snapped him out of it. He sighed irritably; he really didn't want to have to talk to her right now.

"I'm coming in," she called.

As Alucard sighed irritably, Zalith pulled his cape over what wasn't covered of the vampire's back and then he set his eyes on the tent entrance as Varana stepped in.

She stood there, glaring down at them with her arms crossed. "I could hear you fucking outside," she muttered.

Already aggravated, Zalith scowled. "Are you here to join us?" he asked both sarcastically and irritably as Alucard huffed in annoyance and turned his head to face away from Varana. "What do you want?"

Varana rolled her eyes. "Idina's getting fussy, and she wants to know when we're leaving, but she doesn't want to ask."

Sighing, Zalith took his eyes off her and glared up at the tent ceiling. "Twenty minutes."

"Fine," she mumbled, and then, to Zalith's relief, she turned around and left.

Alucard sighed deeply. "I guess ve should get veady to go. Ve need to get to zhe next rendezvous point bevore Liliv's people catch up."

The demon exhaled deeply, nodding as he fiddled with the vampire's hair. "I guess we should."

Neither of them moved, though. Alucard stayed where he was, and Zalith made no attempt to get up. Maybe they could just lay there a little longer.

But Zalith had to be responsible. He couldn't be reckless for the sake of a little comfort. "We should get up," he mumbled sadly.

Nodding, Alucard sat up—but he didn't let Zalith get up. He straddled the demon's lap and asked, "Are you okay?"

"Yeah," he said, stroking the vampire's waist. "I'm just tired of moving from place to place already."

Alucard fiddled with the thin gold chain around the demon's neck. "Ve von't 'ave to do zhis vor much longer, vight? Ve can go to zhe castle any time ve vant to—zhat can be our 'ome now."

The demon shrugged. He was still reluctant to head there despite trusting Alucard that it was a safe haven. "If we can't think of anything else, then maybe," he answered.

The vampire frowned and moved his hand to the side of his face. "Vhat's vrong, Zaliv?" he insisted.

But the demon moved his hand over Alucard's hand on his face and frowned. "Nothing's wrong, baby. I'm just tired," he said. He didn't want to lay there and talk about his despair and dismay. It was time to get moving.

Sighing sadly, Alucard nodded. "Okay. Vell…you're still trying to get better, so…I'll pack everyving up and you can go and vait vith Varana," he offered.

Zalith shook his head. "I don't want to talk to her right now."

"Zhen…you can stay 'ere vith me," he said, smiling. "But I'll still pack everyving up," he said sternly.

"I'd rather stay here with you, but I don't want you to do all the work. You've done enough."

Alucard shook his head. "I'm vine. I just vant you to vest."

The demon sighed reluctantly but said, "Okay."

The vampire got off him and pulled his trousers back on while Zalith got dressed, too. Zalith helped him pick up all the blankets, but then Alucard made him sit on a crate by the wall with his cape as he started to take the tent down. He watched, and when he saw Alucard glance at him, he smiled, trying to hide his despair. But it was gnawing at him like a starved beast. The euphoria of his orgasm had almost completely faded, leaving room for all his negative thoughts and feelings to creep in.

Zalith struggled to fight it. He lowered his head in shame but glanced at Alucard every so often. He didn't want to just sit there and do nothing—he wanted to help Alucard pack everything away, but the vampire insisted he sit there. If he tried to argue with him, he was sure that it would start a conversation Zalith just didn't have the energy to have right now. So he stayed where he was, watching as Alucard packed the tent away along with the blankets as his kitten climbed up onto his shoulder.

When Alucard took the rolled-up tent and an armful of blankets out to where their horses were, Zalith got up and grabbed the blankets Alucard couldn't carry. He followed him outside, rolling the blankets up and attaching them to the back of his horse's saddle. Everyone else seemed to be ready to go, having packed and grouped up around Idina, Greymore, and Freja, who instantly set their eyes on Alucard and Zalith as they emerged from the cave.

With a deep sigh, Zalith finished attaching the last blanket to his saddle and turned to face everyone. "There's a village about thirty minutes south," he called as everyone started standing up, preparing to leave. "We'll head there and pick up a few more horses and some supplies before we head up the mountain to our next safe point."

Nobody had anything to say. They all just mumbled and murmured, waiting to get going. However, as Zalith turned to face Alucard, a crash of thunder rumbled through the greying sky. He was certain that it was soon to rain, and he rolled his eyes. Could the day get any worse?

"Ve should 'ear vrom Tyrus soon," Alucard said, mounting his horse beside Zalith. "And zhen maybe I'll vind out vhy Crowell 'asn't come to me."

"Okay," the demon said, looking up at him. "Hopefully everything's fine."

Alucard nodded in response.

"Considering as you're about to depart, yes…" Opus said, interrupting as Zalith was about to mount his horse. "I feel I should let you know…that my associates and I have decided that we will be joining you, yes."

Zalith glowered at him as he stopped beside Alucard's horse with Camael and whatever the other one was called. "And who gave you the invitation to do so?" he questioned.

"Well, you are yet to tell me whether or not you will retrieve what I asked, yes…and I would like to…study, yes. As I said last night to your…" he paused and looked up at Alucard, "mate…yes. It isn't often I get to see demons so closely in the wild," he said, setting his eyes back on Zalith. "I was going to reach out to you earlier; however, you were busy…mating…loudly, yes," he said with a smile.

The demon rolled his eyes *again.* "Don't you have people you're supposed to be taking care of?"

"Yes. *You* are my current patient. I cannot leave until I know that you have fully recovered."

"I'm fine."

"Regardless, I am still going to accompany you, yes. I am yet to decide what else it is I want from both of you."

Zalith really didn't want to talk to him anymore; he just wanted to get going. "Fine," he grumbled. "Just stay out of the way."

The angel nodded and strutted off.

With an irritated sigh, Zalith mounted his horse and looked back at everyone. "Let's go," he called. He then glanced at Alucard to see if he was ready, smiled as best he could at him, and without further hindrance, he started to lead the way back into the forest.

Chapter Forty-Six

Citadel Overrun

| Crowell |

The very moment he arrived at Fort Rudă de Sânge with the Nefastian Coven, Crowell was stopped by Kristov and Tyrus. Both men looked like they had something urgent to say, so Crowell sent the vampires deeper into the building and stared expectantly, waiting for either of them to speak.

"Aleksei sent me," Tyrus said. "I was initially supposed to help find you and the coven that you were evacuating—"

"But Lord Alucard has sent us a new mission," Kristov interjected. "He wants us to do all we can to keep the disease from spreading across Nefastus; he ordered us to contain the infected and get everyone else to safety."

Crowell only saw glimpses of the horror that had ensnared the Citadel, and as unsettled as the idea of going back made him feel, he wouldn't disobey orders. "All right. I'll create a team and head back there," he replied.

"No need, Baron," Kristov said and looked over his shoulder. "Come," he called.

A group of vampires ready for combat stepped out of the lounge behind Kristov. They each wore their fire-proof robes, their weapons sheathed at their sides—ethos-syphoning swords, silver daggers, and colts with explosive rounds, invented by their Lord himself. They were ready for anything.

Kristov took a spare set of robes and a collection of weapons from Adherent Mirela. He handed them to Crowell and said, "They're ready to head out when you are, Baron." He then looked at Tyrus. "I've been instructed to send you on a continuous journey," he explained as Tyrus frowned. "It has been recently revealed that you are being tracked by the enemy; it is within everyone's best interest to keep you moving until Lord Alucard or Zalith find someone to remove the tracking ethos."

Tyrus looked confused and concerned. He evidently didn't know that he was being tracked. "Where am I going?"

"Lord Alucard has sent me instructions," Kristov answered, taking a map from his pocket. "You'll take this route continuously while my team work to find out who is tracking you. Once we know, we'll find out how to remove the ethos."

"Understood," Tyrus said, taking the map.

Crowell pulled his robes on and made sure that his weapons were secure. "Is there time to send Lord Alucard an owl? I should let him know that I'm here." If telepathic communication with their Lord wasn't a one-way thing, he'd have told him already.

"He's told us to avoid using messengers for now. When he next requests an update, we'll let him know of your arrival and return to the Citadel," Kristov said.

"All right," he said and looked at his team: Adherents Ruxandra, Mirela, Soiman, Gavrilo, Vulpea, Şoimănița, Ştefan, Lilja, and Paladin Cerboaica. They were all very capable vampires. "Where's Lăcrămioara?" he asked, expecting to see her among them.

"Knight Lăcrămioara is already in the Citadel with her own team; I suspect you'll meet up with her not long after your arrival."

Crowell nodded and said, "Okay, let's get moving." He led the way out of the fort and to the dock, where he transformed into an owl and his team into bats, owls, and ravens.

They travelled over the ocean, the cover of the overcast sky granting them greater speed. As they got closer to Nefastus, though, the putrid smell of death and rot filled the dark, smoggy air. Crowell heard the pained, savage snarls of the monsters that had once been human, and he tensed up. But he grasped onto his composure—he was leading this team, and he had to make sure that he was ready.

Once they reached the chaos-ensnared city, Crowell and his team landed in the shipyard, the only place that wasn't thick with smoke, ensnared by fire, or infested by creatures—likely because the massive steel gates were shut at every exit and entrance. He and his team took their original forms, standing there, staring, listening, sniffing. The place was almost reminiscent of DeiganLupus during the bubonic plague.

"Fucking hell," Gavrilo muttered, holding his hand over his mouth and nose.

"What is that *smell*?!" Ruxandra exclaimed.

"Death," Şoiman answered hauntedly.

"Demons," his sister, Şoimănița added, tying her black hair behind her head.

"Baron!" came a familiar voice.

Crowell shifted his senses to the left, setting his eyes on Lăcrămioara. The blood-soaked Knight hurried over with only three vampires behind her, and they all looked horrified. But there was a human with them, too—old, perhaps in her mid-forties, and she wore a plague doctor's mask.

"I can't tell you how relieved we are to see you," Lăcrămioara said when she reached him. "We've waited hours for reinforcements."

"Who's the mask?" Vulpea asked.

"Doctor Moore," the human woman replied. "Your friends here pulled me from the wreckage that was once my private practice."

Crowell frowned at Lăcrămioara, waiting for an explanation.

"Doctor Moore has been studying the infection since the first few cases started popping up," the Knight explained. "It's thanks to her that we've been able to do our job more effectively."

"Explain," Crowell requested.

Doctor Moore stepped forward, strangely brave despite being around a group of vampires. "This infection is…odd," she started. "It evolves quickly, but I've been able to determine that this infection was originally supposed to affect only demons—and it *did.* The demons in the Citadel were infected, and they were transformed into these sort of mindless monsters caught between life and death, starving no matter how much blood or…well, *people* they consumed. The infection moved onto humans when infected demons bit them, and now the whole city is overrun."

"And that's helped deal with the situation how?" Crowell questioned.

"There's a window where they can be saved," the doctor replied. "If given vampire blood and venom before the infection reaches their heart, bitten humans can be turned into vampires. I mean it's not saving their human lives, but it *does* save them from death…well…you know what I mean."

Crowell shifted his concerned gaze to Lăcrămioara. "And Lord Alucard agreed to this method?"

Lăcrămioara looked conflicted. "Not exactly, Baron. We haven't been able to contact him, but this was my call, and I'll take the punishment if he disagrees."

"But the more vampires, the better, right?" Lilja asked. "We lost so many when Dor-Sanguis fell; surely, getting our numbers back up is a good thing?"

"Agreed," Crowell said. "But our Lord has his methods."

"What about the infected that are too far gone?" Cerboaica asked.

"There's nothing we can do to save them," Doctor Moore answered. "Death is a mercy."

"We've been loading the uninfected onto the galleon," Lăcrămioara said, nodding to Lord Alucard's docked galleon. "And the Fledgelings on that trade ship."

With a deep sigh, Crowell glanced at the trade ship docked on the other side of the shipyard and nodded. "All right, let's get moving. Our mission is to contain the spread as best as we can. We'll save whoever possible and kill whoever's too far gone. We're going to have a lot of Fledgelings on our hands, though—they're going to need to feed to complete their transformation. One uninfected human should be enough for five Fledgelings—" he looked at Mirela, "—it's your job to make sure we have blood for them. Take Gavrilo with you. Bring two here for now, store them on that trade ship, and wait for the Fledgelings to begin arriving."

Mirela and Gavrilo nodded.

"Prăvălia, stay here with Doctor Moore to receive and guide the uninfected humans," Lăcrămioara instructed.

Prăvălia nodded.

And then Crowell began leading the way to one of the gates.

"We've been working on the west before we delivered the most recent batch of clean humans," Lăcrămioara said to Crowell.

"We'll get more done if we split into two groups," the Baron replied as he pulled the gate open. "Bogdănel, Ruxandra, Cerboaica, Șoiman, and Șoimănița, head to the west. Everyone else, stick with me."

As instructed, the vampires broke away and headed off to the left as Crowell closed the gate behind them.

Crowell then led the remaining vampires deeper into the Citadel, his sharp gaze sweeping the smoke-choked streets as they advanced. The once-grand city now lay in utter ruin, engulfed by chaos, the eerie glow of flames casting shadows that danced across gilded facades and lavish storefronts. Wealthy residences and opulent shops were shattered and defiled, their carefully curated elegance crumbling under the brutal assault of panic and carnage. Bodies lay strewn across the cobbled streets, some twisted in grotesque death poses, others moving in an unnatural, shuffling gait—infected humans, transformed into monstrous husks hungry for flesh. The scent of burning wood and scorched metal filled the air, underscored by the stench of decaying flesh and coppery blood.

The Baron moved with precision, his mind honed on the task ahead as his senses soaked in every horrific detail. Beside him, Lăcrămioara glided forward with feral grace, her hand hovering near the hilt of her silver-bladed dagger. Teofana and Ștefan flanked them, while Lilja and Vulpea brought up the rear, eyes wide as they scanned for movement amidst the smoke. The clang of horse hooves and the shrieks of desperate animals filled the air, carts overturned and carriages abandoned where they'd been left by those who had fled in terror.

These streets, typically polished and pristine, were now slick with blood and grime, obscuring the gold-trimmed stones beneath. The towering, ornate buildings with their arches and intricate balconies bore scars from fires that had spread across rooftops. Many windows were shattered, some dark and empty, others smeared with claw marks and splattered with blood. Here and there, Crowell could see flashes of gold detailing on doorframes and lampposts, remnants of the city's aristocratic wealth glinting eerily through the smoke. Gasping, trembling figures peered out from narrow alleyways or from behind makeshift barricades, some praying that their hiding places would remain concealed. Others dared to bolt across the cobblestones, only to fall beneath the hands and teeth of the infected.

A sharp sound—a scream cut short—drew their attention down a side street. Ahead, near the boarded-up front of an exclusive-looking pub, a cluster of infected humans clawed and slammed against the wood, trying to break through to the terrified survivors hidden within. Crowell could feel the dread pulsing from inside the establishment, a heartbeat of fear that beat louder with each assault on the barricade.

"Steady yourselves," he murmured, his voice barely audible over the screams and snarls. But his words had weight, grounding the Adherents as they readied their weapons.

In one swift motion, Crowell lifted his hand, calling forth a surge of fire that crackled and roared, encircling his fingers before he flung it towards the infected mob. The flames erupted into the nearest figure, lighting up its vacant, bloodshot eyes before consuming it whole. The others twisted and screeched, some stumbling back as Lăcrămioara took her cue. In an instant, she shifted form, her body flowing into that of a massive black wolf, her fur igniting into dark, seething flames. She charged at the remaining infected, setting them ablaze on contact, her flames spreading like a hungry tide.

Teofana moved in next, her ethos-draining sword drawn and gleaming as she plunged it into a figure trying to claw its way towards her, its flesh sizzling and shrivelling as the blade rendered it motionless. Vulpea and Lilja were quick to flank her, slashing through the infected with their silver knives, each strike calculated and precise. Ştefan took aim with his revolver, the explosive rounds sending two of the infected flying backwards in a burst of blood and ash, leaving only the charred remains of twisted bodies behind.

Crowell watched each of the Adherents in action, their movements efficient, the violence a stark contrast to the noble decorum they usually held. Another infected lunged towards him, but he extended his hand, flicking his wrist to send it hurtling backwards, smashing it into the wall of the pub with a telekinetic force that broke bone and sent it sliding to the ground, unmoving.

As the last of the infected fell silent, the screams from within the pub grew quieter, the survivors stunned into silence by the sight of the vampires standing between them and their would-be killers.

Crowell approached the barricaded door and tapped it with the hilt of his sword. "You're safe now," he called, his voice a mix of command and reassurance. "We're here to help."

The sounds of fumbling and scraping echoed from behind the door, and slowly, a crack appeared as cautious eyes peered out. A dishevelled man, face streaked with dirt and sweat, opened the door further, revealing a cluster of wide-eyed survivors huddled in the shadows.

"Vulpea, take them back to the shipyard," Crowell instructed. "Ensure they make it to safety."

Vulpea nodded and gestured for the humans to follow. They filed out cautiously, clinging to each other as they passed the smouldering remains of the infected. As they departed, Crowell scanned the darkened streets, sensing the weight of despair that clung to the city. But as the survivors disappeared into the distance, he grasped onto the purpose that he'd been given. The Citadel may be shrouded in darkness, but he wouldn't allow it to fall entirely into shadow—not while he still had the power to fight. This city was supposed to be his new home, and he'd do everything he could to save it.

Crowell led his team further into the smoke-laden depths of the Citadel, the flicker of fires casting elongated shadows across the cobblestone streets. The occasional scream pierced the night, quickly stifled by the guttural snarls of the infected. Lăcrămioara prowled beside Crowell, her wolf form shimmering with embers from her earlier transformation, while Lilja kept to his other side, her silver knife ready, eyes glinting with focus.

They turned a corner into a narrower alley lined with elaborate iron-wrought balconies. The once beautiful wrought iron was now twisted, covered in ash and grime, and some doors swung open from where the residents had fled in terror. Flames licked at the wood, sending showers of sparks across the stone path. Among the debris, several figures shambled into view—infected, their eyes vacant but ravenous, mouths pulled into grotesque snarls.

Without a word, Crowell lifted his hand, igniting a fresh surge of flames that burst forth, engulfing two of the creatures in a searing blaze. Lăcrămioara charged forward, her claws swiping with deadly precision as she tore through another infected, its body crumbling beneath her fiery assault. Teofana drew her sword and struck at a creature lunging for Lilja, draining the infected of its limited energy in one swift, ruthless blow. The bodies hit the ground, lifeless.

They moved quickly, and just as they stepped into a small square littered with overturned carts and debris, Crowell's sharp senses caught movement nearby. The flickering glow of firelight illuminated two figures struggling amidst the chaos: a frantic, terrified human being held down by an infected who clawed desperately at him, its teeth bared.

Crowell moved in swiftly, but not fast enough. The infected plunged its rotting teeth into the man's shoulder, a scream tearing through the air as blood gushed from the wound. Lăcrămioara was already there, her claws slicing through the infected's neck, severing its head with ease. The creature crumpled, its teeth still bared in a macabre grimace as it fell away from its victim.

The bitten man staggered back, clutching his wounded shoulder, his wide eyes locking onto Crowell in sheer terror. Crowell stepped closer, his gaze sharp and unyielding as he looked at the wound, knowing the grim fate that awaited the man if left untreated.

"You've been bitten," Crowell said, his voice even but firm. "That bite will kill you—turn you into one of them."

The man's breaths came in ragged gasps, like he was trying to grasp the reality of his situation.

Crowell continued, "The only way to save is to turn you into one of us…into a vampire. But the transformation isn't painless, and it won't be easy—not at first. I'm sure you know what our life involves, so I'm going to ask, do you want that life?"

Desperation twisted the man's features, fear in his eyes warring with the clear instinct to survive. After a moment, he gave a resolute nod, swallowing hard as he choked out, "Do it…p-please."

Crowell placed a steady hand on the man's shoulder. "This will hurt, but you'll survive. Hold on."

Without hesitation, Crowell leaned in, his fangs descending as he sank them into the man's neck. The metallic tang of blood filled his senses, and he drew just enough to weaken the human's body before pulling back; he then bit his own wrist, letting his blood flow as he pressed it to the man's mouth. The man drank reluctantly at first, his eyes fluttering as the potent blood began to take hold. His gulps soon became eager, but just moments later, a low, agonized groan escaped him as he fell to the ground, writhing, his body twisting in response to the violent transformation. The change would be gruelling, Crowell knew, but it would save him from the infection that would otherwise consume him. As the man convulsed, his features contorting, Crowell turned to Ştefan.

"Take him back to the shipyard," the Baron instructed.

Ştefan nodded, slinging the man's limp arm over his shoulder, and then he swiftly carried him back through the burning streets.

Crowell and the others waited in silence, their breaths low and controlled as they kept watch for any further signs of movement in the nearby shadows. The distant screams had quieted somewhat, leaving an eerie stillness, interrupted only by the crackling of flames and the occasional rumble as part of a building gave way to the blaze.

When Ştefan returned, a look of grim determination on his face, Crowell nodded in acknowledgement.

"Let's move," the Baron said, leading them deeper into the city.

They pressed on, their senses sharpened as they hunted for any remaining infected, all the while keeping an eye out for survivors. And not even moments later, his team picked up on a sinister blend of sounds and scents: the metallic tang of fresh blood mingling with the pungent stench of the infected. Ahead, echoes of clashing weapons and guttural roars filled the air, underscored by the unmistakable scent of iron and sweat. Crowell's jaw tightened as he motioned for his team to fall silent, each vampire attuning their senses to the approaching cacophony.

The group crept forward, slipping between the shadows cast by burning buildings, and emerged at the edge of a vast, smoke-filled market square. Flames flickered through the rising murk, casting an orange glow over a frenzied scene. Humans and elves, their faces streaked with grime and their weapons bloodied, fought side-by-side against waves of infected. The infected moved like a relentless tide, driven by the mindless hunger that propelled them forward no matter how many fell.

Crowell quickly took in the scene, his conflicted gaze flickering from group to group. The uninfected fought bravely, but they were clearly outnumbered. He looked at his team and nodded. "We split up. Lilja, take the northern flank; Teofana, the east. Lăcrămioara, with me on the west side. Ştefan, secure any bitten and newly turned—save who you can, but any too far gone are to be killed. If a life can be spared, turn them."

With a final glance of solidarity, the vampires separated, each moving with the precision and lethal grace of their kind. Crowell surged forward, conjuring a burst of fire that cut through a pack of infected, reducing them to smouldering remains. He caught glimpses of his team amidst the chaos: Lilja's blade flashed, severing limbs with every swing; Teofana's movements were fluid as she drained the energy from her opponents, leaving them crumbling to the ground; and Lăcrămioara, transformed into her blazing wolf form, was a whirlwind of fire and fury as she tore into the infected.

Crowell moved with relentless focus, but he took brief moments to glance around, ensuring his team was holding their ground. He noticed Ştefan pulling aside a newly bitten man, his voice firm but reassuring as he spoke to the wounded human, instructing him to drink from a shallow cut on his wrist, saving him from the virus's grip.

The battle intensified, and Crowell's senses were ablaze with the scent of blood and death. Suddenly, a sharp cry split through the din, and Crowell's eyes snapped towards the source. He saw Teofana surrounded by a wave of infected, struggling to keep them at bay. Her blade flashed in swift arcs, but the infected pressed closer, overwhelming her. Crowell's heart clenched as he sprang into action.

With a burst of telekinetic force, he sent several infected flying, clearing a path towards her. He fought his way forward, claws slicing and fire erupting in his wake. He reached Teofana, grabbing her by the arm and pulling her from the crush of bodies. But as he did, a vicious infected sunk its teeth into his side, tearing through flesh and muscle.

Crowell gritted his teeth, fighting through the pain. He dispatched the attacker with a sharp strike, only to feel another set of claws rake across his back. His vision blurred as more infected closed in, striking him from every side. Pain erupted through him, each wound dragging him closer to darkness.

"Crowell!" Lăcrămioara's voice cut through the haze.

As he hit the ground with a painful grunt, Crowell watched through his darkening eyes as Lăcrămioara surged forward in her wolf form, blazing with fury, tearing into the infected surrounding him until only ashes remained.

Returning to her vampire form, she knelt beside him, her face set in grim determination. "Crowell!" she insisted.

He tried to reply, but he couldn't find his voice. The pain was unlike anything he'd felt before, burning through him like fire, forcing him to grunt and writhe and groan.

"H-he saved me!" Teofana wailed, panicking.

"Shit," Lăcrămioara muttered. "Crowell? Can you hear me?"

Crowell managed a stiff nod.

"You're hurt bad," she told him. "We don't have a healer with us."

He scowled confusedly, unsure what she was trying to tell him.

"Lilja!" she then shouted.

Lilja hurried over. "Oh, my God—C-Crowell!" she exclaimed, appearing beside him. "W-what happened?!"

"He's hurt bad—we can't treat him here.," Lăcrămioara said hurriedly. "Take him back to Fort Rudă de Sânge; they're the only ones who can help him."

Crowell opened his mouth to protest, but the agony of his injuries muted him. He looked up at Lăcrămioara, and she met his gaze, her expression fierce and unwavering.

"I'll take over the mission," Lăcrămioara assured him. "We'll handle the rest."

Weakly, he nodded, knowing that she was right but feeling a pang of disappointment pierce through the pain. He had come so far, led his team into battle, and now he was being taken out of it. A flicker of shame gnawed at him, wondering if Lord Alucard would see his weakness as failure.

"Lăcrămioara…keep them safe," he managed, his voice barely a whisper.

She nodded, her hand on his shoulder reassuringly.

As Lilja helped him to his feet, Crowell cast one last glance at the battlefield. He hated that he'd been so badly injured so early into the fight, but staying behind would only make him a burden. He'd done all he could, and he knew that Lăcrămioara was more than capable of leading in his place. He just hoped that once Lord Alucard heard the news, he wouldn't think him incapable of his Baron rank.

Chapter Forty-Seven

Deserters

| Alucard |

Half an hour passed before Alucard and Zalith started slowing. The vampire glanced back at everyone as they stopped; he could see the village just up ahead, but he was certain that it wasn't wise for him or Zalith to be seen.

Alucard climbed down off his horse, as did Zalith, but the demon wandered off to three of his people who had broken off from the rest of the group and started mumbling to them. Staring over at them, Alucard frowned, but he was sure that Zalith was just telling them what to get from the village while Zalith and everyone else waited there.

"Is everyving okay?" Alucard asked quietly as Zalith re-joined him.

"Yeah. I've sent them to get us some different clothes, too. We should wear what regular people do so that we don't stand out so much."

Alucard nodded, but before Zalith could climb back atop his horse, he frowned and took hold of the demon's wrist. He wanted to ask him if he was okay, but…he'd already asked so many times today that he was probably irritating Zalith. So, he let go, picking up Peaches from his horse's saddle instead.

"What's wrong?" Zalith asked, letting go of his horse's reins.

Shrugging, Alucard looked down at his kitten. "I'm just vorried about you," he mumbled.

Zalith sighed as he tucked a loose strand of Alucard's hair behind his ear. "I'm okay, baby."

He wasn't convinced. "Are you sure?"

"I'm sure," he said, and then he leaned closer and kissed him.

Alucard wasn't going to persist; the last thing he wanted to do was annoy Zalith. So, he nodded and scratched Peaches' chin as she purred loudly. He then leaned back against a tree beside his horse and glanced at Zalith, who also leaned against a tree, staring out at the village. The vampire's gaze shifted to Varana, who was scowling skeptically at Camael when he offered to help her down off her horse.

The vampire rolled his eyes before looking down at his kitten again. He couldn't take his focus off Zalith, though. He knew that the demon was depressed, and he wanted to help him, but he didn't know what to do. He never really knew what to do, just like when he had been depressed during Yule. Alucard found himself confused and hopeless, and *that* added to his despondency.

He sunk into his thoughts. He yearned for the comfort of their home, the comfort of their own bed. Just about now, he and Zalith would be waking up—well, *he'd* just be waking up to see Zalith had waited for him. And then they'd lay there and talk or cuddle. He missed that already. But they wouldn't be doing this forever; just another week or so…and then they could head for the castle. *That* would be their home now.

The trio sent to the village returned a while later.

Alucard set his blue eyes on them as they made their way from the village and over to where he and Zalith were waiting. Two of them were pulling two horses each with them, and the other had some folded clothes under his arm. He walked to Zalith, handed the clothes to him, and then he wandered off to join everyone else.

"Alucard," Zalith mumbled.

Taking his sights off the murmuring crowd, Alucard looked at the demon, who made his way behind the cover of a large tree. Alucard placed Peaches atop his horse's saddle and followed.

"We'll change, and then we'll leave," Zalith said, stopping behind the tree as he started to unbutton his shirt, handing Alucard the folded clothes.

"'Ow long until ve veach zhe mountaintop?" Alucard asked.

"Half a day—maybe a little less," he muttered, taking his pocket watch out of his trouser pocket. He then undressed and got into his new clothes—a grey shirt with a black tie, a dark brown leather waistcoat, a black long coat, and black trousers. He then put his pocket watch into his waistcoat's pocket, attaching the chain's end to one of its buttons, and completed his ordinary-citizen look with a brown leather wide-brimmed hat.

Alucard smiled and stroked the demon's coat. "You look like a mysterious vogue," he said with a smirk.

Zalith smiled and leaned his arm against the tree, edging his face closer to Alucard's. "I do? Well, I might just have to wrangle you up and take you out to the pasture later."

The vampire laughed a little. "I'd go villingly."

"And nobody would hear us out there," the demon flirted, tracing his fingers down the side of Alucard's face to his neck. "I'd have you all to myself."

Alucard was starting to feel aroused despite the fact that they hadn't had sex very long ago. But he couldn't let his desires consume him this time. He took the other black wide-brimmed hat and put it on. "Vhat do you vink?"

"Mm," the demon hummed, his eyes hungrily exploring Alucard's face. "I think you look very sexy. I want to do things to you."

The fact that Zalith was flirting with him so much convinced Alucard that maybe he wasn't as distraught as he worried he might be. "Maybe vhen ve get to zhe mountaintop," he suggested quietly, fighting his nervousness. "You can do vhatever you vant to me."

Zalith smiled excitedly and kissed his lips. "It's a date."

With Zalith's help, Alucard then got into the rest of his new clothes: a mahogany shirt, darker brown trousers, and a red necktie that he wasn't going to put on, but the demon smirked amusedly and put it on for him, kissing his lips a single time once they were done.

Before Zalith could leave to return to his people, though, Alucard grasped his hand and pulled him closer. "I love you," he said quietly.

Zalith smiled softly. "I love you, too," he said, and then he kissed him a few times before wrapping his arms around him.

They hugged for a minute, and then the demon led the way back to their horses. When they reached them, though, Greymore and Idina hurried over with concerned, hesitant looks on their faces. Alucard was convinced that they both had something to say that they knew was going to either upset or annoy Zalith—

"So…I have some bad news for you," Greymore started, stopping in front of Zalith.

"Please don't get upset," Idina added, standing beside Greymore.

"What?" Zalith asked with an irritated glower.

Idina and Greymore spoke simultaneously but then silenced and looked at one another.

Idina backed off, leaving Greymore to speak.

"There are some people who are thinking of leaving…for good," Greymore explained.

The demon's expression didn't change. "How many?" he asked—it was almost as if he had been expecting it.

"Eleven," Greymore answered.

Zalith exhaled deeply.

Idina tagged on, "I've been trying to convince them to stay, and they're pretty adamant, but I think we can convince—"

The demon held up his hand, silencing her. "Bring them to me."

Greymore stared at him for half a moment, a hint of dread flickering across his face, but then he nodded. "Okay," he said and raced off to where some of Zalith's people had grouped up away from the rest. The Alpha urged them all to follow, and as he made his way back over to Zalith, the eleven people followed behind him.

All of them looked nervous, glancing at one another and back at Zalith, who invited them to speak with a gesture of his hand.

They glanced at one another again until one man sighed deeply and set his eyes on Zalith. "Look, we're tired," he said bravely. "We've all been doing this for years, and we don't want to keep having to run, hide, and leave everything behind. We just want a quiet life," he explained.

"No more sneaking around, moving from place to place," the woman at his side added.

Alucard eyed each person—the two shapeshifters were among the group, and so was Colt, the little boy Idina had taken to. The rest of them were demons and werewolves. Alucard averted his gaze to Zalith, but the demon didn't seem too bothered, like he'd already decided what to do with them; Alucard felt it was best he didn't get involved.

Zalith exhaled deeply. "Fine. But I'm going to have to wipe your memories."

More than half of the small group gasped and mumbled in discontent.

"Either leave without them or die with them," Zalith said coldly.

The group went back to muttering, but the younger shapeshifter murmured something with panic in his voice, and then he abruptly shifted into a hare and darted for the bushes.

Alucard reacted fast; he held out his hand, immobilizing the hare mid-bounce before it got even half a meter away from where he'd been standing. The hare panted frantically, trying to resist Alucard's ethos, but if *Damien* couldn't break free of the vampire's grip, then what hope did this shapeshifter have?

Everyone gasped or panicked in one way or another, setting their eyes on Alucard and the hare, watching as the vampire's faint, black, constricting snake-like ethos wrapped around the small mammal, slowly starving it of air.

"Kill him," Zalith mumbled.

Without hesitation, Alucard clamped his fist shut, crushing the hare's body, ending the man's life. As the dead hare dropped to the ground, Zalith's people clamoured in shock and fear, and others mumbled words of relief—clearly, not everyone was fond of the man Alucard had just killed. But Alucard stared at his hand for a moment, ignoring the people around him; he heard Varana's voice as she came running, but he cared not to listen to her. Up until now, he had avoided using his demon ethos—why had he just used it without hesitation? He felt the same confoundment he felt last night when Tyrus ignored him. His demon instincts and nature alike hadn't mattered his entire life…why was that changing now?

"What the *hell* is going on?!" Varana demanded. "Who did that?!"

"Alucard," Zalith answered, snapping the vampire out of his thoughts.

Varana glanced at Alucard, frowned, and calmed down. "Oh…."

"Go and tell someone to go to the village and get some fabric," Zalith ordered, looking down at her.

"What?" she questioned.

"We need to make blindfolds."

Varana gawped at him for a moment, glanced at Alucard, and then wandered off—Camael immediately followed her, offering to be the one who did what Zalith asked.

Alucard scowled, looking at Zalith. "'Ow long are zhose angels going to be 'ere?"

"Hopefully not long," Zalith muttered.

"Zalith…" Idina then said, a nervous, almost flustered look on her face. As both Alucard and Zalith looked at her, she frowned in concern. "I was thinking about Colt, and I don't think this is the right environment for him…especially if we don't know what could happen next. So, I was thinking that I might send him away with Elena to live somewhere safe."

The demon frowned, staring down at her.

"I know you have a lot on your plate right now…and I know you're going to want to wipe their memories, but if you could just do me the kindness of having them remember me and altering the situation so it seems like I'm just…away for work or something…that would be amazing," she pleaded. "I don't want Colt to think someone else has left him alone."

Zalith huffed, closed his eyes, and looked like he was thinking about it. After a few tense moments, he opened his eyes and said, "Okay."

Idina pouted sadly—it seemed as if she was about to cry. "Thank you so much," she sniffled—she then leaned in and kissed Zalith's cheek, wiped away her tears, and hurried off to where Colt was waiting with his dolphin toy.

Alucard watched as Zalith sighed and turned his back to his people—all of them were mumbling, whining, complaining—the demon dragged his hand over his face. He was clearly struggling; he obviously had so much on his mind right now, and Alucard just wanted to make him feel better.

"Zaliv?" he asked quietly.

The demon turned to face him, and as he did, Alucard frowned despondently and moved closer, wrapping his arms around him. He held him tightly as Zalith kissed his forehead, nuzzled his neck, and embraced him just as firmly.

It didn't really last as long as Alucard might like, though. After a short while, Camael returned with the fabric that Zalith had asked for. Alucard let go of the demon and leaned back against a nearby tree, observing as Zalith got two of his people to make blindfolds and tie them around the faces of those who wanted to leave. The demon wiped their memories one by one, and then he sent a few of his people off with them to lead them away. Zalith saw to Elena and Colt himself; he altered their memories, put them to sleep, and had some izurets fly them elsewhere.

And then it was time to continue.

As Zalith mounted his horse and everyone prepared to follow, Alucard got on his horse and followed beside the demon as he led the way forward once again.

Chapter Forty-Eight

Mountain

| Alucard |

Rain trickled down onto Alucard's hands and pitter-pattered on his hat. The skies had darkened, and as dusk drew nearer, Zalith led the way up the tree-covered mountain. Nobody said anything since they'd left that village; their group was now eleven people less, and Alucard was sure that, after what he'd done earlier, there might be even *more* people considering leaving.

He glanced at Zalith, who had a vacant stare on his face, and the vampire was certain that he was succumbing to his sullen thoughts; his face might look expressionless, but Alucard could see the distress in his dark eyes. The vampire stared ahead again, tucking the loose strands of his hair behind his ears, which were tucked inside his hat. He then looked down at Peaches, who was sheltering beneath his cape; she was probably hungry, so he'd make sure that someone got her something to eat when they stopped.

When they finally arrived at the mountain-peak plateau veiled by the towering redwoods, Alucard Zalith slowed and dismounted their horses, hitching them to the same tree.

Just as they had yesterday, Zalith's people started to set up camp, making use of the supplies that were already waiting there. Zalith, however, made his way over to the cliff edge, and Alucard followed. Now was a time better than any to ask him what was going through his mind—he knew it would take a lot of attempts for him to finally get Zalith to tell him how he was feeling, but he'd not give up.

"Are you okay?" Alucard asked, stopping beside him.

"Yeah," he said, glancing at him. "I just want to get everything figured out so we don't have to keep living like this."

Alucard frowned, moving closer as he took hold of his hand. "You zon't 'ave to vigure all out vight now. You still need time to veel better, so you should vest."

"Resting isn't going to get us anywhere," he mumbled, staring out at the forest below.

Alucard's concerned frown became a confused one as he slowly let go of Zalith's hand. He didn't seem to be in the mood for his attempts to comfort him right now, and Alucard didn't want to annoy him. So he turned his attention to the ocean of treetops beneath them. But he couldn't seem to let it go. He *knew* that Zalith was hurting, and the fact that he refused to talk to him about it *again* only made him feel irritated—just as it had yesterday. He didn't want to be mad, though… but he didn't want to let Zalith ignore and bottle up his emotions, either. The demon had persisted and made *him* understand that it was better to talk about it, so why wouldn't Zalith do the same?

He frowned at him. "Is zhis you deciding to vorget zhat 'ow you veel matters too? You can't just vocus on vork and noving else—zhe last time you did zhat, you made me veel like I zidn't matter," he muttered.

Zalith turned to face him. "How I feel doesn't matter because it's not going to change anything for us. But I'm not going to do that to you—I promised you that I wouldn't. I'm not going to hurt you like that again."

"Zhen stop acting like 'ow you veel zoesn't matter—matters to me," he insisted sadly. "I vorry about you all zhe time, and zhe last ving I vant is vor you to ignore vhatever is zhat's making you so sad."

"It's nothing worth worrying about; it'll be okay," the demon replied.

There wasn't any getting through to him, was there? Alucard didn't know what else to say, and his continuous failed attempts only made him feel more frustrated. He was partly mad at himself for not knowing what more to do and then partially angry at Zalith for refusing to give in. "Vine," he muttered, looking away from him. "I'll be 'ere if you need me to kill anyvone else, zhen, seeing as zhat's zhe only ving you seem to vant me to do vight now."

Zalith sighed, but before he could say anything, he stopped, seeing that Magnus was making his way over.

Alucard rolled his eyes, convinced that Zalith was about to express his annoyance; it looked like they were now both mad at each other. Alucard wasn't going to apologize, though, because it was how he felt. Zalith made him feel like the only thing he was good for was killing those of his people who tried to leave prematurely. It was the only time Zalith had responded and made him feel like he was doing something he wanted him to do.

"I hope…I am not intruding, yes," Magnus said with a smile, stopping behind them both.

The demon huffed angrily. "What now?"

Scowling, Alucard rolled his eyes. "Maybe you'll tell 'im vhat's vrong," he mumbled.

"What?" Zalith questioned.

"I said maybe you'll tell 'im vhat's vrong," he snarled irritably, glaring at him. "Maybe 'e'll 'ave a cure vor your inability to speak to me."

The demon looked away, closing his eyes—but Alucard saw him roll them.

"So now you're volling your eyes at me, too?" Alucard grumbled. "Is a good ving you zon't get cold; von't bover you vhen you sleep out 'ere by yourselv, vill zhat?" he threatened him.

Zalith frowned confusedly at him, "Are you serious?"

Alucard crossed his arms. "Am I? You 'aven't been taking me seriously lately, so is not a surprise you 'ave to ask. Maybe some time out 'ere by yourselv vill 'elp you understand 'ow I veel vhen you dismiss my vorry vor you like is someving I can just vorget about."

The demon took his eyes off him and looked at Magnus. "Can you excuse us for a moment?"

Smiling, the angel nodded. "Of course," he said, and then he walked off.

Alucard kept his eyes on Zalith. He knew he was about to start arguing with him, but this time, the vampire had no desire to try and defuse the tension. He was *tired* of trying his hardest without success to get Zalith to talk to him after *months* of the demon convincing him that *he* should always speak to him about whatever was wrong.

"Alucard," Zalith started with a stern but almost vacant tone. "I am the kind of person who cannot let themselves be happy unless I fix the problem—and *this*," he said, nodding over at his people as they set up the camp, "this is a problem. And I'm truly not trying to push you away, but no amount of fussing over me is going to change how I feel," he said. "And I love you, and I love that you want to help me—you *do* help me more than you'll ever know—but talking about how I feel isn't going to fix me. I have to fix everything first, and that's why I don't talk."

"You're not *trying* to push me avay, no?" he asked frustratedly. "But you're doing zhat anyvay. Vhat do you vant me to do? Just stand avound and vait until you veel like is time to vemember zhat I can't just vead your mind? You're supposed to tell me vhat's going on vith you zhe same vay I tell *you* vhat's going on vith me. But you zon't do zhat—you punish yourselv, and in doing so, you punish zhose avound you as vell. 'Ow long vill zhis last zhis time? 'Ow long until you vealize zhat not only are you not alone anymore, but zhat zhere are people who care and vorry about you, too," he said, trying his best to keep both his sadness and his irritancy at bay.

"I'm sorry," Zalith said. "And I realize that, but I have a hard time accepting it when all I do is let everybody down."

Part of Alucard wanted to shove his annoyance aside so that he could comfort Zalith, but another part of him wanted to continue expressing how he felt so that Zalith could understand. "So should I just vorget zhat you're zhe most important ving in my life until you decide zhat you deserve me again?" he asked. "I von't just stop trying to 'elp you."

"No," the demon said sadly, looking down at the ground.

"Vight, vell…you do vhat you 'ave to do zhen," he said, unsure of what else to say.

The conversation was disheartening. It was going to be the same again—he could feel it. Zalith was going to focus on his work and end up forgetting that Alucard was there too. And if that was what Zalith needed to do, then…what more could *Alucard* do? The demon didn't want his concern; he didn't want his attempts to comfort him. Zalith wanted to work—it was more important. He hadn't said anything when Alucard just told him that he felt like he was pushing him away, and that made him feel like he didn't matter, just like Zalith made him feel like he didn't matter when the demon had done this before.

But Alucard wasn't going to sit around and suffer this time. If Zalith could forget everything else and focus on what he was doing, then Alucard would also do it. "I 'ave vings to do, too. I guess vor now…maybe ve are better off seeing each ozzer as associates, no? If vixing zhis is more important, and if is all you vant to vocus on, might be easier vor zhe both of us to push each ozzer avay," he suggested as Zalith turned to face him—he felt something cut through his heart as he spoke, like a cold, jagged knife, and as the demon set his confused, astounded eyes on him. Why was he letting himself say this? He didn't want that—he didn't want to put their relationship on hold, but…maybe it was what Zalith wanted—perhaps it was what he needed, and if he couldn't say it, Alucard would say it for him. "I mean…you've alveady pushed me avay; maybe I need to do zhe same until you veel like is time to let me love you again."

Zalith stared at him for a moment; guilt and grief flickered in his dark eyes for the slightest moment, but then he frowned irritably. "Alucard, we have done nothing but spend time together since this started," he exclaimed calmly. "And even before all of this, we were together all the time. *All* I do is worry about you and spend my time making sure everything is perfect for you and that you're going to be okay and safe and happy—and I share *everything* with you," he continued, raising his voice the slightest bit, making the vampire frown confusedly. "But then I keep *one* thing, one little *thought* to myself, and you want to leave?!" he asked, frowning. "Do you want to know what I was thinking?"

Alucard scowled. "Enlighten me."

"I was thinking that everything I do turns out like shit and that you're ashamed of me, that you're going to get sick of me because I'm not good enough in one way or another, and I was too afraid to say it because I didn't want it to become a reality—but look where we are," he said with a derisive laugh.

As he stared at the demon's frustrated, dismal-ridden face, Alucard felt a rush of conflicting emotions. Zalith had snapped at him, and it wasn't something he was used to.

He frowned, sadness, frustration, and regret constricting his heart—his thoughts. He sighed, taking his eyes off Zalith so that he might take a moment to think before acting upon his frustration right away. It hurt his heart to know *that* was how Zalith felt, and he wanted to comfort him—but what use would that be? Zalith had just told him that no amount of fussing over him would help.

Zalith's words repeated inside his head—he didn't know what part to respond to. He didn't really know how to react. He scowled, slowly looking back at him. "If you'd told me zhat vas 'ow you velt, zhen maybe I vould know 'ow to 'elp you. But you just disvegarded my attempts to 'elp, and I took zhat as you vanting me to stop—to leave you alone, and zhat veels like you're pushing me avay. You made me veel like you needed me to go avay so you could vocus on vixing zhis and not 'ave to deal vith me at zhe same time. I'm not ashamed of you, and you zon't 'ave to be pervect eizer. You are more zhan zhe vings you do, and I zon't blame you vor zhis, nor do I expect you to vix zhis all by yourselv. Zhe only ving I vant to do is 'elp you, but you zon't vant zhat, so vhat else am I supposed to do?"

The demon frowned sadly and slowly reached his hand out to lightly grip the side of Alucard's arm. "I didn't want to push you away because I love you… and I'm sorry," he said despondently. "I just want to provide for everyone."

"You matter too, zhough, Zaliv," Alucard murmured, edging closer. "You're doing everyving you can, and everyvone appreciates zhat. But you deserve to be 'appy outside of zhat—you can't just… shut everyving else off until you veel like you deserve to vest."

"I just don't want things to get worse."

"Ve are vine," he asserted calmly. "Ve got avay, ve're both still alive, and nobody died—people might 'ave levt, but zhat's better zhan zhem getting killed by Liliv's people, vight? And I zon't sense any danger, eizer. You got everyvone avay, Zaliv—you need to vest—you *can* vest."

Zalith nodded in response. But then he pulled Alucard closer, hugging him so tightly that Alucard felt like he couldn't breathe.

"Please don't leave," the demon mumbled, burying his face in Alucard's neck. "I never wanted you to leave."

Alucard eased his arms around him, trying his best to fight off the distress that was so quickly gripping him. He didn't want to leave either, but Zalith had made him feel as though he wanted him to go, and that still upset him—that still frustrated him, but he'd let it go. He loved Zalith more than anything and just wanted to help him. "I vill never leave you, my love," he said quietly.

Zalith tensed a little in his grip, and Alucard felt him smile ever so slightly against his neck.

And then they held onto one another in the silence.

Magnus clearly took that as an invitation to return, though. "I assume by your current state that you have solved your conflict, yes." He smiled, stopping in front of them. "And now I must urge you to let us speak."

Zalith backed out of their hug and took his eyes off Alucard, growling in hostility as he glowered at Magnus.

Alucard also glared at the angel. He wanted to focus his anger on Magnus, but he couldn't seem to let go of the fact that he liked it when Zalith made even the slightest aggressive, primal sound. It wasn't often he heard something like a growl or a hiss, and he'd not deny that he loved it. But he shouldn't be thinking about that right now. He was irritated and frustrated—he wasn't going to let a single growl let him forget that.

The angel smiled in response to Zalith's growl. "If I were a demon, I'm sure I would feel the need to submit, yes—but I am not."

Alucard scowled at Magnus. "Vhat do you vant?"

"I'd like to discuss the matter of you repaying your debt, yes."

Zalith sighed. "Fine, if it'll get you off my ass."

"Have you decided whether you'd like to retrieve the Lumendatt for me, yes?" Magnus asked as they both turned to face him.

The demon looked at Alucard as if he wanted *him* to answer.

Setting aside the lingering *arousal* that came from Zalith's primal growl, Alucard frowned and raised his left eyebrow slightly. "What is Erich going to do vith zhis?"

Magnus looked disgusted. "Perhaps it would be best for you to mind your own business, yes."

Zalith seemed to lose any patience he may have had. Before Magnus could comprehend—before even Alucard saw it coming—the demon snatched the angel's throat and forced him down onto the ground.

Alucard stepped back, frowning down at them as Magnus panicked in Zalith's grip.

"What did I tell you about learning some fucking respect?!" the demon growled, glaring at Magnus as he choked.

Alucard glanced at the camp, seeing that everyone had stopped what they were doing to gawp over at Zalith. Of course, Alucard would much prefer to let Zalith teach Magnus a lesson, but as he saw Ulric and Camael *eventually* making their way towards them, the vampire sighed and grabbed Zalith's arms. "Zhat's enough," he said, trying to pull him off the choking angel.

Zalith hissed in Magnus' face and reluctantly let go, and as he stood up, he scowled and growled quietly, watching Magnus struggle to his feet after waving his hand in dismissal towards his two companions.

Magnus stood up straight, brushing the dust off his suit, rubbing his red, bruised neck as he cleared his throat. "The next time you attack me, I might stop being so kind and actually decide to defend myself, yes," the angel threatened, glaring at them both.

"Then I suppose it's in both our best interests that you learn how to behave," Zalith warned.

Alucard exhaled quietly, taking his eyes off the demon for a moment. He still wanted to be mad—he still wanted to be frustrated, but he wasn't. Watching Zalith act so hostile and defensive, so *protective* of him *always* made him feel… aroused. He wasn't going to lie, and he couldn't exactly ignore it, even though he wanted to.

"Quite," Magnus responded. "Do you have an answer for me, yes?"

"Fine," Zalith said.

The angel smiled. "Great."

But Zalith wasn't done. "Is it possible for you to create more of the vaccine for my people?"

"Yes…" Magnus drawled with a slow nod.

That then reminded Alucard that he said he'd send vampires to the Citadel to help clean up the infection and stop it from spreading—but he was *still* waiting to hear that Crowell and his vampires were safe. He wanted to telepathically call to him again, but with all these angels around, he wasn't going to risk leaving his mind so vulnerable.

"Will you?" Zalith asked Magnus, irritated.

The angel frowned. "I will need a lot of pure demon blood, yes…to create the vaccine for *demons*."

"We can get it for you," Zalith said.

"When would you like me to make it, yes?"

"As soon as you can."

"Well, if you get me the blood, I can start immediately, yes."

"How much do you need?"

Magnus glanced around. "How many demons are here?"

"Seven, excluding us," Zalith answered.

"Then I will need seven vials of blood, yes."

"Fine. I'll send people over to you."

The angel nodded. "Yes…I will be in my tent." And then he left.

Before Alucard could say anything, though, Zalith sighed quietly and rested his head on the vampire's shoulder. "I just want to rest," he grumbled.

Alucard glanced at the camp to see that his and Zalith's tent had been put up. He wanted to lead Zalith over there, take him inside, and start kissing him, but he knew that Zalith probably didn't want to do that and that they both had work to do. Zalith had to send people to Magnus, and Alucard had to contact the fort to see if Crowell had arrived yet. That didn't mean he'd completely ignore and forget how Zalith had just made him feel, though. "I 'ave to go and contact some of my vampires—I'll send zhem to zhe Citadel as soon as zhey're veady; zhey'll stop zhe invection vrom spreading out of zhe city and surrounding areas. If you vant to go and send people to Magnus, I'll meet you in zhe tent."

"Okay," the demon said quietly, slipping his hand into Alucard's. He pulled him closer and kissed him. Then, he wandered off, leaving Alucard alone.

The vampire made his way over to his and Zalith's horses; he led them over to their tent, which was actually a lot bigger than the one he and Zalith had slept in yesterday. He took some of the blankets off the horses' saddles, as well as his kitten and his cape, and then headed inside. The tent consisted of two parts; the entrance area had a table in its centre, as well as two blackboards—of course, this location was picked as a base area where he and Zalith would figure out their next moves if they ever had to run—and there they were…running….

Alucard sighed, moving into the back section of the tent that had a cot in it, one big enough for two people. It wasn't as great as a bed, but it would be better than sleeping on the ground. He placed his cape down on a crate, and as Peaches curled up and watched him, he started to lay the blankets out. But all he could think about was Zalith. He wanted to think about what had just happened, he wanted to try and work out how he felt, but…he'd become so distracted.

He sighed deeply, slumping down on the edge of the bed after he finished laying out the blankets. He felt guilty about wanting Zalith's affection after the talk they just had—the argument. He'd upset Zalith, and he knew that the demon was dealing with a lot. He didn't want to make Zalith do something he might not want to do, so Alucard would just have to see if he wanted the same thing he did.

First, though, he needed to contact Fort Rudă de Sânge—and despite being away from the angels' prying eyes, he still wouldn't open his mind. Instead, he used his ethos and summoned a raven, and he told it to fly to Rasmus, one of his newer Paladins, who was responsible for guarding the fort. He ordered it to ask him if Crowell was back or if Tyrus was still out there looking for him. Then, he sent it on its way.

He then stared at the floor and unbuttoned his shirt. At first, he felt a little nervous about it—what if Zalith came in and paid no attention to his attempt to tempt him? He frowned, sighed, and stopped for a moment, looking over at his kitten as she slept silently upon his cape. But he then focused on how *he* felt—on the fact that he wanted the demon's attention, and to get it, he'd have to snatch *his*. So, he unbuttoned his shirt and slowly pulled it off.

Zalith soon stepped into the tent, sighing a deep, heavy sigh as he made his way over, his eyes locked on the ground as he dragged his hand over his face. Alucard looked over at him, and as the demon eventually raised his head and set his eyes on him, his tired, despondent frown became an intrigued smile. "Oh, hey." He smirked, stopping in the doorway to lean on the wooden beam as he started slowly unbuttoning his coat.

Alucard smiled at him, watching as the demon's eyes wandered up and down—clearly, he was enjoying what he could see. "Hey," he replied, glancing down at his belt as he unbuckled it.

"Is this for me?" the demon asked curiously.

The vampire glanced at him and shrugged nervously, leaning forward to rest his arms on his legs. "Maybe," he said.

"Maybe I should join you then," Zalith said with a smirk, pulling off his coat. He started making his way over to him, unbuttoning his shirt as he did.

When Zalith reached him, he took his shirt off. He then leaned forward, starting to kiss the vampire as he rested his hands on the bed on either side of Alucard. The moment Zalith's lips touched his, Alucard felt something satisfying grip hold of him. This was what he wanted—he wanted Zalith's attention, his affection, and his touch. The demon pushed him down onto the bed, crawling over him, still kissing him slowly and passionately as Alucard dragged his hands up and over Zalith's abs, over his chest, and then moved his right hand to the back of his head to grip his hair.

Still kissing him, Zalith stroked his hand down Alucard's body and gripped his unbuckled belt. He pulled it from Alucard's waist and dropped it on the floor. "We shouldn't do this," he murmured through their kisses. "We already had sex today, *and* we did hand stuff at the river," he breathed and lightly bit the vampire's bottom lip. "I don't want you to get tired," he said before kissing him again.

As the demon began kissing Alucard's face, slowly making his way down to his neck, Alucard frowned impatiently. "I zon't care," he breathed, moving his hand down Zalith's body to grip his belt.

Alucard's fingers deftly unbuckled Zalith's belt, the demon's smirk widening as the leather slipped free. Once his trousers were off, Zalith wasted no time in helping Alucard out of his, all the while trailing hot, hungry kisses along his neck and down his chest. Each brush of Zalith's lips sent a thrill through Alucard, who smiled in anticipation, his breath hitching as Zalith's mouth began its slow descent.

The demon's lips teased the sensitive skin of Alucard's waist, his teeth grazing playfully, drawing out a deep exhale from Alucard's chest. With a firm, deliberate hand, Zalith began caressing his growing arousal, each stroke more electrifying than the last. Alucard let his eyes drift closed, his body sinking into the pleasure, a soft sigh escaping his lips as Zalith's mouth finally wrapped around the tip of his dick, the warmth and sensation making everything else dissolve into the background.

But Zalith didn't suck for very long. After just a minute or so, the demon kissed his way back up Alucard's body, lightly biting his neck as he smothered the vampire's dick in lube. Alucard lay there on his back, opening his eyes to stare at the demon as he straddled his lap; Zalith began easing the vampire's dick into his ass, making Alucard grimace in struggle as pleasure ensnared him. He trailed his hands to grip Zalith's waist, pulling him down into his lap, burying his inches in the demon's ass as they both moaned in delight.

Alucard hummed in contentment, holding Zalith's waist a little tighter as the demon slowly moved his body back and forth, pulling the vampire's shaft from his body, moaning as he eased it back inside. It wasn't often Alucard got to feel the enthralling pleasure of Zalith's tight, warm walls around his shaft, but when he did, each time was a little more pleasing than the last. He guided his hand up Zalith's body, gripping his shoulder as he continued to move back and forth—he pulled the demon closer, dragging his hand to the back of his head to grab a fistful of his hair. And then he kissed him—he moaned into the demon's mouth, biting his bottom lip, his body starting to tremble as he did his best not to fidget beneath Zalith.

Zalith sighed in relief, moving his face to nuzzle Alucard's neck as he continued moving his body, moaning quietly every time he eased the vampire's dick back into his body. But he soon started moving faster, and Alucard could feel his trembling body struggling; he tightened his grip on both Zalith's hair and waist, so enthralled in the moment that he didn't even care to control the pleasured moans that left his mouth. The demon groaned just as contentedly—Alucard *loved* to hear his pleased cries, and he loved to feel Zalith's claws as they dug into his skin, trying to grip his chest.

But it never lasted forever. The vampire grimaced when he felt himself edging closer and closer to his limit. The demon stopped kissing him, moaning feverishly as he moved his face to the right side of Alucard's neck—the moment he sunk his fangs into his neck, Alucard felt something so unbearably pleasing constrict him that he almost convulsed, moaning with deep satisfaction as his dick erupted inside the demon's body. And Zalith didn't take his blood, he just let his venom spread through the vampire's body, ensnaring him in euphoria, and he let it take him.

Zalith traced his hands over Alucard's chest and abs, and then he sighed contently as he sat up straight, still straddling his lap. But the demon wasn't done yet. "Do you want me to fuck you?" he asked, smirking down at Alucard as he slowly opened his eyes to gaze up at him.

Alucard could feel his face turning red—but he wanted it, so he nodded.

"How bad?" the demon asked seductively, lightly dragging his fingers over Alucard's abs.

With his body still trembling, with his eagerness to feel Zalith's body against his own becoming a desperate desire, Alucard pouted, glaring up at him. "Veally bad," he replied, his voice an overwhelmed whisper.

The demon leaned closer, moving his fingers up Alucard's body, and as he smirked and leaned into Alucard's face, he lightly pinched his left nipple. "I don't believe you," he mumbled with an unseemly smile on his face. "I think you're going to have to ask me to fuck you so that I know you *really* want it," he teased, pinching a little harder.

Alucard fidgeted, the pinch pushing him deeper into the rapture that had devoured him. He scowled nervously and looked away, but his desire outweighed his anxiety. "I vant you to fuck me," he pleaded.

Zalith laughed quietly, leaning in to kiss the side of his face. "Okay," he agreed, kissing all over his face and neck. "How?"

Still pouting, Alucard gripped Zalith's waist, moving him off him; he then rolled over onto his side, making sure Zalith lay behind him. "Like zhis," he muttered, pressing his ass against Zalith's crotch, and when he felt the demon's thick, hard dick rub against his skin, he closed his eyes and relaxed, letting the desperation take over.

"Okay," the demon replied and kissed the back of Alucard's neck.

Alucard's excitement increased as he rested his head on the pillows, an electrifying, pleasing sensation spiralling through him every time the demon's lips graced his sensitive skin. He exhaled deeply, waiting as patiently as he could as he felt the demon massaging the cold lube into his ass. Zalith then started kissing the left side of his neck, slowly easing his dick inside him. Alucard moaned quietly, pleasure already enthralling him as he felt each wide inch spread his tight walls.

Zalith wrapped his arms around Alucard, hugging him tightly as he began gently thrusting, humming contently as he nuzzled his neck. But the demon quickly sped up; Alucard wasn't going to complain, though; he enjoyed Zalith's eagerness. He grimaced in satisfied struggle, whining quietly and holding Zalith's wrists against his chest. His arching body was already so overwhelmed with euphoric bliss; he felt as if he was reaching a point where he might not be able to take it anymore, a point where he might have to ask Zalith to stop and give him time to recover. However…he didn't want it to stop.

The demon growled quietly, kissing Alucard's neck—but he then bit down *again*. Alucard grimaced, flinched, and grunted, but as the demon's venom spread through his veins once more, the vampire whimpered in ecstasy, gripping Zalith's wrists a little harder. Zalith didn't stop thrusting—in fact, he started fucking him faster, gasping in anticipation into Alucard's ear. The vampire moaned with him, the euphoria swallowing him so abruptly that he started to lose himself to it. But as Zalith suddenly whined loudly into his ear, holding him against his body so tightly that he stopped moving, Alucard closed his eyes and exhaled deeply, trying to calm down. He felt the demon's dick throbbing inside him, and his hot cum sent waves of warmth through the vampire's shivering, overstimulated body.

Zalith began gently kissing his neck, making Alucard smile contently through his frantic breaths. He didn't really have the words to explain how he felt…he was just…relieved, but in a way so pleasing, a way that made him feel as if their world was perfect for a brief while, as if everything was going to be just fine.

The demon exhaled with a pleased groan as he pulled out, and then he gently grasped Alucard's shoulder and made him roll onto his back so that he could smile down at him. Alucard beamed up at him in response, expecting him to say something flirty, but instead, Zalith leaned closer and slowly dragged his tongue over the two small puncture wounds from his bite on the left side of the vampire's neck. Alucard tilted his head to the side, stroking his fingers through Zalith's hair. The demon then moved to the right side of his neck, dragging his tongue over the wounds, licking away the blood.

A deep sigh suddenly broke Zalith's silence, but when Alucard looked up at him, he was still smiling. The demon rested on his back, pulling Alucard closer; the vampire lay his head on Zalith's chest, guiding his arm around him as he tugged the blanket over them both. And then they lay there in the serenity of each other's embrace, listening to the rain gently fall on their tent and the rock outside.

Alucard gradually calmed down, but as the euphoria faded, he began to think—of course he did; why couldn't he control his mind? He thought about what happened before…the things he said to Zalith. He felt awful saying them then and thinking about it now made him feel worse. Zalith didn't deserve to hear that; despite it being how Zalith had made him feel, he felt like he should have just let it go. He didn't want to lose Zalith—he didn't want to spend a moment more away from him than he had to.

He held him a little tighter, closing his eyes. "I'm sorry vor vhat I said earlier," he said sadly. "I vould never vant to leave you."

The demon looked down at him, dragging his hand up and down his arm. "I'm sorry I made you feel like you had to suggest it in the first place," he murmured.

Holding him, Alucard pouted despondently. "I love you, Zaliv," he uttered, burying his face in the demon's chest.

"I love you, too," Zalith replied, stroking his hand up to Alucard's head to start fiddling with his hair.

Alucard smiled. Now, he just wanted to lay there. He felt much better than he had earlier…and he hoped Zalith felt better, too. But he didn't want to lay there worrying. He was content, and he wanted to hold onto that feeling for as long as he could.

Chapter Forty-Nine

Impersonation or Extermination?

| Zalith |

While the rain fell harder, Zalith stared up at the tent ceiling, descending into his thoughts. Now that the thrill of sex and blood had waned, he couldn't keep himself from thinking about what happened earlier. It upset him that he and Alucard argued, and it hurt knowing that Alucard felt like he had to leave. The demon felt like everything was his fault; he always ruined everything, and he was trying very hard to keep his and Alucard's relationship from being something that fell apart because of him. He still felt like karma was catching up with him, like he was paying for all the terrible things he'd done, and losing Alucard was bound to happen because he didn't deserve him, and the universe wouldn't let him have him because he made him happy. He didn't deserve to be happy.

He frowned, sinking deeper. He felt guilty—Alucard wanted to help him, but no amount of talking would make him feel less responsible for what happened and for what was going on. He didn't want to hurt Alucard, though; he didn't want him to feel useless, so he felt as though he'd be better off pretending that he was okay…like everything was fine. If there was anything he would express his sadness about, though, it would be their current situation. He'd rather dwell on and talk about their current predicament rather than face what he was really feeling.

With a despondent scowl, he held Alucard a little tighter, kissing his forehead.

Alucard murmured, slowly exhaling as he woke from his rest. "Are ve going to stay 'ere vor zhe vest of zhe night?" he asked, stroking his hand over Zalith's chest.

Zalith smiled and laughed, fiddling with the vampire's hair. "And do what?"

The vampire shrugged. "Zhis is vine," he said contently.

"I'd lay in bed with you all day if I could. But we should probably start trying to figure things out," he said and huffed. "We can do that here, though."

Alucard moved his head from Zalith's shoulder and to his chest. "You're vight," he muttered. "But vhat do ve start vith?"

"Maybe Tyrus. Perhaps we can leverage that situation into something positive," he suggested.

"Like vhat?" the vampire muttered. "Ve could just get 'im to lead zhose of Liliv's people who are vollowing 'im into a trap…kill zhem. Less vollowers, less power vor 'er, no?"

Zalith thought to himself as he spoke, "That's true…but I wonder if there's a way we can use it more so to our advantage—in a way that's not only going to get rid of some of her followers but get those that remain to turn against her somehow. She can just keep making scions and gathering more followers, but she can't undo something atrocious enough to make people hate her."

Alucard glanced up at him, frowned, and donned a look that made it clear that he was thinking as he rested his head back on Zalith's chest. "So…ve 'ave to shatter 'er veputation. Ve need to…damage zhe invluence she 'as. I vould suggest some kind of set-up…like ve 'ave 'er kill some of 'er people—ve let zhem see zhat she zoesn't care about zhem and zhat she vould kill any vone of zhem vithout 'esitation—because she vould. She zoesn't care about anyvone, not even 'er scions."

The demon shook his head. "I think that might make the extremists more devoted because it's going to seem like she's picking and choosing which of them are worthy and which of them aren't. We need to find a way to make it seem like she's turning her back on *all* of them."

"Do you 'ave suggestion?" Alucard asked.

"We'll think of something," he said confidently. "But what do *you* know about her followers?" he asked, glancing down at him—he was certain that Alucard had to have learned *some* things over his years of spending time with the Numen. "Why *do* they follow her?"

"Hmm…" he murmured in thought, but then he sighed and shrugged. "She is…a zemon queen in 'er own vay, so…she 'as a lot of zemon vollowers, and zhen zhose zemons 'ave a lot of vollowers and vhatever because zhey can go avound and offer just about anyving to zhe people of zhis vorld. Let's not vorget zhat most of Liliv's vollowers are also succubi, and I've seen people do strange vings vor a moment of pleasure, so vollowing some cult in veturn vor a vew minutes of ozzervorldly pleasure probably vouldn't be too uncommon," he explained.

Zalith nodded, listening carefully.

"A lot of zhe people who pray to 'er believe she vill…protect zhem, keep zheir vamilies safe, and provide vor zhem in times of struggle. Take zhe uh…second vorld-vide war, vor example. Zhere vas a lot of vamine—zhe varmers couldn't grow vhatever zhey grow…zhere vas no vood. Liliv sent some zemons to vind zhese people somevhere new to live…and she 'ad zhem kill an entire village of Ephriel's vollowers…but she provided, so…she veally *does* answer zhe people who vollow 'er, vhich is vhy is going to be 'arder to take 'er down zhan say…Zamien. Yes, 'ate is more powervul zhan love and adoration, but people can be turned avay vrom zhe 'ate vhen someving 'opevul enough 'appens. Vhen you 'ave a god who actually answers your prayers, zhen…is not easy to take zhat love avay."

"So, we'd have to find a way to start a wide range of consistent problems and keep her too busy to help those who need her help," Zalith concluded.

"Exactly," Alucard mumbled. "But zhen ve 'ave to vork out vhat vould keep 'er so busy. She 'as a lot of people she could use to solve problems vor 'er."

"Do you have any suggestions?"

He shrugged but then laughed quietly. "Noving vould get 'er up vaster zhan 'earing somevone's trying to get into Luciver's prison; she vinks she's zhe only vone who knows vhere 'e veally is, and a long time ago, she dropped everyving in zhe middle of a war to 'urry and see if somevone 'ad actually vound vhere 'e is. Zhe Numen might 'ave locked 'im up, but zhey zon't know vhere 'e is; zhe Pandorican zhat 'e's locked avay in disappeared. Zhey vant…to kill 'im, maybe—or so Liliv seems to vink, so she is very protective, especially now zhat everyvone knows is possible to kill 'im."

Absorbing everything that Alucard was telling him, Zalith nodded. If they wanted to get Lilith's followers to lose faith in her, then why didn't they just impersonate her—that would be easier than trying to get her to show her face, wouldn't it? And they had a perfectly suitable förvandlare shapeshifter among them. "If we had the means, what's the likelihood of us being able to impersonate her successfully?" he questioned.

Alucard frowned up at him. "Vhy are ve impersonating 'er?"

"If we could get someone to convincingly impersonate her, we could shatter her reputation a whole lot faster than we would by trying to lure her into the open ourselves."

The vampire seemed to be pondering. "Vell…might vork, yes…but…is going to be 'ard to get somevone to impersonate 'er. Zhey vould need to 'ave spent years vith 'er to know 'ow she acts."

"What if we just have someone there who can bear a passing resemblance for a very short amount of time and no one has to interact with this person?"

"Zhat *vould* vork," Alucard confirmed. "If Liliv zidn't intervact vith zhe people she shows 'erselv to. She's not like Zamien; she vill actually speak to people."

The demon nodded. "Fair." He then listened to the rain for a moment. "I need to go pee; I'll be right back."

Alucard nodded. "Zon't get too vet," he said amusedly.

As he got up out of bed, Zalith chuckled softly. "I'll try my best." He pulled his trousers and coat on, and then he left the tent, heading out into the rain.

| Alucard |

While he waited for Zalith to get back, Alucard started pondering. He knew a lot more about the Numen than he let on, and as much as he hated delving into his traumatizing past, he'd have to do it if he wanted to keep both Zalith and himself safe—and their people, too. But he felt so reluctant…not just because of how they treated him but because some of what he learned had left scars upon his very soul.

However, now was the time to get over how the past made him feel and use it to their advantage.

Zalith walked back into the tent a few minutes later. "Sorry. Varana and Idina wanted to know when we're moving on," he said as he took his wet coat and trousers off. He climbed back into bed with Alucard and cuddled up to him.

"I vas just vinking, and…I can share everyving I know about Liliv vith whoever vill be impersonating 'er," the vampire said. "I know…'ow she moves, 'ow she talks—I know zhe vace she makes vhen she's about to snap, too. Zhey'll need to know zhat because she snaps a lot," he muttered. "And zhen if ve vant to keep zhe veal Liliv out of zhe vay, ve can…go to vhere Luciver is," he muttered, dread and *hatred* starting to grip his thoughts—his *heart*. "Zhe moment she veels somevone zhere, she von't leave zhat place vor *years*."

"I don't want you near wherever Lucifer is," Zalith denied, holding him a little tighter. "But we can figure something out."

"Ve zon't 'ave to go. Anyvone could go in zhere and she'd know. Or…" he said, shrugging slightly, "…ve could just lock 'er up…get somevone to pretend to be 'er…and zhen you challenge 'er authority, you vin—obviously—and all of 'er zemons vill vollow you," he said, but sarcastically—they had no way of locking her up; if they did, it wasn't actually a bad idea, was it? Zalith was a powerful demon, and he already had a pack. It might work, but…again, there was no way to lock Lilith up. Or was there?

Zalith turned onto his side so that he could look down at Alucard. "You're so smart," he said with a smirk. Then, he leaned his face into Alucard's and started kissing him.

As they kissed, Alucard's thoughts didn't settle. He had to fight the urge to suggest that maybe *he* could be the one to challenge the fake Lilith. It didn't matter who fought her…they were both demons, and the result would be the same…right? But Zalith was the Apex demon here, not Alucard. He was just…Zalith's boyfriend, so it was probably best that he didn't suggest he did it. He wasn't an Apex, he wasn't even an Alpha—he didn't have a pack. He might argue that every single *vampire* was his pack, but…demons didn't see vampires as other demons, so it didn't matter. Why was he even thinking about it so much?

He sighed as they stopped kissing, staring up at Zalith.

"How do we keep Damien from finding out?" the demon asked him.

"Vell…'e zoesn't pay attention to anyving zemon, so zhe only vay 'e vould know Liliv is not Liliv is if whoever impersonates 'er zoesn't do a good job. Zhey zon't veally spend much time togezzer—zhe only veason she vould 'ang avound vas because I vas zhere, and she vould…see me," he mumbled, the dismay and despair starting to take hold. "She vould disappear vor veeks at a time, too, so…if she vanished, Zamien vouldn't veally…suspect anyving."

"But what if they're working together? They've done so in the past, right?"

Alucard shrugged lightly. "Is possible…so ve need to vind out—but ve still zon't know vhere Liliv is."

"We'll probably have to send someone to investigate—Orin, maybe."

Alucard nodded. The search for Lilith's whereabouts had been put on hold since his castle had been destroyed along with his council. But hopefully Orin would be able to turn something up. "Vine," he agreed. "Vonce ve know vhere she is, ve can vork out 'ow ve trap 'er—given she isn't vorking vith Zamien."

The demon nodded. "That sounds good," he said, and then he offered his hand out to him.

Taking his hand, Alucard frowned slightly. "You zon't 'ave to shake my 'and," he said as Zalith shook it anyway. "Ve've been vorking togezzer on zhis vor almost a year now."

Zalith smirked, letting go of his hand. "But who doesn't love a good business deal?" he asked, and then he leaned in and kissed his lips. "Mine don't normally end like this though," he said with a smile, lightly stroking his fingertips down the side of Alucard's face.

Staring up at him, Alucard smiled as best he could through his flustered gaze.

The demon then ran his fingers through the vampire's hair. "What do you suggest we do about this crystal?"

Alucard shrugged and schemed, "Ve'll take zhe Lumendatt. Ve're trapping Liliv, no? Ve'll take everyving vrom 'er zhat ve can use, including zhat. Ve zon't 'ave to do anyving vor Magnus or Erich—part of me suspects zhat Magnus vants zhe Lumendatt vor 'imselv. If Erich veally vanted zhat crystal, 'e vouldn't ask a scion to vetch vor 'im."

"That's what I'm thinking—either that or Erich is up to something," Zalith muttered.

"I zon't…veally know much about 'im, so…I can't guess. Vhat I do know, zhough, is zhat 'e prevers to keep out of vhatever zhe ozzer Numen are doing."

Zalith nodded, a look of ponder on his face. "What happens if these crystals are destroyed? And what if we were to keep Lilith's? Can we use it?"

Alucard frowned, recollecting what he knew. "Vell…zhey are…crystallized Numen ethos zhat specivically vocuses avound cveation. If ve destroyed zhem, vould be a lot 'arder vor zhe Numen to cveate scions and vorlds and vings like zhat. As vor us using, ve could…I mean zhey do more zhan make scions. Zhey are just…power. Like zhe moons—a vocus…vessel…you get vhat I mean, vight?"

He nodded. "I get it," he said. "Are they easily tracked?"

"Yes," he mumbled.

"We're probably better off destroying them, then…or using them to lure them somewhere."

"You can 'ide zhem, zhough," he added. "Zhe same vay ve 'ide ourselves."

"But then we'd have to get Magnus involved."

"Not veally," Alucard said. "A Lumendatt becomes part of whoever plans to use, so…if zhat person is using ethos to 'ide zhemselv, zhe crystal vill be 'idden, too."

"Interesting… " Zalith said, taking a moment to think. But he then looked back down at Alucard. "What do you think we should do?"

"Could 'elp us. Vone of our current problems is numbers, no? If ve 'ave zhat crystal, zhat von't be a problem. Ve could make our own armies. Is similar to 'ow I make vampires—zhis crystal could give you or somevone zhe ability to make a sub-vace."

Zalith nodded again. "We should consider it," he agreed.

"Okay," Alucard mumbled.

The demon then laid back down beside him, and as he did, Alucard exhaled deeply and moved his arm around him, resting his head on his chest. As they had come to the end of their conversation, Alucard felt like it was soon time for them to sleep. He was tired, and all he wanted to do now was lay with Zalith.

Zalith held him tightly, running his fingers through his hair. "Do you want blood?" he asked quietly—clearly, he could tell Alucard was feeling fatigued.

Did he? Alucard thought about it; he knew blood would make him feel a little less tired, but then again, he *wanted* to rest—he wanted to go to sleep. He didn't feel particularly hungry either. "I'm okay. Vank you, zhough."

"Not even a little?"

Alucard looked up at him, and as he did, Zalith smiled. With a flustered pout, Alucard looked away and thought about it again. Maybe…just a little bit—so that he wouldn't wake up with a headache. "Okay," he mumbled.

He then moved his body over Zalith's, straddling his lap and resting his arms on either side of him as Zalith pulled him closer. But as Alucard moved his face to Zalith's neck, he didn't immediately bite down. He sighed, closing his eyes; he just wanted to savour this moment for a while. Being so close to Zalith—it was something he loved. He moved the side of his face against Zalith's, nuzzling his neck as the demon dragged his fingers through his hair. But he had no desire to sink his fangs into the demon's neck—he wanted to bite him somewhere else—somewhere new.

The vampire kissed Zalith's neck, and as the demon laughed quietly, Alucard slowly kissed his way down his body and to his waist. He thought that was where he wanted to bite... but as he pressed his fangs against Zalith's skin, he hesitated. He felt eagerness in Zalith's touch as the demon guided his hand to the back of Alucard's head—but instead of biting, the vampire kissed the demon's waist, and then he made his way lower.

When he reached Zalith's inner thigh, he edged nearer—he'd decided *that* was where he was going to sink his fangs, and he didn't waste a moment. He pressed his four fangs against the demon's skin, and then he bit down, groaning in satisfaction as Zalith's blood oozed into his mouth.

Zalith flinched but then sighed deeply in delight, moving his hand to the back of Alucard's head once again, gripping his hair. He then hummed quietly, tightening his grip, clearly struggling a little to relax his body as Alucard's venom spread through him. But Alucard didn't want to take too much, nor did he want to get carried away. So, after a few more moments, he pulled his fangs from the demon's thigh and glanced up at him.

"What are you trying to do?" Zalith asked with a smirk.

Alucard took his eyes off Zalith and dragged his tongue over the wounds. Euphoria started consuming him once again as he exhaled in delight, making his way back up Zalith's body and leaning over him. He stared down at the demon's curious face and mumbled, "I'm not trying to do anyving."

Zalith pulled him closer and started kissing him—but his kisses were almost aggressive, and Alucard enjoyed it. He trailed his fingers through Zalith's hair, lightly biting his lip as the demon stopped to breathe. And then they kept kissing.

Eventually, though, Zalith halted, pushing Alucard back a little so that he could stare up at his face. "I want to fuck you again," he said demandingly. "But I won't... because I love and cherish you—and your hot little body," he teased.

Smiling, Alucard rested his forehead against Zalith's. A part of him wanted to tell Zalith to go ahead, but he knew he shouldn't. He was already tired, and his body had been struggling earlier. Instead, he sighed quietly and kissed the demon's lips. "You can fuck me in zhe morning. Is time to sleep now."

Zalith laughed amusedly. "You promise?"

"Yes," he agreed.

The demon smiled. "Okay."

Chapter Fifty

Embers

| **Alucard, *Saturday, Cordus 4th, 960(TG)—Nefastus*** |

Alucard woke what felt like just moments later with a headache so painful that he grimaced and groaned quietly.

"Hey," Zalith said sleepily, stroking his hand over the vampire's chest as he gradually opened his eyes to look at the demon. "Are you okay?"

The vampire nodded, exhaling deeply as he waited for his headache to wane. He then glanced down at his lap, seeing that Peaches had curled up there. He saw daylight shining through the tent walls, the sound of people moving around rather loud outside. "Vhat's zhe time?"

"About ten," Zalith said.

Nodding, Alucard took his eyes off the demon and stared up at the ceiling. But something... something felt wrong. He wasn't sure what it was, but considering that the last time something felt wrong, people had attacked, he began to feel anxious. He sharply turned his head, looking over at Zalith—but the demon was gone. He scowled in panic, sitting up—Peaches was no longer in his lap, the sound of the camp withered into silence, and the air around him... it fell still, cold... and empty.

Alucard glared ahead, his heart racing as a cold breeze made its way past him—through him. And a voice... one so familiar.

"Caedis," it breathed, a low, rumbling growl upon its exhale—and snarling laughter.

The world around Alucard suddenly shifted. The bed beneath him disintegrated into ash, making him stumble to his feet, and the tent disappeared, leaving him standing in complete darkness. And it was a place he knew. The ground was an inch-thick layer of water; the walls were endless darkness, and above, there waited only infinite murk. Silent... motionless... empty... cold... and that feeling. Something was missing, and Alucard had to find it. But what?

He'd have no chance to look for doorways or missing things this time, though. An ominous, thick fog began to spread around him; flickers of red, like embers from a fire, danced around him—this was familiar. Adellum—he'd approached in a similar way, and Alucard knew what Numen ethos felt like. He also knew who lurched nearer with fog as black and night, and the embers... crimson—every instinct in his body told him to run, to flee, but... he stood where he was. He watched as fear scraped at his heart; the fog began to ascend, it began to thicken. Run—he had to, he wanted to... he might. But he held on—he'd been conquering so many of his past traumas, and he wouldn't let this be the fear that defeated him. Lucifer wouldn't force him back into a life of silence.

A grin broke through the dark, spreading across a scaled, harrowing face adorned with ten horns and seven eyes—three on each side of the creature's serpent-like face, and one in its very centre—an eye like hellfire... just like Alucard's. Talons hit the ground, breaking through the fog, cracking the layer of water. Wings as large as a city spread behind his spiked back, and as another rumbling laugh broke through the silence, Alucard glared up at the creature before him.

"Why don't you run?" the beast asked, his voice low, reverberating like a storm upon the horizon.

Alucard wasn't sure if it was fear keeping him where he was, or bravery—maybe a little of both. He knew he should run, but he didn't want to run. He'd run his entire life, and if could stop running from Damien and Lilith and fight back against them, then Lucifer would be no different.

From the dark, Lucifer leaned closer, reaching out his talons so suddenly in what seemed like an attempt to unnerve Alucard—he slammed his hand down but stopped a mere inch above Alucard's head. He couldn't hurt him here... wherever here was. Alucard knew that... Lucifer knew that. But who was to say that this was even him? This was a dream, wasn't it? Alucard was asleep... he knew he was asleep. And Lucifer couldn't find him—he couldn't reach into his mind, he couldn't contact him. This wasn't real, and perhaps that was why Alucard felt so unthreatened.

But then again... why was he seeing this? He and Zalith had mentioned Lucifer in their discussion, so perhaps it was his subconscious reminding him just how afraid he was... how afraid he had been. The very mention of Lucifer brought fear and hatred to his heart, and he felt both right now; it was so confounding that his body wouldn't move—his thoughts wouldn't stop racing. All he could do was stare... his heart racing. He wanted to wake up. He didn't want to see him anymore—to stare into his eyes... that eye.

"It's been... so long," the creature snarled. "You've alluded me for so long—"

Alucard scowled as his thoughts gradually cleared, and his body was beginning to wake up. He'd not waste a moment. He darted—

Lucifer reached out, snatching Alucard in one of his scaled hands before the vampire had a chance to get away. The creature laughed, tightening his grip as Alucard grunted, grimaced, and struggled. "Not this time…" the beast breathed, pulling Alucard up to his face so that he could stare down at him with his one, hell-fiery eye. "Our time will come—your time…." He grinned. "Everything…it's falling into place."

Alucard gritted his teeth in pain, making whatever sound his angst-ridden voice would let him as the creature held him tighter. He could feel his body breaking, he could feel his very being shattering.

"So soon…you'll be mine," the monster grinned—but then he abruptly opened his jaws, and as Alucard's eyes widened in terror, the creature slammed his teeth down shut over him—

Alucard woke with a horrified gasp for air, his heart racing, his body trembling as he gripped the fur blanket beneath him.

Zalith flinched in startlement, dropping the paper in his hand as he gently grasped the vampire's arm. "Alucard?" he asked worriedly.

As Peaches darted off his lap, Alucard looked around frantically; the warmth of Zalith's hand guiding over his shoulder convinced him that he was awake, but his racing heart didn't settle.

"Are you okay?" the demon asked as Alucard looked over his shoulder at him. "What's wrong?"

Staring at him, Alucard slowly calmed. He glanced down at his hands…he looked around the tent…and then he sighed deeply and fell onto his back, exhaling irritably. "I'm…so tired of zhese dveams," he muttered, glancing over at the tent wall as someone outside loudly dropped something metal.

Zalith frowned, putting his work aside so that he could move closer to Alucard. "Maybe we can get or make something to help you with them."

Sighing, Alucard looked up at him. "Maybe. But if ve do zhat, zhen…maybe I von't be able to see vings like I 'ave been."

"I know," he said, "but I'd rather that than you being tormented at every hour."

Alucard shook his head, moving his hand to the side of Zalith's neck. "I'll be vine, I just…need to get used to zhem I guess," he mumbled.

With a saddened frown, Zalith pulled him closer and started fiddling with his hair. "How have you been feeling through all of this?"

Alucard shrugged lightly. He didn't want to think about how he felt—it didn't matter. All that mattered to him was Zalith, but…the demon wanted to know how he was feeling, and he didn't want to lie, nor did he want to refuse to answer. "I just…miss our 'ome…and our bed," he mumbled sadly.

Zalith nodded, hugging him tightly. "Hopefully things will get better soon," he murmured. "We need to work out where we can go," he then said.

"Vrom 'ere? Ve could 'ead down to zhe next village, and zhen if ve're convident zhat ve aren't being vollowed, maybe ve can go to zhe castle?" he asked, undeniably eager to go somewhere he could call home.

The demon sighed, falling silent for a moment. But he then held Alucard firmer. "What if we lose that, too?"

With a quiet exhale, Alucard thought to himself for a moment. He'd already tried to convince Zalith that their castle was safe, that they'd not lose it, and that it wouldn't be found, but Zalith was clearly anxious, and he didn't want to make him go there if he was going to be paranoid the entire time. So…he'd let it go. He'd stop suggesting it, because it evidently wasn't what Zalith wanted, and *he* was fine as long as he was with the man he loved. "Ve zon't 'ave to go," he said, glancing up at him as he looked down at Alucard. "Ve can…vind somevhere else…like a small, discreet place," he suggested.

"I just don't know where, though. I knew so much about Eltaria, but I haven't spent much time learning about Aegisguard because I was so focused on Nefastus and my land here," he said despondently.

"Is vine," Alucard said, looking up at him. "I've been to pretty much every place zhere is to go 'ere…save vor a vew 'ostile places. I can vind somevhere vor us—but vhat about your people? Do ve need to take zhem…or vind somevhere vor zhem?"

"I'm not sure. Having the extra numbers would be good, but if it's easier for us to go off alone without them, then…maybe that's better."

"Is up to you," Alucard said.

The demon took a moment to respond, fiddling with Alucard's hair. But he then sighed deeply and said, "I don't know what I'll want. I'll get back to you in a few hours."

"Okay," Alucard mumbled. He rested his head on Zalith's chest, allowing silence to fall over them.

After a while, and as the sound of people outside began to louden, Zalith lightly trailed his fingertips across Alucard's chest. "Do you want to come to the hot spring with me to have a bath?" he asked quietly.

Alucard smiled up at him and nodded. They'd been following the same river for miles, and here, not only was there a waterfall but a collection of natural hot springs ten minutes away from the camp, and the thought of bathing beneath the falling water and then relaxing in the warm springs sounded enticing.

Zalith smiled, sitting up. He snatched their clothes, handing Alucard his before getting dressed; once they were ready, the demon linked his arm with Alucard's, and they left the tent.

"Oh," Idina called, hurrying over as soon as she saw them.

Zalith stopped walking, watching her as she made her way over, and Alucard stopped at his side.

"Good morning," she said with a smile, reaching them. "Do either of you want breakfast? Nadia just started on some porridge, and Danford found some berries."

"Are they safe?" Zalith asked as Alucard looked over to where Danford was sitting with a handful of blue, rounded berries with black swirling patterns.

"I think so. Danford said they were just Aegisguard's blueberries; he's been working on this um…oh, a field guide to flowering and fruiting plants. He's calling it a plant compendium."

Alucard frowned, watching as Danford threw one of the blueberries into his mouth while he sketched an image of it into his notepad—what an idiot. The vampire rolled his eyes and looked at Zalith. "Zhat's not a blueberry," he said. "Is a soporberry."

"A what?" Zalith asked.

"Soporberry—is a neuroleptic," he said.

Zalith took his eyes off Alucard as Idina gasped and looked over at Danford. The demon frowned…and then looked back at Alucard. "Is he going to be okay?"

"Eh," Alucard said with a shrug. "'E'll sleep vor a vew hours."

"Oh no," Idina panicked, leaving them to hurry to Danford, who was already starting to look as if he was fighting passing out while Freja shook him and asked him what was wrong.

Zalith sighed deeply, and there was an aggravated expression on his face. He and Alucard watched as Idina started snatching the berries from whoever had been handed them.

"He'll be fine!" the demon called as Danford collapsed into Freja's arms, unconscious. Then, he rolled his eyes and looked at Alucard. "Let's go," he said, starting to lead the way away from the camp.

Chapter Fifty-One

The Hot Springs

| Alucard |

Surrounded by the peaceful sounds of the forest, Alucard and Zalith found their way to the waterfall and hot springs. In the silence that had fallen between them, though, Alucard couldn't help but wonder whether Zalith was annoyed at him for letting Danford eat that berry. He could have stopped him…but then again, how could Zalith know he wanted to let him eat it? And he wasn't going to lie…it was funny—it would have still been funny if it were Greymore or Orin or Freja. But maybe there *was* a small part of him that let it happen specifically because it *was* Danford.

He glanced at Zalith as they approached the waterfall, but he didn't look mad; there was a vacant expression on his face, so maybe he was deep in thought.

With a quiet sigh, Alucard followed Zalith out of the woods, but as the sunlight hit his face, the vampire grimaced, pulling his hand from Zalith's and lifting his arm to block the rays. He turned away from it, pain surging through his head as he held his eyes shut tightly.

Zalith gently grabbed his hand and backed off past the tree line with him. "Are you okay?"

Alucard nodded, leaning back against a tree as he dragged his hand over his face. It had never been this bad before—the sunlight on his face had never caused him this much pain, and it wasn't fading as fast as it usually would. Why? He opened his eyes, resting his head back against the bark. "Is just zhe sunlight," he mumbled. "'Asn't veally been zhis bad bevore."

"Is anything making it worse?"

"I zon't know," he grumbled. "Probably all zhis being outside."

Zalith frowned worriedly as he lightly gripped Alucard's wrist and lowered his hand from his face. "Maybe we can go somewhere shadier?" he suggested.

Alucard shook his head. "I'm vine now," he insisted.

"Okay, if you're sure," Zalith said and kissed his lips, slipping his hand back into Alucard's. Then, he led the way towards the waterfall again.

As they stepped out into the sunlight, Alucard averted his eyes, lowering his head to glare at the rocky ground. The pain would wane, he was sure, and as they came to the river bank, they stopped and started undressing. Alucard glanced over his shoulder every few moments, making sure that no one was able to see him despite being far from the camp, and once their clothes were off, Zalith took his hand again and led him into the water.

They stood under the waterfall, letting the water pour down over them. Alucard wasn't one for cold showers, but he *did* appreciate the chance to better wash the dust and remnants of the forest from his hair and skin. And to his relief, Zalith reached into his vault and took out a bottle of shampoo.

"It's always handy to have these spare," the demon said with a quiet laugh, handing Alucard the bottle before taking out a bottle of body wash.

Amused, Alucard squeezed some of the shampoo onto his hand and asked, "Vhat else do you keep in zhere?"

"You'd be surprised," Zalith flirted and started washing Alucard's body for him.

Alucard smiled contently, sinking into the relaxation that came with Zalith's firm but gentle massage. At the same time, he rinsed his hair, and after the last of the shampoo was washed away, he began massaging some into Zalith's hair.

Once they were done washing, they left the river and stood in one of the shallow hot springs. Alucard moved closer to the demon, placing his hands on his waist to pull him even nearer. Zalith smirked, guiding his palms to Alucard's waist, and as Alucard smiled contently, he rested his head on Zalith's shoulder. The warm, steaming pool was a great relief after all that cold water, and as he relaxed, he closed his eyes and exhaled deeply.

The demon, however, started stroking his hand around to Alucard's back, and as he squeezed his ass, Alucard frowned and pouted, leaning back to stare at him.

"Oh no," Zalith said with a smirk. "I think a fish just grabbed your butt."

"Vish zon't 'ave 'ands," he said with a pout. "And zhey zon't live in 'ot springs."

"This one does," he said, glancing down at the water around them. "It was really freaky; maybe we should get out of the water and go make out on the bank over there," he suggested with a flirty smile.

Amused by Zalith's playful mood, Alucard laughed a little as he looked down at the water and then back at Zalith. "Vhat if zhe vish vith 'ands vollows us?"

"If it wants to watch, it can watch, I just hope it doesn't have legs."

"Might," Alucard said. "If 'as 'ands, who is to say zoesn't 'ave legs?"

The demon chuckled as he took him to the bank. "As long as it's respectful and keeps its hands and feet off of you, then I don't mind."

Alucard smiled, and when they reached the river bank, finding a patch of soft grass, Zalith turned the vampire to face him and started kissing him. Alucard returned each of his soft pecks, stroking his hands down Zalith's body as the demon held him firmly and slowly laid him down on the grass. As excitement then gleamed in Zalith's dark eyes, their kiss intensified, and Alucard welcomed the demon's warm tongue into his mouth.

While they kissed and caressed one another's wet skin, Alucard daydreamed a little. He loved hearing Zalith snarl and growl; he deeply enjoyed the fact that his mate was an aggressively protective demon. But there was something he knew he desired more than growls and hisses, more than bites and grabs and aggressive, assertive affection. He wanted to see *everything* that Zalith kept hidden; it wasn't often that the demon would growl, and it was close to *never* that he'd reveal his true self. And Alucard wasn't afraid to admit what he liked anymore, what he *enjoyed*, what he desired. He loved everything about Zalith's hard, muscular body, but he also loved everything about his *demon* form, and witnessing his aggression so much lately had him almost desperate to see it—to see *him*.

Alucard broke their fervent kiss, gazing up at Zalith as a nervous frown surely appeared on his face. "I vant…can I…see you?" he requested unsurely. "All of you."

The demon smirked and laughed slightly as he fiddled with the vampire's wet hair. "I'm already naked. What more is there to see?"

He pouted. "Your zemon vorm," he said—although he didn't really understand why it had come to be called that. With his wings and his horns was Zalith's true form…and this—without them, that was his *human* form. But he wasn't going to get into it. He just wanted to see him.

Zalith edged his face nearer to Alucard's neck, kissed it once, and then leaned into his ear, growling a low, quiet growl. "Are you sure?" he asked, his voice a teasing murmur. "It's scary."

Alucard felt a shiver of anticipation electrify through him. He tightened his grip on Zalith's waist, tensing up as he managed to reply, "Yes."

"Okay," Zalith agreed, ever so lightly tracing his fingertip down from Alucard's neck, over his pec, and between his abs.

As the anticipation slowly transformed into arousal, Alucard stared up at his mate.

Zalith sat up straight, straddling Alucard's lap. He shot a hungry smile down at Alucard before his dark wings and horns appeared on his body, manifesting from a thin black ethos mist as if they had been there all along, simply shrouded.

Alucard gazed up at Zalith as his dark eyes became fully crimson, glowing in the shade of the trees. His black, addax-like horns glistened the ever so darkest shade of purple in the sunlight, protruding from his forehead, and his dragonish wings—as the demon stretched them outwards, freeing them from what was likely a long, long dormancy, their carpels were as dark as night, and the membranes appeared an almost dark red as the sun shined behind them. Zalith then smirked, gradually folding his wings against his back as Alucard moved his hand to his head, running his fingers through his hair between his horns.

"Do you like what you see?" Zalith asked, grinning to bear his two sharp fangs.

Of course, Alucard got to see his fangs all the time, but seeing them paired with the rest of Zalith's demon self seemed to make them look a whole lot more enticing. Realizing that he was just staring, though, the vampire nodded, guiding his fingers around the base of Zalith's right horn. "Yes. But…I vish I could see you like zhis more ovten," he mumbled shyly.

Zalith smiled, leaning his face nearer to Alucard's. "Maybe if you're good," he said, and then he kissed his lips.

"I'll be good," he muttered. "I alvays am."

"You are," the demon laughed. He then kissed the vampire's neck, his chest, and then over to the other side of his neck.

But Alucard wasn't done staring at him. He moved his hands to Zalith's shoulders, sat up with him, and made Zalith lay down. The demon hummed excitedly as Alucard pinned him down on his back, his wings spreading across the grass. Alucard guided his hand up the demon's neck, over the side of his face, and then over his left horn, gazing down at him as he traced his fingertips up to his horn's tip. He remembered what Zalith had shown him—that the base of a demon's horn was such a sensitive area, and he'd not forget how it made him feel when Zalith stroked his fingers around it, just as Alucard started doing to his mate. Zalith murmured in delight, closing his eyes and gripping Alucard's waist as he straddled his lap. As much as he loved Zalith's attention—as much as he enjoyed the demon taking charge—sometimes, Alucard wanted to take control.

As Zalith hummed pleasurably, Alucard kept trailing fingers around the base of his left horn; eventually, he decided to start massaging the space between both his horns with his fingers, and he was sure that Zalith enjoyed it, for he smiled in delight, murmuring pleasurably as his body tensed beneath Alucard's. But the demon then dragged his hands up the vampire's body, guiding his fingers along the defined lines of his muscles; Alucard smiled when Zalith opened his crimson eyes to stare up at him, but Zalith smirked deviously, and before Alucard could respond, the demon rolled over with him and pinned him down again, growling quietly as he did.

The vampire gazed up at Zalith as he stretched his wings out, leaning in and kissing his neck. Alucard turned his head to the side, closing his eyes, sighing contently as the anticipation enthralled him. The demon guided his hand down his tensing body, playfully biting on his neck as Alucard stroked his hand up the side of Zalith's face again to grip his right horn. The vampire then groaned quietly in delight as the demon started massaging cold lube into his ass—Zalith didn't seem to want to drag things out, and Alucard felt the same.

He moved his leg over Zalith's back, pulling him closer, opening his eyes to behold the demon's true form once more, watching as he rested his wings against the grass beside him, gripping the ground with the talons upon their carpals. He then growled aggressively, grasping Alucard's waist with his free hand, smirking down at him as he stared into his eyes, looking like a starved beast about to dig into its meal; it was as if he was telling Alucard that he wasn't going anywhere any time soon. And Alucard meekly gave in. Zalith's possessiveness and aggression made him feel so excited, so *aroused,* and as his dick hardened against Zalith's thigh, he grunted quietly and moved his hand down from Zalith's horn, his arm, and his body to grip the demon's arousal.

As he began caressing the demon's stiffening length, Alucard did his best to contain just how eager he was. Zalith kissed his lips again, sighing pleasurably while Alucard pleased him, and when he slid his tongue into the vampire's mouth, Alucard decided that he couldn't wait a moment longer. He shuffled around a little, moving the demon's shaft down to press its tip against his ass, and then he let go, gripping Zalith's waist as his mate took control once again.

Alucard moaned as Zalith eased his dick inside him; each thick inch brought such intoxicating delight to the vampire's shivering body. He rested his head back against the grass, closing his eyes as he frowned and murmured contently. Zalith moved his face back to Alucard's neck, kissing him, humming quietly in satisfaction as he pushed his shaft deeper.

"Zaliv," Alucard whispered, digging his claws into the demon's skin, pulling him with his leg as close as he possibly could.

"Let it out, baby," the demon commanded as he slowly pulled himself back, moaning quietly into Alucard's ear.

Gripping Zalith's arm, Alucard grimaced in struggle, already becoming overwhelmed. Why it was happening so fast bewildered him, but then again, it could be because Zalith was in his demon form—and his confoundment increased when he glanced down, groaning pleasurably as he set his eyes on the faint, vein-like glows starting to spread up over Zalith's stomach from his crotch, branching outwards. Alucard leaned his head back again, dragging his hands along Zalith's warm skin as the demon assertively thrusted into and out of him. He soon noticed the same glows appearing on Zalith's hands and wrists as he held onto Alucard's body; he'd never seen it before, but he assumed that he was seeing Zalith taking his energy. It made sense—nothing was hidden about Zalith anymore—maybe this was what it looked like when an incubus feasted on someone's energy. And he liked it. Everything about Zalith's body was inexplicably attractive to him, and this new revelation was no different.

Zalith moaned quietly and pinned Alucard's arms above his head as he started thrusting a little faster. He dug his wing talons further into the ground, ripping up the earth, and when he fucked the vampire *deeper*, they both whined pleasurably—and then

Zalith abruptly sunk his fangs into Alucard's neck. With a startled flinch, Alucard winced, and his trembling body quickly fell victim to the overbearing delight of Zalith's venom. He tried to pull his wrists free so that he could grasp onto the demon in an attempt to cope, but Zalith wouldn't let go. His mate growled quietly, biting a little harder as he plunged his dick so deep that Alucard moaned and cried out with each hard thrust.

The demon pulled his fangs from Alucard's body. "You're *mine*," the demon breathed possessively, nuzzling Alucard's neck.

Alucard whined and stammered, "Y-yes."

Zalith dragged his tongue over the bleeding wounds left by his fangs. "Say it," he demanded.

With a struggled moan, Alucard told him, "I'm…yours."

His words clearly pleased Zalith; the demon responded with a satisfied, *relieved* groan before kissing Alucard again. He lightly bit and sucked on the vampire's bottom lip, moaning as he thrusted.

The pleasure spiralling through Alucard's trembling body intensified; he was nearing his peak, getting closer with each deep, rough but delightful thrust. And then Zalith let go of his wrists and instead gently gripped his throat. *That* sent shivers of ecstasy gushing through Alucard; he submitted entirely, opening his eyes to stare up at the demon, who grinned down at him before nuzzling the vampire's neck again.

Alucard's racing heart felt like it might burst out of his chest as he grew ever nearer to his limit. He panted, he whined, and as he tipped over the edge, he cried out in overwhelmed relief, moaning feverishly as he arched his back up towards Zalith and climaxed.

Zalith groaned and breathed deeply against Alucard's neck, thrusting harder and harder until he plunged his dick as deep inside the vampire's ass as he could, making Alucard moan loudly in startled pleasure, and as the demon's warm cum oozed inside him, Alucard hummed in satisfaction, listening to the relived, content moans upon Zalith's breath.

He stroked his fingertips down Zalith's back, and the demon responded with a pleased purr before kissing his way down Alucard's body, gently pulling his dick from his ass. When he reached Alucard's crotch, he used his tongue to clean away the vampire's cum, groaning in gratification as he did. Appeased, the vampire murmured under his calming breaths, and once Zalith kissed his way back up his body, he licked his neck where he'd sunk his fangs, and then he laid down beside the vampire, tearing his wing talons from the ground. He folded his right wing against his back, resting on his right side, and then he moved his left arm and wing over Alucard, hugging him tightly.

"How are you feeling?" the demon asked quietly.

With his arm around him, Alucard gently stroked Zalith's back between his wings. "I veel veally good," he mumbled with a smile.

The demon laughed amusedly, dragging his fingers over the vampire's chest. "Good, I'm glad."

"'Ow are *you* veeling?"

"*I* feel really good," he replied, staring into the vampire's eyes. He then guided his hand to the side of his face, tucking a loose strand of his crimson hair behind his ear. "You're so cute," he murmured, smiling at him.

Flustered, Alucard pouted and turned onto his side so that he could face Zalith, taking his hand off the demon's back and instead moving it to the back of his head. He ran his fingers through his hair, over his head, and to his right horn. And thanks to the euphoria ensnaring him, he didn't feel too nervous to say, "You're zhe most beautivul ving I've ever set my eyes on." He lightly trailed the tips of his fingers around the base of Zalith's horn and down the side of his face.

Zalith looked a little surprised by his compliment but leaned closer and kissed his lips. "You're very sweet. Thank you."

Alucard traced his hand down over Zalith's pecs and abs, and then he sighed as he rested his hand between the demon's pecs. He knew that Zalith loved it when he complimented him, but a part of him suspected that his mate might be upset that he didn't do it as often as *he* did, and that made him feel bad. He loved Zalith so much, and there were so many things he wanted to say to him; he'd just managed to fight his nervousness now, and he'd keep fighting it. He wanted to make Zalith happy, to see him smile, and he also wanted to say the things he wanted to say.

He looked away for a moment but then stared into the demon's crimson eyes. "You make me veel veally good," he started. "And you make me so 'appy. You do so much vor me, and I alvays vant to do more vor *you*, I just…zon't know vhat. And…" he said, moving closer and placing his hand on the side of the demon's face as he stared curiously, "…you vork so 'ard—you do so much vor *everyvone*, and zhey…I zon't know if zhey see 'ow much you do, but *I* do, and…I zon't even know vhat I'm trying to say, I just veally, veally love and appreciate you, and I vant to show you zhat," he said, struggling to find the right words.

Zalith started caressing Alucard's hair, a sad smile appearing on his face. "Thank you," he said. "I don't want you to do anything, though; I'm just happy with you being here with me throughout all of this."

Alucard nodded, shuffling nearer so that he could rest his forehead against Zalith's. "I'm not going anyvhere," he promised. "I'll be 'ere vith you vorever."

"I love you," Zalith said, placing his hand on the side of the vampire's face.

The vampire frowned, unsure why Zalith hadn't said the same thing—but he didn't want to overthink and ruin their moment. "I love you, too," he said and hugged him tightly.

And as the sun climbed higher into the sky, they both lay in the warmth and silence of one another's embrace.

Chapter Fifty-Two

Apples and Sunlight

| Varana |

By the edge of the camp, Varana stood alone amidst a shroud of despair, brushing her horse's mane. She still had no idea what to do with what she knew, with what she was dreading. Ysmay was going to come for her, Zalith, and Alucard…and *she knew*, but she couldn't tell anyone. She felt distraught and afraid; she knew that something terrible was inevitable, and not only could she *not* tell Zalith, but she was terrified to try and do so because she knew he'd react badly. If she *were* able to get the words out, he'd blame her, wouldn't he? Ysmay was *her* sister, after all, and Zalith had warned her countless times of how much he didn't like her, how much he didn't *trust* her…and now, Varana was beginning to understand why.

The whole situation made her feel so lonely and secluded, like the ugliest woman at a party or the widow who no one wanted. The poor farmgirl among a crowd of born-into-money socialites. The ugly duckling. An ugly, wart-faced—

"Is this your horse?"

Varana snapped out of her thoughts and looked over her shoulder to see that Camael, one of the angels, was standing behind her.

The blonde man smiled, glancing at her horse and then staring at her while he waited for an answer.

She sighed sadly and continued brushing her Santana. "Yes," she muttered.

He moved closer. "She's gorgeous. What did you call her?"

"Santana."

Camael nodded, admiring the mare for a moment before shifting his gaze to Varana and adorning a sympathetic expression. "What's wrong?"

Slowing her brushes, she shrugged and mumbled, "I'm sad."

"Why are you sad?"

"I can't say," she complained, still brushing Santana. "Everything's horrible."

"Do you…want to talk about it?"

"No."

He glanced back at the camp. "Well…at least you have your friends."

"I guess."

"And you also have Santana," he said with a smile.

"Yeah," she uttered despondently, moving on to brushing Santana's fringe.

He fell silent for a few moments. "Oh," he then said, reaching into his pocket. "Here."

Varana glanced at him, watching as he pulled an apple from his pocket. He smirked at her and broke the apple in half with his bare hands, offering one half to her. She wanted to roll her eyes—she knew that he was flirting with her, but she wasn't sure whether she liked it or not. So she sighed quietly, taking the apple half.

"Thank you," she replied, feeding it to her horse.

Camael moved closer and fed the other half to Santana.

For a moment, Varana wondered: why was this guy still here? Magnus had done what he'd come to do—he'd cured Zalith. Unless Zalith or his stupid boyfriend had asked the angels to stay for some reason. She didn't know, so she asked, "Why are you still here?"

He chuckled. "With you or in the camp?"

"Both."

"Oh," he said. "Well, Zalith's asked Opus to create the vaccine for everyone, and I'm his…bodyguard, I guess you'd call it. As for being here, I thought that you might be lonely."

She exhaled quietly, brushing her horse again. He *was* flirting with her, and she wasn't thrilled or overly interested, but he seemed okay, and he didn't disgust her like most of the men who tried it on with her. He was actually very attractive, but she wasn't going to sit around and cry about her problems to a stranger—least of all an angel. However, he *was* being nice, and she appreciated it. "Thank you," she replied.

Silence gripped them once more, but Camael seemed keen to talk. "So, who do you hang out with around here? Just your horse?"

She shrugged. "Idina mostly. I'm closest with Zalith, though, but I guess not so much anymore."

"Oh…why's that?"

Varana scowled. "Because my gay ass brother stole him from me!" she snapped.

Camael frowned. "Isn't…Zalith gay, though?"

"Yes…" she grumbled. "But we were still very close."

"How close?" he asked curiously.

"He's my best friend. We've been inseparable for centuries," she murmured sullenly.

He crossed his arms, leaning back against the tree behind him. "Ah…and then he found himself a boyfriend and doesn't spend as much time with you, huh?"

"Yeah," she said despondently.

"That must have been hard for you considering your brother's involved, too."

"He wasn't even in my life until they met, and now everything's so complicated," she complained both sadly and irritably.

He frowned sorrowfully. "I'm sorry that happened. But I'm sure you'll find someone else one day," he said with an assuring smile.

She rolled her eyes, lowering her brush. "Maybe. I'm not focused on that right now anyway."

"Tchh, me neither," he uttered. "Anyway," he then said, standing up straight. "You wouldn't happen to know where Zalith is, would you? Magnus has finished making the vaccine and needs to speak with him."

"Probably fucking my brother somewhere," she grumbled.

He nodded, sighing. "Do you mind if I wait with you until he gets back? I'm tired of Magnus and Ulric," he mumbled.

Varana huffed about it as she tucked the brush into one of the saddlebags. She didn't want to admit it, but some company would be nice. "Sure," she mumbled. "But I don't want to talk about Zalith or his stupid little strawberry-looking boyfriend."

Camael laughed. "All right, no problem."

| **Alucard** |

By the river, Zalith and Alucard still lay side by side. As the sun climbed higher into the sky, Alucard moved his arm over his eyes in an attempt to save himself from the worsening pain it caused him when it hit his face. Zalith didn't fail to notice, and as Alucard grimaced irritably, the demon stretched his left wing over him just enough to block the sun. He then gazed at the vampire as he moved his arm away from his face.

"I veally need to do someving about zhis," he muttered, sighing as he rested his arm down beside him.

Zalith smiled, leaning up on his arm so that he could look down at Alucard. "What *can* you do?"

The vampire shrugged. "I zon't know. I could vink of someving," he said confidently.

"You can," he agreed. "You're very smart." Then, he leaned closer and started kissing him.

Their affection, however, was ruined the moment a screeching bat swooped past, and a cloud of black mist hit the ground a few feet away from them. Rematerializing from within was Toma, Crowell's assistant vampire.

"My Lord," the man said, bowing humbly as Alucard sharply turned his head to glare at him with a horrified look on his face. And when Toma opened his crimson eyes, they widened in terror. "O-oh, my God, I'm so sorry," he exclaimed, swiftly turning his back to them, holding his arms behind his back. "I had no idea—I didn't see a thing," he insisted.

Amused, Zalith laughed, looking back down at Alucard as he pulled on his wing to conceal as much of himself as he could.

"Vhat zhe fuck do you vant, Toma?" Alucard snarled.

"Uh…I…" Toma stuttered, glancing over his shoulder, and as Alucard snarled aggressively, he stood up straight and stared ahead. "Uh…Baron C-Crowell, My Lord."

Alucard sat up slightly, listening.

"Baron Crowell apologizes for his lack of correspondence; he's been incapacitated since yesterday, and—"

"Vhat 'appened?"

"As soon as he arrived at Fort Rudă de Sânge, he took a group to the Citadel to deal with the crisis. He was badly wounded, and we lost Adherents Gavrilo and Mirela," Toma explained. "Adherent Lilja had to bring him back, but the rest of his team, Adherents Ruxandra, Ștefan, Șoiman, Șoimănița, and Vulpea are still there with Paladin Cerboaica and Knight Lăcrămioara's team. They teamed up with a doctor, who found out that humans bitten not too long ago could be saved by being turned into Fledgelings, so they've been turning people, My Lord."

Alucard sighed quietly. This was *twice* now that Crowell had become critically wounded. Was he just not fit for his Baron rank? "Vine. Zhe more vampires, zhe better," he muttered."

Toma continued, "Baroness Păzitoarea has also reported back. Her team found the location of one of Lilith's larger gatherings. No casualties, My Lord."

"Good," the vampire muttered.

"As for the Pandorican, My Lord, Baron Crowell said that he is going to continue his search for it once he has recovered," Toma informed him.

"Vine."

"Your…Tyrus arrived at the fortress, too; we don't exactly know what to do with him."

"'E vas zhere to 'elp Crowell," Alucard said with a frown.

"Oh, yes, sorry, My Lord. He arrived *with* Baron Crowell and the Nefastian Coven. They were able to evacuate every vampire with only minor injuries."

That relieved Alucard *greatly*. He let out a deep sigh and glanced at Zalith, who smiled at him. Then, he set his eyes back on Toma. "Tyrus is being tracked by some of Liliv's people; 'e does not know zhis, and is probably better stays zhat vay. You and Crowell are zhe only two people who know zhis. I need you to make sure zhat vherever Crowell sends Tyrus, 'e is *alvays* moving."

Toma nodded with a humble bow. "Of course. Understood, My Lord. Is there anything else you need me for?"

Alucard thought to himself for a moment. "*Da*. You can 'ead up zhe vay zhere to zhe camp," he said, nodding into the forest towards the camp. "Vait zhere, and zhen I vill come and tell you vhat I need."

"Yes, My Lord." Toma then disappeared into a cloud of black mist and emerged in his bat form. He flew into the forest, heading for the campsite.

Once he was gone, Alucard sighed deeply and laid back in the grass. "Vell… at least now I know vhy Crowell zidn't turn up."

"He doesn't sound like he knows what he's doing," Zalith said.

Alucard exhaled and shook his head. "'E likely zidn't let 'imselv vully vecover vrom vhat 'appened in Dor-Sanguis. May 'ave been a vhile ago, but sometimes, zhe avter-evvects of nightshade can last vor months."

Zalith nodded, fiddling with his crimson hair. "What about the other vampires Toma mentioned?" he asked curiously.

"Păzitoarea is Crowell's vife. She's vone of my best shivters—infățișare, zhey're called; she can turn into a black 'ound. Animal shivting is a vare vampire ability, and zhe black 'ound is vone of zhe 'ardest vorms to master."

"She sounds much fitter for Crowell's job," the demon said with a chuckle.

"I vould 'ave given to 'er if she vas good at gazzering intel; she's more of a vighter."

"Oh."

"Gavrilo and Mirela vere leaders, so losing zhem is a blow, I admit. Cerboaica is vone of my only vemaining shivting Paladins; she can take zhe vorm of a doe. Lilja, Ruxandra, Ștefan, Șoiman, Șoimănița, and Vulpea are some of my oldest vampires and very good vighters. I'm glad zhat zhey're still dealing vith zhe Citadel situation," he explained.

"Do you think they'll be able to contain it?"

"I vink so. Zhey'll veport back to me as soon as zhey 'ave updates."

The demon nodded but then sighed, looking Alucard's body up and down. "I want to fuck you again."

Alucard smiled—

"But we should probably head back soon."

The vampire shrugged. "Ve can stay 'ere vor a little longer," he said, guiding his hand to the side of Zalith's neck.

Zalith smiled, too. "Okay," he said and kissed him again.

Each twirl of their tongues made Alucard feel better, erasing the annoyance that came with Toma's arrival *and* his news about Crowell. Of course, they had to go back to the camp soon, and he was certain that someone or something was going to snatch away the peace that Zalith helped him feel. But for now, he'd enjoy what solitude he and his mate had left.

Chapter Fifty-Three

A Question of Payment

| Alucard |

Once Alucard and Zalith dried off and tidied their hair, they walked back to camp. However, the moment they climbed the rocky slope to the plateau and reached the thick redwood leaves shrouding the entry, Alucard's contentedness withered like a flame in a sudden breeze. Waiting by his and Zalith's tent was Magnus, and the moment the angel saw them approaching, he smiled, keeping his beady little purple eyes on them. Alucard hated him…and there wasn't anything he wanted more than to see Zalith rip his head off, but…they needed him, and they owed him. So that wasn't going to happen any time soon.

"Zalith…yes," Magnus drawled as they stopped in front of him. "I have completed making enough vaccine for each of your people, yes…and we must talk."

"Thank you. We can talk in my tent," the demon invited.

Alucard didn't want to be a part of that. Not only was he through with Magnus and his aggravating personality, but he also needed to go and talk to Toma. So, he looked at Zalith and said, "I 'ave to go and talk to Toma."

Zalith nodded. "Okay. I'll talk to you later," he smiled and kissed his lips.

The vampire then set his eyes on Toma, who was waiting in the shade cast by the massive redwoods. He started making his way over there, and he hoped that by the time he was done with his subordinate, Zalith would have finished with Magnus. The sooner those angels left, the better.

| Zalith |

Zalith led Magnus into his tent. Once they were inside, he turned to face the angel, waiting for him to speak.

"As I said, I have completed creating vaccines for everyone, yes," the silver-haired angel repeated, almost as if he was reminding Zalith of another debt. "I have not yet given it to anyone, but if you would like me to, I will—alternatively, your people can do it themselves, yes."

"It's probably better if you do it so no one makes any mistakes," he said.

"Of course."

"And thank you again."

Magnus nodded. "There is…the matter of my payment, yes."

Zalith sighed deeply. "What do you want?"

"My brother has…seemed to have grown attracted to you, yes…and I am sure that he will ask for sexual intercourse before we depart. I ask that you reciprocate his advances, yes," he said with a smile.

Amused but not surprised, Zalith laughed. "Is that so?"

"Yes."

Still laughing, he shook his head a little. "Unfortunately, you and your brother are three years too late—I don't do these things anymore."

The angel kept his smile. "I am sure you can be convinced, yes. I care about my brothers, so I will try to get you to agree. I assure you, *my* alternatives may not be much better, yes."

"What are your alternatives?" he questioned, completely uninterested in his proposal.

"Well, I am a seeker of knowledge, as you know; I live to learn and understand, and one thing I would like to understand…is your…Alucard."

Zalith scowled in hostility, his protective instincts grasping him tight, intensifying with every passing second. "What do you want from him?"

"I'd like…a sample of his blo—"

"No," Zalith denied.

Magnus frowned. "No?"

"Good to know your hearing works."

"Yes…" Magnus dragged the word out, unimpressed. "I would simply like to learn how he creates vampires."

"That's not for me to tell, and it's not up to me to decide whether or not you get to know."

The angel frowned again, looking confused. "You are…his Apex, yes? You get to decide everything for everyone in your pack. Why would he be an exception?"

"Because he is my equal."

Staring at him, Magnus seemed to be thinking, but then he nodded slowly. "I see. Then…might you ask him if he is willing to share the information I require?"

"I might. What are your other options if he says no?"

"I have no other options, yes."

"You seem creative. I'm sure you'll think of something."

"I don't think I will," Magnus assured him rudely.

Zalith smiled condescendingly. "You shouldn't doubt yourself like that. What about money? I'd be happy to pay you for your services," he offered.

Magnus shook his head. "I'd much rather take advantage of things better than money, yes."

The demon sighed; he already knew he'd say no. "Fine."

"Yes…I will be waiting with my brother for your answers. I will also start giving the vaccine to your people, yes."

Zalith nodded. "Thank you again. You can tell Idina to start rounding everybody up."

The angel nodded, turned around, and then left.

As Magnus left, Zalith rolled his eyes and made his way over to the bed, where he'd left his papers earlier. Alucard was busy, and he had work to do. He wanted to look for somewhere safe for them to go once they left Nefastus…and he had to think over everything that he and Alucard discussed last night.

| **Alucard** |

"My Lord," Toma said, bowing humbly when Alucard reached him.

"I need you to go to zhe closest town and vind some vings vor me," Alucard said as he reached into his pocket and then his vault; he took out a pen and a piece of paper. "You'll most likely 'ave to look avound vor zhese," he muttered, writing down what he wanted. "And make 'aste," he said, finishing his list and handing it to Toma.

Toma took the list, read over it, and then set his sights back on Alucard. "Of course," he said, tucking the list into his pocket. "Is that all?" he asked as Alucard handed him a few Coronam notes.

"Yes," he muttered.

Nodding, Toma then disappeared into black smoke and emerged as a bat, racing into the sky.

With a quiet, deep exhale, Alucard glanced around the camp. His first thought was to return to Zalith and stay with him while he worked, but he didn't want to distract him. So, he looked around for someone to talk to, and his gaze settled on Greymore; the dark-haired werewolf Alpha laughed and slapped some cards down onto the makeshift table that he was sitting around with a few of his packmates. They seemed to be having fun. Maybe he could join in.

The vampire walked over, watching as Greymore handed two cards to each player—Alucard suspected that they were playing blackjack, a game he wouldn't have to put too much effort into.

Greymore caught sight of him as he approached and turned his head to look in his direction, a smile spreading across his face. "Hey buddy," he called, waving his arm, gesturing for him to come closer. "Come join us," he invited—that saved Alucard from having to ask to join.

The vampire sat beside Greymore and one of his friends, and as he made himself comfortable, everyone started placing their bets, using pebbles as chips, and wagering cigarettes, pieces of dried meat, and candy bars.

"We're playing blackjack," Greymore said with a smirk.

Alucard smiled a little, leaning back in his seat. "Someving else vor me to beat you at, 'uh?"

Greymore guffawed and shook his head. "Well, those of us who don't got any cigarettes or shit are playing on an I.O.U basis. That cool with you? Unless you have some fancy, rich-people cigarettes in that coat of yours."

"I zon't smoke," Alucard muttered. "I.O.U is vine."

With a nod, Greymore explained, "The shells are ten bucks, the stones are one buck, and then we found these little limestone-looking rocks, so those are a hundred bucks. You can use these," he said, nodding at everyone's collection of stones and rocks. "Or you can use your real cash," he suggested, nudging his arm.

Alucard watched everyone place a selection of stones and shells into the centre of the table. No one bet over a hundred bucks—he'd heard many a name for the Eltarian currency, but bucks was probably one of the strangest—and he didn't want to show off, nor did he want to get carried away, so he reached into his pocket and placed forward five pieces of gold.

Then, Greymore handed each player two face-down cards, as well as two for himself—one of which he left face-up. He put the deck down and glanced around at everyone as they peeked at their cards. Alucard looked down at his, keeping a vacant expression that even Zalith might not be able to see through—at least he liked to think so, anyway. A two and a nine; he had to get as close to twenty-one as possible to win, but if he went over, he'd lose. And he also had to be precarious; Greymore's face-up card was a seven, so the goal was to keep drawing until he had a total of at least seventeen.

He'd be last to draw, however, as Greymore would go around the table clockwise serving everyone.

"Randy?" Greymore asked, looking at the dark orange-haired man to his left.

"Hit," Randy said.

Greymore passed him a card, and as he took and looked down at it, Randy rolled his eyes and dropped his cards to reveal his king, his six, and his recently served nine. He was out.

With a grin, Greymore took what Randy had bet and set his eyes on the bald man next to him. "Grant?"

The man scratched his balding head, mumbled to himself, and shook his head. "Stand."

"How 'bout you, Tony?"

Tony, the old man with brown but greying curly hair, scratched his silver beard and nodded at Greymore. "Hit."

Greymore slid him a card across the table.

"Hit," he said again, twirling his finger around inside his thick beard, and when Greymore slid another card across the table, Tony took a quick look and let go of his beard. "Stand."

Then, Greymore looked to the man beside Alucard. "Warren?"

Sighing deeply, Warren nodded. "Hit me," he said as if he was taking a risk.

Greymore slid a card across the table.

Warren picked it up, and his eyes widened ever so slightly. "Stand."

"What about you, rich boy?" Greymore smirked at Alucard.

"'It," he answered, and as Greymore slid him a card across the table, he picked it up—a four. "Again," he said, tapping the table with two of his claws. Greymore slid him another—a five. He had twenty…but Grant, Tony, and Warren were still in. Grant didn't seem too confident, Tony appeared content, and Warren had briefly looked surprised—either of them could have twenty-one, and Alucard suspected that Warren did. Tony had settled with what he got—the look on his face wasn't one of assured victory like that on Warren's. "Stand," Alucard said; he wasn't going to take any huge chances just yet.

"All right," Greymore said, and then he flipped his face-down card up to reveal that it was a six. Thirteen—he had to draw. So he took a card and placed it down, revealing another seven.

"God darn it," Grant uttered, throwing down his cards to reveal his eighteen.

Tony sighed and placed down his nineteen, but Warren laughed victoriously and placed down his twenty-one.

Alucard placed down his twenty—he wasn't annoyed. He was pretty sure that he now knew what Warren's tell was—that guy sucked at controlling his face. As for Tony, he fiddled with his beard when he was nervous, and Grant was yet to show his tell.

Alucard would notice it, he was confident. Randy was also yet to reveal his, but once Alucard knew them all, he'd play around with higher stakes.

Warren collected his winnings with a snide chuckle.

Greymore shuffled the deck after returning everyone's cards to it. "So, how's Zalith doing?" he asked Alucard.

"Vine," he mumbled. He was sure that wasn't the case, but he wasn't going to share that with the group.

But then Warren laughed, crossing his arms as he leaned back in his seat. "He's always fine. Guy never looks anything but fine."

"Scared the shit out of that angel guy yesterday—and pretty much all of us, too," Tony said and sipped from his mug of mead.

"Zhen zon't piss 'im off—is simple," Alucard muttered.

"Aye, right," Randy laughed. "That why you two got into a spat yesterday?"

Alucard rolled his eyes. "Is not vhat zhat vas—"

"Nah, man, that's just how they flirt I guess," Warren laughed, and then so did everyone else—except Alucard.

The vampire rolled his eyes again, placing a few more gold coins on the table.

"How'd you two even meet?" Grant asked, placing a few shells and two cigarettes forward.

"D'you just…hook up one night and Zalith decided he wanted more?" Tony questioned, adding a pocket flask to the bet pile.

"No," Alucard snarled. "Ve vere vorking togezzer and decided to keep seeing each ozzer avter ve vere done."

"Wait, wait," Randy then uttered, placing forward his bet: what smelled like jerked meat wrapped in a beige cloth. "Where are you from? I ain't ever heard an accent like that—"

"Stop asking the guy so many questions," Greymore interjected, handing everyone their cards. "Give him some space."

Everyone fell silent on his order, but Alucard didn't want silence.

"I'm vrom Dor-Sanguis," he said, glancing at his cards. "I'm not native Deiganish; is my second language."

"Man, I know a little bit of like…what d'you call it here? Uh…oh, Boszorkian—that's it, man. Fuck learning an entire *whole* language," Warren uttered, peaking at his cards—and that look of surprise flickered through his eyes again.

"I know a bit of Lupanese," Greymore muttered, glancing down at his face-up king. "My mom's side were from Eltaria's Lupa—Tirennia is what it's called back there."

"Do you know enough to 'old a conversation?" Alucard asked curiously.

"I do," Greymore said with a grin before looking at Randy. "What's it gonna be?"

A flicker of hesitation slithered across the orange-haired man's face. "Hit," he said, and as Greymore slid him a card, he deadpanned. "Stand."

"Grant?"

"Hit me," he said, and Greymore slid him a card. He then scratched his head—he clearly did that when he was taking a risk. "Stand," he said. He didn't have twenty-one, did he?

"Hit," Tony then said as Greymore stared expectantly at him. The Alpha slid him a card, and as Tony picked it up, he rolled his eyes and dropped his cards, flicking his stones at Greymore. "Fucking stupid," he complained, revealing his king, his two, and his recently-handed queen.

Greymore chortled, taking his winnings. Then, his brown eyes shifted to Warren. "What you want?"

"Hit," he said.

The Alpha handed him a card.

"Uh…hit," he said. He was handed another card, but then he sighed and placed down his three, his two, his king, and his jack. "Can't fucking win 'em all I guess."

"And you?" Greymore asked Alucard.

"'It," he said—and he was handed an eight to accompany his seven and his six.

Greymore turned over his face-down card to reveal a nine. Nineteen.

Grant threw down his seventeen, sighing deeply.

Randy laid out his twenty with a smug smile. "I'll be taking that—"

"I zon't vink so," Alucard said with a smirk, placing down his twenty-one.

"Ah, ya fucking kidding me," Randy complained, flailing his arms like a stroppy child.

As everyone laughed, Alucard gathered his winnings—at least now he could join in with the shells, stones, and other undesirable rewards.

"How many languages do you know total?" Greymore asked Alucard as he shuffled the deck.

"Six. Lupanese, Aguilian, Boszorkian, Drydenish, Deiganish, and Dor-Sanguian—alzhough Zaliv 'as told me I speak a totally divverent vone in my sleep, so…maybe seven."

"Daaaamn," Warren drawled with a frown.

"Why so many?" Grant questioned.

"I travelled a lot—vas easier to get to know zhe language of zhe people I lived avound."

"True," Randy said, nodding.

Tony then shuffled around in his seat, making himself comfortable. "Are you like…gay-gay…or do you like chicks too?" he blurted.

"Like Danny. Lucky guy," Warren sulked, crossing his arms.

"You're still so mad about that, aren't you?" Greymore teased as Grant, Tony, and Randy chuckled, placing their bets.

"Dude, who wouldn't be? A twink like Danny pulls some smoking hot queen like that? I have no idea how he did it," Warren muttered. "I mean I heard that her sisters all hated him and tried to persuade her to reject him, but somehow, the little guy made it through."

"You're *so* jealous, War" Tony accused, reaching over to whack his shoulder, but the guy fought back and smacked his hand away.

"Whatever," Warren growled. "Anyway, this ain't about me. You into girls?" he asked Alucard, sounding a little insistent.

Alucard frowned uncomfortably, glancing down at his cards as Greymore dealt to each of them. "No, I'm not."

"Mhm, knew it," Tony mumbled.

"Hit me," Randy said, and as Greymore handed him a card, he nodded. "Stand."

"Stand," Grant muttered.

"Hit," Tony said, and as Greymore handed him a card, he huffed and dropped them to reveal his twenty-five. "Shit."

Warren shook his head. "Stand."

Alucard then looked down at his cards—an ace and a three. "'It," he said. Greymore handed him a king. "'It," he said again, and this time, he received a nine. He rolled his eyes and dropped his cards. "Vhatever."

Laughing, Greymore flipped over his card—a three to go with his seven. He drew, placing down a ten.

"Uh-oh," Randy taunted, placing his twenty on the table as Grant chucked his eighteen down.

"Looks like it's time for *sudden death*," Greymore said dramatically, drawing a card for himself and Randy. Then, at the same time, they flipped their cards over. Greymore cheered, laughed, and pointed at Randy, who had a two, whereas Greymore had a queen.

And then *everyone* laughed, even Alucard. He found this amusing—to sit around carefree and play a game with these werewolves.

As he smiled, his laughter fading, Alucard glanced down at his lap. Maybe Zalith would enjoy this too. "Maybe I should ask Zaliv if 'e vants to play," he suggested.

"Yeah, sure man. We can make some room," Greymore concurred. "Want us to wait?"

"You can play a vound vithout me. I'll be back," he said, standing up.

"Gotcha," Greymore said with a wink. Then, he gave everyone their cards.

Alucard headed over to and inside the tent. Zalith, who was sitting at the table, looked up at him, taking his eyes off the few pieces of paper in front of him, and smiled.

"'Ow's going?" Alucard asked, walking around to stand beside him.

Zalith placed his hands on either side of Alucard's waist and pulled him closer. "It's okay," he said with a sigh. "What are you up to?"

Alucard smiled a little and said, "I'm playing blackjack vith Zhomas and some of 'is vriends. I came to see if you vanted to join."

"Uhh…" he mumbled, looking down at his work. But then he looked back up at Alucard. "Sure," he said, but he didn't sound very confident.

"Is vine if you zon't vant to."

"It's okay. I should take a break anyway," he said as he stood up, and then he kissed the vampire's lips.

Alucard's smile grew. "Okay," he said, taking hold of Zalith's hand. He led the way out of the tent. "Are you…'ungry, by zhe vay?" he asked as they walked towards Greymore and his friends.

"A little," Zalith answered. "But I'll be fine. I've been hungrier."

"Hey, boss," Greymore called when they reached the table.

"I heard we're playing blackjack," the demon said as he sat down beside Alucard.

"Sure are," Greymore said. "But on an I.O.U or cigarette and jerky basis," he said with a smirk.

Nodding, Zalith made himself comfortable and took a few coins from his pocket. He placed them on the betting pile.

Once everyone placed their bets, Greymore dealt each player two cards; his face-up card was an eight. He then looked around the table once more, waiting for everyone's choice.

"Hit," Randy said, and as Greymore handed him a card, he deadpanned. "Stand."

"Stand," Grant said.

"Hit me, man," Tony said. Greymore slid the card across the table, and as he lifted it, Tony sighed loudly and dropped his cards. "My fucking god, man. My luck's shit."

"You just suck," Warren sneered with a grin. "Hit me."

Greymore slid a card across the table.

When Warren picked it up, his face flickered with surprise *yet again*. "Stand."

"What's your move, boss?" Greymore asked, setting his eyes on Zalith.

"I'll take another card," he said.

Nodding, Greymore slid a card across the table to him.

Zalith picked it up, and without any reaction at all, he set his eyes back on Greymore. "I'll stand."

Greymore looked at Alucard.

"Stand," the vampire said, sticking with his king and queen.

"All right," Greymore said, flipping over his card to reveal an ace—nineteen.

Randy smugly placed down his nineteen.

Grant revealed eighteen, sighing.

Warren threw his seventeen.

And Zalith calmly showed his seventeen.

"I guess I vin again," Alucard said with a shrug, placing down his cards.

"Are you on a streak, vampire?" Zalith asked with a smirk as he and everyone else handed Alucard their bets—and then, he kissed the side of the vampire's face.

"No," Alucard scoffed amusedly.

Zalith smiled, but as he sat up straight in his seat, he discreetly stroked his hand up Alucard's thigh beneath the table.

Alucard did his best not to react and focused on Greymore, who handed the cards out while everyone placed their bets. The vampire then glanced at his cards, revealing a six and a king.

"Hit," Zalith said.

Greymore slid a card across the table.

Zalith picked it up, glanced at it, and said, "I'll stand."

"'It," Alucard then said, and as he was handed another king, he rolled his eyes and dropped his cards.

The demon smirked at Alucard, making him pout and look away. But the vampire turned his attention back to the game when Greymore lifted his card. A nine and an ace. Everyone else disappointedly put their cards down in defeat apart from Zalith; he revealed his nine, seven, and four.

"Looks like it's you and me," Greymore said with a grin, sliding Zalith a card across the table.

At the same time, they lifted their cards. Greymore had a five, but Zalith had a two.

Greymore laughed stupidly. "Gotcha!" he sneered, slapping the table.

With a slight smile on his face, Zalith rolled his eyes.

Greymore took his winnings. "I see those angels are packing up," he muttered, and once everyone placed their bets, he dealt them two cards again.

"Vinally," Alucard grumbled.

"Good," Zalith said.

"Fucking annoying," Warren complained, looking at his cards. "Kept me up all night yesterday, nattering away in their weird little angel language."

"Hit," Randy said. "I saw one of them tryna work out how to use the cookpot," he then laughed. "Stand." He laughed again and continued, "Fucking idiot burned himself."

Everyone laughed.

But when Alucard snickered, he saw Zalith smiling at him in the corner of his eye, and it made him feel flustered. He couldn't become distracted, though.

"Hit," Grant uttered. "And then they had us all taking that vaccine; wouldn't have done it if Idina wasn't there. Stand," he said as Greymore handed him his requested card.

"Stand," Tony said.

"Well, at least we're all safe from whatever's going around," Greymore said, looking at Warren.

"Hit me," Warren said, and as Greymore handed him a card, he shrugged. "Yeah. Stand."

"Boss?" Greymore asked Zalith.

The demon looked down at his cards. "Hit," he said, and Greymore handed him one. "Again," he said, then he said, "Stand."

"Stand," the vampire said, confident that his ace and queen meant he'd won.

Greymore flipped over his face-down card—he had a nine and an ace.

Randy placed down his eighteen with a sigh, while Grant chucked his seventeen. Tony smirked as he showed them his twenty, and in response, Warren slammed down his nineteen with a huff.

Zalith smiled and revealed twenty-one—a two, a king, a three, and a six.

"Ugh, man," Tony complained.

"Uh-oh," Greymore then drawled as Alucard placed down his ace and queen. "Looks like it's sudden death," he said, dragging out his words as he slid a card each to Zalith and Alucard.

Zalith smirked at Alucard, but the vampire kept his vacant stare. Slowly, as he held the card beside his face, the demon flipped it around to reveal a nine—but Alucard then grinned, flipping his card to reveal an ace.

With an amused chuckle, Zalith shook his head, placing his cards down.

As he took his winnings, a smirk remained on Alucard's face. He was actually enjoying himself; the game was a good distraction from his overbearing thoughts, and it looked like Zalith was having fun, too. He smiled at the demon, watching as he reached into his pocket for his next bet. However, when Alucard felt the approach of a vampire's aura, he sighed and turned his head to look over his shoulder, watching as Toma landed a short distance away. He waved at Alucard, holding a small cardboard box under his other arm.

Alucard sighed again and stood up. "I 'ave to leave you now," he said. "Vank you vor letting me play, zhough."

"No probs, man," Greymore said as everyone else muttered their goodbyes.

"Whoever vins next can 'ave zhat," the vampire said, moving all of his winnings into the middle of the table.

"Sweet," Warren beamed, rubbing his hands together.

Alucard then looked down at Zalith. He wasn't sure whether the demon might want to go with him or keep playing, but the demon almost instantly got up, and after nodding his farewell to Greymore, he followed Alucard away from the table and towards Toma.

Toma bowed when they reached him. "I got everything you asked for, My Lord," he said and handed Alucard the box.

"*Multumesc*," he muttered. "Go now."

"Of course," he said. And then, he transformed into a bat and disappeared into the trees.

"What did you get?" Zalith asked curiously as they walked back to their tent.

The vampire smiled. "Just some vings."

"What kind of things?"

"You'll see," he teased, glancing at him. He then led the way into the tent and placed the box on the table. He opened it and pulled out the bottle of red wine he'd sent Toma to get, along with two glasses, some grapes, cheese, crackers, and a few different slices of meat—everything to make a platter like the one he and Zalith shared all that time ago down by the lake. Once he finished laying it all out, he stepped aside and smiled at Zalith.

"Aw…" the demon said, a sad smile on his face. "Is this for me?"

Alucard nodded, slowly looking down at the table as his nervousness started to get the better of him. "I vanted to do someving nice vor you. You've been vorking so 'ard, and you deserve a treat."

Smiling, Zalith moved his hand to the back of the vampire's head and pulled him in to kiss him. "Thank you," he said sullenly.

With a smile of his own, Alucard pulled out one of the chairs, inviting Zalith to sit. He then sat beside him and poured them both a glass of wine.

As Alucard handed him his drink, Zalith leaned his arms on the table. "So, I was talking to Magnus," he said and took a sip of his wine. "We were discussing what he wanted as payment for what he's done, and he told me that… he wanted a sample of your blood—he wants to work out how you make vampires," he explained.

That made Alucard uncomfortable. "Vhat?" he asked, feeling almost defensive. "Vhy zhe fuck does 'e vant to know zhat?"

"I have no idea," the demon muttered. "I told him I'd ask you, but I knew the answer would be no—even if you did happen to say yes, I still wouldn't let you do it," he said protectively. "I just feel like annoying him and making him think he's actually going to get what he wants," he said with an amused laugh.

Alucard wasn't exactly entertained, though. "Vhy can't zhey just take some money and leave? Vhy does 'e vant vavours and invormation?" he grumbled.

"I offered him money, but he said he'd rather take advantage of things better than money," he said, taking a piece of cheese and a cracker. "His original request was for me to sleep with his brother," he added with an irritated, disgusted look on his face.

The vampire almost choked on his wine and scowled in hostility. "Vhat?" he snarled.

"He said that his brother is attracted to me and would ask for sex before leaving, so he asked that I say yes to repay our debt," he told him, clearly unimpressed yet still amused.

Alucard scowled harder—he *growled* quietly, tightening his grip on his glass as he did his best to try and contain his anger. *That* was a step too far. He didn't care about the belittling stares and the snickering behind his back, but to try and get to him through Zalith? These angels clearly had no idea who and what they were dealing with. "I vant to kill zhem."

Zalith smiled slightly. "Normally, I'd love to see that, but as annoying as he is, I think Magnus might come in handy down the road."

Aggravated, Alucard snarled again. He wasn't just going to let them get away with it, though. "Zhen I'll teach zhem to keep zheir mouths shut," he growled, standing up. He stormed out of the tent as Zalith laughed quietly and followed.

The moment he stepped outside, Alucard set his eyes on Magnus, who was standing over by a tree with Ulric. Camael wasn't too far away either, standing with Varana. Seeing all three of them so calm and comfortable only made Alucard angrier. He marched towards them, claws bared, and fangs ready.

When he saw Alucard incoming, Magnus frowned irritably and turned to face him, but before he could speak, the vampire snatched his throat; Magnus choked and stammered in shock as Alucard forced him back and pinned him against the rock face not far from the tree, dust still flying into the sky as a result of Alucard's sheer speed.

Alucard glared into Magnus' panicked eyes. The angel's brothers surely came running, but that didn't unsettle Alucard. He held up his free hand, and as he did, both Ulric and Camael—who were just a few feet away—stuttered, grabbed their throats, and dropped to the ground as they choked and struggled. Alucard had never done that before; he didn't even know that he was capable of manipulating angels like that, but he wasn't about to stand there and question it. Somehow, he just *knew* that he could do it, almost as if it were yet another once-buried, now resurfacing memory.

"Zhis is zhe vone and only varning I'm going to give you," the vampire shouted furiously, almost roaring as he glowered at Magnus' ugly, stupid little face. "You zon't get to control *anyvone* down 'ere, least of all zhe people *I* love. Erich might 'ave sent you 'ere vith zhe impression zhat zhis vorld is yours to do vith vhat you please, but maybe 'e zidn't tell you zhat *I'm* 'ere—zhis vorld is *mine*, not yours, not 'is, and if you can't accept zhat, zhen maybe you should go back 'ome and beg your pitivul vather to send you somevhere else," he snarled, tightening his grip on Magnus' throat. "If I see you or your brover so much as *looking* at Zaliv—" he warned, glancing back at Ulric who was choking on the ground as most of Zalith's people stared at the scene in confliction, "—zhen I vill not 'esitate to kill you." He edged his face closer to the angel's, glaring evilly into his fear-filled eyes. "Your vather *did* tell you zhat's possible, vight?" he asked, tilting his head ever so slightly as he watched dread smother Magnus' haunted visage. "Zhat's vhy 'e zoesn't vant anyving to do vith me…because I kill vings zhat aren't supposed to be killed."

Ulric then tried chanting a spell, so Alucard began slowly closing his raised fist, his scowl still locked with Magnus; Ulric whimpered and shrieked painfully, all words silenced. Alucard decided to loosen his grip on Magnus' throat at the same time so that he could respond.

"Y-yes," Magnus choked as his brother whined in agony. "I completely understand."

"Good," Alucard hissed. "You can count me sparing your life as payment vor zhe vings you 'ave done. Pack your shit up and get zhe fuck out of my space bevore I change my mind," he threatened him and then let go.

Gulping, rubbing his throat as he took deep, ragged breaths, Magnus dared to scowl. "Of course…" he agreed, but when Alucard's hostile glare struck him again, the angel deadpanned.

Alucard gradually lowered his raised hand, letting Magnus' brothers free. Ulric stumbled to his feet and moved to attack, but Magnus held up his hand and shook his head before taking his eyes off Alucard and hiding his intimidated frown.

As the angels retreated, Alucard huffed frustratedly and wiped the hand he'd grabbed Magnus with on his jacket. On his list of things that utterly disgusted him, grim reapers and angels were near the top.

He didn't want to hang around with all of Zalith's people gawping at him, though, so as the demon smirked and stood in front of him, Alucard hastily took his hand and ushered him towards the tent, hoping that all this business with angels had just come to its end.

Chapter Fifty-Four

Plans

| Zalith |

Zalith followed Alucard back into the tent; he enjoyed seeing his vampire so flustered and bothered—he found it adorable. Of course, he felt bad that he was as mad as he was because he didn't want to upset him, and they were having a nice time, too…but it was cute regardless, and he smirked as he stared at Alucard, who huffed irritably, reaching the table. However, Zalith didn't want to sit down. As the vampire let go of his hand, he took hold of Alucard's other hand and started leading him over to their bed, where he then laid down and pulled Alucard with him.

As Alucard exhaled deeply and rested his body on top of Zalith's, the demon wrapped his arms around him and kissed the vampire's head. For now, he just wanted to lay there with him; Alucard's anger had aroused him, but he wasn't going to do anything about it—he didn't want to take any more of his energy. So he lay there, holding his vampire in his arms, staring up at the ceiling.

He could hear Greymore and his friends laughing loudly outside, but instead of irritating Zalith, it made him feel guilty. When Alucard earlier asked him if he wanted to play cards, he initially wanted to decline and keep working, but he didn't want to upset his vampire or make him feel like he was beginning to drift from him. The feelings of defeat and disappointment in himself began creeping back in, reminding him that he still didn't have answers for a lot of their problems; he needed to do better, and he needed to try harder.

Alucard suddenly snarled under his breath and shuffled around, trying to make himself comfortable, and then he gripped Zalith's shirt a little tighter before sighing deeply.

"Are you okay?" Zalith asked, caressing his hair.

"No," he grumbled.

"What's wrong?"

"I vanted to kill 'im," he muttered stubbornly.

The demon laughed. "I know baby. I'm sorry."

Pouting, Alucard huffed and glared over at the wall.

"You don't have to worry; Magnus' ugly brother can pine for me all he wants—it doesn't matter. I'm yours," he said and kissed the vampire's head again.

Alucard's scowl didn't fade. "Is zhe vact zhat zhey *know* ve're togezzer, yet 'e asked vor zhat anyvay. Zhey 'ave no vespect—none of zhem do."

Zalith frowned, holding Alucard tightly. Part of him agreed—he should just let Alucard kill them. But on the other hand, he knew that he could make use of Magnus someday. However, he didn't want to disrespect Alucard by keeping around people who didn't respect him. He didn't know what to do, but he didn't want Alucard to feel upset. "I haven't really been around angels much," he said, breaking the long pause between them, "but from their behaviour, it would appear that everything I've heard seems to be about right."

"Zhey vink zhey're better zhan everyving and everyvone, and vhen zhey see someving zhat vhreatens zhat idea, zhey'll do vhatever zhey can to make zhemselves veel better."

The demon nodded. "Do you think we can find anyone as knowledgeable to replace Magnus?"

Alucard shrugged. "If ve 'ad zhe time and people to look, sure—but ve zon't."

Zalith sighed again, dragging his fingers down Alucard's back. "I'm sorry, baby."

"I zon't vant to vink or talk about zhem anymore," the vampire muttered. "Do you vant to go back to zhe table? Or maybe ve can just bring zhe vood in 'ere."

He *did* like the idea of relaxing in bed with Alucard and eating their food. So, he nodded and said, "Bringing it in here sounds good. I can get—"

Alucard sat up and made Zalith stay down before he could try to get out of bed. "*I* vill get. You vait 'ere," he said firmly.

Zalith smirked. "Yes, sir."

The vampire then got up and disappeared through the cloth doorway that separated the bedroom from the main part of the tent.

As he sat up, Zalith smiled to himself. Not only did he love it when Alucard was possessive and angry, but he loved when he was bossy, too. He'd not tease him too much so that he could experience the vampire's mood a little more, though; Alucard deserved to rest, especially after what just happened.

| Alucard |

Alucard gathered the food, wine bottle, and glasses from the table, trying to calm down. As aggravated as he was, he didn't want to dwell on his anger. His chosen task was to help Zalith feel better, to do something nice for him, not burden him with snarls and repetitive rants about how much he hated angels.

He walked back through the cloth doorway and set his sights on Zalith, who was sitting up in bed and smiling at him. The vampire carefully placed everything down, and then he got back into bed. He filled his and Zalith's glasses with wine before putting the bottle on the floor, and then he took a sip, sinking into the blankets and trying to get comfortable.

While he lay there, he started thinking about what Zalith said—that the demon was Alucard's, and *that* made him think about what Varana had told him. It still hurt his heart to know that Zalith had already bought an engagement ring, but then disaster struck, and they probably weren't going to be able to get married for a long time. He wasn't sure how long this might be going on, but he was quite certain that Zalith wouldn't propose to him unless he felt like they were safe.

He sighed and ate one of the crackers. The sad reality didn't stop him from wondering, though. He knew what he wanted with Zalith, and he was confident that he knew what Zalith wanted, too—and he wanted to talk about it despite the possibility that their future probably wouldn't be happening for a long time.

With a curious frown, he glanced up at Zalith and shyly asked, "Do you…still vant to 'ave a vamily vone day?"

The demon smiled down at him. "Of course I do," he said—but then he smirked, fiddling with Alucard's hair. "How many kids do you want?"

Alucard looked away nervously. He didn't know. But he *did* want a family with Zalith, and not knowing how long he'd have to wait dismayed him. "I zon't know," he mumbled. "Maybe…vone or two."

"Two sounds nice," Zalith said contently. "We can sit back and watch them play, and maybe we can get a nice house near the beach…and we can take them swimming and have little campfires in the summer. And we can all cuddle under one big blanket and look at the stars," he said almost dreamily.

The vampire smiled sadly, turning on his side so that he could rest the side of his head on Zalith's chest. "I just vant zhis to be over so ve can 'ave zhat."

"I know, baby," he replied, fiddling with Alucard's hair. "I feel the same."

Alucard reached down the side of the bed and placed his glass on the floor. He then got up and straddled Zalith's lap, resting his arms around the demon's shoulders. "Vhat vould ve name zhem?"

"I don't know," Zalith said, placing his glass down on the floor, too. He then moved the platter aside before making himself more comfortable, placing his hands on Alucard's waist. "They're going to have your last name, though, so they have to sound good with Reiner."

As his shyness grew, Alucard shrugged and looked away. "Zaliv sounds good vith Veiner," he murmured.

"It *does*," the demon agreed, lightly stroking his thumb over Alucard's cheek. "I've never had a last name before."

Slowly setting his eyes back on Zalith's face, the vampire frowned nervously. "Vell…is yours vhenever, you know. I vant you to 'ave," he said slowly; although he knew that it would be a while until Zalith asked the question, he couldn't help but attempt hinting at it. His excitement to spend his life with his mate was enticing him more and more with each passing moment.

"Good," the demon replied, "because I want it."

Alucard smiled and picked up his glass.

"What would *you* want to name our kids?" the demon asked.

After taking a few sips of his wine, each an attempt to hide and dismiss his flustered expression, Alucard shrugged and glanced at Zalith's curious face. "Vell, I vould stick to names zhat come vrom Dor-Sanguis—maybe…I zon't know," he hesitated, looking away again.

Zalith laughed a little. "Like what?"

"I zon't know," he repeated shyly. "Zhere are a vew names I like. Zhere is…Sovia," he said. "Vera…and I also like Vaphael vor a son."

"I like Raphael," Zalith said, playing with the vampire's hair. "Vera's nice, too." But then a hint of sorrow flickered across his face. "My family had this sort of…tradition, I guess. We all had names that started with a Z or an X, and…I was thinking that maybe I'd like to keep the tradition going. But it's not entirely up to me. I suppose this is something we should talk about nearer the time, so I—"

Alucard shook his head and said, "No, I like zhat. Zhere are a lot of Dor-Sanguian names zhat can be altered to vit your tradition."

Zalith smiled and traced his hand down over Alucard's chest. "You're sure?"

He nodded. "Like Zovia or Zac. I zon't know." He exhaled deeply and said, "Maybe ve vill see zhem vone day."

"We will," Zalith said confidently. "All in good time."

Alucard then moved from Zalith's lap—

"Where are you going?" the demon asked sadly, watching as he sat beside him, taking his glass and the wine bottle from the floor.

"I'm just villing my glass," he assured him, topping off his wine. He then put the bottle down and sat back in Zalith's lap. "'Ow long are ve going to stay 'ere?" he asked.

The demon chuckled softly. "I don't know. Do you have plans?" he questioned with a smirk.

"No," Alucard said, pouting. "I mean in zhis camp. Vhere do ve go next?"

Zalith smirked again. "I thought that was up to you to figure out," he said with an amused laugh. "I don't know, though; I've been looking at maps and reading up on things all day, but I can't find anything feasible."

Alucard nodded—Zalith was right. He *did* say that he'd be responsible for working out where they could go because he knew Aegisguard better than anyone. "Ve can… get out of Nevastus vor starters. If ve travel to zhe ozzer side of zhe country, ve can take a tvade ship somevhere vemote, maybe. Ve'll vant to leave as soon as possible zhough, no?" he asked, thinking as he spoke. "If ve travel a vew more miles east, ve'll veach a station. Ve can board zhe steam tvain. Vould be much vaster zhan valking, and I'm sure zhat by now, Liliv vinks ve'll vemain on voot," he suggested.

"You just want to go on the train, don't you?" the demon teased, playfully prodding Alucard's side as he flinched and fidgeted.

He snatched Zalith's wrist with his free hand. "No," he denied. "Maybe… vhatever. I like zhem," he muttered.

"I've never had the pleasure."

"Zhen zhat is our plan, no?" he asked.

"Sounds good," Zalith agreed and sipped from his glass. "Anywhere is better than here."

Letting go of Zalith's wrist, Alucard sipped from his own glass before sighing quietly.

"What's wrong, baby?"

"Noving," he said with a frown. "I'm vine."

"Why did you sigh? Are you grumpy?"

"No."

The demon smiled and took Alucard's glass from him. He placed both glasses on the floor, and then he pulled Alucard closer, kissing him all over, hugging him firmly as Alucard frowned, but the demon then laughed amusedly and made Alucard lay down on him. "I love you," he said, relaxing.

"I love you, too," Alucard replied, nuzzling the demon's neck.

Zalith tightened his embrace, gradually moving his hand under the vampire's shirt; he placed his palm on Alucard's abs, and that was where the demon left it.

They lay in silence for a while, content within one another's embrace.

But Alucard suddenly felt the urge to pester Zalith. His mate found it amusing to annoy *him*, so he thought that it was time for some payback. He smirked, sliding off Zalith so that he was lying beside him, and then he leaned up on his arm so that he could look down at the demon's face. As Zalith smiled up at him, the vampire guided his thumb from the demon's jawline to his top lip, and slowly dragged it over his stubbly face. Zalith laughed and grasped Alucard's wrist; he pulled the vampire's hand closer to his mouth and lightly bit his thumb. But Alucard pulled his hand away, his palm stroking against Zalith's stubble-covered cheek.

Zalith, clearly seeing Alucard's reluctance as a challenge, gripped his wrist once more. Alucard tried to pull free, but their playful struggle quickly escalated. Zalith rose, attempting to pin him down, but Alucard wasn't about to submit so easily. He grabbed Zalith's wrist, trying to loosen the demon's firm hold, their laughter mingling with the tension of their playful fight. Despite his efforts, Alucard was gradually pushed onto his side, and then fully onto his back as Zalith's strength won out. He snarled, half in frustration and half in amusement, while Zalith's laughter flustered him, and the demon teasingly rubbed his stubbled face against Alucard's, adding a final playful taunt.

Yielding, Alucard attempted to push him away with a hushed laugh; he tried to growl irritably, but he couldn't because he wasn't irritated, he just hated that he lost every time they got into a friendly brawl. He pouted, turning onto his side with his back to Zalith, who chuckled quietly, dragging his hand over the vampire's arm and back, and then he stopped, leaving him alone.

Sighing deeply, Alucard slid his arm under his pillow, glaring over at the wall as he felt Zalith moving behind him—maybe he was making himself comfortable. He kept his pout but started calming down—that was until he felt Zalith *bite* his ass. He flinched and stammered in startle, rolling onto his back as he sharply turned his head and glared at Zalith.

The demon laughed but patted the vampire's thigh and smiled up at him. "Sorry," he mumbled, smirking amusedly.

Pouting, Alucard rolled back onto his side, burying his face into his pillow. Peaches then pounced up onto the bed, and the vampire started scratching her ears while she purred loudly. He wasn't mad or annoyed, he just knew that acting as though he was would make Zalith try to make him feel better by being affectionate, and that was something he wanted right now.

"Are you grumpy?" the demon soon asked, resting his chin on Alucard's bicep.

"No," Alucard mumbled.

Zalith looked down at his kitten. "What do you think, Peaches—is he grumpy?"

The kitten stopped cleaning her paws and gawped up at Zalith—then, she gazed at Alucard.

"What did Peaches say?" Zalith asked.

"She said you smell vunny," he sneered.

The demon laughed. "She must be smelling *you*," he said, turning his head to look at Alucard's face.

Alucard glared at him from the corner of his eye. "I smell better zhan you."

"Who told you that? The cat?"

"Yes," the vampire jeered.

"She likes to lie."

Alucard then frowned. "Vhat, you zon't vink I smell good?" he asked with a sad pout.

"No," the demon answered, but just as Alucard was about to argue, Zalith smirked and added, "But maybe I like to lie too."

Scowling, Alucard pouted and rested his head back on the pillow. "You're a bad liar," he muttered.

"That's not very nice," Zalith said.

Alucard sighed deeply; he just wanted Zalith's attention—his *physical* attention. He turned onto his back, moving his hand to the side of the demon's face, and as Zalith smiled down at him, the vampire stared into his dark eyes. He just gazed…and Zalith stared back. Alucard was certain that he found it funny, or maybe Zalith was enjoying staring as much as he was. The longer he gazed, though, the clearer Zalith's hidden, rounded pupils became, and seeing them made Alucard smile amusedly—he'd only ever see them if he waited and stared long enough.

"What?" Zalith questioned.

"Noving, I just veally like your eyes," he said, trailing his hand to the demon's neck.

He laughed and asked, "Then why are you laughing at them?"

"Is vunny zhat if I stare long enough, I can see your pupils," he told him. "Zhere vas a time vhen I vhought you zidn't 'ave any."

He laughed again. "Of course I have them—I need to see."

Alucard smiled and stroked his hand down Zalith's body, soon resting his arm at his side. All this talk of eyes reminded him that he needed to do something about the worsening effect that the sunlight had on *his* eyes. He got Toma to pick up some materials when he retrieved his and Zalith's lunch, and he was sure that Zalith wanted to get back to work, so he might as well work, too. "Can I stay in 'ere and vork vith you?" he asked. "Maybe ve can vinish eating and zhen get back to?" he suggested.

"Absolutely," the demon said with a smile, and then he kissed the vampire's lips.

Chapter Fifty-Five

—⊰ † ⊱—

A Walk in the Sunlight

| Alucard |

After an hour of relaxing and finishing their lunch, Alucard and Zalith got to work. While Zalith was sitting at the table with his books and papers, Alucard sat cross-legged on their bed with the materials he'd sent Toma to get.

As he worked, the vampire sunk into his thoughts. There was much to think about, and more to consider. They already had a plan regarding where they were going: they'd travel a few miles to the next town, where a station stood; from there, they'd board a steam train which would take them to the coast, and once there, they could board a trading ship. To where exactly, Alucard wasn't sure, but he did know that a lot of ships leaving Nefastus went to either DeiganLupus or Avalmoor. Alucard didn't exactly want to go to Avalmoor—it was too cold, and there were dragons everywhere. He'd rather go to DeiganLupus. He had people there, he had land, and he knew his way around. It was their best option, but they couldn't stay there; it would simply be an overlay. They'd catch another ship from one of DeiganLupus' many ports; from there, they could get to pretty much anywhere in Aegisguard.

Next was the matter involving Lilith. It wouldn't be long until her people discovered that Tyrus wasn't with them anymore, and Lilith would send her people en masse. Zalith had devised a plan which would involve portraying her—they'd have to get her out of the way first, and Alucard was sure that the only way to do that would be to disturb Lucifer. Once she was gone, he and Zalith could manipulate her followers. They could call all of Lilith's followers into an area, and then he or Zalith could challenge her, defeat her, and win all of her followers…her *influence*, and she would be powerless.

However, they needed to get the crystal from her—the Lumendatt. They'd have to take it before they sent her running after Lucifer, and Alucard wasn't yet sure how. They still needed numbers, and it was high time they stopped *killing* their enemies and began swaying them to their side. After all, a lot of their foes were demons, and demons travelled in packs, which meant they had an Alpha. If he and or Zalith challenged the Alphas and defeated them, then their demons would be his and Zalith's demons. They also had his vampires…but the more the better.

He frowned, trying to focus on the tinted glasses that he was constructing, but he kept scheming—he couldn't help it; the silence had a way of making him overthink.

Once they had all the power and influence that would come from taking out Lilith, they'd target Damien, wouldn't they? Zalith said that he wanted to kill them both, and he'd clearly chosen to focus on Lilith first. After all, it was possible to defeat her without needing Numen ethos; Damien, on the other hand…they'd need Lilith's power. They'd need an army of vampires, legions of demons. They'd need their own cult-like following.

Alucard suddenly felt uncomfortable. He didn't want to think about Damien…but he knew so much about the Daegelus. He knew where most of Damien's influence came from, he knew how to rupture it…he knew how to weaken him. He was even capable of fighting Damien himself, and with Lilith's power and followers, he and Zalith would surely be able to banish him forever. They couldn't kill him, though—not really. The only Numen they could actually kill was Lucifer because he was Alucard's father, and someone who possessed the *blood* of a Numen could kill that Numen. Lilith had no blood children, and neither did Damien, Ephriel, Letholdus, or Erich. But they didn't need to kill the Numen, did they? If they found all of the Obcasus' and Pandoricans…then they could lock every Numen away for eternity.

Sighing, the vampire dragged his hand over his face.

"What are you working on?" Zalith called.

Alucard lifted his head, looking over at the demon, who was gazing curiously across the tent at him. "Uh," he murmured, glancing down at his tinted glasses. "Is someving vor my eyes—to stop zhe sun 'urting zhem so much."

Zalith smirked, putting down his papers. "Come over here," he invited. "Let me see."

Alucard got up and went over to Zalith.

When the vampire reached him, Zalith smiled up at him. "Put them on."

Alucard pouted, sighed, and put the glasses on his face.

The demon smiled and lightly gripped Alucard's chin with his finger and thumb. He then gently turned the vampire's head left and right. "You look very handsome," he said, letting go of his chin. "You did a good job."

"I veel like zhey look stupid," he muttered.

"You don't look stupid, you look nice," Zalith assured him, putting his hands on either side of Alucard's waist to pull him closer.

The vampire shrugged. "I guess I need to see if zhey vork. Do you vant to valk vith me?" he asked, eager to leave the tent for a little while. "You zon't 'ave to," he added. "I know you're busy."

Zalith frowned as he glanced at his work. He sighed before replying, "I'd love to, but…I should keep working."

His answer disappointed Alucard—he didn't want to walk alone, but Zalith had work he wanted to do, and he'd let him do it. "All vight. I'll be back in a little vhile."

"Okay. Stay close to the perimeter," his mate urged him.

Alucard nodded and went to leave—

"Wait," Zalith insisted, grabbing his wrist. He stood up and kissed Alucard before letting go of him. "Okay, you can go now."

Smiling, Alucard left the tent and stepped out into the sunlight…and to his relief, his eyes didn't ache the slightest bit as it hit his face. He stared up at the sky, a sense of satisfaction settling over him as he finally stood in the rays that had tormented his sights since the very first moment he stepped foot in Aegisguard. He felt…free. To stand in the sunlight, to stare up at the sky, and to not have to deal with an aching, drowning headache. How long he'd wished for a day his eyes would see the world in sunlight without him suffering, and today was that day.

He heard someone approaching and took his eyes off the sky, looking over his shoulder. He watched as Idina made her way over.

"Oh," she said with an intrigued smile, stopping in front of him and ogling his glasses. "What's on your face?"

"Zhey're…sunglasses," he named them. "Zhe sunlight 'urts my eyes, so I made someving to stop zhat."

"Oh, wow…you made them?" she asked, surprised. "They look great."

"Vank you," he said before gazing at the horizon.

"How long did it take to make them?"

"Eh…less zhan an hour," he mumbled.

"My my," she said, impressed. "I had no idea you made things."

He shrugged and said, "'As been a vhile. Used to be a 'obby, but I stopped vor a vhile vhen Zaliv and I started seeing each ozzer. Zhen I lost my castle…so…I 'aven't veally 'ad zhe inspiration to make anyving. I needed zhese, zhough, so…I made zhem."

"Are they difficult to see through?"

"Not veally," he said. "Zhey just tint zhe vorld a little darker."

"I wouldn't be surprised if people start asking you to make them a pair, too," she said with a quiet laugh.

Alucard nodded. "Vell…maybe vone day."

Idina paused for a moment. "How have you two been doing?" she asked.

"Ve're good," he answered.

"That's great. I was really worried about you both, especially Zalith…with how sick he was."

"'E's vine; 'e's just vorking," he muttered.

"Good," Idina said with a smile. "I'm glad he's back to his normal self. Anyway, I'll get out of your hair. If you need anything, let me know," she said, and as Alucard glanced at her, she wandered off to join her friends.

Alone again, Alucard sighed and stared at the horizon. He felt as if he was already done with his break—he wanted to head back into the tent so that he could sit and talk with Zalith…but the demon was working, and Alucard didn't want to disturb him. As much as he didn't want to be alone, maybe it was the best thing right now; that way, he could think a little more and consider their options. He already had an idea of where they were going, he just needed to figure out where they could stop. Of course, he wanted to head to Uzlia, but he knew that Zalith wasn't exactly confident about doing that, so he'd give it a little more time before they headed there.

He walked towards the forest; he'd rather walk than stand around.

Where could everybody go? It would need to be somewhere free of Lilith's cultists, Diabolus, and any Numen followers at all, somewhere they wouldn't have to hide or sneak around. But that wasn't possible. Lilith and Damien would have eyes and ears everywhere—he was actually surprised that there wasn't a mole among them. It wouldn't shock him if there was, though. But Zalith would know—his mate was constantly monitoring his people's thoughts in case one of them did so happen to be conspiring, just as Addison was.

Alucard exhaled deeply, slipping his hands into his pockets as he made his way through the woods. The only place they could completely relax would be their castle—he needed to stop thinking about that. He sighed again, trying to concentrate. Almost all of the places that weren't plagued by Numen cultists were instead home to Aegis, which Alucard could just kill, of course, but that would grab Letholdus' attention, and they didn't need that right now…unless they somehow used the Aegis to manipulate Letholdus. Zalith once mentioned pissing off one of the other Numen, getting them to fight against Lilith and or Damien. Maybe they could still do that. If they could avert the eyes of *one* of their enemies, it would be a whole lot easier to deal with the other one.

He kept walking, thinking. Their shapeshifter could pose as Lilith *or* Damien…and the fake could cause a shit storm or meddle with something that would infuriate Letholdus enough to make him hunt down the real Numen. That was an option he'd like to place on the table, so he'd tell Zalith later.

When he reached a small glade, he stopped walking for a moment and leaned against a tree. Their larger plan seemed to be coming together like pieces of a puzzle. Get somewhere safe, get Lilith out of the way, pose as her, steal her followers, increase their own influence thus increasing their power…and use it to lock her away…to lock Damien away…and maybe…kill Lucifer? He frowned, looking down at the ground. He knew that his father would never stop hunting him, but the thought of killing and becoming him…Alucard didn't want that. What if becoming a Numen changed him? What if Zalith didn't like what he became? He'd seen what Numen ethos had done to others, and he knew what it did to him—but *more*? If he had more, he was convinced that he'd become just like his father, and he wasn't going to willingly let that happen.

He dragged his hand over his face. But what option did they have? What option did *he* have? If they truly wanted to eradicate the Numen, they would need pure Numen ethos—they'd need a Numen of their own, and he was certain that Zalith had thought about it…about turning him into a fully-fledged Numen. It was possible, and it would give them the upper hand they needed…but was it what Alucard wanted?

And that wasn't everything. They still needed to find the other Obcasus', they still needed to find the Pandoricans…and they still needed numbers. One thing at a time.

Alucard continued forward, setting his eyes on a cliff edge up ahead. Once he reached it, he sat on a fallen tree and stared out at the ocean of treetops. The only Pandorican he knew the location of was the one Lucifer was trapped inside of. The rest were out there…he just needed to find them. Usually, that was something he'd do himself, but not only was he sure that Zalith wouldn't want him to go, but he didn't want to leave his mate, nor did he want to risk taking him with him. But who could he send? Luther was gone—he wasn't going to think about him. He shook his head and sighed. Crowell was busy, and so were the rest of his capable vampires.

Was it perhaps time to reconnect with old associates? He scowled, pondering. No. Well…maybe. They needed those tools…and Alucard knew just the guy to get them. But he wasn't ready to open that door once again.

Not yet.

Chapter Fifty-Six

The Cliffside

| Zalith |

It was time to take a break. As much as he wanted to keep working—as much as he knew that he *should* keep working, he missed Alucard, and he wanted to spend a little time away from the camp with him. When they were alone at the river, he felt a sense of relief that he just didn't get while surrounded by his people.

He tidied his paperwork up, finished his glass of bourbon, and put it and the almost-empty bottle back into his vault. Then, he grabbed the half-full bottle of wine and the glasses from the bedroom before leaving the tent. Focusing on Alucard's aura through their imprints, he navigated the forest, eventually finding his vampire sitting on a log at a cliff edge. For a moment, he stood there and gazed at the man he loved; he looked completely mesmerized by the setting sun, which made sense—he'd probably never been able to watch the event without pain, had he?

Zalith smiled softly and left the tree line. "Hey," he called.

Alucard snapped out of it and looked over his shoulder, watching as Zalith approached.

When he reached Alucard, he kissed his cheek and sat beside him. "What are you doing?"

"I'm just sitting 'ere. Did you vinish vorking?"

"For now," he said, handing Alucard one of the wine glasses. "I wanted to come and spend some time with you."

The vampire smiled as Zalith filled his glass. "Vank you," he said. "I vas actually vinking," he started, looking down into his wine. "Tomorrow, if ve 'ead vor zhe station, vhen ve get to zhe port, maybe ve can take a ship to DeiganLupus? I know zhat place a lot, and ve can vind somevhere to stay vor a night or two vhile ve vork out vhere to go vrom zhere."

Zalith nodded as he filled his own glass and then put the bottle on the ground. "That sounds good. How long is the trip?"

Alucard shrugged, sipping from his wine. "Zhe closest station vrom 'ere is…'alf a day. Zhen zhe tvain takes avound vhree hours. Zhe ship…a vew days—two to DeiganLupus, I vink."

The demon nodded. "Okay."

Zalith then downed his wine. Alucard's plan made sense—it was smart, it was feasible, and it might very well be what they needed to do to progress in solving this problem. He frowned, sinking into his thoughts for a moment. What if they didn't make it to the station? What if something stopped them? What if they couldn't board a ship? He wanted to make sure he had a plan B and a plan C. He wanted to ensure he was prepared for anything and everything, but as he sat there, his thoughts didn't seem to want to cooperate. He couldn't think straight—he couldn't *concentrate*, and he knew that was probably because he'd been drinking bourbon since Alucard left the tent earlier.

He stared at his glass as he filled it again. Silence had gripped them, and he didn't want that, but…he didn't know what to say. He didn't know what to talk about. His thoughts were…discombobulated.

"So…ve need vings to banish zhe Numen," Alucard said, looking at him. "Ve need to vind zhe ozzer Obcasus', and zhen ve need to vind zhe Pandoricans. I…used to vork vith somevone who is pretty good at vinding vings. I can invite 'im 'ere to 'elp if you vink ve need zhat," he suggested.

"Who is he?" Zalith asked curiously.

"'Is veal name is Gabriel, but 'e goes by Soren Becker in Aegisguard," he said and sipped from his wine. "'E is uh…strange…divverent," he muttered. "'E vas vemoved vrom Erich's Arbiter council a long time ago and 'as been living underground ever since. 'E can still access zhe grim veaper 'ive mind. Seeing zhose angels veminded me…but maybe 'e's dead; I 'aven't spoken to 'im in a long time. Ve zidn't part on zhe best of terms."

Succumbing to the past few hours of drink, Zalith stared at Alucard, blinking slowly for a moment as he absorbed his words. "What happened?" he asked plainly, unable to ponder the information he'd been given. He felt himself slipping away as each moment passed, and with the confusion came a deep, drowning sadness. He could feel it like a weight on his chest…and he couldn't stop it.

Alucard shrugged, finishing his drink. "Vell, an Arbiter decides vhere somevone goes vhen zhey die and end up in Purgatory. So…even zhough 'e vas vemoved vrom Purgatory, 'e zidn't exactly lose 'is desire to judge. I killed a lot of people back zhen, and I turned a lot of zhem into vampires, too. 'E zidn't agree vith my methods, and most grim veapers see vampires as a disgrace to Erich, vor zhey devy 'is laws of death. Soren tried to convince me avay vrom making vampires, but I needed zhem. Vone night, I vent a little too var and turned an entire town in zhe space of an hour—zhat vas vhen 'e decided vas time ve parted vays," he explained, picking up the bottle to refill his glass.

Zalith drank half his glass and nodded. "Why was he removed from the council?"

"'E vasn't zhe best vit. 'E is susceptible to sentiment and guilt trips," he said, amused. "All a soul 'ad to do vas cry and 'e'd let zhem veincarnate. 'E vas...vone of Erich's virst creations, so 'e vasn't so 'eartless and emotionless."

"So, all you have to do is cry and he'll work with you," Zalith said with a smirk.

The vampire sighed. "Probably von't be zhat simple."

"Maybe if we *both* cry."

Alucard shrugged, still with an amused smile on his face. "I'm sure no vone needs to cry. I'll just ask 'im nicely."

Zalith stared into his drink, the world fading further away from his perception. But when he felt Alucard shuffle beside him, he set his sights on him. "Hmm?"

Alucard frowned at him.

"Oh, sorry," the demon chuckled, trying to hide just how drunk he was. "I'm a little tired." But then he carelessly let slip, "I've been drinking all day," before laughing and downing the rest of his wine. He couldn't even control what he said anymore.

The vampire watched Zalith refill his glass. "Vhy...'ave you been drvinking all day?" he asked.

"Because it was there...and I was thirsty," he said with a shrug, placing the bottle down. He wasn't about to tell him that he'd taken a bottle of bourbon from his vault. "I didn't drink a lot, don't worry," he tried to convince him.

With a skeptical frown, Alucard pouted and put his glass down. "Maybe you shouldn't 'ave any more," he said, reaching for Zalith's glass.

Zalith leaned back, holding his glass behind him as he laughed. "I'm fine, baby. Don't worry," he insisted, dragging out his words. But Alucard tried leaning closer to reach his glass, so the demon kissed his lips to fluster and distract him, laughed, and rested his head on the vampire's shoulder. "Tell me more about Bertram," he requested.

"Becker," Alucard corrected, sounding irritated. "Are you drvunk?" he then asked.

"No," he laughed.

Alucard clearly wasn't convinced. "Is not like you to get drvunk at a time like zhis," he muttered.

"I'm *not* drunk," he assured him.

"You *are,* Zaliv," the vampire grumbled.

The demon laughed quietly again, shuffling around, making himself comfortable as he sipped from his glass. "How did you and Becker meet?" he asked, trying to sway him away from the subject.

Alucard didn't immediately respond; he was likely trying to decide whether to persist or not. "'E came to kill me," he finally answered. "Vampires are a disgrace, cut zhem off at zhe source, blah...blah..." he drawled and sighed. "Veality 'it 'im 'alfvay vhrough our battle, and 'e accepted zhat 'e vasn't an Arbiter anymore. I ovvered 'im a purpose, 'e took zhat."

"That was very nice of you."

He shrugged. "Eh, vas business. 'Aving 'im avound made vinding zhe Aegis much easier."

The demon nodded, sipping from his glass again.

"Are you okay?" Alucard then asked, looking down at him.

"I'm okay. Are you okay?"

"No," he said with a pout. "I'm vorried about you."

"I'm okay. I'm right here," Zalith said, smiling up at him.

Alucard sighed deeply and stared back out at the horizon. "Someving's vrong," he murmured. "Vhy else vould you be drvinking vight now? Is not like you."

"I was thirsty," he repeated with a smile.

The vampire huffed and said, "Okay," seeming to give up.

Zalith stared despondently. He knew that he was disappointing Alucard—he was a disappointment because he was always so reluctant and aversive when it came to sharing his thoughts and feelings. Alucard deserved better than that—he didn't deserve someone as unworthy as him. And he was certain that Alucard would start to resent him soon because he kept acting this way, he kept refusing to share his emotions. But it was such a struggle for him to *not* act this way—he'd been like this all his life, over six hundred years, and it seemed impossible to change.

No one had ever really cared about his feelings as much as Alucard did. Usually, he was able to offer what he normally offered—cold shoulders, dismissive subject changes, and flirty distractions—and everyone was fine with that. But not Alucard. Alucard needed more, and he *deserved* more, but Zalith wasn't sure if he could give it to him. He wanted to, but it felt like an unobtainable adaptation. He knew that he couldn't be fixed, and no amount of Alucard's positivity and willingness to help was going to repair his problems.

Did that make them incompatible? No...it didn't make them incompatible at all. But...he felt like it would drive a wedge between them. Where would that leave them in two years? Five years? Zalith knew he was going to make things worse for them without even trying because that was all he ever did. He continuously fucked up everything he had, lost everyone he loved, and let down the people who relied on him. And it seemed like a theme at this point in his life. All he did was work hard and try to make Alucard happy, to make *everyone* happy, but it was never enough. Even when he did good, he knew he could do better, and if he didn't provide, then what was he doing? He had no value beyond what he did for others...and he couldn't even do that right, could he?

Alucard deserved better.

"I'm a failure, Alucard," he murmured sullenly.

Alucard looked down at him. "Vhat? You're not a vailure."

"But I am, though," he insisted. "Because that's all I ever seem to do. I couldn't save my dad. I couldn't save my mom; I can still hear her screaming sometimes. I couldn't save my brother or his daughters. And I had armies that I couldn't save either. Thousands and thousands of lives wasted…and for what? The ones who survived got picked off one by one, and I couldn't save them. And then even in the end, some of them turned on me—but of course, why wouldn't they, right? Because all I've managed to secure for them is their deaths, and then…I bring them here…to give them a home…and then this shit happens. *That's* failure," he said as an awful pain stabbed at his heart, burrowing deep. "And the worst part is—the fucking *worst* part of all of this is that I've been *trained* to succeed all my life; I was the best at everything; I was always so much better than everybody else, and so much smarter than everybody else…and I spent centuries fucking learning and priming myself for this—for *war*, and then I fail…and I let everyone down over and over and over," he uttered through gritted teeth, his sorrow and pain worsening.

The vampire sat him up straight, placing his hand on the side of his neck as he stared into his eyes. "You zidn't vail—I zon't vink you did. You *alvays* do everyving zhat you can—you *alvays* vork so 'ard. And war—you lose people, and you can't save everyvone. Is not your vault zhese vings 'appened. You saved as many people as you could, and zhat's better zhan saving no vone."

"I deserve to have this on my conscience…because I could have done better."

Alucard frowned. "You did everyving you could," he said sadly. "And despite all of zhat, you're still doing everyving you can vor zhese people."

Zalith stared at him for a moment. He wasn't able to accept that it wasn't his fault—he *knew* he could have done better. He knew he hadn't done everything he possibly could have. "Why are you being so nice to me?"

"Because I love you…and I see 'ow much you do—I see 'ow 'ard you vork. You could never be and 'ave never been a vailure, Zaliv," he said firmly, moving closer to rest his forehead against Zalith's. "And zhere is no vone I vould vather spend my time vith."

Guiding his hand to the side of Alucard's face, Zalith scowled in despair. Why? Why had Alucard chosen *him*? Alucard knew so many people; he used to work with and be around so many others before meeting him. Any one of them could do for Alucard what Zalith had already done for him. Did Alucard just love him because he so happened to let Zalith in out of everyone else he'd met? Was he only as devoted as he was because Zalith was his first *everything*…because he had no frame of reference? He sunk deeper into despair. Alucard had imprinted on him…and the marks of so many other demons clung to Zalith's being. The demon knew what he was personally capable of when it came to relationships…and he had to ask himself: what if he'd just manipulated Alucard into imprinting on him? But Zalith loved him so much…he could never manipulate him, he could never twist his very soul like that…to force an imprint. But what if he had? What if he did it without even realizing? It wouldn't be the first time he did something he didn't mean to because of what he was.

He felt his heart break a little. Was it cruel of him to keep Alucard around…entangled in a situation that—with the way things were going—was potentially doomed to fail because of him? He couldn't protect Alucard, and he obviously wasn't meeting his standards. Earlier, Alucard seemed to so easily suggest they take time away from one another, even if he had thought it was what Zalith wanted. But regardless, he knew Alucard would probably be happier with someone else. He didn't *want* him to be with anyone else, and it hurt *so* much to even think about, but…Alucard *deserved to* be happy…he deserved better.

"I love you too, baby," he replied sullenly, taking his forehead off Alucard's. "But I don't want this for you."

Alucard tensed up and frowned confusedly. "Vhat…vhat do you mean?" he asked, keeping his hand on the side of Zalith's neck.

Zalith stroked his hand down to Alucard's wrist. "You need to break up with me…to protect yourself," he lamented, his throat tightening as his heart shattered.

The vampire looked *horrified.* "Vhat?" he instantly snapped, sounding confused, anxious, and *afraid.*

"I don't want this," Zalith said mournfully. "But I don't want something to happen to you because of me. You deserve someone so much better—"

"I zon't vant anyvone else," he refused, moving closer to him.

"I don't want you to want anyone else either, but I'm scared. I just want you to be safe and happy."

Alucard then scowled, clearly at war with his emotions. He shook his head and insisted, "But I *am* safe, and I *am* 'appy."

Zalith shook his head, fighting back his tears. "I'm worried that you only think you're happy because I am the way I am, and we defied the odds at the start; I fear that one day, you're going to regret all of this because all I seem to be doing is frustrating you. And maybe earlier when you said that we should just focus on being associates was you realizing that…I'm not the one—"

"I only said zhat because zhat vas 'ow you made me veel," he interjected. "Zhat 'urt me so much to vink and to say—I vasn't vealizing zhat you veren't zhe vone, and I vasn't deciding zhat I vanted to leave, because I zon't. You vere pushing me avay, and zhat's vhat zhat velt like—zhat's vhat zhis veels like," he said, his voice starting to break, his face smothered with dismay. "Vhy do you veel like zhis? Do I not do enough to make you veel vanted? Vhy do you vant to push me avay so bad vhen all I vant to do is be zhere vith you? Vhen all I vant to do is love you," he questioned, tears forming in his distressed eyes.

With a sullen scowl, Zalith edged closer and placed his hand on the side of Alucard's face. "Alucard, you are more than enough for me," he said quietly. "I'm just afraid that something or someone is going to take you from me because of something I could have prevented," he told him, pressing his forehead against Alucard's. "I love you so much, baby…I don't want you to leave." And then he felt his tears fall. He pulled away from Alucard, trying to hide them. "I just…I just need to take a walk; I need to clear my head," he said as he stood up, and he didn't give Alucard time to respond. He didn't want to be seen crying, and he didn't want to let his despair win. So he walked away, disappearing into the woods, ignoring Alucard's calls.

And there he was…doing it again. Hiding his emotions, running away from his feelings, and pushing Alucard away. The man he loved deserved far better than this.

| Alucard |

Alucard stopped calling Zalith's name and wiped the tears from his eyes, trying to control his dismay. Why was Zalith doing this? Why was he telling him to leave him, and then telling him to stay? It was all so confusing—it *hurt* to feel so confounded by what Zalith wanted. Did he want him to stay? Did he want him to leave? Alucard didn't want to leave. He wasn't going to give up on Zalith—despite everything, he still wanted to spend his life with him. But did Zalith even want the same? Was the demon questioning his feelings—was that…the real reason he hadn't asked him to marry him yet?

He scowled in despair, looking down at the ground. But he didn't want to let his negative feelings win this time, nor did he want to let Zalith get back to camp without hearing what Alucard needed to tell him. So he got up and hurried after him, following his aura. And when he found Zalith stumbling through the woods, heading the wrong way, he hastily caught up to him and grabbed his arm. "Vait," he insisted.

Zalith slowly turned to face him; he'd clearly tried to hide it, but he'd been crying.

Alucard took hold of Zalith's hands and stared into his eyes. "I vill never leave you," he said firmly. "Noving is going to change my mind."

The demon sighed shakily and wrapped his arms around him, pulling him into a tight hug and nuzzling his neck. "I'm so sorry, baby," he murmured sadly.

Alucard wondered for a moment whether Zalith wanted him to stay or leave him to stumble about the forest, but his confusion slowly withered when Zalith took hold of his hand and placed it against his chest. The vampire stared into his mate's tormented eyes, able to feel the demon's erratic heartbeat against his hand, which Zalith held in place. And then he let go for a moment—Zalith let Alucard into both his head and his heart. The vampire could *feel* what Zalith felt, and it was all so overbearing, but so enlightening. He now understood just how profoundly Zalith struggled to express both his love and his guilt; Alucard could feel his remorse, he could feel how *desperately* Zalith yearned for him to stay, how *fiercely* he needed him. And Alucard could feel just how badly Zalith wanted him to understand the things he couldn't say—the things he couldn't express.

He heard the demon exhale a struggled breath riddled with heartbreak. Zalith was so sad—it was a sadness that Alucard knew too well. It gripped him like a snake, constricting tighter and tighter the more he tried to free himself. Zalith was never going to forgive himself—Alucard was sure of that. And the demon was *terrified* that Alucard was going to leave, that he was just going to vanish and start a life with someone else. He feared Alucard would hate him, resent him—he even feared that Alucard would die.

And then there was his love. Alucard could feel that, too. Zalith…he loved Alucard more than he had ever loved anything…*anyone*. The vampire felt just how much he meant to Zalith, and he could feel just how devastated Zalith would be if he lost him…because he didn't want to lose him. Zalith wanted him to be happy, he wanted them *both* to be happy with each other, an eternity filled with only contentment. Zalith still wanted their life together, a family, a world where they were all safe. And his love was so intense that he'd even die to protect Alucard. It burned…the feeling. Alucard could feel it in his own heart. He'd never felt something so vigorous—something so…real. He was Zalith's everything, and Zalith was *his* everything.

"I'm so sorry, Alucard," Zalith repeated, his voice breaking as he held onto him tightly. "I'm sorry."

Alucard felt Zalith's sadness intensifying; he could feel his angst and his fear growing, and if Alucard didn't say something, he was convinced that Zalith was moments from crying, and he didn't want that to happen. Seeing and *feeling* Zalith's despair brought a terrible pain to the vampire's heart; knowing that this was how Zalith felt, knowing how fiercely Zalith loved him, and how deeply he feared losing him forever. It made him struggle to hold back tears again.

He held Zalith in his arms as tightly as he could, a distressed, sullen pout on his face as he buried his face in Zalith's neck. "You zon't 'ave to vorry about me leaving; I alveady decided years ago zhat I vanted to be vith you vorever, and noving vill change my mind. You are everyving to me, and zhere isn't a ving I vouldn't do vor you. Vhatever 'appens, and vhatever comes vor us, ve vill deal vith togezzer. Ve'll get vhrough *everyving* togezzer. You're not alone anymore, Zaliv, and you zon't 'ave to carry all zhis by yourselv. You zon't 'ave to 'ide 'ow you veel, you zon't 'ave to pretend like everyving is okay because no amount of vrustration or convusion is going to drive me avay. Yes, you veally piss me off sometimes, but I piss you off too, no? I gazzer zhat is just a part of sharing your life vith somevone. Von't alvays be pervect, and zhat's okay because ve 'ave each ozzer," he said quietly, able to feel the demon's frantic, panicked heartbeat starting to slow.

Zalith didn't say anything; he held Alucard a little firmer, nuzzling his neck.

Alucard could feel him calming down; he could feel his distress fading. "I love you, Zaliv," he mumbled, and then he leaned back as he placed his hand on the side of Zalith's face.

The demon stared at him for a moment before Alucard kissed his lips, moving his hand to the back of Zalith's head as he kissed back.

"I love you, too," Zalith mumbled.

They kissed again, and again, and once more before resting their foreheads together.

"Let's go back," Alucard said. "Ve can vest, and zhen tomorrow, ve'll 'ead vor zhe station."

With a slight smile, Zalith nodded. "Okay."

Alucard took hold of Zalith's hand and began leading the way back to camp. He was tired, and he was sure Zalith could use some rest, too. He hoped that he felt better; he just wanted Zalith to be happy. Knowing how sad his mate was and how he'd been struggling only made Alucard more desperate to insist that he let him help. It wasn't like Zalith *at all* to drink that much—had he done so to try and ignore how he felt? Alucard frowned, glancing at the demon beside him. He didn't know what else to do or what else to say, but he felt that being close to Zalith right now was the best he could do.

Once they reached the camp, Alucard took Zalith into their tent. He let go of the demon's hand to kill the flames of the few lit lanterns, and then he started undressing on the way to their bed. Wordlessly, they climbed into bed and shuffled closer to one another, and as Zalith embraced Alucard tightly, they both sighed deeply.

"I love you," Zalith whispered and kissed Alucard's forehead.

Alucard smiled, placing his hand against Zalith's chest. "I love you, too."

Zalith kissed his lips, and when he slipped his tongue into Alucard's mouth, their slow kisses grew intense.

The vampire took a moment to catch his breath and asked, "Do you veel better?"

"A little," the demon said, and then he resumed kissing him.

They kissed for a little longer.

"Are you sure?" Alucard questioned worriedly.

"I'm sure," Zalith confirmed, tracing his hand to the side of the vampire's face.

Alucard stared at him for a moment, trying to discern whether his mate was lying or not, and when he was confident enough that Zalith *was* starting to feel better, he let their kissing resume. He was still worried about him; he was certain that Zalith was still distressed, but Alucard wouldn't stop trying to help him through it. Zalith didn't deserve to be so sad, to feel so weighted by the things that had happened. He *always* did the best he could, and Alucard would help him see that.

He sighed contently as Zalith started kissing his neck and down to his chest. He hoped that, maybe tomorrow, Zalith would feel a little better. Alucard would try to talk to him about it…or maybe he wouldn't depending on how Zalith seemed to be doing. Either way, he just wanted to make sure Zalith was okay.

Zalith kissed his way back up to Alucard's lips and pecked them a few times.

When the demon stopped and stared at him, Alucard smiled and said, "Goodnight."

"Goodnight, baby," Zalith replied, stroking the side of his face.

Alucard moved closer, resting his head against Zalith's chest as the demon held him tightly. Tomorrow…they'd be on the move again and on their way out of Nefastus. As relieving as it sounded, it also disheartened Alucard. Nefastus had been his home for the best years of his life…but he was confident that he and Zalith would make their home elsewhere soon enough.

ARC THREE
THINGS LOST, THINGS STOLEN

Chapter Fifty-Seven

Loss

| **Alucard,** ***Sunday, Cordus 5th, 960(TG)—Nefastus*** |

Darkness. Alucard found himself surrounded by it once again. Black in every direction, a thin layer of water on the ground. But it wasn't silent—not this time. An eerie, whistling wind carrying Alucard's demon name upon it, but in a voice he didn't recognize.

His dream didn't last very long though. When he felt a warm hand on his shoulder, he frowned and looked behind for its owner—

The darkness faded as he opened his eyes, setting them on Zalith, who lay beside him, guiding his hand over his shoulder. Alucard smiled, turning onto his right side so that he could lie facing the demon. He then moved his hand to the side of Zalith's face, staring into his eyes.

"Are you 'ungover?" the vampire asked with a smirk and quiet laugh.

"Yes," his mate muttered but then pulled Alucard closer, hugging him tightly.

Alucard smiled. "You shouldn't 'ave 'ad so much to drvink, zhen," he teased.

Zalith smiled, nuzzling Alucard's neck. "Maybe."

They then lay in silence, wrapped in one another's embrace. Alucard noticed that he hadn't woken with a headache for the first time in what might be centuries, and he suspected that it could be because of the fact he'd not had to deal with the sunlight hitting his eyes yesterday. His latest invention had worked *better* than he'd hoped, and the thought of no longer having to deal with that particular discomfort made him feel overly content—but that happiness faded when *Varana* burst into his and Zalith's tent without so much as an announcement.

"I need to talk to you," she said, standing at the end of their bed, glaring down at Zalith.

"About what?" the demon grumbled, still nuzzling Alucard's neck.

"I want to talk alone," she insisted.

Zalith sighed, turning his head so that he could glance at her. "Okay. Give me half an hour—"

"No, I need to talk to you *now*," she demanded.

The demon exhaled deeply, but he didn't have a chance to answer.

Alucard's irritancy quickly increased; he scowled at Varana and snarled, "Vhat zidn't you understand? 'E said not now."

"Okay, and maybe what I have to say can't wait!" she snarled back.

"Make vait," he growled.

"If it wasn't important, I wouldn't be here. I'm sure you can survive without him for two minutes," she snapped.

"Vell maybe I zon't vant to survive vithout 'im vor two minutes!" he snapped back.

Varana scowled in what might be revolt. "Can you stop acting like a bratty little child please?! The world doesn't revolve around you; you two can go back to being disgusting when we're done talking!"

Alucard gritted his teeth and went to yell back at her, but Zalith placed his hand on his chest and sighed quietly.

Then, the demon looked at Varana. "I'll be out soon."

"Thank you," she said irritably, and as she went to turn around and leave, she stuck her tongue out at Alucard.

The vampire growled in hostility, and once she was gone, he pouted and rested his head back down on his pillow.

Zalith huffed but relaxed, too.

Trying to dismiss his aggravation, Alucard stared into Zalith's tired eyes. "You zon't 'ave to go," he mumbled.

"I should. It's probably important."

"But I zon't vant you to go," Alucard mumbled sadly.

"I know," Zalith muttered, stroking his hand to the side of Alucard's neck. "I won't be long." He kissed Alucard for a few moments before dragging himself to the side of the bed, where he sat for a moment with a tired, despondent look on his face.

Alucard sat up. "Are you okay?"

The demon leaned back and ran his fingers through Alucard's hair. "Yeah, I'm just tired," he said with a small smile.

"Vell…ve can alvays vest some more bevore ve start getting veady to leave."

Zalith nodded as he started pulling his trousers on. "I'll come back after I'm done with Varana, and then we can get some more rest," he agreed.

Alucard laid back down and kept his eyes on Zalith as he pulled the rest of his clothes on. Before leaving, the demon smiled at him one more time, and once Zalith had gone, Alucard sighed and stared aimlessly.

Seconds later, Peaches pounced up onto his chest and gawped expectantly down at him.

"Vhat?" he asked.

She meowed quietly.

Alucard was sure that she was hungry, and as much as he liked to lay in bed, he didn't want to make her wait. "Vine," he said with a sigh, sitting up as Peaches shuffled down into his lap. Somebody must have gone to find something for the camp's breakfast by now, so he'd go and see what that was and get some for his kitten.

He pulled on his shirt and his trousers, and then he slipped his shoes on as he picked Peaches up and carried her in his arm. Making his way outside, he set his eyes on a small gathering of people sitting around a fire. Greymore was among them, and when he noticed Alucard walking over, he smiled and stood up.

"Hey, buddy. You hungry?" the Alpha asked.

"No," Alucard mumbled. "But Peaches is," he said, looking down at his kitten.

"I gotcha covered," Greymore said, reaching over to snatch some of the cooked meat off the plate by the fire. "Here ya go," he said, handing it to him.

"Vank you," Alucard replied, holding the food in front of Peaches; the kitten sniffed it and then started eating.

"No problem. Hey, uh…do you know what the plan is?" Greymore then asked.

Alucard glanced at Greymore and said, "Ve're leaving today. Ve're 'eading vor zhe next town—zhere's a station zhere, and ve'll be taking zhe steam tvain to zhe coast, vhere ve'll board a tvade ship to DeiganLupus."

Greymore nodded, a contemplative look on his face. "Sounds good, boss."

"You should tell everyvone to start getting veady to leave soon."

"Gotcha," he said and turned around. But then he quickly turned to face him again as he said, "Oh, one of those angel guys says he's sticking around or something." He nodded to his right.

Alucard looked over there, and when he saw Camael sitting on a log, he scowled in hostility.

"Something about wanting to, uh…I dunno, endure the experience?" the Alpha muttered unsurely. "I guess angels think we're pretty amusing…like mice in a maze."

The vampire snarled quietly. "Angels are fucking parasites." He shot a look at Greymore. "Go and tell everyvone to start getting veady."

Greymore nodded and wandered off to do as he'd been told.

Alucard then turned around, feeding Peaches the rest of her food as he headed towards Camael. "Vhat zhe fuck are you still doing 'ere?" he growled at the angel.

Camael stood up, holding his hands out. "Hey, calm down, all right? I just wanted to stick around and help or whatever. It beats following Magnus around like a lost sheep."

"You are 'is bodyguard, no? Is your job. Fuck off."

He chuckled a little. "Look, I'm not here to pry or babysit. I never get to walk Aegisguard for longer than a few hours. Just…let me linger, would you?" he asked, almost begging…like a pathetic little child.

Alucard gritted his teeth, but his attention was snatched by Varana's echoing, stroppy voice. He glanced over at her and Zalith, and their conversation looked a little heated. He wanted to know what they were talking about, so he snarled and bared his fangs at Camael. "Ve'll vinish zhis later."

Camael huffed. "I'm not doing any harm. I just…." His voice drowned out as Alucard walked off.

When the vampire got to his horse, he placed his kitten on the saddle, letting her finish her food as he reached into his pocket and pulled out his sunglasses. The skies were grey, so he wasn't going to need them for now; he slipped them into one of the saddlebags and sighed deeply, glancing back over his shoulder at Zalith…and he couldn't help but listen in.

"*I'm just so over it, okay?*" the woman insisted, stropping. "*I can't keep dealing with all these bugs and sleeping on the ground, Zalith! I need an actual bed. I'll just go to some backwater town where no one knows anyone.*"

The demon sighed, clearly trying not to lose his patience. "*I told you, Varana. We have to follow the protocol, which means staying together—all of us.*"

"*I hate this stupid protocol! Whose idea even was it?!*"

Alucard rolled his eyes, and when he saw Freja approaching with Danford, he sighed again, certain that whatever they had to say was going to add to his list of things to overthink about later.

"Aleksei," she said, stopping in front of him.

He stared at her, waiting.

"There's something I…*we* need to tell you," she said, glancing at Danford, who didn't look too comfortable about being there.

"Vhat?" he grumbled.

"Well…we only really found out a few days ago, and we wanted to be sure before we said anything…but…."

"Vhat?" Alucard snarled impatiently.

"Well…I'm pregnant," she revealed.

Alucard frowned at her. "Okay…."

"And I just wanted to tell you because it's going to change what I can and can't do in a couple of months," she explained.

"Vine," Alucard muttered. "Ve'll be somevhere more permanent soon anyvay, so you von't 'ave to vorry about moving avound so much," he said, slowly setting his gaze on Danford. He assumed he was the father…and if he was, he felt concerned that it might cause tension with the extended pack. "Are you zhe vather?" he asked.

"Y-yeah," he said, a nervous look on his face. "Right?" he asked Freja.

She slapped his arm and tutted. "Of course you are."

A relieved look banished his frown. "Sorry," he said quietly.

Shaking her head, she then looked at Alucard again. "There won't be any problems at all. Everyone's comfortable with the fact that Greymore and I are just…married."

"Vight," Alucard muttered. "Vell, I just told Zhomas—"

A deafening boom shattered the silence. Alucard barely registered the sound before something sharp and bitter sliced through his neck. His blood sprayed across Freja and Danford, and an excruciating, fiery pain surged through him like venom. His hand flew to the gushing wound, trying to stem the bleeding, but whatever had struck him continued its deadly path, embedding itself in Danford's shoulder. Before he could react further, a rapid series of blasts followed. Two more frozen projectiles tore into him—one cutting through Freja's arm before lodging deep in his chest, while the other streaked from the tree line in a flash of blinding light, plunging into his stomach.

Alucard desperately grasped his bleeding throat as he collapsed to his knees, agony and exhaustion gripping his body like a vice, draining his strength and dulling his senses. The world around him became a hazy, muffled blur—distorted gunfire echoed from all sides, mingled with the shouts and screams of chaos. The acrid scent of blood hung thick in the air, almost suffocating. He couldn't make sense of what just happened, but the sensation was all too familiar—his ethos fading, his life slipping away with it.

And as his last seconds of consciousness poured away with his blood, he was left with one anguished thought.

Where was Zalith?

| Zalith |

The moment the sound of gunshots broke the silence, Zalith felt his heart stop. He grabbed Varana, pulling her behind the closest boulder as everyone started panicking, running for cover.

"Z!" she screeched, leaning over, fussing over the bleeding wound in his arm.

He didn't care. His heart was racing, his thoughts were overwhelming and erratic—where was Alucard? What was going on? Had Lilith's people found them? *Where* was Alucard? He watched as his people fell around him, shots and flashes coming from every direction. But Greymore's voice soon bellowed through the commotion, and those of his men who hadn't sustained awful wounds from the gunfire burst into action, transforming into their wolf forms and darting into the trees to find their attackers.

Zalith wasn't going to waste a moment—he had to find Alucard.

He gripped Varana's wrist tightly, dragging her with him as he sprinted forward, eyes desperately scanning for his vampire. The instant his gaze locked on Alucard, a wave of dread crashed over him, sinking its merciless teeth into his chest, gripping his thumping heart with icy terror. "Alucard!" he cried out, his voice laced with panic as he rushed to his side. Freja and Danford were already there, hunched over Alucard's crumpled form, blood pooling around him as they frantically worked to compress the wounds. The sight of his blood-soaked body felt like a knife to the chest, his pulse racing with a mix of fear and helplessness.

The demon released Varana's hand and darted around Freja and Danford, desperate to get a clearer look at Alucard—and the sight that met his eyes sent a wave of panic so fierce through him that it felt like the air had been ripped from his lungs. Alucard lay on his back, his hands gripping his neck in a futile attempt to staunch the blood gushing between his fingers. Crimson seeped through his clenched teeth as he writhed in agony; Freja and Danford were frantically pressing down on his chest and stomach, their hands slick with blood, their faces twisted in horror. But no matter how hard they worked, Alucard's blood kept pouring, spilling relentlessly as if nothing could stop the life from draining out of him.

Zalith dropped to his knees beside Alucard, looking him up and down in desperation, no words leaving his mouth as he opened it to say something—he held his hands out, no idea where to put them, no idea what to do—

"He's not healing!" Freja cried, Alucard's blood seeping through her fingers.

Mortified, Zalith stared down at Alucard's struggle-ridden face, placing his hand on the side of it.

Alucard tried to speak, but he instead coughed painfully as the blood pooled in his mouth.

"*What do I do?!*" Zalith insisted, speaking into Alucard's mind.

But the vampire didn't reply. He stared up at him, a distressed, terrified look in his eyes, choking on his own blood as he tried to speak words. Could he not hear him? Could he not reply?

His heart racing, Zalith frantically searched around in horror, looking for help, but as a crowd of red-hooded *demons* emerged from the trees and stormed the camp, his panic only increased. He didn't recognize them, and as his people started fighting them off, his fear and shock became overwhelming. He stared back down at Alucard—he didn't want to lose him—what should he do? Was there anything he *could* do? There had to be something! He looked around again, watching as his people collided with the enemy.

"What do we do?!" Freja cried.

He didn't have answers. His heart was beating so fast that it hurt; his thoughts were laced with anguish and horror. The blood…*Alucard's* blood…everywhere. The agonized look on the vampire's face intensified as he took one hand from his neck and reached up to Zalith; the demon panicked, moving his hand to Alucard's wound, trying to stop his gushing blood. But it *just wouldn't stop!*

Why was this happening?

How did this happen?

It was *his* fault…he should have been there with Alucard. And he had no idea what to do—he didn't even know if there was anything he *could* do. But he had to fix it—he had to fix all of this.

He lifted his head, desperately scouring the battlefield. There *had* to be a way to fix it!

| Varana |

Varana observed wide-eyed in horror. She had wanted to flee—maybe if she had just left earlier, this wouldn't have happened. She knew that her sister was here—these were her people…the Diabolus. And Alucard was dying…Zalith was suffering…she had to do something. She had to find her sister, she had to get her to call this off…she couldn't just stand there and do nothing!

So she left. As the panic quickened her breaths and made her limbs tremble, she turned around and darted for the tree line, hoping to find Ysmay before anyone else was killed.

| Alucard |

The world was spinning. Alucard held on as tight as his strengthless body would allow, staring up at Zalith's mortified face. He couldn't speak; all he could do was lay there helplessly as his life slipped from his grasp. When Zalith lifted his head into his lap, holding the wounds on either side of his neck, the pain surging through his body intensified, but he couldn't whine. He couldn't cry or grunt or groan. He couldn't do anything but turn his head and move his eyes.

"Move!" came Camael's distorted voice.

Alucard watched as Zalith lifted his head. He observed through the agony as Camael pulled Danford away from him and dropped to his knees beside him, pulling a small medical kit from his pocket. Camael then ripped apart Alucard's shirt, revealing the two gunshot wounds—one in his chest, one in the side of his waist, both ensnaring the vampire in excruciating pain.

And that pain only got worse when Camael tried removing the bullets.

A tormented cry broke free of Alucard's struggled breaths. He tried moving his arm to push the angel away, but that was when he saw the strange, copper-like marks spreading across his skin from where he'd been shot. Desperation and horror burst through the agony; they were stretching towards his heart, slithering like snakes eager to devour him. And there was nothing he could do but hope that Camael knew what to do.

"What's happening?!" the demon's terrified voice reverberated.

Camael eased a scalpel inside one of Alucard's wounds, but Alucard couldn't cry out. The blood in his lungs made him choke, suffocating him as he writhed and turned his head, unable to escape the unberable pain. He gripped Zalith's shirt in a desperate attempt to seek comfort, cold tears trickling down the sides of his face.

"Deridiuz," Camael's reply echoed. "Anti-Numen metal. I have to extract it before he bleeds out."

An explosion hit nearby, shaking the hard, icy ground beneath Alucard as dirt and wood flew over him, scraping his skin. No relief graced him when he felt the first bullet pulled from his dying body, nor did he feel warmth when his mate gripped his hand. What he *could* feel was death's bitter grip. He knew it was coming—he knew he had but moments left. But why? How? It all happened so fast. He hadn't sensed their enemy—no one had. He stared up at Zalith, the minuscule amount of strength he had left quickly leaving his body. He didn't want to go—not now. In all his four hundred years, this was the only time he wouldn't willingly greet death. He finally had something—*someone*. He loved Zalith, he loved their life together, and he yearned for their future. But Alucard could feel it all slipping away as he sunk deeper and deeper into the drowning agony that had a hold of him.

He tried to say Zalith's name—he needed to tell him that this wasn't his fault, that he loved him…but he couldn't speak through the blood. All he could do was stare, his once-racing heart starting to slow as the infectious metal reached it. Everything was slipping away. He had no fight left—but he tried. He tried with all his might to hold on to whatever will he had, whatever chance he had at making it through this. He had to—he needed to. He wasn't ready to leave—he *never* wanted to leave Zalith. They were supposed to get married, right? They were supposed to have their daughter…their son.

They were supposed to move to their castle and start their life. Was that still going to happen?

No. He wouldn't see anything beyond this battleground. It didn't matter how sorely he wanted his and Zalith's future; there was no fighting this.

With that realization came the last flurry of emotions he'd ever experience. He hated himself for letting this happen, for getting shot, for being the one to fail to live up to his promises. But it was inevitable, wasn't it? He always suffered, he always lost. He was losing the man he loved, he was losing the life he'd learned to appreciate, and he was losing the only chance he'd ever get to be free.

And it came—the poison reached its destination. He felt his heart slowing to a halt, he felt his fading life force stammer. And the cold… it constricted him so tightly that he felt what could only be the grip of Death himself. In what felt like just seconds, everything was torn away… and Zalith… what would happen to him once he was gone? Alucard wanted him to live—he didn't want him to suffer the same fate.

But he couldn't speak the words.

His time was up.

| Zalith |

"Alucard," Zalith breathed, shaking his head, his heart breaking, his *soul* aching as despair enthralled him. Tears built in his eyes as he watched the life of the man he loved fade away before him. Alucard's agonized, desperate stare lifted, his hell-fiery eyes slowly fading to ice blue, and as his hand slipped from Zalith's grasp and hit the ground, he felt a cold, excruciating hole in his heart, in his very being. The connection he had with Alucard—it broke. He could no longer feel his aura, he could no longer feel his existence. It was gone… *Alucard*… was gone. And Zalith… he stared, his tormented heart racing, his thoughts beginning to spiral into dismay. "Alucard?" he asked, his voice breaking, tears falling down his face. With his free hand, he lightly gripped Alucard's shoulder, shaking him. "Alucard?" he asked again. "Don't… don't leave me," he pleaded, his tears dripping onto Alucard's lifeless face as he stared down at him. "Please," he cried, refusing to accept what he knew was true. "Alucard?!"

"I… I'm sorry," came Camael's voice.

Zalith shook his head again, staring helplessly into Alucard's lifeless eyes. The longer he went without a response from his vampire, the further the battlefield drifted away. All the shouting and screaming and gunfire faded until mute, and a protruding question stabbed at the demon's shattered heart as a dreadful emptiness grew inside him. Without Alucard, what did he have left? What was the point in leaving this place if he couldn't take the only man he ever truly loved with him?

And then trepidation hit—a familiar angst. He pulled Alucard into his lap, holding him tightly, staring aimlessly at what he could see of his vampire. The world…everything…everyone…it didn't feel real anymore. None of it was real, was it? This was just the end of another, much longer illusion, wasn't it? He always lost Alucard in the end, and moments later, the world would reset, and he'd be back in the face of Adellum.

Any moment now.

Any second.

But time didn't reset.

He wasn't pulled into the blinding light, he wasn't faced with Adellum again. Alucard was cold, silent, and still in his lap. The fires raged around him, people running, fighting, screaming. The ground shook, horrific creatures running out from the trees, clashing with Greymore's pack.

Was this real? Had all of this been real all along? No…it couldn't be. He wouldn't lose Alucard—he couldn't.

But his despair—the weight of his loss…it dragged him deeper into his dismay.

And then the earth trembled. The ground shattered beneath Alucard, and there was no time for Zalith to react. From the crumbling dirt, twisted, mangled hands clawed their way up, latching onto Alucard with an unnatural force, ripping him from Zalith's grasp.

"No!" Zalith wailed, clinging to Alucard's hand with all his strength, refusing to let go, refusing to let them take him. "You can't have him!" His grip tightened, desperate as tears streaked down his face, but the claws were relentless, stronger than any force he'd faced. They dragged Alucard down into the earth inch by inch until his vampire was swallowed by the dirt, vanishing like a flickering flame consumed by darkness. "No!" Zalith screamed, his voice hoarse with agony, slamming his hands into the cold ground, clawing at the earth as though he could tear it apart, as though he could still save him. He dug frantically, claws shredding against the soil, searching for Alucard's hand, his warmth—anything.

But it was gone.

Alucard was gone.

The emptiness beneath his hands, the silence…it was unbearable. *He couldn't be gone.* Zalith couldn't accept it. He wouldn't. His yells echoed through the chaos, filled with grief, rage, and utter helplessness, his body shaking as he continued to dig, as if sheer will could bring his vampire back.

That will didn't burn for very long, though. The more he dug without finding Alucard's hand, the more he gave in to the inevitable end of this nightmare.

With a defeated, painful huff, he waited, staring down at the dirt.

Any moment now…right? He'd hear the ticking.

None of this was real. He'd seen it all before…it couldn't be real.

But there was no ticking.

There was no light.

Nothing changed.

Alucard was gone.

The world kept on.

And Zalith…

What was left for him?

Anger.

It boiled away his fear…his angst, his horror. His agonizing sadness failed to wane, and it only fuelled his rage. His devastation—it exploded into fury. Why couldn't he save him? Why hadn't he done better? Why had he left Alucard alone?

Who had done this? The demons…the creatures. He slowly lifted his head, glaring around at the battle. These weren't Lilidian demons, they were a cult. They wore sigils on their robes, and it didn't take long for his eyes to meet with someone he knew all too well. Black, bone-straight hair, eyes as red as blood, and a grin of sharp, jagged teeth. He knew who these people were, and he knew who was leading them.

Zalith didn't spare a second thought. He yelled furiously as he burst into action, racing towards Ysmay as she laughed maniacally. He crashed into her, snarling, growling, yelling as they fought. He slammed his fist into her side; she clawed at him, kicking, hissing, and then she screamed when he gripped her arm and flung her across the camp. She collided with a tree, hitting the ground as it fell behind her. But she didn't cower. She laughed, hurrying to her feet in time to catch Zalith's fist before he could hit her again—

"How does it feel to lose everything?!" she laughed, dodging his other fist.

His rage burned inside his chest. He roared as he gave into the anger, baring his claws and slashing her face before she had a chance to evade. Ysmay screamed, and one of her men came running at Zalith, but he sent the man up in white flames in an instant, grabbing Ysmay's throat with both his hands as he did. He pinned the bitch down, squeezing her throat, eager to hear it crack—

He grunted in startle as someone kicked his side with so much force that he was sent tumbling across the ash-covered ground. But he recovered swiftly, standing up, setting his eyes on Ysmay…and Varana. Seeing her defend her sister only made him more furious; she helped Ysmay up, trying to pull her away. Zalith wasn't going to let her go, and if he had to hurt Varana to kill her sister, then he would. He didn't care. That bitch had taken Alucard from him—she had done this, and he was going to make sure she suffered for it.

Zalith burst forward, quickly feeling convinced that Varana had something to do with this; why else would she have tried to leave earlier? She had to know that this was coming, and that forced his anger to become something overwhelming. He'd hurt her if he had to—maybe he even wanted to hurt her intentionally. Either way, Ysmay wasn't getting away. He was going to kill her, and nothing would stop him, not even Varana.

Chapter Fifty-Eight

Prison

| Alucard |

Alucard knew this place—the dark, the cold, the emptiness. His life flashed before him as he sunk deeper, but this time, he didn't relive the awful memories of his childhood; he relived the best memories of his life. Meeting Zalith, slowly falling for him—the day he got to see the demon again after such a long, long time…and the night Zalith had asked that they be together…the night they kissed, danced, and cried a little. Those moments had brought him happiness unlike anything he'd felt before, but now it brought him pain. Agonizing, suffocating pain…because he knew it was over. The happiness…the life he had with Zalith. He'd never live it again, and he'd never see Zalith again. He'd never see anything again.

He drifted down into the dark, no fight left, no will…all he could do was let death take him to wherever he was meant to go. He'd lived a good life—the four hundred years of misery were worth bearing to one day find Zalith. His years of loneliness, of *torture*…he'd live through it all again without a doubt if it meant he got to stumble upon that demon. He might not have got to spend hundreds of years with him, but the near four he had were the best of his life, and if only he could tell Zalith how thankful he was for showing him a world of warmth…of light and love. Zalith had saved him, and Alucard only wished he could have done the same.

Zalith—what would he do now? Alucard could only imagine the torment that his death was causing the man he loved. He knew Zalith would blame himself, and he knew he'd never let it go. Alucard didn't want that. He wanted Zalith to be happy—the demon deserved to live a life without the burden of duty. Maybe now that he was gone, Zalith would be free…he wouldn't have to deal with the weight of Alucard's reality. But he knew Zalith too well—he knew that furiously adamant demon would hunt down the people who had taken him from him. All Alucard could do was hope that it would give Zalith closure…because there was no going back now; Alucard wasn't going back. He watched as the flesh of his human body tore away from him, crumbling into dust. If only…if only he could have told Zalith one last time that he loved him. But time had slipped away…*he* had slipped away.

Thank you—that's what he would have said. *Thank you for loving me, for finding me, and for showing me what it truly meant to be alive.* Alucard still wished they would have got married, he still wished they'd had a family. But he had Zalith—his demon. *He* was his family…he had *been* his family, and the only family he had ever needed. And now that his life was at its very end, he thought…he'd have it no other way. The confusion, the struggle, the wonder…it had all led up to this, to the most joyful moments of his life; what an experience…what a life. *Thank you, Zalith.*

But Alucard's acceptance was quickly diminished. He felt the cold, painful grip of several hands upon him, the feeling returning to his numb limbs. Talons dug into his skin as he felt every inch of his body failing, breaking away into the dark—but what perturbed him the most was the fact that his *true* body formed in place of his crumbling human likeness. His hands became dark and scaled, his black talons shimmering in the darkness. Fire spread over him as he was dragged down faster, able to feel the crushing weight of the earth all around him. And his body continued to break, peeling away until he no longer possessed anything human about him.

And then he fell. The hands let go, the suffocating grasp of the earth lifted, and as a scorching heat scratched against his armoured skin, dread filled his hell-fiery eyes. Red fog thickened as he fell, and a low, rumbling growl broke through the silence. Alucard panicked—he reached forward just in time to dig his talons into the crimson rock above him; he glared into the gaping darkness he'd just fallen from, panting, trembling. And his name—he heard the voice call it. He looked over his shoulder, sheer terror filling his thumping heart as his gaze met with the single, hell-fiery eye…of Lucifer.

This wasn't right—this wasn't death. But…he died…so where was he now?

He had no time to work it out. The seven-eyed creature widened its jaws, reaching up to grab him. Alucard struggled, gripping the rock, but it had been so long since he'd walked in his true form that his scaled, taloned forelegs and hind legs felt foreign. His wing joints were sore from wounds inflicted centuries ago, and his long, jagged spike-covered tail draped, dangling like a lure for the monster below to grasp.

Lucifer snarled as he reached up, his beastly form morphing into something snake-like. He clamped his jaws around Alucard's tail, and when the vampire yelled in panic, a monstrous yelp broke free of his dragon-like jaws in its place, and he was so abruptly yanked from the ceiling, thrown through the air, and met with the ground that he didn't catch a breath until he tumbled to a slow halt.

And then he stared, lifting his head, setting his eyes on the *humongous* monster before him. He watched as Lucifer morphed into a wyvern-like beast, slamming his hooved feet into the ground and roaring ferociously as he set all seven of his eyes on him. It was then that Alucard saw crimson everywhere; dead, black trees, steam spitting up into the foggy air, cracks and chasms in the mahogany ground. Ancient chains remained bound to Lucifer's ankles, scraping along the ground as he charged towards Alucard.

Alucard wasn't going to lay there frozen in fear. As his eyes widened, as terror surged through him, he was possessed by the intense instinct to run—to run, to hide, to survive. With his heart racing, he stood up on his hind legs and darted to his right, setting his eyes on a small gap in the cliff not too far from him. Lucifer's disadvantage was his size; while Alucard's true, wingless dragon-like form stood no taller than a horse, Lucifer was at least twenty times his size, and Alucard would use that to his advantage—and he had but seconds to avoid the monster's jaws.

The vampire sprinted forward, dodging the crash of Lucifer's taloned hand as he slammed it down behind him, trying to snatch him in his jaws before he got away. But that was exactly what Alucard did. With fear spiralling through him, he leapt into the small gap, avoiding Lucifer's snapping jaws by mere inches—but he didn't stop running. He followed the narrow path, veering left as Lucifer roared ferociously, slamming his seven-horned head against the cliff face in a feeble attempt to break his way in.

Alucard collapsed. He lay on the ground, panting, panicking—he was sure he now knew where he was. The black, straight wall not too far from where he lay was smothered in writings and familiar runes. He looked up—the ceiling, although most of it was covered with crimson rock, was also black and straight like the face of a cube. That's what this was—a cube, but not just any cube. He was inside the Pandorican where Lucifer had been sealed for centuries. But how? How had he fallen into this place? How was he going to get out? *Could* he get out?

He scowled, glancing down at his left scaled hand as he only just noticed an aching pain electrify up his wrist. His rings…they were still on his hand, cutting into his skin. His crucifix was still around his neck, and his body…he still had the three wounds that had killed him. Bullet wounds—one in his side, one in his chest, and one through his neck. He wasn't…dead. This was real—*he* was still real…alive…maybe. How else could he feel pain? Why else would the bullets still be inside him? How else would his jewellery still be attached? It wouldn't come with him to Purgatory—to whatever waited after life. He knew the rules—he knew enough of them, anyway. But he didn't want to hope. What if he was wrong?

Lucifer's furious roar broke the silence, and as Alucard looked over his shoulder, he watched as rubble flew past the gap; the wall that Lucifer was savagely attacking would surely soon give way, and Alucard would have to run again. So he set his eyes on a promising path, one that led deeper into the rock. If he had fallen into Lucifer's prison, and if…if this was real…then he had to be able to climb out. He had to be able to return…he had to…he had to get back to Zalith. He'd grasp onto even the slightest little bit of hope—because that demon…he wasn't done living his life with him yet.

Alucard ignored his bleeding wounds, climbing to his feet, both the adrenaline and the hope of seeing Zalith again helping him fight against his numbing fear. He heard Lucifer shifting, the hiss of a snake echoing from the way he'd got into this rock, and as he turned to face the path he would take, his eyes met with those of the snake-like beast his father had transformed into. Fear struck and froze him once more, but he wouldn't let it hold him. As the snake hissed hungrily, the vampire darted forward, and Lucifer followed.

The beast hissed. "Get back here!" he snarled, snapping his jaws shut, missing Alucard's tail by inches.

He had to get away, he had to find the way he'd come into this place, and he had to find a way out and avoid Lucifer as best he could. But his desperate beast of a father trailed behind him, his huge serpent body crashing against the walls as he chased Alucard, snapping his jaws, reaching for him with a taloned hand that sat in place of his tongue. And his rumbling growls—Alucard understood them as speech; all he heard were Lucifer's threats, telling him that he wasn't going to get away this time, telling him that this was where he would die, that he'd never see the sun again—that he'd never see Zalith again.

But he'd not listen.

He darted right and veered left, navigating the maze of narrow paths between the crimson rock. He turned again and again and again, slowly gaining, slowly putting distance between himself and the beast. His heart was racing, his body failing against his injuries; he had to rest…just for a moment. The vampire darted for cover inside a small cave in the rock, its entrance shrouded by twisting red vines. And he stared…panting…waiting. The moment he saw Lucifer's scaled body slither past would be the moment he ran again.

And he heard him coming. He heard Lucifer's mangled body dragging along the rock as he searched for Alucard. Hissing, snarling, calling his name. "Caedis…" he snarled, "you can't hide forever."

This wouldn't be the place Alucard remained. He had no idea how he'd got into a prison that should be completely sealed off from the world outside, but he was determined to find a way out…he just had to do so while avoiding Lucifer's jaws.

And then he froze…watching as his father slowly slithered past, the ground cracking beneath him. Alucard's heart thumped, angst gripping him so tightly. He waited to see the creature's tail drag past…every second feeling like a hundred, but as Lucifer's tail passed by, he let himself relax for just a moment—

"Caedis!" Lucifer jeered, three of his eyes suddenly peeking in through the cave, a wicked smile stretching across his serpentine face.

The abrupt increase in fear was overwhelming, stealing Alucard's breath. He thought he might yelp in startle, in *horror*, but all he could do was stare and try to back off as far into the cave as he could.

Lucifer snickered, morphing into a wyvern-like beast once more and reaching his talons into the cave to try and grab him.

Alucard wasn't quick enough to evade. Lucifer's talon scraped at his skin, breaking through his armoured scales like they were paper. And he whined, the pain unrelenting, tearing his very being away. All Lucifer had to do…was touch him? He gritted his teeth, mustering what strength he had left. He couldn't let his father get hold of him.

Lucifer laughed, digging his talon deeper. "Did you think…did you *really* think you'd get away forever?"

Alucard grunted, trying to back off, but his body was already against the wall. There was nowhere to go. Lucifer was blocking the only way out, but the longer he remained there, the weaker he would get, and the thinner his chances of escape would become. If Lucifer were to win…if he were to devour Alucard, he'd be able to leave his prison…he'd be able to terrorize Aegisguard. And he'd go for Zalith…he'd target everything Alucard loved, and their almost-identical likeness would let his father masquerade as him.

He couldn't let any of that happen. He had to escape, he had to get back to the world where he lived…the world where the man he loved lived. Not even Lucifer would take that from him. But as he stood there, trying to pull Lucifer's talon from his body, he felt loss; as his blood left his body, as his life force drained…so did the things he knew. And what he knew…he knew that he loved someone, he knew there was someone he had to get back to, but Lucifer had taken his name, Lucifer had taken his face; Alucard couldn't remember, and the longer Lucifer held on, the more he would forget—the more his father would gain. And he didn't want to forget. Because that feeling of love, that feeling of desperation to return, it was unlike anything he'd ever felt. It fuelled him, it burnt so ravenously inside him that he wouldn't let it go. He couldn't. He knew he loved this man so profoundly that it had become his very reason for existing, and he wouldn't let his father take that from him.

"It's time to stop running, Caedis. Don't you want to be a part of me?" he growled. "Oh, how we have all missed you so—"

Alucard held onto his determination and darted again. He raced forward, crashing into the side of Lucifer's face and slashing one of his eyes with his talons. Lucifer flinched violently and screeched, stumbling back as blood poured from his face.

Now out of the cave, Alucard sprinted—and Lucifer followed, bellowing a deafening, furious roar as the ground shook beneath each of his loud, slamming footsteps.

Alucard set his eyes on the foggy glade beyond the cliffs. He knew that his escape would be out there. He leapt from the narrow path and into the open, setting his eyes on the rock above, searching frantically for his exit as he raced forward. And when he fixed his sights on the slowly closing crack in the ceiling, a glimmer of hope crept through his suffocating fear. *That* was his way out—but as Lucifer burst out from the rock behind him, he stumbled, the ground shaking—and his beast of a father's tail came swinging at him, smashing into his side, sending him flying across the open ground once again.

When he hit the ground, Alucard unwillingly stayed where he was, the ground under him rumbling as Lucifer drew nearer. He'd lost so much blood; he had no ethos—but neither did Lucifer. If his father weren't locked inside this prison, Alucard would have no chance against him. But even now he was lacking. How was he supposed to get up there—the gap in the ceiling…it was right above him. He stared into its darkness…*that* was his way back to the world…that was his way back to…*him*. The man he loved. Alucard knew that he was waiting for him…and he had to get back.

Turning to face his incoming father, Alucard banished his fear and replaced it with determination. He was leaving, Lucifer wasn't going to have him, and he was going *right now*.

He wasn't the best at mind and perception manipulation, and he was going to have to use his own life force to pull it off in place of his ethos. But when he started charging his attack, the power came from somewhere else. An unknown reserve. Maybe it had something to do with the hole in the ceiling, maybe he was somehow still linked to the world above, a world where his ethos was a strong presence, living inside his vampires, and he'd not waste the opportunity given to him. As Lucifer came just ten feet away, Alucard used his power to break into his father's unguarded mind, and—while desperately grasping what memories he could, whether they were his or Lucifer's—he forced the beast to see not just one but *a hundred* of himself, and they all ran as he did, fleeing in every direction. Lucifer snarled and slammed his tail down over at least ten of Alucard's illusions, but there were still plenty more to keep him hidden.

Alucard veered left, and several of his illusions followed—some in front, some to his left, and some behind. He had to climb, and climb he did. But it took Lucifer no time at all to take out the phantoms he had created—those that were running with him were all that remained, and Lucifer caught up, snarling, growling, yelling. He clearly knew that this was his only chance to snatch Alucard, but Alucard wasn't going to let it happen. Pouncing forward, he dug his claws into the crimson rock wall, climbing up, his phantoms following, some leading. In just moments, he reached the top—but Lucifer morphed into a serpent again and threw himself atop the rock. Alucard's heart pounded in his chest, but he kept his eyes on his way out, he kept his thoughts focused on getting back to where he belonged. And he was so close.

But Lucifer's jaws abruptly snapped through one, two, *three* of Alucard's phantoms…he transformed two of his horns into serpent heads, all three of them snapping and snarling as he dragged his huge body along the ground, chasing Alucard and his two remaining phantoms. Alucard kept his eyes ahead—he was just moments away—all it would take was a leap up onto the ceiling and he could crawl into the gap, he could escape, he could leave with his life…and get back to where he needed to be. But Lucifer was gaining. His jaws snapped shut over another phantom, and as Alucard glanced over his shoulder…he stared into the mouth of the creature that wanted to claim his life.

Was this it? Was this where his life finally came to its end?

Chapter Fifty-Nine

Mantis

| Zalith |

Zalith didn't stop. His heart was broken, his life felt as though it had come to an end. Without Alucard, what did he really have? He had his anger—he had his desire to make Ysmay pay, to *kill* her. *She* had taken his vampire from him, and he wasn't going to let her live. He wouldn't think about anything else. All that mattered now was eradicating Varana's sister, and if Varana didn't get out of the way, he'd go through her.

Varana stepped between him and Ysmay as they ran at each other, but he grabbed her shoulders and threw her aside. As Varana screeched, Ysmay yelled frustratedly, holding out her claw-bared hands as she threw herself at Zalith. He snatched her wrist and pulled her closer as she stumbled—he slammed his fist into her face, and as she stammered backwards, he crashed his fist into her jaw. Ysmay dropped to the ground; Zalith grabbed her throat, and she dug her claws into his wrists, hissing up at him as he snarled down at her. And then he lifted his left hand, extending his claws and aiming for her revolting eyes—

But just like he was before, Zalith was thrown off Ysmay by Varana. But he instantly climbed to his feet and ran at her again, giving her or her sister little to no time to recover at all. He shoved Varana aside again, but she grabbed hold of him.

"Stop!" she screamed, pulling him back.

Zalith growled and sharply turned his head to glare at her. If he didn't care about her so much, he'd kill her in a heartbeat to make his point to Ysmay—but he'd let Varana distract him, and as he pulled free and turned to face Ysmay, she was already right in front of him. She pushed him back with so much force that he was thrown off his feet; his back hit a large piece of rubble, and a jagged metal rod impaled through his back and out through his shoulder. He grunted irritably, gripping the rod, but as he went to pull it from his body, Ysmay launched herself at him, a furious, maniacal grin on her face—and Varana followed, reaching out to grab her sister—

And then light.

Blinding, bright, white light.

As it lit up the area, Zalith felt relieved. It was time for *him* to die…time for this façade to end…time for him to see Alucard again.

The light, however, wasn't directly in front of him. Ysmay still came at him, and the light came from his left—a thick, blinding, humming beam of white light which soon flooded crimson. It collided with Ysmay, who screamed tormentedly, her body bursting into ash. Varana was struck, too, but she was thrown to the side, hitting the ground not too far away…unconscious, unmoving.

Zalith stared as the light died down; it left a devastating path, circular, gaping holes in the rock, steaming, singed…and on the ground lay Ysmay's body. Mangled, skinless, fleshless. Nothing but a revolting mess of bone and blood. And the moment she was destroyed, all of her demons stopped fighting Zalith's people, sharply turning their heads to stare over at their fallen leader.

But that light…where had it come from?

The demon shifted his gaze to the direction the light had come from. He stared at the creature…it looked almost like a drake, standing on all fours, a little taller than a horse. Upon its scaled, dark-purple armoured head were a set of black, dragon-like horns, black spines stretching down its back and folding in at its tail to form jagged spears. The creature snarled, standing up on its hind legs, its forelegs revealed to be arms with four sharp, black talons on the end of each hand. And its teeth—two rows as white as snow, and on either side, two fangs much longer than the others…like a snake, almost. The creature…Zalith knew it was a demon, but it had attacked Ysmay. An ally, maybe?

Zalith looked over at Ysmay's corpse as a revolting hissing came from it, and as he stared, he watched the skeleton of a creature begin to form. She *wasn't* dead, and his determination to make sure she died this time intensified. He gripped the rod in his shoulder, trying to pull it free so he could get up, but the drake-like monster that had hit Ysmay suddenly roared ferociously; Zalith shifted his sights to it, watching as it dropped onto all fours and pounced his way. He tried to pull himself free; he didn't want to fight it, nor did he want to be reduced to blood and bone—at least not before Ysmay had paid for taking Alucard away. But instead of colliding with him, the creature landed *in front* of him, growling aggressively as it glowered at the ashen, horse-sized, mantis-like creature that formed from the bones and crimson goop that had once been Ysmay.

For a brief moment, though…the demonic drake glanced back at Zalith…and Zalith stared into its beautiful, hell-fiery eyes. Within them, he could become lost; within them, he found comfort, he found hope, and he found such heavy, deep relief—he felt so relieved that tears began forming in his eyes once more. This creature—he had scars all along his back and down his arms, and his scent—cedar wood, warm amber, roses, cinnamon—Zalith could never forget it, and he'd recognize it miles away.

The drake standing between him and Ysmay could only be Alucard—*his* Alucard.

Alucard set his eyes back on Ysmay as she slammed her blade-like feet into the ground, roaring a horrific screech as she shook the old, mangled flesh from her demon body. Alucard roared back, standing defensively in front of Zalith. Ysmay started to circle the area in which they stood, and Alucard did the same—and Zalith knew what was going on. He'd recognize a demon's challenge anywhere, and that's exactly what Alucard was doing. Not only was he clearly defending Zalith, but he was also challenging Ysmay and everything she currently had.

Zalith knew he had to back off, but all he wanted to do was revel in his relief. He wanted to hold Alucard, to touch him…but he had to wait. Camael came over to help, and with his assistance, Zalith heaved himself up, pulling the rod from his shoulder—and as Alucard and Ysmay charged at one another, Camael tugged Zalith back, leading him behind a huddle of trees, where most of his people had taken cover after Ysmay's demons stopped attacking.

He watched, holding his hand over his wound as Alucard collided with Ysmay, both of them slashing with their talons, snapping with their jaws. Panic started building within Zalith as he watched them fight; he was terrified that Alucard was going to get hurt again, and he wanted to help, but what if he got in the way? He waited, observing anxiously. But seeing Alucard again…he had no words to explain how he felt. All he knew was that he was *never* going to leave him alone again…and he was going to hold onto him forever.

| Alucard |

Alucard collided with the mantis-like beast; he gripped hold of her arm as she screeched, sinking his teeth into her neck and draining her ethos, taking it for himself; his own ethos was still silent, and he'd take what he could get. He had to kill her—she tried to attack the demon he'd imprinted on, the demon he knew was the one he had to come back for, the one he had to survive for. He didn't remember his name, he didn't remember much at all; he didn't know who this mantis was, he didn't know who *anyone* was…but what he *did* have were his feelings, and he *just knew* that he hated this creature, he loved the man he'd jumped in front of, and he had to protect the people in this camp.

The Mantis screeched, stabbing a blade-like leg into one of Alucard's bullet wounds. He snarled in agony, flinching, losing his grip on her as he stumbled back. And she pounced at him, pinning him down. He'd not yield, though. He slammed his back foot into her stomach, sending her flying back—but she stretched a huge pair of beetle-like wings from her back, regaining balance in the air. But he was fast, despite his wounds; he turned to face her, widening his jaws as he charged his next attack, and as his beam of crimson light burst from his mouth and hit her, she screeched again and dropped to the ground, one of her wings singed off.

With a smug roar, Alucard dropped to all fours. The mantis came at him again, widening her jaws, folding her remaining wings against her back as she leapt up into the air, aiming her blade-like legs down at him as he prepared for her attack. He veered out of the way, and her legs stabbed into the ground; with his jaws, Alucard grabbed one leg, and with his right hand, he grabbed another, and without mercy, he tore the mantis' leg from her body, gripped it in his left hand, and stabbed it into her side.

Purple blood exploded from her body, an agonized cry echoing through the air as he swung around and smashed his tail into her, sending her tumbling across the ground. But she got back up, stumbling, snarling, setting her crimson eyes on him as he stood on his hind legs again, waiting for her next attempt. But he felt as if they'd fought long enough. Right now, he was more concerned about his demon mate. He wanted to go to him…he wanted to remember him…and he couldn't do that with this mantis in his way.

As the mantis pounced towards him again, he jumped, too, and they collided in the air. Alucard overpowered her as they fell, and when her back hit the ground, Alucard savagely tore at her body with his claws. She tried to fight back, but his determination to kill her was too great for her to counter. He started using his teeth; he gripped another leg, tearing it from her body before she could stab it into his side. He clawed at her face, her neck, and her back as she managed to turn around and tried to drag herself away.

Her purple blood smothered the ground, and Alucard was ready to end her life. He held her down, widening his jaws, and then he sunk his teeth into her neck—

Before he had the chance to tear her head from her body, another mantis collided with him, shoving him away from the one he was just moments from killing. The new mantis looked *exactly* the same, and as Alucard climbed to his feet, he watched it try to drag away the twitching corpse of the other. He moved forward to attack, but he stopped the moment the new mantis abruptly disappeared into a rift.

Alucard snarled irritably, dropping to all fours. He then shifted his attention to the mantis' demons. They all stared in what looked like contemplation—what was there to contemplate? Alucard had won, and with a ferocious, deafening roar, he let the mantis' followers know that their leader was gone and that he'd execute every single one of them unless they fled.

No demon fled, however. As he ceased in his victorious roar, he watched as each and every demon who had once followed the mantis began lowering their heads in submission, pledging themselves to him. He'd challenged their leader, he'd pretty much killed her, and now, her people were his.

But his victory didn't bring him contentedness. What *did* spark joy was when he turned around to see that his mate was rushing over to him. He stood up on his hind legs, staring at him, and when the demon reached him, he wrapped his arms around him, holding him tightly. And Alucard didn't fret. This kind of affection…this man's touch…he knew he craved it. As the demon slowly dropped to his knees, Alucard fell with him, succumbing to the demon's embrace, letting go of all his anger, his rage…all that seemed to matter right now was the man embracing him—the man his imprint lay upon.

Yet…he still couldn't remember his name. All he had were his feelings; he knew that he loved this man, he knew that he craved to be with this man, and as he sat there, he felt the desperation to remember very quickly increasing.

He'd stolen handfuls of memories from Lucifer just before his escape, and he sorely hoped that in them, he'd find the things that his father stole.

Chapter Sixty

The Recovered, and the Lost

| Zalith |

Zalith held onto Alucard as tightly as he could, nuzzling his scaled neck, gritting his teeth as he attempted to contain his emotions, but tears still trickled down his face as his knees pressed into the ashy ground. The moments he'd just spent thinking that Alucard was gone forever were the most painful moments of his life, and the relief was so overwhelming that his racing heart couldn't calm. He never wanted to experience that agony again. He'd hold onto Alucard until the end of time, and nothing would take him from him; he'd do whatever it took to keep him safe, because without him... Zalith was nothing but emptiness and rage.

But with his relief came worry. He could smell Alucard's blood *everywhere*, and when he lifted his face from the vampire's neck, he saw the bullet wounds. They still hadn't healed, and Camael had only removed one of the two bullets before Alucard had been dragged into the ground. He leaned back, placing his hands on either side of Alucard's face as he stared into Zalith's eyes. He was certain that Alucard was in pain, and the first thing he wanted to do now was help him. But he felt incredibly anxious; so much had just happened; his heart had been broken, and he couldn't help but dread that something else might be moments away from happening.

First, he'd make sure that Alucard could heal. Then, he'd lead everyone far away from this place. "Camael," he called, looking back over his shoulder and setting his eyes on the angel, who was tending to Danford's shoulder, taking the bullet out of him.

Camael hastily covered up Danford's wound, leaving him and Freja with one of Greymore's men who was also helping the injured. The angel hurried over but with a cautious frown on his face as he eyed Alucard closely.

"Heal him," Zalith demanded, glaring up at him.

But as Camael nodded and moved closer, Alucard snarled defensively and pulled away from Zalith, standing up and backing off—at the same time, Ysmay's demons started to move closer, setting their sights on Camael—

"It's okay," Zalith insisted, standing up and placing his hands on either side of Alucard's face again. "He's just going to help." He then looked around at Ysmay's demons—*Alucard's* demons, for he had challenged Ysmay and won. They seemed to have pledged their loyalty to him now.

Alucard stared at Zalith for a moment but then shifted his gaze to the angel. He growled lowly and backed down, exhaling deeply as he collapsed onto his side. As he lay down, Alucard's new demons retreated, keeping their eyes on Camael as he kneeled beside him, and Zalith sat beside him, gently pulling his head into his lap and making sure that he was comfortable.

"What happened to Varana?" Camael asked as he started cleaning the blood from around Alucard's wound. "I didn't see her come back after your friend here returned."

"She's gone," the demon muttered irritably.

The angel nodded, taking a scalpel from his pocket. "I assume we'll be making haste to leave this area once I've finished removing this bullet, correct?"

Nodding, the demon looked down at Alucard and caressed his drake-like head.

Camael eased the scalpel into Alucard's wound, fishing around for the bullet. It didn't seem to aggravate him—either that or he didn't have the strength to respond to the pain. He just flinched, huffing tiredly as he closed his eyes.

But then he suddenly convulsed violently, snarling angrily as he sharply lifted and turned his head to glare at the angel, who backed off cautiously, holding the deridiuz bullet he'd pulled from Alucard's side.

"You should be able to heal now," Camael said, dropping the bullet. "He's going to need ethos, though," he added, looking at Zalith. "These bullets took everything he had, and considering his species of demon, he will also need blood."

"Thank you," Zalith muttered, looking back down at Alucard as he made him rest his head in his lap again.

With a nod, the angel left.

Zalith gazed at his vampire. He started calming down, his breathing gradually returning to normal. He had to get him blood *and* ethos; he needed to come up with a way to do so and fast—the sooner they could leave this place, the better, but he'd not make Alucard travel if he wasn't capable. "How do you feel?" he asked quietly, caressing Alucard's head—could he even talk? "Can… you talk?" he asked unsurely.

Alucard replied with a quiet, tired growl.

He didn't understand. He frowned despondently, stroking his hand over Alucard's head. "What can I do? What do you need?"

"If he is like our previous queen, then he needs humans in order to regain his human likeness," came the unpleasant voice of someone Zalith didn't know.

He scowled up at the red-robed man—he *hated* that he and the demons behind him had clearly been listening to their private conversation, but now wasn't the time to express his anger. Alucard and what he needed was more important.

Zalith looked down at Alucard and frowned. "Is that what you need?"

"As for ethos, that will slowly return over time, but since you want to leave this place soon, he can take the ethos of others—vampires might be the best idea, considering as they are of his blood and ethos," the same demon interrupted.

Irritated, Zalith scowled up at him. "*Who* are you?" he asked condescendingly.

"Amos," he said. "I served as our previous queen's hand, and now, I serve as his," he said, gesturing to Alucard.

Zalith was skeptical. He knew how demons worked—he knew that a pack would have no choice but to obey whoever defeated their Alpha, but these guys seemed a little *too* eager, and he didn't want them lingering around. "Fine," he said. "Thank you." Then, he waved his hand in dismissal as he looked back down at Alucard.

But Amos didn't leave, and neither did any of the other demons waiting behind him.

Glowering, his impatience increasing, Zalith gritted his teeth but kept caressing Alucard's head. "Is there anything else?" he snarled.

"There is not," Amos answered.

"Then is there a reason you're standing here?" he asked, glaring back over his shoulder at him.

"Yes."

"Which is?" he snapped.

"We now serve him, and so we will protect him until he has recovered."

"I understand that, and we thank you for your loyalty, but I'm sure you and your friends can still do your job just as effectively from over there considering you were the ones who shot him from afar in the first place," Zalith growled.

Amos kept a vacant stare. "We're not going to leave unless he asks us to."

Alucard suddenly woke and snarled irritably, glaring up at Amos and his men.

Staring down at Alucard, Amos nodded and turned around, leading his men away from Zalith and the vampire, leaving them alone.

Zalith rolled his eyes. He was certain that he was going to have to teach Amos some respect very soon; he and this new group of demons needed to understand how things worked here. They might be Alucard's pack now, but Alucard was a part of *his* pack, and where he had his people listen to Alucard, he'd have to make sure Alucard's new people would listen to him.

He then sighed, trailing his fingers over Alucard's head. "Idina," he called, watching as Alucard slowly closed his eyes again, making himself comfortable.

Idina stopped what she was doing and hurried over, stopping beside him.

"How are you doing?" he asked, still caressing Alucard's head.

She nodded. "I'm okay—"

"How is everyone else?"

"They're… a little shaken, obviously. Whatever our attackers used, it didn't seem to have the same effect on anyone else that it did with Alucard," she mumbled. "But…" she said, a concerned look on her face as she looked over her shoulder, "we lost eight of Greymore and Freja's people, and Danford isn't looking too great. Camael took the bullet out, but his wound looks infected," she explained as Zalith looked up at her.

Zalith exhaled deeply. "Okay," he mumbled. "Alucard's going to need human blood and vampire ethos," he said, thinking to himself. There weren't any vampires here, and he didn't want to send anyone out to find some. Amos had said vampires would work best to get Alucard's ethos back, but he knew that demons would work, too. After all, Alucard was a demon, and while vampire ethos might work faster, there simply wasn't any way of getting some. As for the humans he needed to regain his human body… Zalith would *have* to send someone out to get some people for that.

However, he didn't want Alucard to have to take the ethos from some random demon—he'd rather it be his own, and he knew he'd be able to give Alucard enough so that he'd feel better and could possibly even move.

Before Idina could reply, he looked back up at her. "I'll figure it out," he said. "But I want you to keep an eye on that demon… he seems a little too comfortable already," he mumbled, glancing over to where Amos was now standing with his fellow packmates.

"Okay," she said with a nod.

"I also want you to send an izuret to Orin and update him on our situation."

"Okay, I'll do that right now."

"And have you seen Peaches?" he asked, the talk of izurets reminding him that Alucard's hairless kitten was missing.

"I think she ran off," Idina said.

Zalith sighed sullenly and looked down at Alucard. "Okay," he said quietly. "Have someone look for her. I don't want to leave until we find her."

"Okay," she said, and then she went to do as ordered.

With a quiet huff, Zalith gazed at Alucard, still stroking his head while he rested. There was a lot to do; he had to make sure that everyone was okay to travel, and he had to ensure Alucard was also able to walk. He wasn't sure how many humans it would take to help his vampire regain his human body, but he was determined to get it done as soon as possible. Then, they'd head for the station as planned.

Then there was the matter of Ysmay's old pack—what was left of it, anyway. Amos and twenty-five other demons. He didn't trust any of them, despite knowing how demons' loyalty worked when it came to this sort of situation. He'd have to selectively erase parts of their memories, and that was going to take not only a while but a lot of energy. He knew having Orin around would make that go faster, so maybe he'd call him here to help.

For now, though, he just wanted to sit there with Alucard and let him rest. He wanted to sink into the relief that his vampire was okay, and he wanted to regain his composure. He'd almost let go entirely when Alucard was pulled into the ground, and he was still trembling as a result. But he didn't want to think about his fury or his heartbreak. Alucard was okay. He was safe. He was alive. And whatever it took, Zalith was going to get him out of Nefastus as soon as possible.

Chapter Sixty-One

Amnesia

| Alucard |

The lingering pain slowly faded. In the warmth of his mate's embrace, Alucard recovered from his injuries, but the missing pieces that Lucifer had taken from him still waited to be found, and now that his strength was returning, he might be able to sift through what he took from his father when he broke into his mind. He just needed a little more ethos. A little more energy.

"Alucard?" his mate asked quietly.

The vampire murmured a quiet grumble, letting him know that he was awake.

"I want you to have some of my blood," he said, caressing his head.

Alucard opened his eyes, staring aimlessly into the forest across from him. Blood? Of course, he knew that he needed it—he had little to no ethos, and the only way he'd get it would be if he fed, but…he didn't want to hurt his mate. He loved him…and he needed him. Take his blood? He lifted his head so that he was at eye level with his mate and stared into his eyes. He wanted to ask him what he meant, but…he didn't feel as though he was ready to talk. He still felt so tired, so confused, so dismayed.

But then the demon guided his hand to the side of Alucard's face and dragged his thumb over one of his larger fangs. The warm caress of his hand sent shivers through Alucard's body, which remained sensitive while he healed, and it reminded him that they trusted one another with their lives.

"I'm going to cut my arm on your tooth," his mate said, glancing at the fang he'd just dragged his thumb over, "and then you're going to open your mouth and drink my blood," he said, lightly gripping Alucard's bottom jaw in his hand.

Alucard let the demon lightly pull on his jaw, encouraging him to open it—so he did, and then his mate dragged his wrist over his top right fang, slashing his skin, his blood pouring into Alucard's mouth. And its taste was a deep relief, taking a heavy weight off Alucard's shoulders; it filled him with something pleasing, something content.

The demon's sweet, enthralling blood was hard to resist, and as it poured into his mouth, he found it so very hard to fight the urge to bite down. He wanted more, he *needed* more. If he got enough, he'd be able to rummage through the memories he took from Lucifer.

But as the urge to bite intensified, he tried to concentrate on the blood that he was being given. That made it worse, though, because he knew that his mate would never do something like this for anyone else—he knew that this demon did so many things for him that he wouldn't do if it were someone else. And Alucard wanted his memories back. He wanted all the blood that it would take, and he was sure that he could take it.

Giving into the desperation, though, probably wasn't the best idea while he was starved and healing—

His mate grunted in panic as he gripped Alucard's jaw in his free hand. "Alucard!" he exclaimed, struggle in his voice. "That's not what I meant," he told him, staring into his eyes—and it was only then that Alucard realized he had clamped his jaw shut, biting down into the demon's arm, most of which was now trapped inside his mouth.

But his blood—it tasted *so* good. It filled him with euphoria, and he could feel all his concerns fading away. His aching body was numbing, his tiring thoughts were silencing, and the more he swallowed, the easier it was to escape the despair. The panic in his mate's eyes, however, sparked something stronger within him. Regret? He frowned, slowly loosening his grip, letting the demon pull his arm from his mouth. He didn't want to hurt him; he hadn't meant to do that—he wasn't going to tear his arm off... was he?

With a sullen frown on his face, Alucard backed off, taking his eyes off the demon as he turned around—

The demon gently grabbed Alucard's scaled wrist. "Where are you going?" he asked despondently, staring into the vampire's eyes as he looked back at him. "It's okay... you don't have to go—I'm not mad," he assured him.

Alucard wanted to fall back into his mate's embrace; he wanted to give in and let the comfort ensnare him. But now that he'd had blood, he could feel his strength gradually returning, and he wanted to use it to heal his mind. The sooner all the confusion was cleared up, the sooner he remembered his mate's name and could attach memories to these feelings, the sooner he'd feel more like himself, the sooner the despair would leave him.

So he dismissed the desire to give in and kept walking away. It hurt, and all he wanted to do was turn around and run back to his mate, but he knew that he needed time alone to concentrate or neither of them would completely recover from what just happened.

When he reached a large boulder, he slumped down on the grass beside it and exhaled deeply, trying to relax. He glanced at his mate, who, with distress in his dark eyes, headed over to where some of his people were being healed by Camael. Among the people, he recognized Greymore…and Idina. And colt. And Freja. But that was it.

He closed his eyes and concentrated, retreating into his mind. When he found the memories he'd taken from Lucifer, he began searching them. His father had attempted to take away *everything* about his mate, he tried to erase him entirely. But Alucard had gotten away in time. He just hoped he'd taken everything back. If he hadn't, then…he'd have to go back there. To Lucifer. He wouldn't abandon his memories, especially not those shared with the man he loved.

"What would you like us to call you?" Amos suddenly asked, a humble tone in his voice as he appeared in front of him.

Frowning, Alucard lifted his head and glared up at him, snapping out of his thoughts. He didn't want to talk to this guy, nor did he want to talk to any of the demons behind him. All of them gawped at him, waiting for him to answer, but instead of doing so, he snarled irritably and rested his head back on the ground.

Amos frowned—

"Is everything okay?" his mate suddenly asked with an irritated smile on his face, appearing beside Alucard, who glanced up at him.

"Everything is fine," Amos muttered. Then, he looked back down at Alucard, waiting for him to answer.

His persistence only irritated Alucard. He wanted to be alone. But then again, maybe Amos had answers—maybe one of these demons would have knowledge that Alucard was now missing, something that might help him extract his memories from what he'd taken from Lucifer.

He didn't think twice—he needed the blood, too.

In the blink of an eye, he savagely pounced at Amos, who grunted in startle, but he didn't have much time to scream as Alucard pinned him down and sunk his teeth into Amos' throat, tearing his head from his body.

Everyone stood still and watched in silence as he tore at Amos' body—snapping, snarling, tearing into his chest with his talons to reach his heart. He began to feel his fatigue fade once more as he consumed Amos' blood, and as he drained the man's life force, he focused on what knowledge this demon had. And he learnt a lot; Amos knew that the name of Alucard's demon mate was actually Zalith—*Zalith*…of course it was. How could he forget?

Zalith. Such a beautiful name. Such a beautiful man. Such a dangerous, intoxicating demon. Zalith. *Zalith.* He could say it a thousand times, and each would feel like a kiss on his lips, a warm embrace, a long-awaited caress. *Zalith.*

He tried focusing. Where were they? They were in Nefastus, currently on the run, hiding from not only the Diabolus, but Lilith, Damien, and both their cults. He and Zalith had pretty much declared war on the Numen, and the Numen—namely Damien and Lilith—were searching for both him and Zalith.

But then there was Lucifer—*he* was getting involved, too. The Diabolus had recently been handed to Ysmay, one of Lucifer's ethos-created children, and her task was to find him and bring him to Lucifer. Ysmay had very nearly succeeded, but Alucard was alive. And that was all Amos knew.

It was enough. As Alucard focused on Zalith, the confusion started clearing; his stolen memories fell back into place like pieces of a puzzle, but anything involving delving into his memory always yielded moments of his past that he tried to forget, and with remembering the man he loved, the man he wanted to marry, he remembered the things that Damien and Lilith did to him, things that made him grow up believing he'd never be loved. He remembered the pain. The despair. The dismay. The god damn loneliness. That *fucking* loneliness. A feeling he never wanted to experience again. Alone, the only creature of his kind, cursed to exist for as long as the sun lit the world.

But the *love*. Zalith's love took all that pain away. His affection, his embrace, the way he understood Alucard—the way they understood *each other*. They were mated, their lives would forever be entangled, and Alucard would have it no other way.

Yet… the sorrow lingered like a shadow, a shadow that attempted to shroud the light at every turn. Hated. Loved. Unwanted. Desired. Disgusting. Beautiful. Weak. Powerful. The bastard of a cultist whore. The son of an eternal Numen. Banished, cast away. Home in the arms of his beloved.

So many things.

Too many things.

Dark things. Light things.

Horrible things. Wonderful things.

He didn't want to think about any of it. He wouldn't let the dismay ensnare him. His amnesia-like state was loosening its grasp, and the more his mind cleared, the more relieved he felt. He might have lost his human likeness, but he was alive, and so was Zalith. They may have lost people to Ysmay's attack, but they'd saved everyone else, and now they had more demons, too.

Demons that Alucard didn't want to be around right now. He just wanted to be with Zalith.

The vampire snarled, stepping back from what was left of Amos' body. Of course, he'd just killed an important member of his new pack, and he'd have to replace him… so he set his eyes on who he detected as the pack's next strongest demon, and she nodded, understanding that she now had Amos' rank. He then turned around, glancing at Zalith as he started to prowl over to a nearby tree. His mate understood and started following him away from the demons, who watched closely. Alucard just hoped that they'd learn to keep their distance; he wasn't interested in playing Alpha right now.

| Zalith |

As Alucard walked away from everyone else, Zalith followed. The vampire eventually stopped beneath a tree, where he slumped down and sighed tiredly. Zalith sat beside him, placing his hand on the side of his face as he gazed worriedly at him.

"Baby, are you okay?" he asked quietly.

It looked like Alucard wanted to answer, but he frowned in distress. He shuffled closer, lifting his head, and then he rested his forehead against Zalith's.

Zalith understood. Alucard *couldn't* talk in this form, could he? So instead, the demon placed his hand on the side of Alucard's scaled face and connected to him through their imprints, making it so that he could feel what Alucard was feeling—and what he felt was such distressing, agonizing sadness.

He didn't want Alucard to be sad—he wanted to help. "What's wrong?" he asked sullenly, staring into Alucard's eyes.

But the vampire closed them, and so Zalith focused…and what he felt…Alucard needed him, and he was trying to tell him to enter his mind in order to do so. Maybe he'd be able to speak to him that way. And he felt no hesitation. He just wanted to do what he could, and he just wanted to be with him. So, he closed his eyes, concentrating, waiting as Alucard slowly opened his mind so that Zalith could enter.

The demon opened his eyes to darkness, and the moment he set his sights on the crimson-haired vampire standing a small distance away, he felt something so relieving yet so agonizing grip hold of him. Although he'd already seen Alucard, although he'd already been able to hold and embrace him, seeing him as a man gave him an entirely different kind of relief.

His face contorted into a distressed scowl as he hurried forward; he threw his arms around his vampire, hugging him as tightly as he could—and he'd collided with him so abruptly that, as Alucard moved his arms around Zalith, he stumbled back, and they fell to the ground. But Zalith didn't move; he lay there, resting on top of Alucard, holding him firmly as he nuzzled his neck. He did his best to keep his tears back—he'd cried enough today. He was so relieved, though. He'd been terrified that he'd never see Alucard again. But there he was…and Zalith loved him so much. He didn't care what Alucard looked like—man, drake…he was still Alucard, but *this* was what Zalith knew—the crimson-haired, pale-skinned man with a face so beautiful that he could stare at it for eternity. Seeing him the way Zalith knew best gave him such comfort…and he didn't want to let go.

"Zaliv," Alucard said sullenly.

The demon uttered a sound of recognition, still holding him tightly.

"I vhought…I lost you," he murmured, his voice a little shaky.

Zalith shook his head. "I thought I lost you, too," he mumbled sadly. He then kissed Alucard's lips, their soft, warm touch sending more relief spiralling through him. "I love you so much. I don't have words to tell you how glad I am that you're here—that you're alive," he said, gripping Alucard's shirt and pulling him closer.

Alucard ran his fingers through Zalith's hair. "I love you, too," he said, staring into the demon's dark eyes. "Noving vill ever stop me vrom being vith you."

"Nothing will ever stop me from being with you, either," the demon said quietly, holding him firmly.

The vampire buried his face against Zalith's neck. "I vas…vhen…" he paused and frowned before taking a deep breath. "Vhen I vas…gone, I vent to vhere Luciver is—to…'is prison."

Confusion struck Zalith. "How?"

"I zon't know," the vampire murmured. "Vhen zhe ozzer Numen sealed 'im avay, zhey zidn't 'ave 'is Obcasus, so is likely zhat zhe prison's power is veakening. Eizer zhat or 'is scions are able to send vings inside."

With a deep sigh, Zalith fought off the worry that made him feel. They already had enough to deal with. "But he's still locked up, right?"

Alucard nodded. "'E can't get out."

He exhaled, trying to remain calm. "Okay." He then leaned his head back so that he could see Alucard's face again. "Are you okay?"

"I vink so," he replied. "But…Luciver…tried to take my memories avay, and—"

"What?" he panicked.

"I got back vhat 'e took," Alucard assured him. "Vas like zhis sort of…amnesia. Is vhy I vas convused and unsure bevore. But is all coming back, and I vink zhat…I took some vings vrom 'im, too. I vas going to look vhrough everyving, but I kind of just vant to vest vight now."

As relief broke through his abrupt panic, Zalith sighed and pressed his forehead against Alucard's. "You don't have to do anything at all right now," he told him, caressing the side of his face with his fingertips. "You need to rest."

"Ve shouldn't stick avound zhis place vor long, zhough. Zhe sound of all zhe vighting vould 'ave travelled vor miles. Zhe last ving ve need is scavengers or 'unters vinding us."

Although he wanted to give his vampire as much time to rest as possible, Alucard was right. The sooner they got moving, the better. "Yeah. Everyone needs a little time to heal, but we'll head out soon—only if you're okay to travel."

Alucard nodded. "I'll be okay."

"Are you sure?"

"Mm-hmm. Your blood alvays 'elps me veel a lot better."

Zalith pulled him into his embrace again. "Let me know if you need more."

The vampire nodded again. "Vank you."

With a deep exhale, Zalith sunk into the comfort of Alucard's embrace. He knew that they had to start getting everyone to leave, but he just wanted to stay there with him a little longer. He wasn't sure how long it would take Alucard to regain his human form, and he wanted to make the most of being able to hold him like this.

Chapter Sixty-Two

Onwards

| Zalith |

They couldn't stay within the quiet of Alucard's mind forever. Eventually—and reluctantly—Zalith opened his eyes to the real world, relaxing as he stared at Alucard, who, still in his drake-like form, opened his eyes, too. The demon kept his hand on the side of Alucard's scaled face, gazing into his hell-fiery eyes as they burned brightly in the shade of the tree they sat beneath. He felt like this was all his fault…the attack, Alucard's death, and how the vampire had now been forced into what could only be his true form.

But he didn't want to sink into his dismaying thoughts—he couldn't afford to give into his emotions right now. He had a lot to do; he had to manipulate the memories of the demons Alucard had won leadership over, he had to make sure everyone was fit and well to travel, and he also had to make sure that Alucard got what he needed before they headed out. So much to do, so little time…and all he wanted to do was go back into Alucard's mind and be with him there, but he couldn't. It was time to get moving.

The demon sighed quietly and leaned forward, kissing the side of Alucard's face.

"*I'm sorry I bit you,*" Alucard said, speaking into Zalith's mind.

Staring into his eyes, Zalith shook his head. "It's okay," he said aloud. "I'm not mad—don't worry about it," he said, stroking the side of Alucard's face.

Alucard nodded, but the sullen look didn't leave his eyes. "*Vhat do ve do now?*"

"We need to start moving," he said, standing up.

Also standing up, Alucard followed Zalith over to Idina, who was seeing to Danford.

"Has Orin responded?" Zalith asked, stopping beside her.

"Yes," Idina said with a nod. "He said he's ready to help if we need him."

"Good—get him here," he ordered. But then he glanced at Alucard, who looked fatigued *already*. He watched as the vampire slowly laid down on his front, exhaling deeply as he did. His worry grew, but he tried to keep it together. "Is everybody ready to leave?" he asked Idina.

"More or less. But…I'm really worried about Danny," she said, glancing back at the blonde-haired werewolf, who currently looked like a corpse, lying on his back beside Freja.

"What's wrong with him?" Zalith questioned.

Idina shook her head, a perplexed look on her face. "We took the bullet out, but he's not healed from the wound, which is strange because everyone else who'd been shot is fine now," she muttered in concern. "It's like he has a fever, but he's getting colder and colder to the touch every few minutes. We don't know what to do for him."

Zalith frowned, glancing at Danford. From what Idina had said, it almost sounded as if Danford had the same infection he had had. Could that be what it was? He felt a little irritated—they were probably going to need Opus if that was the case. "Has Camael looked at him?" he asked.

"He has," she confirmed. "He doesn't know what it is either."

The demon exhaled deeply, looking around. He knew they didn't have any people here trained in the medical field, and that made him feel stupid for not having been prepared. But then he set his eyes on a few of Ysmay's old demons, glaring at them as they waited behind the tree line, keeping their eyes on Alucard. Could any of them perhaps have the medical knowledge needed to help?

He sharply turned his head, however, when Alucard got up and prowled towards Danford; his first thought was: was Alucard going to devour him the same way he had that demon? But it didn't seem like that was the case. Alucard had a tired, perplexed look on his face, so Zalith stayed where he was, watching alongside Idina as Alucard approached Danford.

When Alucard stopped beside Danford, horror struck the man's face, and he tried to shuffle away, grabbing Freja's hand, but he soon gave up, unable to move much at all.

"Aleksei?" Freja asked worriedly.

Alucard took his eyes off Danford and looked at her.

"Is he dying?" she asked, tears in her eyes.

As Alucard looked down at Danford again, Zalith did, too. He saw the spreading vermillion vein-like marks on his skin, originating from his bullet wound; Zalith knew what a vampire bite looked like, but no vampire had bitten him, so how was he infected with vampirism?

Alucard then glanced at Freja, to Zalith, and down and Danford again.

"What's wrong, baby?" Zalith asked.

Alucard spoke into Zalith's mind, "*Looks like 'e's been invected vith vampirism, but I zon't…vemember if I 'ad anyving to do vith zhis or not.*"

Zalith frowned. "He says he's been infected with vampirism," he relayed to Freja.

Idina frowned strangely. "I don't think he's been bitten…have you?" she asked, looking down at Danford.

He shook his head. "N-no," he said weakly.

"You were standing right in front of him," Freja said, looking down at Danford and then back at Alucard. "The bullet…it went through you before it hit him," she said.

"Oh…" Idina uttered in startle.

Zalith looked down at Alucard. "Is there anything we can do for him?"

Alucard replied, speaking into Zalith's mind, "*I zon't know. As var as I am avare, any vampire zhat tried to turn a verevolf…or any verevolf zhat 'as ingested vampire blood 'as died; our blood is toxic to each ozzer. But…might be divverent vith me—I zon't know. Vampires make ozzer vampires vhrough blood and venom; vith me, takes only my blood, so maybe 'e vill survive—I can't be sure.*"

Zalith exhaled deeply; if there was nothing that they could do, then there was nothing they could do. The fact that Freja would be raising her and Danford's child alone was just another despairing truth to add to the evergrowing mountain. "Is there anything we can do to make him more comfortable?" he asked.

The vampire looked back down at Danford. "*'E looks to be 'alfvay vhrough vhat a transition vould look like. Zhere isn't veally anyving you can do to make 'im veel better, all you can do is keep some 'uman blood avound in case 'e some'ow makes vhrough.*"

"Can't you undo it?" Zalith asked quietly.

Alucard looked up at him. "*I can only take vampirism avay vonce 'as taken 'old of somevone.*"

The demon nodded, looking over at Idina and then down at Freja. "There isn't anything we can do except wait and hope he makes it through. He's going to need human blood if he survives—we'll get some," he said.

With a sullen pout and teary eyes, Freja cried to Danford, "It's going to be okay."

Zalith then looked at Idina. "Get Danford into the wagon and prepare everyone to leave in ten minutes," he ordered.

She nodded. "Of course."

Zalith then led Alucard away from everyone else, and once they reached the same tree they'd been sitting under, Alucard sighed deeply and slumped down, seeming eager for a moment to lay there and rest. And when Zalith focused on his vampire, he could feel that his ethos was still very low, still recovering, still struggling. Alucard needed to sleep, and Zalith wanted to make sure he got as much as possible. But first, they had to get somewhere safe.

He sat beside Alucard, pulling his head into his lap. "Are you feeling okay?" he asked, stroking his head.

Closing his eyes, Alucard exhaled deeply. "*I veel tired,*" he answered, speaking into the demon's mind.

"You can close your eyes for a few minutes," Zalith said quietly. "But we have to keep moving."

Alucard shuffled around, making himself comfortable before closing his eyes.

Zalith let out a hushed sigh, leaning his head back against the tree as he kept his hand on Alucard's head. He looked down at Alucard, slowly examining his scaled, drake-like body with his eyes. The wound in his neck had healed a lot, but those in his chest and side were still open; they weren't bleeding, but he was certain that they were causing Alucard pain. And then guilt warped his thoughts again. Why hadn't he been there to stop Alucard from getting hurt? He should have done better—he *could* have done better.

"Hey, boss," Greymore suddenly called, stopping in front of him.

Taking his eyes off Alucard, Zalith looked up at the Alpha to see that he was holding Peaches.

"I found—woah…" he frowned, looking down at Alucard. "You okay buddy?" he asked in concern but with a surprised look on his face.

Alucard didn't respond.

"He's fine," Zalith said as Greymore handed him Peaches. "Thank you for finding her."

"No problem. She was just south of here hiding under a dead tree," he said with a shrug. "I'll get out of your hair now—feel better, man," he said, glancing down at Alucard. He wandered off to help everyone else finish getting ready to leave.

As Greymore left, Zalith looked back down at Alucard—but he wasn't about to get the time alone with him that he wanted.

Beside him, one of Ysmay's demons appeared, throwing a hogtied, gagged man to the ground. "This is for him," he said, glancing at Alucard before glaring at Zalith.

Taking his eyes off Alucard again, Zalith looked at the terrified human as he tried to wriggle away, and then he looked up at the demon. "Where did you get him from?"

"Does it matter?" he asked with an irritated scowl.

"Yes."

The man rolled his eyes. "There's a small village east of here."

"How did you catch him?" Zalith questioned, concerned. "Did you make a scene?"

With an irritated snarl, the man kicked the human and scowled at Zalith. "Why the fuck does it matter?" he growled. "They're just humans—the hell are they gonna do?"

Zalith adorned a condescending, impatient frown. "Humans talk…gossip spreads; everyone starts to fear the demons from the woods that keep snatching their friends and their family. Maybe they come looking for us and maybe they bring along someone who works with or for the Numen. Suddenly, everyone knows where to find us, every single one of us dies, and all because you thought it didn't matter, and he's just a human," he said, keeping his eyes on the man as his irritated scowl turned into a perturbed one.

But the guy scoffed. "No one saw us."

"How many of you went?"

The man's scowl thickened as he gritted his teeth impatiently. "Would you like to know our fucking names and dates of birth, too?" he snarled.

"Yes," Zalith said with an aggravated smile.

He scoffed again and started to turn around to leave. "Go and fuck yourself—"

With an angered snarl, Zalith used his demonic speed to instantly get up; he lunged at the man, grabbing him by his throat before he had a chance to try and defend himself. Zalith forced him back and pinned him against a tree, glaring into his eyes as he glared back, trying to pull him off. "Disrespect me again—" he warned as the man choked in his grip, "—and I'll kill you. That goes for all your little friends as well," he growled, baring his fangs.

But the man scoffed again. "I'm not afraid of *you*," he laughed.

Zalith tried to resist the urge to kill him. He wanted to make an example of him, but he didn't want to cause drama that Alucard might have to deal with. Instead, he scowled evilly at him. "You should be," he warned. Then, he forced his way into the man's feeble mind; he induced an overwhelming sense of fear and let go of him, watching as he slid down to his knees, holding his hands over his head as he wailed in terror, like he was surrounded by horrific monsters moments from devouring his very soul.

Rolling his eyes, Zalith turned around—but Alucard wasn't where he'd left him. Panic enthralled him as he felt his heart stop; he frantically searched with his eyes, turning his head, but he quickly set his sights on what was unmistakably Alucard's tail giving away his position behind a tree close to the one they'd been sitting under. The human that had been brought for him was missing, and Zalith assumed that his vampire must have taken him.

The demon made his way over, hurrying, and when he stepped behind the tree, he stared down at Alucard. He'd never actually seen what some demons had to do to gain a human form, but now he knew…and as he watched Alucard tear at and chew on the dead man like a savage animal, a smile crept across his face. It relieved him to see that Alucard was fine.

However, the vampire stopped once he noticed that he was no longer alone, and he looked up at Zalith with what looked like startle and embarrassment in his eyes.

Zalith laughed quietly, leaning his arm against the tree. "Are you enjoying your snack?" he asked with a smirk.

Alucard looked away but resumed eating as Peaches—who was sitting beside him—cleaned her paws contently.

The demon kept a smile, glad to see that he was feeling better. But he felt as if Alucard would appreciate some privacy, so he said, "I'll be right back, okay?"

A muffled, "*Okay*," echoed in Zalith's head.

With an amused smile, Zalith turned around and headed towards his people. He'd rejoin him once he made sure that everyone was okay.

| Alucard |

Alucard continued devouring the human. He had once hoped that he'd never have to do this ever again—how revolted it made him feel. But he had no choice. If he wanted to regain his human form, he'd have to drain the blood and the life force of a fair few humans—and he'd have to consume as much of them as he could stomach. Usually, his body would already begin to transform, but he held onto the ethos that would cause his change; he didn't want to end up walking around looking half-human, half-monster. No, he'd wait until he had enough ethos to transform his body as close to his human one as he could, and he knew that was going to take a while.

He stopped eating flesh and focused on draining the rest of his food's blood. Despite desiring the return to his human form, he wanted to be with Zalith. So he pulled his fangs from the corpse and exhaled deeply before getting up. He lazily dragged himself over to where Zalith was standing; the demon smiled at him, and as Alucard reached him, he slumped down onto his front, hoping that Zalith would sit with him. And he did. The demon sat down, leaning back against the tree as he placed his hand on his head.

"Let me wipe your face," Zalith said, pulling off his bloodied, torn shirt.

Alucard waited, gazing at Zalith as he used his shirt to wipe the blood from his scaled face. He couldn't *not* let his eyes wander, however, and stared down at what he could see of the demon's defined body as he continued to clean his face. There was dried blood on his skin; some on his bicep, some on his shoulder and chest. Alucard knew he'd been hurt in the battle, too, but thankfully, deridiuz didn't affect Zalith, and he hadn't suffered.

Once Zalith was done, Alucard sighed and rested his head in the demon's lap. "*Vank you,*" he mumbled into his mate's mind.

"It's okay, baby," he said with a smile, caressing Alucard's head as he chucked his bloody shirt over to the corpse Alucard had almost entirely devoured.

"*I 'ate zhis,*" he uttered despondently.

"You don't like me wiping your face?" Zalith asked with a quiet laugh.

"*No, I 'ate being...zhis,*" he grumbled. "*I look like veatherless chicken,*" he snarled.

The demon laughed amusedly. "No, I think you're beautiful," he said, stroking his fingers over the side of Alucard's neck, along his jaw, and to his chin, which he scratched lightly. "Look at your little scales—they're so cute," he teased.

Alucard huffed in discontent, closing his eyes.

"You'll be back to your usual self soon baby, don't worry. We just need to find you more people," Zalith said, moving his hand over his head. "How many humans do you think you'll need?"

Alucard thought back to the first time he'd had to do this. To regain his human body back then, he'd fed on an entire church—around thirty of the Diabolus. Would it be the same this time? He'd already constructed an appearance, so maybe it wouldn't take as long as when he was a child. He also didn't want to be stuck in his true form for that long, so once he had enough ethos to make himself look as normal as possible, he'd let it transform him.

"*I vink... maybe ten*," he said confidently.

The demon nodded, stroking Alucard's head. "I'll take care of it."

Chapter Sixty-Three

But Hours Away

| Zalith |

It was getting dark.

Zalith hadn't failed to notice that Alucard had been slowing down, nor had he failed to notice how exhausted he looked. He was limping, and the bullet wounds on his body still hadn't healed. As much as he wanted to keep moving, Alucard was more important, so if his vampire needed to stop and rest, then he'd stop and let him rest.

He placed his hand on Alucard's back, frowning worriedly. Then, the demon looked over his shoulder at his people. "We're going to stop here and rest for a short while," he called, and as mumbles of relief and tire broke the silence, Zalith slowed down, bringing the travelling group to a halt.

Alucard followed Zalith over to a tree, where they both sat. The vampire lay on his side, breathing deeply in what was clearly fatigue. Zalith placed his hand on the side of Alucard's head, a sullen, guilt-ridden frown clinging to his face as he lightly stroked his hand down Alucard's scaled neck. He wanted to talk to him; he wanted to see him again, to hold him, to kiss him…but he couldn't. He had to let him rest. So he shuffled closer, leaning back against the tree as he pulled Alucard's head into his lap, trying to help him feel a little more comfortable.

"'*Ow much longer do ve 'ave to travel vor today*?" Alucard asked quietly, speaking into his mind.

Caressing his neck, Zalith stared down at Alucard. "We can stop for the night baby, it's okay," he said. "I don't want you to push yourself."

But Alucard shook his head, exhaling deeply. "*No…ve should keep moving vor a bit longer.*"

"You need to rest, Alucard," he insisted quietly, stroking the side of his face. "Maybe we can keep going later," he said, but he didn't intend on moving again until the morning.

Alucard was clearly utterly exhausted, and he didn't want him to feel like he had to keep going.

The vampire exhaled deeply, nodding as he made himself comfortable, closing his eyes once more.

As Alucard rested, Zalith stared aimlessly into the trees, gently caressing the vampire's head. The quiet mumbles of his people behind him started to drown out as he sunk into his thoughts; so much had happened, and as much as he wanted to ignore how it all made him feel, there were brief moments like this when he simply couldn't. Alucard was hurting, *he* was hurting, and everything just seemed to continue falling apart no matter how hard he tried to make it right.

Varana—he scowled. She'd been telling him that she wanted to leave just moments before Ysmay's attack, and that couldn't be any more suspicious. He couldn't trust her anymore. What did she know? What was she going to tell Ysmay? She knew *too* much, information that might put him and Alucard in *so* much more danger if she were to tell their enemies. How could she do this? After everything he had done for her, after the centuries they had spent together...how could she just betray him like this? He didn't want to think harshly of her, but how could he not? She had turned on him, and there was no telling what might happen next if she decided to share what she knew.

He looked down at Alucard, a sullen frown stealing his angry visage. Why was this happening? It was all his fault. Just like he should have known that Lilith's people would attack the compound, he should have known Ysmay was coming. He had once again let himself become convinced that Alucard was safe with him—but that wasn't true. He had *died*, and if he hadn't come back...Zalith wasn't sure what he might have done with himself. He didn't want to spend a moment without him, let alone live without him knowing that his death was his fault, that he could have done better.

But Alucard was alive and right in front of him...and he'd never, *ever* leave him on his own again. This vampire was the most important thing in his life, and he had to keep hold of him, because if he lost him...what did he have? Varana was gone, his people had lost faith in him, he had no family, and he knew he'd be miserable if he had to revert to living the way he used to—if he had to live a life without the man he loved. He'd rather die than do that, he'd rather end his own life than live one without Alucard.

The exhaustion of the battle, the journey, and his healed wounds was catching up to him. He felt the fatigue strike him like a knife, making him dizzy, making his body feel like stone. As his heavy eyes slowly closed, he tried his best not to give in. Despite knowing that his people knew to be on watch, he didn't want to rest, he didn't want to be so defenceless.

Yet...the exhaustion was winning. His eyes closed...he forced them open. His eyes closed...he shook his head. His eyes closed...and he gave in.

Sleep took him like he was its reluctant but weak prey, slowly swallowing him, his head spiralling, the world spinning. And as all his senses shut off, the darkness enveloped him entirely.

But he woke what felt like moments later. He flinched, looking around anxiously. Everyone was resting, and he couldn't sense danger. But he wouldn't let his guard down.

The demon looked down at Alucard, caressing his head as he slept. That was when he heard Orin's voice, and it was likely *his* arrival that stirred Zalith. He sighed, leaning his head back against the tree behind him. He still had to manipulate and alter the minds of the demons that now followed Alucard, but he just didn't feel like it right now. Not just that, but he'd need Alucard's assistance, and he wanted the vampire to rest. He also didn't want to leave him on his own; he held him tightly, moving his arm around what he could of his drake-like body. He didn't ever want to let him go.

He did, however, have work to do, and as he heard Orin making his way over to him, he looked back over his shoulder, setting his eyes on him, watching as he approached.

"The area's secure, boss," Orin said, stopping beside him. "My pack are still working in my absence."

"Good," Zalith muttered. "I need you here with us for now... or at least until we reach the next checkpoint."

Orin nodded. "Anything you need, boss."

"Make sure everyone's okay, please. Listen to whatever they have to say and relay it all back to me." He wanted to hear their complaints, he wanted to hear that they were disappointed. He deserved it.

"Yes, boss."

Orin then walked off.

Zalith listened for a while, hearing his people say, "Does he know what he's doing anymore?", "How do we know we won't be constantly on the run again like we were in Eltaria?", "I can't do this again. It's all his fault.", "We should've disappeared when we had the chance."

Yes. They should have left. They should have lost their faith long ago.

He let their words pull him deeper into despair. But his fatigue outweighed the sorrow. Of course it did. His eyes were getting heavy again, and this time, knowing that Orin was finally there, he let himself drift off. But he wouldn't be so naïve as to hope that once he woke, things might be a little better. They wouldn't be.

| Alucard |

Alucard dreamed a memory. A fond one. He and Zalith went for coffee—Zalith had just shown up uninvited, but Alucard welcomed him anyway, and they headed to Dargamoore to talk business. But Zalith had other things on his mind; he wanted to get to know Alucard, and Alucard had been standoffish—cautious, even. He sat across the table from the man whom at the time he would have never thought was his mate. He ordered exactly what Zalith ordered; he'd never had coffee before, and it wasn't as great as the humans made it out to be. He'd poured so much sugar into that cup....

But then Lucifer—standing off in the distance at the end of the street, a grin on his face—a face covered in rune-like markings beneath which Alucard knew his father's all-seeing eyes existed. That eye in his forehead, the eye that looked much like his own... that eye could see into the future. His father possessed an ability much like his own—of course, Lucifer had honed such a power, and Alucard was sure that his father could gaze into what was to come at will—yet, it did him no good while stuck within the Pandorican.

And the remaining four eyes on his face—the four hidden beneath the streaking runes on either side of his cheeks; one would show him the extent of someone's power. Another would allow him to peer into one's very soul. The next gave Lucifer the power to see through every existing kind of ethos, illusion, and deception—it even let him see past the barriers between each plane, each world. Nothing could hide from it. And the last eye granted him the ability to see every possible outcome of a situation.

All that power... it surely drove him insane; that was why his siblings sealed him away.

Alucard stared at him, watching the grin on his father's face stretch wider and wider as Zalith spoke in front of him as if everything was fine. Of course it was—Lucifer hadn't actually been there, had he? This was just some sort of illusion—the remnants of Lucifer left behind when Alucard snatched memories and knowledge from his father's mind, taking back everything Lucifer tried to pry from him. And he had to fight it—he had to remove the infection. He had to remember this memory and ignore what shouldn't be there.

So he took his eyes off Lucifer, staring at Zalith, listening to what he had to say. And he remembered how he felt in this moment; despite his uncertainty regarding Zalith's loyalties to Damien, he had found himself enjoying their interaction. He'd never really been a social man, but the more he and Zalith spoke, the more he found he liked it. The demon suggested they met like this between each vampire relocation meeting... and Alucard had accepted—he was glad he had chosen to accept Zalith's invitation. After all, if they had kept things strictly professional, would they be here right now?

He smiled, but the memory before him faded as it came to its end.

And there was no sign of Lucifer.

Was that all he had to do? When he dreamed, when he reminisced when Lucifer tried to steal, did he simply have to ignore his father's infectious presence? That relieved him, that made him feel a whole lot more hopeful.

But then came Zalith's echoing voice. "Alucard?"

A nudge on his arm.

"Alucard?"

The vampire woke; although he wanted to remove Lucifer's infection, he was glad to wake and see his mate's face. "*Vhat*?" he asked sleepily.

"It's getting late, so we're going to move closer to the camp, okay?"

Staring up at him, Alucard nodded. "*Okay*," he said, starting to get up.

Zalith led him over to where his people had set up camp; a few of them were sitting around a small fire, others were already asleep, and some were keeping watch. Zalith sat down beside another tree not too far from where Idina and Orin were; he placed his hand over Alucard's head once more as the vampire slumped down beside him and rested his head in his lap.

"*Zaliv*," Alucard then murmured into Zalith's mind.

He looked down at the vampire. "Yeah?" he asked quietly.

Alucard frowned, staring out into the dark woods. He knew that he was slowing everyone down—he knew how desperately Zalith wanted to get out of Nefastus so that everyone could be safe. Alucard felt like a hindrance. In order to get his strength back, he needed blood, but the energy he got from that would drain the longer he remained in his true form, and now that he had to remove Lucifer's infection from his memories, he wasn't going to be getting stronger any time soon. "*I'm slowing everyvone down," he muttered sadly. "Zhis is all taking too long because of me.*"

"It's not your fault," Zalith said, stroking his head. "You did nothing wrong."

He sighed deeply, glancing up at Zalith. "*I should 'ave been more avare,*" he mumbled. "*But I just... vasn't paying attention—so stupid*," he snarled, disappointed in himself.

"Don't blame yourself, baby," Zalith consoled him. "If you're going to blame anyone, blame me... or Ysmay... or Varana," he said despondently, still stroking Alucard's head.

Frowning, Alucard stared up at him from the corner of his eye. "'*Ow vould zhis be your vault?*"

"If I'd protected you better, then you wouldn't... it wouldn't have happened."

Alucard didn't want to argue with him—he felt far too tired. But he didn't want Zalith to think this was in any way his fault, because it wasn't. "*None of zhis is your vault*," he said, closing his eyes.

"Nothing that happened is *your* fault," Zalith said firmly.

Opening his eyes to stare into the darkness, Alucard sighed quietly. He didn't have the strength to keep going back and forth, nor could he really think of anything else to say. He felt the way he felt, and he was sure that wouldn't change. But what mattered right now was doing something about the fact that he was so exhausted all the time. If he had access to blood—to *humans*—he could reform his human body much faster, and then he wouldn't have to deal with the constant fatigue and rationing of his energy. "*I need more 'umans. Zhe energy I got vrom zhe last vone is alveady vearing vhin; if I 'ad more, maybe I could 'eal vaster, and zhen I vouldn't be stuck looking like a chameleon.*"

The demon smiled slightly. "You don't look like a chameleon, you look like a big handsome dragon," he said, caressing Alucard's head. "I can send someone to get you humans," he then added. "I'll get them to bring as many as you need."

"*I vink I need... maybe nine—but zhen zhey should bring vone vor Danvord, too—'as almost been twelve hours, so... if 'e lives vhrough a vew more, 'e'll need blood to complete 'is transition. Zhen, avter zhat... vell... 'e can decide vhat 'e vants to do.*"

Zalith nodded. "I'll get you both what you need."

"*Vank you,*" Alucard mumbled tiredly, shuffling around, making himself comfortable.

Zalith smiled sadly and kissed Alucard's head. "You should sleep."

"*You need to sleep, too.*"

The demon nodded, stroking Alucard's head. "I will."

Alucard relaxed and glanced up at him. "*Goodnight,*" he murmured, letting his fatigue ensnare him.

"Goodnight," Zalith replied. "I love you."

"*I love you too,*" the vampire replied quietly, drifting off to sleep. When he next woke, he hoped to see all the humans he needed to recover his strength. Maybe then he'd feel like less of a burden.

| Zalith |

Zalith sat there, staring aimlessly ahead. The night was probably going to be long, and he wasn't going to sleep a single hour of it. He didn't care how tired he felt, and he didn't care how much more tired he was going to feel as the night went on. He needed to stay awake—he needed to make sure nothing else happened. And he needed to protect Alucard.

He looked down at his vampire, slowly stroking his hand across the top of his head. All he could really think about was how relieved he was; he'd come so close to losing Alucard forever—*too* close. In the moments he had thought he was gone, Zalith had even considered ending his own life because…without Alucard, what did he have worth living for? Alucard was everything to him, and to lose him would amount to losing himself. He had to do better—he never wanted to go through anything like that again. He had to hold onto Alucard as tightly as he could—he had to make sure his vampire knew just how much he loved him…just how much he needed him. And he wouldn't let *anything* come anywhere near taking Alucard away from him again.

And he knew what he wanted to do…there were a lot of things he wanted to do, come to think of it, but he had to wait. First, he had to help Alucard regain his human body. After that…*then* he could make sure that Alucard knew just how much he wanted him, how much he *needed* him.

With a tired sigh, Zalith leaned his head back against the tree and stared up at the star-filled sky. Tomorrow was but hours away—hours he would spend sitting there in silence watching over his people and the man he loved.

Hours…that he'd spend wondering exactly what he'd say when he saw Alucard's human face again.

Chapter Sixty-Four

The Fledgeling

| **Alucard,** ***Monday, Cordus 6th, 960(TG)—Nefastus*** |

Morning slowly came. The sound of birds and insects woke Alucard, and he opened his eyes to see Zalith staring aimlessly into the forest, his hand on Alucard's head; he was clearly doing his best to keep his senses alert in case of danger, and he looked like hell. He hadn't slept at all, had he?

He spoke into Zalith's mind, "*Did…you sleep?*"

"A little," he lied with a smile, caressing his head; he was *such* a bad liar when he was tired. "How did you sleep?"

"*Vas okay,*" he said, staring at him with concern in his tired eyes.

"Good," the demon said, and then he leaned down and kissed his head.

Alucard knew that Zalith was worried; he was sure that the demon was trying to make sure everyone was safe…keeping an eye out for the slightest glimpse of hostiles. But he needed to sleep; if he was utterly exhausted all the time, and if danger did so happen to turn up, Zalith wouldn't really be able to do much about it, would he? "*Do you vant to get some more sleep?*" he asked, sitting up. "*I can keep vatch.*"

He shook his head. "No, I'm okay," he denied. "Thank you though."

"*You look exhausted,*" Alucard said worriedly.

"I'll be okay," Zalith said, stroking Alucard's head. "I don't think I could fall back asleep anyway—I have a lot to do."

"*Like vhat?*" Alucard asked. "*I can do vhatever you need to do vor you.*"

"No, it's okay. I want you to rest and heal."

Alucard knew there was no use in fighting; Zalith was too stubborn to argue with. With a resigned nod and a quiet sigh, he let his head sink back into Zalith's lap, the warmth of his touch grounding him. The first light of dawn was just beginning to paint the horizon with a soft, pale glow, casting long shadows over the dew-kissed grass. The air was cool, carrying the faint scent of earth and fresh foliage. Above them, the soft trill of birdsong wove through the stillness, a gentle reminder that morning had only just begun to wake the world. Alucard's eyes drifted to the camp, still quiet and motionless, the tents shrouded in mist, their occupants lost in sleep. It seemed no one else had stirred yet, and for now, they had this rare, tranquil moment to themselves. Perhaps they would linger here a little longer—long enough for him to savour this fleeting peace and steal a bit more rest while the world was still wrapped in the soft embrace of dawn.

The rest he so desperately craved wasn't going to come. An uneasy sensation ran down his spine, a familiar feeling of approaching danger that pulled him from the edge of rest. Alucard's gaze snapped to the wagon, where Freja was hunched over, her eyes wide with worry as she whispered to the figure within. He knew it was Danford in there—he could sense it. But then, in an instant, Freja's concern twisted into terror. Danford's voice erupted in a feral snarl, and before she could react, he lunged at her with a savagery that made her stumble back, a half-choked scream caught in her throat. Three of Zalith's people rushed to her side, desperately trying to drag her out of harm's way as Danford sprang from the wagon, his eyes blazing a furious red, his face contorted with a ravenous hunger. Alucard's chest tightened as he watched the scene unfold; he knew that look, he knew the madness that gripped Danford's pale, blood-starved face. And he knew with grim certainty that he was the only one who could stop it.

Two of Zalith's people launched themselves at Danford, each grabbing one of his arms as he thrashed and snarled, his eyes locked on Freja with a desperate, wild fury. The third man managed to pull her back, but even three men weren't enough to restrain Danford's frenzied strength. With a guttural roar, Danford ripped free of their grip, tossing the two men aside like they were nothing. He lunged at Freja again, his fingers nearly grazing her—when Alucard sprang forward, slamming into Danford mid-leap, their bodies crashing to the ground in a chaotic tangle. Freja's scream pierced the air as they rolled across the dirt, limbs locked in a violent struggle.

Danford was on his feet in an instant, his rage undeterred, and he bared his teeth in a savage snarl, ready to attack again. Zalith joined the commotion, stepping in front of Freja, his stance unyielding, but Danford's bloodlust drove him to lunge once more. Alucard moved with lightning speed, pouncing onto Danford's back before he could reach her, driving him face-first into the grass. He pinned Danford down, his grip unrelenting, as the blood-starved vampire-wolf thrashed beneath him. Alucard's muscles strained to hold him there, knowing that one slip could mean disaster for them all.

"Don't hurt him!" Freja cried. "It's not his fault!"

Of course, Alucard knew it wasn't his fault. Danford had been infected with vampirism, and obviously, he survived the process. Now, he was a Fledgeling, and since there was no brood nurse here, Alucard was going to have to take care of Danford himself.... What a misfortunate turn of events. Danford was the last person he wanted to be responsible for…but he had no choice. If he didn't take care of him, he'd die, and he didn't want to doom Freja and her child to a life without a father and mate.

Losing a mate…that was a pain Alucard had almost been burdened with.

Alucard glared down at Danford as he struggled, snarled, and tried so very desperately to escape his grip. The vampire held him down, keeping his left foot on his back and one hand on his head; Alucard snarled before looking over at Zalith, who still stood in front of Freja in case Danford somehow broke free. "*'E vill need blood soon,*" he said into his mate's mind. "*If 'e zoesn't get, 'e vill die.*"

Zalith nodded and then looked at one of his people. Alucard watched as the man Zalith nodded at wandered off and soon returned with a human Alucard had never seen before. Had Zalith sent people to gather humans last night? Probably. The man made his way over to Alucard, holding the terrified human with his hands behind his back.

Alucard wouldn't speak to anyone but Zalith right now…he wasn't going to open up his mind to any other demon. So he looked at his mate. "*Tell 'im to leave 'im 'ere, and zhen everyvone should move avay bevore I let 'im go,*" he said, glancing down at Danford, who was still struggling to get away.

The demon nodded. "Let him go," he said, looking at the man holding the human. "Give him some space," he then said, backing away from Alucard and Danford.

Everyone did as they were told. As the man forced the human to the ground, he let go of him and backed off with everyone else. Alucard then glared down at Danford, waiting for him to switch his focus to the subdued human to the right, but he didn't take his eyes off Freja. Growing impatient, Alucard snarled and slashed his claws over the human's arm—*that* immediately caught Danford's attention; he sharply turned his head, setting his eyes on the whimpering human, and then Alucard let go, letting Danford swiftly turn around and grab hold of the man. As Danford sunk his new fangs into the man's neck, Alucard rolled his eyes and backed off a little.

At least *that* was over…for now. Danford would remain a Fledgeling for a while, and it would take weeks for Alucard to teach him how to control his cravings and sate his hunger without killing his victims. It was a lot of work, and Alucard didn't want to have to do it—Fledgelings were one thing, but *hybrids*? He'd only ever created one other in his life, and it ended very swiftly with the Fledgeling's death—but…he'd do what he had to to keep Danford alive for the sake of Freja and her unborn child.

"*You should keep somevone close to 'im all zhe time,*" Alucard said into Zalith's mind. "*Zhis vill calm 'im down vor now, but… 'e vill get 'ungry again.*"

Zalith nodded, looking over at Greymore. "Make sure someone's keeping an eye on him at all times," he said, and as Greymore nodded, Zalith looked back over at Alucard.

Alucard didn't want to spend a moment longer than he had to with Danford—if he weren't part wolf, it would be different; Alucard would care more. But he disliked werewolves *and* that man too much to give him the attention he would a normal

Fledgeling—so as Greymore and two of his packmates moved closer, Alucard left Danford's side, making his way over to Zalith. The demon then followed him as he led the way back to the tree they'd been sitting under; Zalith sat back down, and as he made himself comfortable, Alucard rested his head in the demon's lap once more.

Rest wasn't the first thing to come to mind, however. He'd just seen that Zalith had most likely sent his people to gather some humans last night, and he assumed that he must have gathered enough for Alucard to use to regain his human body. He knew how meticulous and organized Zalith was, and he was also certain that he wanted Alucard back in his usual form so that they could embrace one another again. Alucard wasn't going to lie...he craved Zalith's touch now more than ever, and being stuck the way he was...it just didn't feel the same. He wanted to feel Zalith's skin against his own...and to feel that, he needed his body back.

He looked up at Zalith and spoke into his mind, "*'Ow many 'umans did you get zhem to bring 'ere?*"

"Ten," Zalith said, confirming that he had in fact made sure to have as many humans as Alucard needed.

"*I could...kill zhem all now...and get my body back.*"

The demon nodded, but then an unseemly smile crept across his face. "Are you going to be naked?"

Alucard deadpanned. "*Yes...*" he grumbled. "*And zhat is vhy you are going to look avay vhen I transvorm,*" he sneered. He then glanced over at Danford as he was pulled to his feet by Greymore and his men. As Freja helped him back into the wagon, Alucard sighed and rested his head back in Zalith's lap. "*I vill also 'ave to 'elp Danvord,*" he grumbled in discontent.

"What if I just take a little peek?" Zalith asked with a smile, disregarding the rest of Alucard's response.

He scowled up at him, unimpressed. "*You 'ave seen me naked countless times.*"

"So that means it's no big deal if I see you naked just one more time."

Alucard sighed, glaring ahead. "*I zon't care if you see me naked,*" he muttered. "*But I zon't vant you to look at me vhen I transvorm zhis body into my 'uman vone—zhe process is revolting,*" he mumbled.

"I want to watch," he insisted.

"*No,*" Alucard grumbled.

"Please?" Zalith asked sadly.

The vampire began to feel uncomfortable thinking about what he'd have to go through. "*Do you veally vant to vatch my body tearing itselv apart? I zon't vant you to see zhat.*"

"I just want to watch and make sure you're going to be okay," he said sullenly, caressing the vampire's head.

"*I'll be vine,*" he muttered... although he remembered how much it had hurt him the first time he'd created his human body, and he was certain that it wasn't going to be any less painful this time. But it had to be done.

"Are you sure?" Zalith asked.

"*Yes,*" Alucard said, looking up at him. "*But... you can still be zhere, just... zon't look at me,*" he said. As much as he didn't want Zalith to see, he also didn't want to be alone once he'd regained his body; he'd need help, and Zalith was the only one he wanted it from.

"Okay," the demon agreed.

Alucard then relaxed. For a moment, he'd rest, and then he'd devour the humans. He wasn't looking forward to the pain, but it would be over swiftly, and he'd finally be back on his own two feet. His *human* feet.

Chapter Sixty-Five

Infected Memories

| Alucard |

The camp was beginning to wake, and Alucard slowly escaped the tight grip of his fatigue. Danford's outburst had disturbed many of Zalith's people, so they were already up and packing, and to Alucard's relief, the Fledgeling hybrid was calm in the wagon with Freja. For now, at least.

He looked up at Zalith and spoke into his mind, "*Vhen should ve start moving?*"

"After you've had your snack," Zalith said with a smirk.

"*Vhat snack?*" Alucard asked with a frown.

"At least *one* of the humans you need to eat."

The vampire sighed, resting his head back in Zalith's lap. Despite wanting his human body back, he didn't feel like devouring anyone right now…but he had to. The sooner he killed them, the sooner he'd be back to his completely normal self. "*Vine,*" he grumbled.

Zalith smiled contently.

"*Vhere are zhey?*"

"I had one of Greymore's guys keep them by the horses," Zalith said, looking back over his shoulder.

Alucard sighed again, slowly pulling himself to his feet. "*I guess I should get zhis over vith,*" he grumbled, starting to drag himself over to where the horses were.

"I'll join you in a moment," Zalith called.

The vampire stopped walking and looked back at him. He watched him step behind the tree, and when he heard him unbutton his trousers, he continued towards the horses. Just like he didn't want Zalith watching his body tear itself apart, he was sure that his mate didn't want him watching him take a piss. He'd give him his privacy.

He reached the horses, and tied by one of the wagons were nine humans. With a savage snarl, Alucard snatched one of the whimpering men from the group with his jaws and dragged him into the cover of the tree line, catching a glimpse of Zalith watching not far away. He stopped when no one was in sight, and he desperately tore into the screaming man, ripping his flesh and gulping down his blood as he devoured his life force. He felt more of his strength returning, and he allowed himself to groan in relief. And when the man's wails died down, and the human took his last breath, Alucard tore only a few more times before backing away from the corpse.

With a satisfied snarl, he licked his maw, shook his body, and headed for the tree line. When he emerged into the camp, he set his sights on Zalith, who smiled and pulled off his shirt. Once Alucard reached him, the demon used his shirt to wipe the blood from his face, and then he threw it atop a pile of old blankets and dirtied clothes.

"I have a question," Zalith then said with a smirk as Alucard used his ethos to pull him a new shirt from his vault.

"*Vhat*?" the vampire asked, watching him pull his new black shirt on.

Zalith laughed slightly but with a curious frown. "What does it taste like?" he asked, nodding over at what was visible of the dead man left in the woods.

Alucard grunted irritably and started leading the way back over to the tree they had been sitting under. "*Disgusting*," he grumbled.

Amused, Zalith laughed quietly and followed behind him. When they reached the tree, the demon didn't sit down. "Alucard," he said, watching him as he sat down.

"*Vhat*?"

"I need to alter the memories of your new friends," he said, and as Alucard scowled irritably, he chuckled amusedly. "Your new demons," he corrected himself. "I need to remove anything that might be problematic for us. I want to remove any recollection they have of working for Ysmay, and I also want to see if any of them possess knowledge useful to us—Orin and I will do it, but I imagine I'd need you to ask them to let me do what I have to do…they don't seem very fond of me."

Alucard glanced at the demon whom he'd elected as his new pack's second-in-command. He felt a little conflicted for a moment…and he was sure his demon instincts were starting to kick in, just as they had when Tyrus had refused to listen to him. Zalith's demons didn't see him as their Alpha, and clearly, these new demons he'd not long taken from Ysmay didn't see Zalith as *their* Alpha. Alucard shifted his sights to Zalith; he and Zalith might be mated…but they weren't *united*, *bonded*; if they were, Tyrus might have listened to him, and *his* demons would listen to Zalith. Having two different packs of demons so close to one another…was that going to cause tension?

He sighed and glared at his new demons, all of whom were waiting not too far away. "*I zon't know vhat to do vith zhem,*" he admitted. "*I zidn't exactly…plan to 'ave a pack of zemons vollow me avound—I'm surprised zhey even chose to vollow me. I'm a disgrace, no?*" he asked with false amusement as he glanced at his wingless back.

"You're not a disgrace, Alucard," Zalith said sternly. "They obviously see that wings are not a measurement of someone's power and worth. You defeated their Alpha, and that's all that matters."

"*Maybe,*" he muttered. "*Or per'aps zhey vere glad vor zhe chance to get avay vrom Ysmay—I can't imagine she tveated zhem very vell,*" he suggested. "*Anyvay, I vill tell zhem to listen to you.*"

The demon moved closer, placed his hand on the side of Alucard's face, and kissed his forehead. "Thank you."

With a quiet sigh, Alucard then led the way over to where his demons were waiting, and as they saw him approach, they all turned to face him, waiting.

Alucard stopped in front of the woman he'd put in charge; he was reluctant to open his mind to these demons; however, not only were they utterly loyal to him and understood that invading his privacy would mean their deaths, but it was also the only way he could give the order. "*Zaliv needs to erase Ysmay vrom your minds; let 'im do vhat 'e must, and do vhat 'e says,*" he told them tiredly as Zalith called Orin over. "*And Orin, too,*" he added.

A few of the demons glanced unsurely at one another, but not one questioned him. They all nodded, setting their eyes on Zalith and Orin.

"*You can do vhatever,*" Alucard then said to Zalith. "*I vill just…sit over zhere,*" he said, looking over at a nearby tree.

"Okay," the demon said with a smile.

As Zalith then moved closer to Alucard's pack, the vampire dragged himself over to the tree and slumped down.

Exhaling deeply, Alucard lay on his side, resting his head in the grass. He didn't know what to do with himself while Zalith worked on altering the memories of the new demons. He could continue to remove Lucifer's infection…but that would require him to use his ethos, and he needed to save as much of that as he could so that he could regain his human body sooner rather than later.

But what if the infection spread? What if Lucifer began invading more of his memories, distorting his past and turning his beloved moments into horrific, terrifying nightmares?

Alucard sighed, closing his eyes. He had to face and remove Lucifer's remnants; he wouldn't take the risk of leaving it too long. He didn't have anything else to do right now, and any ethos he used up, he'd just take from another human. So, as he lay there, he concentrated, searching for traces of his father….

He dreamed. He remembered when he and Zalith were leaving for Avalmoor; they were sitting at a small table atop his galleon's quarterdeck, asking one another questions to get to know each other better. But Alucard's eyes quickly shifted from Zalith to who was standing right behind him…so close that he was sure that Zalith would feel his breath upon his neck if he had actually been there. Lucifer... grinning at Alucard, his crimson eyes staring right into his own. He was closer this time than he had been in the memory before... and Alucard hoped that meant he was getting closer to ridding Lucifer from his mind.

Alucard took his eyes off Lucifer, staring at Zalith, focusing on recalling everything about this memory. And it wasn't hard. He told Zalith that he feared moths; the embarrassment he felt sitting there explaining to him how a moth had flown into his mouth when he was a child, leaving him with a crippling fear. It was stupid, but it was the truth—he felt like he feared moths more in this moment than he feared Lucifer, and that thought alone helped him banish his father's presence.

And he didn't falter moving on to his next infected memory. Zalith and he had stopped in Refroidir; they'd booked a room at an inn... they'd pretty much argued about who got to pay for the stay. But as he turned to hand his money to the inn's owner, his eyes instantly met with Lucifer's—he stood there... barely five feet away, that same maniacal grin on his face.

For a moment, Alucard froze... he felt his heart beat a little faster. Fear? No, he wasn't afraid of him. He was startled... to see him so close; but he set his eyes back on the inn's owner, focusing on her, and once he was handed the room's keys, he set his eyes back on Zalith. And as he focused on his mate, any startle he felt in feat of Lucifer withered, and he followed Zalith into the dark, leaving his now recovered memory of Refroidir.

But he wasn't done. He woke from a restless sleep within the room of his and Zalith's home... a home they'd not get to return to. It brought sadness to his heart; how he yearned to return to the place he and Zalith spent so many wonderful moments. It was the first place that had ever felt like home... the first place he felt so comfortable. Their bed... so familiar, but something was wrong... he remembered.

He didn't want to roll over. He knew what he was going to feel... what he wasn't going to see. But he had to live through his memory, he had to remove the infection, and surely, he rolled over—but fear struck his heart as his eyes met with those of his father—where he should have found a bed empty of Zalith, he found his father lying beside him, a haunting smile on his pale face.

Alucard wanted to move—he wanted to back off, but he couldn't. He felt... paralyzed. In his memory, he hadn't moved, so in his recollection, he couldn't move either. He had no choice but to lay there and stare into his father's eyes. And the longer he remained there, the faster his heart raced, the deeper his fear burrowed into him, and as Lucifer's smile became a grin, his eyes widened in trepidation—

Alucard inhaled sharply, the world around him fading and abruptly reforming the last infected memory. Yule... he sat there... beside the tree, surrounded by opened and unopened gifts; Varana was sitting on a couch not too far away, and Zalith was sitting beside him unwrapping something.

Lucifer wasn't anywhere Alucard could currently see. He sat there, watching as Zalith leaned over and kissed him in thanks for the two rings he got him. Alucard's heart was racing; his angst was holding him so tightly… and he felt as though he was trembling, waiting for the moment he'd see his father's face.

As each second passed, he felt his heart thump a little faster; he felt so anxious… where was he? He watched as Zalith got up, leaving the room—Alucard wanted to tell him not to leave, but… that wasn't how it happened. He couldn't do anything that hadn't happened before—he couldn't alter his memory. He had to live through it… he had to remember it.

But it felt wrong—the longer he waited for Zalith… the gloomier the room became, the colder he felt, and the more intense his angst became. He waited… the walls around him began to tremble, the floor began to swerve, and the world in which he sat started to disorientate. Everything around him swiftly melted into something disfigured—blacks, whites, and greys sapped away the colour; the candlelight became black, the sky outside blood red, and Varana crumbled into ash, every sign of life around him withering.

A whisper—a faint, icy breath—slithered down Alucard's spine, settling into a suffocating chill that tightened around him like a vice. He sat frozen, his muscles locked in place, his voice trapped in his throat, unable to utter even a gasp. His senses twisted, the familiar world around him warping into something unknown and hostile. His eyes flicked to the mirror above the fireplace, its surface warping slightly as though reflecting not just light but something far darker. It showed the ceiling, and there—hanging from it with claws sunk deep into the marble—a twisted creature loomed directly above him.

Its form was grotesque, like a shadow peeled from the abyss, its skin blistered and rotted, raw patches revealing sinew beneath. Alucard's breath caught in his chest as the creature's eyes met his—a pair of hollow voids, black as endless night, filled with a malice that seemed to see straight through him. It let out a low, guttural snarl, a hiss that echoed in the silence like a taunt, and then it twisted its lips into a smile—a grin too wide, too sharp, as if mocking his helplessness. Alucard's mind reeled, disorientation swallowing him whole, the world spinning off its axis as he remained trapped in place, engulfed by the cold, unblinking gaze of the nightmare above.

What was he seeing? He didn't remember this—this hadn't happened. Zalith had brought him a kitten—Peaches… but this… the world around him was black, miserable, and enthralled with suffering. There was no sign of Zalith. And Lucifer… Alucard so suddenly felt a freezing cold hand creep over his shoulder, gripping his skin tightly—Alucard sharply turned his head to his right, his eyes instantly meeting with those so blood-red, and as a grin crept across Lucifer's face, Alucard had no words to explain what he felt—his eyes widened in horror, every instinct within him screaming at him to run—but where could he go?

"*Caedis*," Lucifer breathed, his voice a distant echo despite the fact that he was right in front of him…and he gripped harder, digging his ice-cold claws into Alucard's shoulder. "*Did you really think it would be so easy?*"

And before Alucard could understand, Lucifer widened his jaws and lunged forward—

Alucard opened his eyes, jumping to his feet, backing off as he looked around in utter startle—the trees, the people not too far away preparing to leave….

"Alucard?" came Zalith's concerned voice. "Are you okay?"

He sharply turned his head, looking over at Zalith as he hurried over.

Frowning, he glanced around again. He wasn't within his mind anymore, there was no sign of Lucifer…and Zalith was here. He set his gaze on the demon when he reached him, placing his hand on the side of his face. "*Vhat?*" he asked, the only word he could speak.

"Were you having a nightmare?" Zalith asked quietly.

"*No, I…*" he paused and frowned, trying to calm down. "*Vell…maybe,*" he said confusedly. "*I'm vine.*"

"Are you sure?"

Alucard nodded. "*Are you done vith zhem?*" he asked, glancing over at the demons.

"Not yet," Zalith said. "There's a lot of information to go through."

"*Is zhere…anyving you vant me to do?*" he offered—but what *could* he do? He wasn't willing to use that kind of mind manipulation. The mere idea of it made him nauseous.

"I don't think so," his mate said. "But thank you for asking."

Alucard sighed, resting back down on the grass. "*I vill just…be 'ere,*" he mumbled.

Zalith nodded. "I'll just be over there, okay?"

"*Okay.*"

"Call me if you need anything."

The vampire looked up at him; his mate's affection was already healing the lingering fear that came from his nightmare…or whatever that was. "*I vill,*" he replied.

Zalith smiled, and then he turned around and returned to Orin and the new demons.

Alucard relaxed, though he didn't close his eyes. He wasn't entirely sure if he'd removed Lucifer's infection, but he wasn't ready to jump back in. He'd seen enough of his father's haunting face for now.

| Zalith |

Finished altering the mind of one demon, Zalith prepared to start with the next. He placed his fingers upon the man's face, beginning to change the memories he had of ever working for Ysmay. At the same time, he searched for anything that might be useful to them, but this man knew no more than the man before him.

Maybe Ysmay never told her subordinates anything—perhaps she kept them in the dark for a reason such as this. But then again, Ysmay was arrogant; she would have never thought somebody would challenge her and live to tell the tale. She had obviously underestimated Alucard…and she probably had no idea he'd refuse to stay dead, too.

Zalith sighed, shoving aside the demon in front of him as he finished altering his mind. He didn't want to think about what happened back there; he just wanted to focus on the fact that Alucard was there with him.

With a worrisome frown, he looked back over his shoulder, watching as Alucard shuffled around and curled up like a cat, staring at the camp like a watchful predator on guard. Peaches went to join him, and as Alucard welcomed his kitten to sleep beside him, Zalith smiled. He couldn't let himself become distracted, though. As much as he wanted to stare at and admire his vampire, he had work to do.

The woman Alucard had chosen to replace Amos was next. She stood in front of Zalith with a condescending expression. Zalith didn't care. He placed his fingers on her face, entering her mind. What he found, however, wasn't what he had been expecting. This woman wasn't just some demon—he shouldn't be surprised, though. Ysmay was a Matriarch, so of course, she would have created offspring—and this woman was one such thing. Ysmay's ethos-crafted daughter…one of three.

That didn't matter. Despite Ysmay being her mother, this woman seemed to follow demon laws just like any other demon, so it didn't really matter who she was. She must have some useful information, though—and she *did.* She revealed to Zalith that Ysmay had in fact been put in command of the Diabolus, Lucifer's cult and the very same people who had been hunting Alucard all his life. *And* the Diabolus were in possession of Lucifer's Obcasus, the knife needed to comatose him. Not only did Ysmay possess that weapon, but she also had a Pandorican…a prison that could hold a Numen. How she had come to obtain these items, this woman didn't know, but what she had revealed to Zalith was already so very useful.

Finally, Zalith now knew where Ysmay and Varana were…quite possibly. The Diabolus often converged in one same place—a fort hidden within the mountains of Odessius, an island far out across the seas, a place no one wanted to go. Zalith had never heard of Odessius; Varana had never mentioned it, neither had Alucard, but knowing that

Varana and Ysmay might be there… he had to know more, and he'd ask Alucard once he was done here.

Finished altering her memory, he let the woman go and moved on to the next. There were still a lot of demons to get through, and as tiring as it was, Zalith was glad to have already obtained the information he had.

| Alucard |

Alucard watched as Zalith moved on to the next demon. He wasn't sure how long it had been, or how long it would take… he just wished he could help.

He sighed, resting his head on the grass. He stared at the camp, observing as Zalith's people continued packing everything away, preparing to leave when the time came. Alucard felt as though he should do something, but… what could he do? He was stuck in this ridiculous body looking like the offspring of a gecko and a cat. What could he possibly do? Nothing needed killing… nothing needed tearing apart, so… all he could do was lay there and wait to be told it was time to go.

With an irritated scowl, he looked down at Peaches, watching her as she cleaned her paws. Then, his eyes wandered over to the wagon where the humans were still sitting, tied up and whimpering. Maybe he should just go over there and kill them all now… get his human body back… then he'd be able to do something useful. But the thought of gorging on so many humans at once made him feel sick. That was a lot of ethos to process; he was sure it would leave him feeling every kind of revolted and sick, so he wouldn't do that. But one or two… he could manage it.

Taking his eyes off the humans, he looked over at Zalith. He was certain that the demon would want to come with him—Zalith had become so protective, and there was no question as to why. Alucard would feel the exact same way if it had been Zalith who had died right in front of him. But if he went over there and Zalith followed, it would only make Zalith's work take even longer. He felt conflicted… but then again, it wouldn't take long for him to just go over there and kill one or two of them, would it?

He pulled himself to his feet and made his way over to Zalith, who stopped what he was doing to look back at him. "*I vant to… go and kill vone or two more of zhem,*" he said, nodding over at the humans.

Zalith let go of the man whose mind he was working on. "Okay," he said. "I'm coming with you." And as Alucard started to make his way over to where the humans were, Zalith followed.

Alucard felt no need to falter. He set his eyes on the human closest to him as he reached the wagon, snarled irritably, and lunged forward, sinking his teeth into the man's leg. He dragged him away from the horrified crowd, their muffled screams breaking the silence that had once gripped the camp; Alucard pulled him away and behind a tree, and he didn't waste time. He started devouring him as Zalith leaned back against a nearby boulder, watching.

He felt his fatigue wane a little more as he consumed the man's blood, his flesh, and everything that made him human. To think that he'd have to do this seven more times—he just wanted to be himself again. He hated everything about his true body, and the fact that he had no wings only made him feel all the more ridiculous. Maybe he didn't have to wait until he'd eaten enough humans… maybe he could devour a few more and create himself a human body as best he could. He'd rather that than spend the next few days stuck like this. But what if it went wrong? What if he didn't gather enough ethos and ended up looking like a centaur-lizard-man? He shuddered at the thought. He didn't want that, and he didn't want Zalith to see that.

With an irritated snarl, he pulled his fangs from the withered body of the man he'd been consuming. How many more? He didn't have enough yet, and he was tired of waiting. He sharply turned his head, setting his eyes on another human; Zalith moved closer to him to wipe down his face, but he wasn't done yet. He prowled past Zalith, approaching the group of terrified humans, and he snatched the leg of another, dragging him over to where Zalith was waiting. He started to savagely tear at his body, but just a few moments into consuming his blood, Alucard began to feel nauseous. Trying to rush it really wasn't a good idea unless he wanted to throw up… and he didn't want to do that.

But he soldiered on… consuming the fourth man's blood and life force until he was but an empty husk. And as he lifted his head to glare over at the wagon, he thought… just one more? No… he felt so disgusted. So much blood… as alleviating as it was to his exhausted body, it made him feel sick. Human blood… after years of drinking only Zalith's, human blood tasted something insulting. He'd rather not force himself to consume another drop. He was done for now—until his body could stomach another.

He turned around with an aggravated snarl, setting his eyes on Zalith, who made his way over with the shirt he had earlier used to clean his face, and he used it to do so once again.

"*Did you vind out anyving vrom zhem?*" Alucard asked as Zalith threw away the shirt.

"That woman," he said, glancing back at the woman Alucard had replaced Amos with. "She's Ysmay's child. Ysmay has also been put in command of the Diabolus, and she possesses Lucifer's Obcasus as well as a Pandorican. It is also quite possible that Ysmay and Varana have retreated to a Diabolus hideout on Odessius."

Staring at him, Alucard frowned. Ysmay and the Diabolus had a Pandorican? "*Ve need zhat Pandorican,*" he said without thought. "*Vith zhat, ve can seal Liliv avay vor good.*"

Zalith nodded in agreement, walking at Alucard's side as the vampire started to make his way back over to the tree he'd been resting under. "Agreed, but we'll discuss everything later once I'm finished with all of them," he said, looking over at the demons.

Alucard stopped by the tree and sighed. "*Okay,*" he said. "*Tell me if you need anyving,*" he said, sitting down.

The demon smiled and kissed the side of his face. Then, he made his way back over to Orin, leaving Alucard to rest once again.

Chapter Sixty-Six

Red

| Alucard |

Sunflowers as red as blood stretched as far as Alucard's eyes could see. Two suns—one as blue as ice, and another as red as his own fire brightened up the gloomy, grey sky. Birds flew overhead, cawing something agonizing as rain began trickling down onto his face.

What was this place? He looked back over his shoulder, but the field in which he stood seemed endless. There was no sign of Zalith, and that made him feel anxious. He didn't know this place, there wasn't anyone here, and he had no idea what might happen. But an unsettlingly cold breeze soon rushed past, and as it hit Alucard's skin, he scowled and turned away—only for his eyes to meet those of a familiar face.

The small girl stared up at him, her strawberry-blonde hair floating gracefully in the breeze that had chosen to scorn him. Alucard knew her as the girl who appeared in his dreams roughly a year ago as his and Zalith's daughter. Was that who she was?

She lifted her hands, holding a black cube in her palms, each of its faces decorated with runes and carvings not unrecognizable to Alucard. She didn't speak... and as he took his eyes off her face, he realized that what she was holding was none other than a Pandorican.

Why?

"This is for you," she said, a vacant stare on her face.

"What?" he frowned.

The girl moved closer, reaching up onto her tiptoes. "I found it for you, Papa," she said with a smile, handing him the Pandorican.

Confounded, Alucard looked down at the cube in his hand as he took it from her, and then he set his eyes back on the girl.

"Do you like it?" she asked. "I came all this way to get it for you—and for Daddy."

Alucard's frown thickened.

"You're confused," the girl giggled. "You always make that face when you're confused."

"I... vhy do you 'ave zhis?" he asked, looking down at the Pandorican in his hand.

"You and Daddy sent me to get it," she said proudly. "It was too far away for you—you and Daddy are always so busy," she said with a pout.

"Ve are...." He paused and glanced around. "Vhere are ve?"

"Tengetso," she answered. "How did you not know?"

The vampire looked around again—how did he not know? Those two suns—he had seen them every day for ten years straight, but... that which was blue looked a little closer than what he remembered—bigger, maybe.

"You and Daddy will be okay," she told him, snapping his attention back to her. "And when you wake up, I know you will know what to do," she said, nodding.

"Vhat... to do?" he asked.

"I got this for you," she said, tapping the Pandorican with her hand. "You needed it."

The rain on Alucard's face began to freeze, and as a harsh breeze raced past him once more, the girl in front of him faded away like smoke on water. He felt something painful strike his heart as he reached out to grab her, but in his hand, he still held the Pandorican. None of this made sense—why had he seen this girl again, and why had she handed him a Pandorican? Was it because he hadn't long been told that Ysmay had one and he wanted it so that they could seal Lilith away? Was this his subconscious telling him that it was what he needed to do?

He stood there, staring down at the Pandorican... but as the rain fell harder and colder, the world around him started to slip away....

Alucard opened his eyes, the sound of rain hitting the leaves of the tree above echoing around him. The mumbles of Zalith's people came from the camp just ahead, and beside him...Zalith. Alucard only just came to realize that his head was in the demon's lap—Zalith must have moved him when he came and sat beside him, but Alucard didn't recall that happening. He was so tired.

He stared up at Zalith; the demon looked exhausted, resting with his back against the tree, his eyes closed. Was he sleeping? Alucard hoped so. Zalith hadn't slept in more than twenty-four hours...and he couldn't help him regain his energy like this, could he? He couldn't kiss him, let alone do anything that would help Zalith feel better.

But the demon soon opened his eyes, exhaling a tired sigh as he looked down at Alucard and smiled. "Hey," he said quietly.

"*Good morning,*" Alucard said with a smirk—although he was sure that Zalith couldn't see the expression on his face.

"How are you feeling?" the demon asked.

Alucard exhaled deeply as the rain managed to break through the leaves above and started splashing onto his face. "*I veel okay,*" he said. "*Vhat about you?*"

"I'm okay too," his mate said, placing his hand on the side of Alucard's face.

"*I saw zhat girl again,*" Alucard said, resting his head back in Zalith's lap. "*Our daughter,*" he mumbled.

"In a dream?"

"*Yes. She… gave me someving, but I can't vemember vhat.*"

"Where were you?" Zalith asked, caressing Alucard's head.

Trying to recall his dream, Alucard frowned. "*I vink… ve vere in a vield.*"

"Do you remember what you were doing?"

He thought to himself, struggling to recall his dream. "*I vink… she said she 'ad someving vor me—a Pandorican.*"

The demon smiled slightly. "She's very talented then. She must get that from you."

Alucard shook his head, sighing deeply as the rain continued to trickle down his face. "*No, she vould get zhat vrom you,*" he said, shuffling back a little so that the rain wasn't seeping through the leaves and falling on him—and the mention of a Pandorican… he remembered that he hadn't long told Zalith that he would contact Soren, who might be able to help them locate not only the Pandoricans but the Obcasus', too… those that the Diabolus weren't in the possession of, anyway. He'd bring that up later.

Zalith laughed quietly. "Maybe she got it from the both of us," he said, and then he kissed the side of Alucard's face.

With a quiet, tired huff, Alucard looked over to where his new demons had been, seeing that they were all sitting or leaning against trees, keeping a close eye on him and Zalith. "*Did you get done vith zhem?*" he asked, looking up at Zalith.

"I did," the demon confirmed.

"*Did you vind out anyving else?*"

"Nothing more than what I already told you. Ysmay's daughter seemed to know more than anyone else."

Nodding, Alucard set his sights on the camp. "*So… ve vill leave soon?*"

"We may as well; there isn't really anything else left to do," Zalith said.

"*Everyvone looks veady to go,*" Alucard muttered.

Sighing, Zalith nodded and started to get up. "We best get moving before it gets dark. Wait here, though; I'll make sure everyone's ready. I don't want you wasting any energy."

Alucard nodded and remained where he was, watching as Zalith walked towards his people. The confusion of his dream still remained, and he was certain that it meant *something.* He just needed to decide what.

| Zalith |

The demon headed for the camp, but before he got very far at all, Camael rushed over to him, having been waiting not too far from the wagon. Why was he *still* here? Zalith had been so preoccupied that he'd pretty much forgotten that he'd stuck around.

"Zalith," the angel called, waving his hand above his head as he hurried to catch up with him. "I've been waiting for a moment to talk to you—to both of you, actually," he said, looking over at Alucard, who was prowling towards them. "I'm not just here to make sure you get that crystal to Magnus," he said. "We barely made it out back there—

"*'E told me 'e vas just sticking avound to observe; 'e zidn't mention zhe Lumendatt,*" Alucard told Zalith, speaking into his mind.

Zalith's skepticism grew exponentially.

"—If I knew more about what the plan is here, maybe I could be more useful—I'm here to help," Camael said.

With an aggravated scowl, Zalith replied, "You've been useful thus far without knowing the plan; I'm sure you'll be okay."

"I could have done a whole lot more if I had known what we were up against. I might have even been able to stop Alucard from dying if I had known these people had deridiuz."

Zalith glared at Camael from the corner of his eye. He felt conflicted; he didn't like this guy at all…there was something suspicious about him. He had felt skeptical of Erich and anyone affiliated with him since he met Alucard; he was certain that Erich wanted something from Alucard just like the rest of the Numen, and that he might very well use people like Opus and Camael to try and get to him. Zalith wasn't going to let that happen; he didn't trust Camael, and he probably never would.

"We all learned that they had deridiuz at the same time," the demon said, making his way over to where his horse was as Alucard followed beside him—and Camael trailed them. "So what could you have done? Stopped time so that you could run along home to get something to help? Or better yet, you could have swung by Erich's place and got a few strings pulled so you could talk to Lucifer and see when his last shipment came in—wouldn't that have been something?"

Astonished, Camael scoffed. "For one, Erich has absolutely no contact with Lucifer whatsoever. And if I had known you were running from Lucifer's people in the first place, then maybe I would have known about the deridiuz before you—they've been using demons to harvest it out of hives for the past month," he revealed.

Annoyed, impatient, and tired, Zalith stopped once he reached his horse and scowled at the angel. "You know who Alucard is," he said, "so surely you must have known who we're running from, and yet you decided to keep that information to yourself. I don't know Camael, maybe we should be the ones asking *you* for more information," he said with a condescending, irritated smile. He did his best to keep back as much of his anger and irritation as he could; after all, Camael had helped and might be useful to him and Alucard, so he didn't want to bury any chance at some sort of relationship—but he also didn't want to share anything with him.

The angel sighed, holding up his hands. "All right, got it. I'll leave you alone," he muttered, backing off, and eventually walking away when he realized neither Zalith nor Alucard were going to say a word.

"*Vhy is 'e still 'ere*?" Alucard asked.

Making sure his horse's saddle was secure as Peaches pounced up onto it, Zalith sighed and rolled his eyes. "Because he's persistent."

"*Ve should just leave 'im 'ere*," the vampire grumbled. "*Tie 'im to a tree*."

The demon laughed, amused. "We should," he said, finishing with his horse, "but I wouldn't subject a tree to that; he's very annoying," he laughed—

"Hey," then came Danford's nervous voice.

Zalith frowned and turned around, setting his eyes on the now red-eyed, blonde-haired vampire-werewolf as he stood a few feet from them, staring curiously and wide-eyed at Alucard. What was he doing over here? Zalith frowned—was he attempting to hit on Alucard? That's what it seemed, but…Danford wouldn't do that in front of him, even if he wasn't petrified of Alucard. But fear wasn't what he was seeing right now.

"Uh…" Danford then drawled, his curious, wide-eyed stare becoming a confused frown.

Alucard rolled his eyes. "*All Vledgeling vampires come pining vor my attention,*" he told Zalith. And then he spoke to Danford, "*Vhat do you vant?*"

Zalith was admittedly intrigued. Why could he hear the telepathic conversation that Alucard was having with someone else? Was his vampire purposely allowing him to be a part of it?

With a nervous look on his pale face, Danford twiddled his thumbs together. "Uh…to say…thank you," he said with a flushed stare.

"*Vine, vhatever—go avay,*" Alucard muttered, taking his eyes off Danford to look over at his kitten, who was sitting on the saddle of Zalith's horse.

"Oh…okay, sorry," Danford murmured, slowly backing off. But he then stopped and looked at Zalith. "Oh, hey Zalith," he said, but the demon didn't respond, and so Danford set his eyes back on Alucard. "So…uh…Aleksei…what am I supposed to do now?"

Clearly aggravated, Alucard glanced at him. It looked like he was pondering, but the expression quickly disappeared from his face, and in its place sat a deadpan glare. "*Ve are leaving—make sure everyvone is veady,*" he said.

"Oh, yeah, no…not like…in general," Danford said, dragging his hand over the back of his neck, "but about the uh…vampire…thing—if that's even what it is," he said embarrassedly.

"*Noving,*" Alucard grumbled irritably. "*You live your life, you drvink blood vhen you need to—simple,*" he uttered—but then he sighed, that pondering expression flickering across his face. "*Vhen you veel zhe slightest bit 'ungry, you vill come to me, da?*"

"Are you…going to feed me?" he asked, flustered.

"Oh, my God," Zalith complained, rolling his eyes.

"*Vhat?*" Alucard snarled at Danford. "*No,*" he growled, sounding almost offended. "*You vill come to me so zhat you zon't try tearing your girlvriend's 'ead off again,*" he snapped. "*Idiot.*"

"O-oh," Danford stuttered, his face as red as it could get. "Thank you."

"Danford, I think it's time you went back to your girlfriend," Zalith then said before he could utter another word.

He nodded. "Yeah, okay," he said. "Thank you…and sorry," he mumbled. He then turned around and walked off, leaving them alone.

Alucard sighed as he slumped down onto the grass, and as a rumble of thunder echoed through the sky, he looked up at Zalith. "*Vhen ve next stop, I vill see if I can vinish gazzering zhe ethos I need to 'eal back my 'uman body. Zhen ve can 'ead vor zhe station vor zhe tvain—is okay?*"

"Of course that's okay," Zalith said, smiling down at him. Then, the demon mounted his horse and looked back at his people. "Let's go," he called.

As everyone started to make their way over, Alucard climbed to his feet and followed at Zalith's side as the demon led the way into the forest once more.

Chapter Sixty-Seven

Scales and Horns

| Zalith |

As the sun set over the horizon, and the rain stopped pouring, Zalith stared vacantly into the dark of the forest ahead, still leading the way. A few hours had passed, and the closest town was still six or so hours away. It was late, everyone had been walking for hours, and despite his eagerness to get out of Nefastus, he didn't want to exhaust everyone, least of all Alucard.

He shifted his gaze to his vampire. "How are you feeling?" he asked quietly.

Alucard glanced at him and spoke into his mind, "*I'm vine.*"

Zalith nodded and stared ahead again, gripping his horse's reins. "We'll stop just up ahead here. We'll rest for the night and reach the town tomorrow."

"*Okay,*" Alucard agreed.

Zalith's people began setting up camp when they reached a small glade in the woods, and as they did, Zalith took one of the tents from the wagon and started trying to set it up as Alucard slumped down in the grass under a nearby tree. But Zalith had no idea what he was doing.

"*Are you okay?*" Alucard asked amusedly.

The demon laughed a little as he tried to hide his irritancy. "Yes," he said, wrestling with the tent's strings and pegs.

Alucard continued watching for a short while—Zalith *did* manage to have the front half of the tent stand, but it soon caved in as he moved to fix the rest.

"Fuck," the demon muttered.

"*Are you sure you zon't vant 'elp?*" Alucard asked with a smirk, observing as Zalith dragged his hand over his face in frustration.

"From you?" Zalith asked with an amused smile. "You don't have thumbs," he smirked.

Scowling, Alucard scoffed. "*And yet, I could do a better job zhan you.*"

"That's not very nice," Zalith said as he fiddled with the tent's strings again.

"*Vell, neizer is laughing about my 'ands,*" he sneered, tapping his talons on the grass.

"I'm sorry," Zalith said with a smile as he finally started to get somewhere with the tent. "You know I love your cute little claws."

"*Zhey're not cute,*" Alucard grumbled, looking away.

Zalith smirked as he finished putting the tent up. "They're very cute—you're like a big kitty," he teased, smiling over his shoulder at him as he secured the last tent peg. "Like if Peaches grew fifty times her size and we left her out in the sun a little too long—"

"*I zon't look like zhat!*" he insisted, lifting his head from the grass to glare at him.

"You two look identical," Zalith taunted, sitting down in front of him.

Alucard scowled. "*Vell you look veird,*" he sneered.

The demon chuckled. "I look weird? Where?"

"*Your vace,*" Alucard snarled.

He laughed again. "Why do you always make me have sex with you lying on your back then?"

Clearly embarrassed, Alucard looked away. "*I prever to look avay vrom you,*" he uttered.

The demon scoffed amusedly. "I'll be sure to keep that in mind."

Alucard huffed and looked up at him as he rested his head on the grass again. "*Vill you sleep tonight?*" he asked worriedly, changing the subject.

"Probably," the demon mumbled.

The vampire then sighed deeply, glancing over at the wagon, where two of Zalith's people were securing what was left of the group of humans. "*I vink…I vill kill vone or two more of zhem, and zhen I should be able to 'eal my body back enough so zhat I zon't look like a lizard,*" he muttered.

"Have you eaten enough for it to work?" Zalith asked, looking down at him.

"*Vive should be enough. I just might 'ave some scales or vhatever 'ere and zhere like I did vhen you took care of me zhat vone time.*"

"Okay," Zalith said, placing his hand on Alucard's head. "As long as you're going to be okay, I'm happy."

Alucard nodded and made himself comfortable. "*I'm surprised zhis isn't veird vor you—to see me like zhis.*"

"You are who you are, and I love every version of you," Zalith said quietly, caressing his head. "You could shrink down to three inches tall and I'd carry you around on my shoulder all day," he teased.

Amused, Alucard laughed quietly. "*Vell, I zon't vink zhat's going to 'appen any time soon.*"

"You never know," Zalith said with a shrug.

"*Vhat vould you do if you turned into a lizard?*" he asked, smirking.

"I'd be very confused. Would you be a lizard at the same time in this scenario?"

"*Vhy?*" Alucard asked skeptically, looking up at him.

The demon laughed quietly. "I just want to know."

A little confused, Alucard frowned. "*Yes… I guess.*"

"Interesting," the demon pondered. How could he not think about him and Alucard having sex in their true forms? Well, his would-be true form if he were a Numen.

"*Vhat are you vinking?*" Alucard questioned, glancing up at him.

"Nothing," the demon told him, smiling.

Glaring at him, Alucard frowned and slowly rested his head back in the grass. "*I vill be glad to be vid of zhis vorm,*" he muttered.

"Well, you better go and eat then," the demon hummed, the idea of fucking Alucard quickly consuming his mind. He needed it, but he also craved it. But he couldn't let his primal thoughts take over. He had to focus and stay alert.

As Alucard climbed to his feet and made his way over to the wagon where the humans were tied, Zalith followed. He watched as the vampire snatched the leg of one of the horrified men, dragged him off into the trees, and began his feast, mercilessly devouring his fourth human.

Zalith leaned his shoulder against a tree, smiling while he observed; Alucard's true form fascinated him; among the other things it made him feel, the curiosity was the strongest emotion. Among the captivation, though, he felt tired, and he couldn't really focus on much but the fact that he might just be about to see Alucard back to normal again, and that made him feel relieved—no, relieved wasn't the right word; it didn't do the feeling justice. He loved Alucard no matter what he looked like, but he needed some familiarity, he wanted to touch and hold the man he loved, he wanted to kiss him and feel his body against his own; he couldn't really do any of that while Alucard was trapped in his true form.

He waited, watching as Alucard tore the man apart, devouring every inch of him. And then he snatched the fifth human, but instead of devouring him, Alucard simply sunk his teeth into the man's body and drained every ounce of his life force until he was but a husk. It all happened so fast—maybe Zalith's fatigue made it seem as though time was moving a lot faster than usual, but when he finally snapped out of his gaze, he set his eyes on Alucard, who made his way over to him.

The demon took off his shirt, using it to wipe the blood from Alucard's face.

"*I zon't vant you to see zhis,*" Alucard said to him.

As much as he wanted to observe, he'd give Alucard the privacy he asked for. "Okay," he said, caressing the side of his face. "I won't be far away. Tell me when you're ready."

Alucard nodded.

Zalith then turned around and left the tree line. But he wouldn't wander far. He'd stay within earshot, waiting, desperate to see the man he loved in his human form again. Any moment now….

| Alucard |

Alucard sighed deeply; as eager as he was to return to his human form, he wasn't looking forward to the pain that came with the transformation. But he had no choice but to go through it—he didn't want to spend a moment longer trapped the way he was. He might not have enough ethos to manifest a completely human-looking body, but he knew he had enough to get close.

With a shaky exhale, he closed his eyes and focused, summoning the life force and ethos of the humans he'd killed and stored within himself. The moment he called upon it, his body started to ache; the blood running through his veins felt like fire, and his bones started to feel like weights. He grimaced, trying his best not to utter a sound that might make Zalith run back into the trees—he didn't want his mate to see him like this.

He gritted his teeth, his heart racing as the armour on his drake-like body began to crumble away. His dark, scaled flesh tore and bled, and as his bones started cracking, breaking and reshaping, he grunted quietly in pain. But agony electrified through his changing body; his talons became his fingers, his paws became his hands—everything upon his true form crumbled, broke, and withered, and in its place, his human body began to reform. The blood that trickled to the floor turned to nothing, withering away, and after the stretching moments of pain that was almost unbearable, Alucard could finally…breathe.

And when he opened his eyes, he saw Zalith moving towards him. But the world was blurred, it was spinning, and Alucard became overwhelmed by disorientation. He fell, grunting painfully as pain spiralled through him—Zalith caught him in his arms before he hit the ground, but that only intensified the pain coursing through his tortured body.

"Alucard?" the demon asked desperately.

The vampire trembled in his arms; he felt Zalith place his hand on his naked chest, staring down at him as he struggled to keep his eyes open. The lingering pain was fading; he wished it would leave him faster.

"Are you okay?" Zalith insisted.

Alucard frowned, his once erratically beating heart calming, but he couldn't find his voice. So he nodded, closing his eyes as he exhaled deeply once more. He could feel his horns upon his head; when he glanced at himself, he saw that the claws on the ends of each of his fingers were black, and either side of his waist possessed small patches of dark scales. The ethos was enough; he was human-looking enough.

Zalith then leaned down, pressing his lips against Alucard's, and the vampire welcomed it. It felt as though it had been centuries since he'd last felt Zalith's lips against his own, and they didn't stop with just one kiss. How could they?

Alucard let himself sink into the moment. He could finally kiss Zalith, he could finally feel something. He lifted his trembling hand and placed it on the side of Zalith's neck; to feel the demon's skin against his own…he felt an ache in his heart. He felt as though he had been starved of his touch for far too long. No longer was Zalith's touch unfelt; Alucard could feel *everything*…maybe a little too much. His aching body…just lying there in Zalith's arms began to feel overbearing. It was like his senses were all so suddenly heightened—like a single touch of Zalith's hand to his bare skin would overwhelm him.

He moved his hand to the side of Zalith's face, stopping him from kissing him a moment longer—he needed a moment to breathe.

"How do you feel?" Zalith asked softly, lightly dragging his fingers down the side of Alucard's face.

The demon's touch sent pleasing shivers through Alucard's entire body—why did everything feel so intense? Perhaps it was because he'd only just reformed his body, and like a healing wound would, his body felt overly sensitive to even the slightest touch. And even the faintest breeze made him shiver as if he were freezing.

"I veel…cold," he replied, only just realizing that he was totally naked, and that surely brought an embarrassed look to his face.

"I'm warm," the demon said with a smile, pulling him closer.

Alucard smiled, moving his hand up and over Zalith's chest, lightly gripping his shoulder. Zalith *was* warm—the cold began to wither as he lay there in the demon's embrace, and if he wasn't so embarrassed about being naked, he might just lay there with him for a long while. He sat up, pulling himself a pair of trousers from his vault; he slipped into them and then rested back into Zalith's warm embrace, his once aching, trembling body starting to calm down.

Zalith held him tightly. "Are you okay?" he asked again. "Are you in pain?"

"No, I'm vine," Alucard insisted, looking up at him. "I just veel…I zon't know 'ow to explain; everyving veels…amplivied, maybe. Zoesn't 'urt, zhough," he explained, closing his eyes as he rested his head against Zalith's chest.

"Okay, good," he said quietly, resting his head on the side of Alucard's. "I missed my squishy little vampire," he muttered sadly.

"I missed you, too," Alucard mumbled, dragging his hand down from Zalith's shoulder and over his chest.

The demon laughed quietly. "But I was here the whole time."

"I know," Alucard said with a pout. "I mean…I missed veeling you. I zidn't veally veel anyving like zhis," he said, dragging his hand over his chest. "Everyving velt…muted."

Smiling, Zalith lightly dragged his fingers over the scars that his fangs had left on Alucard's neck years ago. He then leaned down, kissed Alucard's head, and relaxed for a moment, holding him.

Alucard felt content. To be in Zalith's embrace at last—he didn't want to leave, he didn't want to move. He just wanted to lay there in his mate's arms.

"You still smell good," the demon muttered, smiling down at him as he moved a strand of his hair from over his right eye.

The vampire buried his face in Zalith's chest, trying to hide his fluster. "Do I?" he mumbled.

"You do," the demon murmured.

Alucard smiled and moved his hand up to Zalith's shoulder again—but something devious came over him as he stared at the demon's right pec. Zalith wouldn't be expecting it…and he thought he might try to humour himself and Zalith after the past few days of stiffness and sadness. So, with a smirk on his face, he moved closer, and before Zalith could comprehend it, he lightly bit the demon's nipple.

Zalith flinched and uttered in startle, but then lightly grabbed Alucard's cheeks in his hand and lifted his face so that he'd look at him. "Ow," he grunted with a smirk and then laughed a little. "That's not very nice," he said, lightly squishing his cheeks in his hand.

Alucard frowned in embarrassment, but Zalith pulled him closer and kissed his lips.

"I feel like I haven't kissed you in a year," the demon then said sadly, letting go of Alucard's cheeks. He moved his hand to the side of his face and kissed him again, but this time, a whole lot more passionately. And Alucard kissed back, moving his hand to the side of Zalith's neck as they kissed for a long while.

But Zalith soon moved his kisses from Alucard's lips and to his neck, kissing down over his collarbone and his chest, gradually moving back up to his neck which he then nuzzled, wrapping his arms around him.

"I love you so much," the demon purred, holding him firmly.

"I love you, too," Alucard said contently, hugging him just as so.

"Don't leave me ever again, okay?" he pleaded quietly.

Alucard frowned in guilt and sorrow. "I von't," he said. "I'll be vith you vorever."

"Thank you," the demon mumbled, and then he started kissing him again.

Relief swiftly consumed Alucard. For the first time since Ysmay's attack, he felt a lot more like himself. He had his human body back, he could actually feel Zalith's touch—he had missed it so sorely—and each and every kiss they shared in this moment made Alucard feel all the more content. All he wanted to do was lay in Zalith's embrace…to listen to his beating heart and drift off to sleep beside him. But he'd not think about his fatigue yet. He wanted to enjoy this moment a little longer.

Zalith soon stopped, however, and pressed his forehead against Alucard's. He smiled, moving his hand to the top of his head, dragging his thumb over his left horn. "Can you help me finish setting up the tent?" he asked with what might be embarrassment. "Now that you have thumbs."

Alucard laughed quietly. "Okay, city boy," he teased, moving his hand to the side of Zalith's face—but as he caught a flicker of something red in the corner of his eye, he felt his heart stop.

He stared…a glimpse of a familiar face barely visible in the distance through the trees behind Zalith. A face with eyes so crimson, and hair so red. *Here*? *How*? Alucard tensed up, dread starting to fill his heart and soul as Lucifer lingered in the distance, a grin stretching across his face—

"My hero," Zalith laughed.

Taking his eyes off the figure in the distance, Alucard shifted his stare to Zalith's amused face. "Vhat?"

The demon chuckled. "Come on, let's get back," he said, standing up and pulling Alucard to his feet.

Alucard glanced past Zalith, searching the distance for what he'd seen, but there was nothing there. Had he been seeing things? Surely, he was just tired. He'd seen Lucifer so much these past few days that he was bound to think he'd see him again, right? He frowned…what if it meant something? Confliction warped him as he started following Zalith away and back towards where their tent was. He didn't want to panic Zalith over something that might not be anything…so he ignored it. Too much had happened recently…and he just wanted to rest and lay with Zalith.

But if he saw Lucifer again…*then* he'd say something.

Chapter Sixty-Eight

—⊰ ✝ ⊱—

Long-Awaited Embrace

| Zalith |

Zalith led the way towards the tent he'd tried putting up earlier, but it wasn't how he had left it. It looked as though someone had fixed it for him, and he suspected that Idina must have sent someone over to do so.

He sighed, glancing back over his shoulder at Alucard as he held his hand firmly. All he wanted to do was be with him; his vampire had almost died, he'd almost lost him forever, and that had him traumatized. Dread still lingered in his heart, the pain of loss still gripped him so tightly, and he didn't want to let Alucard go. But he still had so much to do; he still had to get everyone somewhere safe—he had to keep everyone safe…and he still had to do better. Right now, though…Alucard. He wanted to lie down with him, talk to him, listen to him…and just feel him with all his senses.

When they reached the tent, though, he heard Idina call his name—so he stopped, looking over at her, as did Alucard.

"I got you both some dinner," she said with a smile, stopping in front of them with two bowls of what looked to be stew. "Oh," she then said, setting her eyes on Alucard, "you're…you again."

"Thank you," Zalith said, taking the two bowls from her.

Idina nodded and then wandered off back to where everyone else was sitting.

Zalith didn't want to sit around the fire with everyone else; instead, he sat down on a fallen log beside his and Alucard's tent, inviting the vampire to sit beside him.

"Vhat is zhis?" Alucard asked as he sat beside Zalith, looking down into the bowl that the demon handed him.

"Some sort of stew," Zalith muttered, stirring the stew in his bowl with his spoon.

Alucard sighed, glaring into his bowl.

"Are you okay?" the demon asked.

"I guess I just…miss being at 'ome."

Zalith sighed, placing his hand on Alucard's arm. "I miss it, too," he said sadly. "It's not even been a week yet and I'm very tired of all of this," he muttered, letting go and picking up his spoon again.

"Vill ve go to zhe castle?" Alucard asked, gazing at him. "Vrom DeiganLupus?"

Zalith exhaled deeply and ate a little of his food. He didn't want to head to their castle—he didn't want to risk losing that, too. But he was tired of living like this, he was tired of walking around the woods, and *anywhere* was safer than here. He had to relent—their castle really was the only place they had left; he wouldn't risk spending too much longer out here where only terrible things had happened. So he nodded and said, "Fine."

Alucard looked relieved to finally hear Zalith agree. "Do you vemember I mentioned Soren?" he then asked.

Zalith rolled his eyes, finishing what he was currently eating. "Becker," he uttered. "I remember."

"Vhen ve get to zhe castle, I can try to contact 'im and see if ve can use 'im to vind out vhere zhe ozzer Obcasus' and Pandoricans are; ve know zhat zhe Diabolus 'ave a Pandorican and Luciver's Obcasus…*I* 'ave Liliv's, so…ve just need Zamien's, vight?"

The demon nodded. "What if he says no?" he asked.

"Zhen…I vill persuade 'im," he said with a smirk.

As he finished the last of his food, Zalith frowned almost irritably. He didn't even know this Soren, but he just knew he didn't like him. *Any* man from Alucard's past who got brought up made Zalith feel aggravated—he didn't know them, and he didn't know what they wanted from Alucard. He felt especially protective now since Attila—who had turned out to be a disrespectful homophobe—and Luther—who had tried taking Alucard from him…who had almost done the most awful things to him. But he wasn't going to give in to such a feeling. After all, Soren could be different. From what Alucard had told him, it didn't sound like this man was obsessed with him.

He sighed quietly. "Truth be told," he said, smiling at Alucard, "I don't know how anyone could say no to your cute little face."

Alucard looked away, staring into his untouched bowl of stew. "I zon't know; Soren vound particularly easy back zhen."

Zalith smiled, placing his bowl down on the ground. He then reached over, taking Alucard's bowl—he hadn't failed to notice that Alucard wasn't eating. "Maybe he's had his eyes checked since then," he said, holding a spoonful of stew out to Alucard. "Or maybe he's straight," he said, smirking.

Alucard looked down at the stew, frowned, and then looked at Zalith. "Or maybe 'e just zidn't let our velationship cloud 'is judgement," he said and then ate the stew off the spoon.

"Well, *I* would let our relationship cloud my judgement, especially considering the way you look. In fact, I did," he said, offering another spoonful of stew out to him.

The vampire sighed, eating the stew before shrugging and looking out at the camp. "I zon't know, maybe 'e 'as changed since zhen. But if 'e does choose to 'elp us, 'e von't do vor vree."

Zalith nodded again. "That's fine. Hopefully he'll just take our money instead of having us sign our lives over to him like Opus."

"I still vink ve should 'ave just killed 'im and 'is ugly brover," Alucard muttered.

"I know," he said. "He may prove useful one day, though—*but*…maybe one day we'll kill him," he said, smiling.

The vampire rolled his eyes. "Vight," he uttered.

"Eat more stew," Zalith teased, holding out the spoon to him again.

Alucard huffed irritably. "I zon't vant anymore."

"You need the nutrients—just one more bite."

The vampire frowned at him. "I zon't get anyving out of eating 'uman vood," he mumbled—but then he sighed. "Sorry," he muttered. "I'm just tired."

"And grumpy," the demon said, amused. But he then put the bowl down, took Alucard's hand, and stood up. "Come lay down," he said, leading the way into the tent.

The vampire followed him in and slumped down onto their bed—which was made up of a pile of furs and blankets once again. He sighed, laying on his back as Zalith lay beside him and rested his head on Alucard's chest, moving his right arm around him. Zalith felt him gradually relax, and as he trailed his hand down Alucard's body and started lightly stroking his fingers over his chest, the vampire closed his eyes. It had been a long day, and he wanted Alucard to get as much rest as he could.

When the vampire sighed tiredly and turned onto his side, Zalith shuffled closer, moving his arm around him, hugging him rightly.

"Goodnight," Alucard muttered quietly.

Zalith hugged him a little tighter. "Goodnight, baby," he murmured, kissing the side of his face before resting his head on Alucard's. "I love you."

"I love you, too."

As contentment enthralled him, Zalith closed his eyes and tried to drift off.

But as the night grew later, he found himself laying there silently beside Alucard, listening to his calmly beating heart as he slept. He wasn't sure what time it was—it had to be early. The sound of birdsong surrounded the tent, and light started to shine through the entrance. He hadn't slept much—maybe twenty minutes or so, and he felt that was enough.

He held Alucard tightly, still resting with his head on Alucard's shoulder, both of them lying on their left sides. All Zalith could really think about was what he wanted and needed from Alucard. He tried his best to resist the urge to allow his hand to wander down past Alucard's waist; he felt as though it had been forever since he'd been able to touch him…to please him and himself, but…he'd wait. Despite his eagerness, despite how much he *needed* it, he disregarded his tired, aching body and waited. He loved Alucard far too much to wake him from his much-needed rest to satisfy himself. But then he thought…maybe Alucard wouldn't mind? No…he'd wait. But…he sighed, holding Alucard a little tighter. He'd wait until his vampire woke up.

ARC FOUR
TO UZLIA

Chapter Sixty-Nine

The Last Camp

| **Alucard,** ***Tuesday, Cordus 7th, 960(TG)—Nefastus*** |

Alucard soon woke from his sleep, the sound of birdsong ringing through his head; he scowled irritably, trying to dismiss the sound. The first thought that came to mind was that he just wanted to be back home in his and Zalith's bed. But here he was…sleeping in a tent in the middle of a forest. It would all be over soon, though…he hoped.

He slowly opened his eyes, exhaling deeply as he moved his hand from under his pillow to grip the arm Zalith had around him.

"Good morning," the demon instantly said—and rather enthusiastically.

With a frown on his face, Alucard slowly rolled over onto his back and stared up at Zalith as he leaned over him, smiling down at him. "Good…morning," he said strangely—why did Zalith have that eager look on his face?

Before Alucard could ask, however, Zalith leaned in and started kissing him. He wasn't opposed to it, though. He hadn't been able to touch or kiss Zalith for what had felt like years, so he moved his hand to the back of the demon's head and kissed back, his normal morning irritation swiftly fading away.

But after a few moments of kissing that had started slowly and swiftly became almost frantic, Zalith pulled his lips from Alucard's and stared down at him. "I need to suck your dick—is that okay?" he asked with a smile on his face.

Fluster quickly gripped Alucard where he lay—as did confusion. Of course, it wasn't a total surprise. Zalith was an incubus; he *needed* energy to keep going just as Alucard needed blood—energy he could best obtain from sex. So he nodded and said, "Okay."

"Thank you," the demon said and kissed Alucard's neck; he hastily made his way down past the vampire's waist, unbuttoned his trousers, and pulled them off him with one hand while he used the other to immediately grasp and caress his shaft.

The frown on Alucard's face soon faded as he let himself relax. Zalith dragged his tongue up his hardening length, and when he started sucking, something pleasing quickly enthralled Alucard where he lay. He sighed contently, moving his hand down his body and over the demon's head, gripping a fistful of his hair as he sucked desperately, humming and groaning. It felt as if it had been so long since he'd felt something so wonderful; his entire, currently overly-sensitive body trembled in anticipation, satisfaction intoxicating him so very quickly.

As Zalith pleased him, Alucard moaned quietly in delight. He no longer cared about the fact that he was somewhere dirty, noisy, and uncomfortable; there was nothing he loved more than waking up to Zalith's affection. But even *that* came to an end. After only a few minutes, he felt like he had no control over his strangely aching body; he grimaced in struggle, moaning quietly as he suddenly climaxed, and Zalith groaned in sheer relief as he eagerly swallowed his cum.

"You taste so fucking good," the demon purred and dragged his tongue up Alucard's dick one last time before kissing his way back up his body to nuzzle his neck.

Alucard exhaled deeply, waiting for his trembling body to calm. It was all still catching up to him.

Zalith then lifted his head, looking down at Alucard. "Hi," he said with a smile, placing his hand on the side of his face. "Did you sleep okay?"

The vampire stared at him for a few moments but nodded as he started to relax. "I did," he answered. "Did *you* get any sleep?"

"I did."

But Alucard was sure that was a lie. Zalith looked exhausted. "More zhan an hour?" he asked doubtfully.

The demon shrugged. "I don't know…probably."

As a concerned frown stole his smile, Alucard sighed and sat up. He made Zalith lie down and leaned over him, staring down at him. "You should get some more sleep."

"I'll be okay."

"No," he argued. "You need more sleep."

"No, I don't," he said with a smirk. "I'm not tired."

"You look exhausted."

"But I feel energized," he replied, moving his hand up to Alucard's left horn, which he then started to stroke with his fingers. "So you don't have to worry."

"But I *am* vorried. You alvays put everyving bevore yourselv. You need to vest, too, Zaliv," he said quietly in concern, placing his hand on the side of Zalith's stubbly face.

"I'm okay, I promise."

Alucard sighed deeply. Was he actually going to get anywhere trying to convince him? He was sure he wasn't, and he wasn't going to lay there forever trying over and over only to get the same outcome. "Vine," he mumbled. "Vhat's zhe plan vor today?"

Zalith gently stroked his cheek with his fingertips. "We'll start moving soon. We should reach the nearest town with a station before dusk."

"Zhe tvains vun by zhere every day at midday—I guess ve vill 'ave to camp nearby and vait until tomorrow," he mumbled irritably.

"I don't want to risk being seen," Zalith denied. "We'll get around half the way there and set up camp, and then we'll leave earlier in the morning. How do you know the train schedule anyway?" he asked with a smirk.

Alucard shrugged. "I know zhat zhe tvain passes vhrough zhe Citadel at ten in zhe morning, and vould take about two hours to get out 'ere," he said.

The demon laughed quietly. "Oh, it does, does it?"

Alucard pouted. "Yes. Vhat's so vunny?"

"I like that you know all about this train that you never go on. You must really like it."

He kept his pout. "As a matter of vact, I do—I 'ave alvays vanted to go on zhis tvain; takes you all avound Nevastus. Ve just never 'ad zhe chance."

"Well, I hope it meets all your expectations and more," he teased.

The vampire sighed deeply. He didn't really know what else to say.

Zalith smiled, pulling him closer so that he could kiss him. Then, he sighed too. "We should probably get going soon. I'll go and see if everyone's getting up and ready to go."

"Vine," Alucard uttered, buttoning up his trousers. He wanted to try and get Zalith to sleep some more, but he knew there was no point—Zalith would just keep insisting he was fine until Alucard had had enough. So, he gave up and moved back to his side of the bed, tidying his hair with his hands.

"What's wrong?" Zalith asked, sitting up to stare across at him.

"Noving," he said…but he then sighed and looked over his shoulder at him. He felt it was better to talk to him than keep how he felt to himself. "I'm just…vorried about you. You 'aven't slept in almost two days."

"I slept a little," he said sadly.

Alucard turned around and shuffled closer to him, moving his hand to the side of his neck. "But you need more," he insisted quietly. "Vhat if someving 'appens and you're too tired to veact?"

"I won't be. I'll be okay—adrenaline will kick in," he assured him.

Alucard stared at him for a moment. He wasn't going to argue with him. So much had happened that he was sure Zalith was far too *afraid* to let himself sleep. As much as he wanted the demon to get some rest, he had to let it go. "Okay," he said quietly, and then he guided his hand from the side of his neck to the back of his head, pulling him into a hug. "I just…you do so much vor everyvone, you deserve to vest sometimes."

"I know," Zalith said quietly, hugging him tightly. "I'm trying. I just want to get out of this forest."

"So do I," Alucard agreed. "Ve'll be out of Nevastus by tomorrow night, no?"

"I hope so," the demon said, leaning back to kiss his forehead.

As Zalith then nuzzled Alucard's neck, the vampire smiled. "'Ave you ever been on a tvain bevore?" he asked, changing the subject.

"No, I haven't had the pleasure," he answered. "Is it fun?"

"Is nice to vatch zhe vorld go by outside vhile you sit zhere."

"It sounds nice."

Alucard smiled as he leaned back to look at Zalith's face. "Should ve get veady to go?"

Zalith sighed deeply. "Probably," he muttered, an irritated look on his face.

"Vhat's vrong?"

"I'm just tired of this."

"So am I," Alucard concurred. "But ve only 'ave to do vor vone more day," he said, trailing his hand to the side of Zalith's face.

"I hope so," the demon grumbled.

Alucard then stood up, taking Zalith's hand. "Come on," he said, handing him a shirt once he pulled it from his vault. "Zhe sooner ve get going, zhe sooner all of zhis vill be over."

Putting the shirt on, Zalith followed him out of their tent and into the camp to see that pretty much everyone was already packing up and getting ready to head out.

However, Alucard's attention was swiftly snatched by the whistles and calls of Greymore and the same three men who had been playing blackjack with him two days ago. Alucard watched as they waved, laughed, and acknowledged his now human-looking self with sarcastic catcalls and whistles alike.

Zalith laughed quietly, and as Alucard scowled and pouted in embarrassment, he led the way over to where his and Zalith's horses were waiting, leaving two of Zalith's people to pack away their tent and its contents.

"Looks like everyvone is almost veady to go," the vampire mumbled, reaching his horse and petting Peaches, who was sitting on its saddle next to his cape.

"Good," the demon said, stopping beside him. "The sooner we get out of here, the better."

The vampire nodded in agreement—

"Hey," Camael interjected, holding up his hand as he stood in front of them, smiling once they averted their eyes to him. "I feel like we've gotten off on the wrong foot," he said with a calm sigh. "I've said it before, and I'll say it again—I'm here to help, and as a gesture of goodwill, I can access the grim reaper hive mind for you and see if anyone knows anything useful about Ysmay and Lilith," he offered.

"Why?" Zalith asked skeptically, beating Alucard by a single moment.

"Because I'm here to help, and it's the least I can do."

Zalith frowned as skeptically as he sounded. "Why? We've done nothing for you."

"You know what they say: the enemy of my enemy is my friend, right? Lilith is Erich's enemy, and I answer to Erich. As far as I see it, your cause is my cause."

Alucard frowned, glancing at Zalith. What the hell did this guy want? Why was he offering his help? Alucard was sure he was up to something, and clearly, Zalith suspected so, too.

"That's quite the risky position you're putting yourself into for two people you don't even know," the demon said.

"Ve vant noving to do vith Erich or anyvone associated vith 'im," Alucard snarled.

Camael sighed. "I understand how you feel about him," he said, taking his eyes off Zalith to look at the vampire. "Honestly, he's a bit of a dick. I'm just trying to find my own way out here; Opus has a job, Ulric has a job, and I'm kinda just…there to watch their backs," he said, crossing his arms. "I don't just want to be the guy that hovers around waiting for you to pay Opus. Let me help—let me be useful," he said, almost *pleading*.

Alucard rolled his eyes, and as he glanced at him, Zalith scoffed in disinterest and turned his back on the angel, diverting his attention to his horse's saddle.

However, Alucard then remembered that he needed to find Soren. He'd lost track of the Arbiter years ago, and a grim reaper might be the best place to start—they were all part of a collective hive mind, after all, so if one had seen Soren, they would all know. "Search your 'ive mind vor me," he ordered.

Camael's eyes immediately lit up with intrigue. "For what?"

"I am in search of a man named Soren—an Arbiter. 'E may 'ave changed 'is name since, but 'e vas vemoved vrom zhe Arbiter Council vor being too gullible. Zon't look at eizer of us again until you 'ave someving usevul," he said, and then he turned his back on Camael just as Zalith had.

"He's going to think you like him," Zalith murmured.

The vampire glanced over his shoulder, watching as Camael wandered off. "No, 'e von't. 'E knows I despise angels."

"I don't know…he seemed pretty desperate."

Alucard leaned on his horse. "Vell, ve may as vell make use of zhat, no? Until ve vind Soren, anyvay."

"I don't like his name," Zalith muttered, leaning on *his* horse to face Alucard. "Soren Becker. What the hell kind of a name is that? Becker."

"Vhy?" Alucard laughed.

"Because it's stupid," he grumbled. "It sounds like pecker."

Amused, Alucard laughed again. "Zhat's not 'is veal name, vemember?"

"Good, because it's unfortunate. We *won't* be naming any of our kids that, either," he said sternly.

Still amused, Alucard frowned. "Vhy do you seem mad?"

"I'm not mad," he said, smiling.

Alucard also smiled, moving closer to him. "I zon't know…you seem mad," he teased, smirking as he moved his hand over Zalith's shoulder to pull him closer.

"I'm not, I just think your friend has a stupid name."

The vampire shrugged, staring into Zalith's eyes with his face just a few inches from his. He wasn't sure what he wanted to say, all he really knew right now was that he wanted to be close to Zalith. He had felt like he'd spent centuries without being able to touch him, and now, he wanted to take every opportunity he had, despite how nervous he felt. Instead of saying anything else, he ignored his nervousness and kissed Zalith's lips a single time; then, he smiled and said, "Vell, zhat may be zhe case, but 'e is not a stupid man. Still, nobody I know is smarter zhan *you*."

Zalith laughed quietly before he leaned in and kissed him. "Thank you."

Alucard then stepped back, fastening his horse's saddle. "Are you veady to go?"

"I'm ready," the demon confirmed—and then, he climbed up onto *Alucard's* horse.

The vampire frowned, but as Zalith held out his hand, he took hold of it and climbed up onto the horse with him, sitting in front of him as Zalith wrapped his arms around him and hugged him tightly.

"Let's go!" Zalith called to the camp, and once everyone swiftly joined them, Zalith tapped the horse's side and started leading the way forward.

Just one last camp…and it would be time to leave Nefastus.

Chapter Seventy

The Katokirinkata Tale

| Alucard |

Peaches curled up in Alucard's lap as he leaned his back against Zalith's chest. The tense, sorrow-ensnared silence was gnawing away at him, and he couldn't take it anymore. He knew that if he let it envelop him a moment longer, he'd start thinking about Lucifer—he'd start worrying about where and when he'd see his father lingering next.

"Zhe ving I'm looking vorward to zhe most is probably 'aving our own bed to sleep in," the vampire said with a sigh. "And I miss cake."

"Ugh, I miss our bed, too," the demon pined, resting his chin on Alucard's shoulder. "And having showers…and shaving—and not being outside so often."

Alucard smirked as he reached back and rubbed the back of his hand on Zalith's right, stubble-covered cheek. "I zon't know, I vink I like your scratchy vace."

Zalith laughed quietly and did the same, stroking Alucard's stubbly face with his hand. "I like yours, too. But I feel like I look too much like my dad," he muttered. "Whom I love, of course, but…."

"I understand zhat all too vell," Alucard mumbled uncomfortably. But then he frowned. "But I zon't love *my* dad, so…at least you zon't 'ave zhat to vorry about."

The demon laughed quietly. "You don't need him."

He didn't want to think about Lucifer. "Vill you tell me about 'im?" he asked. "Your dad."

Zalith nodded, nuzzling the back of Alucard's head as he led the way through the woods. "He was…stoic and very quiet—so quiet in fact that sometimes you wouldn't even notice that he was in the room until he decided to speak up. Everyone always thought this was odd and maybe even rude, but I don't know…he just wasn't a talker. But that being said, he never withheld his opinions if he thought that you were wrong about anything meaningful. He was honestly without a doubt the smartest person I've ever known, and I think that made him very intimidating for many to be around—especially if you didn't understand him, because he spoke very resolutely and very honestly. He'd never show his cards, so it was rare that you really knew how he was feeling…but if he really liked you, every once in a while, he'd shoot you a look, and maybe he'd smile or roll his eyes when someone annoying was talking, and it would make you feel special because just for that tiny little moment, it was like he was letting you into his private little world," he explained fondly. "In many ways, he was the exact opposite of my mother, which was strange because if I knew them separately, I'd never even think to introduce them."

Alucard smiled. "'E sounds a lot like you. All I know about my vather is zhat 'e talks to 'imselv, got locked up somevhere in a Pandorican, and spends 'is days and all 'is vesources 'unting me down," he said with a shrug. "'Ow did your vather veel about your mother's cat obsession?" he then asked curiously.

The demon sighed. "At first, he didn't mind, actually—I think he was the one who gave her her first cat; but then eventually she decided she was going to start breeding them, and there was something about the breed that was extremely desirable in the cat trade, so if you wanted to adopt one, you would have to be either rich or willing to spend a fortune, and *not only* was there a small market for these cats, but she had a notoriously difficult time separating herself from them, so of course, we were soon overrun because she loved the kittens and was trying to achieve something. Initially, it didn't really bother my dad because he'd always be up in his office or what have you, but eventually, they started annoying him in the same way they were annoying my brother and me, and he told her she'd have to get rid of at least fifteen of them. But she said no, so they argued about it for months until ultimately, they decided that the cats would stay exclusively on one side of the house, so she'd be the only one interacting with them."

Alucard laughed quietly as he looked down at Peaches. "Vell, zon't vorry," he said, looking back over his shoulder at what he could see of Zalith. "I love cats, but…I von't be bveeding zhem," he said. "Peaches is enough vor me vight now."

"Thank you," Zalith said in what sounded like relief, kissing the side of his face. "I guess…in a way, we're lucky she's not around because she might try to convince you."

The vampire then frowned as he stared up at the treetops. "If you 'ad zhe power to brving zhem back…vould you?" he asked in what might sound like curiosity, but for some reason, the talk of Zalith's family had him thinking more deeply about life, death, and what it actually was. After all, *he* had died, yet…there he was. Was it possible to bring people back from the dead once they were gone? It had to be, right? After all, death was simply a law written by a Numen…and Numen's rules could be manipulated, defied…. His own blood would create vampires, and vampires had to die to become what they were. He sighed, dismissing his thoughts. "I zon't know vhy I asked zhat."

"Absolutely I would," Zalith answered. "I miss them more and more every day—even though they pissed me off all the time."

"I guess zhat's vhat zhey're zhere vor zhough, huh?" he asked.

"Yeah," the demon sighed quietly. "If Camael wants to do favours for us so badly, he should ask Erich to figure that out," he laughed.

Alucard shrugged. "I'm sure Erich knows 'ow to undo death," he mumbled. "Avter all, 'e *is* zhe vone who cveated vor mortals. Is vhy 'e despises me so much; zhe ethos in my blood devies 'is laws and brvings people back, turning zhem into vampires."

"He shouldn't get mad; he should just try harder to be better," Zalith said.

Nodding, Alucard sighed and leaned his head back on Zalith's shoulder.

"How do you feel about Camael?" the demon then asked.

Alucard sighed again, thinking. "I zon't know. 'E is of Erich, and I'm sure 'e's up to someving. 'E seems a little too desperate to vant to 'elp us. Or…maybe ve are vrong, and 'e veally does vant to 'elp us vor no veason ozzer zhan 'is own—unlikely, but…who knows?"

The demon nodded. "I don't trust him…and I don't want him to know where our castle is, just in case."

"Agreed," Alucard said. "Maybe ve can leave 'im in DeiganLupus vith some of my people—'e looks vairly easy to persuade."

"He does," Zalith agreed quietly, leaning forward, resting his head on Alucard's shoulder once more.

If Alucard didn't know better, he'd say that Zalith was falling asleep. So he didn't say anything—*that* might wake him. Alucard sat there, slowly taking the horse's reins from Zalith's hands as he started dozing off behind him. And then he smiled. Zalith would finally get a little more rest.

Alucard continued leading the way, letting Zalith rest behind him. Every now and then, he felt the demon stir, obviously trying to keep himself from falling asleep. Alucard wanted to tell him it was okay to rest, but he knew Zalith would insist he didn't need it. So he stayed silent, steering the group for the next few hours.

But when a fox suddenly burst out of the bushes, their horse grunted in startle, and Zalith flinched awake. He lifted his head from Alucard's shoulder, looking around at the thinning forest, up at the grey sky, and down at the dried, cracked dirt, which replaced the grass an hour or so ago.

"Oh, hi sleepy 'ead," Alucard said with a smirk, glancing back at him.

Zalith frowned sleepily, dragging his hand over his face. "Is…everyone okay?" he asked worriedly, looking back over his shoulder.

"Everyvone is vine, Zaliv," Alucard assured him. "Ve're almost vhere ve'll stop vor zhe night."

"Okay," he said quietly, and then he leaned forward and nuzzled Alucard's neck again, holding him tightly.

Alucard smiled, coming to a slow halt as he reached a small opening, which he felt would be suitable for the camp. He looked back at Zalith's people, watching as they spread out and started setting up camp.

"Zaliv?" the vampire asked quietly.

"Hmm?" Zalith murmured.

"Ve're 'ere."

"Okay," he mumbled, but he didn't move.

Alucard wasn't going to make him move. He remained where he was, letting his mate rest on him while he watched Idina tell two of Zalith's people to put up their tent. He then watched them do so, and once they had made up the bed within, Alucard gripped Zalith's wrist. "Zaliv," he said, "come on. Ve can go into zhe tent now."

The demon murmured, "Okay." But he still didn't move.

Sighing, and with a smile, Alucard moved around, trying to get off the horse—

"No, stay," Zalith said quietly, tightening his embrace around him.

"Ve can't sit 'ere all night," Alucard said, pulling Zalith's arms from around him.

Zalith sighed and groaned reluctantly as Alucard climbed off the horse. He then offered his hand up to Zalith, and as the demon took it, Alucard helped him down. Keeping hold of his hand, Alucard then started leading the way over to their tent, glancing at Zalith to see that the tired look on his face was worsening.

"Hey, so—" Danford called, scurrying to catch up with and walk beside Alucard, "—Greymore and everyone and I were talking, and I'm just wondering…if I turn into a wolf, will I also be a bat somehow?" he asked, failing to read the irritated look on Alucard's face. "Because I don't know how I feel about that. Or will I have like…bat wings on my wolf body? Or…wolf fur on a big bat body…or…." He grimaced.

"I zon't know," Alucard muttered, stopping outside the tent—because he *didn't* know; Danford was the first *ever* case of lycanthropy bonding with Vampirism.

"Oh…" Danford drawled, frowning.

Alucard sighed deeply, glaring at him. "No, Zanvord, you vill *not* become a volf-bat. Verevolf transvormation and a vampire's bat vorm are divverent. You are a volf…zhis is just your 'uman vorm," he said, looking him up and down. "Vampires turn into bats vhrough years of practicing zhe transvormation ethos zhat comes vith my blood," he explained.

Danford nodded…and then he just stood there…waiting….

But Alucard had no intention of standing around. So, he went to turn around and take Zalith into the tent—

"W-wait," Danford said, stopping him. "Is it true that vampires can't eat garlic?"

Alucard looked back at him.

"Because that would really suck."

"No, is not true," Alucard snarled irritably. "Is stupid 'uman superstition."

"O-oh…okay, cool," he said.

Then, Alucard turned his back on him—

"W-wait…will I have to sleep in a coffin?"

Alucard sighed deeply. "No. Only vampires who can't valk in zhe sun sleep in coffins as an extra precaution."

"O-okay."

The vampire turned around again.

"W-what about…being invited in?"

Alucard clenched his free fist. "Yes, you vill need to be invited into people's 'omes." He went to walk away—

"W-wait—"

"Go away," Zalith growled, rolling his eyes.

Danford frowned sadly. "S-sorry."

"Zhere'll be time vor questions and lessons vonce ve're out of Nevastus," Alucard said dismissively and took Zalith into the tent before Danford could utter another word.

As he emerged inside, Alucard set his eyes on the pile of blankets and furs that made up their bed. He walked Zalith over, helped him to sit down, and then sat beside him, gazing at him as he sighed deeply and made himself comfortable.

"I vink you should get some vest," the vampire said quietly, placing his hand on Zalith's shoulder.

"No, thank you," Zalith denied with a slight smile on his face.

Alucard pouted. If he wanted to get Zalith to rest, he was going to have to make him lay down. He could see the exhaustion on his face, he could hear it in his voice…and all he wanted was for him to sleep for a little. He was going to have to either bribe him into resting or trick him. He'd try the latter first.

He sighed deeply, moving closer. He pushed Zalith down onto his back and straddled his lap, placing his hand on his chest to keep him down. He leaned closer so that his face was just inches from Zalith's…then, he kissed his lips.

The demon laughed and moved his hand to the back of Alucard's head, kissing him back. They kissed for a short while; Alucard wanted to try and tire him out some more, but he was sure that kissing him was only giving him more energy. So he sighed, kissed him one last time, and moved off him. He laid beside him, resting his head on his chest as he moved his arm around him—

"Wait," Zalith said sadly, moving to get up—

Alucard held him tightly, refusing to let him get up.

But Zalith still tried. "I'm not tired," he insisted.

"I know," Alucard said as convincingly as he could. "I just vant to lay 'ere vith you."

"No you don't," Zalith said doubtfully. "You just want me to sleep."

"If I vanted you to sleep, I vould *make* you sleep, Zaliv," he said, still holding his arm around him tightly.

Zalith squinted suspiciously, staring down at him as Alucard looked up at him.

"Vhat's zhat vace vor?" Alucard asked, pulling the same expression.

"Because I think you're trying to make me sleep," he said.

Alucard sighed and sat up, leaning on his arm to stare down at Zalith. "You zon't 'ave to sleep," he said as convincingly as he could. "I just vant to lay 'ere vith you. Veels like I 'aven't been able to touch you or lay like zhis vith you vor so long."

The demon kept his skeptical scowl but relaxed a little more. "Fine…" he said.

With a smile on his face, Alucard laid back down and rested his head on Zalith's chest. All he had to do now was lay there and wait for Zalith to doze off; once that happened, he'd put him into a deeper sleep so that he'd actually get some rest. But for now, he had to make sure Zalith actually dozed off…so…maybe he should talk to him. About what, though? The mention of cats had him thinking….

"Do you 'ave…katokirinkata in Eltaria?" he asked. "Zhe…cat-people?"

"No," the demon answered quietly.

"Vell," Alucard said, making himself comfortable, "I knew an exceptional katokirinkata vonce upon a time. Vas a long vhile ago; I vas probably only about vorty at zhat time. I vas just getting to know zhe vorld I vas born into; I vas completing a job vor Zamien vhen I came across a small group of assassins. Katokirinkata vere common in such a business—avter all, zhey are naturally stealthy. I 'ad never seen a katokirinkata bevore, so I vas obviously vather vascinated." He paused for a moment, exhaling deeply as he recalled the memory, hoping it wasn't infected by Lucifer. "Zhey…vere plotting to take down a rival gang…or someving like zhat. Zhis katokirinkata's name vas Marcusa—she vas old, but vone vouldn't vink zhat considering zhe vay she moved avound," he continued. "I zon't know. Ve veren't vriends or anyving like zhat, I just decided to vun vith zhem vor a little vhile, get to know zheir vorld a little more. Zhe katokirinkata believe in Deities unlike zhe Numen—and not connected to zhem in any vay, eizer—vhich is strange, since zhe katokirinkata are vone of Levoldus' species."

"That's weird," the demon said tiredly. "I imagine Letholdus doesn't like that."

Alucard shrugged. "I zon't vink 'e cares. If 'e did, 'e vould make sure zhey pray to 'im or vhatever. Anyvay…Marcusa. Vas about…vhree veeks into me 'anging avound vith zhem zhat I learned zhere vas a vather 'evty bounty on 'er 'ead. She 'ad stolen everyving vrom velics to monarchs—she vas actually vanted in six divverent countries," he laughed.

"Did…you turn her in?" Zalith asked sleepily.

"No," Alucard said, smiling. "I liked 'er. She vas…vell…I zon't vant to say like a mother, but…she vas like zhat to a lot of zhe ozzer katokirinkata, and she made me veel a lot 'appier zhan I velt vhen I vas vith Zamien. But back zhen, I zidn't veally know better, and zhe second Zamien called me back, I abandoned Marcusa and zhe katokirinkata. I veturned two years later, but…zhere vas no sign of 'er little group of assassins—vitch 'unters 'ad caught 'er a vew months bevore I came back. Zhey 'anged 'er and 'er people in zhe street. I…vas young and easy to enrage, so…I viped zhat village off zhe vace of Aegisguard, and all zhe vitch 'unters, too. Zhat zidn't go unnoticed, zhough. People started calling me zhe Bloody Assassin avter zhat—vas a story zhat vas told vor a long time, but…died out avter a 'undred years or so because no vone else ever saw me—I vas…busy vith Zamien."

Alucard then looked up at Zalith to see that he might have actually dozed off; he lay there with his eyes closed, an almost peaceful look on his face. The vampire smiled, holding his mate tightly. He wanted to make sure the demon got a good amount of rest, though, so as he lay there, he moved his left hand up to Zalith's head—he pressed his middle and index fingers into his forehead and uttered, "Sleep," ensuring that Zalith would sleep for at least an hour or so.

He had nothing better to do, and he didn't want to leave Zalith; he just wanted to lay there with him. So, he closed his own eyes, exhaling deeply as he listened to the slow, calm beating of his mate's heart. Hopefully, tonight would be the last night they had to spend sleeping outside in tents. Of course, they were going to DeiganLupus first, but soon they'd be at their castle and in their own bed. It wasn't their first home, but…it was still a home, and Alucard was sure that Zalith was looking forward to getting there as much as he was.

Chapter Seventy-One

That Dreadful, Lingering Fear of Loss

| Zalith |

Zalith found himself dreaming... reliving a memory from so long ago. He stood there in the lounge of the house he was currently holed up in with Varana and Idina. They had just celebrated their victory in a rather large battle against the humans and their allies, and as he stood there with Varana and Idina—who were speaking to one another of things Zalith didn't really care to listen—he thought about Xurian. He'd sent his brother and his daughters to a safe house a few days prior as he feared the humans might be tracking him, and he didn't want his brother or his family to get wrapped up in it.

He smiled contently as Varana handed him a glass of wine, and when she resumed her conversation with Idina, a rather loud knock came at the door. Despite the fact that Zalith was enjoying his time there, he knew he had to answer it—it could be one of his people, after all. So he left Idina and Varana, made his way to the front door, and pulled it open, expecting to see one of his men... but what he actually saw struck him with such abrupt horror that he felt his heart stop.

At the end of the path that led to the doorway in which he stood, he set his eyes on Alucard; his vampire had been so badly beaten that he would be barely recognizable if not for his crimson hair—he was nailed to a wooden frame with his arms raised, the skin and muscle torn from his back along with what could only be his lungs, positioned to look like feathered wings—and it all looked so familiar. Zalith stood where he was—frozen, struck with everything horrific. His lips moved to speak, but not even an utter escaped—and the pain in his heart only grew as each moment passed him by.

He hadn't even realized he'd dropped his glass, and as it hit the floor, everything around him so suddenly warped into darkness—

Zalith flinched violently, opening his eyes to see that he was still within the tent. Dread filled his heart, but he knew he'd only been dreaming. That didn't calm him down, though; he looked around frantically, unsure of where Alucard was—but as his panicked gaze found his vampire, who was sleeping with his head rested on his chest, he frowned, his rapidly beating heart starting to slow as relief consumed him.

However, anger soon followed; he'd fallen asleep despite his wishes not to, and he wanted to know what time it was, he needed to know that everyone else was okay—so he was going to get up. He carefully moved Alucard off his chest, and as the vampire murmured in confusion, Zalith moved over to the tent's door and peeked outside, his eyes darting from person to person, and as he saw that everyone was fine, the panic began withering.

He looked back over his shoulder, setting his eyes on Alucard as he sat up and stared at him in confusion. *Sadness* gripped Zalith. He felt so paranoid, a feeling he loathed; he didn't want to feel like this…but he was horrified—*terrified* that Alucard might die again. He didn't want that—he didn't want to feel like this…be like this; he just wanted to hold Alucard, so he went back over to the bed, sat down, and shuffled closer to his vampire, moving his arms around him, pulling him nearer as he closed his eyes and grimaced despondently. His heart—it hurt so much; to see what he had seen, and to feel this dread—this harrowing paranoia; he just wanted it to leave him be, but it wouldn't. And all he could do right now was hold Alucard as tightly as he could…as if their lives depended on it.

"Are you okay?" Alucard asked quietly, holding him just as tightly.

Zalith nodded, far too sad to utter a word. He just wanted to sit there and hug him. But his sadness didn't ease up; his heart remained filled with trepidation. He hugged the vampire a little tighter; why did he have to feel like this? Why couldn't he just shut the sadness off?

But the silence wasn't helping. All of his emotions were building up inside him. The sadness, the panic, and the anger—why had he allowed himself to fall asleep? "I didn't want to fall asleep," he said sadly, still hugging Alucard.

"But you needed to vest," the vampire said quietly.

"I don't want you to die," he pleaded, gripping the back of Alucard's shirt with his hands.

"I'm not going to die, Zaliv," he insisted. "I vould never leave you."

"But you *did,*" the demon uttered sullenly. "And we still have so much left to do together," he mumbled, burying his face in Alucard's neck.

"I zidn't…veally die," he stammered. "I just…lost my 'uman body—I can't die, Zaliv. Ve 'ave all zhe time in zhe vorld to do everyving togezzer," he tried to convince him.

"I don't want anything bad to happen to you ever again," he muttered, his voice muffled as he pressed his face into Alucard's neck.

Alucard held him firmly and ran his fingers through the demon's hair. "Ve'll be okay, Zaliv," he said. "I von't let anyving 'appen to you, to me, or to anyvone," he said sternly.

Zalith nodded, hugging Alucard. But as they sat there in silence, he began to feel what might be embarrassment. He didn't want to seem like a needy crybaby, especially in front of Alucard. So he let go of him, moving away. "Sorry," he said—

But Alucard snatched hold of his arms and pulled him back, hugging him so tightly that he couldn't even attempt to try and escape. "You're not going anyvhere," his vampire said. "And zon't be sorry, eizer. I'm 'ere vor you just like you are 'ere vor me."

The demon's sadness still didn't wane, but he was so very thankful for Alucard…and he loved him so much. And he started to think…where and what would he be without his vampire? Alucard meant more than the world to him; this vampire had saved him from himself so many times. If it wasn't for Alucard, Zalith was sure he would have succumbed to his loneliness and enemies years ago. He had no words to explain just how much he loved and appreciated him. All he knew was that he wanted to spend his *entire* life with this man. He wanted to do everything he could for him—he wanted to give Alucard everything he had…and everything he could. Because Alucard deserved it. He was the most beautiful, kind-hearted soul Zalith had ever come across, and he needed him—he was everything to him…and Zalith knew what he wanted to do…and he'd do it before he regretted not doing it sooner.

"I love you, Alucard," he said quietly.

Alucard smiled. "I love you too, Zaliv."

Just then, Zalith heard somebody approaching the tent.

"Zalith, Alucard—I brought you both some dinner," Idina called from outside.

Zalith didn't want to talk, so he simply uttered a sound in response, and Idina leaned in, handing them both a bowl.

"Stew again. Sorry, it's just the easiest to make," she said as Zalith and Alucard took a bowl from her, sitting beside each other.

"Thank you," Zalith said.

"*Multumesc,*" Alucard mumbled.

"Are you two feeling okay?" she then asked.

Zalith shrugged. "We're fine."

Alucard nodded.

"Okay," she said. "If you need anything, let me know—oh…should I…send someone out to get someone for Danford…to eat?"

"No," Alucard said. "Zhere are still 'umans levt 'ere—'e can 'ave vone of zhem."

Idina sighed in relief. "Okay, good—thank you. Should he…have one of them now or wait until he's…hungry?"

"I told 'im to come to me vhen 'e's 'ungry," Alucard replied. "So I'll take 'im to zhem later."

"Okay. Thank you so much Alucard," she said. "I'll talk to you two later." And then, she left, leaving them alone.

But an idea struck Zalith as the woman left. Idina was the perfect person to help him with his plan. "I'll be right back, okay?" he told Alucard.

The vampire nodded. "Okay."

Zalith put his stew aside, stood up, and hurried after the woman, eager to get things prepared for later.

Chapter Seventy-Two

To Bind or Break the Chains of Forever

| Alucard |

Stew. Alucard turned his nose up at it. He didn't want it; the smell alone was turning his stomach. He sighed and put the bowl aside; just as he was about to focus and find out what Zalith was talking to Idina about, though, the demon stepped back into the tent.

"Hey, sorry about that," his mate said, sitting beside him.

"Is okay," he mumbled.

Zalith made himself comfortable, picked up his stew, and ate a little before glancing at Alucard's abandoned bowl. "You don't have to eat it," he assured him. "You can just…eat me."

Alucard pouted, trying not to let him fluster him.

But Zalith reached for both bowls, setting them aside by the tent's exit before turning his attention back to Alucard. In one smooth motion, he crawled closer, straddling Alucard's lap, his weight pressing them together in a way that made the vampire's pulse quicken. Alucard's gaze flickered with uncertainty as Zalith guided his hand to the back of his head, fingers threading through his hair with a touch both gentle and possessive. Without a word, Zalith pulled him closer, his throat exposed, the scent of his skin filling Alucard's senses.

Alucard hesitated, his lips barely brushing against the curve of Zalith's neck. He wanted this—he needed it, the taste of Zalith's blood so close he could almost feel it on his tongue. But the worry gnawed at him; Zalith was already so worn down, his exhaustion palpable, and Alucard didn't want to drain any more of his strength. Yet the look in Zalith's eyes, a silent plea veiled by the sadness he couldn't quite mask…it made Alucard's resistance falter. If this could distract Zalith even for a moment from whatever darkness haunted him, then Alucard would give in, let his fangs find their mark, and take what was being so willingly offered.

He exhaled quietly, staring down at Zalith's neck as the demon waited patiently.

"What?" Zalith asked quietly, sadness in his voice.

"Are you sure?"

"I'm sure," he answered.

Alucard didn't need any more convincing. He widened his jaw and slowly sunk his four fangs into Zalith's neck, and as the demon exhaled in relief, Alucard hummed in delight, his blood almost instantly enthralling his senses, satisfying him deeply as it poured into his mouth. He didn't want to take too much, though, despite his deep hunger. So after just a few moments, he pulled his fangs from Zalith's skin, titled his head back with a satisfied sigh, swallowing the crimson delight, and then he rested his head on Zalith's shoulder.

"How do you feel?" the demon asked, holding him.

"Good," Alucard murmured. "I veel…lighter," he said, noticing that his once aching, heavy body didn't feel like such a burden anymore. "Vank you," he said with a smile, nuzzling the other side of Zalith's neck.

"You're welcome," the demon said, caressing his hair as he kissed the side of his face. But he didn't give Alucard much time to bask in his euphoria. "Come on," he said, slipping his hand into Alucard's. "I want to show you something."

Alucard frowned curiously as Zalith stood up and led him out of the tent. He had no idea where he was taking him or for what reason, but he followed him anyway, and as Zalith took him into the trees and away from the camp, Alucard's curiosity grew.

They soon reached a large black-rock boulder five or so minutes from the camp; Zalith let go of Alucard's hand and placed his hands on his shoulders. "Sit here while I do something—it'll probably take a few minutes, but please don't peek," he said with an *excited* smile, making Alucard sit down.

Intrigued and confused, but delighted to see such an expression on Zalith's face, Alucard sat down and asked, "Vhy? Vhat are you doing?"

"I can't tell you. It's a surprise," he insisted. "But if you peek, you'll ruin it, and I'll be sad, so you have to promise me," he said firmly.

Alucard stared at him for a few moments; he was eager to know what Zalith had in store for him, so he nodded. "Okay. I promise."

"Thank you," the demon beamed, kissing his forehead. And then he wandered off behind Alucard, leaving him to sit and wait.

What was he doing? Alucard had no idea, and this seemed a little abrupt. But it was certainly a change from all the misery and irritation that had come with their trip. He had no idea what it might be, and he couldn't even really start guessing. So he just waited…sitting there…staring into the darkness of the trees ahead until Zalith told him it was time to look.

"Alucard," Zalith then said after a short while, slipping his hand back into Alucard's to pull him to his feet.

Alucard rose to his feet, turning to face him—and in that instant, the light caught his eyes. It shimmered just beyond Zalith, flickering like a secret invitation hidden in the darkness. For a heartbeat, he was still—until he followed Zalith forward, stepping into a small, enchanted space bathed in the soft glow of countless candles. Alucard's gaze swept across the scene in silent wonder. Glistening white candles, their flames dancing gently, adorned the ground, nestled upon the smooth rocks, and even perched delicately on the branches of the surrounding trees. They were everywhere, each placed with deliberate care, their warm light casting an ethereal glow that seemed to make the shadows tremble.

The realization struck him: Zalith must have arranged each one by hand, crafting this moment with an intimacy that touched something deep within Alucard. The effort, the thoughtfulness—it was more than just candlelight; it was a message flickering in the dark meant only for him. Standing within that circle of light, surrounded by the gentle radiance that softened the world around him, Alucard felt a calmness settle over his soul, a rare contentment that made his chest ache with something unnameable. In this place that seemed to exist outside of time, beneath the stars and the glimmer of flame, he felt like he'd stepped into a dream that was only half his own.

In the centre of the circle, Zalith held both of Alucard's hands as he smiled and stared into his eyes. Were they going to dance? No…it looked as though Zalith was about to tell him something—he always had such a serious gleam in his eyes when he was about to say something important. So Alucard stared back, waiting to hear what Zalith had to say.

The demon exhaled quietly, gazing into Alucard's eyes. "Alucard, before you came into my life, I wandered through the centuries—six hundred long years—believing that true, genuine love was something I would never touch, something that would never be mine. I'd wrapped myself in that cold acceptance, wore it like a shield against the world, convinced my heart was untouchable, and for so long, I revelled in that solitude."

Alucard frowned, listening. He wasn't sure where Zalith was headed with his words, but he'd wait to hear it all.

"But then you happened to me," the demon continued. "Like a whisper in the dark, a flicker of light that refused to be extinguished. You unravelled everything I thought I was piece by piece until the person I'd become felt like a stranger even to myself. You made me lose my way in the best possible sense, reshaping my soul in ways I never thought possible. For the first time, I wasn't afraid to change, because with you, it was never about fear—it was about feeling alive, truly alive as if I'd been waiting for centuries just to find you," he professed, squeezing Alucard's hands. And then Zalith slowly pulled his palms from Alucard's, reaching into his pocket as he knelt on his left knee.

Gazing at the demon as he pulled a small black box from his pocket, Alucard felt as if the very world around him halted.

"I have searched for the perfect moment, but time slips through our fingers too quickly, and I can no longer bear the thought of wasting a single second of this eternity without knowing that you are mine in every way for all time. I don't want just to be your lover, your companion in the shadows of night—I want to be your husband, bound to you through every dawn and dusk until the stars fade from the sky. Alucard, my forever, my only…will you marry me?"

Alucard's breath caught, and for a moment, he forgot how to exist in his own skin. The shock of Zalith's words hit him like a heartbeat suddenly too loud, echoing in the silence between them. He stood there, motionless, staring down at Zalith as if this moment were a masterpiece in some forgotten cathedral—a vision he couldn't quite believe was real. His mind went blank, lost in the swirl of disbelief and wonder, every thought slipping through his grasp like wisps of smoke. Was this truly happening? This moment he'd dared not dream of, convinced it could never be his—especially not now…when the world seemed to be on the brink of unravelling.

But it *was* real. It *was* happening. Zalith was down on one knee, his eyes holding a truth that burned brighter than any flame, his hand steady as he offered the ring. He was asking Alucard to be his, not just in fleeting nights and stolen moments, but in every breath of eternity.

As the world came rushing back into focus, Alucard felt a smile stretch across his face—wider, brighter, more unguarded than he ever thought possible. Tears pooled in his eyes, not of sorrow or regret, but of pure, unrestrained joy. He had never felt so certain of anything in all his centuries of existence. He had never been so sure of a single word.

"Yes," he breathed, his voice trembling with emotion, his smile soft and infinite as he met Zalith's gaze. "Alvays and vorever, yes." He reached for Zalith's hand, holding onto him as if he could anchor himself to this moment, this promise of forever. "To spend eternity vith you—zhat's all I've ever vanted. To be yours, *truly* yours, until zhe end of time"

Zalith smiled brightly, a held breath escaping his voice as he slipped the ring onto Alucard's finger. And then he stood up, eagerly throwing his arms around the vampire and hugging him so tightly as he buried his face into his neck.

Alucard struggled to find the words to express how he felt—nothing seemed big enough, nothing seemed right. He was drowning in so much happiness that he couldn't stop the tears from welling up in his eyes. Was he really going to cry? The thought startled him, left him feeling exposed in a way he hadn't felt in centuries. Did people cry when they were so happy that it ached, when the joy inside them felt too vast to be contained? He didn't know, and right now, he didn't care to understand. All that mattered was this—this impossible, wondrous moment where he and Zalith were going to be married. That single thought consumed him, taking over every corner of his mind, wrapping around his heart like a promise carved in eternity.

The demon then moved his face from the vampire's neck and placed a soft, passionate kiss upon his lips before pressing his forehead against Alucard's. "I love you," he told him with sincerity in his voice that sent a shiver of anticipation down Alucard's spine.

"I love *you*," the vampire laughed contently.

Zalith's smile was brief, almost *teasing* before he leaned in and claimed Alucard's lips again, kissing him with a hunger that stole the breath right from his lungs. Alucard had no time to recover, no space to think, just the warmth of Zalith's touch guiding him backwards until his back pressed firmly against the rough bark of a tree. He let himself melt into the kiss, his fingers threading through the demon's hair, holding him close. All he could think about was how utterly content he felt in this moment, how the thrill of spending his eternity with the man he loved made his heart race.

But Zalith's intentions were clearly a shade darker, his desire sharper. Alucard felt the shift as Zalith's grip tightened on his shirt, pulling him down in one fluid motion as he sank to the ground, laying back and bringing Alucard with him. The vampire didn't resist; he wanted Zalith in every way, in every touch and breath until there was nothing between them but the pulse of their shared longing. As Zalith broke their kiss for just a heartbeat and rolled them over, pinning Alucard beneath him, Alucard's lips curled into a smile—a smile full of excitement, a spark of mischief lighting his eyes. This was exactly where he wanted to be, tangled with Zalith, lost in the promise of their forever, wrapped in the heat of a love that even the coldest of nights could never touch.

Zalith's lips moved against his with a slow, deliberate passion, each kiss deepening like a whispered promise as his hand traced a languid path down to Alucard's collar. When Zalith began to unbutton his shirt, Alucard mirrored the movement, his fingers slipping to the buttons of Zalith's own shirt. A fleeting thought crossed Alucard's mind—were they really going to do this, here and now? But as Zalith shrugged off their shirts and pressed his lips to Alucard's bare chest, the question dissolved into the warmth of that touch. Any hint of hesitation melted away, replaced by a yearning that consumed him whole.

The sensation of Zalith's lips trailing across his skin, the heat of his breath against his chest—it was all too much and not nearly enough. Alucard's heart thrummed with a wild need, his mind lost in the intoxicating pull of Zalith's affection. The world outside this moment seemed to fall away, leaving only the two of them tangled in desire and locked in a dance that felt like it had been written in the stars. All Alucard wanted was more—more of Zalith's touch, more of his kisses, more of this eternity they were creating with every shared breath.

And Zalith seemed to sense exactly what Alucard craved. The demon's lips travelled up Alucard's skin with deliberate slowness, each kiss igniting sparks that lingered in his veins. As Zalith reached the side of his neck, Alucard's fingers tightened in his hair, his grip almost desperate. Then, in one swift, heated movement, Zalith sank his teeth into Alucard's neck. The sharp sting stole the breath from Alucard's lips, replaced by a low, shuddering moan as his head tipped back in surrender.

The pleasure was immediate, searing through him like liquid fire as Zalith's fangs pierced his skin. Alucard's eyes fluttered closed, and he let himself drown in the rush of euphoria that coursed through his veins. It was so much more intense this time, almost overwhelming in its bliss, and he realized just how starved he'd been for this—how much he'd missed the exquisite burn of Zalith's venom in his blood. Every heartbeat, every thrum of sensation seemed to pull him deeper into the moment, binding him to Zalith in a way that felt forever.

But eventually, Zalith had to pull his fangs from Alucard's neck, and once he did, he dragged his tongue up from the bottom of Alucard's neck to his ear, where he sighed contently. "You taste really good," he breathed, moving his hand down Alucard's body to grip his belt.

Alucard's smile barely had time to settle on his lips before Zalith's mouth was on his again, the kiss more urgent, almost fevered as if the demon couldn't get enough of him. The shift in Zalith's hunger only fuelled Alucard's own desire, sending a thrill through him that made his pulse race. His hand slid down from Zalith's head, tracing the curve of his back, fingers grazing the hard lines of muscle before wrapping around his waist. Alucard's grip found Zalith's belt, and he eagerly fumbled to unbuckle it, every touch filled with the promise of more.

Zalith's hands were already at work, tugging Alucard's trousers off with a skilful impatience that left the vampire breathless. The moment Zalith's hand closed around his arousal, a jolt of pleasure shot through the vampire, his body tensing beneath the touch, caught between anticipation and need. He hadn't yet managed to free the demon from his own clothes, so instead, he gripped his mate's crotch through the fabric, feeling the heat of him even through the barrier. The friction sent a shiver of excitement down his spine, and all he could think of was tearing away the last of the distance between them, desperate to feel Zalith's skin against his own.

The demon trailed his hand down Alucard's tense body, reaching his own belt. He pulled his trousers off, and then Alucard watched as he reached into his vault to retrieve the lube; he pulled the lid off, slowly squeezed some of the gel-like liquid onto his fingers, and gently massaged it into the vampire's ass. Alucard let out a pleased hum as they started kissing again, and when the demon exhaled deeply and began easing his hard, thick dick inside Alucard, the vampire's quiet moan became a pleased whine. Zalith pressed his forehead against his, and that was when he felt his mate trying to connect with him through their imprints.

Alucard attempted to concentrate, too, but all he could focus on was Zalith's inches moving deeper and deeper inside him. He moaned and frowned, trying his best, and once they connected, once he could feel what Zalith felt, once their connection peaked, the euphoria was unlike anything he'd felt before. He could feel relief—*Zalith* was so relieved that he'd said yes, so happy that they would be spending their infinite lives together for what Zalith hoped was forever—Alucard wanted it to be forever too. He loved Zalith so much, and he could feel just how much Zalith loved *him*. He felt he really couldn't be happier, and all he wanted right now was to enjoy this moment with him. Zalith. His love, his mate, his fiancé. His forever.

The demon then moaned quietly, slowly pulling his body back, lightly gripping a fistful of Alucard's hair in his right hand as he kept his forehead rested on his. He thrusted forward, plunging his dick deep inside Alucard as they both groaned pleasurably. They started kissing once more; Alucard gripped Zalith's left bicep in one hand, moving his other to the back of his head to grip his hair as the demon continued slowly thrusting his shaft into and out of him. The euphoria of his bite, the pleasure of his movements, and the shared feelings he felt from their connection almost had Alucard overwhelmed already. But he enjoyed it—he had never felt so good before, and as he moved one of his legs over Zalith's back, he closed his eyes and tilted his head to the side, inviting Zalith to kiss his neck while he took a moment to catch his breath.

Zalith started by kissing the bite he'd left on Alucard's neck, gradually thrusting a little faster as he decided to focus on one area of his neck, first kissing it several times, now sucking it as he breathed deeply, letting go of Alucard's hair to drag his fingers around the base of his horns.

Alucard couldn't hold back the sound that escaped him; his moan was louder, more desperate than before, his trembling body unravelling under Zalith's touch. He grimaced, caught in the struggle between desire and surrender as the sensations overwrought him. He longed to sink his fangs into Zalith's neck again, to taste him, to draw strength from that bite. His eyes flicked to the spot where he imagined his teeth sinking in, but he hesitated. Beneath Zalith's weight, with the demon's gaze fixed on him, he felt so small, so meek, and the thought of taking that control almost made him tremble more.

His heart raced, each pulse thrumming louder than the last, and when Zalith's hand slid from his hair down to lightly encircle his throat, Alucard's breath hitched. He was utterly captivated, completely lost in that touch. The firm yet unyielding hold made him feel so vulnerable, so completely at Zalith's mercy, and it was exactly where he wanted to be. Alucard's entire being seemed to hum with a heady mix of anticipation and surrender, the thrill of yielding to Zalith's command sending shivers through him. He loved it—the way Zalith's dominance made him feel exposed, claimed, as if nothing in the world could touch him except the demon's will. More than anything, he loved how Zalith could strip away his defences with just a touch, reminding him who truly held the power between them.

Alucard lay there, his body trembling uncontrollably as waves of pleasure surged through him, each one more intense than the last. He felt utterly consumed, his senses reduced to nothing but the heat of Zalith's touch and the rhythm of their movement. Zalith's lips left the tender skin of his neck, trailing back to capture his mouth in a searing kiss, and Alucard melted into it, lost in the raw intensity of it all. He gasped as Zalith released his throat, only to pin one of his wrists above his head, the gesture both possessive and commanding.

Zalith's pace quickened, each thrust driving deeper, more insistent, and Alucard's breath turned ragged. His free hand clawed at the ground as the pressure inside him built, spiralling higher with every movement. He could feel himself teetering on the edge, his entire body taut, trembling, aching for release. Zalith's dominance, his *control* was like a fire burning through his veins, leaving Alucard breathless and utterly captivated. He was so close, so quickly approaching his peak, and the thought that Zalith was the one to bring him to this brink only made his heart race faster.

He reached the edge, and he willingly tipped over, giving himself completely to Zalith. A loud, delighted cry left his gaping mouth as he climaxed, gripping Zalith's hair so tightly in his free hand as he did. His dick throbbed, sending waves of spiralling, consuming pleasure through his sensitive body.

But Zalith kept moving, his limbs trembling against Alucard's—and it wasn't long after that he moaned in satisfaction into Alucard's ear, kissing his neck as he stopped moving, burying his shaft as deeply inside the vampire as he could. Alucard felt the hotness of the demon's cum fill him, the heat spreading around inside him. He lay there meekly, submissively, waiting until the last drop oozed from Zalith's body. Zalith groaned, nuzzling Alucard's neck, and then he slowly pulled his dick from his ass.

The demon exhaled deeply before kissing his way down the vampire's shivering body. He gripped his shaft in his hand, dragged his tongue around, licking up his cum with satisfied hums, and then he kissed his way halfway up Alucard—he seemed to almost collapse as he rested his head on Alucard's chest, sighing deeply as they both tried to calm down.

Alucard stroked his fingertips to the back of Zalith's head, letting free a deep breath as he waited for his trembling, overwhelmed body to settle.

"I love you," Zalith breathed, guiding his hand up to Alucard's head, where he started to caress his hair.

The vampire smiled, staring up at the star-filled sky. "I love you, too," he said, his euphoric, content feeling gripping him so tightly. Everything in this moment felt so perfect; he and Zalith were going to get married, and he couldn't think of anything he wanted more than to spend his life with him.

But he had questions—so *many* questions. As Zalith moved closer, resting his head on Alucard's shoulder, the vampire looked down at him, moving his arm around him. "Zaliv?" he asked.

"Mm?"

"Vhere vill ve get married?"

"Wherever you want, baby," Zalith said with a smile, looking up at him.

"I zon't know," he said, shifting his gaze to the sky again. "I guess I never veally vhought about zhat."

"Well, where's the most beautiful place you've ever been?"

Alucard thought long and hard…where *was* the most beautiful place he'd ever been? The world had recently become scorned by not only fire but famine and poverty, and a lot of the places Alucard had once loved were now gone. Dor-Sanguis, for example—he would have loved to get married in his home country, but that was long gone…for now at least. "Vhat about in Eltaria?" he asked. "I'm yet to see your vorld," he said, smiling down at Zalith.

Zalith sighed, hugging Alucard a little tighter. "If things unfolded a little differently, then I'd show you around, but I'm not ready to go back there yet—it's probably still very dangerous."

With disappointment in his heart, Alucard nodded and sighed. "Vell…ve zon't 'ave to decide vight now vhere ve get married. Maybe ve can look at places vhen ve get 'ome to zhe castle."

"Okay," Zalith said, sitting up slightly, leaning on his arm so that he could look down at Alucard. Then, he kissed his lips a few times and moved a few strands of hair away from his eyes. "Do you like your ring?"

Alucard looked down at the gold, ruby encrusted ring on his left ring finger and smiled contently. "I love. Is my two vavourite colours, too," he said, placing his left hand on the side of Zalith's face. "Vank you."

"Good," the demon said. "I spent a lot of time working on it with the jeweller—does it fit okay?"

Alucard looked down at the ring again, taking his hand off Zalith's face. He fiddled with it, staring at the small diamonds lined around the ring, fascinated by all the tiny, intricate carved details that he hadn't had the chance to see at first. "Vits just vine," he said, nodding with an overly content smile on his face. "I veally love."

Zalith smiled again and leaned closer, kissing him once more.

Alucard couldn't think of a thing more perfect than this to end their night—to end their life on the run, in fact. This time tomorrow, they'd be in DeiganLupus and on their way home. Everything awful that had happened—none of it seemed to matter anymore.

He and Zalith were still alive, and he felt as if they were better and stronger than ever. And soon enough, they'd be planning their counterattacks.

And their wedding.

Chapter Seventy-Three

Celebration…of Sorts

| Zalith |

For a while, Alucard and Zalith lay in one another's embrace, gazing up at the star-filled sky while the candles lit the small opening between the trees. Zalith felt content—as content as he might have ever been. He rested with his head on Alucard's chest, holding his hand as the vampire held his arm around him. He wasn't sure any other moment could be as perfect as this one. He and Alucard were engaged, and he didn't have the words to explain how happy that made him.

His once anxious heart was now filled with utter joy, with relief. After six hundred years, he'd finally found the man he would spend his life with—the man he loved so truly, so wholeheartedly. Alucard was everything to him; he deserved the world, and Zalith would give it to him.

He smiled, glancing up at Alucard's relaxed face. He was sure that his *fiancé* was about to ask him something—he had that same pondering look on his face that he always had when he was trying to figure out how to word something.

"Zaliv?" the vampire asked, obviously checking to see if he was still awake.

"Yes?" he replied, smiling.

"So…do you still vant to take my last name?"

"Of course I do," he said, guiding his hand up to prod Alucard's cheek.

Alucard smiled, resting his head on his arm as he moved it behind his head. "Vhat about…vell…*vhen* vill ve 'ave zhe vedding?"

Zalith sighed quietly as he gazed at the sky. "Well, that depends. We can elope and just do something for ourselves at any time, or we can do something more traditional, which is going to take more time to plan—it usually takes most people about a year to plan a wedding," he explained.

"I zon't…veally know," Alucard said quietly. "Vhat vould *you* prever?"

"I'm not sure either. Eloping sounds more relaxing, but then again, I want to have a beautiful wedding and show you off and make everyone jealous," he said, smirking.

The vampire laughed quietly as he started to fiddle with Zalith's hair. "I vant to show you off, too—a bigger vedding sounds better."

"Can you wait?" Zalith asked, still smirking as he moved his hand up to Alucard's head and started caressing his hair.

"I vill do my best to be patient."

Zalith laughed quietly. "Good boy."

Laughing with him, Alucard shrugged. "Vell, who vill ve invite?"

"I don't know," he said with a frown. "I guess I don't have very many friends these days."

"Me neizer."

"Or family."

"Ve 'ave zhat in common, too," Alucard said with a sigh.

"I guess our big wedding might end up being a small one."

"Is okay," Alucard said. "Ve zon't need to 'ave a million people zhere, just zhose who matter."

"All I need is you anyway," Zalith murmured, looking up at him.

The vampire smiled down at him. "I only need you, too."

As his smile grew thicker with happiness, Zalith sat up, turned around, and rested his arms beside Alucard, staring down into his hell-fiery eyes. Then, he pressed his lips against Alucard's, starting to kiss him slowly.

But the happiness could only mute his other senses and feelings for so long.

After a short while of slow, soft kisses, Zalith began to feel…paranoid, for the lack of a better word. He'd left his people for almost an hour, and realizing that, his heart began to feel as though it was being strangled with angst. What if something happened? He knew it was time to head back—his worry wouldn't let him leave them for a moment longer. As much as he wanted to stay out here alone with Alucard, he knew that his worry would only increase, and that would ruin their time together for both of them.

He stopped kissing his vampire, staring down at his beautiful face for a few moments. "We should head back now. It's getting late."

"Okay," Alucard agreed, sitting up.

Once they got dressed, Alucard took hold of Zalith's hand and followed him through the woods and back towards the camp. Zalith would check on his people, and then he'd retreat into his tent with Alucard—all he really wanted to do right now was relax with him, but first, he had to silence his worried thoughts.

When they reached the camp, Zalith's panic was replaced by relief; all of his people were either sitting around the fire, talking in small huddles, or watching the perimeter—

nothing had happened in his absence. However, just as he was about to head into their tent—

"Why do you two look so happy, huh?" Greymore suddenly asked, stopping beside them.

Alucard smiled contently as he squeezed Zalith's hand. "Ve just got engaged," he said with a smile brighter than Zalith might have ever seen on his face.

"What?!" Greymore gasped enthusiastically. "Bullshit—let me see," he tested with a grin.

Still with a content smile on his face, Alucard lifted his left hand, showing Greymore the engagement ring that sat on his left ring finger, comfortable next to the ring Zalith had given him years ago, the one that had once belonged to his father, the same ring that kept him hidden from the Numen. They looked perfect side by side.

Greymore snatched Alucard's hand, gawping at the ring. "Oh, shit," he grinned, letting go of Alucard's hand. "So, you finally got the old man to settle down, eh?" he laughed.

Zalith rolled his eyes, not exactly in the mood to talk to anyone right now, especially not someone as enthusiastic as Greymore.

"'E's not *zhat* old," Alucard said, smirking at Zalith.

"Pshh, yeah okay," Greymore laughed. "I'm pretty sure he predates time—but congrats brother," he said, patting Alucard's arm. "And you too, Zalith."

"Thank you," the demon said.

"I gotta tell everyone," Greymore said, starting to walk off.

"Tell everyone what?" Idina asked, having just stopped beside Zalith.

"These two geezers got married," Greymore revealed, wandering off into the camp.

Idina took her eyes off him and stared at Zalith and Alucard, tears starting to form in her eyes as she gazed at them. "What?" she asked, a happy but surprised look on her face. "Is he joking?"

"No," Zalith said, smiling.

"Congratulations!" she cried happily. "I'm so happy for you two—" she flung herself forward and hugged them both tightly. "Your parents would be so happy right now," she said, stepping back and looking at Zalith.

He smiled sadly. "They would," he agreed.

"Aw, I'm sorry," Idina said sadly, rubbing his arm.

Alucard moved his arm around Zalith's waist, hugging him slightly. He clearly knew that he was upset by the fact that his parents weren't here to see it.

"Can I see the ring?" Idina then asked.

Alucard nodded and held out his hand again, letting her gawp at it.

"It's so beautiful," she chirped.

Smiling, Alucard glanced at Zalith and said, "Is pervect."

Zalith smiled and guided his arm around Alucard's shoulders, and then he nodded at Greymore, who seemed to be trying to encourage everyone to get up. "I think he's planning something," the demon said, setting his sights back on Idina.

She frowned angrily. "It better not be anything loud—we're in hiding right now," she growled. "Excuse me," she said and stomped over to where Greymore was.

"Vhat's 'e planning?" Alucard asked.

"I don't even want to know," Zalith said, watching as Greymore encouraged someone to start playing a lute.

"I guess…'e is trying to start a party vor us?" he suggested as Greymore riled everyone up, handing out drinks before sitting down to start playing cards with his usual troupe.

Zalith smiled slightly. He appreciated Greymore's efforts, but right now, he just wanted to be alone with Alucard—and he felt as though this 'party' was just an excuse for Greymore to unwind…and he didn't blame him. But Zalith wished they were at home, then he could have planned something much nicer for their engagement party. He also found himself wishing he had more friends with him who he actually liked and didn't just feel responsible for—he might have a better time if that were the case.

He felt…ashamed that he didn't have as many friends as he used to, and he missed Varana—but he didn't want to think about her. He wanted to be alone with Alucard.

"Vhat's vrong?" Alucard asked.

"Nothing," he assured him. "I just want you to have more than this."

Alucard frowned, looking out at the camp as Zalith gestured to it.

"But we'll be at the castle soon. I'm just happy you're here," the demon added, and then he kissed his lips.

Smiling as he stared into Zalith's eyes, Alucard shrugged. "I zon't need anyving else—all I need is you," he said, wrapping his arms around him.

The demon embraced him, too, and kissed his forehead.

"So," Alucard then said, stepping back to smile at him. "Are ve going to join zhem in vhatever zhey're doing, or…do you vant to do someving else?"

"I don't know," the demon said. "What do you feel like doing?"

"I vant to do vhatever vill make you 'appier."

Zalith smiled and then looked out at the camp again. "We should probably be polite and spend time with them since it would seem Greymore is throwing a party."

"Okay," Alucard concurred. "Just let me grab my cape; is getting cold."

The demon nodded and waited while Alucard went into the tent. A smile remained on his face despite the sadness that came with knowing his parents wouldn't see his wedding day. He might tell himself that wherever they were, they were watching over him, but he had no idea where demons went when they died. He didn't want to think about it. He took a deep breath and watched as the once quiet, dismayed camp began waking up, the excitement spreading fast. Tonight was about him and Alucard, his fiancé. He'd not let anything take away his contentedness.

| Alucard |

As he grabbed his cape from the bed, Alucard stopped to stare at his new ring. He smiled as the rubies glistened in the lantern light, his heart fluttering. It finally happened, and there weren't words to describe how overwhelmingly happy he was.

He didn't want to keep Zalith waiting, though. He could admire the ring more later. Once he pulled his cape on, he stepped outside and rejoined Zalith. He took the demon's hand and started leading him closer to the rest of the camp. "Ve can sit 'ere—I'll get us drvinks," he said, making Zalith sit on a fallen log before wandering off to find something for them to drink.

The vampire didn't get very far, though, before Greymore found him and stopped in front of him with two mugs of what Alucard assumed to be mead. "Here ya go, buddy," he said, holding the two drinks out to him.

"Vank you," Alucard said, taking them from him. Then, as Greymore wandered off, Alucard made his way back over to Zalith and handed him one of the drinks. "I vink zhis is some kind of mead," he said, sitting beside him.

"Thank you," the demon said, taking it from him.

Alucard smiled, shuffling closer to him. "So, I guess I should start calling you my viancé," he said.

"I like it better than boyfriend," the demon said with a smile, stroking his hand up Alucard's arm, over his shoulder, and to the back of his head. He then pulled him closer and kissed his lips. "I've never been engaged before—this could be fun," he said, smirking.

"Neizer 'ave I," Alucard laughed. "I never vhought I ever vould be," he admitted.

"What an interesting little path I've led you down," the demon murmured, resting his forehead against Alucard's.

Still smiling, Alucard took hold of Zalith's free hand. "You made my life so much better, and you still do," he said quietly. "I vouldn't 'ave vather 'ad zhis 'appen any ozzer vay."

"Me neither," Zalith replied, and then he kissed him. "I love you."

"I love *you*," Alucard said, running his fingers through Zalith's hair.

Alucard kept his smile, watching as Zalith slouched forward a little, sipping from his drink. The vampire sat up straight and took a sip of his own drink, but as he did, he frowned, perturbed by the sudden vacant expression on Zalith's face as the demon stared forward, watching a few of Greymore's friends dance around the fire. Was something wrong? Alucard was convinced that something must be bothering Zalith—was he still beating himself up over everything that happened? Or maybe…was he not…*happy* that they were now engaged? What if Zalith was thinking he'd made a mistake? Alucard didn't want to think that—he knew Zalith was just as happy as he was.

The vampire stared down into his drink. As it always did, his mind immediately had him think, 'What can I do to help?', but Zalith had told him enough times that sometimes, he just couldn't help him feel better. He wasn't going to ask—the last thing he wanted to do was annoy or upset Zalith. Instead, he started thinking…maybe there was something he could do to put a smile on his mate's face—and staring into his drink gave him an idea. He was sure Zalith would like something better to drink just as much as he would, so he telepathically sent a message to Toma, telling him to bring him and Zalith not only a bottle of wine, but of champagne, too.

However, he then felt the irritating sensation of someone's stare locked on him. He didn't fail to notice Danford creeping around the tree line; the vampire-wolf stood behind a tree less than ten feet away with one of Greymore's men, doing his best to hold a conversation so that the man would remain there with him, making him seem less…creepy. Of course, it was to be expected, so Alucard wasn't mad; he just didn't want to have to deal with it right now—least of all while he was trying to enjoy his time with Zalith. But Danford's ever-irritating presence *did* give him an idea.

Alucard sighed deeply, placing his drink down beside him as Zalith looked at him. "I'll be vight back," he assured him, standing up.

"Where are you going?" the demon asked with both worry and curiosity in his voice.

"I'm tired of Zanvord staring at me vrom avar. I'll go and make sure 'e veeds, and zhen I'll come back," he explained.

"Okay. I'm coming with you," Zalith said, putting his drink down, too.

"No, is vine," the vampire said, placing his hand on Zalith's shoulder to keep him from getting up. "I'll only be over zhere," he said, nodding at the wagon. "*You* can admire me vrom avar," he said, smirking. "And vest, too. Ve've been on our veet all day."

Zalith hesitated, his look becoming one of solely worry. "Can I just come with you, please?" he asked.

Looking down at him, Alucard frowned; he wanted to surprise Zalith with what he had planned, but…he didn't want to leave him there worried and upset. "Okay," he said, holding out his hand for Zalith to take.

"Thank you," the demon said, taking his hand as he stood up.

Alucard then looked back over his shoulder, scowling as Danford tried to hide behind the tree. "Let's go, Zanvord," he called.

Danford leaned out from behind the tree, as did the man he was talking to. "O-oh, okay," he called, hurrying to catch up with him and Zalith, who rolled his eyes.

Alucard silently led the way over to the wagon—but silence was something he wasn't going to get.

"Where are we going?" Danford asked.

"To zhe vagon," Alucard muttered.

"Why?"

"Because you need blood, or you might attack your girlvriend again."

"Oh," Danford said sadly, looking down at the ground. "I feel really bad about that."

"Of all people, Vreja vill understand," Alucard said, looking over his shoulder at him as Danford followed. "She's vorked avound vampires vor years—she vill vorgive you, unless she alveady 'as?" he asked.

"She has," he confirmed. "But I just can't stop thinking about it; I'm worried it's gonna happen again," he blubbered.

Alucard sighed, staring ahead as they approached the wagon. "You vill be a Vledgeling vor a vew months—maybe less if you learn to control yourselv vaster; I vill try to 'elp you, but 'as been a vew 'undred years since I taught anyvone myselv."

"Thanks though, it means a lot," Danford said quietly.

Stopping beside the remaining humans who were tied in the back of the wagon, Alucard said, "Pick vone."

Danford donned a look of startle. "Uh…" he said, slowly taking his eyes off Alucard and Zalith to stare at the humans—but guilt smothered his face. "I don't know."

Zalith sighed quietly, as did Alucard. He didn't want to stand there and wait for Danford to become hungry enough to forget his morals. So, he let go of Zalith's hand and grabbed the collar of the closest human, pulling him from the wagon as he tried to cry through his gag.

Rolling his eyes, Alucard threw him to the ground and waved his hand at him. "Zhere," he said.

Danford looked down at the struggling man and then back at Alucard with an uncomfortable frown. "Do I just…bite him?"

"More or less," Alucard muttered.

"Okay…." He moved closer to the man…but backed off and frowned. He then moved closer again and reached out to grab him as he shook his head in terror—Danford backed off again. He then held his hand to his mouth, looked over his shoulder at Alucard, and then back down at the man. "Where?" he asked. "His neck?"

Alucard now felt impatient. "Yes…" he grumbled. "Or 'is vrist…anyvhere 'e vill bleed vrom," he uttered irritably. "Maybe you can bite and suck on 'is thumb," he mumbled, leaning back against the wagon.

"Like a baby?" Danford asked, wide-eyed.

"Oh, my God," Zalith uttered.

"Just…bite zhe guy bevore I lose my patience," Alucard snarled.

"O-okay, sorry. I think I'll just stick to tradition and bite his neck," Danford said. But as he went to move closer, he looked back at Alucard. "Is Freja watching?"

"Just do it, Danford," Zalith snapped.

With a slight flinch, Danford nodded and knelt, grabbing the man.

As Danford went to bite the human's neck, Alucard rolled his eyes and turned his back on him. "I zon't know 'ow I'm going to get vhrough a veek of looking avter 'im, let alone a month or two," he complained.

Zalith kept an irritated glare, watching as Danford bit the terrified human and started to drink his blood.

Alucard frowned, hearing the hapless sucking and gnawing. "You zon't…bite zhe blood, Zanvord, you suck," he grumbled.

Danford grunted and did as Alucard told him.

"Zhere, like zhat," Alucard said with a sigh as Danford groaned contently, swallowing loudly. He exhaled deeply and focused on Zalith. "Are you okay?" he couldn't help but ask. "You're just…veally quiet."

"Of course I'm okay," he said with a smile, moving his arm around his waist and hugging him from the side a little.

Alucard wasn't sure whether or not he believed him, but he wanted to. He himself was so happy—happier than he might have ever been, but he couldn't help but feel like something was wrong with Zalith, and as much as he wanted to ask, he wouldn't. He knew there was nothing he could do, after all. So, he nodded and sighed. "'E shouldn't be too much longer," he muttered, glancing over at Danford.

"Okay," his mate said with a nod.

Once Danford was done, he sat on the ground and groaned contently, licking his bloody lips.

Alucard sighed deeply and glanced down at him. "You draw, vight?"

Danford looked up at him, an almost dazed look on his face—he was clearly blood-high, and Alucard hoped he'd cooperate. "Y-yeah," he said, nodding, but he soon adorned a delayed look of startle.

The vampire rolled his eyes. "So do you 'appen to 'ave paper and maybe a pen or pencil?"

He shook his head, his eyes wide with nervousness. "N-no, I didn't…have the chance to grab it before we left; most of our stuff is still on your ship, but…I'm sure I can find some."

"Zhen go," Alucard said, taking hold of Zalith's hand. Then, he wandered off with the demon, leaving Danford alone. He'd be fine for the next while.

"What do you want him to draw?" Zalith asked curiously as they reached the log they'd been sitting on.

"I zon't vant *'im* to draw, *I* vant to draw," he corrected, sitting beside him.

"Oh, I like that better," the demon said.

Alucard smiled in response. "I also called upon vone of my vampires to bring us someving better to drvink," he added.

"I like that, too," the demon said with a smirk, and then he moved his hand to the back of Alucard's head, pulled him closer, and started kissing him. He paused after a few strokes of their tongues and asked, "When and where did you learn to draw, vampire?"

He shrugged. "Vell…zhere vasn't much to do vhen I vas vaiting avound in Zamien's castle betveen jobs, so I started drawing vings."

"What are you going to draw?" he asked and sipped from his mead.

Alucard smiled. "Is a surprise."

"Can't I have a hint?"

"No, you 'ave to vait."

"Not even a tiny, baby hint?"

He shook his head. "I'm not telling you."

Zalith laughed quietly as he put his mug down. "It's not a drawing of Danford, is it?"

"No," Alucard grumbled, pouting. "Vhy vould I draw 'im?"

The demon laughed again. "I'm joking. I know you wouldn't," he said, moving his hand to the back of Alucard's head again—and then, he started kissing him once more.

Alucard let them kiss for a little while longer, enjoying Zalith's affection and his company. Maybe Zalith was okay, maybe he just seemed sad because he was tired. He seemed okay right now….

Resting his forehead against Zalith's, Alucard sighed deeply. "Vere you ever intervested in drawing?" he asked curiously, still unaware of what—if any—hobbies Zalith had or once had.

"Yeah, when I was younger," he said with a nod. "But I'm not very good. I love the arts, but I'm not very artistic."

"I zon't believe you're not artistic," Alucard said, smirking. "I vant to see you draw someving," he said. "Vill you draw vith me?"

"I can't promise you that it'll be good."

"I'm sure vill be vine."

And just then, Danford made his way over to them with a few pieces of paper in one hand, and a pen and pencil in the other. "Uh…what do you want me to draw?"

"I zon't vant you to draw anyving," Alucard said with a scowl. "I just vant vhat I asked you to get."

"Oh…" he said, flustered. "Okay," he mumbled, handing the paper, pen, and pencil to Alucard. He stood up straight with an awkward look on his face. "So…I should go, right?"

"Yes…" Alucard grumbled.

"Okay…thanks," he said, and then he turned around and left.

Once he was gone, Alucard handed Zalith half of the paper and the pencil. "Vhat are you going to draw?" he asked curiously.

"What *should* I draw?"

Alucard looked around. "Vell…I zon't know. Vhat did you use to draw?"

"Nothing, really—I'm not very good," he laughed.

"Vhat about Peaches?" he asked, setting his eyes on his small kitten, who was cleaning herself on the saddle of Zalith's horse. "You could try and draw 'er?"

"I'll try my best," the demon said.

Alucard smiled. "Okay."

He watched Zalith stare down at his paper and start to unsurely sketch, and Alucard did the same. He wasn't sure how long Toma would take to get back with the wine and champagne, but at least he and Zalith had something to do in the meantime. And as Greymore and the rest of Zalith's people partied around them, Alucard and Zalith got to work, sketching as best they could with what they had.

Chapter Seventy-Four

Their Last Night in the Woods

| Alucard |

Alucard was almost finished with his drawing of Zalith. He was sure that a short while had passed, and given more time, he knew he could do better, but he was still pleased with what he had accomplished. He put his pen down, turning the paper over so that Zalith couldn't see. He then looked at the demon, curious to see how his drawing of Peaches was coming along.

"Are you done?" Zalith asked, glancing at him as he put his pencil down.

"Yes," he said with a smile. "Are you?"

"I suppose. It's not getting any better."

"Let me see," Alucard said, leaning over.

The demon sighed, looking down at the paper in his lap. "Okay," he said, handing it to him.

Excited to see, Alucard took it from him—and Zalith's drawing of Peaches wasn't actually all that bad…at least Alucard thought so. The cat's body was a little misshaped, and its head was unusually round, but…Alucard loved it all the same. He smiled, taking his eyes off the drawing to look at Zalith. "I vink looks veally good. I vill keep vorever," he said, smirking.

Zalith shook his head. "No, you can throw it out, it's okay," he laughed. "I won't be mad."

"No, I love," Alucard insisted. Then, he picked up his drawing and held it out to Zalith. "And zhis is vor you."

Taking and staring down at it, Zalith smiled appreciatively. "Thank you," he said. "I love it."

Before Alucard could reply, Zalith leaned in and kissed his lips. He kissed him again and again, gradually moving down to his neck—but then he stopped, lifting his head to stare into Alucard's eyes.

"I'll keep it forever," the demon said.

"I vas actually vinking," Alucard replied as a shy frown stole his content visage. "Vhen ve get married…vell…ve should look vor an artist, vight? To draw portraits of us at zhe vedding?"

Smiling, Zalith fiddled with a loose strand of Alucard's hair. "That's a great idea."

"Ve can probably look avound closer to zhe time…or vhen ve are settled in zhe castle."

"Sounds like a plan," the demon agreed.

Just then, Toma's arrival caught Alucard's attention. He looked back over his shoulder, watching as the man landed and rematerialized from his bat form, and then he made his way over with a bottle of red wine in one hand and a bottle of champagne in the other.

"Vell, looks like our drvinks are 'ere," Alucard said, smiling at Zalith.

"And not a moment too soon," the demon replied.

"As requested, My Lord," Toma said, appearing beside Alucard and holding both bottles out to him.

"Vank you," he said, taking them.

As quickly as he appeared, Toma then dematerialized and flew off into the night sky.

"Which do you vant virst?" Alucard asked, showing Zalith what their options were.

His mate took the bottle of champagne from him. "This is fancier," he said with a smirk.

Alucard nodded, putting the bottle of wine down. He then picked up his and Zaliht's mugs of mead and emptied them into the grass. "Vill you open?"

Zalith nodded and carefully pulled the cork from the bottle, letting it fizz and drip to the ground for a few moments. Then, he poured it into both cups before putting it down beside him and taking his cup from Alucard.

They were celebrating, and Alucard wanted to make a toast. "Ve vere…talking about time vonce," he said, looking down into his drink. "You told me I mentioned zhat a lot vor somevone who can't die—but I vealized zhat back zhen, I 'ad never…truly lived," he said, lifting his head to stare into Zalith's eyes. "Not until I met you. You said…ve only 'ave vorever, is not long at all," he laughed. "Vell…I am glad zhat I get to spend my vorever vith you," he smiled, holding up his drink. "To us, and our vorever."

Holding up his drink, Zalith smiled, too. "To us, and our forever," he repeated, and once they clinked their cups together, they both sipped from their drinks. "That was very beautiful," he then said.

Alucard smiled shyly, looking away slightly as he tried to hide his fluster. "I meant zhat," he said, but as the demon moved his hand to the side of his face, he turned back to face him; Zalith started kissing him, and he kissed back, his feelings of contentedness having been so constant since the moment Zalith had asked him to marry him. He felt almost overwhelmed with happiness, and he didn't really know what to do with it. "I love you," he said when they stopped kissing to take a breath.

"I love you, too," Zalith said quietly, keeping his hand on the side of Alucard's face.

However, as Alucard smiled down at his drink, he felt something drip onto his face. He frowned, looking up, and as the rain started slowly falling, he frowned disappointedly, sure that it was going to bring their evening to an abrupt ending. He took his eyes off Zalith, watching as everyone started hurrying to pack their things away, the rain beginning to fall heavier. And Alucard was certain that it was only going to get worse.

"Uh-oh," Zalith said, also watching the camp.

"I guess…is time to 'ead to bed, no?" Alucard asked.

"We don't have to sleep," the demon said, picking up the bottle of champagne as they both stood up.

Alucard smiled, grabbing the bottle of wine. "Vhat…vill ve do?" he asked curiously as he took Peaches from Zalith's horse and followed his mate through the panicking camp while everyone hurried to pack their things away.

"I don't know. I guess we'll have to go inside and see," the demon teased, reaching their tent. He held its door open, inviting Alucard to walk in first.

Alucard made his way into the tent and sat down on their bed, letting Peaches go and wander around. He placed the wine and his drink down, smiling up at Zalith and waiting for him to sit beside him. While he sat there, though, his thoughts danced around the fact that this time tomorrow, he and Zalith might very well be in the comfort of their castle. "So," he said, watching as Zalith sat beside him. "'Ow do you veel knowing zhat ve'll be 'ome maybe zhis time tomorrow?" he asked. "In our own bed."

"It makes me feel better than I've felt all this time, that's for sure," he said with a laugh. But he then leaned forward and lightly gripped Alucard's chin, staring into his eyes. "Aside from today—today is special," he said, and then he kissed his lips.

Alucard smiled, looking down at his drink as he sat cross-legged. "Today is zhe 'appiest I 'ave ever velt."

Zalith moved his hand to Alucard's head, caressing his hair. "I'm glad that you're happy," he murmured. "I was worried that this wouldn't be the best time to do this, but like I said earlier, I didn't want to wait anymore."

Smiling, Alucard rested his forehead against Zalith's. "Now vas a time better zhan any ozzer. Ve've been vhrough so much shit—ve deserve someving good, no?" he said, staring into his fiancé's dark, alluring eyes. "I von't lie…I'd been vaiting; I knew I vanted to marry you a vhile ago, but I zidn't know if you vanted zhe same ving. I 'ear zhat…marriage is scary vor some people, hmm?"

"I'm not scared," the demon said with a content, warm smile. "Are *you* scared?"

Alucard shrugged. "No," he said…but unsurely.

Zalith smirked and teased, "You don't sound so sure."

"Vell…I…zon't veally know about veddings. Vhat if I get someving vrong?"

"You won't get something wrong, baby, don't worry," Zalith assured him. "I believe in you. There's also usually a rehearsal before the wedding anyway to make sure everything goes well."

Alucard nodded, taking a sip of his drink. "Vell…vhat about…" he frowned, something nervous starting to build up inside him. "Ve are both…men…."

"Wait, you're a *man*?" Zalith asked, a dramatic look of shock on his face.

The vampire pouted. "I mean…vill ve both just vear black suit? I know zhat traditionally, zhe voman vears white, so…."

"Well, I don't want to wear white, and we can't put you in white because you're not a virgin, so," he laughed with a grin as Alucard's face surely went red.

He looked away, pouting. "Vhatever," he grumbled.

"It's okay," Zalith said. "Can I tell you a secret?" he then asked quietly.

Still with a pout, Alucard glanced at him. "Vhat?"

"I'm not a virgin either," he said as if it were a revelation.

Alucard rolled his eyes and sighed, finishing his drink. "Anyvay…" he drawled, and as Zalith laughed, he pouted again. "If ve're leaving early tomorrow, ve probably shouldn't stay up too late."

"You're probably right. Although I *was* going to ask you to fuck me; but if it's bedtime, I understand," he flirted.

Flustered once again, Alucard took his eyes off the demon and scowled down at his empty mug. He didn't really know what to say—he hadn't felt this embarrassed in a while, and Zalith was obviously enjoying it. But the question now was, did he want to do what Zalith suggested? He pouted and shrugged. "I can do zhat," he muttered.

"Are you sure?" his mate asked. "You still might be able to wear white at the wedding, but after this, I'm not so positive that you'll be able to get away with it," he grinned.

Still pouting and scowling embarrassedly, Alucard set his empty mug aside and grabbed the front of Zalith's shirt. Before the demon could say anything, Alucard forced him onto his back and glared down at him. "Be quiet," he muttered, holding him down.

"Or what?" Zalith tested.

"Or," Alucard said, lightly gripping Zalith's cheeks with his right hand, squishing them together, "I vill put someving in your mouth so zhat you can't speak," he said, glancing down at the demon's lips, tempted to kiss them, but he didn't, and looked back into his eyes.

"I need more information," Zalith said, his voice a little muffled as he tried to speak with his cheeks between Alucard's fingers.

He fought through his fluster, keeping an almost vacant glare on Zalith. "Zidn't you vonce tell me you vanted me to fuck your vace?"

Zalith laughed. "I don't think I said it like that, but I remember."

Alucard shrugged lightly. "Vell…maybe I vill do zhat."

The demon smirked excitedly. "We're definitely going to have to put you in black for the wedding."

Alucard pouted and took his eyes off him for a moment—he didn't actually know what he had to do, and he felt overly embarrassed about it. But, as nervous as he was, he knew Zalith would have answers for him. "Vhat…do I do?" he asked quietly, looking down at him.

The demon patted his own chest with his hand. "Sit," he said.

With a nervous frown, Alucard did as Zalith instructed and sat on his chest. He watched as Zalith grabbed one of the pillows, propped his head up against it, and then moved his hands to the vampire's waist. He smiled up at Alucard, dragging his hands down and around to his crotch—he didn't waste time at all; he started unbuttoning Alucard's trousers, and then he reached inside to caress the vampire's arousal.

"You're going to have to lean on this," Zalith then said, tapping the crate behind him.

Alucard took his eyes off him and looked at the crate—and he did as Zalith said, leaning forward, resting his arms on it as Zalith continued to caress his shaft with his hand.

"Are you comfortable?" Zalith asked.

The vampire nodded.

"Okay," he said, smirking, and then he took the vampire's dick into his mouth. He twirled his tongue around its tip, stroked its length with his lips, and then he gripped Alucard's thighs with his hands, pulling him closer to his face.

Alucard was sure that he had to move, so he started gently thrusting back and forth, closing his eyes as pleasure began to enthral him. He'd not lie, there was something he loved about the feeling of Zalith's tongue against his shaft; maybe it was how Zalith always knew exactly how to make him feel satisfied, how deeply he pleased him. And as he eased his dick into Zalith's throat, Alucard moaned quietly, his heart thumping a little faster.

Zalith kept hold of his thighs, murmuring sounds of enjoyment and delight as Alucard relaxed, moving back and forth, speeding up ever so slightly. But the demon soon squeezed his legs, nudging Alucard back a little—and Alucard assumed he wanted him to stop, so he did.

The vampire pulled his shaft free from the demon's throat, and as Zalith gripped it with his hand, holding it close to his warm lips, Alucard asked him, "Are you okay?"

"Yeah," Zalith said with a smirk, but he said it with haste, caressing the vampire's wet shaft for a few moments before urging it back into his mouth.

Alucard moaned quietly, resting his head on his forearm as he eased his dick back down Zalith's throat, and then he thrusted. But he never really lasted very long when Zalith used his mouth to please him. And he tried to resist the overwhelming, delightful rush towards his peak, but he struggled. Zalith's muffled, pleased murmurs encouraged Alucard's body to give in; he closed his eyes, grimacing in struggle, but he could feel himself tipping over the edge of his peak—his body was starting to tremble, his heart was racing, and as Zalith moved his hands from his thighs to grip his ass instead, Alucard caved, moaning against his arm as he climaxed, digging his claws into the crate.

Zalith groaned contently as Alucard's dick throbbed in his throat, squeezing his ass tightly. And with a satisfied moan, the demon pulled the vampire back, making him sit on his chest again, easing his shaft from his mouth; he then gripped Alucard's waist, pulling him away from the crate without warning, and swiftly pinned him on his back.

Resting his arms on Alucard's chest, Zalith smiled down at him and wiped his lips with the back of his hand. "You did really good, baby," he said, tucking a loose strand of Alucard's hair behind his ear.

Close to exhausted—which perturbed Alucard—he smiled as best he could, guiding his hand to the back of Zalith's head. He pulled his mate closer, kissing his lips for a few moments, but he couldn't keep it up for very long. He exhaled deeply as Zalith rested his head on his chest, moving his arm around him. He just wanted to lay there and relax.

The demon started stroking his fingers over Alucard's chest, glancing up at him. "You don't have to fuck me if you don't want to," he said quietly.

Alucard looked down at him. He didn't *not* want to, he just needed a moment to rest. "No, I…I vant to," he breathed, trying to calm his trembling body. "I vill. I just…need to lay 'ere vor a second."

"That's okay. Take your time," the demon said quietly.

But then Alucard thought…maybe he *shouldn't* take his time. He felt so very tired, and he knew that if he laid there for as long as he wanted to, he'd end up falling asleep, and he didn't want to disappoint Zalith. So instead of relaxing, he exhaled deeply and gripped Zalith's arms, moving him from over him. Zalith complied as Alucard made him turn his back to him and lay on his side, and as he lay beside him, Alucard rested his head on Zalith's for a moment.

"You'll need this," the demon smirked, reaching behind to hand him a bottle of lube.

Taking it from him, Alucard rested his head on his pillow—and at the same time, Zalith reached behind himself to grip the vampire's shaft, starting to caress it with his hand once again.

Alucard lay there for a short while, stroking his hands down Zalith's back, nuzzling the back of his neck until he felt like he'd mustered enough energy. He gripped the demon's trousers, pulling them off; as Zalith let go of his shaft, Alucard squeezed some lube from the bottle and smothered his dick with it. Then, he massaged a little into the demon's ass, listening to Zalith's quiet, pleased hums. Once he was done, he moved one arm around Zalith, holding him tightly as he started to ease his length inside him.

Zalith moaned pleasurably, gripping Alucard's wrist. Alucard nuzzled the side of his neck, breathing deeply as he started to pull himself back. Despite having only climaxed not too long ago, he was already starting to feel a rapture consuming him. He hummed quietly, thrusting back and forth as he held Zalith tightly.

The demon moaned again, stroking his hand over Alucard's arm and down to his own crotch, where he gripped his arousal. Alucard began moving a little faster when he saw Zalith caressing his own dick; his mate turned his head to the side, and when their eyes locked, Alucard stared for a moment before starting to kiss him.

Alucard's already trembling body started to ache—but he kept going. He breathed deeply through his nose, kissing Zalith, holding him tightly as he thrusted harder. The pleasure spiralled through him, his heart racing—and he had to stop kissing him so that he could breathe, nuzzling Zalith's neck once more. As it always did, a struggled grimace made its way to his face—he could feel himself approaching his peak, but he hadn't heard Zalith climax yet—maybe he wasn't doing it right?

He frowned, still thrusting, still holding him—but he didn't have the strength to hold on for much longer. He was tired, his body was aching, and the longer he kept this up, the worse he knew he would feel. Once more, he grimaced, holding Zalith a little tighter—and as he willingly tipped over the edge and climaxed again, he moaned a struggled moan against Zalith's neck, where he then bit down, but not so harshly as to draw blood. Zalith's pleasured moan followed not too long after, and as he reached back to grip Alucard's arm, the vampire smiled, relieved to know that he'd satisfied his mate.

Alucard rolled onto his back, exhaling deeply as he waited for his trembling body to calm down. He glanced at Zalith, watching as he pulled off his shirt and used it to clean himself before shuffling closer and resting his head on Alucard's chest.

"I…veally love you," Alucard said, smiling down at him.

"I really love you, too," the demon said. "And I hope you had a nice day."

"I did," he said with a nod, closing his eyes as he exhaled deeply again. "Zhis vas…vone of zhe best days of my life."

Zalith hugged him tightly. "Me too," he said quietly. "I can't wait to marry you."

"I can't vait to marry *you*," Alucard replied sleepily.

The demon reached up to Alucard's head and started to fiddle with his hair. "Goodnight baby."

Alucard exhaled tiredly. "Goodnight…Zaliv," he said with a content smile. And then he let himself slowly drift off. He was exhausted but satisfied. It had been a long but wonderful day, and he couldn't wait to wake up tomorrow knowing that he'd be a day closer to not only his and Zalith's new home but the day they'd be married.

| Zalith |

The hours ticked by… and Zalith couldn't sleep.

Laying there, he waited, alone with his thoughts. And his thoughts—they were so heavy, burdened with heartache and disappointment. He thought that asking Alucard to marry him would cure him of the sadness that had gripped him so harshly… and it had, but… it also hadn't. He didn't regret it—of course he didn't. He loved Alucard so much, and all he wanted was to spend forever with him. But what if he died again? What if something or someone took Alucard from him? What if something happened, and Zalith couldn't do anything about it?

He held his vampire tighter. He still felt like he didn't deserve Alucard, like all of the awful things that had been happening were happening because Zalith didn't deserve to be happy—because he had to pay for all the bad things he'd done before he'd met Alucard. What if that was why all of this was happening now? What was next? He'd lost Varana, he'd almost lost Alucard… would he *actually* lose him?

His throat tightened as the heart-breaking dread started to drown him. He missed Varana, and he had no idea where she was or if he'd ever see her again. He'd fucked that up, so who was to say he wouldn't fuck this up, too? He loved Alucard so much… and he deserved the world… not someone as useless and disappointing as Zalith. But… he wanted to hold onto him. Alucard was the only light in his life—he needed him, he wanted him, and he would do whatever he could to keep hold of him. Alucard was his, he was Alucard's… and no matter what the world might throw at him next, Zalith would do his best to fight on—because he had to… for Alucard.

Fighting his sadness, he stared over at the tent's wall. He knew he wouldn't get any sleep, but… at least he could lay here with Alucard. At least he would get to see his vampire wake up to him in the morning… and tomorrow, they'd leave this godforsaken forest and move on with their lives.

At least he hoped so.

Chapter Seventy-Five

Glimpse

| Zalith, *Wednesday, Cordus 8th, 960(TG)—Nefastus* |

Zalith lay silently on his back, staring up aimlessly with his arm around Alucard, who had his head rested on the demon's chest. He wasn't sure how long it had been, but he'd laid there and watched the darkness outside become lighter and lighter, and he was sure dawn was approaching. He hadn't gotten a wink of sleep—how could he? His thoughts were endlessly racing, and his feelings of guilt, of sadness, and of disappointment in himself wouldn't let him settle. He had to stay awake—he had to stay aware. After all, what if something happened? Never again would he let anything happen to Alucard, even if it meant he'd not get an hour of sleep for the rest of time.

He looked down at his vampire, his fiancé, the love of his life, his world, his every single damn thing. The peaceful look on his face brought relief unto Zalith—but only for a moment. He rested his head back against his pillow, resuming his endless gaze into nothing. At least today would be the last day he'd have to spend his time staring at trees. In no less than twelve hours, he and Alucard would be home at their castle; he could shower, he could eat something that wasn't runny stew, and he could sleep in a bed that was his rather than on a cold, damp floor piled with furs. He longed for such things, and he hoped they would help him escape the cold grip of depression that had been drowning him so.

With a quiet, heavy sigh, he closed his eyes for but a moment. How much longer would he have to wait?

But Alucard then stirred, murmuring something Zalith didn't understand.

The demon opened his eyes, looking down at him. "Alucard?" he asked quietly, sure that his vampire was having another nightmare.

Alucard frowned, moving his arm up to Zalith's shoulder; he then opened his eyes, moving his head so that he could look up at Zalith.

"Hey," the demon said, smiling warmly.

The vampire kept his frown, seeming to take a moment to work out where he was. "Vhat's… zhe time?" he asked.

"I'm not sure," he admitted. "I think it's close to dawn." He reached around and found his trousers; he took his pocket watch out and opened it. "Yeah. Almost seven." He put his watch away.

Nodding, Alucard sighed and rested his head back on Zalith's chest, hugging him tightly. "I 'ad a nightmare," he mumbled. "I saw… Zamien. Ve vere back in my castle. Vhen 'e tore your ving all zhat time ago—but zhis time, 'e made me vatch 'im kill you," he explained sadly, his voice laced with fatigue.

Zalith knew that *he* was responsible for Alucard's fatigue. "Don't worry," he said quietly, hugging him. "It was just a dream. Damien has no idea where we are, and he never will," he assured him confidently. But he couldn't not feel skeptical. "Do you think we should be worried?" he asked.

"No," Alucard answered. "Zhis velt divverent. I zon't veel any imminent danger like I did zhose times bevore. Zamien… 'e 'as no idea vhere ve are," he concurred firmly. "I zon't… dream of 'im ovten."

Zalith wanted to tell him that he'd never have to see Damien again, but he couldn't actually promise that. He wanted to tell him that he would protect him from Damien forever, and as much as he would try, he couldn't guarantee it, could he? After everything that had happened, he didn't want to disappoint Alucard any more than he already had. So he wouldn't make promises he felt he couldn't keep.

Instead, he pulled his vampire deeper into his embrace. "Are you okay?"

"I'm okay," Alucard answered, closing his eyes once more.

"I wish I could take away all of your bad dreams," he said sadly. "And replace them with only good things."

Alucard smiled tiredly. "I zon't 'ave as many nightmares vhen I sleep vith you. I used to 'ave zhem pretty much all zhe time bevore I met you."

"Luckily, you'll never have to spend another night alone again," Zalith said.

"Neizer vill you."

Zalith guided his hand to Alucard's head, caressing his hair as he started to fall back asleep.

As Alucard then settled down, Zalith went back to staring up at the ceiling. As much as he wanted to keep talking to Alucard, he wanted his vampire to get as much rest as he could. They had a long journey ahead of them today, and he didn't want his vampire to be exhausted. So, he lay there in silence, staring aimlessly once again.

But Alucard didn't seem to be able to fall back asleep. He stirred, he shuffled around, and with a deep sigh, he leaned up onto his arm and stared down at Zalith.

"What's wrong?" the demon asked, placing his hand on the side of Alucard's face.

"I can't vall back asleep," he said, pouting.

"Are you uncomfortable? Is there something that might help?"

Alucard shrugged, sitting up. "I zon't know," he mumbled.

"Come here," he said, reaching out for Alucard's hand, and as the vampire took hold of his hand, he pulled him closer, making him lay on top of him. "Close your eyes and try not to think about sleeping," he said quietly as he caressed Alucard's hair. "Do you want to hear a story?"

The vampire nodded.

"What kind of story?"

For a moment, Alucard remained silent, likely thinking. "Vill you tell me more about your vamily?"

"Is there anything or anyone in particular you'd like to hear about?" he asked, fiddling with Alucard's fringe.

"Maybe…your brother," he said quietly.

Zalith smiled sadly. It brought sadness to his heart whenever he thought about Xurian, and the nightmare he had about Alucard the night before didn't help. But he was happy to talk about his family; he missed them so much and thought about them so often. He'd take any moment to reminisce about that part of his life.

He took a moment to decide which story he should tell. "When I was about seven, my mother had this friend named…Carlotta, I believe—and I say friend loosely because they were always fighting about one thing or another. She and my mother were fairly similar looking; they had similar tastes and were both very loud and opinionated women, and that sparked some sort of rivalry between them. Since money meant status where I grew up, my mother was the alpha socialite, for the lack of a better term, and up until that point, no one ever really challenged her quite like Carlotta did, and it irritated her to no end.

"So, anyway, one day Carlotta had this *beautiful* custom woven blanket shipped in from overseas, and I don't really remember much about what it looked like except whatever wool it was made from made the blanket look like it was spun from gold, and my mother was *obsessed.* She asked Carlotta where she had the blanket made and what animal the wool came from, but Carlotta *refused* to tell her, and when my mother eventually offered to buy it from her, she declined, which drove my mother absolutely insane. There wasn't a dinner that went by where we didn't hear about this blanket. She would beg my father to hire someone to infiltrate Carlotta's family and look at their records to see where the blanket came from. She wanted to send people across the world just to get wool samples so she could narrow down her search—she even talked about getting someone to break into their house and steal it, or even to get a small thread sample so she could get it analyzed somehow.

"But this blanket obsession went on for about two months or so I think, and soon enough my mother's birthday was right around the corner. I remember Xurian came up to me one day and he looked me in the eyes, and he said, 'We're getting mom that blanket for her birthday', and I remember I felt a little bit sick because I didn't want to steal, especially not from an adult, but he assured me that everything would be fine. Long story short, everything was not fine, and we were escorted off of the property which I remember being very upsetting for me. I cried a lot; I didn't want to get in trouble," he laughed, smiling fondly. "After that, though, my father said that was it, and he didn't want to hear any more blanket talk for the rest of his life, so *naturally* I thought that the whole thing was over…I was wrong." He paused, glancing at Alucard, who was laughing quietly.

"I struggle to picture you crying like zhat," the vampire said with a smirk.

Zalith chuckled. "All I did was cry."

Alucard nuzzled his neck. "Tell me more," he said quietly.

The demon smiled. "About a week later, the day before my mother's birthday, Xurian said he had something very secret to show me, and he took me all the way to the barn where the workhorses were kept. I remember him climbing behind a bunch of barrels and he pulled a huge white blanket out of nowhere like a magician, and he said, 'I got this for mom's birthday from the man with one eye', which in itself is a whole other story, and I thought this was very nice of him because obviously, she wanted a blanket, but the blanket at Carlotta's was gold; I remember him saying, 'That's okay because I kissed Bridget Dewsbury and she said I can go to her dad's farm and take all the flowers I want'. If my memory serves, the Dewsbury's bred racehorses, but they had a large property with thousands of puffy golden wildflowers, so I thought that this was a brilliant idea because we had just learned a few months prior how fabric was dyed.

"So, Xurian and I grabbed some baskets, and we went with his dogs to the field and picked as many flowers as we could carry; we then brought them back to the barn where we mashed up the flowers with rocks and put them in one of the horse troughs. Surprisingly, the water actually almost looked like Carlotta's blanket, so naturally, we thought we were the two smartest children in the country. I remember the two of us talking about starting a fabric dying business and working on a silly little pitch for the Dewsbury's so that they'd let us use their flowers," he told him amusedly.

Alucard laughed again. "Vhat vould you call your little business?"

"I think Xurian suggested 'Dye Guys'."

"Vhat?" Alucard scoffed with a smirk. "No, I love zhat—is perfect," he teased. "I can't imagine you sitting avound dying vabric, Zaliv—I assume zidn't ever 'appen, no?"

"No, but you'll see why soon," he said.

The vampire smiled, waiting for him to continue.

"We let the blanket soak for a few hours, and when we pulled it out of the water, it was extremely uneven and it almost looked like someone had pissed on it," he said with a grimace. "Regardless, it was certainly not the rich golden colour we came to expect;

but that was the least of our worries because the dyed water stained everything else that it touched. We were little slobs, of course, so our hands were stained, our arms were stained, and parts of our clothes and shoes were stained, and I started to get upset because I knew we'd get in trouble. So I was crying, and Xurian, who was already mad about the blanket, was getting annoyed, so he pushed me, which caused me to slip on something while I was catching my balance and I fell *right* into the water," he said as Alucard started laughing again. "I was yellow from head to toe, Alucard—I looked like a banana," he exclaimed, laughing with Alucard.

They both took a few moments to calm down, and Zalith smiled contently; he loved to reminisce, and he found that he loved to do so even more with Alucard. He enjoyed hearing Alucard laugh; he enjoyed knowing that he was making him happy.

"I was very upset," Zalith continued, trying to calm his laughter—but Alucard kept laughing with an amused smile on his face. "So, once I managed to climb out, I pushed Xurian into the water, too—he was mad, of course, so he chased me all the way home, and we ended up fighting in the hallway on top of my mother's very expensive floor runner, which stained much easier than the blanket did. The worst part though was we were having a party the following evening for my mother's birthday, and the runner had actually only been installed a few days prior. She was very excited about it, too; she told all her friends," he laughed. "Oh well. We both got sent to our rooms and weren't allowed to attend the party. We were yellow for about two days."

Still laughing, Alucard shook his head. "You veally 'ad an eventvul child'ood, no?"

"I really did—there was never a dull moment," he said, smiling.

Alucard shrugged, still laughing. "I vish I could say zhe same; I vish I 'ad some vunny stories to tell you."

Zalith hugged him. "If I could take you back in time, I would, baby. We could kiss behind the barn—no one would know," he said, smirking.

With a smile on his face, Alucard lifted his head to look down at him. "I could protect you vrom your mean big brother."

"You'd have to protect me from my big mean brother *and* his big mean friends—and my big mean cousins," he said, fiddling with his hair.

"I vas a very angry little boy at zhat age—zhey vould 'ave all been too scared to be mean to you avter I 'ad dealt vith zhem," he said, flicking Zalith's fringe.

Zalith laughed quietly. "Well, what if they have sticks?"

"Sticks?" Alucard asked.

He shrugged. "Sometimes, they liked to hit each other with sticks."

Alucard pouted. "Zhen… I vould vind a bigger stick and devend you."

"My hero," Zalith smiled, prodding Alucard's cheek.

With a smile on his face, Alucard then rested his head back on Zalith's shoulder. "Can I tell you someving?" he asked quietly, an almost unsure tone in his voice.

"Of course."

"You know zhat…you said you vanted to 'ave a vamily vith me," he said and paused. "Vell…I vink about zhat sometimes, and vor some veason, I veel…avraid, maybe—I vink zhat…because I never veally experienced vhat vas like to 'ave a vamily or grow up vith parents, I veel like I von't…I zon't know…like I von't be good," he muttered, a confounded look on his face. "I never veally got to experience a child'ood, so…I zon't know vhat to do or vhat to give a child," he admitted. "I guess…I'm avraid of vailing zhem," he mumbled despondently.

Zalith frowned sadly, holding him. "You're kind and caring; you listen, and you always do whatever you can to try and help the people you care about. There's going to be a bit of a learning curve, and I'm a little scared too that I won't do a good job, but I think that we can do it together," he assured him.

Alucard smiled. "Okay," he said sleepily.

The demon then kissed Alucard's forehead. "Everything's going to be okay, baby."

Slowly, Alucard moved his hand up to Zalith's neck, dragging his thumb over it. "I love you."

"I love you, too," he said, caressing the vampire's hair as he started to settle once again.

Zalith lay in the silence, staring aimlessly once again. His talk with Alucard had given him a little relief, and he felt as if…maybe he should rest, too. He knew their journey was going to be a long one, and he didn't want to be too tired in case something happened. He'd not let himself sleep though—but he'd rest…he'd just close his eyes for a moment…and let his body relax…only for a few moments….

…But then he woke, snapping out of the sleep he felt so very quickly gripping him. He wasn't where he should be, though. Above him, his eyes were no longer fixed upon the tent roof, but on the roof of the canopy of his and Alucard's bed back home. The sunlight was shining through the windows, the sound of chirping birdsong echoing outside. Confoundment gripped him but so did his worry for Alucard.

Quickly, as he moved his arm to Alucard's side of the bed, he turned his head to look at him, but as his arm could feel and his eyes could see…Alucard wasn't there, and both dread and aching worry struck Zalith's heart. He sat up, his heart racing as he frantically searched their room with his eyes—but then he heard the squeaking of the shower knob turning and the sound of gushing water.

He felt relief—Alucard was just showering. But his dread didn't settle—he needed to see him. So he got out of bed, making his way over to the bathroom. However, as he opened the door…the sound of running water ceased, and the bathroom…it was utterly empty. No sign of Alucard. The lights were off, and the room wasn't filled with steam. In fact, there were no signs that the shower had actually been on at all. And Zalith's worry turned into fear.

But then he heard the floor creak outside—the floor near the top of the stairs could always be heard. He rushed out of the bathroom, hoping to catch Alucard making his way downstairs—but there was nothing. No one. Anything. Anywhere.

Music—the sound of a violin; it played, echoing from below. Alucard had to be in his office playing, so Zalith hurried downstairs, the music becoming louder the closer he came. And he reached out—he grabbed the handle of the door to Alucard's office and pushed it open, but the second he stepped foot in the room, it went silent. The room was empty. The sun shined in through the window behind Alucard's desk, but there was no sign of Alucard or his violin. And Zalith could feel his heart beating so fast that he was sure it might jump out of his chest if he didn't find Alucard soon.

A glimpse of red, however, immediately caught his eye. Out through the window—Alucard? Zalith stared, watching as the crimson-haired vampire walked into the darkness of the forest—although he had only seen a glimpse of him, Zalith knew it was Alucard. So he hurried—he made his way into his own office and pulled open the glass doors, racing out onto the grass-covered lawn.

As Alucard had, Zalith made his way into the forest, but he had no idea where Alucard had gone. He tried to focus on the connection they had to one another through their imprints, but Alucard's location was scattered—all over the place. Zalith just ran—he ran and ran and ran, searching frantically—he felt as if he'd been running for hours, his heart racing, his body aching. But there, behind a tree not too far away, he could swear he saw red. So he changed direction, racing until he saw red once more—no, he saw Alucard. The vampire was walking, moving—Zalith had no idea where he was going, all he knew was that he had to follow. He had to catch up, he had to find him... and as the trees around him seemed to almost laugh in his face as he struggled and panicked, he felt like he was very near to collapse.

But that was when he found him—when he found Alucard. He stopped by a fallen tree to catch his breath; he felt like he'd been running for hours. And as he took his eyes off the leaf-covered ground, his eyes widened in terror. If it wasn't for his crimson hair, Zalith might not know that what lay before him was Alucard—he lay beneath the tree just ahead of him, his body torn, clawed and mangled by what Zalith could only imagine was a beast. Vines had twisted their way through his skin, wrapping around his exposed bones, tying him to the ground that had claimed him. How long he had been there, Zalith had no idea... and when it hit him—when he realized that Alucard was gone, he felt his heart shatter into a billion pieces, his jaw chattering as he tried to find words he couldn't speak, tears escaping from his eyes, trickling down his mortified face—

And then he woke.

Horror smothered his face, dread gripped his heart, and as his hand searched for Alucard's, his vampire was nowhere to be found. He sat up once again, frantically searching the confines of the tent with his eyes—but Alucard wasn't there. He shot up to his feet, pulling on his trousers before he rushed out of the tent. His heart was racing, his body so tense—enthralled by fear and panic. He caught Alucard's scent—and he followed it, leaving the camp, hurrying into the trees—and there he was.

Zalith gave Alucard no time to speak. He flung himself at him, wrapping his arms around him before Alucard could say whatever he was about to say to match the shocked look on his face. He hugged him so tightly, burying his face in his neck—he felt as though he might cry, but he fought it, scowling. "Where were you?" he asked, his voice muffled as he kept his face buried in Alucard's neck.

"I... I vas just peeing," he said, startle in his voice. "What's vrong?"

"I didn't know where you were," he said painfully.

Alucard moved his arms around him and hugged him. "I'm sorry," he said. "But you vere asleep... and I couldn't vait."

Zalith kept hold of him—he didn't want to let go. His nightmare had left him horrifically worried once again, and all he wanted to do was hold onto Alucard for as long as he would let him. But when he rested his head on Alucard's, he stared into the forest ahead—and he already knew that he was too late.

Gunfire—it tore away the silence, and the bullets tore through them both as if they were smoke. He fell back, Alucard slipping from his arms, and as he hit the ground, the pain his body endured was nothing in comparison to that which his heart felt. He didn't care about himself—he could hear gunfire, he could hear his people panicking—but Alucard... he was right there... right beside him. Zalith turned his head, gathering what strength he could to lift his hand and reach out for Alucard, who lay on his front, blood on his face, a still, lifeless look in his blue eyes.

The demon struggled, placing his bloody hand on Alucard's pale, lifeless face. If he could speak, he might plead that Alucard said something—but in his heart, he knew it; he knew that Alucard wouldn't reply—and he knew that he would never hear him again.

Light.

Zalith snapped open his eyes, almost gasping for air as his eyes were struck by the light of day—

"Are you okay?" Alucard panicked, leaning over him, staring down at him with the sun shining over his shoulder through a slight crack in the tent's entrance.

Staring at him, Zalith took a moment to work out where he was. His heart was racing, his thoughts even more so. But then he threw his arms around Alucard, holding him tightly, the horror his dreams had burdened him with having not faded. All he wanted to do was hold onto Alucard, and all he could think was that he didn't want anything to happen to him—he didn't want to lose him... he didn't want to see him die anymore.

"Zaliv?" Alucard asked quietly, worry in his voice. "Did you... 'ave a bad dream?"

Zalith sighed a deep sigh, his paranoia starting to fade. But he didn't want to be a baby about it. "Yeah," he said quietly, trying to make himself sound a lot less afraid than he felt.

"Vhat 'appened?" Alucard asked, still holding him.

"You died," he said quietly. "Twice—the second time, right in front of me, and…I couldn't do anything about it."

Alucard leaned back, placing his hand on the side of Zalith's face as he stared a worried stare. "Vas just a dream, Zaliv. I'm vight 'ere."

"I know," he said sadly, moving his arms back around him. Although he knew they were just nightmares, the dread they had burdened him with hadn't faded much. Two nights in a row now he'd had awful dreams where he'd inevitably see Alucard dead or dying—it was what he feared most, and he knew it was going to stick with him for a long, long time.

But he also felt embarrassed—things like this didn't usually happen to him; he wouldn't let something like a dream get to him, but…he was genuinely afraid. He held onto Alucard possessively, protectively, hoping his worry might wither, and his embarrassment with it.

He laid back, holding Alucard close. And then he let the silence ensnare them. Today was the end of their life on the road. Maybe he should just focus on that.

| Alucard |

They rested there for a while in silence. Tense silence. Silence laced with uncertainty. It was only when voices came from the camp that Zalith let out a sigh.

Alucard hugged his mate tightly. He knew all too well what it was like to have such harrowing nightmares—to see the man he loved die or in danger, to wake up feeling so desperate and confused. He didn't want Zalith to feel any of those things. So he held him, waiting until he knew what to say, or until Zalith told him what he needed. Alucard never really knew what to do for himself when he woke from his nightmares, but he always woke knowing that he needed to feel Zalith's embrace—maybe it was the same for Zalith. Maybe all he needed right now was for Alucard to hold him. So that was what he did.

But when the voices of Zalith's people grew louder, the demon exhaled deeply and glanced at Alucard. "Sorry," he mumbled, placing his hand over his eyes.

Alucard leaned up on his arm and stared down at him, a perturbed frown on his face. "Vhy are you sorry?"

"Because I'm annoying," he replied.

Alucard's frown thickened. "Vhat? You're not annoying. You 'ad a bad dream and I vant to do vhat I can to make you veel better—zhat's not annoying."

"I *feel* annoying."

"Vell, you're not annoying," he assured him. And then he smiled. "Noving you do annoys me…except maybe vhen you make me veel embarrassed vhen ve're trying to be serious," he said, attempting to lift the gloomy mood.

Zalith laughed quietly, gradually moving his hand from over his eyes. He then turned his head and looked up at Alucard." Did you sleep okay?"

Alucard shrugged. "I slept better knowing zhat ve von't 'ave to sleep in a vorest anymore," he said. "Maybe you vill veel better too vonce ve are in our own bed, no?"

"I think you're right," Zalith agreed.

"Zhat veminds me," he then said. "Bevore ve leave, I need to…get vid of zhese," he said, moving his hand over his head to grip one of his horns. "Zhe last ving ve vant is to draw attention to ourselves, and if I step into zhat station like zhis, zhen everyvone vill probably start screaming," he mumbled.

"Aw, but I like them," Zalith said with a disappointed frown, reaching up to touch Alucard's horns.

Alucard pouted. "And I like *yours*, but you zon't let me see zhem so ovten—I vink I've seen zhem…vhat? Maybe vree times since I've known you."

"Are you arguing with me, vampire?" Zalith asked, smirking.

"No. Maybe…. Vhat vill you do about if I am?" he tested.

"It wouldn't be much fun if I told you, would it?"

He kept his pout, not sure whether he wanted to find out. As much as he wanted to stay there with Zalith, he had to get rid of his horns before they left for the station. So, he sighed and sat up. "Maybe you can tell me later vhen ve are 'ome, hmm?"

"I won't have to if you behave yourself," he teased.

Standing up as he pulled his trousers on, Alucard shrugged. "Maybe I vill, maybe I von't," he said, grabbing a shirt. "Who knows?"

"I guess we'll just have to wait and see," Zalith murmured amusedly, also standing up and pulling his trousers on.

Alucard then handed the demon a shirt, and once they were both dressed, they left the tent.

As they made their way over to the wagon, Alucard asked Zalith, "So, vhat do you vant to do virst vonce ve get 'ome?"

"Have a shower…or a nice hot bath," he said, smiling at him. "What about you?"

Alucard shrugged as they approached the wagon. "A bath sounds good. I also just vant to lay in our bed vor a vhile."

"I want to do that, too," Zalith agreed, stopping beside him once they reached the wagon. "I want to fall into bed and stay there for a thousand years."

Alucard smiled, moving his hand over Zalith's shoulder. "Me too."

"I wonder what would become of us."

"If ve stayed in bed vor a vhousand years?"

"Yeah."

"Hmm…vell, I know zhat I vould eventually comatose—if I zon't 'ave enough blood, my body just…switches off," he said with a shrug. "As vor you," he said, smirking and prodding Zalith's shoulder. "Maybe you vill shrivel up like old man," he laughed.

The demon laughed, too. "I don't know. I think we could find a way to survive; you drink my blood, I get energy from you, we live in harmony forever."

Alucard frowned doubtfully. "Vone of us vould vun out of vhat zhe ozzer needs eventually—if ve veally could just live off each ozzer, zhen I'm sure zemons vould 'ave viped out 'umanity years ago."

Zalith smirked and said, "We're smart. We could make it work."

"Maybe," Alucard sighed. "But ve still 'ave a lot to do bevore ve can vink about 'ibernating," he said, looking back over his shoulder at the last few humans tied up in front of the wagon's back wheel.

"We have a lot to do before we do anything," Zalith muttered tiredly.

"Ve'll vigure out," Alucard assured him, smiling. "I mean…*ve* zon't veally 'ave to do anyving—ve just…tell ozzer people vhat to do. Vight?"

"As long as you're out of harm's way, I'll be happy," Zalith said.

"Ve'll keep each ozzer out of 'arm's vay," he said firmly.

The demon smiled, pulled him closer, and kissed his lips. "Eat," he then said.

With a quiet sigh, Alucard snatched the arm of one of the humans and pulled him away from the wagon. Thankfully, he'd only need this single man's blood to hide his horns, and the sooner he drained him of his blood and life force, the sooner they could get on their way to the station and end this part of their journey.

As he reached a tree not too far from the camp, his grip tightened, and he shoved the terrified man back against the rough bark. The human's eyes went wide, filled with frantic desperation, but Alucard didn't sink his fangs in—at least, not yet. He paused, savouring the moment, his gaze locked on the man's trembling form as he struggled uselessly. Alucard's eyes traced the fear etched into every line of the man's face, drinking it in like a fleeting whisper of something sweet. But a shadow of disappointment crept over him, dulling the edge of his anticipation, and he knew why.

This wasn't the hunt. This was a hollow imitation, plucking humans from a camp like ripe fruit on a low-hanging branch. They waited there, frozen and helpless, as if begging to be devoured—easy, predictable, soulless. Boring. Alucard's lips curled into a faint sneer. Where was the thrill in this? Where was the pulse-pounding excitement that once raced through his veins like wildfire?

He missed it—the chase, the delicious tension that thrummed through him as he stalked his prey through shadowed alleyways and moonlit streets. He longed for that intoxicating moment when the herd scattered, when the weakest strayed too far from safety, oblivious to the predator in its midst. There was something electric in those seconds before the strike, the air alive with anticipation as he closed in, silent and unseen, watching his prey step right into his grasp, right into his domain. It was in those moments, with the taste of fear in the air and the thrill of the hunt coiled tight within him, that he felt most alive.

But he didn't hunt anymore. He wouldn't. *He couldn't.* He'd made Zalith a promise—a vow that bound him more tightly than any chain. The thrill of the chase, the hunger that once drove him, was now a forbidden indulgence, locked away. This man before him was the only exception, a singular break in the rule that had shaped his new existence, a necessity. Yet…even as he stood there, gripping his prey, Alucard felt the weight of that promise coil around him like a shadow, reminding him of the lines he had sworn never to cross again.

The man trembled under his grasp, but Alucard's mind drifted to Zalith. The memory of his vow, the certainty with which he had given it—he couldn't betray that. Not for the fleeting satisfaction of a kill, no matter how tempting it might be. This man was an exception, yes, but he would not be the undoing of everything Alucard had fought to restrain.

With a low, guttural snarl, Alucard banished the war raging inside him, shoving aside the last remnants of hesitation. He sank his fangs into the human's neck, the sharp bite silencing the man's scream before it could fully form. The rush of blood met his lips, warm and metallic, its life force flooding through him like a current he couldn't quite deny. He pinned the man against the tree, each pulse of blood drawn into him more necessity than pleasure, a craving he tolerated but never fully embraced.

Alucard's grip remained unyielding as he drained his prey, his eyes narrowing to slits as he felt the man's strength wither, his heartbeat stuttering into silence. When he was finished, he let the lifeless body fall to the ground, the cold, hollow thud echoing in the stillness. He turned slowly, facing Zalith, whose expression was darkened with something akin to disappointment, his eyes a storm of emotions barely restrained.

The vampire's gaze held Zalith's, unflinching, though he could feel the sting of the demon's disapproval like a knife twisting in his gut. He knew Zalith hated seeing him like this—feeding on others, succumbing to the darker part of his nature. But what choice did he have? If he ever hoped to reclaim his human form, to erase the last vestiges of what his fall to Lucifer's realm had turned him into, he needed more than blood—he needed the very essence of life itself. And for that, there was no other way. There were only humans.

"I von't need to do zhat again," he assured Zalith as the horns on his head started to crumble away. "I vink…zhis is enough."

"Okay, good," the demon said, sounding relieved.

"Do you vink everyvone is veady to go?" he then asked, changing the subject. "Zhe sooner ve leave zhis place, zhe better."

"We'll let everyone eat breakfast first, and then we'll head out," Zalith said, starting to lead the way back towards the camp.

"Okay," Alucard said, taking hold of Zalith's hand and following him. He felt relieved that this was the last morning he'd have to wake up in the midst of a camp. He was looking forward to being free of the fear of not knowing what might come next. It had been a long, dreadful week full of so much pain, anger, confusion, and sadness, and Alucard just wanted to rest for a long, long while with the man he loved.

Chapter Seventy-Six

Containment Post

| Alucard |

Alucard felt utter relief when he set his eyes on the entrance to Morronhold just up ahead. He smiled as Zalith leaned forward and rested his chin on his shoulder, sitting behind him atop his horse. And behind them, Zalith's people followed behind the wagon which was being pulled by Varana's and Alucard's horses. The wagon's original Clydesdale was being ridden by Camael—Alucard had thought the stallion might need a break, and the animal looked *very* relieved.

To think that they were just less than an hour away from leaving this place—it made him feel as though a huge burden was being lifted from him. All they had to do was make their way through the town and to the station, where they'd buy their tickets, and then they could board the train, which would take them all the way to the coast. Once they got there, they'd take a ship to DeiganLupus, and then... and then, Alucard would use one of the ships he had stored there to take them home to their castle. *Finally.*

They stopped a small distance from the tree line, where everyone who was riding horses dismounted, and as both Alucard and Zalith dismounted Dimitri, everyone set their eyes on them, waiting for their instructions.

"We'll be going in groups of no more than five," Zalith announced. "We'll all meet at the station, and we'll do our best to avoid crowding as to avoid suspicion."

"Vill be zhe same vhen ve get to zhe docks at zhe coast," Alucard continued. "Zhe ship ve'll all be taking is zhe Vrancesca-Moore—is a tvade ship bound vor DeiganLupus; vill be leaving at six, and ve vill arrive avound vour, so zon't miss."

"When you reach the station, just *one* person from each group will come to either myself, Orin, or Idina, and we will give you what you need to buy your tickets," Zalith continued. "Some of you will also have to take the spare horses—I assume there's a carriage for horses?" he asked, looking at Alucard.

The vampire nodded. "Ve'll 'ave to pay extra vor zhem, but is okay."

Zalith nodded. "Okay. Danford and Freja, you two can come with us—and you two as well," he said, pointing to two of Greymore's men. "The rest of you, get into groups and meet us there."

As everyone started to group up and prepare to head for the town, Alucard took a moment to stare out through the cover of the trees. He set his eyes on a group of four silver-armoured guards standing at the town's entrance—and they were accompanied by a plague doctor; he stood behind the silver-armoured guards like some sort of shadow, fiddling with a fog watch.

"Ve 'ave problem," Alucard muttered, looking back at Zalith.

Zalith frowned worriedly, also looking around behind the tree they were standing in front of, and as he set his eyes on the guards and the shrouded man with them, he sighed and frowned irritably. "I guess we should go and see what's going on," he muttered.

Alucard shook his head. He already knew why they were guarding the entrance with a plague doctor. "Is a containment post. Zhey're making sure no vone carrying zhat invection enters zhe town," he explained. "I imagine 'as probably spread by now," he said slowly. "I zidn't…exactly do enough to stop," he said, looking at Zalith—he knew he could have tried sparing more of his vampires to get the city under control, but he hadn't. "Zhat's my vault," he admitted. "But…" he said, looking out at the guards again, "zhey'll probably vant to check us, and as ve know vone of zhe symptoms shows up in your eyes…" he paused and looked at Danford. "Zhat might be a problem. Zhey'll know 'e is vampire, and ve know zhat zhe people 'ere zon't take too vell to anyvone who isn't 'uman or elv, and I zon't vink 'e vill pass vor an elv."

The demon sighed, a look of disappointment appearing on his face—and Alucard was sure he was blaming himself for the virus having spread.

"Is not your vault," he said quickly before Zalith could look at Danford. But everyone was looking at them, and he didn't want to talk about it here—and he was certain that Zalith would much rather not do this in front of everyone either.

Zalith shifted his sights to Danford. "Use your eyepatch to cover your good eye," he instructed. "We'll say the other one's red as a result of your…accident," he said, grabbing his horse's reins. "Let's go," he then called, starting to lead the way out of the forest as Alucard grabbed the reins of his own horse and followed at his side, and Danford, Freja, and the two of Greymore's men Zalith had selected followed, too.

"Zon't blame yourselv," Alucard said quietly to his mate. "Is not your vault—*I* vas zhe vone who said I vould 'andle containing zhe virus to zhe Citadel, not you," he said in hopes that it might help.

Zalith shrugged. "What's done is done I suppose," he said, an almost despondent look on his face.

The vampire frowned—

"Halt!" one of the guards interjected as they came within twenty feet or so of the town's entrance.

Alucard stopped, as did Zalith and those following them.

"We gotta check you for infection before we let you in—plague's sweeping the whole damn country," the guard spat as the doctor slithered out from behind him, making his way towards them.

"Fine," Zalith said.

As he glanced at Zalith, Alucard felt his worry worsening. He'd expected Zalith to respond with something condescending, but he didn't seem to be putting up much of a fight. Maybe he was tired—of course he was. He hadn't slept much at all last night; Alucard was sure he must have only had an hour or two.

"One of ya at a time, step forward," the guard said, standing beside the plague doctor. "Hey, what's up with him?" he then snapped, nodding at Danford.

"Oh," Zalith said, lowering his voice, "he was attacked by a dog a while back and he hasn't really been the same since unfortunately," he answered quietly—and Alucard assumed he did so to act as though he was trying to spare Danford's feelings.

"I see…" the guard nodded. "What's that?" he then asked skeptically, nodding at Peaches, who was sitting on the saddle of Zalith's horse.

"Just our cat," Zalith smiled. "She's not sick, though, don't worry; she's just a hairless breed. Cats *are* allowed in, aren't they?"

The guard's face shrivelled up into a stubborn glare. "Yeah," he said. "Line up."

Zalith nodded and did as the guard said, and so did everyone else, lining up behind him. The demon then moved forward as he was called by the plague doctor; Alucard was sure these people would think he and Zalith were elves—everyone back in the Citadel had, so why would anyone here think different?

After a few moments, the doctor dismissed Zalith, who returned for his horse and then waited by the entrance as the doctor called Alucard forward.

The vampire let go of his horse's reins and approached the robed, masked man, glaring at him as he stared into his eyes through the goggles of his ridiculous mask.

"Where you guys heading?" the guard asked.

"Osamore," Alucard lied, it being the first place in Nefastus that came to mind.

"What's in Osamore?" the guard asked with what looked like an amused smile on his face.

"Velatives."

The guard laughed.

"What's funny?" Zalith asked.

The guard took his eyes off Alucard and glanced at Zalith. "Oh, nothing," he laughed. "Your friend here—bit of a weird accent. You say you got relatives out here—

they foreigners too?" he asked, setting his eyes back on Alucard, who scowled irritably at him. "Just…never heard no one like you before."

But Zalith then smiled a condescending smile. "Do you usually laugh at things you're experiencing for the first time? Is it a nervous tick?"

There it was. The sass. The attitude. Alucard hid a smile, turning his head away. God, how he loved when Zalith patronized people.

With a frown on his face, the guard looked back at the demon. But before he could speak—

"Because if it's not, we're going to have a problem," Zalith interjected. "And I'm sure that's the last thing you want on your very busy day of being ignorant and searching for germs."

The guard scowled and glanced at his fellow men as they laughed quietly. He embarrassedly rolled his eyes and waved his hand in dismissal as the plague doctor finished staring into Alucard's eyes. "Next," he muttered.

Alucard shook his head irritably and snatched his horse's reins, pulling him with him as he made his way over to join Zalith. "*Tâmpit,*" he snarled, stopping beside Zalith.

Zalith looked back at the guards to make sure they were all distracted and then dragged his hand down Alucard's arm. "Are you okay?" he asked quietly.

"I'm vine," he confirmed. "I just…vant to get out of 'ere alveady."

"So do I," Zalith concurred.

Sighing, Alucard looked back over his shoulder, watching as the guards dismissed and sent Danford their way. "I vorgot 'ow much I 'ate 'umans," he snarled.

Zalith smiled at him, rubbing his shoulder before taking his hand off him. They then stood there and waited for Freja and Greymore's two men to join them and Danford, and once they had all been ogled by the plague doctor, Zalith and Alucard started to lead the way through the town.

The demon took the lead, taking the small group over to the sidewalk. He handed the reins of his own and Alucard's horse to Freja before setting his eyes on Danford. "I need you to *discreetly* send an izuret to Idina warning her of the guards at the entrance—let her know they'll be checking everyone for signs of the virus."

"Y-yeah, no problem," Danford said with a nod and a surprised look on his face.

Then, Zalith took hold of Alucard's hand and led him towards and into a bakery. "What do you want?" he asked, smiling at him.

Surprised, Alucard took his eyes off Zalith and eyed everything before him. It felt as though it had been so long since he'd had something quite like a cake, and every item displayed behind the glass seemed so very appealing. But he wasn't going to ask for everything—as much as he wanted to. He set his eyes on a box of four cupcakes. "Can I 'ave…zhose, please?" he asked.

"Of course," Zalith said, setting his eyes on the baker who was waiting behind the counter—

"And vone of zhose…please," Alucard said, pointing to a tray of shortbread squares.

"Okay. How are you going to eat all of that?" he asked amusedly.

"I vill manage," the vampire said with a content smile.

With a smirk and a nod, Zalith turned to face the baker again. "Can we have one of the boxes of four cupcakes, a shortbread, and a regular white coffee, please," he said, reaching into his pocket to pull out a few silver coins.

Taking Zalith's money, the baker nodded and wandered off to prepare his coffee.

Alucard thought this was a good time to tell Zalith about the ship he had stowed in DeiganLupus—the same ship they'd take to their castle. "I 'ave uh…ship…in DeiganLupus," he said as Zalith shifted his sights to him. "Is anozzer vone of my galleons—could get us to our castle," he said quietly.

"I'm worried that someone who's looking for us might notice that your ship has set sail," he said.

He was right. Alucard frowned and nodded. "Vell…zhe only ozzer ving I can vink of is zhat ve just…buy or 'ire vone of zhe ships docked zhere."

"We'll buy one," Zalith said. "I know that Greymore will be able to sail it."

"Okay," Alucard agreed, turning to face the baker as he returned with Zalith's coffee and put the things Alucard had asked for into a paper bag.

"Thank you," Zalith said as the baker handed him everything, and then, he led the way back out onto the street, where Danford and Freja were waiting with their horses and the two of Greymore's men who had come with them.

And then, they headed for the station.

Chapter Seventy-Seven

— ⊰ ✝ ⊱ —

To the Coast

| Alucard |

To Alucard's relief, everything went by more smoothly than he had expected. They quickly secured tickets for a private cabin and arranged for their horses to be stowed in the livestock carriage. With that settled, they made their way to the platform, the bustle of the station fading into the background. Before they boarded, they left Danford outside the station, providing him with detailed instructions and enough money for the next group of Zalith's people. Danford understood the plan—he'd order someone from that group to stay behind, just as he had done, continuing the cycle to avoid drawing unwanted attention.

After parting ways with their group, Alucard and Zalith boarded the train and made their way down the narrow aisle until they reached their cabin. Zalith pulled the door open with a small gesture, a hint of a smile playing on his lips as he motioned for Alucard to enter first. Alucard stepped inside and let out a weary sigh as he sank into the right-hand seat, which was more like a plush, couch-like bench. The tension in his shoulders eased just a fraction as he settled in, his body finally giving in to its exhaustion.

Zalith drew the curtains over the door and windows, sealing them off from prying eyes in the corridor. The soft click of the curtain rings seemed to wrap them in a cocoon of privacy, the world outside fading into insignificance. He sat down beside the vampire, the warmth of his presence almost comforting as he sipped his coffee in calm, measured gulps. Alucard glanced at him and felt a wave of gratitude—he was glad to finally have this moment to rest, to let his guard down for just a little while.

When the train eventually jolted into motion, the station beginning to blur past the window, Alucard allowed himself to relax completely. The rhythmic sound of the wheels on the tracks seemed to lull him, a gentle reminder that, for now, they were moving forward, away from the chaos and into something that felt almost like peace.

Alucard let out a quiet sigh, tearing his gaze away from Peaches, who was curled up and fast asleep on the seat across from him; the little hairless kitten looked so peaceful, her tiny chest rising and falling with each breath. Alucard's eyes drifted to the window, where the countryside blurred past, fields and distant hills rolling by in a muted wash of green and gold. The coast was still hours away, but he didn't mind; he'd gladly take the comfort of sitting here, cocooned in this moment over walking any day.

With a soft smile, he rested his head on Zalith's shoulder, feeling the solid warmth of him, letting it ground him in the present. The steady rhythm of the train, that familiar clickety-clack of wheels against the tracks became a soothing lullaby, filling the silence between them as they sped towards whatever awaited them at the edge of the horizon.

Once Zalith finished his coffee, Alucard decided to open the small box of cupcakes that the demon had got for him. "Do you vant vone?" he offered.

Seeming intrigued, the demon asked, "What kinds did you get?"

"I vink zhey're just normal sponge cake vith buttercream."

"I'll have one," Zalith said, smiling at him. "But only if you feed it to me."

Gazing at Zalith, Alucard felt his nerves creeping up, threatening to unravel the calm façade he'd been clinging to. He swallowed hard, refusing to let his embarrassment get the better of him. With careful hands, he picked up one of the cakes, peeling the paper from its base, and then broke off a small piece. He held it out to Zalith, trying to keep his touch steady, but his pulse thrummed in his fingertips.

Zalith, however, didn't just take the offered cake with a polite bite. Instead, he reached out and gently gripped Alucard's wrist, holding his hand in place, his touch firm yet teasing. Alucard's breath hitched as Zalith slowly devoured the cake from his fingers, his eyes never leaving Alucard's. But that wasn't enough; Zalith's gaze turned more intense, almost predatory, as he guided Alucard's fingers—now smeared with icing and buttercream—into his mouth.

The demon's lips wrapped around Alucard's fingertips, and he began to suck on them slowly, deliberately, his eyes locked in a smouldering stare that sent heat racing up Alucard's neck. The sensation was electric, almost maddening, and Alucard found himself trapped in that gaze, a mix of vulnerability and excitement tying his stomach in knots. He held on as long as he could, staring back into Zalith's unrelenting eyes, but his resolve crumbled under the weight of his own growing embarrassment. A frown flickered across his face, and he finally broke, looking away, his cheeks tinged with a flush he couldn't hide.

"Does that still do nothing for you?" Zalith murmured with a smirk as he pulled Alucard's fingers from his mouth but kept hold of his wrist.

He pouted and mumbled, "I never said zidn't."

"You made a face like it didn't," Zalith laughed.

Alucard shrugged. "Zhat vas…years ago bevore I knew vhat you vere insinuating," he said, glancing at him.

The demon laughed again. "You're cute."

Looking at him, Alucard couldn't help but smile, too. "So are you," he replied, pulling his wrist from Zalith's grip so that he could move his hand to the side of the demon's neck. But he couldn't exactly ignore the cupcake he had in his other hand—he wanted it so much that he couldn't *not* take a bite out of it as he stared at Zalith.

Zalith smiled, laughing quietly as he watched him.

"Vhat?" Alucard asked, frowning.

"Nothing. You're just so handsome—come here," Zalith murmured, his voice low and teasing as he guided his hand to the back of Alucard's head, pulling him closer. Alucard anticipated a kiss, his heart skipping a beat in the moments before their lips met. But instead, Zalith's tongue lightly traced the curve of his lips, licking away the icing and buttercream that still clung to them.

Alucard blinked, startled for a brief moment, his lips parting in surprise. He stared at Zalith, unsure whether to be flustered or amused. A small pout formed on his lips as he looked down at his cake, his hand slowly sliding from Zalith's neck and back into his own lap, uncertainty tugging at the edges of his composure.

Zalith wasn't done, though. With a playful grin, he leaned in closer and pressed a loud, exaggerated kiss to Alucard's cheek. "Sorry," he said, his smirk widening as his fingers lightly gripped Alucard's jaw, turning his face back towards him. "Let me give you a real kiss."

This time, Zalith's lips met Alucard's in a soft yet passionate kiss, the kind that sent a slow warmth spreading through his chest. Alucard froze for a second, his heart skipping as he returned the kiss, still caught in the unexpected tenderness of the moment. He gazed at Zalith afterwards, a mixture of surprise and something else flickering in his eyes—something deeper, a quiet longing he hadn't expected to surface so quickly.

Zalith chuckled, clearly amused by the reaction he'd drawn out of him. Without another word, he pulled Alucard closer, closing the distance between them, and began kissing him again, more urgently this time, his hands cradling Alucard's face as he deepened the embrace. Alucard could do nothing but melt into him, the world fading away as Zalith's touch consumed him, kiss after kiss.

Eventually, Alucard set aside what remained of his cupcake, his focus entirely on Zalith. His fingers found their way to the back of Zalith's head, tangling in his hair, while his other hand gripped his shirt with a subtle urgency. Their kisses deepened, growing more fervent, and soon, Zalith's hands slipped beneath Alucard's shirt. His touch was slow and deliberate, his fingertips dragging lightly over Alucard's chest before gliding down to his abs, leaving a trail of warmth in their wake.

A flicker of hesitation crossed Alucard's mind—they were on a train, after all. Even though they had their own private cabin, the thought of someone passing by or overhearing something made his pulse quicken with more than just excitement. But as Zalith leaned in closer, his lips moving from Alucard's mouth to his neck, kissing and grazing his skin with tantalizing softness, Alucard's resistance began to waver. The delicate press of Zalith's lips and the way he expertly unbuttoned his shirt made Alucard frown in fleeting confliction. Did he really care if anyone overheard?

The thought melted away as a slow smile spread across his lips. No, he didn't care. He tilted his head to the side, inviting Zalith to continue, enjoying the way his kisses moved up his neck and back to his lips. As Zalith undid the final button and pulled the shirt from his body, Alucard's heart raced with a surge of excitement. He always craved Zalith's attention, and now that he had it, he wasn't going to let anything stop him from indulging in the moment.

Alucard's hands roamed over Zalith's body, his fingers tracing the hard lines of muscle beneath the fabric. His touch was slow but eager, exploring every inch of the demon's form before moving to the collar of his shirt. As their lips remained locked, Alucard began unbuttoning his mate's shirt with a deliberate impatience, pulling it free and tossing it aside, where it joined his own discarded clothing.

The demon's hands continued their path over Alucard's body, the heat of his touch igniting sparks of desire with each caress. The vampire's breath quickened, his own hands gliding over Zalith's chest and down the sculpted ridges of his torso, feeling the raw power beneath his fingertips. He revelled in the closeness, the heat between them rising as their bodies pressed together, every touch, every kiss fueling the fire that now consumed them both.

Alucard felt Zalith's forehead rest against his, their breaths mingling in the quiet intimacy of the moment. He shivered slightly as Zalith's hand slowly traced down over his chest and settled at his waist. The touch was deliberate and gentle, but it carried a weight that made Alucard's pulse quicken. He could sense the intensity in the way Zalith looked at him, the heat in his gaze palpable even without words. The closeness between them, the feel of Zalith's body against his, stirred something deep within him, pulling him further into the moment.

Zalith's lips curled into a smirk, and Alucard noticed the subtle shift in the air as the door lock clicked shut on its own. The soft hum of telekinesis rippled through the cabin as the switch for the 'Do Not Disturb' message flipped into place outside, sealing them in their private space. Alucard didn't need to ask—he knew exactly what Zalith was doing. There would be no interruptions now. For the next few hours, it was just the two of them, alone.

The vampire smiled as Zalith leaned in, their lips meeting again in a slow, deliberate kiss. He felt Zalith's hand trailing down his body, a soft, teasing touch that sent a shiver through him. When the demon's fingers found his belt, Alucard's breath hitched slightly, anticipation tightening in his chest. The quiet sound of the buckle coming undone filled the air as his mate pulled the belt free and let it fall to the floor with a soft thud. The vampire barely noticed, his focus entirely on the way Zalith's hand unbuttoned his trousers and slipped inside, sending a warm jolt through his body.

When Zalith pulled back, their eyes met, and the demon smiled at him, his voice a low, teasing murmur, "Are you liking your train ride so far?"

Alucard pouted, moving his hand up and over Zalith's chest. "Yes," he mumbled, guiding his hand to the back of his head.

"Good," he replied, and then he resumed kissing him, easing his hand into Alucard's trousers to lightly grip his arousal.

The instant Zalith's hand wrapped around his shaft, a surge of excitement coursed through Alucard, sending a ripple of pleasure that heightened his senses. He deepened their kiss, his grip tightening on the back of Zalith's head while his other hand roamed down the demon's firm, muscular body, feeling the heat beneath his skin.

As the rhythmic clickety-clack of the train suddenly jolted them, causing Alucard to frown slightly as he lifted his head, their kiss broke. His breath came in ragged, heated gasps, and without needing to ask, Zalith leaned in, his lips brushing over Alucard's neck. The vampire's eyelids fluttered, his body instinctively arching towards the touch, the warmth of his mate's mouth sending shivers down his spine.

Alucard exhaled deeply, the tension melting away as Zalith kissed his neck, each press of his lips a deliberate tease. His breath caught again when the demon's hand began to stroke his hardening dick slowly, the sensation electrifying. Zalith's caress was firm but unhurried, and Alucard's body responded to every movement, each stroke matching the rhythm of the train as it rattled beneath them. The combination of the demon's touch and the relentless press of his lips sent a pleasurable ache through him, making Alucard sink deeper into the moment, his desire growing with every breath.

As Zalith began to slide Alucard's trousers down, their lips met again in a heated kiss, one that deepened with every moment. Alucard's heart raced, his body responding to every stroke of Zalith's hand as it continued to caress his shaft. The sensation was overwhelming, yet he craved more. They kissed for what felt like a fleeting eternity, the warmth of Zalith's lips sending shivers of pleasure through him.

Soon, Zalith broke away from the kiss, his lips trailing down Alucard's neck, each kiss a slow, purposeful tease. Alucard's breath hitched as Zalith continued his descent, his mouth moving lower and lower until he dropped to his knees before him. The demon's gaze flicked upward, a playful smile curling at his lips before he leaned in and enveloped Alucard's dick with his mouth.

Alucard's head fell back instantly, a quiet, contented sigh escaping his lips as the pleasure coursed through him. His hand instinctively found its way to the back of Zalith's head, fingers tangling in his hair as he guided the rhythm. The sensation of Zalith's tongue slowly dragging over his length sent waves of heat through his body, the slow, torturous pleasure making him hum quietly in sheer enjoyment. He could do nothing but sit there, leaning back, completely lost in the moment as Zalith's mouth worked its magic, each movement pulling him deeper into the intoxicating bliss of their connection.

He turned his head slightly, gazing out the window, the passing landscape barely registering in his mind as his once-relaxed body slowly stirred, awakening under Zalith's touch. When Zalith's tongue moved faster over his dick, Alucard's quiet moan slipped past his lips, his head falling back against the seat as his hand gripped the demon's hair tighter. A smile tugged at his lips, but it was quickly overtaken by the need building within him, his breath coming in quicker, heart racing as waves of pleasure surged through him, captivating his entire being.

His muscles tensed, his body reacting instinctively to the growing intensity of Zalith's movements. Alucard's quiet moans became more urgent, his fingers curling tightly in the demon's hair as he felt himself being pulled towards the edge. He knew he was close—closer than he wanted to admit—and no matter how much he tried to hold back, control was slipping from his grasp.

He frowned slightly, a part of him wishing he could prolong this blissful torment just a little longer, but the sensations were overwhelming, leaving him powerless under Zalith's touch. Every stroke, every flick of the demon's tongue pushed him further towards his peak, and as much as he craved to hold on, he knew there was no stopping it now. His body surrendered to the pleasure, completely under Zalith's spell, and in that surrender, Alucard couldn't help but enjoy the helplessness of it all.

With a quiet moan, he grimaced in struggle, tipping over the edge as Zalith eased his dick into his warm, tight throat—and as he climaxed, the vampire tightened his grip on his mate's hair, leaning his head back as the intoxicating rapture gripped him, a satisfied sigh upon his breath as he exhaled deeply. He felt Zalith's throat stroking his sensitive length as he swallowed his cum with satisfied hums, and Alucard responded with pleased, relieved sighs.

Alucard smiled as Zalith kissed his way back up his body, taking his time to savour every inch of his skin. Each kiss over his neck sent a shiver through him, a teasing warmth that built with every touch. When Zalith finally stood, smirking down at him, Alucard's breath caught in his throat. He could feel the tension, the unspoken promise in that devious smile, and even though fatigue tugged at his body, the gleam in Zalith's eyes intrigued him far too much to resist.

"Stand up," Zalith instructed, his voice low and commanding.

Without hesitation, Alucard obeyed, rising to his feet. As he did, Zalith's arms wrapped around him, pulling him in until their bodies were flush against one another. The demon's lips found his again, their kiss deeper, more demanding this time, and

Alucard's heart raced in response. Zalith's hands slid down his sides, slow and deliberate, before gripping his ass firmly with both hands. The unexpected touch made the vampire frown in surprise, but the moment passed quickly as a wicked smile tugged at his lips. With newfound confidence, Alucard's hands slid down his mate's back, slipping into his trousers to return the favour. His fingers dug into the demon's firm ass, earning him a low laugh from Zalith.

Zalith rested his forehead against Alucard's, their breath mingling as they stood locked in the moment, their hands roaming and teasing. "Turn around," Zalith murmured, his voice thick with seduction as his eyes locked onto Alucard's with an intensity that sent a thrill through him. There was no denying that Zalith wasn't finished with him yet—and Alucard had no intention of resisting whatever came next.

Alucard turned around as instructed, and almost immediately, Zalith's hands were on him, gripping his waist and pulling him back until his body was against Zalith's chest. The vampire shivered at the contact, the warmth of Zalith's skin against his own sending a thrill through him. The demon's lips found the side of his neck again, moving slowly, each kiss deliberate and electrifying, sending ripples of pleasure coursing through his sensitive body like a slow-burning fire.

The vampire let out a soft sigh, his gaze drifting out the window, though he barely understood the passing scenery. The world outside seemed distant, insignificant compared to the sensation of Zalith's hands roaming over him. Those hands traced every line of his body, stroking his skin with a possessive tenderness that made him feel both claimed and cherished. As Zalith's fingers glided up his arms, then down his back, Alucard smiled contently, sinking deeper into the moment.

But when his mate's fingers passed over the raised scars on his back, Alucard frowned, the old wounds stirring a faint, instinctual discomfort. Still, he didn't pull away—he didn't want to. Instead, he leaned his head back onto Zalith's shoulder, breathing deeply as he let himself relax into the demon's touch. Zalith's hands continued to explore him, stroking and caressing, their connection deepening with every breath, every kiss. Alucard closed his eyes, allowing himself to get lost in the warmth, the intimacy, the safety of being completely in Zalith's arms.

The demon kissed the side of his face, dragging his hands down to his waist again, and as he gripped his ass in both hands, he kissed his neck.

"I veally… like vhen you do zhat," Alucard said with a smile, staring at what he could see of Zalith's reflection in the glass.

"Good," his mate murmured, "because I like doing it to you."

Alucard's smile grew. He rested his head on the side of Zalith's as the demon kissed his cheek.

"The veiw's really nice," Zalith then said. "We should ride the train more often," he added with a quiet laugh as he moved his hand down Alucard's body and gripped his dick again, kissing his cheek.

Zalith's touch sent a jolt through Alucard, making him flinch as waves of overwhelming delight rippled through his already trembling body. He hadn't fully recovered from his recent climax, but the lingering sensation only made him crave more, unable to wait. A deep groan escaped his lips as Zalith's hands dragged slowly down his back, the demon's touch both comforting and electric. Each kiss Zalith pressed against his skin sent more sparks of pleasure through him, his lips tracing a path up Alucard's spine. When Zalith's fingers brushed over the scars again, Alucard shivered, the intimate gesture striking a balance between tenderness and temptation.

As his mate reached his neck, he kissed the back of it slowly, then the side, each touch making Alucard's breath hitch. Zalith's chin came to rest on the vampire's shoulder, a quiet, possessive gesture, as his hands slid down once more to grip Alucard's waist firmly. The vampire exhaled, his right hand moving down instinctively to cover Zalith's, their fingers intertwining for a brief moment of connection.

The demon leaned in, his warm breath brushing Alucard's ear before he pressed a teasing kiss against it. His lips moved softly over the sensitive skin, and then he nipped at Alucard's earlobe, drawing a quiet laugh from him. But the playfulness didn't last long—Zalith's foot nudged between Alucard's legs, tapping lightly against his ankle, urging him to part his legs a little more. Alucard complied without hesitation, and when Zalith guided him to bend forward slightly, Alucard's hands rested against the cool glass of the window, his reflection barely visible as his breath fogged the surface.

Zalith's smile widened into something wickedly devious as he kissed the nape of Alucard's neck again, slower, more deliberate this time. Every kiss seemed to promise more, and Alucard's body responded with growing anticipation, his pulse quickening as his mate's hands roamed possessively over his waist.

Alucard, with his hands against the window, exhaled deeply. He smiled contently as Zalith kept kissing his neck, dragging his hands down his body. His excitement only grew when he heard Zalith pulling off his trousers—and even more so as the demon started to massage the cold, viscous lube into his ass.

He waited, leaning his arm on the window so that he could rest his forehead against it—and as Zalith started slowly easing his thick, hard dick into his body, Alucard frowned and moaned quietly, something pleasing gripping him where he stood. Zalith held onto the vampire's waist, pulling himself back as a content sigh of pleasure sat upon his breath. He leaned into Alucard's ear, kissed the side of his face, and started to breathe against the vampire's neck as he began pushing himself forward, pulling himself back, guiding his intoxicating length into and out of Alucard's body as the vampire moaned quietly, as the demon hummed and groaned in delight.

Zalith began thrusting faster, each movement sending deeper waves of pleasure coursing through Alucard's body. But it was when Zalith pressed his right index finger into his side that everything shifted—an almost overwhelming sensation rippled through him, a surge of pure ecstasy that made him tremble. Alucard tensed, his body instinctively arching into the pleasure, completely enthralled by the intensity of the demon's touch. It wasn't just the quickening rhythm of Zalith's thrusts that consumed him, but the pressure from that single point, amplifying every wave of sensation.

A moan slipped past Alucard's lips, his voice shaky, almost breaking into a whispered version of Zalith's name. His breath came in ragged gasps, his chest rising and falling as he struggled to keep up with the onslaught of pleasure. The sensation was intoxicating, every nerve alight, making it nearly impossible for him to form words.

Zalith's own moans of pleasure filled the air, a deep, excited sound that only spurred Alucard on. The demon's movements became more frantic, faster, harder, and Alucard's breaths grew more frantic in response. His mind felt hazy, teetering on the edge of control, and just when he thought he couldn't take any more, his mate leaned in and sank his fangs into his neck.

The sharp bite sent a white-hot pulse of pleasure straight through Alucard, blending with the already overwhelming sensations, and he couldn't suppress the loud moan that tore from his throat. The combination of Zalith's fangs and his relentless thrusts was almost too much, his body tightening in response, completely surrendering to the bliss that flooded his senses.

Alucard grunted, his body trembling as he felt the tension coil tighter within him. The venom from Zalith's bite coursed through his veins, spreading like fire, claiming every part of him that the demon's touch hadn't already dominated. The pleasure was all-consuming, pulling him deeper into a haze of euphoria. Another moan escaped his lips, this one louder, rawer, as he clenched his fist against the glass window, trying to brace himself against the sheer exhilaration overwhelming him.

Zalith's thrusts quickened *even more*, his breathing becoming just as frantic as Alucard's. His grip tightened around Alucard's waist, fingers pressing into his skin with a possessive urgency, driving them both further towards the edge. Alucard's body ached, every muscle straining with the intensity of the moment, but none of it mattered—he welcomed the ache, the relentless pace, the heat that surged through him with each thrust.

His teeth clenched as another moan slipped from his throat, his breath hitching in an effort to stifle the sounds of his pleasure, but it was a losing battle. The intensity of Zalith's bite, the demon's hands anchoring him, and the rapid movements of his dick pushing into and pulling out of his body seemed to blur the line between pain and bliss—everything entwined in a storm of sensation. Alucard could feel himself spiralling towards the peak again, his body trembling uncontrollably as he teetered on the brink.

The pleasure, the euphoria—it tangled around him, pulling him under, each thrust pushing him closer to that overwhelming release. His body was caught in a frantic, desperate struggle between holding back and surrendering completely, but he knew it wouldn't be long. He could feel it building, surging through him, and there was no escaping the inevitable, no matter how hard he tried to contain it.

Zalith's grip on Alucard's waist tightened, his hand sliding around to wrap firmly around Alucard's shaft. The added sensation made Alucard grimace, his body trembling as a surge of intense satisfaction rippled through him. The demon's relentless pace—thrusting into him while caressing his dick—sent wave after wave of pleasure crashing over him, each one more overwhelming than the last.

Alucard could feel the inescapable approaching, the sensation twisting through his body like a wildfire he couldn't control. With one final, deep thrust and the expert movement of Zalith's hand, Alucard's climax ripped through him. His moan broke into something closer to a whine as the intensity of the release took hold, pleasure and exhaustion mixing into one overwhelming sensation. His body draped with fatigue almost immediately, but he stayed where he was, chest heaving as he struggled to catch his breath, still lost in the lingering pleasure, feeling the demon's hot cum fill him.

Zalith let out a soft, satisfied moan of his own, pulling his fangs gently from Alucard's neck, the sharp sting followed by a lingering warmth that coursed through his veins. Alucard's body was still trembling slightly, the aftershocks of his climax leaving him breathless. His mate groaned softly in bliss as he pulled Alucard closer, wrapping his arms around him in a firm, possessive hug. Alucard leaned into him, still panting, letting the comfort of Zalith's embrace ground him as the intensity of the moment slowly ebbed away.

Alucard leaned his head back, resting it against the side of Zalith's as he exhaled deeply, the weight of fatigue crashing over him all at once. His body felt heavy, utterly drained, and all he wanted now was to sink into something soft, to lay down and let the exhaustion take him. But there was no real comfort to be found here, not in their small cabin on the train. He sighed quietly, resigned to his weariness, and waited as Zalith cleaned them both with a few of the complimentary tissues, his touch gentle and unhurried.

Once they were cleaned up, Alucard pulled his trousers back on and slumped into the seat, sighing deeply, his body feeling almost boneless with tire. Zalith sat down beside him, wrapping an arm around his shoulders and pulling him close. He nuzzled into the side of Alucard's neck, his breath warm and comforting against his skin. For a long moment, they simply sat there in silence, the world outside the cabin fading into the soft rhythm of the train's movement.

Alucard closed his eyes, letting the quiet settle over them like a blanket. He could feel the pull of sleep tugging at him, the desire to just drift off and rest for the remainder of the journey. Maybe he would, if he could find a way to get comfortable. His body ached with the need for rest, and as he leaned into Zalith's warmth, he wondered if he might just manage to steal a few moments of sleep, held securely in his mate's embrace.

"How are you feeling?" the demon asked quietly.

He sighed and shuffled around, turning to face him. "Tired," he answered.

Zalith hugged him tightly. "I'm sorry," he said quietly. "You can have a nap if you want."

Although he wanted to sleep, he felt…reluctant. He pretty much *always* fell asleep after they had sex, and he wanted to enjoy sitting there in Zalith's embrace. "I'll be vine," he assured him, stroking his hand up Zalith's body and to his head so that he could fiddle with the demon's hair.

Zalith smiled, staring at him for a while. But he soon took hold of Alucard's left hand and lifted it so that he could look at the engagement ring. "It looks good on you," he said contently.

Alucard smiled. "I veally love," he said happily. "Vank you," he murmured, shuffling closer and resting his forehead against Zalith's.

"Anything for you, baby."

With a tired sigh, Alucard then leaned his head on Zalith's bare chest, fiddling with the thin gold chain around his neck. "I vish ve vere in our own bed alveady."

"Soon," Zalith said, caressing his hair. "We're only a train and boat ride away."

"Two boats," Alucard muttered.

"Two boats," the demon said with a nod.

Just then, a quiet knock came at their door. Alucard lifted his head, and it didn't take him long to determine that it was Camael waiting outside; he could feel his angel ethos like a sickly chill in the air. He watched as Zalith sighed, stood up, and pulled on his shirt before unlocking and opening the door.

"I have news for Alucard," Camael immediately said.

Alucard rolled his eyes and pulled his own shirt on as Zalith looked back at him. "Vhat do you vant?" he muttered, crossing his arms to conceal his chest, for he couldn't be bothered to sit there and tie every button his shirt had.

Zalith opened the door enough so that Camael could see Alucard.

"I've been searching the hive mind for your…Becker," the angel said.

"And?" Alucard questioned.

"His last recorded sighting was in Divinos," he said.

Alucard rolled his eyes again. "*Of course* 'e'd be 'anging avound vith zhe vizards," he grumbled. "Anyving else?"

"He killed a couple of guys—he's been looking for someone…a wizard."

"Do you know vhich vone?"

"No. All I know is that he's been making his way through the ranks of a widely-known clan—the Darkhearts."

Alucard rolled his eyes so hard that they might fall out of his head. *Of course* Becker was getting himself tangled up with something so bothersome as a particular clan of wizards Alucard had hoped he'd not have to deal with. "Vhy is 'e pissing zhem off?"

Camael shrugged. "Seems like the wizard he's after took something from him."

"Vight," Alucard muttered. "As if zhere's anyving levt vor somevone to take. Go avay," he mumbled, waving his hand in dismissal as he leaned back in his seat.

Before Camael could utter another word, Zalith shut the door in his face and locked it again.

The demon sat down beside Alucard, moving his arm around him and pulling him close as the vampire sighed deeply. He was sure that Zalith was about to ask him about what he had said to Camael, and he had no reason not to tell him. "Zhe Dark'earts are…more or less a cult of vizards zhat vollow Ephriel," he mumbled. "Zhey delve a lot in dark practices—necromancy and blood magic," he said. "Zhat's anozzer ving Becker 'ated about me," he laughed. "I used to use a lot of blood magic, too—I still do sometimes."

"I don't want us to get ourselves involved in Pecker's business if we can avoid it," Zalith said.

"Ve von't be getting involved," Alucard said firmly. "I'll make sure 'e zoesn't bring 'is vork vith 'im vhen ve meet."

"Good, because the last thing we need is more problems."

The vampire glanced up at him but then made himself comfortable, resting his head on Zalith's chest again. "Ve'll 'ave a whole lot less of zhem vonce ve get 'ome," he mumbled tiredly.

Zalith sighed, hugging him a little tighter. "I hope so," he murmured. Then, he kissed Alucard's forehead, making himself comfortable.

Alucard wasn't sure how long was left of their journey, but he was certain that it was more than an hour, and he felt *exhausted.* He didn't want to fall asleep, but he knew he inevitably would. If he slept the rest of the train journey, maybe he'd feel a whole lot less sluggish once they were on the boat to DeiganLupus. He wanted to make sure that he was awake and aware once they arrived—he'd have to find a suitable ship, after all. So, as he lay there, he let himself slowly drift off, knowing that he was safe with Zalith. And when he woke, he hoped that their journey to the coast would be over.

Chapter Seventy-Eight

—⊰ ✝ ⊱—

Goodnight

| Zalith |

Zalith gazed out of the train window, watching as the once-blue sky faded to a dark, gloomy purple. As dusk approached, the train started to slow, and the demon assumed it was because they were nearing their journey's end. He felt glad that this part of their trip was coming to a close, but he wasn't exactly looking forward to the rest of it; two boats sounded straining, but then again, it could go by much faster than he felt. Either way, this was better than being stuck in the woods.

He looked down at Alucard, who was sleeping beside him, having moved his head from his chest to his lap not too long ago. He smiled as he fiddled with the vampire's hair, gazing down at his peaceful face. He really loved Alucard…so much. Just looking at him made him feel a whole lot better—and he didn't want to have to wake him up, but the train was slowing, he could see the sea outside. Zalith didn't want to hang around any longer than he had to.

With a tired sigh, he stroked his fiancé's head, moving his hand down to his shoulder. "Alucard?" he asked softly.

Alucard murmured quietly.

"We're here," he said, rubbing his back.

"Alveady?" the vampire mumbled.

"Yeah," Zalith said, smiling. "It's only been four hours."

The vampire sighed deeply and sat up but leaned his head on Zalith's shoulder. "Zoesn't veel zhat long."

"Because you were sleeping, darling," he said and kissed the vampire's head.

"Did you not get any vest?"

"Some," Zalith lied. "But I didn't want to fall asleep and miss our stop."

"Okay," Alucard said quietly as he moved his hand up and over Zalith's chest and to the side of his neck. "Zhe boat trip isn't zhat long—zhey use steam on zhose, too, so…maybe an hour or two."

Zalith stroked his hand over Alucard's and held it. "That's not too bad. I was expecting longer."

"Is not long to zhe castle vrom DeiganLupus, eizer," Alucard said, smiling up at him. "An hour or two if zhey 'ave zhe steamships to 'ire or buy or vhatever ve do."

"Perfect," the demon said, relieved. "I can't wait to shower. And shave."

"Me too. And to be in our own bed again."

"All in good time, I suppose," Zalith mumbled and kissed his head again.

Just then, the train's breaks screeched loudly…and the train came to a gradual halt. Now that one-third of their journey was over—and now that they were leaving Nefastus—Zalith felt a whole lot more relieved, especially since he knew the journey from here wasn't as long as he'd been dreading.

"Come on, baby," he said, moving his hands to Alucard's shoulders, making him sit up. "It's time to go."

Alucard sighed tiredly, yawning as he picked up Peaches. He also went to pick up the small box of cupcakes and his wrapped-up shortbread, but Zalith smiled and took them from him, carrying them for him as he opened the cabin door and started leading the way towards the closest exit.

Once they disembarked from the train, Zalith and Alucard retrieved their horses from the livestock carriage and made their way towards the station's exit. The platform was simple, a stretch of concrete with worn paths leading away from it, where the other passengers were already filtering off in clusters. Zalith guided his horse forward, following the flow of people for now, his eyes scanning the area for direction.

At the end of the platform, a signpost caught his attention, and after a quick glance, he followed the road it indicated would lead them to the docks. As they started along the path, Zalith spotted Idina and Orin not far ahead, but their plan was to remain separated for now, so he kept his distance, steering his horse towards the quieter edge of the cobblestone road.

The crowd around them was bustling, people fanning out from the station in all directions. The faint glow of what seemed to be a city flickered in the distance, its lights piercing through the evening haze, but Zalith had no intention of heading that way. He and Alucard kept to their path, moving away from the flow of people and towards their own destination.

Eventually, the road ahead split into a fork, and Zalith reined in his horse, taking a moment to assess which way to go next.

"Is zhat vay," Alucard said, nodding to the furthest, right road.

With a nod to Alucard, Zalith led the way down the narrow dirt path, the soft crunch of hooves on earth filling the quiet between them. The path wound through the landscape, eventually bringing them to a steep hill that required careful navigation. But after a few minutes of descent, they found themselves on a brick road, which soon transitioned into wooden planks, the sound of their horses' steps changing with the surface beneath them. The planks creaked softly as they approached a short set of steps that led up onto the docks.

They weren't alone—several other travellers had followed behind them, their figures scattered along the path. Zalith's people, too, had arrived in separate clusters, keeping to their own groups and maintaining a deliberate distance from one another, just as planned.

Zalith's gaze shifted to a small cabin near the docks, where a couple was already speaking to the ticket vendor and exchanging coins. It was clear that this was where they needed to go as well. He nudged his horse forward, his focus set on the task ahead, silently preparing for the next stage of their journey.

"Evening," the moustached vendor said, smiling at Zalith as he and Alucard stopped in front of his window. "What can I get ya?"

"Two to DeiganLupus—the horses, too," Zalith said.

"Sure," the man replied and pointed over his own shoulder. "It's the Maryloo—she's right at the end. The crew'll tell you where to put your horses," he said, placing two tickets on the counter. "Two gold."

Reaching into his pocket, Zalith retrieved two gold coins and placed them on the worn counter with a quiet clink. He accepted the tickets, giving a brief nod in thanks before turning back to Alucard. Without a word, he led the way down the docks, the wooden planks creaking beneath their steps. His eyes scanned the row of ships until they landed on the one they were meant to board, its sails catching the faint breeze.

When they reached it, one of the crew approached them. "Horses this way," he called.

The demon and vampire followed the dockhand onto the ship, their boots thudding softly against the wooden deck. They were led to a small stable-like compartment, where several other horses had already been stowed. After hitching their own horses securely, Zalith and Alucard made their way below deck, navigating the narrow corridors until they reached the cabin marked on their tickets.

Once inside, Zalith shut the door behind them with a quiet thud, pulling the curtains closed to block out the noise from the deck above. He let out a deep sigh as he slumped down into the nearest seat, the tension of the day finally slipping from his shoulders. For a brief moment, the world felt quiet, and the cabin provided them a small reprieve from the journey still ahead.

Alucard sat beside him. "Ve'll be zhere sooner zhan you know," he said with a smile, letting Peaches curl up in his lap.

Zalith smiled at him. "Do you think we can get something to drink?"

"Zhere's probably a bar. Vhat do you vant? I'll go and get," he offered.

"It's okay, I'll go with you," he said—he didn't want Alucard to go anywhere alone…just in case.

"Okay. Vill…she be okay 'ere?" he asked, looking down at Peaches.

"I don't want to leave her here on the off chance a stranger comes into our room," he said, standing up. "She's family."

Also standing up, holding Peaches in his arms, Alucard smiled. "Okay. Zhere should be a bar usually…at zhe end of zhe 'allvay," he said as Zalith opened the cabin door and stepped out into the corridor.

Nodding, Zalith led the way down the narrow corridor. As the ship jolted into motion, he instinctively gripped the handrail and reached for Alucard, steadying them both before they could lose their balance. He rolled his eyes with a small huff of amusement but continued down the hall until they reached a coach area with a bar and several tables scattered within.

Zalith made his way to the bar, leaning against it as one of the bartenders approached with a pleasant smile. "Water, please," the demon requested, then turned to Alucard. "Do you want anything?"

Alucard returned the smile and shook his head. "No, vank you."

Once he had his glass of water in hand, Zalith led them back to their cabin, the gentle sway of the ship accompanying their steps. As they settled in, Zalith took a seat by the window, sighing deeply as he watched the water rushing by outside. Alucard leaned into his shoulder again, and Zalith smiled, comforted by his presence. He could tell that Alucard was fighting against the fatigue that clung to him, his head dipping now and then as he dozed off, only to stir and try to stay awake.

Zalith rubbed his hand gently over Alucard's shoulder, resting his head against his as he sighed. Soon, they'd reach DeiganLupus, and Alucard could finally get the rest he needed—this time, in the comfort of their own bed, away from the exhaustion of travel.

| Alucard |

Alucard flinched awake, blinking against the heaviness of his fatigue. Every time he forced his eyes open, the sky outside seemed to have grown darker, sinking the world around them into deeper shadows. He tried to stay alert, but his eyelids kept drooping, the rhythmic motion of the ship lulling him back towards sleep. That was…until Zalith's voice snapped him out of his haze. He sat up straighter, his pulse quickening as he realized where they were, the familiar sight of the DeiganLupus docks just outside the window.

Rubbing his eyes, Alucard stood and carefully scooped Peaches into his arms, the small, hairless kitten stirring sleepily against his chest. With Peaches nestled securely, he followed Zalith out of the cabin and up onto the deck. The cool evening air hit his face as they stepped out, refreshing his tired senses. Together, they retrieved their horses, and Alucard couldn't help but feel a wave of relief wash over him as their hooves clacked onto the dock. Home was finally within reach.

"Ve can…go zhis vay," Alucard said sleepily, nodding to his left. "Zhere's a guy down zhere who loans ships out—at least zhat's vhere 'e vas last time I vas 'ere. Ve should send Zhomas to 'im to get a ship. Ve zon't vant anyvone to vecognize me, and ve should probably keep our names off vings, too. Ve can vait in zhere," he said, nodding over at a small alleyway.

"Sounds good," the demon said.

"You'll need to tell 'im to ask vor a steam tvader—zhey're zhe vastest," he said, leading them into the alley and out of sight.

"Okay," Zalith said with a nod.

As Zalith telepathically sent a message to Greymore, Alucard took a moment to glance out at the docks, the crisp air carrying a faint scent of saltwater and smoke. The area wasn't as bustling as he had anticipated, but it still thrummed with activity. A handful of workers moved about, loading crates onto ships that bobbed gently in the murky water, their lanterns casting flickering golden light over the wooden planks. The docks stretched out into the river, framed by the hulking silhouettes of larger vessels moored in the distance, their sails dark and heavy in the dimming light.

Small, smoke-choked buildings lined the edge of the waterfront, their brick facades streaked with soot and grime from the nearby factories. Narrow alleyways between them twisted into shadows, the faint clatter of horse-drawn carts echoing faintly through the fog that had begun to roll in off the river. Alucard's sharp eyes caught sight of a few figures lingering by the taverns, their faces obscured by the low-hanging mist and the warm glow from within the pubs.

Despite the movement around them, there was a certain stillness to the place, the quiet hum of the evening settling in. Alucard's gaze shifted back to Zalith, who seemed focused on his task, but the vampire's mind remained tethered to the scene before him—a place both familiar and distant, cloaked in an eerie calm as the day surrendered to night. But then he remembered Camael. He didn't want that angel knowing where his and Zalith's castle was, and he was certain that Zalith felt the same. So, he connected with Toma and telepathically told him to have someone pick Camael up immediately and take him to one of the hotels he owned in the city. He'd figure out what to do with him later.

"Depending on vhere zhis ship is zhat Zhomas gets, ve'll probably be better off using zhis alley to get zhere," the vampire then said.

"All right," the demon replied.

"Did you tell Zhomas?"

"Yeah," he said with a nod.

"Okay," Alucard said, leaning back against the wall as he patted his horse. "Vell," he sighed, "vonce ve get back 'ome, maybe avter ve've been zhere vor about a veek or so, I'll contact Soren and 'ave 'im start looking vor zhe ozzer Obcasus' and Pandoricans."

"Hopefully he's sorted out his shit by then."

"'Opevully," Alucard agreed. "I vill make sure 'e 'as bevore ve get 'im to do anyving."

"Okay," he said, smiling at him.

Alucard wasn't sure how long they stood there, waiting for Greymore's call. Time seemed to stretch, the quiet rhythm of the docks filling the space between them. Finally, the signal came in the form of an izuret, and with a shared glance, he and Zalith began pulling their horses towards the end of the docks. The ship Greymore had hired awaited them, its shadowy silhouette against the misty waterfront. Once aboard and after Zalith's people had gathered, they set sail into the dark waters.

As the ship cut through the water, Alucard handed Greymore the detailed instructions he'd need to navigate to their island. With everything in place, they were finally on their way, the city and its looming secrets shrinking behind them as the night carried them forward into the unknown.

↞❖↠

For nearly two hours, the ship sailed through the dark waters. Alucard kept his gaze fixed on the horizon, the salty breeze cooling his skin as they neared the warded island nestled between Avalmoor and DeiganLupus. When they finally docked, Greymore took the lead, following Alucard's instructions to navigate towards the on-island village.

As they disembarked, Edwin came rushing out onto the black-sand beach, eager to greet them. Alucard and Zalith handed off their horses, watching Edwin's familiar figure as the weight of the journey began to lift. He and Zalith exchanged a glance before turning towards the towering black-brick castle that loomed in the distance, its silhouette bathed in the silver glow of the six moons. The sand beneath their feet shimmered like the night sky, an ethereal beauty that stretched out before them as they approached the grand stairway leading up the side of the mountain to the castle gardens. Once they reached the top, they followed the stone pathway towards the patio, their long, exhausting journey finally coming to an end at last, and the repose was palpable.

Alucard unlocked the door with a touch—one of the few who could, along with Zalith and Edwin. As soon as the glass door creaked open, a deep sense of relief washed over him. The familiar warmth of the interior greeted him: the gold-panelled walls gleamed beneath the light of the crystal chandelier, the red carpets soft underfoot. He took it all in, remembering how the last time they stood here was for Zalith's birthday, though it felt like years had passed since then.

Suddenly, a loud, excited bark echoed through the hall. Alucard turned just in time to see Sabazios charging towards him, the massive hellhound's paws thudding against the floor. Peaches, startled by the commotion, hissed and leapt from the vampire's arms, scrambling beneath a nearby table for safety.

Alucard chuckled, his heart warming at the sight of Sabazios bouncing with excitement in front of him, his massive tail wagging furiously. Zalith stepped back slightly, a smile tugging at his lips as he watched the reunion, clearly amused by the hellhound's enthusiasm. Despite the fatigue clinging to his bones, Alucard couldn't help but feel a deep contentment as he stood there, finally home, surrounded by those he cared for.

"I 'aven't been gone *zhat* long," the vampire said with a smirk, scratching the dog's ears as he slipped his shoes off. "I'll see you tomorrow. I need to go to sleep," he sighed, patting Sabazios' head. Then, as the dog calmed down, Alucard took hold of Zalith's hand and started to lead the way through the castle.

He longed for the comfort of their bed, but he knew Zalith would prefer to wash first—it was always his way. So, without a word, Alucard led the way through the dimly lit hall, the shadows clinging to the walls like old memories. They passed through the gloomy corridors, the soft echo of their footsteps the only sound breaking the stillness. The winding stairs creaked beneath them as they ascended to their room, nestled in the tallest and widest tower of the castle.

Once inside their en-suite bathroom, Alucard gently released Zalith's hand and walked towards the bath. The room was cool, the polished stone underfoot sending a slight chill up his legs, but the thought of warm water soon washing away the remnants of the journey made him relax. He reached for the taps, his mind already drifting towards the peace that awaited them.

"Do you still vant a bath?" he asked, looking over his shoulder at the demon, who pulled his shirt off and threw it into the laundry basket by the door.

"I'd love a bath," he answered.

Nodding, Alucard turned the taps and let the water run as he made his way over to the counter, where Zalith had taken out a razor and some shaving foam. He leaned against it and asked, "Do you know vhat you vant to 'ave vor breakvast in zhe morning?"

As Zalith spread the shaving foam on his face, he glanced at him. "You," he said with a smirk, picking up his razor.

Alucard pouted, looking down at the counter.

The demon laughed quietly, starting to shave his face. "And maybe some eggs and some bacon," he said. "And some fruit, too."

"Zhat sounds good," Alucard said. "And pancakes."

"That sounds nice," the demon agreed.

Alucard nodded, shifting his gaze to the bath as it filled. He thought about shaving, too, but he was so tired; he just wanted to take a bath and head to bed. "Vhat…do ve do tomorrow?" he asked, looking at Zalith again.

"Do you have anything in mind?" he asked, still shaving his face.

He thought to himself for a moment. So much had happened this last week, and all he could really think about was how much he wanted to rest. They were home now…and they could do whatever they liked, couldn't they? And he did love to spend his time with Zalith. "Maybe ve can just…vest. Vor a day or two. I zon't know…ve could put some music on…sit avound and enjoy our time avay vrom zhat godvorsaken vorest."

"That sounds like a wonderful idea," his mate said, wiping his face with a towel.

"Maybe ve can even get a drvink and talk about zhe vuture," he mused.

"One of my favourite things to do with you," the demon said, scooping some shaving foam onto his hand.

As Zalith then rubbed it onto Alucard's face, the vampire frowned. "Vhat are you doing?"

"Shaving your face," he answered, picking up his razor.

Alucard pouted, glancing down at the razor as Zalith started shaving his face. He didn't want to say anything and distract him—the last thing he wanted was a cut on his face, so he stood there…waited…and let Zalith do what he wanted.

Once Zalith was done, he used the towel to clean his face and smiled. "There," he said. "You look as handsome as ever," he teased.

The vampire smiled shyly. "Vank you. But you are more 'andsome zhan I am."

"I think we're tied," the demon laughed, starting to unbutton Alucard's shirt.

Alucard frowned doubtfully. "No," he said as Zalith pulled his shirt off. "You 'ave zhose dark, captivating eyes and zhat scary, mean expression on your vace—zhat I love, by zhe vay," he said with a confident smile, stroking the side of Zalith's clean-shaven face.

"Well, I could say the same for you, but your eyes look just like fire," he replied, resting his forehead against Alucard's as he pulled his own shirt off. "Or ice, depending on where you are." He then pulled off his trousers, and once they were both undressed, he took Alucard's hand and led him over to the bath.

As they climbed in, Alucard switched off the water and relaxed, leaning his back against Zalith's chest. "Do you vink…if ve 'ave a child, zheir eyes vould…change like mine?"

"Maybe," the demon murmured. "I guess we'll find out when we have our daughter," he said, rubbing his hand on the vampire's chest.

Smiling, Alucard sighed and gripped hold of Zalith's hand. "I'm excited to 'ave a vamily," he said, but as he thought about it, sadness gripped his heart. He didn't know what it felt like to have a family—Zalith was the closest thing he'd ever had, and he still felt like his lack of experience might cause him to struggle once they had a child. But he was still excited nonetheless, and he'd do his best.

"With who?" the demon then asked.

Alucard pouted, sure that Zalith was playing dumb. "Vith you."

"With me?"

"Yes," he grumbled.

"Oh, since when?"

Alucard kept his pout, thinking for a moment—but he knew the answer. "Ever since I virst saw our daughter in my dream," he mumbled.

Zalith stroked his hand up and over the vampire's chest and started to fiddle with his hair. "I wonder if I'll see her in my own dream one day."

The vampire shrugged. "Maybe she'll show 'erselv if you ask nicely."

"Maybe," the demon said.

With a content smile, Alucard then turned to face his mate. He stared at his face for a moment, but then he reached over and grabbed one of the shampoo bottles. He poured some into his hand and started washing the demon's hair for him. "Maybe ve vill see 'er vor veal vone day, hmm?" he asked quietly.

"I hope so," the demon smiled.

Once he was done washing Zalith's hair, Alucard sighed a tired sigh and smiled at him. Zalith looked tired, *he* felt tired, and it was getting late. Maybe it was time they headed to bed. "Do you vant to go to bed?"

"Are you tired?" the demon asked.

"A little," he said with a shrug.

Zalith smiled and took hold of his hand. "Okay, let's go," he said, standing up and leading Alucard out of the bath.

They both grabbed their towels and dried off before heading into their bedroom; they both immediately climbed into bed, and once he used his telekinesis to turn the lights out, Zalith pulled Alucard close and rested his head on his chest.

As he lay there, Alucard glanced down at the new ring on his finger. "Are you avraid?" he abruptly asked, it being the first question that came to mind.

"Afraid?" Zalith questioned quietly.

"Of zhe vuture. I zon't know vhat to expect, and zhis is all new to me. Sometimes, I veel…avraid about, but…knowing zhat I 'ave you makes me veel better," he murmured, hugging him tightly.

"You don't have to be afraid, baby," Zalith said softly. "I'm sure everything will work out just fine."

"Okay," he mumbled and kissed Zalith's head. "I love you. Goodnight," he said sleepily.

"I love you, too," the demon replied. "Goodnight, darling."

With a contented smile on his face and a deep sense of relief in his heart, Alucard closed his eyes. It had been a long, gruelling week—so much had happened, and both he and Zalith had endured unimaginable pain and struggle. But now it was finally over. They were home, where they belonged, and for the first time in what felt like ages, Alucard allowed himself to breathe freely.

Here, in the safety of their castle, they could start to rebuild, they could put their lives back on track piece by piece. He thought about their future, the wedding they would soon plan, and the joy that would come with it. The excitement stirred within him, but for now, all he wanted was to savour the simple comfort of being home with the man he loved by his side.

But as much as the thought of their future filled him with hope, Alucard couldn't shake the concern that lingered in the back of his mind. Zalith had been through so much—Alucard had seen sides of him he'd never seen before, glimpses of torment that haunted him still. He knew Zalith wasn't fully healed, that the trauma of everything they had endured still clung to him like shadows. All Alucard wanted was to help him, to be there for him in every way possible.

He wasn't sure if he could heal Zalith on his own, but he would try. He would do whatever it took to help them both recover from the sorrow and torment that had gripped them so tightly. Because in the end, Zalith was everything to him—his heart, his world. And there wasn't a single thing Alucard wouldn't do for him.

With that thought, Alucard exhaled softly, allowing the quiet peace of the moment to wash over him. The future awaited them, but for now, they had each other. And that was enough.

THE NUMEN CHRONICLES
SERIES ONE

Nosferatu
The Numen Chronicles | Volume 1

✝

Demon's Fate
The Numen Chronicles | Volume 2

✝

Light
The Numen Chronicles | Volume 3

✝

Demon's Bane
The Numen Chronicles | Volume 4

✝

Ascendant
The Numen Chronicles | Volume 5

✝

Icarus
The Numen Chronicles | Volume 6

✝

Demon's Curse
The Numen Chronicles | Volume 7

✝

Renascence
The Numen Chronicles | Volume 8

✝

Demon's Reclamation
The Numen Chronicles | Volume 9

✝

[And more…]

THE NUMENVERSE
OTHER SERIES/STORIES

Aldergrove Chronicles

Set in the year 1176 after Aegisguard's second world war. After being told he has only six months left to live, Clementine decides to track down his sister's murderers, leading him to Aldergrove Academy, a place where a hundred students must fight to the death to earn their right to travel to the New World. But he soon learns that the students aren't the only ones prowling the corridors at night in search of blood.

†

Where The Wild Wolves Have Gone

Set in the year 1330. Following Luan, a young transman werewolf who belongs to a pack owned by Lyca Corp., a military-focused organization. The pack have served them for generations, but after a mission goes sideways, Luan begins to learn the horrifying truth about the people they serve.

†

Greykin Chronicles

Set in the year 1332, following Jackson, a journalist who heads to the snowy mountains of Ascela in search of his missing best friend, Wilson. But he discovers that not only is there a whole different world hidden out there, but death isn't necessarily the end for some creatures.

†

The Numen Chronicles Series Two

Set in the year 1335. While hunting for his missing friend, Elijah stumbles upon a fiery journalist, who so happens to be looking for the same people as him: the doctors who experimented on him when he was a child. But when the two are forced to go on the run together, Elijah's healing wounds are opened, and he realises that Lyca Corp. took more than his childhood.

To stay up to date with future releases, follow the author through their website!

www.numenverse.com/

Milton Keynes UK
Ingram Content Group UK Ltd.
UKHW040439031224
452051UK00005B/25

9 781917 270052